John Dillon

Frontispiece
John Dillon at the time of his marriage in 1895

JOHN DILLON

A Biography

by
F. S. L. LYONS

Professor of Modern History
University of Kent at Canterbury

'. . . it would really be a tragedy if the history
of that party were allowed to perish as so much
in Irish history has perished' (John Dillon to
T. P. O'Connor, 12 Apr. 1925, on the Irish
parliamentary party).

'The story of his life is, for the greater part,
the story of the nationalist movement' (*Irish
Times*, obituary of John Dillon, 5 Aug. 1927).

LONDON
ROUTLEDGE & KEGAN PAUL

First published 1968
by Routledge & Kegan Paul Ltd
Broadway House, 68–74 Carter Lane
London E.C.4

Printed in Great Britain
by W & J Mackay & Co Ltd
Chatham, Kent

SBN 7100 2887 3

TYPOGRAPHER: Keith Kneebone

Contents

List of Illustrations

Preface

During the ten years of preparation for this book I have received a great deal of help from many different sources. My greatest debt is to John Dillon's family, not only for allowing me to undertake the work, but for placing at my disposal, without restriction or interference, the entire and formidable mass of their father's papers. I wish particularly to thank Mr. James Dillon for his interest and his valuable recollections; John Dillon (grandson of the subject of this biography) and his wife Jean for transcribing and typing the diary of Elizabeth Dillon (née Mathew); and above all, Professor Myles Dillon who first suggested the project to me, who has encouraged me at every turn and to whose scholarship and infinite patience I am indebted beyond measure.

For permission to make use of, and to quote from, other collections of papers, I am grateful to the following: the late Lord Beaverbrook for making available to me some important items from the Lloyd George Papers, Mr. A. J. P. Taylor, Mrs. Elton and the Beaverbrook Library for supplying me with photostats and Beaverbrook Newspapers for allowing me to quote from them; the Director and Trustees of the National Library, Dublin and the Public Record Office, London; the Trustees of the British Museum and the Director of the State Paper Office, Dublin; the Director of the National Library of Scotland; Mr. D. F. Porter and the Librarian of the Bodleian Library, Oxford; the Marquess of Salisbury; Mrs. D. Gill; Mr. Mark Bonham Carter; Sir Shane Leslie; His Eminence Cardinal Conway; Dr. and Mrs. Michael Tierney; Mr L. P. Scott; Mrs. E. H. Nathan; and the Macmillan Company of New York for permission to quote from Lionel Trilling's introduction to Henry James's *The Princess Casamassima* (Macmillan, 1948 ed., New York), the passage which appears at the head of chapter one.

Every effort has been made to get in touch with the owners of copyright material. If there is any instance where this has failed, it is hoped that this general acknowledgment will be accepted as adequate.

Since the publication of this book brings to an end twenty years of work on the history of the Irish parliamentary party, I wish to record here the names of those, some, alas, now dead, who helped me in various ways at various stages in my studies. I have been particularly indebted to the following for permission to use copyright material. Mrs. Sophie O'Brien (widow of William O'Brien); Mrs. W. A. Redmond (daughter-in-law of John Redmond); Mrs. Maev Sullivan (daughter of T. M. Healy); Colonel N. Harrington (son of T. C. Harrington). Above all, in completing these labours I remember my father, who gave me the encouragement and help that alone made it possible for me to think of becoming an historian.

I wish also to express my thanks to the Directors, Librarians and staffs of the Bodleian Library, the Manuscript Department of the British Museum, Christ Church, Oxford, the Library of the University of Kent at Canterbury, Liverpool

University Library, the National Registry of Archives, the National Library of Scotland, the Public Record Office, the Royal Dublin Society, the State Paper Office, Dublin Castle, and the Library of Trinity College, Dublin. To two libraries in particular I am especially grateful. I should like to acknowledge the unfailing courtesy and assistance I received from Miss Bondfield and Miss Donnellan of the Royal Irish Academy, where the Dillon Papers were housed while I was working on them. And, as always, I have pleasure in recording my gratitude to the former Director of the National Library, Dr. R. J. Hayes and to his staff, amongst them I must specially mention Mr. P. Henchy (the present Director), Mr. John Ainsworth, Mr. D. MacLochlann and Mr. T. P. O'Neill.

Many scholars have helped me most generously with suggestions, criticism and information. Among them I wish particularly to thank Mr. David Ayerst, Professor L. P. Curtis, jr., Mr. R. P. Davis, Mr. Owen Dudley Edwards, Mr. A. C. Hepburn, Dr. R. B. McDowell, Reverend Professor F. X. Martin, Professor K. B. Nowlan, Dr. Owen Sheehy Skeffington, Dr. David Thornley and Professor T. Desmond Williams. My debt to the friendship and scholarship of Professor T. W. Moody is in this, as in anything of substance I have ever written, incalculable. To him also, to Professor Myles Dillon, to Mr. Richard Langhorne, and to Mr. A. C. Hepburn, I owe much valuable help in the thankless task of proofreading.

The typing of this book was an arduous business and I am most grateful to those who relieved me completely of the task—Miss A. Pooley, Miss C. Aungier and Miss M. Spencer-Payne. To Miss Spencer-Payne in particular, who combined this with many other kinds of assistance, I am deeply thankful.

Finally, it gives me great pleasure to acknowledge that this book could not have been written without my wife's readiness to take all sorts of burdens off my shoulders; for this, and for her patience during so many years, I have no words adequate to express my feelings.

F. S. L. LYONS

Juniper Rough,
Upper Hardres,
Canterbury.
April 1968

Abbreviations

B.M., Add. MS	British Museum, Additional MS
D.P.	Dillon Papers
F.J.	*Freeman's Journal*
I.H.S.	*Irish Historical Studies*
L.G.P.	Lloyd George Papers
N.L.I.	National Library of Ireland
P.R.O.	Public Record Office
R.P.	Redmond Papers
S.P.O.	State Paper Office
U.I.	*United Ireland*
W.F.J.	*Weekly Freeman's Journal*

NOTE ON TERMINOLOGY

In the course of this book I have spelt the words 'nationalist' and 'nationalism' with a small 'n' when referring to general matters connected with the needs and demands of Irish nationality. But I have used Nationalist with a capital 'N' to denote the Irish parliamentary party and their supporters. This is not intended to suggest that that party had a monopoly of Irish nationalism, which they obviously had not; it is simply used, as contemporaries frequently used it, for purposes of quick and easy identification.

F.S.L.L.

I

The Young Man
From The Provinces

The defining hero may be known as the Young Man from the Provinces.
He need not come from the provinces in literal fact, his social class may
constitute his province. But a provincial birth and rearing suggest the
simplicity and the high hopes he begins with—he starts with a great demand
upon life and a great wonder about its complexity and promise. He may
be of good family but he must be poor. He is intelligent, or at least aware,
but not at all shrewd in worldly matters. He must have acquired a certain
amount of education, should have learned something about life from
books, although not the truth . . . Thus equipped with poverty, pride
and intelligence, the Young Man from the Provinces stands outside life
and seeks to enter.

Lionel Trilling, 'The Princess Casamassima'
in *The Liberal Imagination*

(i)

This is the story of a man who spent nearly fifty years in the forefront of
Irish politics, but who lived to see his party destroyed, himself unhonoured
and forgotten, and everything he had lived and fought for discarded as
irrelevant. Yet his career, which ended in disillusionment and in what the
world calls failure, is an important chapter in the modern history of Anglo-
Irish relations. His own experience ranged from the earliest days of the
Home Rule movement to the rise of Sinn Fein, from Butt and Parnell to
Griffith and de Valera. And through his ancestors and his posterity the
name of Dillon spans the period from famine to affluence, his father, John
Blake Dillon, having been one of the founders of Young Ireland, while his
son, Mr. James Dillon, has been a Minister of Agriculture in the Republic
and until recently leader of one of the two largest political parties in the
State.

In later life John Dillon used sometimes to say that he was the son of an
Irish rebel and the grandson of an evicted tenant. This, though not
absolutely correct, defines accurately enough, if not his origins, at least
the formative influences of his life. The Dillon family had lived for unnumbered generations at Lisyne in County Roscommon. They had the sole
tenancy of a farm or small estate belonging to the French family and

bordering on the lands of their namesakes (but not, so far as can be ascertained, relations) the Viscounts Dillon at Costelloe. The first member of the family to emerge from the almost total obscurity in which the absence of records has shrouded their history is John Dillon's grand-father, Luke Dillon. The date of his birth is unknown, but he was already grown to manhood at the time of the 1798 rising, and family tradition has it that he was a member of the revolutionary organization, the United Irishmen, though the same tradition suggests that he had a well-developed sense of survival, since he not only drilled the United Irishmen at night but the Yeomanry by day. His sympathies, however, were firmly on the side of the insurrection and he is said to have taken part in the 'Castlebar races', when a small French contingent, with some Irish auxiliaries, dispersed a much larger British force. In person, Luke Dillon seems to have been athletic and vigorous, known in his own county as a hurler and as a horse-man. Indeed, his horsemanship may have been responsible for the connec-tion of the Dillons with a prolific and influential Galway family, the Blakes of Dunmacrena. At any rate, it is also part of the family legend that when Anne Blake saw him vault into the saddle after visiting her father she declared, like Deirdre in the saga, that she would marry none but him, and she kept her word.

But although Luke Dillon survived the exciting days of '98 he became, early in the nineteenth century, a victim of the system of land tenure then prevailing in Ireland. When his lease fell in he was unable to pay the fine for its renewal and was obliged to leave the family holding. He moved to the small market town of Ballaghaderrin[1] and died there in 1825. One of his sons, Thomas, sought to repair the family fortunes by starting a small shop. This prospered and in time became a substantial business which was to play an important part in John Dillon's life and which is still in the family possession. Thomas handed it over as a going concern to his widowed sister, Monica Duff, and she in her turn passed it on to her daughter, Anne Deane, also widowed after a brief and not very happy marriage. Anne Deane was a woman of great business ability and remark-able force of character. Under her régime, not only did 'Monica Duff' prosper and expand, but it became a second home for her cousin John, while she herself, as will be seen, for many years was like a second mother to him—so much so that on her tombstone he wrote simply that he owed everything to her.[2]

The immediate consequence of the move to Ballaghaderrin was that Luke Dillon's son, John Blake Dillon, the father of the Dillon who is the subject of this biography, was born (in 1814) a Mayo man, thus establishing a family connection with the county which was to be of great importance in the future. John Blake Dillon was educated privately, mostly by the old

---

[1] Nowadays this is generally spelt Ballaghadereen, but I have kept to the old form which the Dillons themselves habitually used.

[2] For sympathetic portraits of Mrs. Deane, see Wilfred Scawen Blunt, *The land war in Ireland* (London, 1912), pp. 59–60, and Sophie O'Brien, *My Irish friends* (London and Dublin, 1937), pp. 102–11.

country 'classical' masters who were common in those days, and went first to Maynooth with the intention of becoming a priest. Finding in due course that he had no vocation, he went instead to Trinity College, Dublin. There, as a Catholic, he was to some extent a *rara avis* in an environment which was essentially (and at that period stridently) Protestant, but it was at Trinity nevertheless that he made the most important friendship of his life —the deep attachment to Thomas Davis which was cut short only by the latter's early and sudden death in 1845. Both Dillon and Davis became interested in politics even while they were at Trinity and both were active in the College Historical Society, then as now a training-ground for budding lawyers and politicians. Dillon read ethics and mathematics at the university, but the law was his destination and he was called to the Bar in 1841. By that time he and Davis had already begun to dabble in political journalism, writing for the Whiggish *Morning Register*, but it was in 1842 that they, together with another young man of great promise, Charles Gavan Duffy, took the momentous decision to start a newspaper of their own. This paper, the *Nation*, opened a new door for a whole generation and provided the basis for a coherent political philosophy of Irish nationalism which was to have immense influence then and for many years to come.[1]

Since this was the tradition into which John Dillon was born, we must be clear about the doctrines to which his father and Davis and Gavan Duffy were committed. They were best summed up by Davis in the prospectus he wrote for the new paper, describing the aims of himself and his friends:

> Nationality is their first great object—Nationality which will not only raise our people from their poverty by securing them the blessing of a domestic legislature, but inflame and purify them with a lofty and heroic love of country—a Nationality of the spirit as well as of the letter—a Nationality which may embrace Protestant, Catholic and Dissenter—Milesian and Cromwellian—the Irishman of a hundred generations, and the stranger who is within our gates: not a Nationality which would prelude civil war, but which would establish internal union and external independence; a Nationality which would be recognised by the world, and sanctified by wisdom, virtue and prudence.[2]

To those who know anything of the history of romantic nationalism in nineteenth-century Europe much of this will have a familiar ring, and it is certainly true that Young Ireland, as Davis and his friends soon came to be called, had obvious affinities with Young Italy. Davis, especially, whose insistence on the necessity of recalling the people to their language, literature and history led Patrick Pearse rightly to describe him as 'the first of modern Irishmen to make explicit the truth that a nationality is a spirituality', reminds one very strongly at times of Mazzini. But it would

[1] Dillon Papers (hereafter cited as D.P.), 'Life of John Blake Dillon by his wife'. This is a fragment written in impeccable copper-plate in a school copy-book and is unfortunately incomplete.

[2] *Thomas Davis: Essays and poems, with a centenary memoir* (Dublin, 1945), p. 13.

be misleading to regard Young Ireland merely as a regional variant of a European pattern. It expressed itself, naturally enough, in the contemporary mode, but it sprang directly from Irish conditions and it was fully as conscious of economic and political realities as it was of national ideals. This was true even of Davis, but it was still truer of John Blake Dillon, who was less literary and more practical than either Davis or Gavan Duffy. Duffy himself in later years drew a striking distinction between his two friends. The passage in which he did so is worth quoting, because both the physical description of John Blake Dillon and the analysis of his ideas might be those of his son John:

> In person he was tall and strikingly handsome, with eyes like a thoughtful woman's, and the clear olive complexion and stately bearing of a Spanish noble. His generous nature made him more of a philanthropist than a politician. He was born and reared in Connaught amongst the most abject and oppressed population in Europe and all his studies and projects had direct relation to the condition of the people. Codes, tenures and social theories were his familiar reading, as history and biography were an inspiration to the more powerful imagination of Davis. He followed in the track of Bentham and de Tocqueville and recognised a regulated democracy as the inevitable and rightful ruler of the world and he saw with burning impatience the wrongs inflicted on the industrious poor by an aristocracy practically irresponsible. Davis desired a national existence for Ireland that an old historic state might be raised from the dust, and a sceptre placed in her hand, that thus she might become the mother of a brave and self-reliant race. Dillon desired a national existence primarily to get rid of social degradation and suffering which it wrung his heart to witness without being able to relieve. He was neither morose nor cynical but he had one instinct in common with Swift, the villainies of mankind made his blood boil. . . .[1]

It is not surprising that in 1842 John Blake Dillon's blood should have boiled when he contemplated the plight of 'the industrious poor'. The population of Ireland was then over eight million and repeated famines earlier in the century had indicated that, given the backwardness of agriculture and the viciousness of the prevailing system of land tenure, the soil would simply not support anything like that number. The great mass of farmers occupied small and uneconomic plots of land as tenants often rack-rented, liable to frequent and speedy eviction, and depending for the sustenance of themselves and their families mainly upon the potato. It only needed the failure of that staple crop to push this fatally vulnerable society over the brink. Such a failure was only three years away when the *Nation* was first started, and all the political manoeuvrings of the time have to be seen against this vast impending national calamity.

In retrospect it seems extraordinary that apart from the writers in the *Nation* so little attention was paid to the fundamental economic problems

---

[1] Sir Charles Gavan Duffy, *Young Ireland* (London, 1880), i. 60–61.

1. John Blake Dillon

2. John Dillon in 1869

of the country. The political stage was still dominated by Daniel O'Connell' old now, and surrounded by inferior and unlovable men, but gathering himself for one last attempt to secure Repeal of the Act of Union and the re-establishment of a separate Irish Parliament. So long as he seemed to have some prospect of success the Young Ireland group supported him. By 1843, however, it was clear that his bid had failed miserably and re-criminations soon broke out between the young men, impatient for reform, and the old man and his followers, content to bide their time and play the opportunist game which had often served so well in the past. Occasions of friction multiplied—the most notable, perhaps, being the rejection by O'Connell and a majority of the Irish hierarchy of a well-intended proposal of Peel's to create university institutions in Ireland in which Protestants and Catholics might mingle. Davis and his friends protested bitterly at the doctrine of segregation—religious apartheid, we might almost call it—which those who denounced the 'Godless colleges' seemed to be advocating and the divergence between Young and Old Ireland grew steadily more marked.

That particular quarrel came to a head in 1845—the year of Thomas Davis's death, the year in which the failure of the potato crop launched Ireland on the long nightmare of the Great Famine, and also the year in which John Blake Dillon's health began to take an ominous turn. Over-strained and disheartened by his failure to heal the breach between the rival factions, he fell ill, and while recuperating in the country learnt of Thomas Davis's sudden death after what had seemed only a mild attack of scarlet fever. Dillon's condition deteriorated rapidly and he began to spit blood. To save his life he was sent to Madeira for the winter, but when he returned to Ireland in the summer of 1846 he found the divisions in Irish politics even more intense. As before, he tried to reunite the forces of Repeal, but there was no doubt where his sympathy lay. When in January 1847 William Smith O'Brien, like Davis a Protestant nationalist, but a landlord and at that time a Member of Parliament, founded a new body, the Irish Confederation, John Blake Dillon speedily identified himself with it.

Up to this time it had been easy to say what Young Ireland stood for. It looked backward to an ancient tradition and forward to the resurrection of a nation which should not only be conscious of that tradition but should also be served by Irishmen of all creeds and origins in the common pursuit of social justice and political independence. That political independence of England should be the prelude to this brave new world all could equally agree. But whether independence should come by moral suasion or physical force was harder to decide. Most, probably, were prepared to wait upon events, but with the formation of the Irish Confederation and the growing influence of the more tough-minded among them, most notably John Mitchel, one of the most outstanding political journalists to emerge in nineteenth-century Ireland, a more militant note began to predominate. The contemporary observer who, asked to define the 'tone' of the *Nation*, replied briefly 'Wolfe Tone' was as perceptive as he was concise. By 1848 the spirit of 1798 was again abroad in the land and the exciting news from the continent encouraged Mitchel and his friends to believe that a successful rising might indeed be possible. But the Government was well informed and the conspirators, if that is not too grandiose a term, were incorrigibly amateur. Mitchel was seized in May, and although a sporadic, sputtering rising did break out shortly afterwards it was a total failure and two of the other most prominent leaders, William Smith O'Brien and Thomas Francis Meagher, were taken prisoners.

John Blake Dillon, although married only the previous year to a young wife who was now pregnant with their first child, joined in the rising, but avoided capture and after some adventurous weeks on the run escaped to the United States. He was joined soon afterwards by his wife Adelaide with the daughter whom he had never seen and they settled on Long Island while he began to practise law in New York. It was there, in 1850, that their eldest son, William Dillon, was born. His younger brother, John, was, however, born not in America but in Blackrock, just outside Dublin, on 4 September 1851, when his mother was home visiting her family. She returned with the child to New York and another daughter was born there in 1854 The next year, under a Government amnesty, the family came back to Dublin and John Blake Dillon began yet another legal career. Four more children, three boys and a girl, were born between their return and 1862. But poor health dogged the family from the start and it is important to remember, when considering the crucial problem of John Dillon's own health, that two of his sisters died of consumption at the ages of 18 and 20 respectively, that the third sister died when she was 12, and that of his four brothers one died at the age of 6 and another aged only 3. Of the two survivors, apart from John, his elder brother William was threatened with tuberculosis and went out to Colorado in his mid-twenties; he made America his permanent home and he, too, became a lawyer, dying in 1935. The younger surviving brother, Henry, seems to have been the healthiest of the lot. Having been called to the Bar and practised for a short time, he entered religion and became a Franciscan, taking the name Father Nicholas; he lived until 1939.

Because of the family's unexpectedly early return from America, John Dillon's most impressionable years were spent in Dublin, where he was to make his home for the rest of his life. They lived first in what was even then a fashionable part of residential Dublin, 51 Fitzwilliam Square West, only a few yards away from Adelaide Dillon's old home in Fitzwilliam Place. Her father, Simon Hart, was a solicitor, whose firm, Hart and O'Hara, is said to have been one of the first, if not the first, Catholic law partnerships to begin practice after the relaxation of the penal laws. In the summer-time the Dillons used to leave the city, as many Dublin families then did, for the seaside. Usually, they occupied a house at Killiney, Druid Lodge, belonging to John's great-uncle, William O'Hara, and this, rather than Dublin, impressed itself upon the young boy as his real home. All his life he loved

Killiney, which is indeed the most beautiful part of the coast south of Dublin, and he returned to it again and again in later life. From a fragmentary memoir his brother William wrote in old age it is clear that for both brothers Druid Lodge held a very special place in their affections. It was an ideal house for boys to grow up in, with a field where they played cricket and football, and the sea only ten minutes away.

> My earliest distinct recollection of my brother (wrote William Dillon) dates from this period. We had an open sailing-boat, in which we used to go sailing . . . My brother was more daring and adventurous than I was. On several occasions, he came pretty close to ending our lives there and then. On one occasion there was a stiff wind from the shore and we sailed out quite a long distance, almost out of sight of land. The wind came on to blow a gale, and we had a very hard time, indeed, in beating back to Dalkey Island . . . The old boatman who lived at the landing-place at Dalkey Sound . . . reported to my grand-uncle [sic] that it was nothing short of a miracle that we escaped with our lives.[1]

It was not all play, of course. The family background was a bookish one, and although the children received little regular schooling, they were privately taught by a succession of tutors. One of these, James Stephens, was subsequently to become one of the Fenian leaders, and it was only a few years after his employment with the Dillons that he was imprisoned in Richmond jail, from which he was spectacularly rescued by John Devoy, another Fenian who was to cross John Dillon's path more than once in later life. When John was about 13 years old he and his brother William went to Dr. Quinn's School in Harcourt Street, Dublin, in preparation for the university.[2] Even as early as that John was showing a mathematical bent, and he was to continue this with distinction at the Catholic University, which he entered at the age of 15.

But at that point, when he had barely begun his career as a student, the family suffered a disastrous blow. His father had lived quietly for several years after the return from America, devoting himself to the law and keeping out of politics. The presence of James Stephens in the house was, it seems, less an indication of a relapse into extremism than a simple gesture of goodwill and assistance towards a man who had been 'out' with John Blake Dillon in '48'. Nevertheless, it proved impossible for a man of Dillon's reputation to avoid public life altogether and in 1865 he took a prominent part in founding the National Association.[3] This was a broadly based body

---

[1] 'Recollections of the early life of John Dillon, by his brother, William Dillon', p. 3 (D.P.). This is a typescript corrected in William Dillon's hand, but undated. It belongs to the period between 1927 and 1935.

[2] Ibid., p. 6. It appears from a recent life of James Stephens that Stephens taught in the Dillon household only for a few months in 1858. See D. Ryan, *The Fenian Chief* (Dublin, 1967), p. 82.

[3] For John Blake Dillon's connection with the National Association see E. R. Norman, *The Catholic Church and Ireland in the age of rebellion* (London, 1965), chaps. 4, 5 and 7.

of moderates which had the blessing of the Church and was designed partly as a counterweight to Fenianism and partly to promote certain specific reforms—for example, the disestablishment of the Church of Ireland, improved conditions for tenant-farmers and the setting up of a genuinely national university. It was worthy, laborious and much given to internal disputes, but it brought Dillon back to the familiar world of politics to the extent that in that same year, 1865, he agreed to stand for Parliament and was duly returned for Tipperary. Within little more than twelve months he was stricken by cholera and died on 15 September 1866 after only a few days' illness.

His death left Adelaide Dillon with a young family to support and educate and it seems unlikely that she could have sent her three sons to the university without considerable help from her own family. At any rate, when she herself died in May 1872, probably from tuberculosis, it was the Harts and O'Haras, together with Anne Deane, who looked after the Dillons. John thenceforward divided his time between the O'Hara house at Killiney, his uncle Charles Hart's house in 2 North Great George's Street, Dublin (which became his own permanent home), and Ballaghaderrin. He was still at the university when his mother died, because, having first taken his Arts degree, he had then, after a brief spell in the office of a Manchester cotton-merchant (which was, however, long enough to give him a lifelong distaste for business as an occupation), entered the medical school in Cecilia Street, qualifying in 1875.

His university career, like that of his two brothers, William and Henry, was distinguished. He won many prizes and played a prominent part in the most famous of the college societies, the Literary and Historical, of which he became Auditor in 1874–5, his final year at the university.[1] As Auditor, it was his duty to deliver an inaugural address and this in due course became his only published work. Dillon's choice of subject was 'The utility of debating clubs and societies such as the present', but his real theme was the function of a university. When he first entered 86 St. Stephen's Green, Dr. Newman had already departed, but the memory of him remained and some of those whom he had appointed were still professors. However, the general control of the university had passed to clerics more rigid in their views and more rigorous in their discipline, and Dillon, who in the previous year had already been concerned in presenting a memorial to the bishops about this and also about inadequate attention to scientific subjects, took the opportunity in his inaugural to recall his audience to 'the idea of a university' set out by Newman in his famous discourses. Starting from Newman's dictum that a university 'is not a convent, it is not a seminary, it is a place to fit men of the world for the world', he protested against the tendency of the university authorities to wish to insulate students against the snares and pitfalls of exterior reality. As his first considerable public utterance this speech has a special interest, the more so since its forthright-

---

[1] James Meenan (ed.), *Centenary history of the Literary and Historical Society of University College, Dublin, 1855–1955* (Tralee, n.d.), chap. 1.

ness and almost brutal logic anticipate with remarkable exactness his mature style:

> Would you say [he asked] that the best way were to keep a young man in total ignorance of what the world is, up to the very day when he must go forth to encounter it, unexperienced and unprepared? Or would it not, on the other hand, be wiser to keep him for some few years in a state of transition, so to speak—a state which would bring him into constant contact with the world around him, but which would, at the same time, surround him with influences powerfully tending to induce him to choose what is good in that world in preference to what is bad? . . . Unfortunately, it sometimes happens that, alarmed by the wide spread of corruption and the success of doctrines which seem ruinous to all that they hold most dear, the authorities of a university forget the world for which they are preparing their students and think that by shutting out the evil they will best prepare young men to meet it. They ostracise from their teaching all of literature that seems to have an immoral tendency, all of science and philosophy that seems to run counter to their faith, and make it one of their most earnest cares to protect their students from all contact with, or even knowledge of, the spirit of the age.
>
> In so acting, they fail most miserably in one of their most important duties, which, as I have already said, is to surround with wholesome influences a young man whilst he is making himself acquainted with the spirit of his age and the busy intellectual world in which he must take a part, be it obscure or illustrious. It seems to me that such a system of protection is as unreasonable and childish as if a man were to spend two or three years in a hot house as a preparation for an expedition in search of the North Pole . . . What can it avail to keep a student in ignorance of the Darwinian theory, or of the doctrines of Huxley, or Herbert Spencer when, on leaving the university, he must find the intellectual atmosphere full of the opinions and writings of these men? Is there not a danger that on looking back he will lose respect for the teachers who, while they professed to offer him every kind of knowledge, kept from him much that was true and wonderful; and that as a consequence a strong reaction will set in in favour of the new theories—half false, half true —which are so striking and so captivating?[1]

Part of his address has a more than academic interest, since it marked his first attempt to grapple with a problem that haunted him for many years until it was resolved by Act of Parliament in 1908. This was the need, essential as he saw it, for the creation of a truly national university. 'Gather together', he pleaded, 'the youth of a country in a great national university. See that it be favourable to the formation and free interchange of opinion. See, in fact, that it encourage all those qualities which go to make a true man, and you will produce this result: at least one half of those differences which, in after life, lead to friction and animosity, will be fought out peaceably, but in all earnestness, among the students; while three-fourths of the

[1] *Nation*, 21 Nov. 1874.

prejudice which, like a thick fog, shuts out the light of truth, will vanish in so clear and bracing an air.'[1]

Youthful idealism, we may say, though it was an idealism, tempered no doubt by many disappointments, which remained with him to the end of his days. At the time, however, what most impressed his audience was the freedom, indeed the ruthlessness, with which he contrasted Newman's 'great and glorious undertaking' with the sad reality around them:

> So far [he said] these glorious hopes have borne but little fruit. Their failure is due to causes, both external and internal, which I am not called on here to discuss. But because we have failed so far, must we, therefore, relinquish all hope of ever obtaining a National Catholic University for Ireland? God forbid that we should ever be so false to our country and our faith. It rests with the Catholics of Ireland, and with them alone, to determine whether the hopes with which this universe was founded shall yet be realised.[2]

By some contemporaries this was regarded as a deliberate attack upon the university authorities for their obscurantism and the Unionist *Dublin Daily Express*, in particular, made great play with this intelligent young man struggling to free himself from his cage. 'He knows', observed the editor with unction, 'that no man is well educated who has not studied the great philosophical and scientific theories at present before the world, and that this timorous, careful adjustment of the curriculum upon a narrow theological principle, reflects dishonour upon his university and renders its degree valueless. He sees clearly that the heads of his university love their religion a great deal better than they love truth, and would endeavour to shut out the light, in order that their own peculiar opinions may have the greater chance of being accepted, their real nature not being seen in the darkness.' Dillon at once indignantly repudiated the sentiments the newspaper was fathering upon him and took the occasion to declare his own 'unalterable allegiance' to the Catholic University.[3] Nevertheless, he had allowed himself to be publicly critical of his academic superiors and, although no one at the time could have guessed the significance of the incident, this was the first brush with ecclesiastical authority of one who was to become perhaps the most outspoken opponent of clerical influence in his generation.

(ii)

But if an incipient anti-clericalism could be read into the speech, did that imply some more fundamental crisis of belief? The answer is that it did

---

[1] This passage was not reproduced in the newspaper accounts of his inaugural, but it is cited by P. J. Hooper in his 'Life of John Dillon', pp. 27–28. This is an unfinished typescript, begun shortly after Dillon's death and no more than a sketch for what might have become the official biography. But Hooper had access to early letters and documents which have since disappeared and his fragment remains an important source; it is cited hereafter as 'Hooper narrative'.

[2] *Nation*, 21 Nov. 1874.

[3] For these exchanges, see *Dublin Daily Express*, 18, 19 and 21 Nov. 1874; *F.J.*, 18 and 23 Nov. 1874.

not, but that there is some evidence to suggest that in the year or two before his inaugural Dillon had undergone a period of acute religious doubt. During his student days he began to keep a diary, a habit which he tried fitfully to prolong into later life. The earliest of these diaries are no longer extant—the survivors begin in the autumn of 1876—but the late Senator P. J. Hooper, who began to assemble material for a biography soon after Dillon's death, included in his unfinished manuscript several passages from the period before 1876 which throw some light on this problem. From these it appears that from time to time during his university career he was subject to fits of black despair and that during these he was assailed by all kinds of scepticism and frustration. This may partly have been the not unnatural reaction of an intelligent and introspective young man to the cloistered and sometimes suffocating atmosphere of Newman's university, but it seems most likely that it was directly connected with a mysterious deterioration in his health. Up to the time he entered the university there is plenty of evidence of sheer physical exuberance—he loved sailing, swimming, fencing, boxing, skating and football. But from about 1870 onwards these pleasures were constantly interrupted by illness and before long had to be almost completely abandoned. He had trouble with his eyes (a major disaster to such an insatiable reader), and worse still, he began to be plagued with dyspepsia, an ailment which faithfully returned to him at every crisis of his life up to the very end. Added to this was a threat, eventually unrealised, of varicose veins and some degree of heart trouble.

In the face of these torments, individually not overwhelming, but collectively a heavy burden, it is not surprising that a note of despondency began to enter his diaries. In 1870–1 the contrast between his own stagnation and the exciting events in France and Italy during and after the Franco-Prussian war seemed almost intolerable. 'It is wretchedly humiliating', he wrote on 23 June 1871, 'to think how subject the soul is to the body. How gladly would I charge to the cry of "Viva Pia Nono". That is the one advantage of youth, the recklessness of death. God grant that I may have a chance before this time next year.' To sacrifice his life for the decaying secular régime of the papacy was hardly an ambition characteristic of John Dillon and the mood soon passed. Later that year another entry (6 September) showed that his thoughts were turning nearer home. 'I feel sure', he recorded, 'that if I live I shall do something to make my name remembered, but this cursed heart of mine will kill me before long; I don't much care anyway, if only it does its work quickly. One thing I do wish for, that I may give my life for Ireland; then I would die content.'[1]

It would be easy to dismiss this mood as a kind of Byronic posturing, but, although no doubt there was an element of self-conscious exaggeration, it is a mood which recurs so often as to suggest some deep-seated malaise. His very youth, which had seemed so full of promise, now seemed no more than a Dead Sea fruit. In June 1870 he recorded his emphatic agreement with John Mitchel's dictum that it is 'the most disgusting por-

[1] 'Hooper narrative', p. 21 (D.P.).

tion of a person's existence'. And in other (undated) entries he asks: 'Will I conclude my life in the shady groves of a lunatic asylum? After dinner I, who am naturally of a phlegmatic disposition, felt a strong inclination to jump up, smash a considerable quantity of glass, curse a good deal and rush out of the room. From that time until bed-time I endured a kind of hell upon earth without pain. I cannot keep quiet for ten minutes. Yet I feel too weary and weak to walk and my eyes are too sore to read.' 'My nerves are in an abnormal condition, accursedly abnormal, yet I am rarely in that state meant by "in pain" . . . I tell you that the poor hypochondriac suffers more in one week than was ever dreamt by the strong, brave and healthy.' And again: 'On, on, tearing through a wild rushing sea, surrounded on all sides by shoals and black rocks, sick in head and weary in arm . . . looking back with tearful eyes to the pleasant waveless sea on which I sailed in youth.'[1]

Hypochondria, as he was perfectly well aware, was indeed part of his trouble, and a serious part, for the settled gloom which accompanied it led him inexorably towards a spiritual crisis. An entry in 1871 indicates that he was already having to struggle to hold on to his faith: 'As to the next world I cannot see any fixed principle and I must trust more to the mercy of God and my holy mother than to myself.' He continued for a while longer to go to confession, but found himself increasingly unable to distinguish between guilt and innocence. And it was about the same time that in another undated entry he wrote: 'I am still at sea, so far as knowledge of the truth is concerned [about] the exact difference between good and evil and though I sometimes wish to know it, yet I fear the knowledge . . . Thank God my faith is strong.' But it was not as strong as he would like to have believed and a year later (2 September 1872) he had this to record: 'I have nearly completed my twenty-first year, I look back on the past without regret, to the future with little hope, but with an increasing calmness. I realise to the fullest its utter hollowness, the constant gnawing want of something that is not here. I imagined that the want was supplied by the beautiful theories of religion, but the enthusiastic faith of my youth is fading . . . I will read up the stoics.' Such self-questioning was not so abnormal as he imagined and a spasm of Welt-Schmerz is a common enough episode in the intellectual development of eager, intelligent and frustrated romantics. But Dillon, with that uncompromising honesty which was an essential part of him from the very beginning, carried his doubts to the confessional, where he informed the astonished priest that he was 'half an infidel'.[2]

Under pressure from his religious adviser he agreed to continue at any rate the outward practice of religion, and although for a few months longer he still wavered, by the end of 1873 his doubts seem to have subsided. On 18 November his diary contained this passage: 'Wanted. The best book on the relation of the Catholic Church to science and modern thought, liberty, etc; also the most recognised history of the Church and the most authentic and able treatise on moral philosophy as taught by the Catholic Church.'

[1] Ibid., p. 23.   [2] Ibid., p. 24.

It is not possible to chart the stages of his journey home, but by the following March he was so safely back in harbour that we find him in charge of a catechism class and at no subsequent crisis of his career, even in moments of deepest sorrow, is there any indication that his faith ever again deserted him.[1] Yet there is evidence from much later in his life that the struggle had left its mark upon him and that certain tensions had not been completely resolved. Thus, in July 1890, when he was approaching middle age and in the very forefront of Irish politics, a reading of *The Kreutzer Sonata* set him brooding on a question which had troubled him for years:

> It revived in my mind [he noted in his diary] problems which used to exercise and torment me, before my life became too muddy for any problems. Went to 11 o'clock Mass and heard a priest, an Englishman I should judge from his accent, speak of the 'fetid sewer' of pagan life, applying the term to the Greece and Rome of St. Paul's day. Alas! Alas! What good can come of this? What Tolstoy seems to see and what has been forced on me with agony and inexpressible suffering is that Christianity is incompatible with the enjoyment of beauty, and the infinite joy of life; the supreme of beauty being the human body in youth. We make a kind of compromise, but essentially and logically they are exclusive of each other.[2]

A few years after this, when he had married Elizabeth Mathew, a calm and joyous Christianity entered his life and relaxed these tensions, but this period, as we shall see presently, was tragically brief and after her death he reverted to the austere, almost Jansenist, religion of his youth. He was, indeed devoted to his family, and his intimate friends found him, as they had always done, a gentle and a cultivated man, but in matters of the spirit he remained a solitary, facing with stoic fortitude a universe which, in many of its aspects, seemed to him harsh and forbidding.

But there was another reason, apart from physical weakness and spiritual stress, for the frustration and sense of guilt which pressed upon him so constantly in these student years. In an entry for November 1872 his diary gives us an indication of it. I have set up two altars in my heart,' he wrote. 'On the one is enthroned knowledge, on the other duty and my country.'[3] It is, in fact, clear from the diaries that for many years, and not just while he was at the university, he was obsessed by the pursuit of learning. One of his first intellectual heroes was Francis Bacon and the young disciple seems from the outset to have resolved to take all knowledge for *his* province. In his time at college, and even after he had taken his degrees, he read with a frenzied desperation literature, history, philosophy, medicine, and science, as well as exploring all sorts of by-ways which suggested themselves in the course of his reading. For much of his life he was an inveterate buyer of books and his diaries are full of resolutions—regularly broken—to curb his bibliomania. The result was that he built up a splendid library which, while reflecting a remarkable diversity of interests, was especially

[1] Ibid., pp. 24–25. [2] Diary of John Dillon, 6 July, 1890 (D.P.).
[3] 'Hooper narrative', p. 24 (D.P.).

rich in editions of the English poets and among these Shelley in particular of whom, as also of Swift, he claimed to have read every line.

From time to time he would work out regular schemes of study in the hope of canalising and controlling this voracious appetite for knowledge. Such schemes usually broke down, but, ironically enough, the only occasions when they came anywhere near success were when Her Majesty's Government withdrew him temporarily from other distractions. Then box after box of books would pour into Kilmainham jail, or those of Dundalk and Galway, and sheet after sheet of foolscap would be covered with lists of yet more subjects to be investigated, yet more volumes to be acquired. In later years the passion somewhat abated, but only because he had then become a compulsive reader of newspapers, working his way through six major papers (Irish and English) every day, and reading them with such attention that almost every one of them was marked with a blue pencil for subsequent clipping. Unfortunately, the disposal of this vast mass of newsprint never kept pace with his reading of it, and the piles of paper would mount in his study until desk and reader alike would disappear from view, whereupon the family would make a concerted raid to clear the room and the process would begin all over again.

While he never did succeed in bringing his grandiose schemes for acquiring universal knowledge to fruition, he seems to have made a rough-and-ready division of his reading rather on the lines of de Quincey's distinction between the literature of power and the literature of knowledge. For Dillon the books that contributed to his knowledge were his medical and scientific textbooks and whatever came his way of history, biography and philosophy; quite apart from these were works of literature—mostly poetry and the novels ('dream-books', he called them) which he read when he no longer had stamina for anything else and which he seems to have regarded as a kind of self-indulgence, culpable but irresistible. Here is a typical entry (4 July 1870) concerning his more serious reading:

> There are so many things I want to read if my eyes get alright—all about Frederick the Second, about Manfred, about Roger de Lona, etc. I must look out for Giannoni. Then I must finish Sismondi, read Smith's *Wealth of Nations*, the rest of Michelet's *History of France*, Döllinger's *History of the Church*, Sully's *Memoirs*, Froissart, etc. etc. . . .[1]

This bare list, which is only one of many, suggests something not only of his appetite, but also of the dangers of indigestion awaiting him. He was not unaware of this himself. 'My chief sin', he wrote in another (undated) entry, 'is love of knowledge, and selfish though I am I at least can see and despise it.' And again: 'The pursuit of knowledge is a strange and confounding chase. Sometimes, as I sit in the library blinking over a book . . . sick at heart, sick of stomach with the peculiar indescribable distress of dyspepsia . . . sick in my eyes, for they, too, are sore and weary, the vast

---

[1] Ibid., p. 18.

spirit of universal knowledge rises up before me and mocks my feeble efforts.'[1] Certainly, if to engage in such a pursuit was to be guilty of the Faustian sin of presumption, John Dillon was adequately punished for it.

(iii)

It would, however, be misleading to think that because he was by nature introspective, inclined to hypochondria, and absorbed both in his health and in his studies, he had no time for the outer world of politics. As his father's son he could not help meeting with, and hearing the ideas of, the men who had belonged to the Young Ireland group and who resumed old friendships when the Dillons returned from America. One of the most intimate of these was John Martin, married to a sister of the John Mitchel who had been one of the most resolute rebels of '48 and had been sentenced to transportation. Mitchel had made a dramatic escape from Australia and had then settled in New York. Although he did not approve of John Blake Dillon's transformation into a liberal-minded moderate, the Mitchel, Martin and Dillon families remained close friends, and it was through this connection that John Dillon made his first entry into Irish politics. There can be no doubt that at the outset of his career it was the tradition of militant nationalism represented by John Mitchel which captured his imagination. Although he had been too young to be drawn into the Fenian outbreaks of 1867 he had, after all, known James Stephens and there are indications, as we shall see, that when he began to emerge into public life the Fenians were aware of him and that he was aware of them. There is, however, no evidence that he actually joined the Irish Republican Brotherhood. That very acute Dublin policeman, Superintendent John Mallon, probably found the right phrase when he described him in 1880 as 'a cool Fenian', meaning one in general sympathy with, though not involved in, Fenian activities, for, as Dillon was many times to make clear, his objection to physical force was its inexpediency and its impracticality rather than its essential wrongness.[2] It is, however, ironical that it was not until 1896, when he had left these youthful ardours behind him and was the leader of a large and eminently respectable parliamentary party, that the police at last came to the solemn conclusion that he 'does not appear to have been at any time a member of the I.R.B.'[3]

Nevertheless, in his student days the idea of an armed uprising haunted his thoughts and in 1870 the outbreak of the Franco-Prussian War inspired him for a brief moment with the wild hope that England might be drawn in. 'I hope it may be true', he wrote, 'for then there would be a chance for Ireland.'[4] But that year was significant for Ireland in a quite opposite direction, for during the course of it Isaac Butt founded his Home Govern-

[1] Ibid., p. 19.
[2] Cited in C. Cruise O'Brien, *Parnell and his party* (London, 1957), p. 30 n. 1.
[3] S.P.O., 'Crime Branch Special Papers', 11426/S, biographies of 'home suspects' reviewed in March 1896.
[4] 'Hooper narrative', p. 34 (D.P.).

ment Association. Quite where it would lead and what forces it would liberate no one could then foretell, but Dillon at the start was inclined to be condescending about it. In September 1871 he admitted that the movement for Home Rule seemed to be doing very well 'not that I believe they will ever get it, but then it will prepare the way for something better'.[1] And again, early in 1872: 'Let others do the talking; I will prepare for the day which I hope is approaching, when the sharp edge of the sword will decide the quarrel of seven hundred years.' And he added a verse from Thomas Davis's 'Song for the Irish Militia':

> The tribune's tongue and poet's pen
> May sow the seed in prostrate men
> But 'tis the soldier's sword alone
> Can reap the crop so bravely sown.

'Meanwhile', he concluded, 'I have found two congenial spirits, Mitchel and Davis, enough to turn a race of slaves into the wildest lovers of their country.'[2]

Yet, by a curious twist, it was Mitchel who first directed his thoughts towards the possibility of parliamentary action. In 1873 John and his brother William were largely responsible for raising £2,000 by subscription for the relief of Mitchel's poverty. Naturally, this drew them very close to him and in June 1874 Mitchel wrote to John Dillon that he had it in mind to return to Ireland and offer himself for election to parliament. He had no intention of taking his seat if elected, but he knew that as a still unpardoned rebel his candidature would arouse controversy and he was anxious to use the machinery of parliamentary elections to remind the Irish people that there still existed an alternative policy to that peaceable pursuit of a moderate measure of self-government which Isaac Butt was then so ineffectively pursuing in the House of Commons. Later that year he paid a brief exploratory visit to Ireland, where he met the two brothers, but he had returned to America by the time a vacancy occurred in Tipperary. His name was at once put forward and as there was no opposition he was declared elected. The election was thereupon quashed on the ground that he was an unpardoned felon who had escaped from justice and a second election had therefore to be held. Mitchel was determined to attend this one in person, but when he arrived at Queenstown early in 1875 it was immediately obvious that the old rebel was mortally sick. It fell to others to fight the election for him and the burden of speaking and canvassing in the constituency was carried by two known Fenians—John Daly of Limerick and Charles Doran of Queenstown—as well as by the 23-year-old Dillon.[3]

It was during this campaign that Dillon met for the first time the man who was to become first his closest political friend and then his bitterest political enemy. This was William O'Brien, a young journalist from Mallow, who was reporting the election for the *Cork Daily Herald*. O'Brien

---

[1] Ibid., p. 34.   [2] Ibid., pp. 34–5.
[3] William Dillon, *Life of John Mitchel* (London, 1888), vol. ii, chap. 7.

later became a devoted Parnellite and constitutionalist, but at this time his sympathies were much more with the physical force movement and he had even been for a while a member of the I.R.B. Thirty years later he recorded his impressions of the encounter in his *Recollections*. It has to be remembered that when this volume appeared O'Brien had quarrelled violently with his friend. This accounts for the touches of malice which he knew so well how to insinuate into the most innocent-seeming descriptions, but allowing for that his portrait of Dillon on his first public intervention in Irish politics is clearly recognisable, even through the peculiarities of the author's style:

> His great height looked all the vaster for his thin and wasted limbs, upon which the languor of death seemed to be fastening. His soft, dark eyes, slowly waking up to a perception of the persons introduced to him and the things they said, somehow gave me the impression that they had already gone far on the road to unconsciousness, and found some difficulty in returning to life from behind the heavy eye-lids. His white and still face on a background of black hair of singular intensity might well indeed have seemed to be a face in a black coffin, if it were not for a tinge of rich Spanish colour about the handsome features, and the light of vivid apostolic passion that flamed in his eyes, once they were kindled to their work. It was, I think, one of the young medical student's first public speeches, and made up by its earnest ring for the difficulty which he found in sustaining his voice or even his limbs during its delivery.[1]

Mitchel did make one personal appearance in Cork at the end of February, but he was too unwell to deliver his address himself and John Dillon read it for him.[2] Despite the candidate's evident illness, he was nevertheless elected by a large majority. But it was an empty gesture. Mitchel had barely time to issue one more declaration that he would never sit in Parliament before death took him at his word. He had travelled painfully to Newry to stay with his brother, and there he died in March 1875. John Dillon was beside him at the end and was one of the chief mourners at his funeral.[3] At the graveside his other old friend, Mitchel's brother-in-law, John Martin, collapsed and was taken to the Mitchel's Newry house, where he, too, died within a few days. Dillon was deeply marked by these events, as his diary shows: 'Of the scenes which I have passed through, glorious and sad, I cannot write now. I must leave some other time when my mind shall be more healthy to write of the Tipperary election and of the noble friends that I have lost.'[4]

Martin's death had one consequence which was to have an incalculable effect upon Dillon's own career. Martin had for some years sat for the county of Meath as one of Isaac Butt's supporters and it may well have been his influence that persuaded Dillon to take the Home Rule movement more seriously than he had done in the past. At any rate, when in 1873 the

[1] William O'Brien, *Recollections* (London, 1905), p. 110.   [2] *Nation*, 6 Mar. 1875.
[3] *Nation*, 13 and 20 Mar. 1875.   [4] 'Hooper narrative', p. 39 (D.P.).

old Home Government Association was replaced by the Home Rule League which seemed to promise a more active policy, Dillon became a member of it, though for some time to come a very passive member. But in 1875 a new star rose on the horizon when Charles Stewart Parnell succeeded to Martin's vacant seat in Meath. Almost from the moment of his arrival at Westminster Parnell seems to have grasped the futility of Butt's respectful and elaborately constitutional methods. He determined to attract attention to Ireland's needs by making it difficult, if not impossible, for the House of Commons to transact English business. In this policy of 'obstruction' he gathered round him a small group of resolute men, some of them recent recruits from Fenianism, and soon not only transformed the role of Irish nationalists at Westminster, but split the Home Rule movement down the middle.

These events, which were ultimately to change the whole course of Dillon's life, had no immediate effect upon him at all, and it was not until 1877 that he moved further into public life. Indeed, it almost seemed for a while that the Tipperary election had been a flash-in-the-pan and that he had become involved in it out of filial piety rather than from any deep-seated political conviction. Nothing could be further from the truth. His abstinence from politics during 1876 was not voluntary—it was caused by a serious relapse in his health. It is difficult even now to be sure what it was that was fundamentally wrong with him. He still suffered from his eyes and from dyspepsia, but in addition to this he had an internal, or intestinal, complaint which he himself tried to diagnose in page after page of his diary and which he also tried to mend by a series of outlandish and drastic experiments. It seems, in fact, to have been some form of infection of the colon—he himself complained repeatedly of what he called a 'restriction' or 'blockage' of the colon, and there were moments when he feared it would be incurable. There were other, and even worse moments, when he feared a loss of control of his bodily functions and looked forward to a hideous future of physical and mental degeneration. Yet at the same time he was still consumed by his thirst for universal knowledge. He was immersed in Bacon's *Advancement of Learning* ('here I have discovered a philosopher whom I would call divine if that were no impiety'), but divided his homage between that and Berkeley's *Principles of Human Knowledge*. 'It is the subtlest, clearest, most exquisitely written and most sublime book which I have ever read.'[1] And in the same month as these entries occurs a list of books to be ordered on his next visit to Dublin. It includes an edition of the *Arabian Nights*, George Sand's *Histoire de ma vie*, a note to 'find out about Norse literature' and, more ominously, one volume on *Functions and disorders of the reproductive organs* and another on *Diseases of the rectum*.[2]

[1] Diary of John Dillon, 18 and 27 Oct. 1876 (D.P.).

[2] Ibid., 31 Oct. 1876. The first of these books, William Acton's *Functions and disorders of the reproductive organs* (London, 1857), was almost a Victorian classic. Acton himself was a pioneer in the study of sex. For his work, see Steven Marcus, *The other Victorians* (New York, 1966), and Brian Harrison, 'Underneath the Victorians', in *Victorian Studies* (Mar. 1967), x. 239–62.

For the remainder of 1876 he continued to be haunted by this mysterious disease which by November had reduced him to asking himself this question: 'Whether it would not be wiser for me to apply myself to face the idea of death and strive to rob it of its terrors?'[1] But this was hard to do and a few days later there was another despairing outburst prompted by the dread of an incurable malady. 'Alas against such terrors as this all steelings of the heart are absolutely useless. Of what avail is it to tell a man that he ought not to think about it when his mind is made a blank for all things else? Oh, no man who has not felt it can *conceive* what it is when the world within is blotted . . . I can make no better effort to give an idea of it than by comparing it . . . to the blotting out of a beautiful [view] of Killiney Bay dancing in a summer sun with its lovely strand [and] beauteous mountains by a damp sea fog.'[2] Living mainly at Killiney, as he was at this time, he was a good deal isolated from society and this accentuated his tendency towards introspection and the solitary life. Consider, for example, the mode of existence revealed by this entry only three days later:

Get up at 9.
9½–10 breakfast, one cup of tea and two rounds of toast.
10–12 read.
12–1½ walk.
1½–2 lunch—a chop generally.
2–3 read.
Then if I am very tired lie down for an hour.
4 if I could get in the hot water I want to put in [the] bath this would take about half an hour and then half an hour's walk before dinner.
6–6½ dinner and novel or paper.
6½–7¾ work with Chrissie [his sister Christina].
9–10 read with Chrissie.
10 walk down for the *Times*.
10–12 anti-dream book and then dream book.
But all this can be of no avail if my colon be restricted.[3]

This is the régime of an elderly hermit of valetudinarian habits rather than of the romantic, passionate young man he really was. It seems clear enough, certainly, that Dillon, despite his enthusiasm for medicine, was precisely the type of student whom it is most dangerous to introduce to the detailed description and analysis of disease. And, at bottom, he seems to have known it himself. 'Hypochondria', he wrote later that same night, 'I will track that direful word through the history of the wretched race of men. O word laden with groans, coming down through long ages ghastly with *degrading* wretchedness of innumerable god-like beings.'

The narrative of his ailments continues into 1877 and 1878, but it is evident from his diary that, despite sometimes severe relapses, he was slowly getting better. The references to his colon first diminish and then almost disappear, though without reference to any specific cure. We do not know what happened to improve his health in this respect and it may

---

[1] Ibid., 27 Nov. 1876.   [2] Ibid., 1 Dec. 1876.   [3] Ibid., 4 Dec. 1876.

not even have been a permanent improvement—ten years later eminent doctors were still diagnosing what they liked to call 'intestinal catarrh' and of course he remained acutely susceptible to dyspepsia—but this may be the place to record a fact which was known only to his family, and indeed not known even to his children until after his death, that at some point in youth or early manhood he had suffered a rupture and for much of his adult life was obliged to wear a truss. It is not clear when he was first affected by this, but some of the symptoms he describes belong more obviously to this than to his suspected colitis, and there is some evidence from early 1877 that he had begun to realise this himself, for in January his diary had a note headed 'prevention of hernia . . . a subject on which I must make investigations'.[1] It is perhaps not altogether a coincidence that these were also the years when his addiction to violent exercise disappears. Whatever be the explanation of his illness and of his partial recovery, the fact of the disability must never be forgotten when the extraordinary outbursts of sustained activity in his later career come to be considered. These were only made possible by a reckless expenditure of painfully acquired energy and they had always to be paid for by a physical reaction of one kind or another. That he should have been able to lead the life he did lead, and to conceal this weakness from his closest friends and colleagues, indicates not merely that he had conquered his hypochondria, but that he had gone forward from that to cultivate a truly stoical fortitude and a formidable power of mind over body.

(iv)

The immediate consequence of recovery, even partial recovery, was that his interest in politics rapidly revived. One sign of this was his close involvement in the affairs of the newly founded Society for the Preservation of the Irish Language, of which in 1877 his brother William became treasurer and he himself a member of the Council.[2] One of John Dillon's achievements was to introduce Isaac Butt into the Society and a letter still survives in which the veteran leader wrote that to do something for 'the grand old language' had always been 'one of my dreams, as I must call projects which, in the multitude of work that is forced upon me I am compelled to cast aside with a vague hope of some day realising them.'[3] This letter, characteristic in its ineffectiveness as well as in its friendliness, might well have struck an answering chord in Dillon, for he, too, was full of good intentions about the language which were continually being thwarted by the pressure of events. Just about this very time he made the second of two resolutions to learn Irish, but it does not seem that he ever succeeded in doing so.[4] Nevertheless, he remained deeply attached to the movement, later joined the Gaelic League, encouraged—but did *not* compel—his children to learn it, and before he died had the satisfaction of seeing his son

---

[1] Ibid., 6 Jan. 1877.   [2] *Nation*, 17 Feb., 7 and 21 Apr. 1877.
[3] Isaac Butt to Dillon, 31 Mar. 1877 (D.P.).
[4] Diary of John Dillon, 29 Nov. 1876 and 29 Jan. 1877 (D.P.).

Myles well along the road to becoming one of the foremost Gaelic scholars of his time.

In 1877 the language revival seemed hardly more than a forlorn hope and for more practical purposes Dillon pinned his hopes to two bodies, both of which he joined at this period. One was the Tenant Right Association, derived from an agitation of the 1850s, and although Gladstone's Land Act of 1870 had altered the terms of the problem, it was still set upon its initial and central aim of securing more effective protection for the tenant in his holding. It was not, at this stage of its history, very effective, and it was becoming clear that the only way in which it could hope to realise its programme was through the pressure it might bring to bear upon the Home Rule League. Dillon, as we have seen, had joined the League at its foundation, but it was only in 1877, when the Parnellite policy of obstruction was first fully developed and applied, that he began to grasp the possibilities of parliamentary action. More or less consciously he had been looking for a strong man in politics for some time and the events of that summer convinced him that he had found one. On 31 July, near the end of an exhausting and acrimonious session, Parnell and a handful of supporters, including Joseph Biggar and John O'Connor Power, mounted an obstructive debate that lasted all night and into the afternoon of 1 August.[1] This was in its way a historic episode, since it precipitated a final and decisive breach between Butt, who greatly deprecated such unseemly action, and the young activists who were now making all the running. Dillon immediately recognised it as such and that same day, 1 August, he made this note in his diary: 'This day I mark as the beginning of a new era in the history of Erin. And I wish to have in my room the portraits of the three men who pointed out to Ireland her way to freedom—Parnell, O'Connor Power, Biggar.'[2] And another entry a little later reveals that he had understood completely the central issue posed by the new policy. Parnell, he noted, had incurred criticism for calling it 'a policy of retaliation'. But what did he mean by this? Simply that, whereas English legislation passed easily through Parliament when English Members were agreed that it was in the English interest, Irish legislation did not do so even when it was vital to Ireland and when the overwhelming majority of Irish Members demanded it:

> But what is to be done then to put an end to this state of things which would be ludicrous if it were not so fatally serious a matter to Ireland?
> This is the question we have been asking ourselves since the Union. Mr. Parnell and Mr. Biggar have solved this problem simply and effectively and here is their solution. If Englishmen will persist in preventing us from doing our business, why then let Irishmen inter-

---

[1] For this phase of the obstructionist campaign see David Thornley, 'The Irish home rule party and parliamentary obstruction', I.H.S. (March 1960), xii. 38–57; David Thornley, *Isaac Butt and home rule* (London, 1964), chap. xii; Lawrence J. McCaffrey, 'Irish federalism in the 1870's: a study in conservative nationalism', *Transactions of the American Philosophical Society* (1962), new series, vol. 52, part 6.

[2] Diary of John Dillon, 1 Aug. 1877 (D.P.).

fere in English business too. If they vote down our land bill, why we will kill their education bill with amendments.

This is simply the philosophy of the policy of retaliation. And if the Irish people do not quickly come to understand it and put it in practice, they will very much belie their reputation for intelligence which they have heretofore enjoyed.

By means of following this policy of retaliation the Irish can, if they choose, very rapidly get whatever measures they desire—Home Rule included. And let me add, not in the mutilated and modified form that some bills are now presented with a view to placate the English parliament, but in that form precisely in which the Irish people desire them to be cast.[1]

That Dillon was not merely an academic observer is clear from the fact that in February of 1877 he was elected to the Council of the Home Rule League, and even more so from the fact that Parnell was beginning to consult him on electoral matters and also to write to him very freely about the split inside the Home Rule movement. Thus, in April, when a vacancy occurred in Tipperary, he asked for help in choosing a *working* member. 'Do you know of any such person whom the extreme party would be liable to support? . . . I think with twenty such men here we can have things at our mercy. Please let me know what you think and who you would suggest.'[2] A few months later came a further appeal for aid in electing a new member for Clare and this time Dillon actually went down to the constituency to give what assistance he could.[3]

It is significant that Parnell, even at this early date, should have regarded Dillon, still only 26, as providing a link with 'the extreme party', but in reality Dillon's own position was much more complicated than this. It was true, of course, that his friendship with John Mitchel and his activities during the Tipperary election of 1875 had associated him in many people's minds with extra-parliamentary agitation. But at the same time he was torn between a genuine affection for Butt and a growing belief that Parnell had at last provided a justification for electing men to sit in the House of Commons. And as the rift between the two leaders widened it was this and not 'extreme' politics that occupied him most. 'Question of the hour', he noted in his diary at the end of July 1877, 'how to make Parnell's policy the national platform without giving any room for a split.'[4] But it was not a situation in which neutrality was possible and inevitably he moved more and more on to the side of the young and rising men. He indicated this by helping to organise a demonstration at the Rotunda to greet Parnell and Biggar on their return to Dublin at the end of that crucial session of 1877. Dillon himself spoke at the meeting and went to some pains to explain how a follower of John Mitchel's could find anything good in a parlia-

---

[1] Ibid., about 25 Aug. 1877; he repeated some of these phrases in an open letter in the *Nation*, 1 Sept. 1877.
[2] Parnell to Dillon, 20 April [1877] (D.P.).
[3] Parnell to Dillon, 25 July, 6, 9, 11 Aug. 1877 (D.P.).
[4] Diary of John Dillon, ? July 1877 (D.P.).

mentary policy. 'John Mitchel', he was reported as saying, 'had often re-marked to him that of all the infernal machinery by which the British Government had degraded, demoralised and kept down the Irish people, the most effective was the sham of parliamentary representation. When sitting in the gallery night after night he had often formed the opinion that Mitchel was right, but he believed now that an opportunity for effective parliamentary action had at last arisen and that, if the Irish people were now faithful, freedom was secure.'[1]

In retrospect this can be seen to mark a turning-point in John Dillon's political career, the first clear public statement of his conversion from militant to constitutional nationalism. But at the time it was not so clear even to himself. What appealed to him about Parnell's policy was that it was a policy of attack, and it was to be a long time yet before he, who was to become one of the greatest 'House of Commons men' of his generation, thought of Westminster other than as a place where Irish members made more or less piratical raids to carry off whatever legislation they could under threat of disrupting the entire proceedings of Parliament. Indeed, so far was he from complete acceptance of the constitutional line, even in its advanced Parnellite form, that his diary, at the end of 1877 or early 1878, contains a sketch of quite a different policy. It is an astonishing anticipation by twenty years of the Sinn Fein doctrines of Arthur Griffith and one of the supreme ironies of Dillon's own life that before he had even entered Parliament he should have outlined with such uncanny accuracy the programme which was in 1918 to end his own political career. Here is what he wrote:

> A plan for bringing about the final crisis between England and Ireland, by withdrawing our representation, setting up a parliament in Dublin and obstructing the carrying out of English acts. Avoiding as much as possible an armed collision, but setting on the people to resist carrying out English laws.[2]

At the time this was the merest day-dream, no more realisable than his pursuit of universal knowledge, but when we turn, as we must now do, to consider one of the most painful episodes of his life, his attack upon the sick, ageing and bewildered Isaac Butt, we have to bear in mind that Dillon himself, besides being far from well, was also much confused and uncertain of his future direction, caught in mid-passage between two quite different traditions of nationalism. Butt's biographer has written critically of the younger man's 'self-righteous nationalism', and has described him as having 'like some beautiful and rather dyspeptic bird, swooped upon his victim and savaged him'.[3] To those who look at the quarrel from Butt's point of view this may seem indeed to have been the case, but the tortured and introspective student whose painful odyssey we have followed through

---

[1] *F.J.*, 22 Aug. 1877.

[2] Diary of John Dillon, undated but from internal evidence falling between late 1877 and February 1878 (D.P.). For an earlier precedent see T. W. Moody, 'Irish-American nationalism', in *I.H.S.*, xv, no. 60 (Sept. 1967).

[3] Terence de Vere White, *The road of excess* (Dublin, 1946), pp. 366, 374–5.

his diaries was hardly 'self-righteous', whatever else may be said of him. The violence with which he was now to assail Isaac Butt can be explained partly by the ruthlessness, repeated every generation, with which the young replace their elders, but partly also by the very fact that Dillon was such a new and hesitant convert to parliamentary action. John Mitchel had been until this the guiding star of his life. If he was to desert that star, he must at the very least be assured that the battle to be fought in the House of Commons was a real battle and not a sham. He believed that Parnell offered this assurance and that Butt did not. Therefore Butt had become a brake upon the wheel of progress and must go. It was the familiar, pitiless logic of youth—harsh, certainly, to those who suffered from it, but as natural as life itself and as inexorable.

The quarrel began to come to a head in 1878. The previous August, after the obstruction crisis, Butt had been displaced by Parnell as President of the Home Rule Confederation of Great Britain, but although this was an indication that he was losing ground fast he still had a considerable parliamentary following and many supporters in the Home Rule League itself. However, when in January 1878 a Home Rule Conference assembled in Dublin, Irish affairs had been pushed on one side by the Balkan crisis originating in the Russo-Turkish War of 1877. There seemed for a time a possibility that England might be drawn in and Dillon came to the conference anxious to convert the Home Rule movement to a policy of non-cooperation. He therefore proposed a resolution calling on the parliamentarians to demonstrate that Ireland, while deprived of self-government, could have no 'community of interest' with England in her dealings with foreign powers, by leaving the House in a body before a division on the Balkan crisis was taken. He did not mince his words in proposing the resolution. 'What is necessary to be brought home to the English people,' he said, 'is the reality of our demand for Home Rule and the sternness of our demand to have it.' 'There is nothing that we can do,' he continued, 'not even a repetition of the scenes of '67 [*Applause*] that could more rapidly convince the English people we must have Home Rule than a blow struck on this occasion—a demonstration of Irish nationality in the House at a moment so eventful in the Eastern debate, when the eyes of Europe are attracted to the House of Commons with an interest greater than ever in the memory of living man.'

Butt was utterly appalled and implored Dillon to withdrew his motion, which, if passed, would be 'the death-knell of the Home Rule party'. 'For what does it do? It affirms that we have no common interest with England. How many of the Home Rule League will follow you in that? How many of the clergy will follow you in that?' Moreover, he added, it would be the height of folly to decide to walk out before they knew how the question might come before them. If, for example, 'there was in the Queen's speech that the Government were prepared to grant Home Rule for Ireland, or even some great measure dear to Ireland, such as the improved tenant Bill, do you mean to say, if you were able by a party vote to keep them in power you would not do it?' It was a valid point and it is the measure of Dillon's political immaturity at this time that he should have left himself open to it. In the end Parnell, stepping in between the young man and the consequences of his impetuosity, as he was to do more than once in the years ahead, secured a compromise resolution, recommending the party, in the event of the Eastern question being raised, 'to consult together and carry out as a party a united line of policy and action'.[1] But this barely even papered over the cracks, and when the issue did come up in the new session, not only was the Home Rule partly hopelessly divided, but Butt himself, by voting with the Government, emphasised the differences between him and his assailants. For Dillon, on the other hand, the immediate consequence of this eruption was that he failed to secure re-election to the Council of the Home Rule League in 1878, though he did regain his seat the following year.[2]

By that time, however, many things had changed in Irish politics. During 1878 Butt steadily lost ground and Parnell, in his letters to Dillon, no longer troubled to disguise his contempt for the old leader. In June, explaining that in order to secure the passing of an Irish Intermediate Education Bill, he would try to contrive that the estimates for the Queen's Colleges should not be taken until after the bill was safely through, he added: 'Butt, of course, as usual will want to surrender everything.'[3] Sure enough, two weeks later he had to report the failure of these tactics owing to Butt's arrival at the last minute. 'He, I have reason to believe, has persuaded the Chancellor to take these estimates on Monday and has promised him there shall be no opposition.' And he continued:

> I shall protest against these estimates being taken before the bill has been passed, pointing out that it would never have been introduced but for the threatened opposition to these estimates and that it is madness to throw away our weapons before we have won our battle.[4]

All common ground between Butt and his critics had now disappeared, but it fell to Dillon to deliver the most violent and almost the last attack the old man had to suffer. Significantly, it was again a question of foreign policy which set him in motion—all his life this was to be an area of politics which interested him profoundly. On this occasion it was the outbreak of war with Afghanistan in which, unlike the previous crisis, England was directly involved and which therefore offered exceptional opportunities to Irishmen to make the traditional capital out of England's difficulty. Butt, however, would have none of this, and in the autumn made it publicly known that he would deprecate any Irish amendment to the Address which might have the effect of embarrassing the Government in its war effort. Dillon erupted violently in a letter to the Press from which these are the key sentences:

[1] *F.J.*, 16 Jan. 1878; *Nation*, 19 Jan. 1878.   [2] 'Hooper narrative' (D.P.), p. 48.
[3] Parnell to Dillon, 28 June 1878 (D.P.).   [4] Parnell to Dillon, 13 July 1878 (D.P.).

No honest Irish nationalist can any longer continue to recognise Mr. Butt as leader. In his letter he openly acknowledges that the interests of the British Empire are more to him than the sufferings of the unhappy people who have trusted him as leader only to be betrayed by him in the hour of trial. The only hope that now remains for the country is that Mr. Parnell and the active party will take an independent line of action and openly denounce the monstrous piece of traitorism which is about to be enacted.[1]

In this he spoke for a growing body of opinion and similar protests came from many different quarters. The Council of the Home Rule League, on the other hand, although increasingly impotent, were still faithful to Butt after their fashion and blocked various attempts by his antagonists to force a decision. But this could not go on for ever and when at last a full meeting of the League was held at the beginning of February 1879 the storm broke. Dillon came armed with resolutions calling particularly for a strong policy on the land question and for a parliamentary demonstration to be made against English rule in Ireland by an attack on the constabulary estimates. These were ruled out of order, but when T. D. Sullivan moved what was in effect a vote of no confidence in Butt and called for a stronger line in Parliament, Dillon used this as the opportunity to say what was almost uncontrollably rising up within him:

> I don't want to call Mr. Butt a traitor [he said], and I tell you so for this reason—he is getting no *quid pro quo*. I don't believe Mr. Butt is a person who would sell the cause. Far from it. Let no one suppose it gives me gratification to have to speak in this way. God knows I never felt a task more miserable. For a long period I loved and trusted Mr. Butt. But Mr. Butt has invited free speech. I speak my belief and I assert that he has turned his back on the principles which he enunciated at the conference of 1874 [*sic*] . . .[2]

Butt replied to this charge, which meant in effect that he had surrendered the parliamentary independence of his party to suit the needs of the Government of the day, and had entered into unbecoming negotiations with Ministers, in an emotional speech which contrived to be both dignified and exasperating. He still had sufficient support to secure a form of words, similar to the call for united action that had been agreed on the previous year, which considerably softened the impact of Sullivan's amendment. Yet even this was only passed by thirty two votes to twenty four and Parnell, Biggar and Dillon were all in the minority. Butt left the meeting a beaten man. Already ill, he declined very rapidly, and by May he was dead. The way was at last clear for younger men to launch the Home Rule movement on a new course from which the dead leader would have turned in horror. And although Dillon was more inexperienced than many at that crucial

[1] *F.J.*, 2 Dec. 1878.
[2] *F.J.*, 5 Feb. 1879. Dillon was referring to the meeting of Irish M.P.s on 3 March 1874 when they resolved to act as 'a separate and distinct party in the House of Commons' (*Nation*, 7 Mar. 1874).

conference and was still outside the parliamentary circle, there was one passage in his speech against Butt in which not only did he lay down a doctrine that was to be central to his own policy for many years, but he spoke also for all those who were tired of stagnation and parliamentary bowing and scraping and longed for an active, fighting policy. Starting from the assertion that 'the adoption of a mere policy of redress of grievances is a crushing out of the nationality of Ireland', he contrasted Butt's speeches— 'when he was really Mr. Butt'—with the sorry spectacle of the last two or three years:

> Instead of demanding our national rights as rights unquestionable, all that was sought for was an inquiry, as if any inquiry was needed. Good God! is not the very fact of asking the English Parliament a lowering of the national flag. But even that motion for an inquiry is thrust into the background and the whole attention of the party is turned to the redress of grievances, and in the redress of grievances, there are always compromises to be made between the demands of the Irish people and the prejudices of the English nation. But is not that a selling of the principle of Home Rule? That principle is that Ireland should make the laws which are to rule Ireland . . . I maintain that seeking to influence the public opinion of England is of no use. If they resist our just demand for Home Rule we should make them feel our resentment.[1]

It was a new voice, speaking for a new generation, demanding a new policy. The young man from the provinces no longer stood outside life, seeking to enter. He had arrived.

[1] *F.J.*, 5 Feb. 1879.

2

The Land War:
First Phase

If Dillon wanted a new policy which should be a real, fighting policy, the basis for it was staring him in the face, since by 1879 it was clear for all to see that the land question was once more in ferment. In this, indeed, there was nothing surprising, since the problems of landlord and tenant had run like a red thread through Irish history since the Union. The Famine, though in one sense it might have been expected to ease the problem by the depopulation it caused, had proved to be only the most extreme outbreak of a deep-seated disease and not its cure. The disease was complicated in its origins and almost beyond the wit of man to mend, but its consequences for the peasantry, who formed the great majority of the population of Ireland, were all too painfully obvious. In the seventies the Irish land problem was essentially twofold, though the two aspects were interrelated. It was a problem of insecurity and also a problem of incipient starvation. The insecurity arose from the fact that the tenant—and the vast majority of small farmers were tenants—had no proper security in his holding. In parts of the north, it is true, the 'Ulster custom' had given him some rudimentary rights of compensation for disturbance and for improvements he might have made on his farm. Gladstone's 1870 Act had tried to confirm these rights and give similar protection to the rest of the country. But that legislation had proved a disappointing failure. Gladstone had hoped to make the unsavoury business of eviction so expensive that landlords would hesitate to use it. 'The policy of the Bill is this,' he explained to Cardinal Manning, 'to prevent the landlord from using this terrible weapon of undue and unjust eviction by so framing the handle that it shall cut his hands with the sharp edge of pecuniary damages.'[1]

But what was undue and unjust eviction? The Act of 1870, under the influence of the House of Lords, merely defined this as eviction following the failure of the tenant to pay 'exorbitant' rents. As might have been expected, the courts, in various rulings, adopted an elastic interpretation of 'exorbitant'. Unfortunately, this was only part of the trouble. Ireland, within a few years of the passing of the Act of 1870, was deep in the trough

[1] J. L. Hammond, *Gladstone and the Irish nation* (London, new impression, 1964), p. 100.

of agricultural depression. Prices of farm produce declined sharply and, since the depression was affecting Britain also, so did the earnings of the migrant agricultural labour upon which many Irish families depended to eke out the meagre living they scratched from the inhospitable soil at home. Some idea of the scale of the problem may be gathered from the official statistics, which indicated a decline in the value of the principal crops produced between 1876 and 1879 of nearly £14 million and for the people of Connaught alone a loss of earnings from England of £250,000 in the single year 1879.[1] Desperate for money, they had recourse to their usual last line of defence—the banks for the more prosperous, the village money-lender or 'gombeen-man' for the mass of poorer tenants. But this credit, at best precarious, did not last long, and soon it proved impossible for many farmers to pay the ordinary rents which even a sympathetic court might have hesitated to call exorbitant. Failure to pay brought with it the inevitable consequence of eviction, and eviction produced its inevitable crop of outrages, including the maiming of cattle and the burning of hay-ricks and farm buildings, the attempted, or sometimes actual, assassination of landlords and their agents, and the even more deadly, because inward and secret, village vendettas against the 'land-grabber' who was brazen enough to take a farm from which another had been evicted.

And so the dreary cycle revolved—not new, but aggravated in its consequences by the prevailing depression. Unhappily this general economic malaise was accompanied in several parts of Ireland by actual starvation, especially in the west, where despite the decline of population, caused by the Famine thirty years before, too many families were still trying to win a livelihood from the bogs and mountains and stony land. So backward were these unfortunate people that they still, like their fathers before them, depended upon the potato for their staple food, and the potato, though normally fertile and prolific enough, was vulnerable to the wet summers so frequent in that part of the world. Such summers there had been in 1877 and 1878 and now again, in 1879, the crop was threatened in the south and west of the country, where many thousands of families faced the possibility that, unless something was done to aid them, they might die of hunger. Where the crop in 1876 had amounted to over 4 million tons and had been valued at nearly £12½ million, in 1879 it declined in quantity to just over 1 million tons and in value to less than £3½ million.[2]

Poor and helpless as they were, these people, left to themselves, might well have relapsed into that fatal apathy which in the forties had preceded and accompanied death on an appalling scale. But this time they were not to be left alone. Long ago, in the shadow of the Famine, James Fintan Lalor, perhaps the most original mind among the Young Irelanders, had pointed out that the land question was, or could become, the key to national

[1] *Preliminary report on the returns of agricultural produce in Ireland in 1879* [c. 2495], 1880, table V, p. 899; statement by W. N. Hancock to the Statistical Society reported in *Evening Mail*, 28 Jan. 1880; see also N. D. Palmer, *The Irish Land League crisis* (New Haven and London, 1940), p. 64.

[2] *Preliminary report on the returns of agricultural produce in Ireland in 1879*, table V.

regeneration.[1] That prophecy was now to be fulfilled, mainly through the agency of a young Fenian, Michael Davitt. Davitt (born, like Parnell, in 1846) was five years older than Dillon, with whose life his own was to be closely intertwined at many points, and by 1879 already had much harsh experience behind him. His family had been evicted from their Mayo farm and had migrated to Lancashire, where the young Davitt had gone to work as a child-labourer in a factory, losing an arm in an industrial accident when only 11 years old. He remained passionately attached to his native land and as a young man was drawn almost inevitably into the Irish Republican Brotherhood. He acted as an arms agent for the organisation, was arrested in 1870 and, on the unfounded suspicion that he had been concerned in an assassination plot, received the savage sentence of fifteen years' penal servitude. Released in 1877 on ticket-of-leave, he at once rejoined the I.R.B., but although this in itself suggests that he still looked to total separation from England as the final goal, he had, according to his own subsequent account, begun during his imprisonment to move towards the idea that before this distant objective could be achieved it was necessary to put 'more immediate issues' before the people.

But his own account may be misleading, and recent scholarship tends to place his conversion to a policy of co-operation between revolutionary and constitutional nationalists *after* his release from prison. Visiting America in 1878, Davitt found that some of the most advanced nationalists, hoping apparently to celebrate the coming centenary of Grattan's constitution of 1782 with some striking manifestation, were impatient to launch out in a new direction. This new direction, defined by John Devoy, who took a large share in formulating it, as a 'new departure', envisaged that extremists would work with parliamentarians to obtain reforms—specifically the abolition of landlordism—but on the understanding that when the right moment arrived the parliamentarians would combine with the extremists to bring about a political revolution, by force if necessary. Who really deserved the credit for the new departure and what precisely it meant to the different participants are questions still disputed by historians, though most would agree that Parnell, while negotiating with Devoy and Davitt, and eventually throwing his influence behind the land agitation, avoided committing himself to a hard-and-fast alliance with the American Fenians to achieve their ultimate and highly visionary aims. For the biographer of John Dillon, however, it is sufficient to record that by the spring of 1879, not only were Davitt and Devoy thinking along the same lines, but the first tentative steps had been taken towards framing concerted action with Parnell, who was already watching the critical agrarian situation very carefully.[2]

[1] See especially the article 'To the Confederate and Repeal Clubs in Ireland, (January 1847) in L. Fogarty (ed.), *James Fintan Lalor, patriot and political essayist, 1807–49* (Dublin, 1918), pp. 67–83.

[2] T. W. Moody, 'The New Departure in Irish politics, 1878–79' in T. W. Moody and D. B. Quinn, *Essays in British and Irish history in honour of James Eadie Todd* (London, 1949). See also T. N. Brown, *Irish-American nationalism* (Philadelphia, 1966), chap. 5, and T. W. Moody's review of that book in *I.H.S.* xv, no. 60 (Sept. 1967).

No development could more exactly have coincided with Dillon's hopes and ambitions. His father's record on the land question, his personal knowledge of conditions in the west, his membership of the Tenants Defence Association, all inclined him towards an agrarian movement. Indeed, A. M. Sullivan of the *Nation*, who knew him well, wrote a few years later that long before Parnell had taken up the land agitation 'Mr Dillon had been of opinion that it was upon this question of land the national struggle would essentially have to be fought out'.[1] This may perhaps be crediting him with too much foresight, but it certainly appears from his diary that as early as 1877 he was much preoccupied with the problem, for in August of that year he made the following notes: 'To gain a thorough knowledge of the land question and plan a bold campaign for next year', 'motion to prevent increase of rent until question is settled', 'short bill to gain fixity of tenure at present rent'.[2] Since he was still very much an outsider at that time these jottings, though they anticipate very strikingly at least part of the policy Davitt was soon to pursue, had no immediate application. And when the land movement did get under way in the spring of 1879 the initiative rested not with Dillon but with Davitt, and after him with Parnell. It was on 20 April that Davitt held at Irishtown, in County Mayo, the first of what was to be a series of land meetings in the west. In June, Parnell accepted an invitation to attend one of these at Westport, ignoring the Archbishop of Tuam's warning to him to keep away, but it was not until 13 July at Claremorris that Dillon's fragile health allowed him to make his first contribution. At that meeting he had charge of a resolution calling upon all nationalist Members of Parliament 'to demand with firmness, perseverance and obstructive force when necessary, the redress of those grievances which affect the agricultural classes', and pledging those outside Parliament 'to strengthen the hands of our representatives by continued salutary and vigorous action'. This was vague enough to mean anything from passing resolutions to shooting landlords, but Dillon made it very clear in his speech that no appeals for justice in Parliament would have any effect unless backed by strong pressure from without. What kind of pressure? No doubt there were hungry and desperate men present who would have been glad enough to hear him suggest physical force. But, young and ardent as he was, this was a solution he was not prepared to recommend, though, as he made plain, his objection to it was practical rather than moral. 'He was against physical force at present,' he was reported as saying, 'because there was too much physical force against them. They had no rifles, while the Government had thousands of their fellow countrymen [he meant the armed Royal Irish Constabulary] to oppose them. They had, therefore, only to look to Parliament, where a man had arisen who had shown the Irish people a method by which they could win all their rights, and although that man was a landlord, he was not inclined to turn him out. That man was Charles Stewart Parnell.'[3]

[1] A. M. Sullivan, *New Ireland* (London, 1882 ed.), p. 441.
[2] Diary of John Dillon, about 20 Aug. 1877 (D.P.).   [3] *F.J.*, 14 July 1879.

This speech, the very first of all the hundreds he was to deliver in the land war, reveals strikingly some of his most deeply and most permanently held convictions. That agitation was the key to success, that physical force was not justified against overwhelming odds, that the parliamentary party must be vigorous and obstructive, these were ideas that were to remain with him all his life. Even his qualified acceptance of Parnell—that he was a worthy leader *though* a landlord—expressed that innate hostility towards the landowning class which he kept to the very end.

Yet there was no immediate sequel to his fiery beginning. Dillon was not present when Davitt formally launched the Land League of Mayo at Castlebar on 16 August, and although he was at Ballaghaderrin in September when John O'Connor Power addressed a meeting, he is not reported as speaking again himself until 5 October.[1] On that day he was at Maryborough, warning the farmers that the real test of their capacity of organise and endure would come after the November rent demands. He urged them to avoid outrage, to combine as much as possible, to offer their landlords a rent reduced by 50 to 60 per cent and, if this were refused, to pay no rent at all. Remorselessly, he followed out the logic of this suggestion, foreshadowing what was to become a central feature of the agitation in the months ahead. A tenant who paid no rent would, he said, no doubt receive notice to quit. But his fellows 'must put a ban on his land'. 'If any man then takes up that land let no man speak to him or have any business transactions with him.'[2] Here, more than a year before the incident which gave it its name, was the principle of boycotting laid down in all its stark simplicity.

In the same issue of the *Nation* which reported this speech, Dillon was mentioned as a possible parliamentary candidate for Queen's County, the constituency where the speech had been delivered. This evoked from him a curiously enigmatic letter in which he said that he had hoped to stand for another county [Tipperary] with which he had close ties, but, he added, 'recent circumstances in connection with my private affairs have made this impossible, and rendered it necessary for me to leave this country for some years'. There is nothing in his papers, admittedly very scanty for these early years, to indicate what the 'recent circumstances' were, but almost certainly he was referring to the state of his health. We know from his diaries up to 1878 (they cease for the time being in 1879) how constantly his health preoccupied him and how often he was actually ill. With his family history tuberculosis was always a possibility, and the necessity of seeking a healthier, drier climate hung over him constantly during these years.

Eventually, as we shall see, he had to yield to this compulsion, but in 1879 the mood of despondency soon passed. He flung himself with a kind of febrile energy—in itself suspect—once more into the work of the agitation, and when the national Land League was formed in Dublin only three weeks later he and his brother William were elected members of the com-

[1] *Nation*, 7 Sept. 1879.   [2] *Nation*, 11 Oct. 1879.

mittee.[1] The objects of the League had gradually become more clearly
defined since Davitt had first raised its standard in the west. Essentially,
they were twofold. In the long run, and as the final objective, 'the land of
Ireland for the people of Ireland'—that is, the creation of a genuine peasant
proprietary. But in the short run, and as a matter of dire urgency, the
protection of the tenant against excessive rents and against eviction for
failure to pay such rents. What the League leaders aimed to do was to
persuade the tenants, in Parnell's famous phrase, 'to keep a firm grip of
their homesteads', by organising amongst themselves a refusal to pay
'unjust' rents (which in any given case the League was prepared to assist in
defining) and by agreeing not to take farms from which their fellows had
been—again 'unjustly'—evicted. Thus, by disrupting the normal landlord-
tenant relationship, they hoped to bring the landlords to a realisation that
it was in their own interest to adjust their rents to the capacity of the tenants
to pay.

Implicit in this agitation, however, was nothing less than a strike against
rent, and since to advocate such a course could be construed as an attack
upon property—Davitt, for one, made no secret of the fact that he stood
ultimately for 'the abolition of landlordism'—those who spoke in that
sense left themselves open to the counter-stroke of the law. At the beginning of November, Dillon attended a meeting at Gurteen where Davitt
and several other speakers used precisely this kind of language.[2] Just two
weeks later three of the speakers—Davitt himself, a journalist, James Daly,
and J. B. Killen (or Killeen)—were arrested. At once a protest meeting
was held in Dublin at which Parnell and Dillon were the main speakers.
Dillon launched a passionate attack on the Government for its refusal to
admit the existence of famine conditions in the west and charged the
authorities with arresting Davitt and his friends not for what they had said,
but because 'they stood between a cold-hearted and remorseless Government . . . and a starving people'.[3]

With this speech, and with Davitt's temporary removal from the scene,
Dillon began to emerge as Parnell's principal lieutenant in the land war
he now seemed bent on pushing as far and as fast as he could. From Dublin
they went together to Balla in County Mayo, where evictions were scheduled
to take place. They succeeded in halting the evictions (though only for the
time being) and in doing so demonstrated the undeniable power that a
mass agitation could generate. But how was that power to be used? Inciting
hungry and desperate men to pay no rent was a dangerous game. How long
could this pent-up force be used only for moral suasion? How soon would
it boil over into actual violence? This was the problem Parnell faced during
the next two years, and he balanced between extremism and moderation
with, on the whole, remarkable skill, losing neither his nerve nor his judgement. Dillon was younger, more impulsive, more passionate, but it is clear

[1] Michael Davitt, *The fall of feudalism in Ireland* (London and New York, 1904),
p. 173.
[2] *F.J.*, 4 Nov. 1879.   [3] *F.J.*, 22 Nov. 1879.

even from these early meetings that, although some particular incident or evidence of suffering was liable to sweep him off his balance, Parnell's policy had gone far towards convincing him intellectually. At that same Balla meeting, for example, even though it was an indignation meeting called to protest against evictions, he asked whether they ought to use violence. He answered his own question with an uncompromising negative —again, not because he disapproved of force, but because it would merely lead to the suppression of the movement by greater force. The weapon they must use, he urged, repeating this next day at Swinford, was the organised pressure of public opinion, so that 'no man would dare to take a farm from which there had been an eviction'.[1]

How long Dillon could have walked this tightrope between advising tenants to pay no unjust rent, but at the same time to use no violence, it is impossible to tell, for at this point his career took an unexpected turn. It was decided that he should accompany Parnell on a special mission to the United States, and a few days after attending Davitt's farcical trial at Sligo (where the Government had to drop the prosecution when it became obvious that no jury would convict) the two emissaries sailed for America. Leaving Ireland just before Christmas, they had ten stormy days at sea, most of which Dillon spent below decks. Always a poor sailor even when crossing the Irish Sea, he found the Atlantic in midwinter unmitigated torment. It was his first adult visit to the United States and there were many who were eager to see John Blake Dillon's son, but almost from the beginning the mission ran into difficulties. Their main object was to raise funds for the League and for the starving families of the west, but they had also, naturally, to devote much of their time to the important but delicate business of convincing Irish-American audiences that the land agitation was not a deviation from the national struggle, but a vital and integral part of it. It was the money-raising aspect of their activities that caused them most difficulty, for when they arrived in America there were already two other funds competing for subscriptions for famine relief—one launched by the Duchess of Marlborough (wife of the Lord Lieutenant) and the other, the Mansion House Fund, under the auspices of the Lord Mayor of Dublin. It was unfortunate that the Lord Mayor, E. D. Gray, happened not only to be a nationalist M.P. of moderate views, but also the owner of the *Freeman's Journal*. He was not pleased to find yet another fund in competition with his own, and one consequence of this was that the Parnell mission did not get the kind of coverage that might have been expected from the principal national newspapers.[2]

However, despite these domestic bickerings, Americans were certainly eager to see and hear Parnell. He and Dillon were plunged at once into an orgy of meetings culminating in Parnell's speech to Congress. On most of these occasions Dillon, understandably, played second fiddle and in the

---

[1] *F.J.*, 24 Nov. 1879.

[2] For this rivalry see especially the leader in *F.J.*, 25 Feb. 1880, and the attack on the *Freeman* in the *Nation*, 28 Feb. 1880.

Irish newspapers his speeches were generally reported very briefly. But on one occasion at least, as Parnell liked to recall, his lieutenant's contribution came less from what he said than from how he looked. Throughout his life he was always very thin for a man of his height (he was 6 ft. 2 in.), but at this particular time, with the threat of serious illness never far away, his haggard features, white face and dark eyes made an immediate impression on all who met him. Thus, at one of their western meetings, after both had spoken and the hat had gone round, the Governor of the State remarked that he had been moved to subscribe not by Parnell but by Dillon. 'Parnell didn't impress me a bit,' he said. 'When I saw this sleek young dude, as well fed as you or I and a damn sight better groomed, I said to myself: "The idea of sending out a man like that to tell us they are all starving!" But when the other man, poor Dillon, came along, with hunger written on every line of his face, I said, "Ah! that's a different thing. There's the Irish famine right enough." '[1]

The burden of these mass meetings, interspersed with strenuous travel and even more strenuous American hospitality, was very heavy, and for Dillon it was much increased by the fact that, since Parnell never put pen to paper if he could avoid it, most of the secretarial work fell upon him. Later in life, when he had become the complete professional, he would have taken this in his stride, but in 1880 he was altogether too inexperienced and it became necessary to send for help. The man chosen was Timothy Healy, then only 23 years old, but already making himself invaluable to Parnell as the Parliamentary Correspondent of the *Nation* (Healy was related directly and by marriage to the Sullivans, who owned the paper) and already bent upon a political career. When he arrived near the end of February he found things better than he had been led to believe, but he quickly realised that the correspondence had got very much out of hand. Healy was at once taken in tow by John Devoy and, even more formidably, by Parnell's two sisters, Fanny and Anna, both intransigent nationalists, but entirely lacking their brother's coolness and judgement. It was Fanny who laid the blame for the confusion upon Dillon, partly because he had left his slippers in one hotel and his nightshirt in another, which, she argued, was evidence of general disorganisation.[2] It was, in fact, evidence only of lifelong inability to control the small, insistent details of daily existence, but it was true, nevertheless, that Healy's quick wit and powers of rapid and intensive work did a great deal to relieve the strain.

Healy had not very long arrived before word came from home that Parliament had been dissolved. Parnell at once returned to Ireland for what was certain to be a crucial general election. At the time he left the mission had raised about £26,000, most of it for the relief of distress, but it was decided that, although Healy should go back with him, Dillon should stay on in America to keep up the momentum of the tour. His main function was to bridge the gap between Parnell's departure and the arrival of

---

[1] William O'Brien, *Recollections*, p. 239 n.
[2] T. M. Healy, *Letters and leaders of my day* (London, 1928), i. 80–81.

Michael Davitt and to prepare the way for what was to be Davitt's chief
preoccupation—the extension of the Land League organisation to the
United States. In these latter meetings, therefore, Dillon's emphasis was
less on distress (which was, indeed, well catered for by the various funds)
than on the long-term aims of the League. 'The ultimate object of the
Irish Land League', he explained in New York at the end of March 1880,
'is to bring it within the power of every Irish farmer to acquire possession
of his own farm.' In the meantime, of course, demands for excessive rent had
to be resisted. If the harvest was bad next year, he dared not contemplate
what would happen, but even if it was good they must make sure that the
food was not sent out of the country, lest the threat of famine return. 'The
doctrine we teach is—let no man pay his rent if that payment will leave his
wife and family in starvation.'[1]

(ii)

He remained in America until July, overlapping with Davitt for about two
months, and then returned home to an Ireland which, though this might
not have been immediately apparent, had undergone a political revolution.
The general election had been a personal triumph for Parnell, not only in
that he had himself been returned for three seats, but because the number of
new, active Members who looked to him for leadership had been considerably
increased. Correspondingly, there was a decline in the strength of the old-
style, conservative or 'Whiggish' Home Rulers of the type which had dominated Irish representation under Butt. The new Members were numerous
enough to secure the election of Parnell as chairman of the party, but the
balance between old and new was still fairly evenly distributed. Parnell, it
has been reckoned, could not count with certainty in the early summer of
1880 upon more than twenty-four Irish Members as against twenty-one
unrepentant Whigs; the scales were held by fourteen uncommitted Members, most of whom, however, were gradually drawn over to the Parnellite
side as time went on.[2] Dillon, in his absence, had been elected as one of the
Members for Tipperary, coupled with P. J. Smyth, who ranked as a Whig,
but a more reputable one than many, since in years gone by he had had
connections with Young Ireland. What the Irish Home Rulers might do in
the House of Commons was a very open question, for the election had
returned Gladstone to power at the head of his second ministry. He was
known to be concerned about Ireland, he might even translate this concern
into beneficial legislation, and so the first months of the new Parliament
were allowed to pass quietly enough, the Irish Members watching events
at Westminster, the agrarian agitation simmering, but by no means ex-
tinguished, at home. The main aim of Parnell and his immediate following
was to extract from the Government some promise of redress for evicted
tenants. A private Member's Bill to this effect attracted such support that

---

[1] *Nation*, 17 Apr. 1880.
[2] C. Cruise O'Brien, *Parnell and his party* (London, 1957), pp. 25–6.

3. John and Christine Dillon

4. John Dillon in early manhood
(*undated drawing by Edward Clifford*)

in June the Government substituted for it its own Compensation for Disturbance Bill, the essence of which was that certain classes of distressed evicted tenants might be compensated out of the Irish Church surplus. Irish nationalist Members of all persuasions joined in supporting this and on 26 July it passed its third reading and was sent to the House of Lords. That House, with extreme foolhardiness, rejected it on 3 August.[1]

It is against this background of studious parliamentary moderation brought to nothing by the action of the House of Lords that the reappearance of John Dillon in Irish politics must be seen. The first speeches he made on his return echoed what he had been saying before he left America—that if 1880 turned out to be another famine year the people must 'hold the harvest' or, where the harvest had failed, they must at least not pay rents—'Any attempt,' he said, 'to levy rent for a year of famine must be met with a stern and desperate resistance.'[2] And a few days later (26 July) he returned to the same theme, but with a significant variation, inspired perhaps by his distaste for the fund-raising aspect of his American tour. It was time, he told his audience, to stop thinking about charity, and the report of his speech continued: 'His desire was so great to put an end beggary and the distribution of relief that he felt inclined to say on behalf of the Land League of Ireland that the time for relief was at an end and the time for the people to secure food for themselves—the time to help themselves—had come.'[3]

Immediately after this he crossed to London to enter for the first time as an elected Member the House he was to come to know and love so well and where he was to spend so much of his life. And since, in his earliest days there, he established a reputation for being one of the wild men of the left, it is worth recording that his first intervention in debate reflected not the uncompromising public man, but the fastidious, bookish scholar he was in private. Why was it, he asked, breaking into a discussion of the Civil Service Estimates, that the British Museum received an annual grant of £118,000 whereas the National Library of Ireland got only £2,000? 'That,' he observed, 'was an entirely insufficient sum and the consequence was that the National Library of Ireland was a disgrace to Ireland and most inconvenient to every student in the city of Dublin.'[4]

These preliminary courtesies over, it was not long before he gave the House a taste of different metal. On 10 August, after the Lords had rejected the Compensation for Disturbance Bill, he warned Members that a dangerous situation was developing in Ireland and that there might be 'bloodshed and massacre' to come.[5] He then returned to Ireland and delivered at Kildare a speech which made him famous—or notorious—

[1] For these events see Cruise O'Brien, op. cit., pp. 36–50.
[2] *Nation*, 24 July 1880.
[3] *Nation*, 31 July 1880.
[4] Hansard, H.C. Debates, 3rd series, vol. 254, col. 2052. His first recorded words in Parliament were three questions he asked earlier the same day on behalf of Parnell (ibid., cols. 1946–8).
[5] Ibid., vol. 255, col. 786.

overnight. It has been described as 'a one-man New Departure', and so, in a sense, it was, for it was the most explicit statement made by any responsible Irish leader up to that time in favour of a general strike against rent. Dillon's bitterness against the ineffectiveness, as he saw it, of parliamentary action overflowed, and the whole burden of his speech was to urge the farmers to organise, organise, organise. In every parish, he said, 'two active young men' should visit each farmer who was still outside the League and persuade him to join it. The farmers should then march to their meetings in good order and 'let the word go out that no farm from which any man had been evicted should be touched or used for human purposes until its rightful owner was put back upon the soil'. Then came the passage which was to reverberate across the Irish Sea:

> When they should have enrolled 300,000 members of the League, if the landlords should persist in refusing the moderate demands of the people, they would give out the word to the people of Ireland to strike against rent altogether and pay no more until justice was done to them . . . In the meantime, the representatives of the people could paralyse the hand of the government and prevent them from passing laws that would throw the people into prison for organising themselves. They could obstruct the passing of coercive laws and set the people free to drill themselves and organise themselves . . . They had a right to march to their meetings and to obey the commands of their leaders if they chose to do so. They would see that every man in Ireland had a right to have a rifle if he liked. All he could say way that if the manhood of Ireland was not enough when they had their rights to win their freedom and put down landlordism, then he should be ashamed to call himself an Irishman.[1]

This speech, though it clearly suffered in reporting, is of crucial significance for several reasons. First, it indicates how far to the left Dillon stood at that moment. In fact, of all the new men elected in 1880 under Parnell's shadow, he was, again at that moment, the most extreme. Just four days before the speech was delivered Superintendent Mallon of the Dublin Metropolitan Police had made that diagnosis already quoted—that Dillon, in his opinion, was 'a cool Fenian'. After reading the speech he might well have wondered if 'cool' was the *mot juste*, and even though, as we have seen, no direct connection between Dillon and the I.R.B. has ever been established, it remains true that he received, then and afterwards, the respect of John Devoy and other 'extreme men', and that for that reason, if for no other, he was a legitimate object of police curiosity. But the speech not only exhibited his extremism, it also indicated that while he might call himself a Parnellite he had so far only absorbed the obstructionist side of Parnell's parliamentary technique. Parnell, indeed, was at this very time pondering another obstructive campaign, but he was anxious not to have to use it except as a last resort. Dillon, on the other hand, seemed to be thinking of parliamentary action solely in obstructionist terms and to regard

[1] *F.J.*, 17 Aug. 1880: *Nation*, 21 Aug. 1880.

Westminster as a place where an Irish Member came mainly to register angry protests.

And here was the third and perhaps the most significant aspect of the Kildare outburst. It announced, no doubt unintentionally at this stage, that here was a new Member who was not amenable either to parliamentary conventions or to party discipline, who represented in his own person the elemental force of agrarian revolt, and who was therefore an unpredictable and explosive factor in the extraordinarily complex situation in which Parnell was involved. For, as Dr. Cruise O'Brien has well shown, Parnell was at this very time feeling his way towards some kind of constitutional-agrarian balance, which would free him from timid Whigs on the one hand without leaving him dependent on 'bold Fenian men' on the other. This balance Dillon's passionate speech threatened to destroy, and the divergent paths of the two men, and the mounting tension between them, so evident during the next two years, possibly have their origins at this point.

This was not immediately apparent, however, for the Chief Secretary, W. E. Forster, contrived quite unwittingly to allow Dillon to escape the worst consequences of his incendiary speech. It was natural that Forster should denounce the speech, but the terms he used in the House of Commons were such as to bring Irish supporters of all kinds flocking to Dillon's side. The speech, said Forster, had been 'a most dangerous piece of incitement'. 'Its wickedness,' he added, 'can only be equalled by its cowardice.'[1] Thereupon Dillon moved the adjournment of the House in an attempt to induce Forster to explain why he had called the speech 'wicked'. The imputation of cowardice was, he said, something he could ignore, but wickedness was another matter. 'This is so intensely English that I will not pass over it in silence. What is it he found wicked in my language? He found it wicked because I encouraged the people to resist, to the best of their ability, a law which he knows, in his soul, works the foulest injustice in Ireland.' In Ireland, he added bitterly, the law always worked to protect the rich, but 'if the landlords do as they did in 1849 and 1863, as regards clearing out the people, from what I know of the temper of the people, such a course will not be pursued without desperate resistance and more or less bloodshed'.[2]

Forster's reply to this was simply to say that, for him, Dillon's speech was wicked and cowardly because, whatever consequences it might have for those who heard and acted upon it, it was so phrased that the speaker could not himself be prosecuted for it.[3] This might have been more telling if Dillon had not been arrested later in the year for language which was certainly no more violent than that he had used at Kildare, and if Forster had not chosen the very next day to remark of the situation in Ireland—which had become extremely tense after the rejection of the Compensation for Disturbances Bill—that 'it looked as if we could wait a few months to see what could be done'. This was altogether too much for Dillon, who took

[1] Hansard, H.C. Debates, 3rd series, vol. 255, col. 1373. [2] Ibid., cols. 1870–3.
[3] Ibid., cols. 1873–4.

it as an invitation to Irish members to redouble their pressure on the government, and in a short outburst, so passionate as to be almost incoherent, threatened during the coming winter to put the question to the test—whether Irishmen should or should not have the right to possess a rifle. 'He thought it likely', adds Hansard, 'that after he went back to Ireland he would start a series of rifle clubs in every part of Ireland and they would then see if it was foul treason and rebellion in Ireland to arm the Irish people and teach them how to shoot . . .'[1]

So ended Dillon's first parliamentary session. It was, however, only the prelude to an autumn of intensive agitation. He had no sooner got back to Dublin than in a speech to a Land League meeting he set the tone for the coming campaign in a phrase which anticipated the famous remark Parnell was to make at Ennis a few days later. Warning the people against the base atrocities, such as cattle-maiming, which always reappeared in any active phase of the land war, he urged them nevertheless to organise, for whatever land reform they might get from the government next session would be the measure of their exertions in the coming winter.[2] Parnell, though he had by no means abandoned his policy of constitutional-agrarian balance, was quite content to develop this line of attack. The session of 1880, fruitless as it was, had revealed only too clearly the limitations of parliamentary pressure. Had he continued to rely on this the two halves of his alliance would have fallen apart and the agrarians, led by Dillon and probably by Davitt also, would have emerged as a formidable and potentially uncontrollable combination. Moreover, the central thesis on which Dillon was operating—that the only way to move the Liberal Government towards a real land reform was through Land League agitation—seemed unanswerable. True, it involved the danger that the Liberals were as likely to be moved towards repression as towards reform, but this was a risk that had to be taken; indeed, a little coercion might supply precisely the cohesion needed to keep Parnell's heterogeneous forces together.

At Ennis, therefore, on 19 September, Parnell made the speech which was to become as celebrated as any he ever delivered. The Government land reform of next session, he told his audience, would be 'the measure of your determination not to pay unjust rents; it will be the measure of your determination not to bid for farms from which others have been evicted, and to use the strong force of public opinion to deter any unjust men amongst yourselves—and there are many such—from bidding for such farms'. What he meant by this, he explained, was that a transgressor should be placed in a 'moral Coventry', shunned by all his neighbours 'as if he were a leper of old'.[3] A few days later this treatment began to be applied not just to tenant-farmers but to Lord Erne's agent, Captain Boycott, thus providing not only a new word for the language but an object-lesson which

[1] Ibid., cols. 2033, 2039–44.
[2] *Nation*, 11 Sept. 1890.
[3] For this speech and its background, see R. B. O'Brien, *The life of Charles Stewart Parnell* (3rd ed., London, 1899), i. 236–7.

was closely marked by the peasantry. 'Moral Coventry' proved to be a powerful weapon and one easily abused by unscrupulous men. And as the land war developed the authorities became increasingly convinced that this kind of suasion was, in fact, no better than intimidation and set themselves to break it. The leaders of the League had therefore a difficult task. Since they could not recommend open violence, they had to rely on the boycott, but there was always the risk, of which they were fully aware, that the boycott, in irresponsible hands, could develop into an intolerable village tyranny.

Dillon, as one who had already become identified in many people's minds with a policy of violence, was particularly conscious of the dilemma and his speeches that autumn showed it. On the one hand he had to drive home the need for organisation, on the other hand he had to restrain these sometimes desperate men from acts of physical violence. Not unnaturally his hearers sometimes failed to discern exactly where the shadowy border-line was to be drawn. At Carrick-on-Suir, for example, in his first visit to his constituency since his election, his attempt to combine a warning with advice met with almost total incomprehension. The advice was the standard advice that Parnell and the other spokesmen were giving Sunday by Sunday up and down the country—that if a landlord would not accept a fair rent, then his tenants should pay no rent at all, and should not occupy farms from which men had been evicted for acting on this advice. But, Dillon added, people had been saying that the League had been instructing tenants not to pay rent in *any* circumstances. 'More power to the Land League,' came a voice from the crowd. On the contrary, said Dillon, they had not, in fact, ever advocated that debts justly incurred should not be paid. 'I never told a man,' he said, 'not to pay a debt he had contracted by his own free will.' 'Oh,' interjected a voice in the crowd, 'devil a landlord more we'll pay.'[1]

Here in a sentence was the fatal oversimplification liable to befall a policy too sophisticated to be readily grasped by an ignorant and passionate peasantry. And even though, at this same meeting, Dillon persevered in his efforts to drive home to his audience that the League discountenanced assassination and violence of all kinds, it was part of his dilemma that he could not press this too far without making the League appear to the landlords a less dangerous and effective threat than they had feared. Perhaps the formula he used at Cork early in October came as near as anything to defining his true position. 'I wish to tell the Irish landlords,' he said, 'that while we use every endeavour . . . to keep the people within a defensive line and to prevent every act of outrage or attack upon their class, that if they undertake . . . to repeat the deeds of past years and to break the laws themselves, without boast I think I can say that we have at our disposal means which will make them bitterly repent the day that they broke the peace in Ireland.'[2]

Not unnaturally, the Government was rather more concerned about the threat to peace which the League seemed to present and in November

[1] *Nation*, 9 Oct. 1880.   [2] *Nation*, 16 Oct. 1880.

prosecutions were instituted against the ringleaders on charges of conspiracy to prevent the payment of rents. Those prosecuted—the 'traversers',
to use the official language of the subsequent State trial—were Parnell
himself, Dillon, Biggar, T. D. Sullivan, Thomas Sexton (a rising member
of the Parnellite section), together with Thomas Brennan, one of the secretaries of the Land League, and Patrick Egan, one of its treasurers. The
court proceedings did not begin until after Christmas, but then occupied
some twenty days. The outcome was as might have been expected. The
League was given ample free publicity, money poured into a Defence Fund
for the conduct of the trial, the jury—inevitably—disagreed and the
traversers were discharged. Their freedom of movement had been little, if
at all, restricted, and while the trial was in progress important meetings of
both the parliamentary party and the League executive were held in Dublin
to take due precautions lest the leaders should be imprisoned. What
happened at the party meeting throws an interesting light on Dillon's
attitude to questions of political discipline, questions which in one form
or another were to occupy him for most of his life, but to which later he
was to give rather different answers. Parnell, having been re-elected chairman, proposed that a committee should be elected to act virtually as the
cabinet of the parliamentary party, with power to shape and direct the
policy and action of the party in any emergency, or to take specific steps
when the party, for one reason or another, could not be consulted. He was,
obviously, preparing to delegate authority in case he should fall foul of the
law, but Dillon countered with an amendment which, if accepted, would
have given the committee a much more precise role and much more actual
power than Parnell's rather vague motion envisaged. Dillon wanted a committee of nine members, in addition to the chairman, to plan and direct the
policy of the party on all occasions not sufficiently urgent to require a full
party meeting, but *also* with power to alter in emergency decisions already
taken by the party, with the sole reservation that when the emergency was
very great, then the party should be consulted. And not only this, he
further proposed that any member who refused to follow the policy laid
down by the committee should be asked to explain himself at the next
meeting of the full party.

At the time he made these suggestions Dillon, aged 29, had been effectively a member of the party for less than six months—yet already he was
seeking to make it a more disciplined and unified body. Not surprisingly,
this somewhat dictatorial approach roused much angry opposition and the
senior Member for Tipperary, P. J. Smyth, probably spoke for many when
he denounced this attempt to tighten the bonds of discipline as 'a deface-
ment of the rights of conscience' and 'a violation of the fundamental
principles of liberty'. Clearly, some members, at least, still thought of
themselves primarily as representing a constituency rather than as units in
a highly centralised party. Parnell might well have derived some amusement from the discussion. Within five years he was to create a party far
more disciplined than Dillon at this stage conceived, and it was to be a

party dominated by its chairman, not by any standing committee. But the time was not yet, and it was characteristic of the two men that, while both saw the problem, Dillon's instinct was to rush in to solve it there and then, whereas Parnell's reaction was to wait until circumstances played into his hands. He had no difficulty in demonstrating that Dillon's resolutions bound individual members too tightly and gave the committee too much power. Dillon, therefore, withdrew his amendment and Parnell's original resolution was passed. In the balloting for the committee Dillon was placed equal third with the former Fenian, Arthur O'Connor. E. D. Gray headed the poll and T. P. O'Connor was second; the other members were Biggar, John O'Connor Power, John Barry and Andrew Commins. Not a single 'Whig' gained a seat and this itself was an indication that the party was moving to the left.[1]

Parnell, as it happened, by outmanoeuvring his lieutenant on this occasion, saved him from what might have been a difficult situation, for as things developed in the crucial early weeks of 1881 Dillon would almost certainly have found himself at odds with the kind of committee he had proposed, and would have had to do a good deal of explaining to the party at large. At the beginning of the new session Gladstone and the Chief Secretary, Forster, were faced with a double responsibility—to restore order in the country and to provide the kind of legislation which would so transform the land question as to cut off disorder at its source. The Land Bill Gladstone had in mind was not to be the final solution of the problem—far from it—but it was to work a revolution nevertheless. Based on the principle of co-partnership in the soil between landlord and tenant, it proposed to give the tenant the famous 'three Fs'—fair rents, fixity of tenure and free sale; that is the right, when he vacated his holding, to get a fair price for the improvements he had made to it. Over and above this Gladstone proposed to set up Land Courts to which the tenants would be encouraged to apply, so that the rents payable to their landlords might be fixed by judicial action after all circumstances had been taken into account.

Such a measure, if given a fair chance in Ireland might indeed, as Gladstone hoped, undermine the whole land agitation. But before the carrot could be dangled, the stick had first to be applied. The opening days of the session were occupied, not by redress of grievances, but by the Government's attempt to secure special powers to deal with disorder and by the Irish party's furious struggle to thwart this intention. They could not succeed in doing that, but they could—and did—succeed in holding up all other parliamentary business. Amendment after amendment was moved to the Address and the debate did not end until eleven exasperating and angry nights had passed. Dillon took an active share in these debates, concentrating chiefly on drawing attention to the dangers that might follow if, under its special powers, the Government were to sanction the use of troops to help in evictions. Evictions, he forecast, were soon going to be numerous and if they were carried out by force would be met by force.

[1] *Nation*, 1 Jan. 1881.

'What use', he asked amid noisy interruptions, 'did the right honourable gentleman mean to make of the troops, unless it were the extermination of the people?'[1]

No sooner was this debate out of the way than the Chief Secretary, on 24 January, introduced the Protection of Person and Property (Ireland) Bill—the threatened measure of coercion. Forster justified this interference with the ordinary course of law by the evidence of unrest which had reached him from all over the country. Dillon, complaining bitterly that the liberties of the Irish people were to be voted away on the evidence of 'a lot of police spies', pointed out that the deterioration in the situation on which Forster had laid such emphasis had only become critical after the harvest had been gathered in. 'As soon as the harvest was reaped,' he said, 'the struggle for life and death began, the question being whether it should go to pay arrears of rent, or whether it should be used as food by the people.' He then gave a solemn warning that if because of this evictions were multiplied a great social convulsion would follow:

> He declared deliberately [runs the report] having spent most of his life among Irish farmers that if the House drove the Irish farmers to a state of despair, they could not expect anything but outrage and murder; and it would take the form, not of intimidation, but of the revenge of despairing men.[2]

This speech, which seemed to give notice that boycotting was only a prelude to something much worse, helped to confirm his already established parliamentary reputation as an extremist. His next outbreak, barely ten days later, certainly did nothing to remove that impression, for this time he embarked upon a deliberate interruption of the prime minister after the Speaker had called upon the latter. Dillon refused to give way to Gladstone, and amid great uproar he was 'named' by the Speaker. His suspension was voted by 395 votes to thirty-three, but, since he refused to leave voluntarily, he was removed by the sergeant-at-arms. Gladstone attempted to resume his speech, but Parnell now intervened to move that the Prime Minister 'be no longer heard'. He, too, was named, suspended and ejected. 'From this incident forward', the report continues, 'the business of the House proceeded under indescribable confusion.'[3] But for a long time it could not proceed at all, since Member after Member rose from the Irish benches until in all thirty-six had been suspended and ejected.

This scene—unique in the history of the Irish parliamentary party—has to be seen in relation to two crucial events. One was the Speaker's decision —taken on the previous day on his own initiative—to end a sitting which had continued, thanks to Irish obstruction, for forty-one hours. By so doing he had in effect broken the back of the obstructive policy and thus much reduced the force of Irish opposition in the House of Commons. The

---

[1] Hansard, 3rd series, vol. 257, cols. 875–82.
[2] Ibid., cols. 1248–60.
[3] Ibid., vol. 258, cols. 69–72, for the Dillon and Parnell episodes.

other event was the announcement, on the very day of Dillon's interruption of the Prime Minister, that Michael Davitt, who had returned from America to resume the chief direction of the Land League, had been arrested. As Dr. Cruise O'Brien has pointed out, this episode was a turn-ing-point for Parnell and his party. The excitement of the scenes in Parlia-ment, the imminence of coercion, the likelihood of numerous evictions—all these things had stirred opinion in Ireland to boiling-point. There was a strong temptation, therefore, for Parnell to treat the suspension of the thirty-six Members as a virtual expulsion from the House of Commons and to lead his friends back to Ireland, where the agitation might well have led to a general strike against rent. Indeed, only a few weeks earlier (on 16 January) he had stated publicly that the first arrest under the Protection of Persons and Property Act would be the signal for such a general strike.[1] True, Davitt was not arrested under the Act, which had not yet become law, but his arrest and the broader policy of coercion were obviously part of the same pattern, and the Government's seizure of the founder of the Land League could perfectly well have been made a *casus belli*—if Parnell had wished to make it so.

But it was not just a question of leaving Parliament *en masse*; it was a question of where to go from there. Just before Davitt's arrest the execu-tive of the Land League had met in London—ironically enough, in a room in the House of Commons. There, Davitt had expounded what Andrew Kettle (one of the League secretaries) described as his policy of dispersion—that is that Parnell and three or four others were to go to America to collect funds, that some were to stay in England and try to work upon public opinion there, and that the remainder—Davitt, Dillon and the League staff—were to proceed to Ireland and fight the battle against coercion. Kettle's own view was that a better policy would be for the whole party to concentrate in Ireland, face the consequences of coercion, and prosecute the no-rent campaign with full vigour. The meeting adjourned to the next day, at the Westminster Palace Hotel, with the decision between 'disper-sion' and 'concentration' still in the balance. Then Parnell, according to Kettle's account, produced his own solution. The party would fight coercion in Parliament as long as they could. They would then cross to Ireland, where every Member would go at once to take charge of his own constituency and Parnell would announce that the first arrest under the Coercion Act would lead to a general strike against rent. This, it seems, was enthusiastically accepted and E. D. Gray, though not a member of the League executive, was called in to see if he would pledge the support of the *Freeman's Journal*, which he did.[2]

From all this it might seem that Parnell was strongly committed to the

---

[1] C. Cruise O'Brien, *Parnell and his party*, p. 60. But for a different view see M. Hurst, *Parnell and Irish nationalism* (London, 1968), chap. 4.

[2] A. J. Kettle, *Material for victory* (Dublin, 1958), pp. 38–42. These memoirs were written in old age, probably about 1914, and have therefore to be used with caution, but they form a valuable supplement to the account of this important meeting in Davitt, *Fall of feudalism*, p. 302.

policy of concentration. And no doubt if, after the suspension of the thirty-six members, he had chosen to put it into effect, he would have carried a number with him, perhaps twenty by Dr. Cruise O'Brien's reckoning, though the same authority doubts if more than five (including, of course, Dillon) would have actively advocated secession.[1]

In reality, however, nothing of the sort occurred. Dillon, acting presumably on instructions, hastened back to Dublin, and there, on 4 February, he urged the League not to be stampeded into violence, but to maintain rigorous self-control. If the organisers of the League were arrested wholesale in any particular locality, he advised the members of the League in that area to pay no rent until their organisers were released, but he was careful to add: 'I do not think it would be wise to advise the people to anything like a general strike against rent, because I wish to give every landlord the opportunity of taking his stand either for or against coercion.'[2] It appears that at that same meeting he was charged to convey to Parnell the view of the League that he should go to America, that is, follow the Davitt plan of dispersion.[3] Dillon's papers throw no light on his personal attitude at this crisis, though, given his deep involvement in the affairs of the League, it is reasonable to suppose (as, indeed, Davitt has indicated) that he would have been for the policy of concentration and the strike against rent. But Parnell, characteristically, had decided neither to disperse nor to concentrate, but to carry on with parliamentary opposition. If, he said in a Press interview on 5 February, the party consulted their own feelings, they would indeed retire from Westminster, 'but we have been sent here by our own people to do very disagreeable but necessary work, and we must do our duty in fighting this Coercion Bill step by step as best we can'.[4]

(iii)

In rejecting the proposal to secede from Parliament, Parnell, as Dr. Cruise O'Brien has shown, was opting firmly for a constitutional rather than a revolutionary role, and doing so, not merely because the Coercion Bill had yet to be fought through its various stages, but because there still hovered in the wings the Government's Land Bill, which might provide a solution for the agrarian problem. But he had to convince the Land League executive that he was right. Its next meeting was held, for safety's sake, in Paris, whither the League funds had already been transferred. Mainly because of the need for security, the entrances and exits of the members were mysterious and one incident in particular remains baffling to this day. The only substantial report of it we have is from T. M. Healy, written long afterwards and not very reliable, supplemented by brief references in a life of Parnell published by T. P. O'Connor in 1891 and in Davitt's account which appeared in 1904, but as Dillon was involved in it, it must be men-

[1] C. Cruise O'Brien, op. cit., p. 61.
[2] *Nation*, 12 Feb. 1881.
[3] *F.J.*, 15 Feb. 1881.
[4] *Nation*, 12 Feb. 1881.

tioned. Parnell failed to arrive in Paris at the time arranged, and as the days passed with no sign or word from him the executive grew alarmed. Healy, who was not a member of the executive, but who was acting as Parnell's secretary and had come to Paris to meet him, was asked whether he had any letters which, if opened, might give a clue to Parnell's whereabouts. With great reluctance he handed over a letter in a woman's hand and Dillon and Patrick Egan were deputed to open it. Having retired to another room, they did so and came back with a Holloway address. According to Healy's account, the letter was from a barmaid who had had a child by Parnell and was now asking for money. It was decided that Healy and Biggar should set out for this address next day, but as luck would have it they met Parnell coming from the station to their hotel just as they were starting. He never referred to the incident, but Healy resigned his post as secretary forthwith. The Holloway barmaid was almost certainly an invention of Healy's, but that a letter from a woman was opened in Parnell's absence seems to be beyond question. And, since we know that Katharine O'Shea herself wrote several letters to Parnell at the Paris hotel, to postulate a mysterious barmaid may perhaps be unnecessary. Both T. P. O'Connor and Davitt refer to the incident as the first overt sign of the O'Shea affair, and Katharine O'Shea herself stated in her book on Parnell that her liaison with him first became known to his colleagues when they opened one of her letters. It would scarcely be surprising, in view of all this, if the coolness between Parnell and both Dillon and Healy which later was to become a factor in the relations of the three men with each other was to some extent connected with this strange episode.[1]

When they eventually got down to business Parnell made it plain that he was not going to accept either the Davitt policy of dispersion or the Kettle policy of concentration. Instead, he read out a document which in all probability was the basis of the open letter to the Land League he published shortly afterwards and in which he made three points. First, he deemed it his duty to stay at his post, not go to America. Second, he did not agree with the view taken by some members of the League that little was to be gained by parliamentary action. And finally, having, after the suspension of the thirty-six members rejected one alternative—to withdraw from Parliament—he was committed to 'go on widening the area of the agitation' and to effecting a junction 'between the English masses and Irish nationalism'.[2] According to Kettle, who was present, this was agreed to with only the party of concentration—himself, Brennan and Dillon— dissenting.[3] Before they separated they took one further important decision

[1] T. P. O'Connor, *Life of Parnell*, p. 136; M. Davitt, *The fall of feudalism in Ireland*, p. 306; Katharine O'Shea, *Charles Stewart Parnell*, i. 178–80, ii, 165; T. M. Healy, *letters and leaders of my lady*, i. 107–10. See also the remarks of Jules Abels, *The Parnell tragedy* (London, 1966), pp. 112–14. It should be added that when I showed this to Mr. James Dillon, he mentioned that he had some recollection of his father saying that an illegitimate child was involved, though Mr. Dillon thinks the address was Birmingham, not Holloway. The mystery, therefore, remains.

[2] *Nation*, 14 Feb. 1881. But this, as Mr. Hurst points out (op. cit., pp. 71–4) involved no loss of political dynamism.   [3] A. J. Kettle, *Material for victory*, p. 45.

—Dillon was designated to succeed Davitt as the League's chief organiser in Ireland.[1] Thus Parnell emerged from the crisis not only with his parliamentary policy intact, but with his most impetuous and uncontrollable lieutenant committed to the work of the League in a way that would keep him fully occupied in Ireland, if indeed it did not end by landing him in prison.

Back in Ireland, Dillon lost no time in resuming the campaign against 'unjust' rents, and his first major speech after the Paris meeting—it was in Tipperary on 27 February—was an even more emphatic and explicit defence of boycotting the land-grabber than Parnell had attempted at Ennis. 'If you meet him in the fair, walk away silently. Do him no injury, offer him no violence, but let no man have any dealings with him. In the same way, when he lives in the country, let every man's door be shut against him. I would always have you remember that when a man has been made to feel the anger of his neighbours, you should always let him know that the moment he consents to conform to the rules of the Land League . . . you are willing to forgive him and to hold out the right hand of fellowship to him again.'[2] A few days after this the first arrests were made under the Coercion Act, which had passed through its remaining parliamentary stages very rapidly, and although Dillon, perhaps to his surprise, was not among the earliest victims, the fact that repeatedly during March he used similar language suggested that his span of liberty might be short enough. While it lasted he used it to go over to London to make his protest against a second coercive measure, the Peace Preservation (Ireland) Bill, more commonly known as the Arms Bill. In his speech on the second reading, still rather inexperienced and in a highly excitable state, he allowed himself to be tempted into a defence of American Fenianism, of John Devoy in particular, and of extremism in general. Wrought up as he was, he, in fact, went much further, both in manner and in content, than he had yet allowed himself to do in Ireland. He adopted, says the usually favourable *Nation* report, 'an indescribable contemptuousness' in his tone and bearing. The storm burst when he declared bitterly that he wished Ireland had the means of waging a civil war, but even after it had died down he remained unrepentant. 'For a moment quietness reigned', continues the report, 'and something very like a shudder ran round the House as he stated that if he were a farmer about to be evicted he would open fire and shoot as many as he could of the evicting party.'[3]

This was, indeed, wild language for a responsible leader of the tenant-farmers to use. It must be seen as the measure not only of his immaturity, but also of the almost intolerable tensions to which he was being subjected. With Davitt in jail, he was now in virtual control of the Land League, and yet, although one Coercion Act had been passed and more repressive legislation was pending, although arrests and evictions were increasing,

---

[1] Healy, op. cit., i. 109.   [2] *Nation*, 5 Mar. 1881.

[3] *Nation*, 12 Mar. 1881; for the speech and for Parnell's attempt to minimise its effect next day, see Hansard, 3rd series, vol. 259, cols. 156, 336.

from Parnell came no sign that he had moved one iota from his dogged determination to persevere with parliamentary methods.[1] It was not surprising, therefore, that sharp divergences of attitude began to emerge. For Dillon the League was still all in all and he viewed the prospect of Gladstone's promised Land Bill with extreme scepticism. For Parnell, on the other hand, the Land Bill was the principal, almost the sole, justification for keeping the party at Westminster and the one hope of preventing a collapse into anarchy in Ireland. The promised Bill was introduced on 7 April and, with its concept of dual ownership, it did, as we have seen, offer substantial concessions. Parnell, for tactical reasons, treated it with reserve at the outset, but did not reject it out of hand. Dillon, on the contrary, condemned it absolutely from the moment of its publication. He pointed out that several large categories of tenants would be excluded from its benefits, alleged that the proposed land courts would favour landlords, and emphasised especially that it did not help those who were in arrears of rent and therefore most likely to be evicted.[2]

For the moment, mainly because Parnell temporised, an open split between them was avoided. Indeed, they both attended a League meeting in Dublin and Dillon seconded Parnell's motion calling for a convention or large representative meeting of the League to consider the measure thoroughly and decide what policy to adopt towards it. But though he seconded the resolution, Dillon was under no illusions about the dilemma in which Gladstone had placed people like himself. 'If,' he said, 'on the one hand we advise the tenantry on the rack-rented estates to go into court, and the court decides against them, what will be their and our position as regards the strike against rent? On the other hand, if we don't advise them to go into court, can we pursue the policy which has worked such good all over the country, which has affected so much in the reduction of rent—the policy of a united strike against unjust rents . . . I very much fear that this Act was drawn by a man who was set to study the whole history of our organisation and was told to draw an Act that would kill the Land League.' It was a penetrating and indeed a prescient analysis, but it did not affect his own policy in the slightest. He would not, he said, oppose the Bill if the Land League decided it was not to be opposed, 'but no consideration, not even the call of my own constituents, would induce me to vote for this Bill, knowing as I do that I would be only helping to rivet the collar of the master around the Irish tenants'.[3]

The Land League Convention did not meet until 21 April and in the interval Dillon's dislike of the Bill if anything intensified. Recognising the temptation the land courts would be to the tenants, he warned them that if they agreed to any measure which put power into the hands of the judges to fix rents 'they were going blindfold into a worse state of slavery than they ever were in before'.[4] When at last the Convention met it took two

[1] For the arrests see *Nation*, 12 and 19 Mar. 1881.
[2] *Nation*, 16 Apr. 1881, speech at Ormonde Stile.   [3] *F.J.*, 13 Apr. 1881.
[4] *F.J.*, 19 Apr. 1881.

days over its deliberations. On the first of these Dillon was absent, speaking against the Bill, ominously enough, at a meeting in County Tyrone, but he was there on the second day and was as uncompromising as ever. The outcome of the debate was that, after passing a highly academic resolution to the effect that the only final solution to the problem would be the abolition of landlordism, the Convention in effect threw the ball back to Parnell by agreeing that the party should be left free to support the Bill or not as they thought fit, though with the proviso that they would work to improve it in the committee stage. Dillon would have none of this. Borrowing a phrase of Davitt's, he declared that 'fixity of tenure' (one of the Bill's most alluring concessions) meant 'fixity of landlordism'. The Bill was 'thoroughly dishonest' and it was 'perfectly hopeless and silly' to expect that it would be amended in committee. However, he found himself very much in a minority and had to acquiesce in the decision to allow the party its freedom of action, though he did secure a promise—which subsequently turned out to be worthless—that a second convention would be held before the third reading to judge if the amendments obtained in committee were satisfactory.[1]

But now at last he was to be removed, if only temporarily, from the scene. Immediately after the Convention he went to Grangemockler in County Tipperary and delivered one of his most intransigent speeches, urging the tenants to stand by the League, not to pay excessive rents, and to punish any man who assisted the landlords to levy such rents. If they were faced with eviction, he prophesied, 'the people would resist, and the next time a man was shot in Ireland for refusing to leave his home peaceably, the verdict would be . . . wilful murder, not against the policeman who shot him, but against Gladstone and Forster who sent the police there'.[2] On 2 May he was arrested for this speech and taken at once to Kilmainham prison in Dublin. The immediate, though short-lived, reaction of his family was one of relief. 'God', wrote his grandmother to his brother Henry, 'has placed him where he is to save him from something much worse', and Mrs. Deane, who visited the prison soon after his arrest to organise the gifts of pictures, flowers and comforts of all kinds that were flowing in from his admirers, reported that 'the consideration and politeness of the governor . . . filled her with gratitude'.[3] But upon the public at large the effect of the news was profound. Not only because Dillon was the first M.P. to be arrested under the Coercion Act, but because it was widely realised what imprisonment might mean for him. He was, as the *Freeman's Journal* pointed out, 'a gentleman notoriously in a state of health which must be seriously affected by incarceration, no matter how light in character', adding sententiously: 'Unhappy land, where the objects of popular affection are also the objects of State punishment, where the ivy of devotion twines not around the palaces of kings, or the assemblies of statesmen, but around the scaffold and the prison.'[4]

[1] *Nation*, 30 Apr. 1881.   [2] *F.J.*, 29 Apr. and 3 May 1881.
[3] Mrs. Hart to Henry Dillon, 9 May 1881 (D.P.).   [4] *F.J.*, 3 May 1881.

There was, however, at least one object of popular affection still at large and still much more concerned with the assemblies of statesmen than with prison. In one sense, Parnell's mastery of the constitutional-agrarian balance was strengthened by the temporary disappearance of the fiery agitator who might before long have become a rival rather than a follower. On the other hand, Dillon's arrest was a challenge he dared not ignore without risking the loss of the left, or agrarian, wing of his precarious combination. Here, after all, was precisely the situation he had envisaged earlier in the year and to which the proper answer, as some still thought, should be a massive withdrawal from Parliament and an all-out campaign for a general strike against rent in Ireland. But he could not do this without losing the right, or constitutional, wing of the movement and alienating both the priests and the powerful *Freeman's Journal*. He resolved, therefore, to confine himself to a gesture which would register disapproval of the Government's action, but would not endanger Gladstone's Land Bill. This was to abstain from voting on the second reading of the Bill. Even that was only carried at a party meeting by eighteen votes to twelve after Parnell himself had threatened to resign if his policy was not adopted. And in the event, so reluctant were some of his supporters to make any demonstration against a Bill which seemed such a great advance on any land reform yet achieved, that no fewer than fourteen of them voted for it on the second reading in spite of the party resolution on abstention.[1] Once it had reached the committee stage, of course, they had the sanction of the League Convention for their attempts to improve it by amendment, and one Member at least, T. M. Healy, laid the foundation for his brilliant parliamentary career by his extraordinary mastery of the details of this most complicated measure. When the time came for the third reading (no more was heard of a second Convention to consider the amendments in committee) Parnell no longer tried to coerce his party and twenty-seven of them voted for it. On 22 August, after some changes by the House of Lords, it at last became law.

Parnell's conduct that session suggests strongly that he was deliberately modulating the tone and temper of the party so as to secure the passing of the all-important Land Act. But there still remained the danger that too much parliamentary emphasis would cause an uproar on the left and during the summer of 1881 he showed signs of wanting to navigate back to his old position of balance. To do this he had to re-establish contact with the more extreme wing and, having got himself suspended from the House by a well-timed outburst on 1 August (when his absence could do no harm to the Land Bill), he came back to Ireland with this end in view. For some time past, indeed, he had been meditating one highly effective way of achieving it, which was to found a nationalist newspaper that would be entirely under his own control and would thus free him from dependence

---

[1] *F.J.*, 11 May 1881; C. Cruise O'Brien, *Parnell and his party*, p. 67, where the figure for those opposing abstention at the party meeting is wrongly given as eleven, O'Donoghue having been omitted in error.

on the existing, and on the whole moderate, Press. As editor for the new paper, *United Ireland*, he chose the young journalist William O'Brien, who, since his coverage of Dillon's campaign in the Tipperary election, had gained a national reputation by his heartrending reports of midwinter evictions on the Galtee Mountains and had graduated from Cork to the *Freeman's Journal*.

But if *United Ireland* was to be a genuine organ of the left, Dillon's support, as Parnell well realised, would be essential. Absent as he was from the battle while the land legislation was passing through Parliament, Dillon had never been out of mind, though public attention had been concentrated on his health rather than his policy. And of his health the reports were generally bad. 'At an age when healthy young men are in the full prime and vigour of their strength', the *Freeman's Journal* gloomily reported, 'Mr. Dillon has, in fact, been kept alive only by the careful watching of his medical attendants.'[1] The danger which everyone dreaded who knew his family history was tuberculosis, for not only had his mother and one sister died of it years before, but in December 1880 his favourite sister Christina had succumbed to it very rapidly and his brother William had recently had to leave the country for Colorado in order to avoid the same fate.[2] Although it was not publicly known at the time, the *Freeman's Journal* paragraph prompted the Under-Secretary (T. H. Burke) to request a report from the General Prisons Board on the state of Dillon's health. The reply, though guarded, was on the whole encouraging and certainly indicated that the prisoner's health was being closely watched. On the request of his own doctor, Joseph E. Kenny (later a prominent Parnellite M.P.), who was allowed to visit him regularly, he was soon moved to the Infirmary, where for a time he had a room to himself. When the Infirmary became too crowded he was moved back to a cell which was about twice the average size.

Nevertheless, the mere fact of confinement, combined with insufficient air and exercise and a prison diet which, however supplemented from private sources, was a torture to his dyspepsia, brought about a slow but steady deterioration. In June another report was called for, and although Dillon himself insisted he was all right, two doctors from outside gave it as their opinion that his health 'requires to be watched with anxiety'. Only two weeks later, set in motion this time by the Lord Lieutenant, the Under-Secretary demanded further information. The authorities replied (8 July) that, although Dillon appeared delicate, he seemed no more so than when he had first entered the prison three months earlier. But at the beginning of August the prison doctor (Dr. J. Carte) reported that Dillon was suffering from 'feeble respiration', as well as a bowel complaint. He continued: 'Loss of weight amounting to nine pounds (since imprisonment), dullness

[1] *F.J.*, 18 May 1881.

[2] These facts seem to have been quite widely known. See the comments of Joseph Chamberlain's correspondent, W. H. Duignan, writing to Chamberlain, 14 Nov. 1881, cited by C. H. D. Howard (ed.), 'The man on a tricycle,' in *I.H.S.* xiv. no. 55 (Mar. 1965).

over chest, impaired respiration, and general anaemia, lead me to believe that imprisonment, if continued, will endanger his life.' Independently, his own doctor, Kenny, was bombarding the General Prison Board with demands that Dillon should be released at once before he was attacked by the family bogy of tuberculosis. The loss of nine pounds, he pointed out, was particularly serious for a man whose height was 6 ft. 2 in. and whose normal weight was less than 10½ stone. The Under-Secretary's response to these various pressures was to direct that two independent doctors, 'of undoubted eminence', should examine Dillon. However, when they arrived, he politely but firmly refused to be examined, insisting that the prison doctor had already provided sufficient data about his case. The eminent visitors had therefore to content themselves with observation and with a study of the reports already made by Carte and Kenny. In their own statement they stressed Dillon's pallor and emaciation and regarded the loss of weight as 'of grave significance'. Given all this, and taking the family history into account, they had no hesitation in asserting that his life was in danger and that no further improvement or relaxation of his prison régime would be any substitute for release. On 5 August therefore it was decided that he should be discharged on the ground of ill health and he was released the next day.[1]

Even if there had been any disposition on the part of the authorities to make life unpleasant for him—and this was not the case—the state of his health would have precluded it. One consequence of this relative lenience was that he was allowed frequent visitors and that correspondence passed in and out of Kilmainham quite freely. Thus, when Parnell was preparing to launch his newspaper it was perfectly easy for him to get word to Dillon that he hoped he would become a director of *United Ireland*.[2] But William O'Brien, the prospective editor, and still at that time an admirer rather than a friend of Dillon's, was flabbergasted to learn from him that he would not allow his name to be associated with the paper in any way. He had always, he wrote on 12 July, been opposed to the idea, though O'Brien as editor would have gone far to remove his objections, But, he added ominously, within the past two months a gulf had opened between himself and some of the League executive on the one hand and Parnell and his parliamentary supporters on the other. It concerned—inevitably—the Land Bill, then on its way through committee. 'I am quite clear', wrote Dillon, 'that I cannot allow the people to suppose that I regard the course adopted by the parliamentary party towards the Land Bill as satisfactory. You will see then, that it is quite impossible for me just now to allow my name to be identified with a newspaper which must of necessity put the best face on Parnell's action.' He was not at all clear, he said, what his own course would be when he came out of prison. 'It is not unlikely that I shall retire from politics.'[3]

---

[1] The full file on his case is in S.P.O., Chief Secretary's Office, Registered Papers, 15406/82.

[2] R. B. O'Brien, *Parnell*, i. 300–1.   [3] William O'Brien, *Recollections*, pp. 304–5.

Here was the most explicit sign of the danger always inherent in the movement—that its two wings would split apart. Naturally, those who had gone to prison because of their League activities (and they included besides Dillon, another M.P., Matt Harris, the League official, Thomas Brennan, and an able and popular priest, Father Eugene Sheehy) regarded with hostility and suspicion a policy which seemed likely to end in undermining the League completely. Imprisonment intensified rather than diminished their militancy, and this aggressiveness of 'the Kilmainham party', as they were now beginning to be called, was perhaps the most difficult aspect of the difficult situation in which Parnell found himself that autumn.

(iv)

With Dillon's release on 6 August the situation came rapidly to a head. A week later *United Ireland* made its first appearance and showed from the outset that moderation was a word missing from O'Brien's vocabulary. And a week after that again Dillon made his first speech to his constituents since his imprisonment the previous May. He was as intransigent as ever and went out of his way to connect Land League activities with the Fenian tradition, asking the young men in his audience to pledge themselves 'that if in the future far greater sacrifices should be asked at the hands of our people than have been asked by the Land League, there will be found in Tipperary and in all Ireland hundreds and thousands who will be ready to venture in the paths which John Devoy and Michael Davitt trod before them'.[1] This *may*, of course, have been a reference to the New Departure, but it is safe to say that not many of those who heard him would have thought so. Finally, on 29 August, at a banquet in Dublin to celebrate his release (from which Parnell was absent—he was in Tyrone on by-election business), Dillon, while reiterating his belief that the Land Act was a fraud and that the League was still the only sure hope for the people, announced that since he was in a minority and did not wish to cause dissension, he would be retiring from politics 'for many months'. He ended this sensational speech with a passage which admirably defined the fundamental purpose of the agitation and which drew, with painful clarity, the distinction between the agrarian and the parliamentary wings of the movement:

> We taught the people in the beginning [he said] to turn their faces from London and look to Dublin; and we taught them that as long as the centre of action, the centre of gravity and power, instead of lying on Irish soil, lay in London, so long would there be weakness, corruption, treachery, and that the lesson we must draw for the future of Ireland is this, that if we want power, if we want earnestness and reality in any Irish movement, the controlling power must be here in Ireland, in the ancient capital of our nation, under the influence and in the midst of Irishmen . . . If you sent angels into parliament, unless they are controlled by a public body sitting in Dublin they

[1] *F.J.*, 22 Aug. 1881.

will betray the people. Let us then resolve that for the future we will never trust any parliamentary party who will not make it their highest duty and pride to conform their action and seek their inspiration at the hands of men who have come up fresh from the manhood and brain of Ireland.[1]

The *Freeman's* comment on Dillon's resignation was an almost audible sigh of relief. 'We respect the line which Mr. Dillon has adopted, and those who will grieve over the absence of such a man from the councils of Ireland will rejoice at the thought that he is gaining strength and vigour under milder skies and in balmier atmospheres than ours.' But such relief was premature, though Dillon tried hard to keep his word, staying away from the Land League Convention which met in September to consider how best to confront the *fait accompli* of the Land Act. At that Convention it was agreed, despite violent appeals from America to ignore the Act and 'hold the harvest', to test its operation. Parnell proposed that the tenants in general should be restrained by the League from rushing into the land courts to try to secure rent reductions until certain selected cases had been taken to the courts to show whether the Act was really beneficial or not.[2] In order to placate the left wing, both in the United States and in the League executive in Ireland, Parnell explained in a telegram to the American Land League that these test cases were intended to expose the 'hollowness' of the Act, and in a series of speeches in late September and early October he repeated this theme, launching violent attacks on Forster and even on Gladstone. Gladstone retaliated by warning him in a speech at Leeds on 7 October not to use the League to frustrate the Act. 'He desires to arrest the operation of the Land Act, to stand as Moses stood, between the living and the dead; to stand there, not as Moses stood, to arrest but to extend the plague.'[3] Parnell replied unrepentantly at Wexford two days later—it was then that he described the Prime Minister contemptuously as 'a masquerading knight-errant'—and on 12 October the Cabinet, fully convinced that Parnell was bent upon ruining the Act, took the momentous decision to arrest him. On the following day he was seized in Dublin and taken at once to Kilmainham.

It has been said with truth that by doing this the Government got Parnell out of most of his difficulties, since his imprisonment enabled him to bid once more for the support of the left wing. At the same time, from his own standpoint as a constitutional leader, there was much to be said for being removed temporarily from the scene, for he could go to jail pretty certain that the agitation would die down and that the land courts would soon begin to yield their fruits.[4] As he himself wrote to Katharine O'Shea on the very day of his arrest, with as much insight as cynicism: 'Politically

---

[1] *F.J.*, 30 Aug. 1881.

[2] *F.J.*, 16, 17 and 18 Sept. 1881; C. Cruise O'Brien, op. cit., p. 70, where the opening date is incorrectly given as 11 September.

[3] *F.J.*, 8 Oct. 1881; J. L. Hammond, *Gladstone and the Irish nation*, p. 249.

[4] C. Cruise O'Brien, op. cit., pp. 70–2.

it is a fortunate thing for me that I have been arrested, as the movement is breaking fast, and all will be quiet in a few months, when I shall be released.'[1] But on the short run it did not seem so, and Gladstone's action provoked a storm of protest, uniting the various sections as they had not been united for months. Indeed, by a piece of almost unearthly psychological maladroitness he had even, in his Leeds speech, contrived to bring Dillon back into the fray. Gladstone had singled him out as 'a man of the most extreme opinions upon every question connected with the nationality of Ireland', but also as 'most devotedly attached to his country'. Now, said Gladstone, supposing you believe that 'your beloved Ireland was entitled to complete independence of national existence, which I think is what he believes—what would you do about the Land Act? Would you stand between the people and its operation? Would you reject it?' And he proceeded to answer his own question in a passage which deserves to be remembered as a classical instance of English incomprehension of Irish realities:

> No, you would not. You would say you were not justified in intercepting the benevolent legislation of a measure like the Land Act, and that is what Mr. Dillon, alone, I am sorry to say, among his friends, has done. He will not give up his extreme national views, but neither will he take upon himself the fearful responsibility of attempting to plunge his country into permanent disorder and chaos by intercepting the operation of the Land Act. I claim him as an opponent, but as an opponent whom I am glad to honour.[2]

This attempt to discriminate between Dillon and Parnell, and, as some contemporaries were convinced, to drive a wedge between them, could have had only one result. Four days later Dillon broke his self-denying ordinance and took the chair at a Land League meeting in Dublin. He would not have been there, he said, but that he owed his country an explanation for being praised by Gladstone, and praised on false grounds. So far from *not* standing between the country and the Act he would have attacked it in Parliament had not Gladstone's Government kept him in Kilmainham while it was being passed. 'If it be',' he added, 'that the Act is worthless and the old fight is got up again, Mr. Gladstone will have an opportunity of judging whether he is still glad to honour me or not.'[3]

So far from any wedge having been driven between the two Irish leaders the events of the next few days seemed to draw them steadily closer together. On 13 October, immediately after his arrest, Parnell wrote to Dillon asking him to preside that night at a meeting of the Land League executive. He warned him that 'some of our friends' were anxious for a change of policy (by which, presumably, he meant a general strike against rent), but that this must be resisted:

[1] Katharine O'Shea, *Charles Stewart Parnell; his love story and political life* (London, 1914), i. 207.
[2] *F.J.*, 8 Oct. 1881.
[3] *F.J.*, 12 Oct. 1881.

I am, however, very strongly of opinion that no change should be made, at all events until we can see whether we can keep the tenants out of the court. I would recommend that the test cases be proceeded with . . .

If we can do this, and if the government do not suppress the organization, we can I am sure maintain and strengthen the movement.

Everyone who had to do with Parnell experienced at one time or another his complete disregard for personal susceptibilities when the cause was at stake. And now, at this crucial moment, he did not hesitate to appeal to Dillon, who had all along been the foremost critic of his policy, to take the responsibility for it in his absence. 'I should hope', he concluded, 'under the altered circumstances that you would feel yourself in a position to resume your place at the head of the movement and give the Convention resolutions [relating to the test cases] a fair trial.'[1]

This placed Dillon in a cruel predicament. The city was in a fever of excitement and it would have been fatally easy to encourage some great explosion of popular feeling which might have precipitated that social convulsion he had so often prophesied. Yet instead he was asked to swallow his own feelings, disregard his own resignation and press upon the League the policy of moderation he had so recently attacked. The strain upon him was intense and his speech that evening showed it. 'It has more than once been painfully felt by me,' he observed bitterly, 'how humiliating it is sometimes, and how trying it is to a man's patience, to be mixed up in the politics of a country which is not very prosperous and not very strong. The result is that we are compelled to submit peaceably to insults which other countries would know how to answer in the proper way.' Nevertheless, he rose to the occasion and showed leadership of a high order. Throwing all the weight of his great influence behind Parnell's policy, he urged the League to remain calm, to stay within the law and to carry out the operation of testing the Act.[2]

But it was hard to remain calm and law-abiding when the arrests continued. Next day—14 October—Thomas Sexton and the acting secretary of the League, J. P. Quinn, were seized and sent to Kilmainham. That evening a vast indignation meeting was held in the Rotunda, where, inevitably, the key issue was whether or not the time had at last arrived to apply the final sanction of the Land League and order a general strike against rent. Dillon once again urged calmness and circumspection. The executive, he said, had agreed not to launch an all-out 'No Rent' campaign—it was too grave a step to take without further consideration. But, he added, if any county liked to take the lead in initiating such a policy, it was free to do so, and no doubt its example would be followed. Then, in one of the most masterly understatements of his career, he observed: 'We wish it distinctly

[1] Parnell to Dillon. 'Thursday' [13 Oct. 1881], (D.P.) On the envelope is a note in Dillon's hand that it was written 'morning after Parnell's arrest', but in fact it seems to have been written on the morning *of* his arrest; this would be perfectly possible, since he was taken at breakfast-time.

[2] *F.J.*, 14 Oct. 1881.

to be understood that the executive of the Land League have no intention of coercing or intimidating people into paying rent'.[1] Yet, by a most extra-ordinary irony, at the very moment Dillon was counselling caution Parnell had decided to throw caution to the winds. That same day, 14 October, he wrote as follows from Kilmainham:[2]

My dear Dillon,
    I wrote you yesterday that so long as the Government refrained from suppressing the organization of the League that I thought we ought to hold by the resolutions of the Convention. The action of the Government, however, today, in arresting Messrs. Sexton and Quinn and in issuing warrants for the arrest of Messrs. O'Connor and Healy, renders it impossible for the resolutions of the Convention to be carried out, as the absence of our central officials and the certain arrest of any who may take their place will render it impossible to work out the details of the policy recommended by the Convention. I am therefore with great reluctance driven to admit that there is no resource save the adoption of a strike against all rent, and suggest that you should announce the adoption of this policy at the meeting to-night and the withdrawal of test cases.
                                                    Yours very truly,
                                                    Charles S. Parnell.

    This letter had a strange history. According to William O'Brien's *Recollections*, Parnell had smuggled it out from Kilmainham intending that it should be read at the Rotunda meeting. Dillon, however, he says, thought it wiser not to make it public until the executive had discussed it. After the meeting was over, therefore, a number of the leading figures in the League—amongst whom he mentions, besides Dillon and himself, Dr. J. E. Kenny, Joseph Biggar, T. D. Sullivan and J. J. O'Kelly—met at the Imperial Hotel in Dublin. They talked until midnight, and separated without any decision being taken about whether or not to launch a No Rent campaign. O'Brien was for it, so also, he thought, was Dr. Kenny. The others for various reasons were against it, except that Dillon, as O'Brien recalled, did not commit himself one way or the other, and seemed inclined to leave the issue, as he had just suggested in his speech, to local initiative.[3] And they were still in this state of indecision when on the following day—Saturday, 15 October—O'Brien, O'Kelly and Dillon were all arrested and taken to Kilmainham.[4]

    Now, the curious thing is that Dillon apparently never received the letter, or rather, received it in odd circumstances forty years later, when Parnell was in his grave and he himself had retired from politics. Mr. James Dillon has recently told the present writer that one evening in the early 1920s he was sitting in the family house in North Great George's Street with his father and an old friend and former member of the parliamentary party, John Muldoon. A letter addressed to John Dillon was

[1] *F.J.*, 15 Oct. 1881.   [2] Parnell to Dillon, 14 Oct. 1881 (D.P. photostat copy).
[3] W. O'Brien. *Recollections*, pp. 353–6.   [4] *F.J.*, 17 Oct. 1881.

handed in at the door and brought to him in his study. He glanced at the envelope and handed it to Muldoon. 'Whose writing is that?' he asked him. 'Why, the Chief's, of course,' replied Muldoon without any hesitation. This, when opened, proved to be the letter of 14 October 1881 from Kilmainham. It had been given to a friendly warder who had had no chance to get it out to Dillon before the latter's arrest next day. He then, it seems, put it in a drawer at home and forgot all about it. Many years later, after his death, his house was being cleaned out and the letter was discovered. It was then taken to Dillon, reaching him long after the last echoes of the land war had died away.

Why, then, should O'Brien have suggested that Dillon had received the letter before the Rotunda meeting? It has to be remembered that in his memoirs he is frequently inaccurate, except when quoting actual documents, that this particular volume was written nearly twenty-five years after the events it purports to describe, and that the account he gives of the letter is meagre and in some respects inexact. The mostly likely explanation is that, since both he and Dillon were swept into Kilmainham immediately afterwards and came face to face with Parnell, the letter and the whole No Rent policy would obviously have been the burning topic for discussion. No doubt O'Brien and Dillon would then have heard the terms of the letter and would have explained what had happened at the Rotunda meeting. The juxtaposition of these two series of events on two successive days would certainly have made it easy for O'Brien to confuse them. And it has to be added that in 1905 it suited his book to confuse them, consciously or unconsciously, since he was then in the midst of his quarrel with Dillon and anxious to exhibit him as lacking 'imaginative insight' and tending to view any new departure in the land question with 'a suspiciousness, an indecision, a certain revolutionary toryism of mind, which fails to perceive that "old methods" cannot always continue to be the most effective ones'.[1]

At any rate, once they were all in Kilmainham it was relatively easy to decide what policy to pursue. There is, however, a conflict of evidence about Parnell's own attitude. O'Brien, in his memoirs, maintained that Parnell was 'most resolute' for extreme measures—that is for a general summons to the tenants to pay no rent.[2] Katharine O'Shea believed that he was 'really opposed to it'—and Dillon 'openly so'—but agreed to it as the wish of the majority in Kilmainham.[3] Parnell's principal biographer, R. Barry O'Brien, who came to know him a few years after these events, used the same phrase. 'Parnell', he wrote, 'was really opposed to the manifesto', but reluctant at that time to stand out against his left wing, for the No Rent policy was being pressed by some of the Irish-Americans, notably Patrick Ford, and by Patrick Egan from Paris.'[4] The evidence of the letter of 14 October, already cited, suggests that Parnell had already, though reluctantly, made up his mind to issue a No Rent appeal or mani-

---

[1] W. O'Brien, *Recollections*, p. 305. For the relations between the two men in 1905, see chapter 8 below.
[2] Ibid., p. 365.   [3] K. O'Shea, *Parnell*, i. 209.   [4] R. B. O'Brien, *Parnell*, i. 319–20.

festo even before Dillon and O'Brien joined him in prison. It is unlikely, therefore, that the anxious discussions in Kilmainham did much more than confirm him in a decision already taken.

The No Rent manifesto, announcing this policy to the country, was written, all accounts agree, by William O'Brien, as indeed is easily deduced from its superheated style. And all accounts equally agree that Dillon was firmly opposed to it. Barry O'Brien is more specific than the rest in suggesting that his opposition was due to his conviction that a strike against rent could not be carried out without the help of the priests, who could not possibly support 'so bare-faced a repudiation of debt'.[1] Andrew Kettle, who was probably closer to his agrarian views than anyone else in Kilmainham, noted that 'it took O'Brien all he knew to induce John Dillon to sign it'.[2] Dillon's opposition was certainly not based solely on the probable failure of the priests to participate—this was never a decisive factor with him at any stage of his career—but the fact that they could not be expected to participate was only part of a wider complex. If his speeches before his imprisonment are carefully studied, it will be apparent that under the responsibilities of leadership he was maturing fast. They were still fiery, they still throbbed with that hatred of landlordism which was one of his most abiding passions, but they were not irresponsible in the sense that his Kildare speech of 1880 might be said to have been irresponsible. He was, in fact, deeply conscious of the terrible dangers in which rash action might involve large numbers of poor, simple people who looked to their leaders for guidance. And because of this he advised them repeatedly to organise by all means, and to use the boycott, but to remain peaceable and resist the sometimes overwhelming temptation to resort to violence. If this was sound sense when their leaders were among them in the flesh, it was doubly sound when they had been spirited away to Kilmainham. Without central organisation, without national leaders, a genuine No Rent campaign was impossible and to provoke any such campaign was to risk—as events were soon to show—the degeneration of a disciplined struggle into a series of squalid, anarchical, agrarian outrages.

Dillon, however, was in a minority in Kilmainham and the No Rent manifesto, signed by all the leaders then in the prison, went out on 18 October, appearing next day in the Press.[3] It produced immediate results, results which were easily predictable, and which Parnell must have anticipated. It was condemned by the *Freeman's Journal*, more gently deprecated by the *Nation*, and denounced by Dr. T. W. Croke, the 'Land League Archbishop' of Cashel, famous for his sympathetic support for the tenants. Finally, on 20 October the Government moved to suppress the Land League, and the manifesto, lacking any organisation to propagate it, fell upon the deaf ears of tenants who were instead preparing to 'test the Land Act' by the simple expedient of taking full advantage of its terms. An heroic phase of the land war was over.

[1] Ibid.   [2] A. J. Kettle, *Material for victory*, p. 56.   [3] *F.J.*, 19 Oct. 1881.
[4] *F.J.*, 20 Oct. 1881; *Nation*, 5 Nov. 1881.

3
Withdrawal And Return

(i)

For Dillon this second spell in jail, after only two months of freedom, was a serious matter. His previous sentence had been short, and served during the summer, yet even this had endangered his health. Now he was faced with a winter's imprisonment and no one could tell when the ordeal would end. Almost from the beginning he was in and out of the Infirmary and within a month his condition was such as to strike one visitor very painfully. This was W. H. Duignan, an Englishman (though probably of Irish descent), who was at that time touring Ireland and reporting his impressions to Joseph Chamberlain. On 12 November he visited Kilmainham and had this to say of Dillon:

> I never spoke to Dillon before but his appearance deeply affected me. He is *in* consumption and to keep him in Kilmainham for a winter means the sacrifice of his life. I am no judge of Irish prisons but if Kilmainham is a fair specimen of them, I shall henceforth pray very heartily for 'all prisoners and captives'—especially Irish. But what I want to say to you just now is that Dillon is on the way to death and that keeping him confined, especially where he is, is simply hastening his end. It needs no doctor to see this for it is written in his eyes and on his face.[1]

This was ominous enough, but unfortunately there were to be other complications. Within ten days of Duignan's visit it was announced in the nationalist Press that to save the very considerable expense of providing special food (estimated for Land League prisoners generally, and not only in Kilmainham, at £400 a week), all political prisoners were to go on prison diet.[2] Although Parnell's sister, Anna, at once set about raising a sustentation fund, the prisoners duly went over to the diet on 1 December. Upon Dillon, actually dyspeptic as well as potentially tubercular, the results were immediately disastrous. He was seized with serious illness and vomiting and was at once confined to bed.[3] His health continued to cause alarm and Dr. Kenny was even reported as having said that the diet was killing him. Frank Hugh O'Donnell, a member of the parliamentary party, but not a Land Leaguer, visited the prison on 8 December and learnt from

[1] C. H. D. Howard (ed.) 'The man on a tricycle', in *I.H.S.*, xiv, no. 55 (Mar. 1965).
[2] *F.J.*, 21 Nov. 1881.
[3] *F.J.*, 3 Dec. 1881.

Parnell that the food was indeed extremely disagreeable. And on the very next day Parnell himself had a note inserted in the *Freeman's Journal* stating that Dillon's health was 'seriously undermined'.[1] However, by Christmas-time the food situation began to improve again, since the appeal for funds had raised about £9,000, and from this it was calculated that it would be possible to provide every prisoner (or 'suspect' in the jargon of the Crimes Act) with one good meal a day for another seventeen weeks, provided there was no great addition to their numbers. By a curious coincidence, if it was a coincidence, this period of seventeen weeks extended to the end of April 1882, precisely the time, as we shall see, when Parnell negotiated the Kilmainham 'treaty' which ended their imprisonment.

To this extent at least conditions could be said to have improved by the end of the year, though captivity could never be less than irksome. The worst deprivation was probably lack of exercise and fresh air. The cells were small and the furniture the barest minimum. Prisoners were woken at 7.30 a.m., allowed out until eight o'clock, locked up again for breakfast, and exercised, weather permitting, from about ten until midday. They went to their cells for dinner, were allowed out once more at three o'clock, but were shut up finally at five, lights being put out at nine.[2] In these cramped conditions it was not surprising that even with better food Dillon's health continued to give cause for anxiety. On 19 January the faithful Dr. Kenny, himself an inmate of the prison, noted in his journal that Dillon still continued 'very poorly' and that this was due partly to anaemia and partly to 'intestinal catarrh'. Two days later, after the prisoner had been attacked by a sudden fever, Kenny wrote to the authorities that Dillon's condition had so alarmed him that he had had to sit up most of the night with him.[3] And, although Dillon himself explained to his brother Henry that he hoped to be out and about soon, it took him several days to get over the attack.[4]

Naturally his family were deeply worried, and so also, it seems, was the Chief Secretary. At any rate, Forster sent for Dillon's brother, William, who was home on a visit from Colorado, and the following exchange, recorded by the Crown Solicitor, took place:

> He, Mr. Forster, would not have arrested him if it had not been absolutely necessary . . . As to his health, he is not in any immediate danger, but he might be. 'Now, we don't ask any promise from him, we simply say, if he likes to go to the continent, he may go. We take his word at once'. Dr. [*sic*] Dillon: 'I don't think, in fact I am sure he would not, give any promise, but if he were released I would use my influence with him to induce him to go and I am sure I would succeed'. Mr. Forster: 'That won't do. The doors of Kilmainham are open if he likes to go to the continent, but he must not stop here. You will tell him that.'

[1] *F.J.*, 9 and 10 Dec. 1881.
[2] *F.J.*, 29 Dec. 1881; *United Ireland*, 7 Jan. 1882.
[3] S.P.O., Chief Secretary's Office, Registered Papers, 15406/82.
[4] John Dillon to Henry Dillon, 24 Jan. 1882 (D.P.); *U.I.* 11 Feb. 1882.

William did pass on the message, but John's reaction was much as might have been expected. Not only did he repudiate the proposal indignantly, but he persuaded William to take out of Kilmainham with him a copy of his reply to the Chief Secretary and to have it published in the Press. In the letter he was careful to make it clear that the suggestion was made entirely without his consent or knowledge. Two months previously, he said, Captain Barlow of the Prisons Board had made a similar suggestion. 'I stated upon that occasion to Captain Barlow that under no circumstances would I enter into any conditions with the Government and that I wished to have no further communication with him on this matter.' The same applied now to the Chief Secretary and he, Dillon, had not altered his position in the slightest.[1]

This affair caused considerable excitement in Government circles and Dillon was cross-examined as to why he had given the letter to his brother in the first place. He replied simply that he had not considered the message from the Chief Secretary to be 'of a private nature' and had therefore had no hesitation in making it public. By making it public, of course, as both he and the authorities very well knew, he had contrived to show the Chief Secretary in an unflattering light, as one who was only anxious to bribe an incorruptible patriot to remove himself from a situation in which he was nothing but an acute embarrassment to the Government. It may have been a consequence of this, or it may have been because Dr. Kenny protested overmuch, that the prison doctor, so amenable on the previous occasion, was this time less inclined to believe that Dillon's condition was serious. Thus on 31 January, the day on which Dillon's letter to Forster appeared in the Press, he reported that Dillon's life had not been, nor was then, in danger, and in the teeth of Kenny's complaints, he repeated this emphatically a week later. Kenny did not see his patient at all between 12 February and 19 March, but on the latter date he found him 'looking extremely delicate' and recovering with obvious difficulty from an attack of influenza.[2] Dillon himself, it seems, was sufficiently concerned to make a formal protest to the medical officer, Dr. Carte, against his continued imprisonment, but although this letter was published in 1896 by his enemies to make it seem that he had been suing for terms, there was in fact no question of negotiations or conditions of any kind.[3] Indeed, in the letter itself he stated that he had asked his doctor not to make any further reports on his health, and Kenny's Kilmainham journal shows that although he thought Dillon was looking 'extremely ill' he did not intend to refer to the matter again.[4] Clearly, therefore, unless there was some catastrophic deterioration,

[1] S.P.O., Chief Secretary's Office, Registered Papers, 15406/82; *F.J.*, 31 Jan. 1882. In an autobiographical note written in 1932 William Dillon recalled the interview as 'one of the most peculiar experiences' of his life (D.P.). He did not, however, mention the proposition Forster made to him.

[2] S.P.O., Chief Secretary's Office, Registered Papers, 15406/82.

[3] *Irish Catholic*, 28 Mar. 1896. This was part of a series of violently partisan articles entitled 'The New Leader', which were almost certainly written by T. M. Healy.

[4] S.P.O., Chief Secretary's Office, Registered Papers, 15406/82, entry for 29 Mar. 1882.

Dillon's release would depend not upon his health but upon other factors.

These other factors were part political, part agrarian. Parnell is alleged to have said at the time of his arrest that 'Captain Moonlight' would take his place, meaning that the withdrawal of his leadership would leave the field open for all kinds of violence and outrage. This was precisely what happened. Some of the blame for this may be laid at the door of the Ladies' Land League, which had been founded early in 1881 as an auxiliary to the Land League proper, but which came into its own when the main organisation was suppressed. Dillon's cousin, Mrs. Deane, was president of it, but the real driving force behind it was Parnell's sister Anna, who, with some of her colleagues, made a series of provocative speeches in the winter of 1881–2 which would certainly have landed them in jail had they not been women. But more sinister than the ladies' movement, which in the last resort Parnell could—and did—bring to heel, was the work of the secret societies and other unlawful agencies or individuals during that dark winter. It seemed indeed that the Coercion Act, instead of banishing agrarian crime, had only intensified it. Thus, where for the ten months March to December 1880—i.e. before the Act was passed—the number of 'outrages' had been 2,379, the number for the corresponding period of 1881—with the Act in full operation—was 3,821, while cases of firing at the person, as well as actual murders, had trebled. Equally, whereas in October 1881, when Parnell went to jail, the number of outrages for the month was 511, the number in March 1882 was 531. Even more telling was the fact that while in the first quarter of 1881 the total number of cases of homicide and firing at the person had together been seven, the comparable figure for the first quarter of 1882 was thirty-three.[1]

The growth of this unrest was just as much a danger to Parnell as it was to the Government, and the longer he stayed in prison the more difficult it would be for him to re-establish his authority afterwards. But was there any reason why he should stay long in prison? Gladstone had put him there because he had seemed to stand between Ireland and the beneficent operation of the Land Act. With the Land League suppressed and its leaders in Kilmainham the Act had at least a fair chance to work and within a few months was, in fact, working well. Once it was established and flourishing he needed only an indication of future good behaviour from Parnell to let him out again. And Parnell, for his part, in addition to his reasons for wanting to be free to put the constitutional movement on a sound footing once more, had the strongest personal motive for release, since Katharine O'Shea in the spring of 1882 was nursing their dying child and he desperately wanted to be with her.

As early as December 1881 Parnell, it seems, was turning over in his mind the possibility of some kind of arrangement with the Government, though, as he wrote to Mrs. O'Shea, he could not make one at that stage without retiring from politics altogether. By the following February his letters to her were becoming more emphatic of the necessity for a settle-

[1] R. B. O'Brien, *Parnell*, i. 329–30.

ment, but it was not until April that highly secret negotiations, in which Captain O'Shea (of all people) played a prominent part, were at last opened.[1] The details of these negotiations and of the so-called Kilmainham 'treaty'—it was not, in fact, a treaty—need not concern us, and have been many times described and analysed elsewhere. Here it is only necessary to indicate their effect upon Dillon and upon his political future. There is some disagreement as to whether Parnell played a solitary game or whether —and if so, how far—he took his colleagues into his confidence. Davitt later maintained that their leader, inscrutable as ever, kept them all in the dark.[2] Admittedly, he was himself in prison in England at the time and therefore not an eyewitness; on the other hand, he was in close contact with the prisoners immediately after their, and his, release and no doubt they all discussed the events of the previous weeks in detail. As against this, Captain O'Shea told Gladstone on 5 May that Parnell *had* consulted his friends and had, not unexpectedly, come up against difficulties, especially with Dillon. 'He intimated', runs Gladstone's note of the conversation, 'that he (Parnell) had now got his hand upon Dillon, who is difficult to manage and intensely ambitious.' No student of the period is likely to fall into the error of regarding Captain O'Shea as an unimpeachable source for anything and even Gladstone must have had some difficulty in reconciling this statement with Dillon's own speech in the House of Commons the previous day, in which he had emphasised that he personally had had no communication, direct or indirect, with Ministers or with the Irish Government. 'I now feel myself just as free,' he had added, 'to take any course which may seem right and judicious to me as I did when I went into Kilmainham jail.'[3] Perhaps the truth may be that Parnell did confide in him to a limited extent, but that Dillon refused to consider himself bound by his leader's commitments, even if, out of loyalty, he refrained from attacking them in public.

When one considers the terms it is easy to see why Dillon should have reserved his freedom of action. Briefly the understanding, thus tortuously arrived at, was that the Government would take up the question of arrears and would amend the Land Act in certain particulars, notably by extending the benefit of its fair rent clauses to leaseholders. In return, Parnell undertook to use his influence against intimidation and agrarian outrage in Ireland—in effect to end the land war as far as he could end it—and, given that coercion would be dropped and the Land Act amended, to agree to regard the Act as 'a practical settlement of the land question' which would, in its turn, enable the Irish party 'to co-operate cordially for the future with the Liberal party in forwarding Liberal principles and measures of general reform'.[4] As a result of these negotiations and in the teeth of Forster's pro-

---

[1] K. O'Shea, *Parnell*, i. 226, 235–6; C. Cruise O'Brien, op. cit., pp. 75–6.
[2] Davitt, *Fall of feudalism*, p. 353.
[3] Hansard, H. C. Debates, 3rd series, vol. 269, cols. 129–30; C. Cruise O'Brien, *Parnell and his party*, pp. 75–6.
[4] Ibid., p. 77, and sources cited.

tests, who thereupon resigned as Chief Secretary, the Cabinet decided on 2 May to release the three principal prisoners—Parnell, Dillon and O'Kelly—others having been set free earlier on compassionate grounds. Later that same day the trio left Kilmainham, intending to go straight to Parnell's Wicklow home. They got no further than Kingstown that night and next morning Dillon returned to his own house in North Great George's Street. 'The long confinement', noted a reporter, 'has preyed very much on his appearance', but nevertheless he plunged immediately into hectic activity.[1] That evening—3 May—he was rejoined by Parnell and O'Kelly and they all left for England, where, after a brief but triumphant appearance in the House of Commons, they proceeded to Portland prison to meet Michael Davitt, who was due to be released on 6 May.

On that very day, as the four Irish leaders were travelling up to London, the new Chief Secretary, Lord Frederick Cavendish, who had only just arrived in Ireland, was killed with his Under-Secretary, T. H. Burke, by a band of assassins who fell upon them while they were walking in the Phoenix Park in Dublin and stabbed them to death. The murderers belonged to a secret society, the Invincibles, just the kind of society Parnell himself had feared would proliferate in his absence, and the assassinations came as a deadly blow to him and to the other released prisoners, for it seemed as if they must destroy at one stroke the whole basis of the Kilmainham understanding.

Yet in reality this was not so. It was not so partly because neither Parnell nor Gladstone wanted it to be so and were able to continue in remarkably close contact after the initial shock of the murders had passed, and partly because the natural upsurge of English hostility imposed upon the Irish party a unity they might otherwise have found it difficult to maintain. Both Dillon and Davitt had differed sharply from Parnell in their view of the land question before their imprisonment and nothing that had happened since had brought them any closer together. Indeed, even while they were in prison the police, whose sources of information were ubiquitous, had reason to believe that friction was arising between Parnell and Dillon over the treatment of Land League agitators who had been promised payment for their activities. In some cases, it seems, the Ladies' Land League, with Parnell's approval, was withholding payment, whereas Dillon maintained that all financial pledges should be honoured. The details are obscure and the matter dropped once the 'suspects' were released, but since at least one of those whose case Dillon supported was a suspected Fenian and regarded in his own locality (Mayo) as a dangerous man, there was a clear implication that if there were two parties in Kilmainham Parnell's was the moderate one and Dillon's the more extreme. When they came out of prison Parnell lost no time in bringing the activities of the Ladies' Land League to a close by cutting off their funds. In a letter he wrote to Mrs. O'Shea on 20 August he commented that 'the two D's' (Dillon and Davitt) had quarrelled with him because he

[1] *F.J.*, 4 May 1882.

would not sanction any further expenditure by the ladies. This was certainly true of Davitt, but it is clear from Parnell's letters to Dillon earlier that month that the business of winding up the Ladies' Land League was, in fact, carried out by the two of them jointly.[1] As for the 'treaty' itself, though it could be, and no doubt was, presented to Dillon and his friends as a tactical necessity, it was a more bitter pill to swallow, since it registered in effect Parnell's acceptance of the Land Act having defeated the Land League. When the prisoners emerged from their various jails these differences might have been expected to open up still further the gap between agrarians and parliamentarians which had been inexorably widening during 1881. But English revulsion from the Phoenix Park murders provoked such strong anti-Irish feeling that Gladstone had no option but to bring in a fresh Coercion Bill. Equally, the Irish Members had no option but to oppose it, and in doing so were able to retain for a few months longer their own precarious solidarity.

This largely explains why Dillon's break with Parnell was so long delayed. Immediately after the murders he joined with the other Parnellite members in resisting the Coercion Bill, and this and other parliamentary business kept him in England for two months. It was not until 23 July that he made his first speech in Ireland, and even then he went out of his way to pay tribute to Parnell. No leader, he said, was ever 'more tolerant of difference of opinion, less anxious to take credit for himself and to give all possible credit to the men under him'. The moral he drew from this was that Parnell's hand must be strengthened in Parliament by sending him back after the next election with at least eighty members at his back instead of the small group—Dillon put it at thirty-three—which was all he could count on at the moment.[2]

The union of hearts between Parnell and his fiery and unpredictable young lieutenant lasted, however, for only a few weeks more. In mid-August they were together in Dublin for the opening of the Irish National Exhibition of industry and on 16 August they both received the freedom of the city. Each took as the theme of his speech the need for the development of Irish industries and Dillon especially emphasised that intensive industrial development would be impossible until Ireland, under Home Rule, had her tariff autonomy. Much more was to be heard of this protectionist argument in the years ahead, but Dillon could not resist giving it one characteristic twist which indicates both the extent of the difference of attitude between Parnell and himself and also the direction his own mind was still inclined to take. 'The great movement which led to the independence of America,' he remarked, 'originated in a trade dispute, and let us hope that this will be a good augury for Ireland, and that a movement to establish the national

---

[1] S.P.O., Registered Papers, 33858/82, reports by Superintendent Mallon, 22 Apr. and 4 May 1882. For the later history of the Ladies' Land League, see Parnell to Dillon, 9 and 11 Aug. 1882 (D.P.); R. B. O'Brien, *Parnell*, i. 364–5; K. O'Shea, *Charles Stewart Parnell*, ii. 51.

[2] *U.I.*, 29 July 1882.

independence of Ireland will originate in a trade dispute, perhaps, with the manufacturers of England.'[1]

(ii)

But this, though it seemed as intransigent as ever, was in reality a swansong. Dillon did, it is true, attend, again with Parnell, a meeting in connection with a new body in which Davitt was much interested—the Irish Labour and Industrial Union—but after that there was a silence. Then, early in September he was reported to be at Avondale with Parnell, Davitt and Brennan to consider how best to consolidate the various movements which were beginning to compete for public attention—Home Rule, land, labour, evicted tenants and home industries.[2] Nothing was made public from this conference, but we know from Davitt that it was then that Parnell revealed his intention to launch a new national organisation in the autumn. It was to be 'open'—that is, constitutional—and, while embracing the nationalist cause as a whole, it was to be dominated by the parliamentary party and dedicated to the winning of Home Rule. This new body, the Irish National League, was proclaimed with much ceremony in October 1882, but a few weeks before it was launched the country learned with a shock that Dillon was not only resigning his parliamentary seat but leaving Irish politics altogether 'for the next few years'. The reason he gave his constituents, in a letter published on 25 September, was the state of his health, which for some time, he wrote, 'has been such as to make it impossible for me to discharge satisfactorily the duties of an Irish representative'.[3]

That his health was poor and that he needed time for recuperation everybody recognised—the evidence of it had been all too visible in Kilmainham, and there had been little improvement since Kilmainham. His brother William, writing to him in August to tempt him out to Colorado, referred with concern to a letter John had written him on 31 July in which he had admitted to being 'very ill indeed' and 'frightfully knocked up'. William's response to this was to urge him to keep a promise he had made to the family that if his health had not improved within a year he would have done with Irish politics altogether.[4] Clearly, then, this was no diplomatic illness, but what astonished his friends was the apparent finality of his action. To depart for a few months, or even a whole session, was one thing, but to withdraw 'for the next few years' suggested that something more than ill health lay behind this sudden resignation. As Justin McCarthy put it with his usual discreetness: 'Of course your health is beyond all other considerations, but you can take as much time as you like—your constituents and your colleagues alike will, I am sure, be ready

---

[1] *F.J.*, 17 Aug. 1882. For the general background to this speech see F. S. L. Lyons, 'The economic ideas of Parnell', in M. Roberts (ed.), *Historical Studies* (Cambridge, 1959), ii. 60–78. At this stage Parnell regarded tariff autonomy as impracticable and urged 'voluntary protection' upon the country.
[2] *U.I.*, 16 Sept. 1882.
[3] *U.I.*, 30 Sept. 1882; Davitt, *Fall of feudalism*, pp. 371–2.
[4] William Dillon to John Dillon, 27 Aug. 1882 (D.P.).

to meet your wishes in every way. We consider you quite worth waiting for; we want to keep you on any terms. I am sure your retirement now would be quite misunderstood and would have a very bad effect.'[1] Another parliamentary friend, Richard Power, whose disquiet was all the more striking since he was a loyal Parnellite, did not even pretend to believe that ill health was the real reason for Dillon's departure. He was, he wrote, quite in the dark about the proposed 'new departure' (the Irish National League) and was anxious to have Dillon's views and advice:

> You know [he wrote] how I have always feared and hated private treaties and government negotiations and I would much prefer to follow your example and resign at once than remain a member of a party which was not thoroughly independent and perfectly indifferent to English interests.[2]

The press reaction was, naturally, more guarded, but it was obvious that journalists, as well as politicians, found the coincidence of Dillon's illness with the establishment of the Irish National League difficult to credit. The *Freeman's Journal* conceded that if health reasons were the cause of his retirement, then he could not be pressed to stay. 'But if it be not a fact that Mr. Dillon's retirement is in this sense a necessity, we put it to him plainly that he has no right to resign at this moment and that the reason he has given is not a sufficient one.' These were stern words, though sweetened no doubt by the tribute which followed and which revealed something of the hold Dillon then had upon his countrymen. 'Mr. Dillon is not only beloved by the Irish people, perhaps more than any other man, not excepting even his own leader, Mr. Parnell, but he is, though not the leader, a trusted leader of the popular party.'[3]

No public sign, either of approval or disapproval, came from Parnell, and there is no evidence in the Dillon Papers of any private exchanges between the two men on this subject, but Parnell's mouthpiece, William O'Brien, affirmed in *United Ireland*, with just that degree of overemphasis likely to convince his readers of the opposite, that it really was Dillon's health which had forced him to this step. 'Shattered health, and that alone, is the reason for his retirement. Between him and Mr. Parnell or Mr. Davitt there is no shadow of division. They are as perfectly agreed as to the future as they were bound together in the past. The policy which is about to be recommended to the country was devised by them in concert and has the hearty adhesion of all three.' Leading articles in *United Ireland* were anonymous, but the impassioned appeal to Dillon not to go was unmistakably the work of O'Brien both in its urgency and in the unblushing hyperbole which was the hall-mark of his style. Dillon, he wrote, ought to realise before committing himself irrevocably, 'that the country recognises in him a unique figure whose place no other man can quite fill, whose translucent

---

[1] Justin McCarthy to John Dillon, 25 Sept. 1882 (D.P.).
[2] Richard Power to John Dillon, 26 Sept. 1882 (D.P.).   [3] *F.J.*, 25 Sept. 1882.

purity and chivalry have a certain magic, such as the silver casket once borne before the Irish hosts used to be endowed with'.[1]

Dillon, however, remained unmoved by these appeals and held firmly to his decision to withdraw from politics utterly and completely. He was absent from the meeting which launched the Irish National League and he was not in his seat when Parliament reassembled in November. A few weeks later he left for Malta and a brief paragraph in the papers reported that he was going to winter in the Mediterranean, before going out to Colorado in the following spring to join his brother William.[2] His movements then become difficult to trace, but he seems to have stayed in Malta until February 1883 and then moved on to Sicily, and probably to Rome, before settling for some time in Capri. A brief note he wrote exactly a year later in America indicates that this nomadic life did not suit him and that he found the change from furious action to almost total inaction hard to bear—it was, he recollected, 'a period of acute misery', and it lasted until he came home to Ireland on his way to America.[3]

It was the early summer of 1883 before he left for Colorado, but once he had finally gone he disappeared out of history for just over two years. It is an extraordinary fact about a career otherwise so copiously documented that, apart from a few letters to Mrs. Deane, one notebook and a small cash-book, there is nothing at all among his private papers to show that such a person as John Dillon even existed. Nor did any reports about him reach the general public. He might have been on another planet for all that was heard or known of him in Ireland. The surviving notebook is little more than a scrapbook, interspersed with newspaper cuttings, but it does yield one or two items of information. It is clear, for example, that his bibliomania returned in all its vigour and that he bought and read books as insatiably as ever. His range, as always, was prodigious—Thucydides (for the first time), Bishop Stubbs, Carlyle, Ruskin, review articles, medical textbooks, histories and biographies in the greatest variety and profusion. His taste for languages revived and he worked hard and successfully at German, though he seems to have made no progress with the other three he most wanted to learn—Greek, Norse and Arabic. Politics apparently impinged on him hardly at all. He took some interest in what was going on in the United States and speculated as to why the Irish vote was habitually Democrat, but he did not mix with Irish-Americans and when he read of their activities they 'called up again that feeling of disgust for Irish politics which has often almost made me forswear them for ever'.[4]

When he reappeared in the world after his two years' withdrawal the Press let it be known that he had spent the whole of that time with his brother William on a ranch about fifty miles from Denver and near the little town of Castlerock, where William had a law practice. This was substantially correct, for, although the notebook and the account-book indicate that he was away from time to time on short trips to other parts

---

[1] *U.I.*, 30 Sept. 1882.   [2] *U.I.*, 6 Dec. 1882.
[3] 'Notebook, 1883–4', entry for 17 Feb. 1884 (D.P.).   [4] Ibid., entry for 4 Feb. 1884.

of the West, his main object was to rest and to throw off if possible the threat of tuberculosis which had hung over him for so long. In this he can be said to have succeeded, though with two reservations. One was that for many years to come he continued to be highly susceptible to coughs, colds and influenza and, as we shall see, as late as 1902 a serious illness resurrected the danger of tuberculosis. And the other was that, although he returned with his lungs restored, the other ailment which had plagued him from his student days and which he and his doctors persisted in calling dyspepsia (it was, in fact, gall-bladder trouble) remained to trouble him and was liable to become acute whenever he was under strain.

But this only gradually became apparent. When he re-emerged in June 1885—his first interview was at Lincoln, Nebraska—on his way home to Ireland, he appeared fit and relaxed, being described as much bronzed and dressed in Western fashion in a flannel shirt, blue suit and white sombrero. Asked for his views on the political situation, he would say only that Parnell was succeeding admirably in bringing the Home Rule question to the fore and that the next general election, fought under an extended franchise and a new register, would surely give him a party of more than eighty.[1] He left New York on 20 June, but his ship was delayed by engine trouble and did not arrive at Queenstown until 5 July. A reporter came upon him fast asleep in his cabin and, on waking him, found him, predictably enough, 'not in a very communicative mood'. Dillon insisted that he was returning home on private affairs, and when asked if he would stand for one of the marginal northern constituencies, merely replied that he had not come back with that object and did not know what he would do if the contingency arose.[2] He did not disembark at Queenstown, but sailed on to Liverpool and thence to Dublin, arriving home late on the evening of 6 July. He was met by Davitt, T. D. Sullivan, Dr. Kenny and a large and enthusiastic crowd. Briefly returning thanks for the welcome, he said he was astonished that anyone still remembered him and that he only expected to be home for about a year. He would not comment on politics, being, as he said, 'outside' them, but he did let fall that even though he had only passed through Liverpool he had been asked to stand for the Scotland division—a constituency, despite its name, with a large Irish vote.[3]

He had come back to a situation which seemed at that moment to be full of astonishing and exciting possibilities. While he had been away Parnell had consolidated the policy of constitutional pressure and had firmly established the reputation of his party as a formidable and on occasions a constructive force, so much so that in October 1884 the Irish hierarchy had called upon them to urge the educational claims of Catholic Ireland in the House of Commons. This was respectability indeed, but there remained another side to the coin. Agrarian agitation continued because the root causes of agrarian discontent had not been removed. Farmers still suffered from depressed prices and, because they did not own their own farms, they were still vulnerable to eviction. Parnell himself did not this

[1] *Nation*, 4 July 1885.   [2] *F.J.*, 6 July 1885.   [3] *Nation*, 11 July 1885.

time become involved in their fate, but some of his colleagues did, as did also the Irish National League. Faced with this problem, Gladstone's Government, which by 1885 was stumbling under an accumulated load of burdens and mistakes in various parts of the world, had no resource but coercion. For some months previously the radical wing of the Liberal ministry, represented in this instance by Joseph Chamberlain, had been exploring the possibility of settling Ireland's constitutional demands by conceding to her a 'central board' which would have controlled local government, but was a far cry from legislative independence. Chamberlain overestimated Irish support for this scheme, partly perhaps because he attached too much importance to the apparent approval shown by the Irish hierarchy, and even more because he most unwisely relied too heavily on the advice of Captain O'Shea, who misled him into thinking that Parnell would accept these proposals as a final settlement, which, of course, the latter was not prepared to do.[1] But even this modest scheme was too much for some of Chamberlain's Cabinet colleagues, and when Chamberlain found that they were bracing themselves for a fresh Coercion Act, without having remedial legislation to offer at the same time, he, Sir Charles Dilke and G. J. Shaw Lefevre all laid their resignations before Gladstone. These had neither been accepted nor withdrawn when on 8 June the Government was defeated in the House of Commons by an ominous coalition between the Conservatives and the Parnellites. The latter had already received a strong hint from Lord Randolph Churchill that a Conservative Government would not find it necessary to renew coercion. Accordingly, Lord Salisbury took office, forming a caretaker administration until the general election could be held nearer the end of the year. And not only was coercion dropped, but a promising beginning was made—in the Ashbourne Act—towards a solution of the land question by helping tenants to purchase their holdings from their landlords.[2]

It was becoming clear, despite Gladstone's emphatic denials, that the two great English parties were drifting into the position of bidding for Irish support—support, that is, from the Irish voters in English constituencies and from the much-enlarged Irish party it was expected Parnell would lead back to Westminster after the election. At the moment of Dillon's return it seemed that the Conservatives had more to offer, and *United Ireland*, with greater gusto than sense, had just celebrated the 'Conservative alliance' with a virulent attack upon Chamberlain which, before very long, was to bring its own nemesis. It was this situation that explained why, the moment they could interview him, reporters had tried to extract from Dillon what he thought of the possibility of Irish votes being cast for Conservative candidates in Britain. His reply, given on board

[1] C. H. D. Howard (ed.) 'Documents relating to the Irish "central board" scheme, 1884–5', in *I.H.S.*, viii, 237–63 (Mar. 1953); also the same author's article, 'Joseph Chamberlain, Parnell and the Irish "central board" scheme, 1884–5', in *I.H.S.*, viii, 324–61 (Sept. 1953).

[2] C. Cruise O'Brien, *Parnell and his party*, pp. 86–98; L. P. Curtis, *Coercion and conciliation in Ireland, 1880–1892* (Princeton, 1963), chaps. 2 and 3.

ship at Queenstown, was eminently satisfactory. The Irish vote should be cast where it would do most good, 'irrespective of parties'.[1] This was precisely the point William O'Brien was trying to drive home in *United Ireland* at that very time and he used Dillon's return to emphasise the theme. 'His translucent [that word again!] sincerity and classic chivalry of character', he wrote, 'have always given his words a tone of sacredness—a something appertaining to the priest rather than the politician—in the estimation of the Irish people.' But, acting on the well-established principle that in Ireland it helps to have the priest as well as the politician on one's side, he continued:

> The childish suspicion that the Irish party are about to turn Tory disquiets him no more than the old accusation that they had turned Whig. He knows that they esteem Whig and Tory with the utmost impartiality precisely in proportion to their usefulness to Ireland for the moment. He feels, in short, that Mr. Parnell is to be trusted . . .[2]

These were characteristically large and optimistic assumptions, but for the time being at least they seemed not far wide of the mark. Shortly afterwards Dillon received a deputation from the Irish National League—which, incidentally, repeated the hope that he would stand for a northern constituency—and in replying to them he confessed that the change in Irish politics was even greater than he had imagined and that for this the credit was due to 'the extraordinary and never-to-be-too-much-praised parliamentary skill of the Irish party'.[3] Clearly, at this stage he was going out of his way to indicate that he had not returned to Ireland with any disruptive intentions and, so far from thrusting himself forward, it was not until October that he signalised his re-entry into politics by agreeing to be elected on to the Central (Dublin) Branch of the Irish National League. There is nothing in his private papers to show why and how he reached this decision, but the important speech he made to the Central Branch on 6 October offers a significant clue. In this, the first serious statement he had made to the Irish people for nearly three years, he said almost nothing about the burning question of the hour, Home Rule, but returned inexorably to his old theme of the land question. He paid a slightly grudging tribute to the Ashbourne Act, but anticipated a line he was to pursue at intervals for the next twenty years by warning the tenants not to be inveigled into paying too much for their land. This led him on to one of the most interesting passages in all his public speeches—an explanation of his hatred for the landlord class, the hatred that throughout his career provided him with most of his political dynamism. It was due, he said, partly to his long family tradition, partly to his reading of Irish history, partly to the evidence of his own eyes:

> I learned to hate them [he said] because I saw that they had this country by the throat. I learned to hate them because I saw that throughout all the long time since they were planted here by William [III] and by Cromwell, they never showed the faintest interest in the

[1] *F.J.*, 6 July 1885. [2] *U.I.*, 11 July 1885. [3] *U.I.*, 1 Aug. 1885.

welfare of the country; and I learned to hate them because I know that wherever the name of Ireland is held up either in England or foreign countries to opprobrium and derision . . . you are almost sure to find an Irish landlord, or some stripling who will become a landlord, in the very foremost of Ireland's foes. I learned to hate them because I read and saw with my own eyes that every effort in favour of Irish nationality was stamped and crushed out with all the savage brutality of a class who knew that they were hated by the people, and who knew that that hatred was just.

For these reasons, he concluded, it was a waste of effort to overthrow English rule until the landlord class had been smashed. 'I believe it was that', he said, 'fully as much as, perhaps more than, any theory as regards the different systems of landholding . . . that induced me first to go heart and soul into the land movement . . .'[1]

For the immediate future, however, his advice was what it had been before, to conduct their agitation within the law, but to be ready to resist coercion when it came. Parnell, he observed, had said that the people must pay for the land or fight for it, and he agreed that they should certainly pay what was fair. This was an important qualification, but still more important was his addendum—that if, by insisting on rents which the tenants could not pay, the landlords once more plunged the country into chaos, then the fight would be on again and they, the League, should not feel bound by their peaceful resolutions.

What gave this remark its real significance was that the signs were already beginning to appear—scattered, as yet, but visible all the same— that agricultural depression was bearing heavily upon the farmers and that an increasing number of them were finding even the judicial rents fixed under the Act of 1881 an impossible burden. The landlords' answer to un- paid rents in the past had always been eviction and evictions were beginning again. What could be done to help the tenants? Curiously enough, it was T. M. Healy—not generally to be classed as an agrarian—who suggested a possible solution, at a meeting in Monaghan two days before Dillon's speech in Dublin. He advised the tenants in that area to ask a reasonable abatement of rent from their landlord. If they were refused they should lodge their rents in a bank in the names of three or four trustees (including the parish priest) and use the money to help those whom the landlord might evict. This scheme was not entirely novel—one similar case in County Cork has been traced as far back as 1881—but what was novel was Healy's further suggestion that for such a manoeuvre to be successful it would need to be adopted on a national scale. The suggestion did not attract much attention at the time and was only briefly reported in the Press under the modest headline—'A Plan of Campaign'.[2] More, much more, was to be heard both of the scheme and of the headline. Indeed,

[1] *U.I.*, 10 Oct. 1885.
[2] *Nation*, 10 Oct. 1885. I owe the reference to the 1881 precedent to Mr. Richard Hawkins. It was reported in the *Cork Examiner*, 12 May 1881, and was noted by the authorities—see S.P.O., Chief Secretary's Office, Registered Papers, 19099/1881.

within a fortnight *United Ireland* was giving similar advice which Dillon at once urged the tenants to follow. 'In many instance where the landlords were not wealthy,' he said, 'it would be absolutely impossible for them to evict any great number of tenants, and those evicted could be supported liberally out of the rent they might have given to the landlord.'[1]

(iii)

These were the first mutterings of a coming storm, but for the moment they passed unnoticed in the general excitement of the imminent general election. In Dillon's absence the party and the League had worked out a system of county conventions whereby nationalists in the various constituencies could meet to select the parliamentary candidates to fight the election. Many of these candidates were recommended by Parnell and a small inner group, or caucus, of the party, and most conventions were presided over by M.P.s, but even though control by the politicians was very much a reality, yet the conventions did associate the people with the electoral process and worked, on the whole, very well. Since the selected candidate then took a pledge before the assembled convention to 'sit, act and vote' with the parliamentary party, it was clear that a much more cohesive and disciplined body was going to emerge from this election. Once Dillon had committed himself to re-entering politics he was in constant demand at the conventions and was soon deeply immersed in the old, wearing routine of incessant travelling and speaking up and down the country. The difference, of course, was that now the issue was Home Rule much more than the land question and that on Home Rule he accepted completely the leadership of Parnell.

Parnell himself had by this time had his celebrated secret interview in London with the Earl of Carnarvon, the incoming Lord Lieutenant, and had received a favourable impression—altogether too favourable, as it turned out—of the Conservative attitude to Home Rule, while Carnarvon for his part was apparently convinced of what was *not* the case, that his views and those of the Irish leader were remarkably close together. Carnarvon, in fact, spoke only for himself, and his sympathetic view of the Irish demand later received short shrift from his Cabinet colleagues, but Parnell seems to have come away from the interview strengthened in his inclination to see what could be won from the Conservatives. This was sound policy on several grounds. The Conservatives were more likely to settle the land question satisfactorily, since they had more influence over Irish landlords than the Liberals could ever hope to have. Again, the Conservatives controlled the House of Lords, which was certain to massacre Liberal legislation. And further, the Conservatives were the more congenial party for Irish Catholics living in Britain to vote for, since in educational matters they were the champions of the denominational schools.[2]

[1] *U.I.*, 24 and 31 Oct. 1885.
[2] For a recent authoritative account of the Carnarvon interview see L. P. Curtis, *Coercion and conciliation in Ireland*, chap. 3.

At all events, Parnell had little difficulty in carrying his party with him, and even Dillon, whose hackles might have been expected to rise at this close co-operation with a landlord party, made no reservations. 'I don't believe,' he said in Dublin in October, 'there exists in the world a large party who worked under a leader and were proud to follow his leadership, who have always exercised a greater freedom of speech and a greater independence of thought than the men who call Mr. Parnell their leader . . . and I say that it is to this great quality is due a great deal of the loyalty which I have borne him from the first moment he entered public life . . .'[1] And Parnell, after his fashion, returned this loyalty. Since Dillon had agreed to stand for one of the marginal constituencies—North Tyrone—it was thought advisable to find him a safe seat as a reserve. Mayo, with all its local and family associations, was an obvious choice. There were four divisions and four candidates to be chosen. But there were five names to choose from, including one of the original Land Leaguers, J. J. Louden, whose chief defect in Parnell's eyes seemed to be that he had learnt nothing and forgotten nothing since 1879. With characteristic ruthlessness and ingenuity, Parnell, who presided at the convention, put forward three names and declared them selected on a show of hands. For the fourth seat —East Mayo—he asked the convention to choose between Dillon and Louden. Naturally, Louden had no chance whatever, and though his supporters protested loudly at the time, and he himself wrote bitterly to the papers afterwards, Dillon was selected. In this curious way began his connection with the constituency he was to represent until the end of his political career thirty-three years later, for in 1885 he lost North Tyrone (though only by twenty-three votes) and had to fall back upon his second line of defence.[2]

When the dust settled after the election it was found that in Britain the Liberals had a lead of eighty-six seats over the Conservatives and that the Irish party (including T. P. O'Connor's Liverpool seat) had precisely the same number of members. Parnell was bitterly criticised by some at the time for having committed the Irish vote in Britain to the Conservatives, but, apart from the fact that the effect of this may have been exaggerated by contemporaries, the closer the balance between the two parties the greater the leverage for the Irish. And even Parnell could scarcely have anticipated the amount of leverage he had actually achieved. Right up to the election Gladstone had not revealed his mind and it was only after the results were out, but before Parliament reassembled, that his son Herbert let it be known that his father was thinking along the lines of Home Rule. This 'Hawarden Kite' was technically unauthorised, but if it revealed that Gladstone at least was moving towards Home Rule, the opening of Parliament on 21 January indicated that the Conservatives were moving rapidly away from it. At once the Government dropped even the pretence of an alliance with the Parnellites and announced its intention of reintroducing coercion, whereupon Parnellites and Liberals combined to defeat it.

[1] *U.I.*, 24 Oct. 1885.   [2] C. Cruise O'Brien, *Parnell and his party*, pp. 131–2.

Gladstone then took office and settled down to the delicate—and, as it soon proved, impossible—task of carrying the whole of his party with him on Home Rule.

While he grappled with this problem Parnell's own control of *his* party was suddenly threatened by an incident which might easily have paralysed the Irish forces at that crucial moment. T. P. O'Connor had been returned for Galway city as well as for Liverpool. Since he chose to sit for the latter there was a vacancy in Galway. For this Galway seat Parnell recommended none other than Captain O'Shea, whose wife's lover he had been for several years past. What his motives were, and by what sort of pressures he was driven to this desperate expedient, is no part of this story. What is relevant, however, is that his action immediately provoked a virtual mutiny in the party. O'Shea was intensely unpopular, he was not a pledge-bound member, he had a very poor parliamentary record, and to inflict him again on an Irish constituency (he had previously sat for Clare) seemed an intolerable insult. Moreover, although the rank-and-file most probably did not realise the true inwardness of the O'Shea affair at that time, those who were most prominent in the revolt—T. M. Healy and Joseph Biggar—certainly did so. What made their revolt so serious was that together they proceeded to Galway with the declared intention of blocking O'Shea's candidature. Other leading members of the party, however, though no friends to O'Shea, placed the unity of the party and loyalty to Parnell above all else. Telegrams flowed in a mounting tide to Galway, urging Healy and Biggar not to press their opposition, but they stood their ground until Parnell descended on the constituency in person and exerted his full authority to secure the selection of O'Shea.

Where did Dillon stand in all this? He was at Ballaghaderrin when the crisis broke and was kept informed by William O'Brien. As he afterwards used to tell the story, his impulse had been to go to Galway to take his place beside Healy and Biggar, and he had even reached the point of ordering the carriage to take him there when a telegram came from O'Brien telling him not to go.[1] This was followed on 7 February by a letter in which O'Brien thanked him for his action, or rather, inaction. Of course, he said, they all shared Dillon's loathing for O'Shea, but they could not afford to indulge their feelings. 'The question was, in the special circumstances of the moment, whether we should swallow O'Shea or utterly destroy our movement and party at its brightest moment for a personal reason which we could not explain. It was a bitter and scandalous alternative, but it seemed to us an alternative between accepting an odious personality and chaos.'[2]

The next day O'Brien, and those acting with him, sent off telegrams asking each member of the party to authorise the attachment of his name

---

[1] Family information. Dr. Cruise O'Brien is incorrect in stating (p. 177) that Dillon's intention had been to support O'Shea.

[2] T. W. Moody, 'Parnell and the Galway election of 1886', *I.H.S.*, ix (Mar. 1955), pp. 319–38.

to a public declaration in support of Parnell. On 9 February the names of fifty signatories were published, but Dillon's, most conspicuously, was absent. To Harrington, the secretary of the League, he had sent this reply: 'Regret deeply but cannot give my name. I shall say nothing unless Healy is attacked.'[1] His contribution to the crisis was, therefore, negative throughout, but not less important for that. If he had openly sided with Biggar and Healy the result would have been incalculable and the party might not have survived such a split. On the other hand, he could not bring himself to express public enthusiasm for Parnell. O'Brien's letter to Dillon is studiously discreet, but it carries the strong implication that both he and Dillon were aware of the relationship between Parnell and Mrs. O'Shea. Dillon, whose standards were high and austere, could never have brought himself to back O'Shea's candidature, which he could only have regarded as contemptible in itself and as pressed upon the party for degrading reasons. But, from Parnell's point of view, his silence could be construed as ominous rather than forbearing, since, after all, he had *not* signed the declaration of support. He who was not with him might be presumed to be against him and it may well be that this, more than Dillon's recent declarations of loyalty, were what registered most with his leader.

Nevertheless, the loyalty persisted. In the first speech he delivered after the crisis (16 February) Dillon warned his audience that it was a time for silence and restraint. True, he was speaking about Home Rule, but it was a phrase to which many present could have given a different interpretation; and even silence, he suggested, had its limits. By their silence at this crucial point in the struggle they could convince the world that Parnell was 'fully authorised to speak on behalf and negotiate on behalf of the Irish people'. If Parnell thought the moment ripe for Home Rule, farmers and others with grievances would be prepared to make sacrifices. But, if 'Whig promises' proved false, and Home Rule did not materialise, then there would be nothing for it but to take up the fight once more.[2] Since he had drawn attention a fortnight earlier to the grave plight of the farmers and had forecast that there would be more evictions which would have to be resisted, it is clear that his mind was already running on a resurrection of the land struggle should Home Rule not go through.[3]

How it failed to go through is a familiar story which need not concern us here. Gladstone, having shed Hartingtonian Whigs on the right and Chamberlainite Radicals on the left, struggled gamely on against impossible odds, but his Home Rule Bill, after a tense and sometimes bitter debate, was defeated on the second reading by thirty votes. Parliament was at once dissolved and the ensuing general election was fought very largely on the Home Rule issue. It did not essentially change the Irish representation— eighty-five nationalists (later restored to eighty-six) were returned—but in Britain the outcome was very different. The Unionists (including both Conservatives and Liberal Unionists) won 394 seats, the Liberals 191.

[1] C. Cruise O'Brien, op. cit., p. 178 n. 1.   [2] *F.J.*, 17 Feb. 1886.
[3] *F.J.*, 3 Feb. 1886.

Even with the support of the Irish party, Gladstone thus began the new Parliament in a minority of 118. But the defeat of Home Rule meant not only the postponement of Irish aspirations to a distant future. It involved with it the defeat of a thoroughgoing measure of land purchase which Gladstone, much to the disquiet of some of his own party, had insisted was an essential part of a final settlement. It followed, therefore, as Dillon had prophesied, that the inability of the Liberals to redeem their promise of Home Rule brought the land problem once more into the foreground. Indeed, Dillon himself had explained to that ardent and poetic supporter of lost causes, Wilfrid Scawen Blunt, as early as 2 June—five days *before* the decisive vote on Home Rule—that if Gladstone's gamble did not come off and Lord Salisbury returned to power in the autumn 'all were prepared for a new land campaign'.[1] While Home Rule hung in the balance Dillon had observed meticulous restraint and had pledged his full support for Gladstone's Bill, but after the issue was decided he was free, like Gladstone on an earlier and famous occasion, to come among his people 'unmuzzled'.[2]

Once he did so it began to appear from his speeches that the Home Rule crisis had left him with two overwhelming impressions. One was that there now did exist in England a genuine fund of goodwill towards Ireland. 'In spite of all we have suffered from the English democracy in the past,' he said in Dublin just after the Bill had been defeated, 'in their present attitude they have established a claim to our friendship and our gratitude.'[3] His discovery of 'the English democracy' was carried further during the election campaign, which he spent mainly speaking in England and hardly at all in Ireland, and the favourable opinion he formed in 1886 of the English people, as distinct from their rulers, was one he never wholly abandoned thereafter. Indeed, in years to come his relations with the rank-and-file of Liberal supporters in England were to become closer than those of almost any other Irish Member.

The second impression he carried away from the events of that exciting summer was that Gladstone's cardinal mistake had been to couple land purchase with the Home Rule settlement. In future, he suggested (in a speech at Dublin when the full extent of the swing against the Liberals had become known), the two issues should be separated—preferably in such a way that land purchase could be dealt with after Home Rule had been achieved. 'We found', he said, 'that it swamped the boat at the last election and there is nothing for it now but to throw it overboard.'[4] In the long term this was no doubt realistic, but most Irish farmers were more interested in the short term, and in the short term they were faced with intensifying agricultural depression and with its inevitable concomitants of unpaid rents and ruthless evictions. We know from the findings of a Royal Commission

[1] W. Scawen Blunt, *The land war in Ireland* (London, 1912), pp. 197–9.

[2] Ending his contribution to the Home Rule debate, he had ominously remarked: 'It is true that there is a truce of God in Ireland at the present time, but how long will it last?' (Hansard, 3, cccv, 1004–9).

[3] *U.I.*, 19 June 1886.

[4] *U.I.*, 31 July 1886.

(the Cowper Commission), which collected evidence in the latter part of 1886, but did not report until early in 1887, that for the previous two years prices of crops and of livestock had been falling catastrophically and that this was due partly to American competition, partly to soil exhaustion and partly to the restriction of credit by Irish banks, shops and moneylenders.[1] Because of the depression even the judicial rents fixed under the Act of 1881 were proving impossible to pay, while, of course, on those estates which had so far not been affected by the Land Act the position was even worse. As far back as January 1886 there had been ominous signs on the Galway estates of the miserly Marquess of Clanricarde that in these harsh circumstances the instinct of the people was to resist eviction. At that time, and so long as Home Rule remained a possibility, Parnell had tried through the Irish National League to damp down the agitation, but in the absence of Home Rule and with the approach of autumn it was unlikely that he could restrain the tenant-farmers much longer.[2]

It was with this situation in view that on 4 August the Irish party passed a resolution warning the Government that payment of the judicial rents would be impossible. When Parliament reassembled later that month Parnell moved an amendment to the Address—which was seconded by Dillon—calling attention to the plight of the tenants, especially those on the Clanricarde estates at Woodford, where evictions were again in progress. In September, Parnell returned to the attack by introducing a Tenants' Relief Bill which was intended to enable the land courts to suspend evictions where a tenant paid half the rent due, to admit leaseholders to the benefits of the Act of 1881, and to give the courts power to reduce even the judicial rents already fixed. Predictably, this was rejected by the strong Conservative majority in the House of Commons and the way lay clear for a renewal of the land war.[3] Parnell's immediate reaction was to authorise an appeal to America for funds to assist the tenants who would soon be flocking in large numbers for relief. The tone of the appeal was studiously moderate, the aid being requested to 'assist in preserving for our movement that peaceable character which had enabled it to win the most recent and almost crowning triumph'.[4]

But would the movement remain, could it possibly remain, peaceable? If Parnell had his way, perhaps it might. For him, the supreme objective was still Home Rule and this could only be won by building on that foundation of Anglo-Irish goodwill that had been laid in 1886. A renewal of the land war, with all the outrage and violence this entailed, might shatter this goodwill at the outset and set back the national cause for many years. But there were others who were nearer to the mind and heart of rural Ireland than Parnell and for them the Government refusal even to admit the existence of a crisis was a challenge to action they were in no mood to refuse.

[1] *Report of the Royal Commission on the Land Law (Ireland) Act, 1881, and the Purchase of Land (Ireland) Act, 1885* [C. 4969], H.C. 1887, xxvi, 8, para. 16.
[2] Cruise O'Brien, *Parnell and his party*, pp. 165, 197–8.
[3] Curtis, *Coercion and conciliation in Ireland*, pp. 142–4.
[4] *U.I.*, 2 Oct. 1886; Cruise O'Brien, op. cit., pp. 200–1.

It must therefore have been with a sense of inevitability that members saw Dillon rise from the Irish benches after the Tenant's Relief Bill had been rejected and heard him pour out his indignation and scorn in language that powerfully recalled the days of the old Land Leagué:

> I go back to Ireland [he said] to tell the tenant that if he wishes to live he must trust his own exertions; and so long as I have life and liberty . . . so long shall I tell the people of Ireland to continue in that course of persistent and determined agitation by which in the past they have won every single liberty and every single concession which has been granted to them, and by which in the future, if they will only show perseverance and bravery, they will win in spite of the Irish landlords and in spite of this House, the right to live as freemen in the land of their birth.[1]

And on this note, as surely a declaration of war as any speech he ever made, he left for Ireland.

[1] *Hansard*, 3, cccix, 1223–47; *U.I.*, 25 Sept. 1886.

4
The Land War:
Second Phase[1]

(i)

Dillon's dramatic departure from the House of Commons not only sym-
bolised the re-emergence of agrarianism as the dominant theme in Irish
politics, but also marked an important, if temporary, shift in the leadership
of the movement. Parnell's career up to that time had been a strange
chiaroscuro, hesitating between the extremes of brassy publicity and almost
total inaccessibility. Now, in the autumn of 1886, he melted once more into
the shadows, remaining there for the better part of the next eighteen months,
and appearing fleetingly and enigmatically only when driven by absolute
necessity. The vacuum thus created was filled by a triumvirate—the three
men who, through the National League, *United Ireland* and the apparatus
of public meetings, exercised most influence in the country. These were
Dillon himself, William O'Brien, and the secretary of the League, Timothy
Harrington. Using the National League as their base of operations, they
met in Dublin to frame a policy that would give the tenants the kind of
protection which the Government, following the rejection of Parnell's
Bill, could not or would not afford.[2] Parnell later claimed to have no knowledge of what was in the wind, but, although there is a conflict of evidence
about this in the recollections of his followers, it is clear enough, both from
his own warnings to the House of Commons and from the fact that he
sponsored the appeal for American funds, that he was fully aware that
another crisis in the history of the land question was looming.[3] On the
other hand, it is quite possible that he did not learn the details of what was
proposed by his lieutenants because he did not wish to learn them. Apart
from his own ill health, and his obsessive preoccupation with Katharine
O'Shea—both factors tending to withdraw him from public life at this

[1] An earlier version of this chapter appeared as an article, 'John Dillon and the Plan
of Campaign', in *I.H.S.* (Sept. 1965) xiv, 313–47. The present version is considerably
altered, but I am grateful to the editors of *Irish Historical Studies*, Professor T. W.
Moody and Professor T. Desmond Williams, for permission to include material used in
the article.
[2] It is difficult to fix precisely the date of their meetings, but they were all in Dublin
during September and October, and O'Brien's recollections indicate that they began to
discuss their plans soon after Parnell's Bill was defeated (W. O'Brien, *Evening memories*
(Dublin and London, 1920), pp. 157–8).
[3] C. Cruise O'Brien, *Parnell and his party*, pp. 202–3.

period—there were obvious political reasons why he should prefer not to know too much. As a constitutional leader bent upon nurturing the tender plant of Liberal friendship, the last thing he wanted was to become involved in a new land war which, with its inevitable outrages and attacks upon property, was bound to disturb peace-loving Englishmen of all parties.

At all events, whatever his reactions might or might not be, the leaders in Ireland resolved to proceed on their own. As early as 28 September Dillon, speaking in Dublin at the Central Branch of the League, advised the tenants to organise themselves by estates for the coming struggle, and on 17 October, speaking at Woodford, in the heart of the already restless Clanricarde country, he gave the first glimpse of what this might mean in practice:

> When we meet with an estate where the people are courageous and determined, we advise them to meet together, each estate by itself, and decide what [rent reduction] is fair to ask, and ask that together, and if they are refused there is but one course open to them if they mean to fight according to the policy of brave men—that is, to pay a portion of the rent which they have offered to the landlord into the hands of two or three men in whom they place trust. That must be done privately and you must not inform the public where the money is placed. Thus every man who is evicted can get an allowance from them as long as he is out and, believe me, if the landlord sees that he won't go very far . . .[1]

This advice has, of course, a familiar ring. It is substantially the same advice which, as we saw earlier, first Healy and then Dillon had given the tenants the previous year. And even since then, in January 1886, the police had noticed that in east Galway branches of the League had been trying to put a similar policy into practice, though not, apparently, to any great effect except on the Clanricarde estate, where little or no rent was paid after the landlord had refused a request for a 50 per cent abatement.[2] But two things gave Dillon's speech a significance lacking in these earlier precedents. The first was that evictions were increasing rapidly both in number and in geographical extent—at the end of September they were reported not only from Galway, but also from Clare, Cork, Kerry, Limerick, Kildare, Kilkenny, Wexford and Roscommon—while it was morally certain that widespread failures to meet the November rent demands would swell their number still further. And the other new factor in the situation was that Dillon's speech was not an isolated incident, but the prologue to something much more serious. How serious was indicated by the document which appeared in *United Ireland* on 23 October. It was entitled 'A Plan of Campaign', and in it the author (anonymous, but known to have been Timothy Harrington) recommended the scheme put forward by Dillon a week earlier as one suitable for adoption by the tenants generally. The tone

---

[1] *U.I.*, 2 Oct. and 23 Oct. 1886.
[2] S.P.O., Chief Secretary's Office, Registered Papers 1888, no. 26523.

was business-like rather than emotional and Harrington had much practical advice to offer as to how the tenants should go about their collective
bargaining. He warned them, for example, not to make the elementary
mistake of frittering away their funds in defending tenants in the courts,
and, on behalf of the Irish National League, he offered to help tenants to
guard against embezzlement by dishonest trustees. Even more important,
he stated that the League would maintain grants to the evicted tenants
after the estate funds had been exhausted. Finally, he reminded them of the
power of the boycott. 'That the farms thus unjustly evicted will be left
severely alone, and everyone who aids the evictors shunned, is scarcely
necessary to say.'[2]

Immediately the Plan was made public Dillon, O'Brien and other M.P.s
descended upon various key points, mostly in the south and west, to explain
it to the tenants and to help them carry it out. The most critical situation
was in Galway on the Clanricarde estates, and it was there, in the little
town of Portumna, that Dillon and O'Brien together gave the first demonstration of the new tactics. On 18 November the landlord's agent was in
his office waiting to receive the rents from the tenantry. To his astonishment, four hundred of them marched into the town with banners flying
and a brass band blaring to greet the two exponents of the Plan who had
just arrived. After speeches from the visitors explaining what the tenants
should do, the procession marched to the land agent's office and told him
they would pay their rents less a 40 per cent reduction, and even that only
if the Woodford farmers evicted the previous August were reinstated. The
agent, flabbergasted, replied that he had no power to agree to any such
terms. 'This means war!' exclaimed one of the tenants' representatives and
the four hundred moved off again to the strains of 'The minstrel boy', back
to the hotel where Dillon and O'Brien were staying. There, they paid over
to the two leaders the rents less 40 per cent, on the agreement that these
would be lodged in the bank on the tenants' behalf. And that night, with
a torchlight procession and the inevitable band, they escorted their distinguished guests triumphantly out of the town.[3]

The Portumna rent collection naturally received the utmost publicity
in the nationalist Press, and it provided the model for a number of others
in different parts of the country. Within a matter of weeks it became clear
that, unless checked, the organisers of the Plan had hit upon a device which
could make life very difficult for a great many landlords. Yet the reaction
of the Government was curiously hesitant. We know now that those on
the spot were more sympathetic to the hardships of the tenants than was
realised at the time. Both the Chief Secretary, Sir Michael Hicks Beach,
and General Sir Redvers Buller (who had been sent over to reclaim Kerry
and Clare for law and order) tried hard to dissuade landlords from pre-

---

[1] *U.I.*, 2 Oct. 1886.
[2] *U.I.*, 23 Oct. 1886.
[3] *F.J.*, 19 Nov. 1886; there is a vivid but inaccurate account in O'Brien, *Evening
memories*, pp. 171–4.

mature or harsh evictions and in some cases even went so far as to resist requests for official aid in carrying them out.[1] Perhaps because they had not a very high opinion of Irish landlords, perhaps because they were reluctant to face the implications of a recrudescence of the land war, they did not take alarm as soon as they might have done, and up to the end of October seem to have been under the impression that the country was 'settling down'.[2] But after Portumna this comfortable illusion vanished and the Chief Secretary, writing half apologetically to Lord Salisbury, explained that originally the Irish Government had been advised by its law officers not to take action against the Plan or those who published or propagated it. 'There seemed reason, too, to hope', he said, 'that the Irish tenants would not care to deposit their money with "trustees" against whom they could have no remedy, if they bolted with it. But Dillon and Co. *have* been strong enough to get them to do this already in several instances . . . And as more meetings are held in different parts . . . the example is spreading rapidly and, if not checked, may too probably lead to a suspension of the payment of rent, very generally, in the west and south.'[3]

By the time this letter was written Hicks Beach had already taken the first decorous steps in the formal legal ballet which always preceded the real clash between Government and agrarians in Ireland. On 26 November 1886 Dillon was cited before the court of Queen's Bench to give bail for 'good behaviour' and at the same time a meeting due to be held in Sligo to advance the Plan was 'proclaimed'. Neither of these moves affected the situation in the slightest. Dillon secured an adjournment, the Sligo meeting was held and the rent collections continued.[4] When Dillon's case eventually came to trial on 13 December he used the courtroom as the platform for a powerful speech in defence of the Plan, making the point, which came uncomfortably near the bone, that the kind of pressure he was urging the tenants to bring to bear against the landlords was not markedly different from that which the Chief Secretary had already tried to exert upon them:

> I want to know [he asked] if it is going to be the decision of this court, that where we are engaged in an attempt to do, perhaps to a greater extent, what the executive government have endeavoured to do—where we are engaged in an attempt to save the people from ruin and extermination . . . not by encouraging lawlessness and crime . . . but by endeavouring to induce the people to substitute, for the methods which they had always adopted in the past . . . the methods of public and open organisation . . . we are to be brought up before this court, and held to bail for good behaviour, as being persons of ill-fame?[5]

[1] Curtis, *Coercion and conciliation*, pp. 140–2, 148–9.
[2] Lord Ashbourne to Lord Salisbury, 24 Oct. 1886 (Salisbury Papers).
[3] Sir Michael Hicks Beach to Lord Salisbury, 30 Nov. 1886 (Salisbury Papers).
[4] *F.J.*, 27 and 29 Nov. 1886.
[5] J. J. Clancy (ed.) *Mr. Dillon and the Plan of Campaign* (London, Irish Press Agency pamphlet, 1887).

The short answer to these largely rhetorical questions was 'yes' and the outcome of the case was not only that Dillon had himself to give securities for £2,000 bail, but that the court pronounced the Plan to be 'an absolutely illegal organisation'. This was the signal for which the Government had been waiting. Two days later the police swooped on a rent collection at Loughrea and seized the rents, the books and the trustees, among whom were O'Brien and, inevitably, Dillon.[2] Although they were released immediately afterwards, the Plan was duly proclaimed on 18 December as 'an unlawful and criminal conspiracy', and on 4 January Dillon and the other Loughrea rent collectors were brought to trial in Dublin on the charge of criminal conspiracy. A state trial of this kind was always a form of ritual exercise and this one was no exception. The Crown spent many days trying to find a jury that would convict, while Dillon used the frequent adjournments to come over to London to protest about the way his trial was being handled. The end result was entirely predictable—the prosecution failed to get the jury it wanted and in February 1887 the traversers went free amid great nationalist rejoicing.[3]

In the weeks following this success for the organisers of the Plan their agitation reached what was probably the high-water mark of its success. Rent collections, although driven underground, continued to be effective, and the Plan itself, which in the early weeks had only been adopted on ten or a dozen estates, spread rapidly. Indeed, Dillon himself later reckoned that most of the 116 estates ultimately involved had been affected by the early spring of 1887.[4] But at this point he and O'Brien had to face two new threats—one, as was to be expected, from a renewal of coercion by the Government, and the other, more immediately ominous, from Parnell. On 6 December 1886 Parnell emerged from his obscurity (he had been ill) to ask John Morley, his main link with Gladstone, what effect he thought the Plan was likely to have on English opinion. Morley told him frankly it was having a very bad effect and Parnell, who insisted that the Liberal alliance was 'the fixed point in his tactics', undertook to send for 'one of his lieutenants' and to press for an immediate end to violent speeches. The lieutenant—William O'Brien—duly arrived and had his interview (of which he has left a vivid but probably unreliable description) with his chief in a dense fog at Greenwich Observatory. According to O'Brien's account, he promised that the Plan would not be extended beyond its existing limits 'unless under special circumstances' and that violent speeches would be avoided in future.[5] This preoccupation with violent speeches is explained by a letter John Morley was writing at that very time to Dillon. At Castlerea, on 5 December, Dillon had used language which could be interpreted as meaning that a day of reckoning would come for policemen

[1] *U.I.*, 18 Dec. 1886.
[2] O'Brien, *Evening memories*, pp. 192–3.
[3] *Hansard*, 3, ccx, 847–67, 1826–30; Curtis, op. cit., pp. 164–5.
[4] *Report of the commissioners appointed to inquire into the estates of evicted tenants in Ireland*, H.C. 1893–4 [c. 6935], xxxi, 422, para. 14791.
[5] O'Brien, *Evening memories*, pp. 178–3.

and others who helped with evictions when Ireland had a government of her own.[1] Morley warned him that such speeches were liable to frighten off English supporters of Home Rule. 'Anyhow, it would be of enormous value—if we are, as I trust, to keep up the goodwill between you and the English Liberals—if you could see your way to some effectual explanation of your words.'[2] The clear implication here was that Gladstone (who described Dillon's speech to Morley as 'very bad') could not, as the responsible leader of the Opposition, give any sympathy to a movement which involved direct or indirect illegality.[3] This was made clear to Parnell when he came to see Morley again on 12 December, though Parnell, for his part, brought reassurances that discipline had been restored.[4] This was, in fact, very far from being the case, but for Dillon and O'Brien these exchanges were serious, since they indicated that however much sympathy their efforts on behalf of the tenants might excite in unofficial breasts, they would get no public backing either from Gladstone or from their own leader.

(ii)

Just how serious this might be events were soon to show. At the end of January 1887 the Cabinet decided that it would be necessary to deal with the Plan of Campaign by an unprecedentedly severe Coercion Act. Sir Michael Hicks Beach, whose heart had never been in the work of defending Irish landlords, was clearly not the man for this job, and he was replaced by Arthur Balfour. Balfour's appointment was received by the Irish Members with incredulous laughter, but he was to show himself before long to be one of the ablest and toughest Chief Secretaries Ireland had ever had. Like Gladstone in 1881, he saw the problem of the Irish agitation as twofold, requiring on the one hand the restoration of law and order and on the other hand the granting of substantial land reform. The Coercion Bill which was his answer to the first of these problems was introduced in March, but was so bitterly opposed by the Irish Members that it did not pass into law until July. Its effect (at least as Balfour applied it) was greatly to strengthen the executive in dealing summarily with boycotting, conspiracies against rent, intimidation, resistance to eviction, rioting, unlawful assembly and the inciting of others to commit any such crimes. In addition, there were provisions enabling the Attorney-General to transfer cases involving trial by jury from a disturbed district to one where, in his opinion, a fair and impartial trial could take place. Further, the Lord Lieutenant, acting in conjunction with the Irish Privy Council, was empowered to declare by proclamation that the provisions of the Act were in force in any specified part of the country. And finally, and bitterest pill of all, it was intended that the Act should be 'perpetual', that is, should become a permanent part of the Irish legal code.

[1] *F.J.*, 6 Dec. 1886.   [2] Morley to Dillon, 9 Dec. 1886 (D.P.).
[3] John Morley, *W. E. Gladstone*, iii. 280.
[4] Ibid., iii. 281. For further evidence of Liberal uneasiness about the Plan of Campaign, see Michael Hurst, *Joseph Chamberlain and Liberal Reunion* (London, 1967), p. 94

The sugar that was intended to coat this pill was the Land Act, which also passed slowly through its various stages during 1887. It attempted (too late) to put into effect some of Parnell's suggestions of the previous autumn and it also owed something to the recommendations of the Cowper Commission. Although it was contemptuously dismissed by Dillon as totally inadequate, it did allow for the scaling down of the judicial rents and for further revisions at the end of three years, and it marked an important step by bringing 100,000 leaseholders within the provisions of the Act of 1881. It was in no sense a revolution, as the 1881 Act had been, but it was nevertheless a substantial reform.

For Dillon, however, the crucial question was not whether Balfour could mitigate the hard lot of the tenants, but whether he would succeed in crushing the Plan of Campaign. His accession to office brought new heart to the landlords and a new vigour to the administration of the law in Ireland.[2] But, since the Coercion Act took so long to pass into law, it was not until August that the real clash came. First, Balfour 'proclaimed' the Irish National League as a dangerous association and used his special powers against it to such effect that between then and the end of the year nearly 150 branches (mostly in the south-west) were suppressed.[3] Next, prosecutions were initiated against William O'Brien and John Mandeville, a leader of the Tipperary tenants. On the day appointed, 9 September, O'Brien did not appear for trial at Mitchelstown, but Dillon, accompanied by several English M.P.s, including Henry Labouchere, arrived in the town to be greeted, as he usually was wherever he went in Ireland at this time, by a large, enthusiastic and not readily controlled crowd. He seems himself to have sensed almost at once that trouble might easily break out. 'Let us cut this as short as possible,' he said to Labouchere; 'they will send the police and military into the town. They will attempt something and something may occur if we go on long. I suggest we say a few words and ask them to disperse.'[4] About what happened next there are many different accounts, for inquiries and investigations continued for months afterwards. But the main outline is clear enough. Dillon climbed up on a brake to address the crowd which was densely packed around him. Seeing this, a body of police tried to force their way through to allow an official note-taker to come within earshot of the speaker. Almost immediately scuffles broke out between them and the audience and soon a savage set-to, blackthorns against batons, was in progress. Outnumbered and confused, the police broke off the fight and fled back to the barracks which overlooked the meeting-place. Despite Dillon's effort to clear the ground a seething mob still filled the market-square and stones were thrown at the barracks.

[1] Curtis, *Coercion and conciliation*, pp. 180–3.

[2] Harrington to Dillon, 23 Mar. 1887 (D.P.), for the improved morale of the landlords; *U.I.*, 19 Mar. 1887, for the first arrests of priests, the most striking sign of a new toughness at Dublin Castle.

[3] For details see F. S. L. Lyons, 'John Dillon and the Plan of Campaign', *I.H.S.* (Mar. 1965), xiv, 322.

[4] A. G. Thorold, *The life of Henry Labouchere* (London, 1913), p. 332.

Thereupon the police opened fire and before the crowd could scatter three men were killed and two wounded. This was bad enough, but much worse might have followed if Dillon, with great personal courage, had not walked alone across the now deserted square up to the barracks gate and urged the officer in charge to desist.[1] The matter was immediately raised in Parliament, and although Balfour stood by his policemen, the episode had two major consequences. In the first place, English public opinion was profoundly shocked and Liberals in particular began to show a much more active sympathy for the Plan—many of them were to be found at Irish meetings in the months and years ahead, with the result, certainly not expected at the outset by either Gladstone or Parnell, that the land war in its new phase strengthened rather than weakened the Liberal-Nationalist alliance. And secondly, even though Balfour in public still insisted that the nationalists had provoked the riot and that the police had only acted in self-defence, he himself revised the police regulations to prevent a repetition of the incident and also set on foot a secret investigation to distribute the blame for the undoubted panic which had led to the firing. Writing to his uncle, Lord Salisbury, Balfour admitted that it was perfectly clear that there had been great mismanagement by magistrates and officers, but hoped —rightly as it turned out—that his new instructions would avoid this in the future.[2]

On the short run the Mitchelstown affair made no difference whatever to the ruthlessness with which Balfour pressed home his attack upon the Plan. In November O'Brien, after many adventures, was lodged in Tullamore jail, where he immediately began his fight, half-comic but potentially tragic, against the wearing of prison clothes. His disappearance meant that the main burden of continuing the fight now fell upon Dillon. It was an almost crushing responsibility. True, the National League still retained the loyalty of the people, the tenants remained in remarkably good heart, and, best of all, there was extraordinarily little outrage or violence, except—as at Mitchelstown—in the face of police provocation, or where passion overflowed, as now and then it did, at some particularly harrowing eviction. There was, indeed, some boycotting, but this was implicit in the whole organisation of the Plan and it was tolerated by the leaders as a necessary weapon which they felt able to control. Dillon himself, indeed, was well satisfied during 1887 that the agitation had won 'an immense triumph' in the suppression of agrarian crime. This, at any rate, was the view he expressed to Wilfrid Scawen Blunt in July, but already by September he was beginning to wonder how long this could last. Walking with Blunt one day along Killiney strand, and this was after Mitchelstown, he observed that if any of the organisers of the Plan were to be killed in the course of his work it would open the way for reprisals by extremists, and that if there were to be any large-scale seizure of the leaders by Balfour it might throw

[1] *U.I.*, 10 and 17 Sept. 1887; *F.J.*, 10 Sept. 1887; Hansard, H.C. Debates, 3rd series, col. 331; Thorold, op. cit., pp. 331–6.
[2] Curtis, *Coercion and conciliation*, pp. 197–200, 435–8.

the entire movement into extreme hands. 'We have,' he explained, 'a very delicate and difficult task before us. It will not do for us *all* to be locked up, for that would leave the people without proper guidance. They would then be led by violent and imprudent men and we should have a repetition of the Phoenix Park murders, which would put us back to the position we occupied in 1882. On the other hand, we cannot turn tail or cease to hold our meetings . . . We must hold our meetings as best we can, and only resist when the police, as at Mitchelstown, put themselves clearly in the wrong.'[1]

(iii)

In the history of Irish agitation the traditional counterpoise to extremism had always been the influence of the Church and it was of great significance to the leaders of the Plan that almost from the beginning that influence, with one or two important exceptions, had been thrown behind them. Both the Archbishop of Dublin and the Archbishop of Cashel had come out in support of the tenants and many priests up and down the country had taken an active part in the movement.[2] The fact that Balfour did not scruple to send some of them to prison increased rather than diminished the commitment of the Church to the cause. Nevertheless, from the Government's point of view, there could be no more effective way of combating the Plan than to bring about a massive withdrawal of ecclesiastical support. If this could not be done by jail sentences for erring priests, there were other methods. One, which was highly secret, and in the nature of the case probably not very widely attempted, was to invite the co-operation of the more conservative bishops by suggesting to them the desirability of removing exceptionally troublesome parochial clergy from one part of a diocese to another. We know from the police records that, at a later stage, such co-operation was sought from, and given by, the Bishop of Waterford. By April 1890 it appears that he had moved no fewer than seventeen priests and the Divisional Commissioner of the R.I.C. reported that the Bishop, if carefully handled, could generally be relied upon to help. 'Although the Bishop has not made a clean sweep of all the troublesome priests,' he wrote, 'he has effected some very judicious transfers and is doing very well. His Lordship gives his attention to any matter represented to him, but, I think, he does not like to be pressed. I have therefore been very cautious in having him approached.'[3]

Such co-operation was, however, necessarily sporadic and haphazard

---

[1] W. S. Blunt, *The land war in Ireland*, pp. 292–3, 311. The following month he expressed much the same point of view to R. B. Haldane, one of his closest friends among the younger Liberals. 'We did over and over again repudiate separatism and denounce crime', he insisted; but at the same time added that they could not confine their meetings to the passing of harmless resolutions—if they did, they would be despised as cowards by their own people (Dillon to R. B. Haldane, 12 Oct. [1887], Haldane Papers, National Library of Scotland, MS. 5903, ff. 35–8).

[2] *F.J.*, 2 Dec. 1886; O'Brien, *Evening memories*, pp. 194–200; F. S. L. Lyons, 'John Dillon and the Plan of Campaign', *I.H.S.*, xiv, 324 n. 42.

[3] S.P.O., Crime Branch Special Papers, 120/35, reports from the Divisional Commissioner, 21 Mar. and 1 Apr. 1890.

and the Government aimed at something much more ambitious. As early as the spring of 1887 the Cabinet began to consider the possibility of sending a mission to Rome in order to enlist the Pope's support for an ecclesiastical ban on the agitation. But in this they had been anticipated by Dr. John Healy, Coadjutor Bishop of Clonfert, who the previous December had complained to the Vatican that boycotting was rife again in Ireland and that the clergy were becoming altogether too closely involved. The Pope therefore decided to send over his own representative to find out the true situation, and in July 1887 that representative, Monsignor Persico, arrived in the country.[1] He listened to both sides and was not unsympathetic to the nationalist cause, though in Limerick at least, where the Bishop, Dr. Edward O'Dwyer, was a most uncompromising opponent of the Plan, there seems to have been a feeling among the junior clergy that their point of view was insufficiently represented. However true this was, they were, it seems, firmly told by their Vicar-General that Persico, having ascertained that they were in danger of prosecution, had written urging that no priest should do anything to bring himself within reach of the new Crimes Act.[2] This did not mean that he was completely opposed to the agitation, nor even that the action the Vatican was soon to take was the action he himself would have recommended or wished. No less a person than Cardinal Manning, indeed, was quite convinced that the Persico report alone would not have moved the Pope to action, and when in April 1888 the Papal Rescript condemning the Plan was published, Manning sent a note to Dillon and O'Brien stating quite categorically his belief that 'Monsignor Persico has had no part in this late event. I do not say this lightly.'[3]

Nevertheless, the pressure against the Plan began to build up. In September Dillon had an angry interview with the Bishop of Limerick, who denounced the combination of tenants on the Herberstown estate in that county as 'highway robbery and plunder'. To this Dillon replied, according to Wilfrid Scawen Blunt, who was there, 'with great courage and frankness', pointing out that the local priests themselves had been in favour of action and that he could not possibly now go back on his pledges to the tenants.[4] This was the first direct clash between Dillon and this strong-minded cleric and there were to be many more. But in the immediate sequel the initiative lay not with a local bishop but with Leo XIII. As 1887 drew to a close it became known that an English mission, headed by the Duke of Norfolk, was going to Rome. Dillon, like most other people, leaped to the conclusion that the Government was planning to use papal influence to coerce the Irish clergy into withdrawing from the agitation. At once he reacted furiously in a speech that was aimed as much at Protestant Englishmen as at Catholic Irishmen:

[1] For the Persico mission see P. J. Walsh, *Archbishop Walsh*, chap. 13; P. J. Joyce, *John Healy, Archbishop of Tuam*, chap. 5; C. Cruise O'Brien, *Parnell and his party*, pp. 213–16.

[2] Dillon to Harrington, 12 Dec. 1887 (D.P.).

[3] Blunt, *The land war in Ireland*, p. 435.

[4] Ibid., pp. 319–21.

If [he said] Mr. Balfour imagined he was going to better his position by applying for the pope's assistance, he misjudged the Catholics of Ireland. These very men who were now calling in this strange assistance to the back of the English government in Ireland were the men who only a short time ago used to say to Englishmen that Home Rule meant Rome Rule. What kind of rule meant Rome Rule now? He said as an Irish Catholic, that although they revered the Pope in Rome as the head of their religion, they would no more take their political guidance from the Pope of Rome than from the Sultan of Turkey.[1]

These were brave words, but, in fact, at that moment Dillon was playing from weakness, not from strength. It is clear from his private papers that he was finding the strain of leading the movement virtually single-handed almost intolerable. With O'Brien in prison he dared not risk being caught himself and had accordingly to spend most of his time in England, where week after week he addressed meetings at which he stressed both the absence of serious crime in Ireland and also the fact that for the Irish tenant the Plan of Campaign represented a form of combination not essentially different from the trade-union organisation of the British working-man. This was valuable work and in doing it he was laying the foundations for the high reputation he enjoyed in England, especially among Liberals, for the rest of his life. But it was also wearing work, and in the short run not obviously rewarding. It is not surprising, therefore, that he turned with relief to one house where he was always certain of welcome. This was the home of Sir James Mathew, a judge of the High Court and on close terms not only with most of the legal luminaries of his day but also with many of the rising men in the Liberal Party. Sir James was himself an Irishman (in fact, a nephew of the famous Franciscan apostle of temperance, Father Mathew) and a graduate of the University of Dublin. He, of course, took no part in politics, but the general atmosphere in his house was warmly sympathetic to Home Rule. His daughter Elizabeth, indeed, went much further and was a passionate nationalist. To be more precise she was a passionate admirer of John Dillon, whom she was eventually to marry. In 1887 he was not yet in love with her, but he was greatly drawn to her and to her family, relaxing among them as he did nowhere else. By the end of November she thought him, not surprisingly, 'very tired and wan' and recorded with horror in her diary that he spoke 'with desperate calmness of the certainty he felt of being arrested directly he goes back to Ireland'.[2]

This, however, was only one of his worries. His own personal safety was never his main concern, but what did drive him almost to distraction was the realisation that if he and O'Brien were arrested simultaneously the movement might collapse altogether. Unless, of course, Parnell were to emerge once more from his chosen obscurity. But of this, as Dillon wrote bitterly to Harrington a few days later, there was no sign:

---

[1] *F.J.*, 19 Dec. 1887.   [2] Diary of Elizabeth Mathew, 27 Nov. 1887 (D.P.).

The situation has become very serious indeed. I have utterly failed to get any word of him. He plainly means to boycott us till the opening of parliament at all events. I would have no fault to find with his not appearing publicly to communicate with us. But it is an extraordinary line of policy to go off without a word—and most of all without so far as I know making any arrangement to secure that we shall not be stranded for money . . . it will be simply monstrous if we run short of money in a crisis like this.[1]

To add to his problems he had heard from John Morley, so he told Harrington, that Balfour was contemplating a deal with the Irish bishops— a Catholic university in exchange for episcopal support against the Plan. The idea filled him with rage and he planned to block the scheme by publishing a rumour of it in *United Ireland*, together with a note that no Catholic Irishman would for a moment believe that an Irish bishop would enter into such an infamous transaction. Morley's information was close enough to the mark. We now know that in October 1887 a group of English and Irish Catholics led by the Duke of Norfolk, and including the anti-Plan Bishops Healy and O'Dwyer, asked Balfour to approach the Vatican with a view to establishing and endowing such a university. Balfour, who was always interested in the possibility of broadening the base of higher education in Ireland, took the suggestion seriously enough to write a memorandum on the subject, but, as he explained to Salisbury, it should be made plain that such a concession would be granted only 'when, by the efforts of the Holy Father, the Irish priesthood shall have learnt the ten commandments'.[2] At that precise moment Balfour did not see his way clear to bring the project forward and it therefore lapsed for the time being; but the incident was instructive, revealing as it did how far the Government was prepared to go to bribe the Irish Church, and also how quick Dillon was to realise the threat implied in a manoeuvre of this kind. The inescapable fact that faced him whatever way he turned was that the attitude of the Church was of absolutely crucial significance to him, yet at the same time was something which it was beyond his power to control.

It was predictable, therefore, that when the crisis came to a climax with the publication at the end of April of the papal rescript condemning the Plan he should react with vehemence, indeed with passion. The rescript took the line that the Plan was to be discountenanced on three grounds: that it was unlawful to break contracts such as tenants had voluntarily entered into with their landlords, that the courts were available for those who sought rent reductions, and that the funds for administering the Plan had been extorted from those contributing.[3] In meeting this threat Dillon took the principal part, first discussing with Archbishop Croke on 28 April the proper line to be pursued. Three days later an article appeared in the Press, apparently inspired by Croke, which argued ingeniously that the Plan would indeed deserve to be condemned if it fell within the categories

[1] Dillon to Harrington, 12 Dec. 1887 (D.P.).
[2] Curtis, *Coercion and conciliation*, pp. 275–6, 387–8.   [3] *F.J.*, 27 and 30 Apr. 1888.

mentioned in the rescript, but as, in fact, it did not, and since the whole document was based on a mistaken view of the landlord-tenant relationship, it could not possibly be regarded as applying to Irish conditions.[1] Following on this, Dillon, in concert with Dr. Kenny and William O'Brien (and with Parnell's agreement), arranged for a meeting of Irish Catholic M.P.s to be held on 14 May. But he dared not wait so long without himself voicing some sort of protest. On 7 May, therefore, at Drogheda, he made a major speech in which, very characteristically, he went beyond the immediate issue of the Plan and the rescript—*that* could be left to the theologians, who, he was confident, would rule that the rescript was inapplicable to Ireland. What he was concerned with was its political significance. It was, he suggested, an insult to the Irish Church, the more so because it indicated, in his belief, 'that in the hour of our difficulty the voice of Catholics in England—a miserable crew—prevails at Rome over the voice of our bishops'. Nor could the papacy itself escape a share of the blame for the timing of this blow, 'when we are engaged in a life-and-death struggle with a cruel Government, when priests are in prison and treated as criminals for no other reason than that which they were taught by their Master . . . to sympathise with the oppressed, the suffering and the poor . . .' And then, in a remarkable peroration, which far transcended the matter immediately at stake, he memorably defined his own view of the relations between Church and State:

> Are we to be freemen in Ireland or are we to conduct our public affairs at the bidding of any man who lives outside Ireland? We owe it to ourselves, we owe it to our friends in England, we owe it to the ancient traditions of our country, we owe it to our Protestant fellow-countrymen, who expect they are about to share with us a free Ireland, that it will not be an Ireland that will conduct its affairs at the bidding of any body of cardinals. I take my stand upon that principle, and I will stand or fall by that principle, and I assert here today that in the conduct of our national affairs, the defending and asserting of our rights, we Irishmen—Protestant and Catholic alike—should be free from any interference; whether it comes from Italy or any other country. That is the principle of Irish liberty, and I say without fear that if to-morrow, in asserting the freedom of Ireland, we were to exchange for servitude in Westminster servitude to the cardinal who signs that document or any body of cardinals in Rome, then I would bid good-bye for ever to the struggle for Irish freedom.[2]

On the day following this outburst Parnell at last broke silence. Speaking at the Eighty Club in London, to an audience mainly composed of Liberal notabilities, he contemptuously dismissed the papal rescript as bound to be 'a disastrous failure' which he was prepared to leave to his Catholic colleagues to deal with. As to the Plan of Campaign, itself, while not actually throwing it overboard, he told his listeners that he had been ill

---

[1] *Irish Catholic*, 5 May 1888.   [2] *F.J.*, 8 May 1888; *U.I.*, 12 May 1888.

when it was started and that he would have advised against it because of its bad effect upon public opinion. By the time he did know of it, early in 1887, it was too late to disavow it, since Dillon and O'Brien were then under arrest—a curious chronological error this, since it was in December 1886 that O'Brien had come to London to see him, at a time when both he and Dillon were still free men. Parnell admitted, however, that the restrictions on the spread of the Plan which he had then imposed had been observed on the whole, though he would have preferred to replace it gradually by a new 'method of organisation' which he was at that moment contemplating. 'But,' he added ominously, 'we shall now have to wait.'[1]

This speech has been described by one authority as a masterpiece, and perhaps it was, in the sense that Parnell achieved his main purpose of placing both Plan and rescript in perspective and reminding, not merely his London audience, but anxious Irishmen at home, that compared with Home Rule these were peripheral issues and that, to win Home Rule, the cultivation of the Liberal alliance must continue to be the cardinal point of nationalist policy. To the protagonists of the Plan, naturally enough, it seemed anything but masterly. William O'Brien, who, in Dillon's view, was about at the end of his tether,[2] regarded the speech, critical as it was of the Plan, as tantamount to a sentence of death. In a passion he dashed off an almost incoherent article for *United Ireland*, lamenting the demise of their agitation, but bowing to Parnell's authority, since he was 'the only man living who has the right and the power to wound the Plan of Campaign in a fatal spot'. The article, fortunately for all concerned, never got beyond the proof stage and the envelope containing the proof is still in the Dillon Papers marked in Dillon's own hand: 'This article was stopped by Tim Harrington and me. Had it been published, it would have utterly ruined our movement and driven me and others out of public life.'[3] Both the article itself, almost abject in its submission to 'the chief', and the action of O'Brien's colleagues in stopping it, were remarkable manifestations of loyalty to Parnell and of determination to preserve at any rate the façade of unity in the movement. Yet it is difficult not to feel that for Dillon at least, who, as we have seen, had been complaining bitterly five months earlier about Parnell's neglect, this was one more step along the road of disillusionment. His loyalty in this crisis was real enough, but it may well have been loyalty to the tenants who depended on him, rather than to the leader on whom he himself found it increasingly difficult to depend.

(iv)

As it turned out, neither the rescript nor the Eighty Club speech were as devastating in their effects as might have been expected. True, when the bishops met on 9 May Dr. Croke had a hard job to prevent them from passing a resolution of censure upon Dillon, but this was more for his

---

[1] *F.J.*, 9 May 1888.   [2] For evidence of this, see below pp. 102–3.
[3] Cruise O'Brien, *Parnell and his party*, pp. 218–20.

criticism of the Vatican than for his agrarian activities, and when at the end of the month the hierarchy produced its own commentary on the rescript, it was clear enough—to those who could read between the lines of its respectful and platitudinous prose—that the Church was reluctant to commit itself to out-and-out opposition to the tenants' movement. Indeed, it would have been difficult to do this without risking a collision with the Catholic members of the parliamentary party, who, at their meeting of 17 May, had come out strongly in favour of the Plan and against interference by the Holy See 'with the Irish people in the management of their political affairs'.[1] So far as the question originally at issue was concerned—the participation of the clergy in the agitation—it is probably fair to say that the rescript gave the more cautious clergy an excuse either to withdraw or to stand aside, but there is little sign that those who were already deeply committed felt any less committed. As late as July the Under-Secretary wrote to Balfour that 'certainly the rescript has had no effect as *yet*', and in October he was reduced to the extremity of suggesting that priests convicted of forwarding the Plan should be put into prison dress.[2]

It took time, of course, before the crisis of May 1888 could be seen in perspective, but time was precisely what Dillon had not got. His presentiment that his return to Ireland would lead to his conviction had been speedily fulfilled. At his very first public meeting in April, when he was exhorting the tenants of Lord Massereene, whose estates were not far from the town of Drogheda, to join the Plan he was at once arrested and soon afterwards was sentenced to six months' imprisonment. By using the machinery of appeal he was able to stay out of jail until 20 June (when he was sent to Dundalk prison), but throughout the crisis over the rescript he had to act with the knowledge that in a matter of weeks he was going to be removed from the scene.[3] This largely explains the note of urgency in his speeches during his last days of liberty. In the short space that was left to him he had to rivet the attention of the tenants to the need for upholding the Plan and to inspire them with his own conviction that not merely rents but fundamental principles of liberty were involved in the struggle. The rescript was still his main theme and he attacked it in some of the most passionate speeches of his career. 'We are here to declare,' he said to a mass meeting in Dublin on 20 May, 'that we will not submit or bow to action like this and that we will assert in spite of the Tory Government, in spite of English intrigues at Rome, our civil rights and show to the whole world that we know how to distinguish between spiritual and political affairs.' And at this same meeting, referring to the possibility that priests might in future be prohibited from political activity, he insisted on the right of the priest to be a citizen as well as a spiritual leader:

[1] Ibid., pp. 221–4.

[2] Sir J. W. Ridgeway to A. J. Balfour, 3 July and 5 Oct. 1888 (Balfour Papers, B.M. Add. MS. 49808, f. 172, and 49809, f. 2).

[3] For his arrest and imprisonment see S.P.O., Chief Secretary's Office, Registered Papers, 1888, no. 8259; *U.I.*, 21 Apr. 1888, 23 June 1888.

Look over the whole of Europe to-day. Point me out a single country in which the Catholic priest occupies the same position that he does in Ireland. Why is that so? That is so because we have vindicated throughout our history the right of the Catholic priest to be a citizen as well as a priest . . . The attachment of the Irish people for their priesthood and for the See of Rome has survived the rack and the gibbet, but I doubt very much whether it would survive if we were to see the priests forbidden to sympathise with the poor and, as they were told to do by the Great Master, to denounce iniquity even when it was in high places. I say woe to the Catholic Church in Ireland if the priests are driven by the court of Rome from politics, and woe still more if we know it has been done at the bidding of a corrupt English ministry.[1]

This was strong language, but Dillon did not hesitate to repeat it week after week before his disappearance into Dundalk prison. Nowadays, when passions, agrarian and religious, have subsided, it is difficult to appreciate the courage that was needed to make such speeches. But in the Ireland of the 1880s he was a brave man who would face not merely the Irish hierarchy, but the papacy itself, on an issue of this kind. No doubt he had much intelligent lay sympathy behind him (though equally, no doubt, he shocked many timid souls to the core), but no other leader spoke out as consistently and boldly as he did. Indeed, few other Irish Catholic laymen in responsible positions have ever taken their stand so openly, or defined the proper relations of Church and State with so much clarity and force. Through it all Dillon remained personally devout—after the crisis of his youth his faith was absolutely central to his existence—but that did not prevent him, either in 1888 or afterwards, from attacking undue clerical influence wherever he found it. In 1888 he was on the side of the parish priest against higher ecclesiastical authority. In later years, as we shall see, he was just as ready to rebuke parochial presumption whenever that seemed necessary. But at all times he was true to his fundamental belief that democratic government demanded a sense of personal responsibility from the individual and that Ireland would never be fit for Home Rule unless her people were able to exercise that responsibility free from supernatural solicitings. This belief he never abandoned and so remained to the end of his life that *rara avis* in constitutional politics—a liberal, independent Irish Catholic.

Once Dillon went to prison the old general concern about this health, which had been so evident in the Kilmainham period, reasserted itself. Nor was this concern limited to his friends. The Chief Secretary warned his officials that any serious breakdown in the prisoner's health would be 'almost a national calamity', and even Lord Salisbury was driven to remark, in his brutal but perceptive way, that Dillon would be 'far more formidable dead than alive'.[2] From the moment he entered Dundalk jail, therefore, a close watch was kept upon his condition. There was no question of his fighting, as O'Brien had done, against the indignity of prison dress; on the

---

[1] *U.I.* 26 May 1888.   [2] Curtis, *Coercion and conciliation*, pp. 226, 229.

contrary, so far from any severities being inflicted upon him, he was admitted at once to the Infirmary, where, as Sir West Ridgeway reported to Balfour, 'there certainly seems a tendency to treat him as an honoured guest'.[1] This was quite true, for not only was the warder a sympathiser of Dillon's but so also was the prison doctor, who contrived to reconcile his conscience to supplying official reports to the General Prisons Board and private bulletins to Dillon's cousin and solicitor, Valentine Dillon, through whom they were relayed to his friends and, usually, to the nationalist Press. During July he bore up apparently fairly well, even though it was an exceptionally cold and wet summer, but by August, despite all precautions, there were ominous signs that he was beginning to lose weight. About the middle of the month the prison doctor became seriously worried and on 23 August warned Valentine Dillon that if the prisoner's weight went on decreasing he could not accept responsibility for what might happen. 'As he says himself, the alarming point is that he is getting lighter although he is so well circumstanced.'[2] Dillon himself admitted, in a letter smuggled out to his cousin, that he was 'losing ground very fast', but that this must be kept strictly private to avoid distressing his friends. If he was not released by the end of August, he added, he would consider further steps.[3]

But September came and he was still in prison. However, near the middle of the month he was visited by Dr. G. P. O'Farrell of the General Prisons Board and this inspection revealed a marked deterioration. What worried Dr. O'Farrell, as it had worried his colleague a month earlier, was that the deterioration should have continued despite the relaxed régime under which Dillon was living. In his report, therefore, although not anticipating any immediate crisis, he took a grave view of the long-term prospects for the prisoner who, when he visited him, had served slightly less than half his sentence. Here is the essence of his findings:

> Dillon suffers, as I have previously pointed out, from an unhealthy condition of the mucous membrane lining the digestive tract, producing that form of chronic dyspepsia which Sir Andrew Clarke [a Dublin consultant] calls 'chronic gastro-intestinal catarrh', and the symptoms of this gastric affection [sic] seem latterly to have become aggravated. He suffers from uneasiness after food and occasional attacks of sharp pain for the relief of which he has to have recourse to opiate pills. He has lost 5 lbs. in weight and the Prison Governor states that Dillon's appetite is rapidly failing so that he now 'pecks at his food rather than eats it'. The white of the eye was, I noticed . . . slightly jaundiced and the facial lines, producing an habitually haggard expression, seemed to me more marked than before.
>
> Dillon has now been three months in prison and during all this time not only has he not been subjected to any prison discipline, but his surroundings have been made as favourable as possible—he has been treated as a hospital patient and allowed, when the weather per-

---

[1] Ridgeway to Balfour, 27 June 1888 (Balfour Papers, B.M. Add. MS. 49808, f. 168).
[2] Dr. H. MacDonnell to V. B. Dillon, 13 and 23 Aug. 1888 (D.P.).
[3] John Dillon to V. B. Dillon, 20 Aug. 1888 (D.P.).

mits unlimited exercise in the hospital grounds. He takes daily, on the lines laid down by his private physician, Sir Andrew Clarke, tonics and laxatives and occasionally opium for the relief of pain. Notwithstanding all this, the Prison Medical Officer, Dr. McDonnell, is of opinion that Dillon is losing ground and, speaking officially, he told me that unless a material improvement takes place before the end of the month (a probability so remote that it may be discounted) he will consider it his duty to submit a report . . . that the prisoner's life is endangered by further confinement. Remembering the gastric affection from which Mr. Dillon suffers and having regard to his personal medical history in, and out of, prison, it would be easy for Dr. McDonnell to justify the course he proposes to adopt. Further, although I don't consider Dillon's life immediately endangered by his imprisonment, yet I fear from the failure which has already shown itself that there is now a risk, an accumulative risk (increasing day by day) in his further detention . . . To wait before recommending Dillon's release, for any serious loss of strength . . . would be in all human probability to wait too long.[1]

The prisoner himself, meanwhile, was as tranquil as it was in him to be. Indeed, a time was soon to come when he would look back nostalgically to the peace he enjoyed in Dundalk jail. Although at first he had not been allowed books and paper, that regulation was soon relaxed and bibliomania reigned once more unchecked. So solicitous were the prison officers for his comfort that his ruling passion was even indulged to the extent of the white walls of his cell being tinted and candles substituted for gas-light, so that no glare should trouble his eyes.[2] A notebook which he kept for the last two weeks of his imprisonment shows the uses to which he put such privileges. He seems in that short period to have been reading Robert Burns, Macaulay's *History*, the Icelandic sagas, a great deal of Burke, whose 'exquisite felicities of phrase' led him to copy out whole passages, most of them relating to the very theme of his own speeches before his imprisonment—the nature of political liberty and how to preserve it.[3] Apart from all this there were the usual periodical articles to be read and the by now familiar schemes for future study to be drawn up—the life of Garibaldi, the history of France in the seventeenth century and Ireland in the eighteenth, the history of political economy, German socialism, Australian aborigines and so forth. It is scarcely surprising that, caught once more in the toils of universal knowledge, he should have looked on almost indifferently at the exciting events outside, which included not only the continuing struggles of the tenants, but also the unfolding of the strange drama of the special commission appointed to inquire into the conduct of the whole Irish movement, following the *Times*'s allegations of the previous spring that Parnellism and crime were inextricably linked together. 'It is a curious sensation', he wrote on his last day in prison, 'to watch the fight from a place like this,

[1] S.P.O., Chief Secretary's Office, Official Papers, 14 Sept. 1888.   [2] Ibid.
[3] For example the entry for 15 Sept. 1888 (D.P.).

as I am doing now, to see how the tide of fortune varies and how the battle eddies backwards and forwards.'[1]

Such Olympian remoteness was a luxury that could not last. Next morning before breakfast the governor appeared in his cell 'in a high state of delight' and read out the order for his release.[2] Balfour had accepted the recommendation for Dillon's discharge (with the more alacrity because it was rumoured that the special commission was going to demand it anyway, so that he could give evidence) and on 15 September had directed that he should be allowed to go at once.[3] Back at his house in Dublin, Dillon suffered an understandable reaction. The all-devouring present came crowding in upon him again and he had to brace himself once more to the making of speeches, the travelling, the exhortations, the taking of decisions which might mean life or death for many families. 'Utterly upset and unable to fix myself to anything', he recorded only three days after his release. 'I expected this, but what a maddening and inexplicable tangle my life is in.'[4]

He might have used the very same words about the Plan of Campaign. During his absence the situation had undoubtedly deteriorated. The number of League branches was steadily declining (in April 1888 there had been 1,031 and a year later there were 975, the decrease being entirely accounted for by suppressions), and although O'Brien had done his best to carry on single-handed, the task had been too much for him, especially as he was always liable to be rearrested. Even the apparently comforting fact that evictions had slowed down was to some extent an illusion, partly because the Government was bringing pressure to bear upon landlords to hold back, but partly also because 10,000 notices had been served which could become actual evictions if the landlords' strategy demanded it. Dillon himself, it is true, drew a rather different conclusion. In a speech he made in Dublin a week after his release he emphasised the reduction in evictions (leaving aside the pending notices of eviction), but ascribed this solely to the effect of the Plan of Campaign upon landlords and of boycotting upon land-grabbers—bold words, not altogether justified by the sequel.[5]

But even if evictions, for whatever reason, were temporarily less burdensome than before, there were other adverse factors to contend with. One was the emotional state of Irish opinion after the death of John Mandeville. Mandeville had been imprisoned in Tullamore jail and, like O'Brien, had fought against the authorities' intention to treat him as an ordinary prisoner, suffering considerable hardship in the process. Six months after his release he had died of a throat infection and it was widely believed in Ireland that this was a direct consequence of his imprisonment, a belief in no way diminished when Dr. Ridley, the prison doctor, cut *his* throat just before he was due to give evidence at the inquest.[6] A second difficulty

[1] 'Note-book', 17 Sept. 1888 (D.P.).
[2] Ibid., 19 Sept. 1888, written when he was back in North Great George's Street.
[3] S.P.O. Chief Secretary's Office, Official Papers, 15 Sept. 1888.
[4] 'Note-book', 21 Sept. 1888 (D.P.).
[5] F. S. L. Lyons, 'John Dillon and the Plan of Campaign', *I.H.S.*, xiv, 331, nn. 70, 71.
[6] O'Brien, *Evening memories*, pp. 327–36; Curtis, *Coercion and conciliation* pp. 223–7.

5. 'Force No Remedy', Dillon and Parnell in
Kilmainham, 1881, *Vanity Fair*, 1881

6. 'The Plan of Campaign', *Vanity Fair*, 1887

was financial—the cumulative strain of having to maintain their movement on a much bigger scale and for far longer than had originally been anticipated. The funds subscribed by the tenants had either all been spent or were being held for use on particular estates, so that the promoters of the Plan had had to fall back upon the resources of the National League, together with such other occasional sums as could be raised from time to time. Even at the beginning of 1888 Harrington had warned Dillon of impending financial ruin and the situation had not improved in the course of the year.[1] During his time in Dundalk Dillon made up his mind that a major effort would have to be made to raise funds overseas and that this must be combined with a deliberate policy of limiting their commitments. Just before he was released he explained his ideas and fears to William O'Brien:

> I need not tell you [he wrote] how much I sympathise with you for the frightful load of responsibility that is thrown on you. There can be no doubt that we have to look forward to a year of desperate exertion and desperate anxiety. I am sure we shall pull thro' all right if you can keep out of prison, but I should feel anything but confident if you were caught again. You must remember that it will certainly be six months next time. I foresaw long ago what it would come to in the matter of expense. It is largely a question of the biggest purse and our expenses during the next year will I fear run up to twenty thousand at least. That is if we fight to win. The only way in which we can hope to get this money is for one of us to go to Australia, and I am willing to go if you can manage to keep at liberty. My notion with regard to our policy during the winter is that we should not try to extend the movement but concentrate all our resources and all our energy on the estates where the war is now going on. . . .[2]

But, and here was yet another critical factor, could Dillon, who had lately been so ill, survive the wear and tear of a mission to the other side of the world? Certainly his diary that autumn suggests that he was in no fit state to go. It was not that he was in a state of physical collapse, rather that he was plunged in the deep depression and lassitude that always accompanied his dyspepsia. Even such a simple operation as furnishing his room paralysed him. 'Often the feeling has come over me that I am enchanted,' he wrote in October, 'and that I who cannot manage to carry out the simplest arrangements in a house am trying to manage the affairs of a whole nation—sometimes the whole thing appears to me a ghastly absurdity.'[3] Ten days later—'not gaining ground. I am in a terrible state.'[4] Again, on October 26: 'If I cannot reorganise my living arrangements and better my health somewhat I *must* soon become utterly stupefied and hopeless. I have not far to go.'[5] And finally, when he crossed to London for the opening of the parliamentary session he reached 'the lowest stage of misery'

[1] T. C. Harrington to Dillon, 14 Jan. 1888 (D.P.).
[2] Dillon to O'Brien, 14 Sept. [1888] (D.P.).
[3] Diary of John Dillon, 12 Oct. 1888 (D.P.).
[4] Ibid., 23 Oct. 1888. [5] Ibid., 26 Oct. 1888.

in his lodgings. 'Life in ordinary London lodgings is *impossible* for me. It would mean first imbecility and then death.'[1] These entries, it is obvious enough, mark a re-emergence of the hypochondria he had himself diagnosed in his student days, but they can be read not merely as leaves from the journal of a dyspeptic man but as leaves from the journal of a disappointed man. For the real root of the trouble in the winter of 1888–9 was that the Plan was not going well. On 5 November Dillon and O'Brien had spent two gloomy hours discussing it. 'We both agreed', recorded Dillon, 'that if P[arnell] maintains the attitude he has for the last year we could not see how it would be possible for us to maintain the fight over another year. The situation is doubtless one of tremendous difficulty. It will take at least £25,000 to run our movement to this time next year.'[2] By Christmas the outlook was even bleaker. Eviction notices were being served on the de Freyne estate and it was not certain whether the tenants could be held to the Plan. Then came word that troops were to be billeted at Falcarragh in County Donegal, where evictions were being carried out on the Olphert estate, and that the whole district was threatened with starvation because of the failure of the potato crop. Altogether it is not surprising that when he and O'Brien and Dr. Kenny met over the holiday to discuss the position all three were at the end of their tether.[3]

In these desperate circumstances Dillon turned at last to Parnell, explaining the situation and begging for funds. When he had been imprisoned in June, he wrote, he had reckoned that £6,000 would have seen them through to the end of the year, provided there was no exceptional expenditure. But his going to jail, and the issuing of the papal rescript, had been the signal for a stiffening of the landlords' attitude, for a sharp rise in evictions (though, as we have seen, this curve soon flattened out) and, inevitably, for an increase in expenditure which had gone up from £750 a month in June to £1,200 in October, resulting by the end of 1888 in a total deficit of £7,000. If, he declared, in the face of this financial pressure they ceased to make regular payments to the evicted tenants, the result would be 'utter ruin and collapse'. 'This movement', he added, 'is to a great extent a game of bluff on both sides, and if any idea got abroad that we were short of money [that] would cause an immediate disaster.' In short, he needed £5,000 at once and the promise of another £5,000 not later than the beginning of March. After that, he reckoned, his Australian mission, and possibly an American tour by O'Brien, should set them on the road to success.[4]

We know from a letter Dillon wrote to Harrington about this time that he had very little hope of moving Parnell. When in London he had indeed tried to see him, but as usual without success, and had not even succeeded in finding out whether Parnell would advance money for the expense of the Australian mission. It is a measure of Dillon's desperation that he was apparently considering calling a meeting on his own initiative of those

---

[1] Ibid., 15 Dec. 1888.   [2] Ibid., 5 Nov. 1888.   [3] Ibid., 23, 24 and 27 Dec. 1888.
[4] Dillon to Parnell, 14 Jan. 1889 (D.P.).

members of the party who had taken an active part in the Plan of Campaign, 'so that a decision may be come to whether the movement can be carried on'. He did not actually do this, but, as he reminded Harrington, they both bore a heavy responsibility 'for having put pressure on O'Brien last spring to continue the movement instead of abandoning it, as he at that time was inclined to do. I have no doubt that we did the right thing. But from that day to this nearly the entire burden of the movement—and a terrible burden it has been—has [been] borne by him. And had it not been for our action last May he would not be in the situation in which he is.'[1]

The situation O'Brien was in at that moment was painfully familiar. Faced with yet another prosecution, he was sentenced later that month to four months' imprisonment and sent to Clonmel jail. There he renewed his fight against prison dress and for some weeks suffered harsh treatment in consequence. This almost caused Dillon to cancel his proposed Australian mission until he received a note from O'Brien, whose spirit was truly indomitable, that the worst was over and that money was all they needed for victory.[2] Since Parnell had in the meantime promised to 'scrape together' £10,000 as a stop-gap measure, the way was at last clear for Dillon to depart, and he sailed on 6 March on the mission which was to take him away from Ireland for the next thirteen months.[3]

(v)

This tour, the longest he was ever to make as a political leader, was an exhausting experience, but, although his dyspepsia and consequent depression continued to attack him at intervals, his health seems actually to have improved. His insatiable curiosity was aroused by nearly everything he saw, and although he was critical of a good deal, especially the hotels, he was impressed by the vigour and forthrightness of Australian life. Sydney he did not much care for, but the more he saw of Melbourne the more he liked and admired it, especially 'the vast and immensely costly works that are being carried out, the evidence of almost incredible works which have been carried out during the last few years'. And when the time came to move on he was sorry to go. 'For the first time since I came to Australia I was beginning to feel a little bit at home.'[4] As a politician—and he met most of the leading figures in Australian politics—he was most struck by the progress the Australian colonies were making as self-governing entities within the Empire. In several notable speeches he drew a moral from this which might have surprised those at home who still thought of him as a Jacobin, but which, in fact, followed logically enough from the way his mind had been moving before the land war had flared up again. Indeed, even the Plan of Campaign had only deflected his energies, not changed

[1] Dillon to Harrington, 'Tuesday evg', probably between 14 and 26 Jan. 1889 (D.P.).
[2] W. O'Brien to Dillon, undated, but the context indicates Feb. 1889 (D.P.).
[3] Parnell to Dillon, 26 Jan. 1889 (D.P.).
[4] Diary, 2 and 4 Oct. 1889.

his mind. The effect of the Home Rule crisis of 1886 had been to convince him utterly of the rightness of the point Parnell had ever since been trying to drive home—that the one hope for the peaceful attainment of self-government for Ireland was that the Irish party should strengthen their alliance with the Liberals and do all they could to win the sympathy of the English masses. In his very first speech after his release the previous September, Dillon had gone out of his way to emphasise the importance of this policy:

> I am not ashamed to say here to-day [he had declared in Dublin on September 25] that I can find in my heart not the slightest trace of bitterness against the people of England, that while I can recollect the day when the name of England, and the power of England . . . were hateful to my heart, that feeling is dying away and I can hardly now find any trace of it in me. It may be that I have been demoralised by the countless acts of personal kindness that I have received from Englishmen, but I cannot find it in my heart to regret that that feeling of hatred is passing away.[1]

In Australia he was to repeat many times this doctrine of the union of hearts, stressing repeatedly that separation was not the Irish goal. At Port Adelaide, soon after his arrival, he made this crystal clear. 'All that we ask,' he said, 'is that we in Ireland shall stand in the same relation to the Empire as you in Australia . . . We are willing and anxious to form a part of the British Empire, but never will we consent to form part of that Empire on terms that are dishonourable to free men, nor allow strangers to make our laws and administer them.'[2] And in Melbourne, where he was criticised by some for importing Irish quarrels into Australia, he retorted that the cause he stood for was the cause 'of everyone who lives in the English Empire'. All they wanted, he added, was what Australia had got, 'and I say that it is not right for any man in Australia to call us "separatists" because we mean to struggle for the very rights which you possess'. Indeed, as he was careful to point out, Ireland in 1886 had been prepared to make concessions—'of rights you in Australia would not forgo'—and those concessions they were still content to abide by.[3] It is doubtful if, in fact, Dillon would have been content to leave Ireland permanently in a position of inferiority to the other white self-governing territories. On the contrary, the longer he stayed in Australia the more he seems to have become aware of the wider problems of imperial organisation which were awaiting solution and of which Irish Home Rule was an integral part. The precise form imperial organisation would take in the future he did not pretend to forecast—though in Australia and still more in New Zealand he was exposed to the ideas and pressures of those who were working for federation—but it is interesting that as early as 1889 he had arrived at the germ of what was later to be the concept of free association. 'Our policy,' he said at Newcastle, 'is laid down on the great principle that there can be no union between two peoples unless that

---

[1] *U.I.*, 29 Sept. 1888.   [2] *U.I.*, 25 May 1889.   [3] *U.I.*, 29 June 1889.

union be based on the liberty of both, and that any forced union, which has as its root, as the principle of its existence, the domination of one portion of a great empire over another, is doomed sooner or later to extinction.'[1]

In New Zealand, where he was enthusiastically received, he took the same line—equality within the Empire was the path of progress. 'Over and over again,' he told an important meeting at Wellington, 'the [Irish] party had declared their anxiety to remain a portion of the Empire, but they would never accept a subordinate position, and must be put on a footing of equality with the remainder.'[2] This doctrine fitted very well with the ideas of one element in New Zealand politics which, while it did not relish the possibility of being absorbed into some kind of Australasian grouping, did look forward eagerly to a broader imperial federation. New Zealand imperialists, not unlike Cecil Rhodes, who saw in Parnell a man after his own heart and had just presented him with £10,000, regarded Irish Home Rule as a step on the road to a larger policy.[3] But this was always provided that a self-governing Ireland would not be separatist. Dillon's affirmation of an Irish future within the Empire was therefore sweet music to New Zealand ears. It has been suggested that in another and more questionable sense he may also have appealed to those who felt that imperial federation would make the Empire a more formidable force in world affairs and thus provide a strong shield behind which they could further their annexationist ambitions in the Pacific; and that, when Dillon declared at Auckland that the Irish deserved self-government 'because we are white men', he was appealing, consciously or unconsciously, to an emotion deeply felt by many of his hearers, who, however sympathetic to Irish Home Rule, had no intention of applying that exhilarating doctrine to the people of Samoa.[4] It would, however, be easy to read more into this phrase than Dillon intended. He was not a 'racist', but he was a realist. At that point in time the only working assumption a practical politician could make was that for as far ahead as one could see, self-government was likely to be the preserve of white-settled colonies, and Dillon, so far from enunciating any colour theory, was only stating a political cliché, though, of course, one which would arouse special enthusiasm in a country where the workers (many of them Irish and low in the social scale) stood in constant dread of Asiatic immigration.

But although he was as always, fascinated by other countries' politics, these issues, large as they were, were peripheral for him. His business was to explain the Plan of Campaign and to raise money for the evicted tenants. Again, as with Home Rule, he was careful to maintain a moderate tone. The Plan, he readily admitted, was 'a strong and extreme policy', but, he added: 'It was an axiom amongst all men who loved liberty that many

[1] *U.I.*, 6 July 1889.
[2] *U.I.*, 9 Nov. 1889.
[3] For the exchanges between Rhodes and Parnell see R. B. O'Brien, *Parnell*, ii. 184–9
[4] I am indebted for this reference to Mr. R. P. Davis, who is engaged on research into the support for Irish Home Rule in New Zealand.

things could be done amongst people who were denied liberty that would be immoral and unjust among a free people.'[1] Wisely, in a part of the world where landowners were an important section of the community, he restrained his habitual violence in speaking of the Irish landlords and concentrated his audiences' attention on the plight of the evicted tenants. 'We do not wish to ruin the landlords,' he explained; 'we are quite willing that they should reap a fair interest on their outlay, but we do protest, and always shall, against their present policy of extortion.'[2] To the end of his political career he was never to come to terms with the landlords about what was a fair interest and what extortion, but on the short run his newfound moderation paid handsome dividends. The financial result of the tour was £33,000, an achievement without which the Plan of Campaign could not have been carried on.[3]

(vi)

Early in 1890 he turned for home, but since he travelled by way of Honolulu and the United States, he did not arrive back until 20 April. By then the situation had changed in several important respects. Not long after Dillon had set out on his mission Balfour decided to force the issue on half a dozen 'test estates' by throwing all his influence behind the landlords. That this did not just mean Government assistance for evictions was shown by the case of the Ponsonby estate. So that it should not capitulate to the Plan, Balfour secretly encouraged the formation of a syndicate of English and Irish landlords to take over the property and run it by means of a committee of management.[4] To meet this threat O'Brien did his utmost to draw Parnell into the fray. The immediate result of his efforts was the announcement, in mid-July 1889, that a Tenants' Defence Association would be formed to protect the tenants against the landlords' combination. Writing to Dillon to explain this new development, O'Brien said he had presented Parnell with two alternatives. If Parnell would take the responsibility of surrender, then he, O'Brien, would wind up the organisation and try to secure the best terms he could for the tenants. But, on the other hand, 'if he wanted the fight to go on he must openly help us and initiate a fund that would give us £30,000 in addition to the £30,000 we count upon you for'. Parnell, he reported, was still reluctant to involve himself in agitation, but if he could be persuaded to launch the new organisation and its appeal for funds, all might yet be well—if not, 'the situation is full of danger'.[5]

His next letter to Dillon—a month later—revealed the full extent of the crisis. O'Brien had gone again to urge Parnell to lend the immense weight of his prestige to the new organisation and had received a flat refusal, despite the grim details O'Brien had given him of imminent collapse

---

[1] *U.I.*, 15 June 1889.
[2] *U.I.*, 11 Jan. 1890.
[3] *U.I.*, 17 June 1890. This was his own estimate.
[4] Curtis, *Coercion and conciliation*, pp. 239–52.
[5] William O'Brien to Dillon, 14 July 1889 (D.P.).

on several key estates. Then, after more fruitless exchanges, the state of tension between Parnell and the agrarians was suddenly lit up as by a lurid flash of lightning. Here is how O'Brien described the incident:

> I told him I had considered the matter carefully and no longer felt equal to the individual task of carrying on the new movement in face of his attitude—that it was plain that instead of relieving us the new League would simply be an additional burden which we were expected to work, while he continued to look on in an attitude of cold apathy. I told him plainly that the moment I could communicate with you, we would have to consider whether we could any longer remain in so intolerable a position. He said with the most brutal frankness that we could not get out of it—that we had got ourselves into it, adding 'you forced me to say that'. I said 'I am glad that I forced you to be frank, but I think you will find you are mistaken in supposing that you have tied us to the stake and that you can leave all the responsibility on our hands, while you take all the advantages and none of the labour.'

This letter, an extraordinary outburst from so devoted a Parnellite as O'Brien, ended with the suggestion that for the time being they should 'retort Parnell's policy of silence upon him'. Although O'Brien himself was soon due to be sent to prison again (a prosecution was already hanging over him), he would arrange for the key estates to be looked after in his absence, while the Australian money Dillon was raising would carry them through financially. O'Brien's calculation was that by seeming to withdraw altogether from the struggle himself he would in effect coerce Parnell and the party as a whole into activity, out of which would come a big enough fund to relieve their anxieties. 'If you were here,' the *cri de coeur* ended, 'of course the difficulty would not have arisen, for between us we could have struggled along, but alone *I cannot stand it any longer*, and it is full time to force him out of a most cruel and infatuated policy of veiled hostility.'[1]

Dillon's reaction to this letter, when it reached him near the end of September, was strangely detached—perhaps at that distance even O'Brien's superlatives lost some of their force. 'Not surprised,' he noted laconically, 'only it has come sooner than I looked for. Shall be very curious to see how P. will act. He is a wonderfully calculating and astute politician. This business may end in driving both O'B. and me out of public life. I wonder how I should feel. I fancy rather a relief, but it is impossible to say.'[2] In the result, however, O'Brien's calculations had proved remarkably accurate. Parnell, indeed, still held aloof personally, but after the Tenants' Defence Association had been launched in October the party rallied round it and at the county conventions which were held all over the country between then and the end of the year no less than £61,000 was raised for the relief of the evicted tenants.

Simultaneously with this revival of support, partly indeed contributing to it, went an intensification of the agrarian war itself. It centred round the

[1] William O'Brien to Dillon, 14 Aug. 1889 (D.P.).   [2] Diary, 25 Sept. 1889 (D.P.).

estate of A. H. Smith-Barry, the most active member of the syndicate that had taken over the Ponsonby estate. That autumn Smith-Barry's tenants began to withhold rent out of sympathy with the Ponsonby tenants and he responded with evictions. The town of Tipperary was part of the estate and soon it, too, became involved in the traditional pattern of boycotting and eviction. To thwart the landlord, many of the shopkeepers moved out of the town altogether and a kind of shanty town, 'New Tipperary', was hastily constructed near by. This venture, which began while O'Brien was in prison, was eagerly taken up by him after his release in December, and with his prestige once committed to it, it became a central factor in the situation which faced Dillon on his return.[1]

It was a situation of mingled light and shade. On the one hand, funds were more plentiful than they had been, the tenants were apparently in good spirits, and it now seemed possible to hold out until the general election, when, as it might be hoped, a sympathetic Liberal Government would return to power. On the other hand, Parnell remained cold and, since his citation in the O'Shea divorce case in December 1889, his future was uncertain, at least until the case came to trial. Again, New Tipperary was proving costly, the landlords seemed in at least as good heart as the tenants, and Balfour was as determined as ever to beat the Plan of Campaign. The pattern, in short, had not changed, though the scale had apparently diminished. Police reports in the summer of 1890 indicated that the country was quietening down and, although it remained true that evictions and boycotting continued wherever the Plan was in operation, it was beginning to be clear that it suited both sides to confine the struggle to the selected estates where the issue had already been joined.[2]

For Dillon himself the old, dreary round soon began again, almost as if he had never been away. There were financial details to be straightened out; there were meetings to be addressed and New Tipperary to be encouraged; there was boycotting to be defended in and out of Parliament; there were the attentions of the police and the scufflings and riots that were always liable to break out whenever he was addressing crowds large enough to attract official note-takers; there was even, to remind him that he was thoroughly at home once more, another violent dispute with the Bishop of Limerick, who chose to issue a further public condemnation of the Plan at the precise moment when evictions were being carried out in his diocese.[3] But all these familiar incidents of the struggle were rapidly coming to seem marginal. Two great questions hung over the future and to some extent they were interrelated.

The first concerned Parnell. In a sense, it was the same question that had been haunting Dillon since the Kilmainham period—what was to be the relationship between a constitutional leader and an agrarian movement

[1] *U.I.*, 14 Dec. 1889; O'Brien, *Evening memories*, pp. 431–6; Curtis, *Coercion and conciliation*, pp. 252–4.

[2] For the situation in midsummer, 1890, see Curtis, op. cit., p. 269.

[3] For this clash see F. S. L. Lyons, 'John Dillon and the Plan of Campaign' in *I.H.S.* (Sept. 1965), xiv, 339–41.

from which he had publicly dissociated himself, which was in some ways an embarrassment to him, but which could not be abandoned without serious loss of prestige and general discouragement amongst nationalists both parliamentary and agrarian? Linked with this was the second problem—the perennial problem of money. By the summer of 1890, despite Dillon's mission, and despite the efforts of the Tenants' Defence Association, funds were again running out. A police report of July estimated that the organisers of the Plan were supporting over 800 families at a cost of £32,000 p.a. Added to this was the cost of New Tipperary, which the police reckoned at £40,000.[1] Both these estimates were, in fact, below the mark. since the cost of New Tipperary was probably nearer to £50,000,[2] and Dillon himself admitted privately that they were maintaining upwards of 1,000 families.[3] To cope with these demands Parnell's help was essential, but once again it was difficult to be sure where he stood himself. He was prepared to authorise a second levy in Ireland and also to permit a fund-raising mission to America, but beyond that he would not move.[4] It seemed, therefore, that the burden must remain, as before, on the shoulders of Dillon and O'Brien.

In absolute terms it may not in retrospect seem to have been such a heavy burden, though it has always to be seen in relation to the meagre resources available to carry it. For all practical purposes the Plan of Campaign lasted from October 1886 until the Parnell split in December 1890.[5] During that period 116 estates in all were affected by the operations of the Plan. On sixty of these settlements were reached without a struggle and on a further twenty-four after a clash; on fifteen estates the tenants capitulated and went back on the landlords' terms; on eighteen of them no settlement had been reached by May 1891 and seventeen were still in dispute at the end of 1892, including the Clanricarde estate, where all the trouble had started.[6] Estimates of the number of tenants evicted with their families as a result of these conflicts naturally vary a great deal, since the figures fluctuated in the course of the struggle. By 1889 the police estimated about 1,000 were involved, in the summer of 1890 they put the figure at 1,314 (including 470 evicted before October 1886 and therefore the responsibility of the National League), but by the autumn of 1891 their estimate had dropped to 1,094. Dillon, it is true, stated in November 1891 that 1,400 families had been dependent on aid during that year, but this may have been an exaggeration, due partly to the very confused conditions in the

---

[1] S.P.O., Chief Secretary's Office, Registered Papers, no. 4208.

[2] Curtis, op. cit., p. 253.

[3] Dillon to John Fitzgerald, President of the Irish National League of America (copy in Dillon's hand), 21 May 1890 (D.P.).

[4] F. S. L. Lyons, 'John Dillon and the Plan of Campaign', *I.H.S.*, xiv. 342–3.

[5] For the Parnell split see chapter 5.

[6] S.P.O., Crime Branch Special, Secret /3408. 'List of estates on which the Plan of Campaign was originally established and on which settlements have not as yet been completed', 19 May 1891; *Report of the commissioners appointed to inquire into the estates of evicted tenants in Ireland* (hereafter cited as *Evicted tenants commission*), H. C. 1893–4 [c. 6935], xxxi, 422, appendix V, pp. 95–96.

year of the split and partly to a natural desire to paint the picture in its
blackest colours so as to stimulate subscriptions. At any rate, when testi-
fying later before the Evicted Tenants Commission he gave the number of
families still dependent on grants as about 800.[1] All of these had been
directly involved in the Plan of Campaign and, although they were drifting
back to their former holdings from 1892 onwards, some of them, or their
descendants, were not reinstated until after the passing of the Evicted
Tenants Act in 1907.

It is clear from these figures that the 'wounded soldiers of the land war'
hardly constituted a mighty army, even if one includes (as in practice up to
the split the organisers of the Plan did include) those who had become
casualties before October 1886. But these unfortunate people had to be fed
and housed and this cost a great deal of money. In the spring of 1892 the
Under-Secretary tried to find out just how much. After exhaustive investigation the police suggested the grand total might be approximately
£194,000, including in this the maintenance of National League tenants as
well as those directly connected with the Plan of Campaign.[2] But even this
was an underestimate and Dillon's own figure, which is convincing because
of the wealth of detail accompanying it, was £234,000 from November
1886 up to the time—December 1893—when he gave evidence to the
Evicted Tenants Commission. Most of this came from the various special
funds already mentioned, the only other large item being £42,000 from the
original estate funds which had formed the basis of the Plan in its early
stages. Of the grand total of £234,000, grants to tenants accounted for
£126,000, building and repairing houses for them cost £50,000, and legal
expenses of one kind or another amounted to £11,500.[3]

To meet demands of this kind proved, as we have already seen, a constant nightmare for Dillon and O'Brien. And it was to end this nightmare
once for all that they planned a major tour of the United States in the
autumn of 1890. From the Government's point of view there was obviously
much to be gained from preventing them and it seems that Balfour's
thoughts were turning in this direction from the beginning of September.[4]
It only needed one rash speech or disorderly meeting to provide grounds for
a fresh prosecution and, as might have been expected, the efforts of the two
men to keep the pot boiling in New Tipperary soon gave the authorities all
the scope they needed. They were arrested separately, O'Brien at Glen-
gariff (where he was staying with his newly-wed wife), and Dillon at
Ballybrack, where he was taken into custody early on the morning of 18
September.[5] 'Should Messrs Dillon and O'Brien now be convicted of the

[1] S.P.O., Crime Branch Special, Secret /4208. 'Memo. by R. E. Beckerson as to
present condition of nationalist funds', undated, but minuted by the Under-Secretary,
27 Nov. 1891: *Evicted tenants commission*, evidence of John Dillon, p. 421, para. 14955.

[2] S.P.O., Crime Branch Special, S/4697, 13 May 1892.

[3] *Evicted tenants commission*, p. 421, para. 14995.

[4] S.P.O., Registered Papers, no. 17063, case for prosecution presented for legal
opinion, 4 Sept. 1890.

[5] *U.I.*, 20 Sept. 1890.

charges now pending against them,' minuted a Castle official with some complacency, 'it will be most difficult to supply their places with men having power in America.'[1]

The trial opened in the town of Tipperary with a menacing mob demonstration and equally menacing baton charges by the police. Following their usual tactics, the accused gave bail and continued at large, travelling down to Tipperary from time to time as the exigencies of the case demanded. Meanwhile, they were intensively shadowed by the police and the surviving reports show that they were under continuous surveillance from 20 August until 8 October.[2] But the next day both men disappeared suddenly and completely from view. For nearly a week no word or sign of them could be traced. Then, on 15 October, came news that they had turned up at Cherbourg. Gradually the mystery became clear. Having agreed with their sureties that they would break bail, they decided to make a dash for France and from there to go to America as they had originally intended. Their escape was carefully organised down to the last detail by John Clancy, sub-sheriff of Dublin and an ardent Parnellite. They were driven through the city in broad daylight ('there was nothing suspicious about their movements', reported a hapless constable) and spent the evening in a friend's house at Dalkey. At midnight they walked a few hundred yards to the small cove grandiloquently called Dalkey Harbour, rowed quietly out to a small fishing-vessel, and slipped away under cover of darkness. The voyage, though in fact uneventful, was not without its hazards. In rapid succession they were becalmed, fog-bound, driven before a gale, and nearly boarded by a revenue cutter off Guernsey. Finally, when they reached port they had only one day's supply of water left.[3]

It had been a dramatic episode, though in sober fact a quite unnecessary one, since, as Sir West Ridgeway explained to Balfour, the legal technicalities were such that the police could not have touched them until they had actually failed to appear in court at the appointed time, 'even if we had seen them stepping aboard an Atlantic steamer'. He reserved his worst blame for the magistrates who had allowed bail in the first place, but he had to admit that the police had been very negligent.[4] It was, of course, this aspect of the matter that caught the eye of a delighted public. William O'Brien had long accustomed the readers of *United Ireland* to see the Plan of Campaign as part of the struggle of an oppressed nationality against a brutal and alien Government, and in such a struggle any victory over the authorities (such as this was immediately felt to be) achieved a moral effect far beyond the intrinsic importance of the particular event. O'Brien, in short, had grasped a crucial fact about politics in an unsophisticated country—that colour, movement, emotion and legend have great power over simple men. Each clash with Dublin Castle, each riot, each baton

[1] S.P.O., Chief Secretary's Office (unnumbered), 22 Sept. 1890.
[2] S.P.O., Crime Branch Special, Shadowing returns, Aug.–Oct. 1890.
[3] Ibid., Shadowing report for 9 Oct. 1890; *U.I.*, 18 Oct. 1890.
[4] Sir W. Ridgeway to Balfour, 10 Oct. 1890 (B.M. Add. MS. 49809, ff. 200–2).

charge, each imprisonment, was celebrated as an incident in an unending crusade, and the leaders of the Plan were correspondingly invested with the heroic qualities a generous and passionate people were only too ready to ascribe to them.

Such adventures were meat and drink to an incurable romantic like O'Brien, but for Dillon, dyspeptic and always prone to sea-sickness, the voyage to France was just one more sacrifice to be stoically endured. Yet, as it turned out, this was the last time he was to be called on to risk his life and health for the tenant-farmers of Ireland. Had he but known it, he was sailing away from an entire and completed phase of his career. Never again would the land war be the central theme of his life, for with the dramatic explosion of the O'Shea divorce case in November, Parnell was to resume the centre of the stage and agrarian politics, which had filled so much of the last ten years, were suddenly to seem, if not irrelevant, at least peripheral. When Dillon next saw home the familiar landmarks of a decade had been all but obliterated and the once-great Irish party brought to ruin. Nothing was ever to be quite the same again.

5
The Break With Parnell

(i)

After only three days in France in which to recover from their escapade, Dillon and O'Brien set off once more. On 25 October they sailed for New York, arriving there on 2 November and joining forces with the other delegates on the fund-raising mission—T. P. O'Connor, Timothy Harrington, T. P. Gill, and T. D. Sullivan.[1] For the next few days they were busily engaged in collecting money for the evicted tenants and it seemed virtually certain that the tour would be a resounding success. But before they had been in action for much more than a week the thunderbolt of the Parnell-O'Shea divorce case struck them with devastating force.

The divorce case itself, of course, was not unexpected. Captain O'Shea had filed the petition seeking a divorce from his wife and citing Parnell as co-respondent as far back as December 1889, and long before that, as we have seen, the leading members of the party had become aware of, or had at least suspected, some of the circumstances surrounding the mysterious affair. But between the time when the petition was filed and their own flight from Ireland a month before the case was due to come on both Dillon and O'Brien had heard conflicting reports about what was likely to happen. Parnell's own line, so far as he bothered to indicate that he had one at all, was that he would emerge from the ordeal without a stain on his honour. This, apparently, he had said to Michael Davitt and had written to both William O'Brien and T. P. Gill. What he seems to have meant by this was not that he had not committed adultery, which scarcely anyone in the inner circle of Irish politics could have been persuaded to believe, but that the divorce case would collapse, as the *Times* case had previously collapsed after the exposure of the Pigott forgeries. And, indeed, right up to the end, if we are to believe the story Katharine Parnell told the young M.P., Henry Harrison, after Parnell's death, there was a possibility that O'Shea might be bought off, and even of a final twist to the situation in which, instead of the husband divorcing the wife, the wife would have been able to divorce the husband.[2] Parnell's lieutenants were certainly not privy to the manoeuvres that preceded the bringing of the action, but it is a legitimate criticism of them that they seem to have accepted passively such ambiguous

[1] *U.I.*, 18 and 25 Oct., 8 Nov. 1890.
[2] For this aspect of the divorce question see F. S. L. Lyons, *The fall of Parnell* (London, 1960), chap. 2.

assurances as reached them and to have made absolutely no provision against a possible disaster.

Yet Dillon for one was not without warning that if the worst came to the worst there would be trouble ahead. While he was away on his Australasian tour he received from his old friend, Dr. J. E. Kenny, a letter written on New Year's Day 1890, only a few days after the petition had been filed. Kenny had already been trying to mobilise opinion for some gesture of support from the party members and he wrote to Dillon expressing a view of which much more was to be heard in the months to come:

> Now I don't know whether there is any truth in the allegation and personally I don't care, except in this sense that I should be truly sorry poor P. should be in a position in which he must suffer more or less mental annoyance which a charge of that kind, true or false, should necessarily cause him. I believe he is much more sensitive than he gets credit for, but this is in my opinion our plain duty, that come what will we are bound to stand to him as one man and show that no amount of obloquy will displace him from his position as our leader. It is quite plain that, true or false, the matter has been timed by that vile hound, O'Shea, who, if it is at all true, sold her as a matter of sale and barter, so as to serve the enemy who are up to some new game to revenge themselves for the defeat over the forgeries.[1]

What Dillon's reaction was to this, which anticipated by nearly a year the classical pro-Parnell line, we do not know. In any case, when he returned to Ireland in the spring of 1890 he was immediately engulfed in his Plan of Campaign responsibilities and had more to do than speculate about a hypothetical crisis. But in September of that year, with the divorce suit only a couple of months away, in the course of a conversation with John Morley, after Gladstone the most devoted of Liberal Home Rulers, Dillon committed himself to the prophecy that proof of the charges against Parnell would make no difference to his authority in Ireland 'provided there was no disclosure of nauseous details'.[2] And in America in November, after the crisis had broken, Dillon's own instinct was to separate the leader's political position from his private life. On 16 November he was reported as having declared that in the existing state of affairs—he had in mind the immediate needs of the evicted tenants rather than the long-term prospects of Home Rule—Parnell's retirement was impossible.[3] Interviewed two days later, not only he, but also William O'Brien, T. P. O'Connor and T. P. Gill, all expressed their support for Parnell.[4]

By that time, however, the case, which had indeed disclosed 'nauseous details', had received enormous and, from the Parnellite viewpoint, extremely adverse publicity. Because he wanted to marry Katharine O'Shea, Parnell made no move to defend himself and allowed her counsel only a

---

[1] J. E. Kenny to Dillon, 1 Jan. 1890 (D.P.).
[2] John Morley to Gladstone, 17 Nov. 1890, cited in Lyons, op. cit., p. 82.
[3] *F.J.*, 17 Nov. 1890.
[4] *F.J.*, 20 Nov. 1890.

watching brief. The result was that Captain O'Shea was able in the witness-box to build up a picture from which it appeared that for nine long years he had been an innocent victim cruelly deceived by his wife and his former leader. This, it is true, was not a view of Captain O'Shea which would leap unbidden to the minds of those who knew his history, and many years later that devoted and passionate Parnellite, Henry Harrison, published a very different story, based upon what Katherine herself told him immediately after Parnell's death. The essence of his story was that O'Shea, so far from having been deceived, in reality connived at the relationship between Parnell and his wife, and did so, partly in the hope of political advance-ment and partly in the hope of financial gain. Which version—the hus-band's or the wife's—was the true one has been much argued by historians and will continue to be argued so long as the materials for a final judgment remain as sparse and unsatisfactory as they are now.[1] But what is more important for our purpose is that, whatever may have been the inner truth of the affair, Parnell stood forth, in the lurid light of the divorce-court evidence, not merely as a proven adulterer, but as one who had for many years resorted to every kind of low stratagem to pursue his squalid intrigue in secret.

Yet even with this seemingly damning weight of evidence against him his own people refused—at first—to throw him over. True, there were excep-tions. Amongst the laity the most formidable was Michael Davitt, who considered that he had received from Parnell the clearest assurances that he would emerge without dishonour from the case. When the details of the trial appeared to show exactly the opposite, Davitt lost no time in calling publicly and privately for Parnell's retirement from the party chairman-ship, to which, in the ordinary course of events, he was due to be re-elected on 25 November. Even Davitt, however, only asked that he should 'efface himself, for a brief period, from public life', in fact until such time as the law permitted him to marry Katharine O'Shea.[2] Potentially more influen-tial than Davitt, though temperamentally more cautious, the Irish hier-archy was bound to take a similar view. We know from correspondence that passed between various bishops that feeling ran very high against Parnell from the outset and that some were for influencing the parliament-ary party against voting him into the chair at their crucial meeting on 25 November. On the other hand, there were obvious political dangers in exerting too open or too obvious a pressure. For the time being, therefore, the hierarchy—guided very largely by Archbishop Walsh—held its hand, hoping apparently that the party would give Parnell a quick and decent burial without need for episcopal interference.[3]

---

[1] Harrison's version has recently been attacked by an American writer, Jules Abels, in *The Parnell tragedy* (London, 1966), but Mr. Abels has no new evidence to offer and the question remains open. For the present writer's view, which Mr. Abels's book has not changed, see F. S. L. Lyons, *The fall of Parnell* (London, 1960), chap. 2.

[2] Lyons, *Fall of Parnell*, pp. 78–9.

[3] Lyons, *Fall of Parnell*, pp. 76–8; Emmet Larkin, 'The Roman Catholic Hierarchy and the fall of Parnell', in *Victorian Studies* (June 1961), iv. 315–36.

But the party seemed to have no such intention. First, the Irish National League was rapidly mobilised in his support and then, on 20 November, at a large and emotional gathering at the Leinster Hall in Dublin, important parliamentarians, among them Tim Healy and the vice-chairman, Justin McCarthy, rallied behind the chief. Beyond question one of the factors which influenced opinion in general, and that meeting in particular, was the arrival of a cable backing Parnell from four of the Irish delegates in America—Dillon, O'Brien, Gill and O'Connor. In the excitement of the moment few were prepared to attach overmuch importance to the fact that the fifth delegate, T. D. Sullivan, had refused to sign on the moral ground that Parnell's adultery made him impossible as a leader, though this was an ominous forecast of an argument that was to loom larger and larger in the weeks to come. Moreover, it was an argument that could be used by English Nonconformists as well as by Irish Roman Catholics, and since both were bound together in the Liberal-Nationalist alliance, it was likely to be a very powerful argument. Gladstone, though he was also under pressure from other quarters, was especially sensitive to Nonconformist protests, since Nonconformist votes were so essential to his party, and there is evidence that the strength and volume of these protests had considerable influence upon his own actions during the critical days immediately following the divorce case.[1] After an initial hesitation, he decided to exert his immense authority and prestige in an effort to persuade the Irish leader to resign. Failing to make direct contact with Parnell, he saw the vice-chairman, McCarthy, on Monday, 24 November (the eve of the Irish party conference), and told him that if Parnell continued in the leadership this might involve the loss of the next general election and the postponement of Home Rule. Later that night he followed this up by a letter which may or may not have reached McCarthy, and also by a letter to John Morley—intended to be shown to Parnell—containing an unmistakable warning that if Parnell remained at the head of the Irish party, Gladstone's own leadership of the Liberals would be rendered 'almost a nullity'.[2]

So far the effect of the crisis on the delegation in America had not been catastrophic. True, they had called off their programme of meetings and they stayed close to the big cities where they could get news quickly, but up to the time of the party meeting there was still no reason to suppose that things might not right themselves in some way yet to be determined. Dillon, however, was not so sure, and after the first public intimations of Liberal misgivings he at once scented danger, noting in his diary on 23 November, even before Gladstone had begun to move, 'I don't believe Parnell can weather the storm now that the ministers [he meant the Nonconformist ministers] have opened fire on him.'[3] This was remarkably early to have anticipated Parnell's defeat and at the time there seemed

---

[1] J. F. Glaser, 'Parnell's fall and the nonconformist conscience', in *I.H.S.* (Sept. 1960), xii. 119–38.

[2] Lyons, op. cit., pp. 83–9.

[3] Diary of John Dillon, 23 Nov. 1890 (D.P.).

little to justify such a prognostication. On the contrary, Parnell, having eluded all attempts to intercept him before the party meeting of 25 November, was at that meeting duly re-elected chairman. But some at least of the Irish members present apparently expected that, having received the homage of his party, Parnell would then gracefully retire. When it became plain that he had no intention of doing anything of the kind, a reaction began to set in. But even when John Morley read him the famous letter from Gladstone—*after* the party meeting—he remained entirely indifferent and simply insisted that he would not resign the leadership. Gladstone then took a very grave step. Although his letter had not been known to the Irish party when they re-elected Parnell, and although they had had no subsequent opportunity to discuss it, he decided to publish it. By so doing he confronted his Irish allies with an appalling choice. Either they held to Parnell and thus took the responsibility for jeopardising Home Rule, or they came to the painful decision that Home Rule was more important than any individual and threw over their leader, leaving themselves open to the accusation that they had done it at the bidding of an English statesman.

Dillon, of all men the least open to the charge of amenability to English dictation, was profoundly impressed by the threat implicit in Gladstone's letter, and Timothy Harrington, who was with him in New York when they first learnt of it, noted that his friend 'regarded it as a most important and momentous document, and I could see that his view of the present position of Irish politics is very much altered by it'. By this time (26 November) the Irish delegation had dispersed again and it was difficult to frame any concerted policy. Dillon and Harrington therefore set out for Cincinnati, where they were to meet O'Brien. By the time they had linked up with him all three of them had heard from home that the party had not had Gladstone's letter before them when they re-elected Parnell. O'Brien's impulse was to urge the party to open negotiations with Gladstone, still apparently in the hope that an agreed solution might somehow be reached. 'Dillon and I', recorded Harrington, 'had warm discussions as to the wisdom of this course and I can easily foresee that should it come to a choice between holding by Parnell or trusting to Gladstone, we are very likely to take opposite sides.'[1] They agreed to send a cable home urging the responsible members of the party to ascertain Parnell's reaction to Gladstone's letter before taking any further action, but Harrington could see that already Dillon anticipated some kind of break-up. Indeed, he even asked Harrington what he would do in such a case, to which Harrington replied miserably that while he would not be against private pressure being put upon Parnell to retire *temporarily*, on no account would he participate in any public manoeuvre to oust him.[2]

Dillon was only too accurate in his prediction. Gladstone's letter *had* put the Irish party under an intolerable strain and almost immediately it

---

[1] Diary of Timothy Harrington, 26 Nov. 1890 (N.L.I. MS. 2195).
[2] Ibid., 27 Nov. 1890.

began to show signs of falling apart. On the day following the letter's publication a second meeting was held at which Parnell made it perfectly clear that he was not going to resign. But it was also clear that many members wanted him to do so and the upshot of this inconclusive exchange was a decision to adjourn until the following Monday (1 December) to allow time for the delegates in America to make their views known. In the interval both sides worked feverishly to prepare for the coming battle and Parnell, in particular, used the breathing-space to prepare and issue, in time for Saturday's newspapers, an extraordinary manifesto 'To the people of Ireland'. This was his counterstroke to Gladstone's letter and it purported to reveal to an astonished public that Parnell's private discussions with Gladstone (which had taken place a year previously and with which Parnell had then expressed his complete satisfaction) had shown the Liberals to be fundamentally unsound both on the details of their proposed Home Rule settlement and on the equally vital question of land purchase. For good measure he also threw in a reference to a conversation he had had with John Morley in which he alleged that Morley, in addition to further equivocation about land purchase, had conveyed to him 'a remarkable proposal' that he, Parnell, or another of his party should be Chief Secretary in the next Liberal administration and that one of the law offices should be held 'by a legal member of my party'. These 'disclosures' need not detain us here, for they were immediately refuted by both Gladstone and Morley, but what was important was the tone, which was defiantly and provocatively hostile throughout, and the consequences, which were catastrophic.[1]

In launching this blistering attack upon his former allies Parnell was probably aiming to appeal over the head of the party to Irish public opinion, which so far had remained extraordinarily loyal to him. It is also possible that he intended the manifesto as a grand diversionary tactic so that when the party met on Monday it would find itself discussing not Parnell's fitness for the leadership but Gladstone's reliability on the question of Home Rule. As we shall see, the latter gambit very nearly succeeded, but the price was astronomically high. For one thing, this distorted version of strictly confidential private conversations finished him absolutely with the Liberals. But more important, it accelerated the growth of opposition to him not only within his own party but also in Ireland. Of this the most striking and ominous indication was the fact that at last the Church began to show its hand. On 1 December condemnatory statements from both Archbishop Walsh and Archbishop Croke appeared in the Press. Both these influential archbishops had, in fact, already been in private contact with Parnell's opponents in the party, but they had hitherto exercised the utmost caution. Now, however, Dr. Walsh wrote to Tim Healy making it clear that in his view the leadership was 'practically vacant'. 'If there was any doubt, or room for doubt, on that point up to this,' he added significantly, 'there will, I trust, be none tomorrow.'[2] Healy

---

[1] Lyons, op. cit., chap. 4 and appendix I.
[2] Ibid., pp. 115–17; Larkin, op. cit., pp. 326–8.

himself had rapidly abandoned his earlier pro-Parnell position once it became plain that Parnell's continued leadership would jeopardise the Liberal alliance and, although barely recovered from typhoid, he had crossed to London in time for the party meeting, where he immediately became the centre of resistance to his former chief.

But, from the point of view of the balance of power within the party, the most important factor was the reaction of the delegates in America. They had been converging on Cincinnati and by 28 November had reached the point of sending a private cable to Parnell urging him to retire—a cable signed by all save Harrington, who set a simple loyalty to the leader above all other considerations. Next day came news of the manifesto and even Harrington had to admit that the effect was devastating. 'My colleagues', he noted in his diary, 'are more enraged than ever and characterise it as a breach of faith which makes it impossible for Gladstone ever to touch Parnell.' 'With intense pain', he added, 'I hear that Dillon and O'Brien declare that on no account will they ever serve again under the leadership of the man who could issue such a manifesto.'[1] In fact, they viewed the matter so gravely that they decided to issue a statement of their own, but even before settling down to write it they dispatched a cable home in which they declared that the manifesto had convinced them that 'Mr. Parnell's continued leadership is impossible'. Their counter-blast, when it came, was partly a repudiation of Parnell's insulting language, partly an insistence on the necessity of the Liberal alliance, but above all an absolute repudiation of Parnell himself.[2] This reaction, though predictable, was nevertheless a deadly blow to Parnell's chances of success, for it meant that almost all the senior and experienced men in the party—Healy, McCarthy, Sexton, and now Dillon and O'Brien—had taken sides against him. And since Dillon and O'Brien had carried the burden of the agrarian war, and even in a sense of the leadership, over the past four years, their renunciation of Parnell was bound to have immense effect. Not indeed, that their individual attitudes had been at all similar. O'Brien, as Harrington had been shocked to observe, had become extremely bitter not merely against Parnell but against any one who supported him. This was perhaps an inevitable swing of the pendulum for a volatile and impulsive man who had worshipped his leader and now, in his disenchantment, veered to the other extreme. But Dillon was very different, formidably different. Harrington found him 'calm, unimpassioned, but resolute, and I fear that no consideration will bring him and Parnell together again'.[3]

However, for the moment the decision lay with the party meeting which began, as planned, on Monday, 1 December, but which continued, as had certainly not been planned, throughout that week. This protracted ordeal in Committee Room Fifteen of the House of Commons was a landmark in the history of the Home Rule movement—indeed, it could be said that the

[1] Diary of Timothy Harrington, 29 Nov. 1890 (N.L.I. MS. 2195).
[2] *F.J.*, 1 Dec. 1890.
[3] Diary of Timothy Harrington, 2 Dec. 1890 (N.L.I. MS. 2195).

movement never completely recovered from it. It very soon turned out not
to be merely a debate as to whether or not Parnell should resign, but rather
a wide-ranging discussion about the policy and function of the Irish party
at Westminster. Should they be independent of all English parties, or rather,
could they be independent since the events of 1886? Alternatively, if, as
some said, alliance with the Liberals was essential, could the party preserve
their self-respect if to maintain that alliance they agreed to sacrifice their
leader? And if they did agree to sacrifice him ought they not at least (as
Parnell himself suggested) to secure from the Liberals suitable guarantees
that Home Rule, whenever it might be passed, would be satisfactory to
Ireland? So potent was this last argument that even after two days of
general debate had revealed that a majority of the party had turned against
Parnell, his supporter, John Clancy, succeeded in carrying a motion that
the party whips be instructed to obtain from Gladstone, John Morley and
Sir William Harcourt their views on two vital points connected with Home
Rule, points which had been thrown into prominence by the version of
them, flatly contradicted by Gladstone, that Parnell had given in his manifesto. These concerned the future control of the semi-military constabulary
force in Ireland and also the way in which the land question was to be dealt
with when the time came to pass a Home Rule Bill. When he heard that the
party had agreed to this manoeuvre Dillon was flabbergasted, even though
it was accompanied by a pledge, given by Clancy on his leader's behalf,
that Parnell would retire if satisfaction were obtained. Dillon could never
suffer fools gladly, but neither could he withhold admiration from a political expert, and his diary makes it clear that while his misgivings about
Parnell were as great as ever, he regarded the party as falling into the
former category and the leader as still very much the expert. Even before
it was known whether or not the party were going to accept the Clancy
resolution, Dillon observed to Harrington that the worst thing that could
now happen would be that Parnell should retire, since this would place his
successor in a hopeless position.[1] And in his diary he wrote on 4 December,
when it seemed as if the resolution would be accepted, that the party had
been caught in a 'rat-trap'. 'And it seems to me that the only way out of the
imbroglio is that Parnell should resume the lead, and all members of the
party who can reconcile it to their conscience and honour to follow him
should fall into line again.'[2] Two days later, on Saturday, 6 December,
before he had heard how the negotiations finally went, he still could not
understand 'how our men can have been so silly as to fall into the trap set
for them by Parnell'. And he continued:

> This idiotic piece of tactics seems to me to have handed over the
> opposition bound hand and foot to Parnell. The question at issue is
> entirely changed and the minds of the people drawn to a new
> issue . . . Every fresh development only increases my admiration for
> the infinite political skill of Parnell, his power of planning a cam-

[1] Ibid., 4 Dec. 1890.   [2] Diary of John Dillon, 4 Dec. 1890 (D.P.).

paign, of *seeing* what ideas will take hold of the minds of the people, of diverting discussion from the real points in controversy.[1]

But Parnell was not the only political genius in action in those fateful days. The success of his manoeuvre depended in the last resort upon Gladstone and Gladstone refused to be drawn. He met the party delegation courteously, but was entirely non-committal at first; later, having conferred with some of his chief colleagues, he wrote firmly declining to enter into details of his proposals for Home Rule until after the Irish party had themselves settled the question of the leadership. This rebuff meant that the debate in Committee Room Fifteen was brought back inexorably to what was, after all, the crucial issue—the future of Parnell. And at last, on Saturday, 6 December, after a final session in which nerves were overwrought, tempers out of control, and angry, indeed unforgivable, words spoken, the party split in two. Justin McCarthy, the vice-chairman, led forty-four of his colleagues from the room. Parnell, surrounded by twenty-six of his supporters, still sat in the chair. He claimed this as a victory, but in reality it was a mortal blow. A great force in Irish and British politics—a united, pledge-bound party led by a man of genius—had been shattered into fragments and all the high hopes of imminent success were as if they had never been.

(ii)

Unhappily, the clash in Committee Room Fifteen was only the opening phase of a war which was now carried into Ireland, where a pending by-election at Kilkenny suddenly assumed crucial importance as the first opportunity of testing how opinion was running in the country. Both sides began hurriedly to prepare for the struggle. On Monday, 8 December, the anti-Parnellites, as we may now begin to call them, elected a committee of eight (which included Dillon, O'Brien and T. P. O'Connor—all still in America) while their new chairman, Justin McCarthy, issued a manifesto to the Irish people justifying the break with Parnell and asserting that allegiance to Ireland was more precious than allegiance to any one man, especially when that man had made further co-operation with the Liberals impossible so long as he remained leader.[2] Even before he had written his manifesto, McCarthy cabled to Dillon and O'Brien asking for authority to add their names to the signatories. They hesitated, however, to come out so strongly at this stage.[3] This was partly because they were so far from the scene and not yet in possession of all the facts, but partly also because a new possibility was beginning to take shape. By the time McCarthy's manifesto had appeared in print, William O'Brien had taken an initiative of his own and messages were already passing between him and Parnell about a possible meeting in France to try once more for a peaceful settlement. With O'Brien thus poised for the highly congenial role of *deus ex*

---

[1] Ibid., 6 Dec. 1890; Lyons, *Fall of Parnell*, p. 180.   [2] Lyons, op. cit., p. 154.
[3] Ibid., p. 180.

machina, both he and Dillon were reluctant to commit themselves. They approved, it is true, of McCarthy's election as 'chairman of the Irish party' and were in general sympathy with what the anti-Parnellites had done, but, they said in a cable to McCarthy, 'we desire, as hitherto, to leave the responsibility to you, co-operating by methods we believe best to secure Mr. Parnell's withdrawal and the reunion of the party'.[1]

This was almost a declaration of neutrality, but events were making it increasingly hard for them to remain aloof. On 10 December Parnell arrived in Dublin, broke into the offices of *United Ireland* (which had been following an anti-Parnellite line), dismissed the editor, gave an interview to an American correspondent which breathed defiance in every word, and warned a large and enthusiastic meeting at the Rotunda that the limits of constitutional action might be very near. From Dublin he travelled to Cork to address his constituents in the same vein, and from there, with almost incredible energy and *élan*, went straight to the main battlefield of Kilkenny. When this news reached Dillon and O'Brien in New York they were profoundly affected by it, so much so that, together with T. P. O'Connor, they issued a statement of their own in an effort to counter the effects of Parnell's remarks in Dublin. This statement was largely written by O'Brien, who, characteristically, had now swung from his initial bitterness to something like a return to his old tenderness for Parnell—perhaps the incorrigible romantic in him was stirred by the spectacle of the once-omnipotent leader fighting for his political life against what already seemed to be overwhelming odds. Consequently, the declaration, though firm in its insistence upon the vital importance of the Liberal alliance, was studiously moderate towards Parnell.[2] This moderation itself, however, was due not only to lingering affection for the fallen chief but also to active revulsion from the language already used against him by Healy in Committee Room Fifteen and which was at that very moment being given a much wider currency—by Healy and others—during the Kilkenny election. So greatly were the delegates in America depressed by this evidence of deterioration that they all, and especially Dillon, grew increasingly despondent and began to think seriously of resigning.[3] Certainly, there was not much point in remaining in America. Their mission had been paralysed from the start of the crisis and was now disintegrating rapidly. Parnell had sent for Harrington, who departed on 13 December; on the same day William O'Brien and T. P. Gill sailed for France; and on 17 December T. D. Sullivan left for Ireland. Only Dillon and T. P. O'Connor stayed on in New York and on both of them the strain of prolonged isolation and inaction was beginning to tell.

However, isolation and inaction for a few weeks longer would be a small price to pay if, by some miracle, O'Brien were to bring off a settlement with Parnell in France. Two days before the ebullient optimist sailed he, T. P. O'Connor and Dillon discussed the terms he should offer Parnell

[1] Ibid., pp. 180–1.   [2] *F.J.*, 12 Dec. 1890.
[3] Diary of John Dillon, 10 Dec. 1890 (D.P.).

when they met in Boulogne. Dillon wrote them out twice on hotel note-paper, retaining one version himself and giving the other to O'Brien. The two versions differ slightly, but O'Brien's is the more authoritative, since it was the one on which he based his conversations with Parnell. Briefly, it was proposed that the majority should agree that their election of Mc-Carthy as chairman was 'informal' and that, if Parnell wished it, the reunited party should formally re-elect McCarthy. Parnell was to be given some personal satisfaction in the form of a public declaration by the party enumerating the mitigating circumstances which had encouraged him to make his stand—the Leinster Hall meeting, his initial re-election on 25 November, Gladstone's overhasty publication of his letter. Also, an attempt was to be made to induce Archbishops Croke and Walsh to retract their denunciations of him. It was further to be suggested to Parnell that his personal influence would continue to be dominant, that his retirement would only be temporary, and that his return to the leadership would be welcomed under certain (unspecified) conditions. In addition to these sops to his *amour propre* he was to be left with substantial authority. Thus, he was to share with the new party chairman in all future discussions as to the provisions of the coming Home Rule Bill; he was to have the right to nominate an equal number of members on the party committee, or, if he preferred, that committee could be 'thrown overboard' completely; he was to remain president of the Irish National League; above all, he was to be—with two others elected by the party—a joint treasurer of all party funds, cheques to be signed by any two treasurers. These were very large con-cessions and it is perhaps a measure of the isolation of the delegates in America that they failed apparently to realise how vigorously they would be resisted by the majority of the party, even if Parnell himself could be persuaded to accept them. Certainly, if he had accepted them, and if the majority had acquiesced in them, it is hard to see how his successor could even have begun to function with this still powerful figure looming in the wings.

But suppose one or other of these numerous conditions failed to be met and the negotiations broke down—what was then to be their course? Dillon's own preference would probably have been to get out of the whole miserable business—he was at this time oppressed again by dyspepsia and plunged, as a necessary consequence, into deep depression. But, at the same time, conscious of their responsibility for the evicted tenants, he and O'Brien were both prepared to make it a condition of their remaining in the party that further money should be raised for these poor people and that the party would undertake to look after them. And to this they added two other conditions—that there should be an assurance of enough funds being available to enable the party as well as the tenants to carry on, and that the *Freeman's Journal*, which was still obstinately Parnellite, could either be 'spiked' or else brought round to the majority viewpoint.[3]

It was easy to write of the majority viewpoint, harder to define what it

---

[3] Lyons, op. cit., pp. 183–7.

was, at least in the country at large. In fact, this could not begin to be determined until the Kilkenny election had run its course. It was savagely fought on both sides. There was mob violence in some parts of the constituency and both Parnell and, in the other camp, Davitt, were physically assaulted. When the result was declared the anti-Parnellite candidate won by just over 1,000 votes, but Parnell made it clear that he would not accept this verdict as final and went out of his way to repeat the warning he had given in Dublin that 'when constitutional struggle, if it ever does (I don't say it ever will), becomes useless and unavailing, at that moment I will declare my belief to you and I will take your advice and be guided by your judgement'.[1] This was a typically Delphic utterance, but, taken in conjunction with the so-called 'appeal to the hillside men' made by his supporters during the campaign, and the open sympathy shown him by men of known Fenian inclinations, it was understood by many to mean that he was shaping his course away from the parliamentary movement and back towards the old chimera of physical force from which, more than anyone else, he had sought to turn away his fellow countrymen.

Dillon, waiting tormented in New York, could only watch the spectacle with mounting disgust and try to make what sense he could of the conflicting accounts reaching him from Ireland. Not surprisingly, there was some divergence between what he said in public and what he wrote in private. Publicly he still took the line that Parnell ought not to be leader and on 15 December attacked him, for plunging Ireland into a conflict for 'purely personal ends', and for using 'language and base accusations, revolting to every free man, which, unless altered, shows that he is unfit to be the leader of a nation aspiring to be free'. A few days later he followed this with an appeal to the Kilkenny voters to support the anti-Parnellite candidate and so demonstrate to Parnell 'the futility of all further opposition to the majority of his party and the will of his country'.[2] Privately, however, he was sickened by the whole affair and sent a letter after O'Brien on the very day of the latter's departure which showed, even thus early in the crisis, how little love he had for Parnell's opponents. 'Healy', he wrote, 'is maddening. And I expect Davitt will be as bad. And it infuriates me to read of Parnell being hounded down by the priests.'[3] Letters from home only confirmed his worst fears. His own cousin, Valentine Dillon, who had come out for Parnell, wrote that some of the leading Parnellites—Dr. Kenny, J. J. Clancy, John Redmond—were open to compromise, provided Parnell was not harshly treated, but that the very savagery of the attack upon him was making it difficult for his more moderate followers to do anything to build a bridge.[4] And it did not help to hear from one of these moderates, Dr. Kenny, of the 'awful thirst' shown by some of the party members to destroy Parnell from the very beginning of the crisis. Kenny was inclined to put most blame on Thomas Sexton and John Barry and to excuse Healy's

[1] *F.J.*, 24 and 25 Dec. 1890.   [2] Lyons, op. cit., p. 188.
[3] Dillon to O'Brien, 13 Dec. 1890 (Gill Papers).
[4] V. B. Dillon to John Dillon, 13 Dec. 1890 (D.P.).

behaviour in Committee Room Fifteen on the grounds that he had not fully recovered from his illness. 'Remember', he added, 'not one of them can plead the manifesto *which seems to have so much influenced you and William, because they had declared their position two days before a word of it was written or before a whisper of its being about to be issued was heard.*'[1]

These letters struck gloom into Dillon's heart. 'I have not felt utterly beaten until now', he noted in his diary. 'But after reading the *Freeman* of December 10—and 5 and 6—and seeing the class of men who are going with Parnell, I do believe the game is up and unhappy Ireland must pass thro' the valley of death into which Parnell is dragging her. I have been miserable and sick, and have no stomach for any fight, much less for the sordid, beastly fight which is before us in Ireland.'[2]

This mood was reflected in the detailed analysis of the situation he sent to O'Brien next day. He was, it appeared, absolutely convinced that the situation was hopeless and still thought the best thing he and O'Brien could do would be to resign. Inevitably, he regarded the Kilkenny election (then working up to its angry climax) as the key to the situation. He anticipated, quite rightly, that Parnell, even though beaten, would fight on and Dillon thought it probable that 'with private encouragement from him' the Fenian movement would again become formidable. Imagine, then, the situation of the anti-Parnellite majority. Relying on the bishops and priests for support, and having Parnell and the extremists on its flank [they] would soon become utterly contemptible and would be either at the mercy of the Liberals or would be obliged to break with Gladstone and the Liberals and therefore justify Parnell's action and put themselves in a position from which *no* amount of explanation would ever extricate them'. The upshot would be the certain loss of the coming general election and, to Dillon's jaundiced eye, it seemed quite possible that if the Liberals saw they could not win an election on Home Rule they would drop the whole policy. 'And this again would fully justify Parnell in the eyes of the multitude.' It was, he admitted, just conceivable that Parnell would come to terms with O'Brien and agree to withdraw, but unless at the same time he gave some sort of pledge of support to the party the position would be no better and the fate of the election would be extremely dubious. 'All cordial relations between our party and the Liberals are hopelessly broken.'[3]

For Dillon, then, still marooned in New York, unable to return to England or Ireland without the immediate certainty of arrest, and denied any other possibility of action until he heard the outcome of O'Brien's mission, these were among the darkest and loneliest days of his life. His illness continued to depress him, he was sick, dyspeptic and wakeful, and kept more and more to his hotel bedroom, reading Lowell's critical essays and waiting, waiting, waiting for news from France. 'I long with an unspeakable longing', he wrote in his diary on 20 December, 'to get out of

[1] J. E. Kenny to Dillon, 13 Dec. 1890 (D.P.).
[2] Diary of John Dillon, 17 Dec. 1890 (D.P.).
[3] Dillon to O'Brien, 18 Dec. 1890 (Gill Papers).

politics and have done with the sordid misery of that life, and get to read
and think and live at least for a few years before I die, but I fear it is too
late now.' It was indeed too late, for while Dillon languished in New York,
O'Brien at last made contact with Parnell and from their meeting new and
far-reaching developments began almost at once to flow.

Although O'Brien had actually reached Boulogne on Christmas Day, it
was not until 30 December that he had his first—and highly secret—interview with Parnell. He found his former leader, not surprisingly, in one of
his more frigid moods, but plunged bravely in with the terms he, Dillon
and O'Connor had agreed upon in New York. Characteristically, Parnell
swept this elaborate document on one side and took the wind completely
out of O'Brien's sails by making a new condition of his own—that he
would only consider retirement if O'Brien and *not* McCarthy, were to
succeed him as chairman of the reunited party. O'Brien, naturally seeing
in this an obvious tactic to divide him from the majority, or even from
Dillon, tried to laugh the proposal out of court. But when he found that
Parnell was perfectly serious he made his own counter-suggestion, which in
its turn was calculated to give Parnell pause—that not he, but Dillon,
should be the new leader. They then parted, each promising to think over
the other's terms, and Parnell carrying away with him a document which
embodied most of the concessions drafted in New York, but which contained in addition a promise that O'Brien would have nothing to do with
any new (anti-Parnellite) newspaper, and also the strange idea that an
effort should be made to get Gladstone to acknowledge that he had erred
in publishing his famous letter so precipitately.[2]

O'Brien, of course, had to consult Dillon before he could make any
reply and the latter was astounded to receive on 31 December a cable from
his friend announcing Parnell's extraordinary *démarche* and seeking his
advice. It was hard to know what best to say. It *seemed* a trap. On the
other hand, it did just possibly offer a way out. His diary reflected his
bewilderment:

> I never imagined it was possible that I could be put into such a
> position of perplexity as I am now placed in by cable from W. O'B.
> this afternoon. Men say here that Parnell is mad, but it seems to me
> that his astuteness is absolutely infinite, and in all the reflections on
> the possible outcome of the situation which have passed thro' my
> head in the last few days what has now happened never occurred to
> me. The moment I read the cable I felt that P. had executed a master-
> stroke and all my reflection since has only deepened my conviction—
> and increased my alarm and uneasiness.[3]

At length, after consulting T. P. O'Connor and receiving in a further cable
a favourable account of the Parnell-O'Brien meeting from John Redmond
and T. P. Gill, Dillon (with O'Connor) sent back an encouraging reply,

[1] Diary of John Dillon, 20 Dec. 1890 (D.P.).   [2] Lyons, op. cit., pp. 193–202.
[3] Ibid., p. 203.

though warning O'Brien not to lose touch with the anti-Parnellite majority. But Dillon was still extremely uneasy. A second cable from O'Brien that same day (31 December) explained that Parnell had refused to allow him to tell the majority leaders, McCarthy and Sexton, about his offer until Dillon's reaction was known, 'which', noted Dillon, 'confirms my suspicions'. 'My *strong* impression is that Parnell has executed another *coup* similar to when he got the party to go to Gladstone and demand definite pledges.'[1] In this Dillon was nearly, but not quite, correct. What Parnell had in mind was not just a similar *coup* but precisely the same one.

On New Year's Day, while Dillon was still recording his confused emotions in his diary, Parnell wrote an important letter to O'Brien. In it he completely transformed the whole basis of the negotiations. Declining the terms offered to him by O'Brien, he reverted to the proposal he had made in Committee Room Fifteen and now proffered it anew in a slightly different form. What he suggested was that McCarthy (who was, after all, the elected leader of the anti-Parnellites) should obtain an interview with Gladstone and ask him for a memorandum expressing the views of his colleagues and himself on the questions put to him in vain by the Irish delegation from Committee Room Fifteen—the two questions being, of course, the settlement of the land question and the control of the police. Assuming he got such a document, McCarthy was to transfer it to O'Brien, after which O'Brien and Parnell (*not* McCarthy, who throughout seems to have been regarded by Parnell as no more than a messenger) should consult together as to whether or not it was satisfactory. If it was satisfactory, then Parnell would forthwith announce his retirement from the chairmanship of the party. But the terms of the Liberal memorandum were not to be disclosed to any other person until after the introduction of the Home Rule Bill, and not then unless the Bill failed to embody the terms of the memorandum; however, if the Bill did embody them, then Parnell should be allowed to publish the memorandum after the Bill had become law.[2]

The scheme bristled with difficulties and O'Brien's first inclination was to regard it with the deepest suspicion, especially since further inquiry revealed that McCarthy as well as Parnell was to retire and that Parnell still clung to his proposition that O'Brien was to be chairman of the reunited party. On the other hand, he was prepared to risk a great deal to bring about Parnell's peaceful withdrawal. Accordingly, he met Parnell again at Boulogne on 6 and 7 January and made three counter-proposals of his own—that Dillon should be chairman, that McCarthy and Sexton should be told of all that had passed so far, and that McCarthy should join with Parnell and O'Brien in deciding upon the adequacy of the Liberal guarantees. After hard and sharp argument Parnell conceded the first two of these points, but still insisted that only O'Brien and himself were to be the judges of the Liberal guarantees.[3]

All now depended upon the reactions of those who were to be drawn

[1] Diary of John Dillon, 1 Jan. 1891 (D.P.).   [2] Lyons, op. cit., pp. 204–5.
[3] Ibid., pp. 207–11.

into the negotiations—McCarthy, the Liberal leaders, and, above all, Dillon. Dillon was still eating his heart out in New York, thinking almost longingly of the peace he could find simply by going back to Ireland and serving his prison sentence when, late on 6 January he was flabbergasted to receive this cable from O'Brien:

> You elected chairman if McCarthy first obtains from Gladstone private guarantees constabulary and land satisfactory to Parnell and myself on lines previously defined. We agreeing side with Parnell if guarantees refused. If McCarthy consents this course much preferable. Question arises if McCarthy refuses what should be our action. Myself think resign.[1]

To Dillon this astonishing communication pointed to only one conclusion —that the situation had got completely out of O'Brien's control. He replied:

> Could not think of accepting chairmanship; proposed terms in my judgment intolerable; not bona fide. Consider proposal about Gladstone trap. Would never bind myself any course in event of refusal by Gladstone. I sail France Saturday. Insist truce till I arrive.[2]

This, though more economical than O'Brien's telegraphic style, seemed clear enough. But what it could not convey was his exasperation at the new turn of events which, as he noted that night in his diary, was 'bad as bad can be'. O'Brien, he wrote, 'seems to have walked into the very trap into which the party walked before, and for doing which we all blasphemed against the party in Chicago. Now the proposal is that I am to get the chairmanship on terms such that I would rather earn a living by blacking shoes than accept. Yet, judging from William's cable he has agreed to these terms and thinks I should accept them.' Naturally, he discussed the matter with O'Connor, who was later to record in his memoirs that at this time, like others who had been devoted to Parnell, he regarded Dillon with some suspicion as the only possible rival to the leader, but that at the critical moment he saw not a sign of personal ambition in him.[3] Dillon himself, indeed, found O'Connor less worried by the prospect than he was, but finally got him to agree that it was out of the question to accept the conditions, though O'Connor apparently clung to the hope that Gladstone might be induced to give the required guarantees. 'I *cannot* think there is the slightest reason to suppose that he would entertain the idea. Very seedy tonight and very hopeless in every direction.'[4]

A night's reflection brought not optimism, but at least a pause to despair. On 7 January Dillon again cabled to O'Brien to beware of Parnell and repeated that he would be no party to exacting guarantees from Gladstone. However, if O'Brien and McCarthy thought the scheme had even a faint chance of success he would not stand in the way, though he would prefer them not to come to any final decision until he arrived in France. O'Brien,

[1] Ibid., p. 211.   [2] Ibid., p. 212.
[3] T. P. O'Conner, *Memoirs of an old parliamentarian*, ii. 294–5.
[4] Diary of John Dillon, 6 Jan. 1891.

now cock-a-hoop, replied that in his view Parnell *was* genuine and that there was a real possibility of success. But Dillon was not so easy to persuade. He still thought it wrong to press McCarthy to go and see Gladstone, though if it could be arranged he would not interfere. Accordingly, on 10 January, the day of his departure for France, he issued a studiously moderate statement appealing for a truce while the talks were proceeding. 'I believe', he said, with an optimism he was far from feeling, 'it is still possible to reunite the party, save the general election and secure Home Rule within three years.' Privately, however, he regarded the situation as 'practically hopeless'. In his diary he noted that Parnell had in effect 'captured' O'Brien, 'and I fear P. has succeeded in dividing O'Brien from me'.[1]

(iii)

It was not a cheerful augury for their reunion, but, strangely enough, while Dillon was at sea the situation began, almost miraculously, to improve. On the face of it, it hardly seemed likely that the Liberal leaders would even agree to see McCarthy, let alone make binding, and possibly embarrassing, pledges about a still hypothetical Home Rule Bill. Indeed, the Liberals that Christmas had been fully as depressed as Dillon, and defeat at the first by-election since the split in the Irish party had plunged them still further into gloom. It was not surprising, but from the Irish viewpoint extremely ominous, that some of them at the end of the year began to turn their eyes towards alternative policies which the electorate might find more enticing than the bleak prospect of handing over the government of Ireland to a set of politicians who seemed to concern themselves with nothing but a mutual passion for hounding each other to death. Yet there were some who continued to believe in Home Rule and of these the most sympathetic was John Morley. On 12 January he agreed to receive an emissary from O'Brien. It was T. P. Gill, who explained the background of the situation fully and urged Morley to explain to Gladstone that his help was the one hope of ending the *impasse*. He then provided Morley with details of the Parnell-O'Brien proposals on the understanding that they were to be shown to Gladstone. But Morley, although sympathetic in public as well as in private—the very next day he went out of his way to make a speech emphasising friendship for Ireland—was not hopeful on the delicate question of guarantees, 'a desperately childish sort of device if ever one was', as he described it to Gladstone when forwarding the proposals. Gladstone's response, predictably, was full of objections. He could only deal with the *de facto* leader of the party and the Irish did not seem yet to have made up their minds who that was; a document binding colleagues would present 'great difficulties'; and he could say nothing about the land question until the extent of the Government's measure to be introduced next session became known. Morley passed these discouraging comments on to Gill when the latter came to see him again on 16 January. But Gill

---

[1] Lyons, *Fall of Parnell*, pp. 212–14.

was not easily put off and made one point which impressed Morley considerably—that if Gladstone saw McCarthy he would not be officially aware that the latter was about to abdicate and therefore could without impropriety discuss Home Rule details with him. Reporting this conversation to Gladstone, Morley added that if the negotiations did break down, then he judged 'that Dillon and O'Brien will throw all up; will go to prison and will come out to find the whole movement in pretty complete collapse, or else Parnell practically master of a demoralised party'. It was this apprehension which in the end weighed most heavily with the Liberals and even cancelled out Sir William Harcourt's vehement protestations against any kind of dealings with the Irish party until the leadership issue had been finally settled. The fact that a few days later a Unionist seat (West Hartlepool) was actually captured by a Liberal who fought primarily on the issue of Home Rule also helped to steady the Liberals' nerve and to dispose them to go at least some way towards helping to bring the crisis to a peaceful and satisfactory conclusion.[1]

By the time Dillon landed at Le Havre on 18 January the atmosphere had thus become so hopeful that he was himself, if only for a while, infected by the prevailing optimism. In a note he made in his diary he listed the factors which inclined him to believe that a settlement might really be possible. One was that he found that McCarthy and Sexton had practically agreed without pressure from him that guarantees *should* be sought from the Liberals; another was Morley's sympathetic attitude; a third was O'Brien's absolute conviction that Parnell was genuinely anxious for peace; a fourth was the information O'Brien had given him about the situation in Ireland 'which confirmed in me the conviction that there was absolutely no other way in which it would be possible to save the movement except by a treaty with Parnell'. Added to all this was the negative effect on him of the bishops' hostility to Parnell, combined with 'the scandalous attempts made by Healy and others to misrepresent W. O'B. and to thwart his attempt to make peace.'[2] These last two factors indicated to him the way in which the struggle might further degenerate if it were allowed to continue and undoubtedly influenced him in throwing all his weight behind O'Brien's peacemaking, however far-fetched it might seem.

Shortly after he arrived Dillon had two further encouraging communications. McCarthy wrote agreeing to visit Gladstone, and Gladstone himself sent a friendly letter promising every support in his power to the parliamentary party, while emphasising that 'the British Liberal party, loyal as before to Home Rule, refuses to follow Mr. Parnell'.[3] Nevertheless, when it came to the point Gladstone was still intent upon preserving his freedom of action and, as he told his own followers, his inclination was to have no secret agreement, no dealings with Parnell, and to keep the question of Home Rule guarantees quite separate from the leadership question. Moreover, as he observed to his old colleague, Lord Granville, he was disappointed in Dillon, who 'does not seem to be a bit stiffer in the back than

---

[1] Ibid., pp. 223–9.   [2] Ibid., p. 230.   [3] Ibid., p. 231.

O'Brien'. 'I should like,' he added ominously, 'to hear something of Healy, who is of stiffer material.'[1] John Morley, by contrast, who knew from his previous dealings with T. P. Gill that the guarantees could not in practice be separated from the leadership, saw Dillon and O'Brien, not Healy, as the key to the situation, for if the negotiations fell through and they went to prison to serve the sentences outstanding against them, Parnell would have unlimited opportunities for mischief during the six months they would be out of action. On the other hand, as he explained to Dillon, it was not possible to push the Liberals beyond a certain point. A secret agreement such as that proposed, he said, 'is a thing absolutely out of date in our politics at this time of day, even if we knew for certain that the secrecy would be honourably observed, and that is what, after past experience, we cannot possibly feel sure of'. And in any event, how could Gladstone treat officially with McCarthy 'when he knows from every newspaper that he opens that this very treaty is to be the preliminary and the price of his deposition'?[2]

This was serious enough. No less serious was a long letter Dillon received a few days later from Archbishop Walsh. In the course of it the archbishop gave an unequivocal warning against negotiating with Parnell. 'I feel really bound to let you know', he wrote, 'that the indignation of the country is rising; that, strange as it may seem to you, confidence in you two may easily be lost; and that, even at present, if any open protest were to be made against the further continuance of the negotiations, it would carry with it, I am satisfied, the hearty and open concurrence of *at least* three-fourths of the nationalist forces of the country'. And he continued:

> While it is (at all events generally) felt, then, that neither of you two will in any way consent to any arrangement involving his continued leadership, it is almost universally feared that he may succeed in drawing you both into an acceptance of some arrangement which will put him in a position to take the field at the general election.
>
> No matter what arrangement the party may come to, the opposition to him will go on, and, I feel satisfied, I am well within the mark when I say that there are fully one half of the seats now safely held by nationalists in which neither he, nor any one supposed to be in his favour, that is in favour of him as leader, will have the smallest chance of success at the general election.
>
> The only way to save the elections, and to save the cause, is *to get rid of him at once*. Whether he is willing to go or not, should not make a particle of difference in the case.[3]

This was plain speaking and it came from an expert in Irish public opinion. Neither Dillon nor O'Brien was likely to underestimate the force of what the archbishop had to say, but it still remained true that whether there would ever be any negotiations or not depended on the Liberals. They, largely influenced, it would seem, by Morley's plea that if they did

---

[1] Ibid., p. 232.   [2] John Morley to Dillon, 23 Jan. 1891.
[3] Archbishop W. J. Walsh to Dillon, 26 Jan. 1891 (D.P.).

not give assurances they would lose Dillon and O'Brien, and that 'the
battle against him [Parnell] will be hopeless unless we have Dillon and
O'Brien with us', eventually agreed, on 28 January, upon a statement to
be handed over to the Irish intermedaries who duly transferred it to O'Brien
in France. The assurances, or 'guarantees', concerned both the land and the
police. As regards the former, it was stated that the land question must
either be settled by the imperial parliament simultaneously with the
establishment of Home Rule, or within a limited time thereafter specified
in the Home Rule Bill, or else power to deal with it must be given to the
Irish legislature. As for the police, it would be for the Irish government to
set up a civil police force 'to take the place of the present armed and semi-
military police'; while this was being done the existing force would undergo
rapid reduction and transformation, disappearing completely when the civil
force was completed.[1]

O'Brien and Dillon discussed these terms on 30 January and found them
satisfactory. O'Brien at once wired to Parnell to come and clinch the issue,
and on 3 February, having travelled non-stop from Ireland, he met the two
peacemakers at Calais. Parnell was tense, irritable, overtired, and this may
have contributed to the stormy atmosphere which soon enveloped the meeting. We have unfortunately no exactly contemporary account of what
occurred and are largely dependent upon O'Brien's various subsequent narratives. When in November 1891 he published in the Press a history of the
French negotiations he simply stated that Parnell read the document, suggested certain amendments, and departed next day for England.[2] Four years
later, defending Dillon from a charge made during the 1895 general election
campaign that he had been primarily responsible for the breakdown, he
said this: 'So far from the breakdown of the arrangement at Boulogne
being due in any way to John Dillon, he played a more unselfish part and
faced a more cruel misrepresentation and injustice than probably any man
ever faced before.'[3] But in 1910, having in the meantime quarrelled bitterly
with Dillon, he laid the blame for the catastrophe upon his former friend.
In this version—a volume of his memoirs entitled *An olive branch in Ireland*
—he said little about Parnell's suggested amendments or his own reaction
to them and concentrated instead upon an exchange which took place
between Parnell and Dillon not at the main meeting but the following
morning, when Parnell was about to go on board ship. At first all went well
Parnell, O'Brien claimed, being so amiable that he volunteered to resign
from the presidency of the National League as well as from the chairmanship of the party, and then went on to give Dillon some expert advice on
how to manage the party. Next they discussed the disposition of the old
Land League money still stowed away in France—the so-called 'Paris
Fund'—which Parnell suggested should be lodged in future in his name

[1] Lyons, op. cit., pp. 234–5.
[2] *F.J.*, 4 Nov. 1891.
[3] *F.J.*, 24 July 1895; see also W. O'Brien, 'Was Mr. Parnell badly treated?' in *Contemporary Review*, lxx (Nov. 1896), 683.

7. William O'Brien
from the portrait by William Orpen
(*Courtesy of the Municipal Gallery of Modern Art,
Dublin*)

8. Charles Stewart Parnell, from a drawing made by
J. D. Reigh in 1891. In the left hand corner is
Parnell's own verdict: "That Reigh is the only one
who can do justice to my handsome face"
(*Courtesy of the National Gallery of Ireland*)

and in Dillon's. According to O'Brien, Dillon bleakly objected that the first time he was in need to pay salaries Parnell would be in a position to cut off his supplies and render him helpless. O'Brien's dramatic narrative continues:

> Parnell rose to his feet, white with passion. 'Dillon,' he said, with that power of his to produce the effect of ice and fire at the same moment, 'Dillon, that is not the kind of expression I had a right to expect from you after the way I have behaved to you.'

Almost at once he recovered his poise and they continued to talk until his boat was about to leave. 'But we all spoke', O'Brien recalled, 'with the unreality of physicians prescribing for a patient who had already expired under our eyes.'[1]

The account is highly coloured and the bias unmistakable. Nevertheless, it does seem from fragmentary comments let fall by various parliamentarians that the conference had not gone well. John Redmond, for example, wrote to O'Brien a few days after it had taken place that 'John's interview with P. at Calais had a *very bad effect*'. Harrington, too, wrote in the same strain: 'I think John said something to him about the funds in Paris which wounded him terribly.' And later in the year, when he, like O'Brien, was publishing his recollections of the crisis, he stated—and was not contradicted—that Dillon had asked that Parnell should release and place at his disposal as much of the Paris Fund as would sustain the parliamentary party for three years. 'I have it both from Mr. Parnell and Mr. Dillon', said Harrington, 'that the latter gentleman declined to take the chair if this was not done.' And even Tim Healy, who, though certainly not privy to the dicussions, always had his ear close to the ground, was able to write to Archbishop Walsh a few days later that Parnell had 'blasted' Dillon to Gill when they were going back on the boat. 'I never could get on with that man,' he was alleged to have said; 'you know O'Brien was the man I wanted.'[2]

It seems clear therefore that there *was* some friction at the meeting and probable that it was about money, since Dillon had always regarded a sufficiency of funds as essential to the conduct of the movement. The fact of friction in itself, of course, was hardly surprising. Temperamentally, the two men had always been poles apart, and by the time they met at Calais both had been in a state of high nervous tension for three months on end. Parnell had always found Dillon an able but not very amenable lieutenant, while Dillon, though respecting Parnell's political mastery, had never succumbed to his dominant personality. For each the course of events since the divorce must have confirmed the mistrust he had of the other.

Yet, despite these obvious and long-standing incompatibilities, it would not be correct to say, as it later suited O'Brien to say, that the negotiations in France foundered on the clash between Dillon and Parnell. On the contrary, when he got back to England, Parnell showed every sign of taking

[1] W. O'Brien, *An olive branch in Ireland*, pp. 46–8.   [2] Lyons, *Fall of Parnell*, pp. 236–8.

the Liberal guarantees seriously, sending for T. P. Gill—the harassed and slightly inadequate Mercury of all these transactions—and impressing upon him the necessity of amending the guarantees so as to make them more watertight. Unfortunately, at this interview with Parnell (on 4 February) Gill seems to have allowed him to receive the impression that the Liberal leaders had laid it down as a condition that it should be O'Brien who should pronounce on the guarantees and that O'Brien would be asked to bind himself to accept them before they could be published. While this was no doubt an accurate enough rendering of the Liberal position—they had always insisted to Gill that they would not deal with Parnell—it was disastrous to convey it to Parnell, whose nerves were already overstretched and whose fierce pride was ready to flare up at the slightest indication that he was being slighted or by-passed. Naturally, he reacted strongly. He would be placed, he said in 'a humiliating and disgraceful position' which neither his own self-respect nor that of the Irish people would allow him to occupy for a moment.

But was wounded pride the only explanation for his outburst? Or was it that at bottom he wanted the negotiations to fail, knowing that if they succeeded they must result in his retirement? We do not know enough of his inner mind to be sure of the answer, but it is at least suggestive that apart altogether from proposing amendments which the Liberals were very likely not to accept, he followed this by introducing a new element into an already tangled situation. Writing to Gill the day after their interview, he alleged that information had reached him (he did not say from what source) that *all* the Irish Members would be retained at Westminster even after Home Rule had been achieved. This prospect—with its implication of some continued oversight of, or even veto upon, Irish legislation— was,he declared, 'ominous and most alarming'. In this supposition he may not, in fact, have been far wide of the mark, but that he should introduce it at this stage in the form of an unsubstantiated rumour was itself 'ominous and alarming'. Or so at least it seemed to Gill as wearily, and fruitlessly, he set himself to remove these latest apprehensions of Parnell's. But since at the same time he learnt from the Liberals that they would not 'alter a comma' of their original guarantees it was clear that hope of an agreed settlement was fast disappearing.

On 7 February, Gill crossed once more to France, bringing with him the letter Parnell had written him two days previously about the future position of the Irish representatives at Westminster. Until they actually met him and read the letter both Dillon and O'Brien had apparently genuinely believed that a peaceful solution was within their grasp. But once Gill had brought them up to date their disillusionment was rapid and complete. O'Brien, indeed, went through the motions of assuring Parnell that the alleged new conditions were 'absolute rubbish' and Gill, in a further interview with the fallen leader on 10 February, thought he had made some headway in overcoming Parnell's anxieties. Since, however, he had also to tell him that the Liberals refused to amend their guarantees, the final result was the same—the negotiations had reached the end of the road. A few more polite but ineffectual letters were exchanged on both sides before, on 12 February, Dillon and O'Brien crossed to Folkestone, There, as expected, they were duly arrested and taken to Scotland Yard as the first stage of a journey which for both of them led straight to six months in Galway jail.[1]

(iv)

To analyse Parnell's motives for entering into these negotiations and then breaking them off just when they seemed to be reaching fruition does not belong to the biography of John Dillon.[2] Whether he used them as a tactic to try to divide his enemies or whether he sincerely sought a settlement, these are questions which puzzled contemporaries then and have puzzled historians since. Here we are only concerned with Dillon's attitude to the crisis and with the effect of the breakdown of the negotiations upon his subsequent career. He was never, as we know, an unqualified optimist where public affairs were concerned and he had had his doubts about the 'treaty' with Parnell from the beginning. Once he got to France, however, and within range of O'Brien's all-devouring enthusiasm, he does seem to have allowed himself to hope that they might indeed reach agreement. Twenty years later, discussing the affair with Wilfred Scawen Blunt, he pointed out that the terms offered were so generous that Parnell might reasonably have been expected to accept them; he himself, he insisted, had assured Parnell that he would resign the chairmanship back to him after six months and would in effect be a working vice-chairman during the leader's retirement.[3] Twenty years efface many memories and this was certainly an oversimplification. But his diary of those events written at the time corresponds with his recollection twenty years later—that Parnell was on the verge of compromise. Even as late as 7 February, before he learnt the worst from the unhappy Gill, Dillon still, it seems, thought that the gap between Parnell and the Liberals was so 'absurdly small' that the negotiations could not fail, and so also thought some of Parnell's own closest followers.[4] It was only some days later, when he had had time to estimate the difficulties and to gauge the cross-currents of passion and interest, that he was able to reach a more balanced judgement and to write in two sentences the epitaph of the famous negotiations in France. 'I never could bring myself to look with hope or satisfaction on the proposed arrangement. It might have come off alright, but I could not see how it could.'[5]

Whatever doubts may remain about Parnell's motives there can be none about the consequences which ensued. The negotiations were his last chance to reach a peaceful settlement on favourable terms, and his failure, or

[1] Ibid., pp. 238–44.
[2] Ibid., pp. 244–50, for an attempt at such an analysis.
[3] W. S. Blunt, *My diaries*, ii. 381, entry for 10 Mar. 1912.
[4] J. J. Clancy to William O'Brien, 4 and 5 Feb. 1891 (Gill papers); John Redmond to William O'Brien, 5 Feb. 1891 (Gill Papers); V. B. Dillon to W. O'Brien, 6 Feb. 1891 (Gill Papers); Diary of John Dillon, 7 Feb. 1891 (D.P.).
[5] Diary of John Dillon, 12 Feb. 1891 (D.P.).

refusal, to seize that chance was, in the literal sense of the term, fatal. With the two peacemakers out of the way, he and his enemies sprang at one another with renewed ferocity. But this time the unevenness of the struggle was much more apparent. When Dillon and O'Brien went to prison in February, Parnell was still a formidable force. When they came out in July he was a long way down the road to ruin. In the interval he had lost two further by-elections, his opponents had had time to organise, and their Irish National Federation had begun to draw the people away from the still Parnellite National League. In addition, and more serious, Healy had launched a newspaper, the *National Press*, which waged the most savage journalistic warfare against Parnell, even to the extent of calling him, in one celebrated article, a 'thief' who had failed to account for moneys committed to his charge. Parnell himself, meanwhile, carrying almost the whole burden of the campaign on his own shoulders, had visibly begun to fail in health and vitality, though losing nothing of his inflexible determination to fight on, if need be alone.[1]

Throughout their time in Galway Dillon and O'Brien watched the struggle from afar with fascinated horror. For them, indeed, prison at this point was a real haven of refuge. Both had been under intolerable strain for many months and the jail, as administered by its friendly and compliant authorities, was almost a rest-cure. They were comfortably lodged, could take what exercise they wished and could get up and go to bed when they pleased. Their diet was carefully supervised by the prison doctor and it is remarkable that Dillon, for whom previous spells of imprisonment had involved grave physical risk, this time throve during his sentence and came out fitter than when he went in. Both men used their unaccustomed leisure characteristically. O'Brien poured his volcanic energy into a novel—later published as *A queen of men*—while Dillon, as usual, read voraciously, mainly in German literature and philosophy, and especially the works of Heine and Schlegel. They were, of course, kept apart and seem only to have met once during their confinement. This was a serious deprivation, as was also the enforced absence of newspapers. On the other hand, the prison warders were, to say the least, sympathetic, and one way or another the prisoners managed to keep abreast of what was happening in the great world. They got over the problem of being separated by writing to each other on small scraps of paper enclosed in tiny envelopes which could be smuggled from one cell to the other. It is this correspondence—most of it belonging to the five or six weeks before their release—which allows us to know with fair accuracy how they reacted to the developing crisis outside. Few of O'Brien's notes have survived—Dillon's letters to him are much more numerous—but from the evidence available it seems that they were more or less agreed on the broad strategy of what they should do when they came out.

On one thing, certainly, there was no difference of opinion between them. They would *not* serve under Parnell in any circumstances whatever. But

[1] Lyons, *Fall of Parnell*, chap. 10.

this apart they were still as anxious as they had been in France to bring about some general peace which, on the basis of his retirement, would enable the two wings of the party to unite. O'Brien's notion was to bring about a meeting of the whole party—by what magic this was to be done he seems not to have specified—where Parnell would agree, or be persuaded, to retire, subject to his reserving the right to criticise the Home Rule Bill when it was eventually introduced. If, in the meantime, the general election occurred (and it was widely expected to be imminent), it should be agreed that no sitting Member should be disturbed, except where two-thirds of the party voted that he should stand down. Any casual vacancies at by-elections should be filled by combined conventions of the National League and the Irish National Federation, which in any event should be united under a new name without delay. Finally, to protect the party against schism in the future, the old parliamentary pledge should be reinforced by a definite rule that whenever two-thirds of the party demanded it, any member should forthwith vacate his seat. In the light of Parnell's known attitude, which had not grown any less inflexible as the year proceeded, these proposals may well have seemed chimerical, and O'Brien himself does not appear to have expected Parnell to accept them. What he was really aiming at was to separate him from his more moderate followers, amongst whom he numbered John Redmond, Dr. Kenny, J. J. Clancy and Patrick O'Brien.

Dillon agreed that it would be wise to approach some of the more moderate Parnellites—but what if they rejected such overtures? O'Brien's reaction was that he would throw up the whole business in disgust and retire from politics. Dillon, however, was made of sterner stuff. It might, he thought, be six months or a year, before they could say the position was 'utterly hopeless', and if they did not, on their release, take the decisive step of siding with the anti-Parnellites by joining the National Federation, they would in effect be handing the whole movement over to Healy. In an undated letter, which seems to have been written soon after the notorious 'Stop Thief' article in the *National Press*, Dillon commented: 'I cannot doubt that this last outburst of filth has been a plot of Healy's with the view of getting things into what he considers a wholesome condition for our release—which of course he looks forward to with considerable uneasiness.'[1] He pursued this line of thought further in another letter written at the time of the Carlow by-election, and belonging, therefore, to late June or early July:

> You seemed the other evening to be under a very false impression as to my estimate of Healy's power. I consider Healy a most formidable element in the situation. And by a little mismanagement he might easily be made so influential as to render it perfectly hopeless to rescue the [country?] from the extreme faction. But consider how it has been that Healy acquired the influence he now has. I believe it has been largely due: (1) to the outrageous language used by Parnell and some of his men towards the majority of the party . . .

[1] Dillon to O'Brien, 'Tuesday', probably June 1891 (W. O'Brien Papers, N.L.I. MS. 8555/1).

and (2) to the foolish, most unwise attacks made by Harrington and Joe Kenny against the priests and bishops, which have thrown them more into Healy's hands than would otherwise have been the case. If we were to stand aloof from the Federation and adopt an attitude of 'outside' hostile criticism of Healy and his set, I am convinced the result would be to make Healy even more formidable than he now is. And it is just because I think Healy and the spirit which he is gathering round him so dangerous that I consider it essential, if we are to remain in public life at all, that we should without delay get into the party and try it out with Healy and his gang.[1]

At about the same time Dillon also drew up for O'Brien's approval a memorandum suggesting the conditions on which might depend their decision to join the anti-Parnellites. Part of it is missing, but the surviving fragment has this significant passage:

> I think it would be possible to carry on the movement successfully in the face of Parnell's hostility given the following. 1st. That you have control of a paper. 2nd. That the *Freeman* [still Parnellite] was neutralised or brought over . . . 3rd. That we find ourselves able to control Healy or to isolate him with a small following and for my part—if we could secure O'Connor, Sexton, and the majority of our side—I should not object to come to an open rupture with Healy, it might be the occasion of a junction with some of the other side. Given these conditions I believe it would be possible to face Parnell and carry on in spite of him, altho' of course he would for a time at least be able to do fearful mischief.[2]

It seems from this—and it is a measure as much of his perception as of his desperation—that in addition to the original split Dillon now envisaged a further clash among the anti-Parnellites which, he hoped, would justify itself by the creation of a moderate centre party, leaving the extreme Parnellites and extreme Healyites to do their worst on either wing. But even so he doubted if the moderate Parnellites could be won over. 'I have given this matter no end of consideration', he wrote in the same memorandum, 'and I am utterly unable to imagine any scheme by which we should be able to work with them, much as I should desire it. The situation appears to me to be too simple. There is absolutely only one point of difference between us —will they give up Parnell's leadership? Unless they do we cannot work with them—and *can* they do it now? Parnell has been too clever, he has bound them so that I cannot for the life of me see how they can escape from him.' As for Parnell himself, Dillon was convinced that 'his master passion now is to have revenge on Gladstone, the Radicals and his enemies in general', so that they had only to expect his implacable hostility 'the moment we commit ourselves to *any* course calculated to preserve the alliance with the Liberal party'.

[1] Cited in Lyons, *Fall of Parnell*, p. 285.
[2] Dillon to O'Brien, undated memorandum June–July 1891 (William O'Brien Papers, N.L.I. MS. 8555/1).

There was, however, one further factor which bedevilled the situation and which weighed very heavily with Dillon in particular. This was the fate of the evicted tenants and the impossibility of carrying the Plan of Campaign any further. Parnell was sure to realise the extent to which these agrarian difficulties embarrassed his opponents and, as Dillon rightly anticipated, 'he will of course hold like grim death to the Paris Fund if we commit ourselves against him'. O'Brien had previously suggested that one solution would be to go back to America and devote themselves to raising funds for the tenants. But Dillon would have none of it. It would be 'a miserable failure' and would merely make them scapegoats. 'The two factions would be only too glad to unload on our shoulders the responsibility of a state of things entirely due to their own misconduct. Whoever remains in Irish politics will have to face the responsibilities connected with these estates, and for my part if I retire I will state this distinctly and shall take the best possible care to cut myself off from all other responsibility in connection with them.'[1]

O'Brien was less ready to give up the idea of reconciliation with the moderate Parnellites than Dillon, and even the Carlow election, which if anything intensified the bitterness between the two sides, did not immediately affect his optimism. 'It takes away the last hope of P's securing a majority by fair means', he wrote within a few days of the result, 'and brings his moderate supporters nakedly face to face with the question—are they going to help him to defy the country and wreck everything in mere vengeance?'[2] He still felt, therefore, that an attempted junction between moderates on both sides was worth while. If the Parnellites refused, then Dillon and O'Brien could join the majority with a clear conscience and if the majority refused, then they could, with an equally clear conscience, wash their hands of the whole sorry business and retire.

Dillon took a different view. Where O'Brien wanted to approach the moderate Parnellites *before* he and Dillon took sides, Dillon maintained that they must first declare where they stood. 'And having once definitely taken sides, we would then be in a position to exert ourselves to form a party of moderation and to act as a rallying-point for all who desire to put an end to the fight.' At least in this way they would be able to test opinion and judge whether or not it was possible for them to continue in politics. But, he pointed out, if the Parnellites still turned a deaf ear to their proposals, then the situation might develop in two possible ways. On the one hand, if Parnell were to succeed in holding together his followers and in carrying on the struggle, then it was quite likely 'the majority party would become a Healy-bishops' party, and if I found that their forces were too strong for us, I should then with a good conscience retire and have done with Irish politics'. On the other hand, they might well find that if they joined the majority their combined influence would be too strong for Healy, while their policy of opposing Parnell and giving the Liberal alliance a chance to produce its expected fruits, would rally to them a great deal of public

[1] Ibid.　　[2] Lyons, *Fall of Parnell*, pp. 285–6.

support, in the face of which Parnell's party might begin to crumble away. 'And if a movement of that kind set in it would be extremely rapid.'

Therefore, Dillon suggested, when they were released they should simply say to the Press that they had no intention of opening further negotiations, but that they would do their best to bring about peace in whatever way they could. Then, they should try to see Redmond, whom they regarded apparently as their best hope among the Parnellites, and put their proposals for reunion to him. And only after that, if they found from him that enough Parnellites were willing to come over, should they lay their proposals for reconciliation before the majority. 'I am strongly of opinion', he wrote, 'that after what took place at Boulogne, we have no right to call upon McC's men to agree to any terms, unless we come with full authority from the other men, they having all read and accepted them as written out.' But, and Dillon was careful to make this absolutely clear, he would not agree (as O'Brien had suggested) that one of their terms should be that Dillon should replace McCarthy as chairman of the party:

> . . . it is utterly out of the question to make my being elected chairman a condition of our joining the McCarthy party. I have thought over that point carefully and *nothing* would induce me to consent to such a proposal. I believe it would be exceedingly bad policy. It would be taking up a position utterly indefensible before the country and which might lead to a hideous disaster, to say nothing of the intolerable position in which I should be personally put. The chairmanship under present conditions is a position of hideous and frightful responsibility and nothing would induce me to have anything to say to it, except such a general and spontaneous call from the party and the country as would give me sufficient weight to have some hope of carrying on the party successfully.
>
> To sum up then—my proposal is: immediately after we have seen Redmond, if a number of Parnellites don't accept our proposals, that we should frankly and without conditions of any kind throw ourselves in with the McCarthy party. Then define our position and endeavour to rally a party on the platform of fighting Parnell, giving Gladstone a fair chance, and a friendly welcome to all who will join from the other side. If H. objects, fight him inside the party. If we are beaten, leave public life. If we win, I believe we should succeed in disintegrating Parnell's following and that all would go right.[1]

This long and powerful statement clinched the matter. O'Brien replied accepting Dillon's arguments and agreeing that they should signal their adhesion to the anti-Parnellites by joining the Irish National Federation as soon as possible after their release—'always provided that if the *vae victis* policy triumphs, that is if any of P's men are willing to come over and are repulsed and insulted, we shall clear out'.[2]

---

[1] Dillon to O'Brien, 'Monday', probably 20 July 1891 (W. O'Brien Papers, N.L.I. MS. 8555/1); part of this letter is cited in Lyons, *Fall of Parnell*, pp. 287–8.
[2] Lyons, op. cit., pp. 288–9.

(v)

Perhaps the most interesting thing to emerge from this correspondence was the fact that the prospective clash with Healy preoccupied the prisoners quite as much as the actual conflict with Parnell. And certainly, in their absence, Healy had become more and more the mainspring of the entire anti-Parnellite resistance, while his paper, the *National Press*, assailed with unprecedented bitterness and rancour all who still retained any vestige of loyalty to Parnell. Nor was there any guarantee that Dillon and O'Brien would escape his venom if, when they emerged, they showed the slightest sympathy for the Parnellite point of view. Indeed, on the very eve of their release he published an ominous article, warning them quite distinctly to have no dealings with Parnell or his followers. But Dillon, speaking to a Galway crowd within a few hours of his release on 30 July, refused to be provoked into controversy. He did, however, come out unequivocally against Parnell's continued leadership, and he insisted as firmly that the essence of Irish policy should still be support of the Liberals—it would be time enough to turn on them if the Home Rule bill proved inadequate. From this, he went on, as was only to be expected, to condemn the violent language used on both sides, though he blamed Parnell for beginning it in his manifesto. But then, after a pledge of his support to the evicted tenants, came the key sentence: 'I say deliberately that my voice shall always be given in favour of welcoming any rational, patriotic and reasonable offer which comes from any quarter—I care not where—and which points towards a reunion of the national ranks in this country and the banishment of the demon of discord from the ranks of the people of Ireland.'[1]

The varied reactions to their release and to the tone of their speeches—for O'Brien had spoken in the same sense as Dillon—indicated, as if they had not been aware of it already, how appallingly complicated was the situation in which they now found themselves. One hopeful sign, about the only one, was the declaration of E. D. Gray junior, the owner of the *Freemans' Journal*, that he was bringing the paper over to the anti-Parnellite side, a course which, as he had anxiously been assuring Archbishop Croke for some weeks past, he had long been nerving himself to adopt.[2] This could not formally happen until a shareholders' meeting was held a few weeks later, but at least it served notice on Parnell that he was about to be deprived of the principal nationalist newspaper in the country. Against this, however, had to be set further warnings from the *National Press* against negotiating with the enemy; an angry speech from Dr. Kenny (one of the 'moderates' they had been hoping to capture) asking them why they did not admonish clerical intolerance on the anti-Parnellite side; and above all, a savage riposte from Parnell on 2 August, in which, while speaking of

---

[1] *National Press*, 31 July 1891; *F.J.*, 31 July 1891.

[2] For Gray's vacillating conduct, see his letters to Archbishop Croke in July 1891 (Croke Papers, N.L.I. microfilm, P.6012); the dilemma of the Freeman's Journal at this point is well described by E. Larkin, 'Launching the counter-attack: part ii of the Roman Catholic Hierarchy and the destruction of Parnell', in *Review of Politics* (July 1966), xxviii, 359–83.

O'Brien with marked affection, he accused Dillon of various acts of indiscipline in the past and of 'throwing away his sword' now, before the
Liberal promises had been tested by performance.

In these circumstances the fond hopes Dillon and O'Brien had nursed of
a centre-party coalition of moderates soon vanished. It is not even clear if
they actually succeeded in seeing John Redmond. No mention of such a
meeting was made afterwards, and no documentation of it has come to
light, but if, as is on the whole likely, it was held, it produced no results.
Redmond may have been a moderate, but he was also deeply attached to
Parnell by personal loyalty and affection, and this was probably the de-
termining factor. Neither he nor any other Parnellite came over to the
majority in these critical days and Dillon and O'Brien had therefore no alternative but to take the decisive step of throwing in their lot with the anti-
Parnellites. They chose to do so at Mallow on 9 August before what was
said to have been the largest anti-Parnellite demonstration yet held. Both
went out of their way to be calm, dignified and moderate. Dillon, in his
speech, admitted readily that in the past he had greatly admired Parnell and
had even been bound to him by close ties, but, he said, it was impossible
to follow him when by his conduct he was endangering not merely the
evicted tenants but the whole future of Home Rule. He was careful, however,
not to extend his strictures on Parnell to the Parnellites. Even at this late date
they would be welcome if only they would leave him and join the majority.[1]

The offer was never to be repeated again in such favourable terms. Three
days later, when it had still failed to elicit any response, Dillon presided
at a meeting of the Irish National Federation in Dublin and in so doing
showed to all the world that he—and O'Brien—had come down decisively
on the side of Parnell's opponents. It was a delicate position he found himself in—doubly so since Healy was in the audience—and it is scarcely surprising that his speech was not one of his happiest. With his habitual
frankness he felt compelled to say that both sides had committed serious
mistakes in the past. This, of course, was a sure way to earn the disapproval
of Parnellites and anti-Parnellites alike, and the fact that in rebuking them
he took a lofty and dispassionate tone did nothing to soften the impact of
what he said. Worse still, and very strangely for a man of his experience,
he yielded to the temptation to follow Parnell's ugly precedent of raking
over the past history of the movement to find evidence discreditable to the
other side. All that he achieved by this was that he became embroiled in an
acrimonious public correspondence with Parnell, which lasted until the
latter's death, over the release of the Paris Fund for the relief of the suffering evicted tenants[2].

As was only to be expected, this decisive step by Dillon and O'Brien
ended abruptly whatever hope they might have had of forming a moderate
centre party from their own sympathisers and refugees from Parnell's camp.[3]

---

[1] *F.J.*, 10 Aug. 1891.   [2] *F.J.*, 13 Aug. 1891.
[3] For an abortive attempt by John Devoy to make peace, see Lyons, *Fall of Parnell*,
pp. 301–2.

Privately, they clung a little longer to the hope that John Redmond might yet come round, but Healy's newspaper was always there to insult him in good time to prevent that happening. Thus on 8 September, Dillon, in the scrappy diary he had again begun to keep, noted 'an abominably stupid attack on John Redmond' in that morning's *National Press*. 'Damn it. Could not Healy have the sense to let him alone. He must root up the whole family when things were going on well.'[1] Not surprisingly, when Redmond broke silence a few days later—for the first time since their release—he reproached them for having let slip 'a golden opportunity' in having joined the majority and thus lost the power to influence either side. No doubt, he conceded, they detested the methods used against Parnell, but they seemed to lack the courage to denounce them. 'Allied to the party led by Mr. Healy, their power for good was absolutely nil.'[2] Although O'Brien soon afterwards replied regretting that 'after a long period of deliberation' Redmond should have chosen to speak in this way, the damage was done—damage which, as we shall see, had consequences that stretched far into the future.[3]

Meanwhile, there was nothing in Parnell's own behaviour that autumn to suggest that things were ever going to be any different. Although his health was deteriorating rapidly, he did not abate his furious energy one jot. Week-end after week-end he still came over to Ireland, addressing meetings in all parts of the country. To his immediate followers he refused absolutely to admit the possibility of defeat, and although the defection of the *Freeman's Journal* was an almost mortal blow he at once sought to repair the loss by launching a new paper, to be called the *Irish Daily Independent*. Yet the policy, if it could be called that, which he was laying before the Irish people was appalling in its bleakness and hopelessness. For, when he was not abusing his enemies, he was proclaiming the cause of 'independent' nationalism which, it seemed, was coming to be increasingly identified in his mind with a turning away from constitutionalism. 'If I were dead and gone tomorrow,' he said at Listowel in mid-September, 'the men who are fighting against English influence in Irish public life would fight on still. They would still be independent nationalists.'[4] As O'Brien commented to Dillon, the whole speech showed 'that he is almost desperate and as incoherent as in the wildest of his Kilkenny speeches . . . and that he is falling back more and more on the hillside boys'.[5] And at Creggs a fortnight later, with the mark of his fatal illness already upon him, his admonition to his followers to fight on against all odds was submerged in a whole series of rambling attacks upon his enemies, ranging at large over the Plan of Campaign, the Boulogne negotiations, even the Kilmainham 'treaty'.[6] To Dillon all this was inexpressibly tragic. And in his diary he made this comment on his once great leader's last speech in Ireland: 'Parnell at Creggs yesterday, incoherent scurrility—sad, sad. He must positively be going mad.'[7]

Eight days later Parnell was dead.

---

[1] Diary of John Dillon, 8 Sept. 1891 (D.P.).   [2] *F.J.*, 15 Sept. 1891.   [3] *F.J.*, 21 Sept. 1891.
[4] *F.J.*, 14 Sept. 1891.   [5] William O'Brien to Dillon, 15 Sept. 1891 (D.P.).
[6] *F.J.*, 28 Sept. 1891.   [7] Diary of John Dillon, 28 Sept. 1891 (D.P.).

6

The Wasteland

Parnell's death, though an uncovenanted mercy for his opponents, brought no real relief to Dillon. Ever since his imprisonment in Galway, if not before, he had been at least as much concerned about the struggle for power within the anti-Parnellite camp as about the overthrow of the former leader, and Parnell's removal from the scene made it all the more likely that the warring factions, lacking a formidable antagonist to unite against, would fall upon each other still more fiercely. As for the remnant of Parnell's 'faithful few', whatever faint hope there might have been that they would agree to be reconciled over his grave was dashed before he was even buried. The Parnellite newspaper, *United Ireland*, in its first issue after Parnell's death, made it quite clear that peacemaking was far from his followers' minds. Parnell, it declared, had been 'sacrificed by Irishmen on the altar of English liberalism . . . Murdered he has been as certainly as if the gang of conspirators had surrounded him and hacked him to pieces.'[1]

Something had to be allowed to the Parnellites in the first hysterical anguish of their grief, but the dead chief's funeral, which took place in Dublin on Sunday, 11 October, the day after this newspaper article appeared, showed how widely that grief was shared. It was an immense, solemn and most moving demonstration of affection for Parnell. Feeling in the city ran so high that his leading opponents were in actual physical danger and could not, if they had wished it, have attended the ceremony. Most of the animosity was probably directed against Tim Healy, but Dillon did not escape it either, and on the previous Friday, for the first and only time in his life, a Dublin crowd had hooted him as he passed in the street.[2] Immediately the funeral was over the Parnellites issued a declaration pledging themselves to continue the policy of independent opposition and the fight, it seemed, was on again.

The immediate arena was Parnell's vacant seat in Cork city. John Redmond, who succeeded him in the leadership of the minority, was overwhelmed by the weight of anti-Parnellite strength thrown against him and was decisively defeated. A month later another vacancy occurred in Waterford city and here, after a hectic and sometimes violent campaign, Redmond

---

[1] *U.I.*, 10 Oct. 1891.   [2] Diary of Elizabeth Mathew, 11 Oct. 1891 (D.P.).

just scraped home against no less a candidate than Michael Davitt. These two encounters demonstrated all too clearly that the bitterness of the struggle had if anything been intensified since Parnell's death. But they also showed that the Parnellites were still a force to be reckoned with, and it is not surprising that some well-intentioned Nationalists began to feel that in order to avoid a lacerating conflict at the general election (which could not be far away) some kind of accommodation between the two sides should if possible be reached. The indefatigable Gill, despite his harrowing experiences as a go-between during the Boulogne negotiations, stood ready to take the initiative. Early in January 1892 he wrote to Dillon enclosing an elaborate scheme for reunion, for the allocation of the Paris Fund, for the future conduct of party affairs, and for the election of Dillon himself as chairman. Gill was driven to intervene partly because he was concerned—as Dillon, of course, was, too—for the fate of the evicted tenants, but partly also because he felt, quite rightly, that an Ireland deeply divided at the general election would be a poor advertisement for Home Rule. 'What a commentary that will be', he observed, 'upon our claim to manage the affairs of a country full of conflicting interests and prejudices where the chief problem of the statesman for the first twenty years after Home Rule will be conciliation, his chief art conciliation, his chief work conciliation.' Gill's notion was that Dillon and Redmond should meet privately without consulting any of their colleagues (except, in Dillon's case, William O'Brien) and see if they could agree. If they could not, then the matter need go no further; if they could, then Gill believed, with his usual facile optimism, that each would be able to carry his own party with him. The text of Dillon's reply seems not to have survived, though his own bleak comment, written across the top of Gill's letter, indicates his reaction clearly enough: 'Wrote advising him not to interfere.'[1]

Yet, if nothing came of this particular manoeuvre, evidence continued to reach Dillon that others, too, contemplated some sort of deal with the Parnellites. William O'Brien, also looking at the matter largely from the viewpoint of the evicted tenants, was pressing independently for a settlement within a few days of Gill.[2] And later in January Dillon heard from his Parnellite cousin, V. B. Dillon, that Timothy Harrington was anxious to discuss possibilities with him.[3] On top of that came another letter from Gill with the revealing news that Harrington was being secretly approached by Tim Healy and his henchman, P. A. Chance. The news came from John Redmond and, for Dillon's delectation, Gill quoted this passage from Redmond's letter to him: 'Harrington yesterday received a letter from Chance . . . asking if John Redmond and he would dine with him (Chance) "to meet and shake hands with the wicked Tim", and plainly hinting that they were anxious to make terms with us behind Dillon's back . . . I could scarcely contain my indignation and I need not say I regarded

[1] T. P. Gill to Dillon, 7 Jan. 1892 (D.P.).
[2] W. O'Brien to Dillon, 12 Jan. 1892 (D.P.).
[3] V. B. Dillon to John Dillon, 25 Jan. 1892 (D.P.).

the letter as an insult. It shows, however, the straits the "antis" are in—
what a happy family they are and what class of men Dillon took to his
bosom and must rely upon.'[1]

It is scarcely surprising, in the light of this anti-Parnellite intrigue, that
Redmond and his friends should have proved evasive. Thus, although at a
meeting of the committee of the anti-Parnellite party in February 1892
Dillon carried—against the votes of Healy and Arthur O'Connor—a re-
solution proposing further negotiation with Redmond, nothing came of it.[2]
Later in the year, with the general election imminent, Dillon tried once
more. He and T. P. O'Connor attempted to make contact with the
Parnellites through the agency of a prominent Irish-American, P. A.
Collins. Collins was presumably deemed to be impartial, and though
Dillon later learnt that even before he arrived in Europe he had been
approached to undertake the negotiations by Healy's friend, John Barry,
he certainly exerted himself to make peace.[3] But when a meeting was held,
it was not a fully representative one, and it was designed not to lead directly
to reunion, but merely to avoid unseemly wrangles at the election by
apportioning seats among Parnellites and anti-Parnellites in advance. And
even this meeting was only arranged with very great difficulty and not without additional assistance from the English radical, Henry Labouchere. It
was first proposed that the general election should be managed by a
committee on which all three sections—Dillonite, Healyite and Redmondite
—should be equally represented. This committee was to go through the list
of sitting members and decide whether each was to continue as a candidate
at the next election. The criterion was simply to be whether or not he was
the man most likely to win the seat, though it was also envisaged that if they
pressed for it the Parnellites should be left with an unspecified minimum of
safe seats.[4]

This was far too elaborate a scheme to have the slightest hope of success
and when the conference did take place in Dublin at the end of May, 1892,
it was much more restricted in its scope. Neither Healy nor any of his
associates were present, and though Redmond was consulted the only
Parnellite actively engaged in the negotiations was Harrington. On the
other side, Dillon and T. P. O'Connor were directly involved—together
with the Irish-American, Collins—and William O'Brien and Davitt were
also kept informed. Dillon found Harrington 'thoroughly sincere and
anxious to save the cause', but also 'utterly unreasonable and impracticable'. He claimed twenty-five seats for the Parnellites, asserting they were
sure to win at least twenty at the general election.[5] Since Dillon himself did
not consider they were likely to win more than thirteen, and four more

[1] T. P. Gill to Dillon, 27 Jan. 1892 (D.P.).

[2] T. M. Healy, *Why Ireland is not free* (Dublin, 1898), p. 56.

[3] P. A. Farrall to Dillon, 19 May 1894 (D.P.).

[4] The scheme was outlined in a letter from J. J. Clancy to John Redmond, 24 May
1892 (Harrington Papers, N.L.I. MS. 8577/1); there is a typed copy of this letter in the
Dillon Papers.

[5] Diary of John Dillon, 1 June 1892 (D.P.).

doubtful, there was little chance of agreement.[1] But behind Harrington stood Redmond and Redmond was not to be wooed. Whether he mistrusted Dillon's ability to sway the anti-Parnellites, whether he thought the terms inadequate, or whether too much bitterness had accumulated to allow reconciliation, the end result was the same. Late on 1 June, Collins and Harrington, having been to see Redmond, came back to Dillon and gave, he recorded, the 'worst possible account of his tone. He spoke to them as a wrecker and pretended to, if he did not actually, contemplate the ruin of the Home Rule movement.'[2]

The consequence of these abortive negotiations was that when the election came in July Parnellite fought anti-Parnellite in a number of constituencies. At the time of the election the Parnellites numbered thirty and they put forward candidates in forty-five seats. When the election was over they were reduced to nine sitting members as against seventy-one anti-Parnellites. It was a crushing defeat, but it was not annihilation. They continued to maintain their separate organisation; they possessed their own newspaper, the *Irish Daily Independent;* they even shared control over the Paris Fund and Harrington joined with Dillon and Davitt in distributing the money from the Fund to the evicted tenants after protracted law-suits had cleared the way for this in 1894. Nevertheless, the election of 1892 had defined with cold clarity the limits of their influence. Nor was their position more than marginally improved three years later, when in the general election of 1895 they returned ten M.P.s. They could not be ignored and sooner or later would have to be dealt with, either by negotiation or by all-out war. But the time for dealing with them was constantly deferred and did not come until 1898, when the entire political situation had been drastically changed. Meanwhile Ireland drifted towards the second great crisis of Home Rule still deeply and miserably divided.

(ii)

Unhappily, however, the most serious division was not between those who had been for and those who had been against Parnell, but within the anti-Parnellite majority. Essentially, it was a division between Dillon and Healy and one that was to keep them apart for the rest of their lives. It is hard to avoid the suspicion that it was partly temperamental, though, of course, much else entered in as well. Healy was a self-educated man who had risen in the world largely, though not entirely, by his own undoubted talents. He was a formidable advocate—indeed, one of the most outstanding of his day—and a scarcely less formidable parliamentarian, with an almost unique knowledge of House of Commons procedure and the wit to exploit this to the full. On the other hand, he was a very difficult colleague. Undeniably able, fertile in ideas, indefatigable in action, he was at the same time intensely ambitious. His running fight with Parnell, first at the Galway

[1] Note in Dillon's hand, 2 June 1892 (D.P.).
[2] Diary of John Dillon, 1 June 1892 (D.P.).

election in 1886 and then during the split, had demonstrated very clearly two of his dominant characteristics. One was that he was an unpredictable subordinate who played second fiddle with an ill grace. Yet his other characteristic helped to ensure that, if others could contrive it, second fiddle would be precisely what he would always play. He possessed to an unusual degree the sharp Irish tongue and was quite unable to resist the clever but unforgivable remark that festers, maybe for years. The struggle with Parnell had given him full scope for this unsavoury gift and it was undoubtedly one of the things Dillon liked least about him.

But there were also things about Dillon which were liable to irritate Healy. For one thing, Dillon had in a sense been born into the purple. At any rate, even as a student he had been marked out as a coming man, and although his own abilities would have taken him far in any case, it was no disadvantage that he was his father's son. Moreover, he had had leisure to acquire an elaborate education and from early manhood had been able to devote himself to politics as to a profession. To Healy, clawing his way painfully up the ladder of success, this could easily have been galling. And in other important ways the two men were totally different. Dillon was deliberate, Healy impulsive; Dillon was pessimistic, Healy mercurial; Healy thought Dillon authoritarian, Dillon was sure Healy was irresponsible. Even in Parliament their styles clashed. Dillon approached the House of Commons with a high seriousness and his speeches, often sombre in tone, were usually deeply informed and carefully prepared. Healy, by contrast, was a brilliant improviser, but shared to the full the witty Irishman's tendency to sacrifice substance to the pleasure of planting his banderilla in his tormented opponent.

So long as Parnell lived the animosity which was probably unavoidable between two such incompatible characters was kept below the surface, though, as we have already seen, Dillon was well aware that he was soon likely to have a fight with Healy on his hands. And Parnell was not long dead before the quarrel began to develop. Ostensibly it arose out of the newspaper war which was a legacy from the last months of Parnell's career. There can be no question that before the *Freeman's Journal* deserted the fallen leader at the very last moment, Healy's *National Press* had carried the main burden of the struggle against him. The cost was met largely by Healy's friends and he himself had allowed his lucrative law practice to go to pieces while he conducted the paper almost single-handed. He had made it, of course, a vehicle for the most ferocious criticism of Parnell and in return had been savagely attacked in the *Freeman's Journal*. As a result of one of these attacks he took a libel action against the *Freeman*, which was still pending when that newspaper came over to the anti-Parnellite side. With its conversion the case for maintaining the *National Press* as a second anti-Parnellite daily was obviously much weakened, especially as the *Freeman* had a large circulation, a distinguished tradition and a substantial revenue from advertisements.

Healy, naturally, could not see it like this. Instead, he fought tooth and nail against the obvious solution, which was the amalgamation of both papers. He, and his friend William Martin Murphy, the wealthy industrialist, who was the principal financial backer of the *National Press*, both urged on Dillon that the *Freeman's Journal* had lost its claim to be regarded as 'the organ of the party' and that this title now belonged by right to the *National Press*. 'You and O'Brien,' Murphy warned Dillon near the end of November, 'must see that the country is against you on the subject.'[1] Healy himself was much more outspoken. 'Of course,' he wrote to Dillon, 'I feel very deeply and bitterly the results of the line adopted by O'Brien and yourself. It is the Boulogne business over again with Gray [the young and much-confused proprietor of the *Freeman*] substituted for Parnell. But for you and O'Brien he was utterly crushed and your parleying has resuscitated the *Freeman*.'[2] This was a clear enough indication of the gap between them. The whole endeavour of Dillon and O'Brien, both before they went into Galway jail and after they came out, had been to reconcile the opposing parties and such reconciliation in their view must extend just as much to an erring newspaper as to an erring individual. This, especially, had been the main emphasis in the speeches they had made in Galway, immediately after their release, and a little later in Mallow. Healy's comment on this was that in those speeches they had seemed to attach altogether too much importance to the conversion of the *Freeman* and too little to the position of the *National Press*. 'To save the risk of the *Freeman* becoming a freelance, you risk everything in our office, on the excellent African principle of devil-worship, because God is so good he needn't be placated (pardon the parallel) . . . You reply it is converted. I say its place is filled and there is not room for a second chair in the National Library.'[3]

Dillon was hardly likely to fall into the error of confounding Healy with God and he had no intention of placating him. His answers to these letters have not survived, but we know from the correspondence he and O'Brien had carried on in prison that they both regarded a newspaper independent of Healy as absolutely essential to their own political survival.[4] Dillon therefore stuck to his guns and the plans for amalgamation went ahead. The negotiations were protracted and bitter, all the more bitter because in July 1892 the *Freeman's Journal* had to pay Healy £700 arising out of his libel action. Nevertheless, once amalgamation was completed, the reconstituted *Freeman's Journal* became once more the principal means of influencing nationalist, or at any rate anti-Parnellite, opinion in Ireland. Whoever controlled the board of directors had therefore gone a long way towards winning a decisive advantage. The struggle for power on the board became correspondingly acute. For the most part it was conducted in the secrecy, or semi-secrecy, of board meetings, but occasionally it spilled over into the press and it figured with monotonous regularity in the proceedings

[1] W. M. Murphy to Dillon, 23 Nov. 1891 (D.P.).
[2] T. M. Healy to Dillon, 24 Nov. 1891 (D.P.).
[3] T. M. Healy to Dillon, 30 Nov. 1891 (D.P.). A further letter from W. M. Murphy (also in the Dillon Papers) written on the same day made the same point equally forcibly.
[4] See pp. 137–40 above.

of the parliamentary party. It was intricate, tedious and squalid; worst of all, it dragged on through 1892 and right up to the time of the Home Rule debates in the summer of 1893. In the end, the Archbishop of Dublin was asked to mediate and he devised a board on which both sections were represented, but with which neither was satisfied. Healy later described it as 'moulded' to include a majority of Dillon's supporters, but for a time it was very evenly divided. Thomas Sexton became chairman, and although he inclined on the whole to Dillon, he was so sensitive to criticism that at one crucial moment during the Home Rule debates he threatened to withdraw from Westminster until the parliamentary party rescinded a motion (proposed by Healy) which they had passed by thirty-two votes to twenty-five to the effect that they should take no further part in the *Freeman's Journal* business. To bring Sexton back, the party hurriedly held a second meeting which reversed the previous decision by thirty-three votes to twenty-seven, whereupon he countermanded his resignation. To some observers, especially those who knew what was really happening, this bickering at a critical moment in the country's fortunes was the last straw. Davitt, who thought Sexton wrong in having yielded to provocation, remarked to Dillon that the Liberals could easily lose a by-election because of these Irish dissensions, 'and such a blow at the Government would in my judgement justify Gladstone in dropping the Home Rule Bill for the present and in proceeding with his British programme'.[1] Archbishop Walsh, who was even nearer to the heart of the struggle, was still more outspoken. 'The action taken', he wrote, 'is disgraceful to the Irish parliamentary party. I should like to know how anyone could now regard them as a body in whose hands any public interest would be safe . . . So far as I am concerned, the party has committed political suicide.'[2]

Nevertheless, despite these heartrending disputes, Dillon continued to fight the battle for control and his tenacity in the end brought its reward. Gradually the opposition began to weaken and after Healy's virtual expulsion from the board in 1894 Dillon's influence was predominant.[3] The real significance of this went far beyond the battles on the board. The newspaper quarrel, indeed, was only part of a much wider issue. For what was at stake was the whole future of the constitutional movement. In Parnell's prime that movement had displayed three outstanding characteristics— unity, discipline, loyalty to the leader. And this was true not only of the parliamentarians but of the country at large. With Parnell at the head of both the party and the Irish National League there was a close and generally

[1] Michael Davitt to Dillon, 11 June 1893 (D.P.).

[2] Archbishop W. J. Walsh to Dillon, 11 June 1893 (D.P.).; for the Archbishop's earlier involvement, and growing impatience with all parties, see his series of letters to Archbishop Croke in the spring and early summer of 1892, especially those of 14 March, 'Holy Saturday', and 10, 12 and 16 May (Croke Papers, N.L.I. microfilm, p. 6013).

[3] Healy's view of the quarrel is given at length in his nearly contemporary account, *Why Ireland is not free*, pp. 59–98. This is an exceedingly polemical pamphlet, but the facts are generally, though not always, accurate. Later, he supplemented this in *Letters and leaders of my day*, ii. 391–4. There is also substantial documentation in the Dillon Papers, especially in his diary, July to December 1892 *passim*.

harmonious relationship between the men who went to Westminster and the constituencies that sent them there. True, whenever his authority was temporarily withdrawn, as after 1882 it increasingly tended to be, frictions and difficulties were apt to arise, but so long as he was leader, and so long as the tide continued to flow towards Home Rule, such incidents remained exceptional and to all outward appearances the movement was as formidably monolithic as ever.

The dissensions which broke out during and after the overthrow of Parnell shattered the framework within which his rule had been imposed. It was not only that there were now two leaders, two parties, two national organisations. This was bad enough, but what was infinitely worse was that inside the majority section entirely divergent interpretations of the future role of the parliamentary party began to emerge. Dillon's attitude was essentially simple and straightforward. What he wanted to do—and what, from the moment he re-entered politics in the autumn of 1891 he never ceased to work for—was to restore, at least among the majority, the Parnellite conception without a Parnell. What he aimed at was a unified control, a strong leadership, a vigorous discipline—above all, perhaps, a reassertion of the primacy of the parliamentary party in the national movement, with the inevitable corollary that compared with the party the constituencies would occupy a subordinate position.

Healy's standpoint was fundamentally different. We have seen already how he chafed at Parnell's leadership and he was certainly even less willing to accord the same sort of authority to any of his former fellow lieutenants. Politicians who resent centralised party discipline are likely to appeal to the constituencies and Healy was no exception. But he had a very special reason for believing that such an appeal might be successful. As the fight against Parnell had progressed it had increasingly taken on the appearance, in Ireland especially, of a struggle in which a fundamental issue of morality was involved, and it was primarily on this issue that the weight not only of the Irish hierarchy, but also of the parochial clergy up and down the country, had been thrown against him with devastating effect. Now Healy, as *par excellence* the opponent of Parnell, and especially as the man who, above all others, had dared to drag the divorce-court proceedings into the foreground from Committee Room Fifteen onwards, was the obvious rallying-point for all this clerical opinion. And it was precisely in the constituencies that this clerical opinion was most important and influential. For Healy, therefore, the support of the constituencies was his trump card.

Neither Dillon nor O'Brien could hope to compete in this particular field. Dillon was strongly anti-clerical in some of his attitudes and had demonstrated this repeatedly during the Plan of Campaign. William O'Brien though perhaps less outspoken, had nevertheless incurred ecclesiastical censure as editor of *United Ireland*, so much so indeed that one of the last important communications Parnell received before the split was a formal complaint from the hierarchy about what they called the lack of supervision over that newspaper.[1] Both Dillon and O'Brien were, of course, well aware of the possible long-term consequences of the involvement of the clergy in the fight against Parnell and we know that even in Galway jail Dillon had expressed his anxiety lest the anti-Parnellite majority should become a 'Healy-bishops' party' which would be the signal for his own retirement from politics.[2] Nor, apparently, had Parnell's death done anything to diminish this danger. Certainly, Healy continued to receive the almost embarrassingly violent support of the *Irish Catholic*, a weekly newspaper which was not, it should be said, in any sense the organ of the hierarchy (in 1894 Archbishop Walsh threatened to denounce it publicly if it did not moderate its tone),[3] but which represented the extreme clerical point of view and circulated widely among the presbyteries. It was ominous, also, that in the Cork and Waterford by-elections there had been intense activity by the clergy on behalf of the anti-Parnellite candidates and this was to occur again on a more extended scale at the 1892 general election.

Here, then, was a factor Dillon had constantly to take into account, Against it he could pit his personal prestige—which stood high—and the support of many of the senior men in the party. Most of these, in fact, had at one time or another been alienated or insulted by Healy, but with some of them it was a question whether he did not frighten them more than he exasperated them. Justin McCarthy, for example, the party chairman, was totally incapable of standing up to Healy, or for that matter to Dillon. He was ageing, in poor health and trying by his writing to discharge a mountain of debts. Thomas Sexton, too, though he had no love for Healy, was not cut out for rough-and-tumble politics and Dillon was never able to rely implicitly upon him. William O'Brien was made of tougher fibre, but he was egocentric to a degree and quite unable to take a broad view of the movement as a whole. Whatever aspect of it engrossed him at the moment *was* the movement and nothing else mattered. In the nineties he was still an unrepentant agrarian. Since he was out of parliament from 1895 onwards (having, quite reasonably, chosen to go bankrupt rather than accept personal liability for certain legal expenses arising out of the evicted tenants' affairs) and living in the west of Ireland, he became more and more absorbed in rural problems and less and less touched by Dillon's anguished letters from the scene of battle. Nevertheless, he remained for a few years longer a staunch friend and the man to whom of all others Dillon revealed most of what was in his mind.

After 1892, it is true, he gained unexpectedly two powerful allies. One was Michael Davitt, who at last, though reluctantly, agreed to enter parliament and at once became a key figure in the party. Dillon, of course, had worked closely with him in the Land League days, but it was only in the stress and strain of the nineties that a much closer friendship was forged between them. Davitt fully shared Dillon's views about Healy and his clerical propensities and in 1893 warned him—as if he needed any warning

[1] F. S. L. Lyons, *Fall of Parnell*, p. 267.   [2] Ibid., p. 287.
[3] Archbishop W. J. Walsh to Dillon, 6 Apr. 1894 (D.P.).

—that Healy was 'paving the way for a "clerical" (a Healy) party at the next general election. The *Irish Catholic* has been moving on such lines for some time and it is generally understood in the country now that the miserable sheet speaks for Tim.'[1] On the other hand, Davitt, though an honourable man driven remorselessly by an exacting sense of duty, was also an impatient man, who lacked Dillon's almost infinite resource and tenacity in manoeuvre and who, anyway, was never happy either in the House of Commons or in the parliamentary party. He was, besides, a poor man with a living to earn by writing and lecturing and with little time to spare for political wrangles. All the same, he brought to Dillon's aid great national prestige and high moral courage, both invaluable in the morass of Irish politics in the nineties.

Dillon's other ally was the Irish-Canadian, Edward Blake, who, also with many misgivings, accepted a safe seat (in County Longford) at the 1892 general election. Blake had had a brilliant career in Canada both as a lawyer and a politician. Indeed, he could have been Canadian Prime Minister but for a curious defect of temperament which led him to mistrust his own powers and to 'solve' difficult problems by handing in his resignation. The Irish party in these years of dissension was hardly the place for a man with a chronic urge to resign and scarcely a year went by without Blake offering, indeed pleading, to be released. He was persuaded, however, to stick it out for fifteen years, in the course of which he became one of Dillon's closest political friends. Although they were very different in temperament —Dillon was much more positive and intense—they thought alike on most questions and both had the same kind of stoical integrity. Blake came to Westminster with a great reputation and there can be no doubt that his speeches on major constitutional issues—such as Home Rule, Irish taxation or the Australian Commonwealth Bill—though they now seem wordy and dull, shed some much-needed lustre on the Irish benches. He was also exceedingly generous, and though his personal income suffered from his involvement in Irish affairs, he subscribed heavily to the almost non-existent party funds and was instrumental in raising money in the U.S.A. and Canada. He became one of Healy's favourite targets and, being both sensitive and melancholic, was driven almost to distraction by the bitter arguments at party meetings, where in O'Brien's words, he 'could but lay his head on the table covered by his clasped hands while he listened to the mean disputations in which he found himself immersed'.[2] But he remained loyal through everything and he was one of the few upon whom Dillon could rely unreservedly.

Dillon himself, however, was in no state to undertake the kind of fight that would be needed to deal with Healy and, had he known how long it would last, might well not have undertaken it at all. His health (as was always liable to happen under strain) had cracked once more and he was haunted by the familiar devils of dyspepsia, sleeplessness and depression. In

[1] Davitt to Dillon, 6 Sept. 1893 (Davitt Papers).
[2] William O'Brien, *An olive branch in Ireland*, p. 73.

August 1891 he resumed his intermittent diary and managed to keep it
going until the end of 1892. Throughout that period dismal references to
his condition abound. And even the presence of Elizabeth Mathew at
Killiney could not raise his spirits. He dragged himself out there to dinner
one day in October 1891 after having been 'miserably ill' the night before.
'I was in a condition of indescribable distress', he wrote in his diary. 'I felt
as if I would go out of my mind. This cannot last long.'[1] Not surprisingly,
she found him 'dreadfully thin and worn' and she was gravely worried
about him.[2] That winter (1891–2) he had an attack of influenza—it was to
be an annual visitor for years to come—and, so he told O'Brien, one of his
lungs had been 'slightly touched' by the severe cough he had developed.[3]
A month later he was still feeling the effects and—ominous sign, indeed—
could hardly bring himself to read a book. 'The lethargy and *vis inertiae*
from which I suffer is phenomenal', he recorded.[4]

These extracts could be paralleled by many others and there can be no
doubt that the cumulative effect of so much illness was very serious. It
was not merely that he was physically run-down, but that he became increasingly dissatisfied with the sort of life he was living and filled with longing for a more ordered kind of existence, where he would have time to sit
and read or to enjoy nature without being oppressed by details of political
management and all the petty quarrels and vexations arising therefrom.
'Absolutely necessary to reconstruct my life', he noted in April 1892, 'so as
not to fritter it all away in these cursed politics.'[5] But, with the struggle
for power over the *Freeman* reaching a climax and the general election
imminent, 'these cursed politics' held him tighter than ever and he grew
correspondingly more desperate. 'Extremely seedy,' he recorded in mid-
May, 'life still in hopeless confusion . . .'[6] By the end of that month, after
a speaking engagement at Bradford, followed by a hectic rush back to
Dublin for the fruitless 'seats deal' with the Parnellites, he was stricken,
inevitably, by dyspepsia. '*Horribly* bad all Saturday night and ever since,'
he wrote. 'Worse I think than I have ever been yet. I don't see how I can
hold out for the general election.'[7]

(iii)

Yet hold out he did, because, if he wanted the movement to continue the
way he thought it should, there was no alternative. The general election was
arduous and unpleasant, but at least rivalries among the anti-Parnellites
were stilled while they dealt with Redmond and his followers, and Dillonites

[1] Diary of John Dillon, 15 Oct. 1891 (D.P.).
[2] Diary of Elizabeth Mathew, 17 Oct. 1891 (D.P.).
[3] Dillon to W. O'Brien, 9 Jan. 1892 (O'Brien Papers, N.L.I. MS. 8555/3).
[4] Diary of John Dillon, 25 Feb. 1892 (D.P.).
[5] Ibid., 26 Apr. 1892.
[6] Ibid., 15 May 1892
[7] Ibid., 30 May 1892.

and Healyites co-operated peaceably enough on a joint committee which directed the campaign with reasonable efficiency.[1] The outcome, as we have seen, was more satisfactory to the majority party than they could have dared to hope and their seventy-one Irish seats (seventy-two if T. P. O'Connor's Liverpool constituency is included) left them in an almost unassailable position so far as their Parnellite rivals were concerned. Indeed, since the Parnellites, too, were a Home Rule party, the total Home Rule representation of eighty-one seats, though falling short of Parnell's peak figure of eight-six, was a remarkably small decline in the nationalist strength, considering the buffetings the party had undergone in the interval. Satisfaction was tempered, however, by the poor showing of the Liberals, who were outnumbered by Conservatives and Liberal Unionists and whose precarious overall majority of forty depended entirely on the Irish nationalists of both wings, together with one Independent Labour Member. Earlier in the year Dillon (with McCarthy and Sexton) had had two interviews with Gladstone and had found him as fully committed as ever to Home Rule and eager to plan in advance how the Bill of 1886 might be improved when they returned to office. But office with such a tiny majority was a daunting prospect and although Gladstone himself remained as loyal as ever to the cause which had become the dominant theme of his life, his fellow Liberals would not have been human if they had not begun to think that other issues —including the succession to the leadership—were more urgent.

From the Irish point of view, therefore, it was essential to bring pressure to bear upon their English allies as quickly as possible. The Tories would remain nominally in power until parliament reassembled briefly at the beginning of August and this meant that all the crucial Liberal decisions would have to be made in the last weeks of July. It was particularly ominous that John Morley, Gladstone's automatic choice as Chief Secretary for Ireland, was—as a letter he wrote Dillon in mid-July plainly indicated— badly shaken by the smallness of the Liberal majority.[2] Dillon, although 'horribly seedy' after the campaign, went over hurriedly to London to stiffen his ally and learn what he could of the prospects for Home Rule. On 27 July he saw Morley just before the latter went off to dine with Gladstone, and gathered from him that the situation was '*extremely* serious'.[3] Next morning he had breakfast with Morley and found Lord Spencer there. Spencer was at his most discouraging and even put it to Dillon that Gladstone might announce that he was unable to form a government. 'I urged strenuously how impossible it would be for Mr. G. to justify such a course before the public opinion of the world, and Lord S. appeared to agree. I stated that in the event of Mr. G. refusing to form a government our position in Ireland would be a very terrible one—that the only choice open to us would be either to attack the Liberals, or retire from public life altogether, leaving

---

[1] For an account of the campaign, see F. S. L. Lyons, *The Irish parliamentary party*, pp. 144–7.

[2] John Morley to Dillon, 16 July 1892 (D.P.).

[3] Diary of John Dillon, 30 July 1892.

the field to the Parnellites, or to hold on in parliament attacking every government.' And the note in his diary continues:

> I told them that unless we had a distinct declaration from Mr. G. that the Home Rule Bill would be introduced the first thing next session and kept to the front as *the* foremost gov. measure till passed thro' the Commons, we could not hold our own in Ireland. That we did not require them to state what they would do if the Lords rejected it, but gave my view of what would be best.[1]

That afternoon there was a meeting of the Liberal leaders at Gladstone's house and on 29 July Dillon saw John Morley yet again, when 'he said it was all right about the Home Rule Bill—after a stiff fight'.[2] How effective Dillon's intervention was, it is, of course, impossible to say, but such a firm declaration made at that particular moment by a man whose party had it in their power to turn the Liberals out at the first sign of backsliding was impossible to ignore. And while there is no evidence for the rumour later spread about by Healy that Dillon himself was offered a seat in the cabinet then being constructed, his advice on the central issue of whether or not to proceed with Home Rule was certainly taken very seriously at ministerial level.

It remained true, however, that even if the Liberals could be brought to screw their courage to the sticking-point, the prospects for success were faint. On 23 August Dillon, together with McCarthy and Sexton, had a further interview with Gladstone, accompanied by John Morley. It was a depressing experience. The old man was much cast down by the election results, which, in his opinion, had reflected a widespread feeling in the constituencies that it was time to turn to domestic legislation. Moreover, the smallness of the Liberal majority would make it certain that the House of Lords would be used ruthlessly against the Home Rule Bill. And he declared 'with great sadness that in view of his age and of the way in which the election had turned out he had no longer any hope of being in at the death'. He rejected as 'absurd and not to be thought of' the suggestion of passing the Bill through the Commons and sending it up to the Lords to be massacred session after session, though he seemed to have no notion what to do if the Lords did throw it out. 'But I fancied I noticed indications', wrote Dillon, 'that the idea of hanging up the Bill for a session or two so as to make the election safe, by proceeding with imperial legislation, before appealing to the country, was in Mr. G.'s mind.' Even so, before the meeting ended they did get from him what seemed a satisfactory statement of the Liberal commitment to Home Rule and with that they had to rest content.[3]

The Home Rule Bill could not be introduced until 1893 and in the meantime John Morley addressed himself as Chief Secretary to the evicted tenants question, which for Dillon was second in importance only to Home

[1] Ibid., 30 July 1892.
[2] Ibid., 30 July 1892.
[3] 'Memorandum of conversation with Mr. Gladstone on Wednesday, 3 August 1892' (D.P.).

Rule. Morley agreed, after some prodding, to set up a judicial inquiry and although Dillon would have preferred a Royal Commission, he was to some extent placated by the fact that the presiding judge was Sir James Mathew, who, three years later—though neither of them realised it yet—was to become his father-in-law. The commission met in Dublin towards the end of 1892 and collected a great deal of evidence about tenant-landlord relations in general and the Plan of Campaign in particular. Dillon himself was briefly interrogated—and very tenderly handled—but he soon realised that the commission was too lightweight for its job. 'I am extremely uneasy about the report of the E. T. commission', he wrote to O'Brien at the end of December. 'I fear it will be a feeble business. And I know that Redmond and Co. are determined to support the view that nothing can be done for the tenants and that the Commission was a piece of humbug. And I am sorry to say that Healy and co. will also . . . do their utmost—as far as they dare—to discredit the Commission.'[1] This was perhaps a little unfair, since the real trouble was that Dillon and O'Brien wanted from the commission something no government—least of all one with such a precarious majority —would at that time have been prepared to implement. This was to recommend that the State should take compulsory powers to restore tenants and should provide money for rebuilding houses and restocking land. The commission, though condemnatory of the landlords and certainly in favour of reinstating the tenants, balked at such a thoroughgoing policy.[2] The sequel was bitterly disappointing. A private member's Bill to reinstate the tenants got nowhere, and although the government did push an Evicted Tenants Bill through the Commons in 1894, it was, of course, rejected by the Lords.[3] The issue was then shelved and a proper solution did not come for another thirteen years, until the Liberals were once more in power. Worse even than this, John Morley, before he relinquished office, found the mantle of Balfour descending upon him. When tenants went outside the law in resisting eviction he had no option but to use the resources of the law against them. He had no love for landlords, indeed, but even less idea how to stand up to them. 'The thing is the last desperate device of the enemy', he wrote to Dillon. 'They [he meant, apparently, the landlords] may destroy us. But you and I foresaw this all along. They have been able to drive us towards coercion whenever they liked.'[4] It was a melancholy epitaph upon a well-intentioned but ineffectual term of office.

But all these disappointments and frustrations sank into insignificance compared with the central issue—the fate of Home Rule. During the winter of 1892–3 the cabinet anxiously considered what form the promised Bill should take and Morley remained in close and constant negotiation with the leading anti-Parnellites, especially Dillon, Sexton and Edward

---

[1] Dillon to O'Brien, 29 Dec. 1892 (W. O'Brien Papers, N.L.I. MS. 8555/3).

[2] *Report of the Evicted Tenants Commission*, 1893–4 [c. 6935], xxxii, 13–30.

[3] For these abortive attempts, see Hansard, H.C. Debates, 4th series, vols. 23, 27, and 28; Dillon's most considerable intervention is in vol. 27, cols. 740–58.

[4] John Morley to Dillon, 6 Nov. 1893 (D.P.). See also Morley, *Recollections* i. 354–5, 377–9, 387, and ii. 38–9; T. M. Healy, *Letters and leaders of my day*, ii. 400–1.

Blake, whose Canadian experience of self-government soon proved invaluable. As a result of all this preparation Dillon came to the session of 1893 with some hope that the Bill would be a satisfactory solution to the Irish problem. Up to a point no doubt it was. As Gladstone introduced it on 13 February, it provided for a bicameral legislature, the smaller house (the Legislative Council) consisting of forty-eight members elected for eight-year terms by voters with substantial property qualifications, the larger house (the Legislative Assembly) consisting of the 103 members elected by the existing constituencies, though this would be subject to change according to the future distribution of population. Some provision was made for a limited veto by the smaller chamber and also for joint sessions on critical occasions. The powers conceded to this Irish legislature followed broadly the precedent of the 1886 Bill, but what chiefly strikes the modern eye is the amount still reserved to the Imperial Parliament—it included matters affecting the Crown, regency and viceroy, peace and war, defence, treaties and foreign relations, external trade, coinage, customs and excise, and some other less important spheres of government. The intention, in short, was to entrust to Ireland only what could be construed as exclusively domestic, though even this was subject to the major reservation of the land question. In 1886 Gladstone had hoped to carry land purchase on a large scale *pari passu* with Home Rule. In 1893, more cautious, he proposed to retain imperial responsibility for this for a period of three years. The fact that so much still remained within the purview of the Imperial Parliament brought up once more in all its fearsome complexity the problem of what to do about Irish representation at Westminster. Gladstone's original plan was to retain eighty Irish Members with the right to vote on Irish or imperial issues, but not on purely British ones. The imagination boggles at the difficulties this would have caused, but, in fact, Gladstone had to abandon it in committee and ended by agreeing to retain the eighty Irish Members for all purposes.

More contentious even than this were the financial clauses of the Bill, which were the ones the Irish Members found least satisfactory. It was proposed that all fiscal and commercial legislation for the British Isles would be under the control of the Imperial Parliament. From customs and excise duties levied on Irish trade would be extracted an annual sum which would be regarded as Ireland's contribution to the Imperial exchequer. The newly created Irish executive would levy and collect most other taxes and would take over the whole of the civil government charges, except the constabulary charges, of which it would bear two-thirds. These proposals, which even in their embryonic form had led to a sharp clash between Sir William Harcourt (Chancellor of the Exchequer) and John Morley, aroused strong protests from the Irish Members about the amount of the Irish contribution, especially in view of the fact—so they asserted—that Ireland had been consistently overtaxed since the passing of the Act of Union.[1] It was partly to meet this objection that Gladstone, in the course of the de-

[1] A. G. Gardiner, *The life of Sir William Harcourt* (London, 1923), ii. 220–3.

bate, agreed to set up a special commission to study the financial relations between Britain and Ireland and to concede meanwhile that the financial provisions of the Bill should be valid initially for only six years, to allow of their being revised in the light of the commission's report.

The Home Rule session of 1893 was one of the longest in parliamentary history. More than eighty days were devoted to the Bill itself, yet in retrospect all those words, all that effort, all that time seem to have been spent in pursuit of a phantom. The majority for the Bill in the Commons could never be large—it was forty-three on the second reading and thirty-four on the third—and when it reached the House of Lords it was summarily rejected by 419 votes to forty-one. Gladstone, had he been younger and in better health, or had a more enthusiastic Cabinet behind him, might perhaps have gone to the country on the issue of the Lords' veto, but this was not possible, and both Home Rule and the question of democracy versus aristocracy vanished into limbo, only to reappear, linked together as inextricably as ever, fifteen years later.

Much of the burden of fighting the Bill through the Lower House was carried by Gladstone himself, for it was the deliberate policy of his Irish allies not to take up parliamentary time by long set speeches. Their point of view was put by a few selected speakers and—except for interventions in committee—the rest remained almost entirely silent. Dillon shared in this self-denying ordinance and confined his general appraisal of the Bill to a short speech on the third reading. It was not one of his more remarkable performances, but it did register beyond all possible doubt his own acceptance of the measure as 'a great charter of liberty to the people of Ireland', and also his conviction that the Irish would accept it as a just settlement which they would try to carry out in all good faith.[1]

With the shadow of defeat hanging over it from the moment of its introduction the Home Rule Bill is sterile ground for the historian. The speeches of individuals were largely academic exercises, but one feature of that hot and angry summer has survived when all else has been forgotten—the recrudescence of party passion. Much of it centred round Joseph Chamberlain, whom the Irish could never forgive for the part he had played in the defeat of the Bill of 1886, and it was he, in the course of the 1893 debate, who inflicted on Dillon the most acute embarrassment he ever suffered in the House of Commons. On 3 July Chamberlain, making much of the unfitness of the Irish for self-government, taunted Dillon with a speech he had made at Castlerea early in the Plan of Campaign in which he had incautiously said that when the Irish Parliament had the police under their control they would 'remember those who had been the enemies of the people'.[2] Dillon defended the speech as having been delivered 'under circumstances of cruel and extraordinary provocation', that is, immediately after the Mitchelstown affair. The recollection of these events was hot in his mind, he declared, when he made the speech in question. It was a disastrous

---

[1] Hansard, H.C. Debates, 4th series, vol. 16, cols. 1651–62.
[2] For the disquiet this caused among Liberals at the time see pp. 86–7 above.

error of recollection, for the speech was actually made in December 1886, whereas Mitchelstown did not take place until September 1887. Chamberlain, sensing at once that something was wrong, sent his son Austen off to check the reference. Meanwhile, Dillon's own colleagues realised with horror what was happening. According to Healy, whose account naturally extracts the maximum pleasure from Dillon's discomfiture, Sexton passed Dillon a note while he was still speaking, warning him that he had got his dates wrong. But perhaps it came too late, or perhaps Dillon was too confused—at any rate, he sat down without attempting a correction. Chamberlain, now fully armed, at once sprang to his feet and made the correction for him. We know nothing of Dillon's private reaction to this—his diary is completely silent for 1893—but the next day he had to make his apology to the House. He admitted, rather lamely, that while he had recently consulted the newspapers to recall the speech he had become confused as to dates:

> While reading the speech the impression conveyed to my mind with singular force was that I had alluded in that speech to the incident I related to the House yesterday, and also to the events at Mitchelstown. I cannot now offer any explanation how that impression arose in my mind except that I must have made in the autumn subsequent to the events at Mitchelstown a speech of the same character, and reading a speech six years old the impressions from the two speeches got mixed up in my memory.

He had then, he continued, thrown away the newspaper and when Chamberlain had raised the matter afresh, 'I admit that without inquiry and without investigation, I spoke from memory of that old transaction, and was betrayed by my memory into a gross mistake'.[1] It was a most unhappy incident, but it is not necessary to read into it the implication Dillon's enemies were only too ready to suggest, that he was deliberately making a false statement. Apart from the fact—to put it at its lowest—that no experienced Irish politician would voluntarily deliver himself into Chamberlain's hand in this way, Dillon, unlike many Irish Nationalists, cared deeply for the House of Commons and, once his Land League days were over, treated it with great respect. Parnell, when charged before the special commission with having told Parliament in 1881 that secret societies had ceased to exist in Ireland, was able to say with perfect indifference that 'it is possible that I was endeavouring to mislead the House of Commons on that occasion'.[2] To Dillon, such an attitude was utterly inconceivable and—knowing what we do of his health and of the constant strain he was under—we do not need to go any further than the explanation he gave the House, that he had genuinely confused two separate incidents.

---

[1] Hansard, H.C. Debates, 4th series, vol. 14, cols. 717–21 and 814–15; T. M. Healy, *Why Ireland is not free*, pp. 81–3; Sir Charles Petrie, *The life and letters of the Right Hon. Austen Chamberlain* (London, 1939), i. 57.
[2] See J. L. Hammond, *Gladstone and the Irish nation*, p. 591.

(iv)

The rejection of Home Rule and the retirement of Gladstone in March 1894 plunged the Liberal Party into disarray.[1] After a short, sharp struggle Lord Rosebery emerged as Gladstone's successor. He immediately signalised his accession to power by a speech in the House of Lords in which (following a line already marked out by Lord Salisbury) he made what rapidly became a notorious declaration, that before Home Rule could be granted to Ireland, 'England, as the predominant partner in the Three Kingdoms, will have to be convinced of its justice and equity'.[2] This was a remark well calculated to appeal to the Liberal rank and file, many of whom had been chafing for long enough at the postponement of domestic reforms, while Gladstone went tilting at the Home Rule windmill. But at that particular point in time, when Rosebery was stepping into Gladstone's shoes, such a statement was bound to inflame all devoted Home Rulers—British as well as Irish—and to offer the Tories the pleasing spectacle of Liberalism apparently in full retreat from the policy which had been central to its programme for the past eight years. 'I blurted it out,' Rosebery remarked contritely to John Morley, of all men most likely to be dismayed by such a *démarche*. And he added: 'You know that you and I have agreed a hundred times that until England agrees, H.R. will never pass.' To which Morley justly replied: 'That may be true. The substance of your declaration may be as sound as you please, but not to be said at this delicate moment.'[3]

Retribution followed immediately. In the House of Commons next day the radical, Labouchere, moved an amendment to the Address which, with support from Redmond's and Healy's supporters, was carried by two votes. The Government eventually got out of its predicament by the undignified expedient of negativing the amended Address and substituting the old one, but serious damage had been done—to Rosebery's standing as Prime Minister, to the Liberal Party in general and to the Liberal-Nationalist alliance in particular. From that time forward the parliamentary attitudes of Parnellites and Healyites were very similar. Both groups were prepared to consider Irish reforms on their merits, regardless of what party introduced them, but the corollary of this was that they held themselves equally free to attack the government of the day, whether Liberal or Conservative, if any tactical advantage was to be gained by doing so. Dillon, however, did not share this opportunist outlook. For him, however uncongenial Rosebery—or for that matter, Harcourt—might be, the Liberal alliance was still the foundation of his political system, because only the Liberals could or would concede Home Rule. From this it followed that, taking the long view, he could not afford the luxury of denouncing Lord Rosebery, tempting though it might

---

[1] The struggle for power that resulted has recently been described in fascinating detail in R. R. James, *Rosebery* (London, 1963), chap. 9, and P. Stansky, *Ambitions and strategies* (London, 1964), chap. 2.

[2] Hansard, H. L. Debates, 4th series, vol. 22, cols. 22–5.

[3] Morley, *Recollections*, ii. 21.

have been to do so. Instead, he went a few days later to Edinburgh, where
Rosebery was due to make an important speech. The Prime Minister did
certainly try to correct the impression left by his House of Lords declaration
when he observed that he had not meant that they should wait for an English majority before attempting to pass Home Rule, but that 'if we wanted
to carry Home Rule we must carry conviction to the heart of England',
adding that he believed there would *be* an English majority anyway. As a
restorative this was not particularly invigorating, but Dillon professed himself 'firmly convinced that in Lord Rosebery the cause of Ireland had an
honest and an honourable champion who would be false to no pledge which
was given by the government to which he belonged as Foreign Secretary
and to no pledge given to the people of Ireland by the statesman of England
into whose place he had stepped courageously'. This was optimism indeed,
and it seems to have occurred to Dillon himself that perhaps he was over-
doing it. At any rate, in a second speech the following night his tone was
more characteristically cautious. Lord Rosebery's explanation had, he said,
'to a considerable extent' removed all doubts from his mind.[1]

Whether it had or not, the hard necessity of clinging to the Liberal
alliance remained, even though, as an unpleasant incident later that year
showed all too clearly, it involved real dangers to the independence of the
party. The anti-Parnellites were, of course, desperately short of funds, and
in the spring of 1894, about the same time as Rosebery's speech, though in
no way connected with it, Lord Tweedmouth, who as Edward Marjori-
banks had been Liberal Chief Whip under Gladstone, approached Edward
Blake and offered the party, as a private gift, the sum of £2,000. This was
generous and well intentioned, but to have accepted it would have been a
kind of political suicide. The offer was, therefore, politely declined, only
Blake knowing the donor's name. There followed an appeal for funds in
Ireland which allowed the party to stagger on into the summer. But in
August, at a meeting in London at which Justin McCarthy, T. P. O'Connor
and Dillon were all present, it was decided to launch an appeal to the Irish
in England and also to British sympathisers with Home Rule. A circular
letter was accordingly sent out by the treasurer, J. F. X. O'Brien, and copies
of this circular reached a number of prominent Liberals. They responded
generously and among the cheques which began to come in were two for
£100 each sent by Lord Tweedmouth, one from himself and one from Gladstone. These, following the usual practice, were acknowledged with other
subscriptions in the *Freeman's Journal* at the beginning of September. Immediately there was an uproar and Healy and his followers were loud in their
condemnation of this apparent bartering of the independence of the parliamentary party. The same line was pursued with relish by the Parnellites and
by some Irish Unionists. Dillon's reaction was to dismiss the outbursts as
largely manufactured by Healy for the purpose of embarrassing them. To
him the real issue, as he wrote to O'Brien, was not whether the cheques
should or should not have been accepted, but whether Healy's protest was

[1] *F.J.*, 19 Mar. 1894.

not an act of disloyalty to his colleagues and 'the root and cause of the scandal and evil that have resulted from the controversy'.[1] In this, however, he was surely mistaken. A serious error of judgement had been committed, and although the treasurer tried to shuffle out of it by attributing the circularisation of the Liberals to a clerical mistake, this carried little conviction and few episodes of these years of disunion did more to damage the anti-Parnellites. To the very end, indeed, the affair was grossly mismanaged, for after a long and semi-public wrangle as to whether or not the cheques should be returned, all were sent back except Gladstone's, which it was felt to be ungracious to refuse.[2]

The 'predominant partner' speech and the Tweedmouth fiasco both showed the difficulties inherent in the Liberal-Nationalist alliance once Home Rule had been shelved. Moreover, the failure of Rosebery's Government to produce any constructive social legislation for Ireland weakened still further the position of those who held, like Dillon, that Liberals and Nationalists were indissolubly wedded and must cleave to one another in sickness and in health. Not surprisingly, therefore, the months following these dismal incidents saw an intensification of internal strife. Dillon's own attitude remained consistent. He stood, as always, for a disciplined, united, firmly led party and, as he said near the end of 1894, while some seemed to think the Parnellite system was a bad system because of what had happened in 1890, 'I hold that to be the height of treason and folly towards the Irish cause'.[3]

But a return to the Parnellite system was impossible under existing conditions. It was impossible under the weak chairmanship of McCarthy, impossible so long as Healy retained strong support in the Irish National Federation, impossible, above all, so long as he and his followers were so evenly balanced with the Dillonites both in the parliamentary party at large and in the parliamentary committee in particular. In a crisis Dillon could generally manage to scrape together a majority in the party and his control of the committee was usually firm, but to get these majorities involved constant manoeuvring and anxious analyses of the list of members so as to ensure that 'his' voters would, on any critical issue, be strong enough to overwhelm the enemy. 'Nothing', wrote O'Brien later, looking back upon the nightmare with cold distaste, 'could induce him [Dillon] to give up the tactical advantage of having a majority, even nominally, on our side, no matter how narrow or ineffective that majority might be, or what humiliating complaisances were necessary to keep on the right side the three or four trembling weaklings whose votes turned the balance. The committee continued to reign, but only by ceasing to govern.'[4]

There are signs that Dillon, from the time of the incident of the Tweedmouth cheques, was bracing himself to come to grips with his adversary.

[1] F. S. L. Lyons, *The Irish parliamentary party*, p. 49 n. 2.
[2] For this entire episode see M. Banks, *Edward Blake, Irish nationalist* (Toronto, 1957), pp. 86–108.
[3] Cited in Healy, *Why Ireland is not free*, p. 110.
[4] W. O'Brien, *Olive branch*, p. 73.

'I think', he wrote in September 1894 while on a cure in Marienbad, 'we are very close to a final struggle with Healy and his gang, and I dare say this would be as good a time to have it fought out as any that could be selected.' It would come, he thought, probably at the Irish National Federation elections in October or November. If this could be tied in with a meeting of the party, so much the better. 'Then if all our friends turn up it will be possible to strike a decisive blow and to do something to revive the [parliamentary] fund.'[1]

Alas for these careful calculations. Healy was still much too strong to be touched that autumn and the anti-Parnellites drifted on towards the general election of 1895 as deeply divided as ever. Yet, curiously enough, that election, though in one sense it marked the nadir of the parliamentary party, in another sense prepared the way for Dillon's victory by bringing on the decisive battle with Healy. The election itself did not mark any great shift in the balance between parties. The Parnellites went up from nine to eleven, the anti-Parnellites went down from seventy-one to seventy, but this was offset by the return of one Liberal Home Ruler. Nor was it an election fought on a wide front—where twenty-one seats had been uncontested in 1892, the figure was sixty-one in 1895. What gave the campaign its drama was not the clash of party with party, but the boiling over into full public view of the bitter internal feud among the anti-Parnellites.

The trouble began when Healy attacked the proposal to run the campaign through the committee of the parliamentary party, which would be charged with fixing the dates for county conventions to select candidates, consulting with the constituencies about suitable choices, and appointing party members to act as chairmen of the conventions. Healy made the point—technically correct—that the committee in 1892 had not been confined to the parliamentary party, but it is not unreasonable to suspect that his real objection was that earlier in the year he had committed the tactical blunder of refusing to serve on the committee after having been elected. It had, therefore, become a thoroughly Dillonite body and it was an obvious move for Healy to deny its competence and to suggest instead the summoning of a national convention.[2] It was perhaps significant that he voiced his complaint at a branch meeting of the Irish National Federation, and even more significant that when the executive of the Federation met a few days later Dillon found himself in a minority. To his intense chagrin the meeting condemned the party committee's conduct of the election as 'an usurpation of authority', claimed for the Federation the right to summon the local conventions, demanded that these conventions should have the right to nominate their own chairmen, denounced the dates already fixed for many of the conventions as unsuitable, since many clergy were on retreat, and repeated Healy's demand for a national convention.[3]

This was an emphatic statement of the doctrine of 'the freedom of the

---

[1] Dillon to W. O'Brien, 2 Sept. 1894 (W. O'Brien Papers, N.L.I. MS. 8555/4).
[2] *F.J.*, 29 June 1895.
[3] *F.J.*, 3 July 1895.

constituencies' with which Healy had repeatedly identified himself. If it had carried the day, it would have shattered the whole system Parnell had set up and which Dillon was trying to preserve. At one stroke it would have destroyed the primacy of the parliamentary party in the national movement and would in effect have reduced its members to the status of mere delegates from the constituencies. It was a threat that had to be faced and the committee went ahead with its plans in the full knowledge that there would be trouble. How much trouble could hardly have been anticipated. Healy reacted to the challenge partly by using his majority on the Federation to summon rival conventions, partly by making as much mischief as possible at those summoned by the party. In the result, of the forty conventions which met to select candidates three-quarters were called by the party, but at twenty-three out of the forty, irrespective of which side summoned which convention, controversy of one kind or another broke out. These quarrels —supposedly secret, but in fact widely publicised—were tedious and squalid beyond belief. Each faction fought hard, neither was overparticular about its methods, and the country, it may fairly be said, was sickened by both of them.[1]

At one convention, however, the issues raised were so fundamental that it cannot be passed over. On 8 July the Nationalists of Tyrone met at Omagh. Dillon was to preside, but as Healy also attended it was clear from the outset that with the two rivals face to face an explosion was likely. The proceedings were intended to be private, but, in fact, received full and sensational coverage in the *Irish Times* and the *Irish Daily Independent*—the *Freeman's Journal* remaining discreetly silent. It appears that Dillon had some difficulty in taking the chair at all, but after he had done so Healy asked whether a candidate for North Tyrone would be selected on that occasion. This was always a marginal seat and had traditionally been the preserve of Liberal Home Rulers (admittedly an increasingly rare species in Ireland) rather than of Irish Nationalists. Dillon accordingly replied that he understood that the Nationalists of North Tyrone had decided to adopt a Liberal Home Ruler, Serjeant C. H. Hemphill, as their candidate. This brought from Healy an apparently devastating retort. He jumped up and began to read from a letter purporting to have been written by Edward Blake on behalf of the parliamentary committee to Thomas Dickson, the Liberal Home Rule organiser, in June of the previous year. From the summary of the letter in the newspapers next day it seemed that Blake had been instructed to inform Dickson that the executive of the Irish National Federation could no longer subsidise Nationalist activities in North and South Tyrone, or in North and South Londonderry, and that these four seats must become the responsibility of the Liberal Home Rulers at the next election. In addition, the letter appeared to indicate that Blake had also been instructed to ask Thomas Ellis, the Liberal Chief Whip, if the Liberals

---

[1] For some of these incidents see W. O'Brien, *Olive branch*, p. 84; Healy, *Why Ireland is not free*, pp. 116–21; F. S. L. Lyons, 'The machinery of the Irish parliamentary party in the general election of 1895', *I.H.S.*, viii, No. 30 (Sept. 1952).

would be willing to subscribe £200 p.a. towards the cost of fighting each seat. Ellis was said to have agreed to this on condition that the seats should be regarded as specifically Liberal, not Home Rule seats; this, the newspaper report continued, had been accepted by the committee of the Irish parliamentary party.

It would be hard to imagine anything more calculated to destroy all confidence in the Irish party than such a charge—that they had in effect sold four Irish seats to the Liberals for £800 a year. No wonder that Dillon, as Healy gleefully reported to his brother Maurice, was 'livid with rage'.[1] He, of course, categorically denied that any such compact had been made. This denial was soon followed by others—from the Liberal Chief Whip, who said there had been no such transaction, and from Justin McCarthy, who denounced the accusation as 'an absolute and most scandalous falsehood'. But the damage had been done and only one thing could have repaired it—the publication of Blake's original letter to Dickson. This the committee steadily refused to sanction, partly on the principle that private correspondence ought to *be* private, but partly, one may suspect, because it was just near enough to the version that had appeared in the Press to make explanation very difficult. However, it is quite evident from the text of the famous letter, which has since been published, that there was, in fact, no sale of seats to the Liberals.[2] What Blake's letter did do was to serve notice upon the Liberal Home Rulers that if the work of registration was to be carried on in Tyrone and Londonderry—which would involve a *total* of £200, not £800 as stated in the Press reports—it would have to be paid for by the Liberal Home Rulers with the logical corollary that the seats would be fought at the general election as Liberal Home Rule seats. From this it was clear that there was no question of their being handed over unconditionally to the Liberals and that they were still to be regarded as part of the Irish Home Rule forces. Nevertheless, it was an embarrassing letter, because it revealed so obviously the poverty and weakness of the party. Naturally, the committee did not wish to expose their nakedness any more than they could help, and this was a further reason for declining to publish. But equally naturally, the aura of secrecy which surrounded the whole affair led the party's numerous critics to suppose the worst. Blake would have much preferred his letter to have been published, as this alone could have exonerated him, but he allowed himself to be overborne by his fellow committee members and contented himself with a justificatory speech at Cork which, however, lacking the essential document, carried little real conviction.[3]

Dillon's instinct was always to meet an attack with a counter-attack and, as he wrote to O'Brien, if Justin McCarthy were to issue a strong manifesto

<hr>

[1] T. M. Healy, *Letters and leaders of my day*, ii. 422, letter wrongly dated 8 June 1895.

[2] F. S. L. Lyons, 'The Irish parliamentary party and the liberals in mid-Ulster', in *I.H.S.*, vii, no. 27 (Mar. 1951).

[3] For Blake's part in the affair, see M. Banks, *Edward Blake: Irish Nationalist*, pp. 112–37.

laying the blame for the 'Omagh scandal' upon Healy it might be possible to muster enough support to expel him. On the other hand, as Dillon had to admit, numbers within the party were still very evenly balanced. Even on any ordinary motion and allowing for some absenteeism, he reckoned that thirty-three would vote with him and twenty-four with Healy, with six doubtful. And if the motion were one to expel Healy the majority would only be two or three, which would not be decisive. 'The result', as he pointed out to O'Brien, 'would be to rehabilitate H. and earmark every man who voted against his expulsion as a follower of his—also to fix upon us the responsibility of any further misfortunes which may happen to the party.'[1]

Much clearly depended on the party meeting which was to be held in August. Blake was absent in Canada, but before he went he briefed Dillon to make his case for him. Dillon for his part prepared very carefully for the occasion, as his manuscript notes show. From these it appears that he based his speech on two arguments. The first was that Blake had acted with the full authority of the committee, and he was able to show from the committee's minutes that this was so. The other argument was that all the committee had done was to recognise a long-standing condition of affairs. Of the four seats in question he pointed out that North Londonderry had never been a Nationalist seat, that South Tyrone had occasionally been won by a Nationalist, but had been marginal since 1885, as had also been the case with North Londonderry. As for North Tyrone, he, Dillon, had fought it in 1885, but had been beaten, albeit narrowly. 'After this defeat,' he said, 'the local leaders in North Tyrone had preferred to try their chance with a Protestant Gladstonian Liberal.' The policy of running Liberal Home Rulers had therefore been begun in the election of 1886 and had continued ever since; from this it followed that the costs of registration should properly be borne by them.[2]

The debate that followed was not reported in detail, but it seems to have emerged quite early in the proceedings that the two sides were still very closely matched. Healy could not carry a motion to publish the documents in the case, but neither dared his opponents risk a vote of censure on him. Even Dillon conceded that Healy's support was about twenty-five, and, in fact, when a motion approving the action of the chairman and committee was carried it was only passed by thirty-three votes to twenty-six. When the meeting proceeded to the election of the committee Dillon's vulnerability was underlined. Blake, Davitt, Sexton and William O'Brien were all absent, and though Dillon rated his own hard core of supporters at twenty-five—the same as his estimate of the Healyites—he was unable to prevent the election of Healy himself and two of his supporters, Arthur O'Connor and E. F. Knox. Most members were probably reluctant to take sides too openly and perhaps it was a sign of the general desire for peace at all costs that the three members most directly concerned with the recent

[1] Dillon to W. O'Brien, 30 July 1895 (W. O'Brien Papers, N.L.I. MS. 8555/5).
[2] F. S. L. Lyons, 'The Irish parliamentary party and the liberals in mid-Ulster'.

controversy—Dillon, Blake and Healy—jointly headed the poll with thirty-one votes each.[1]

Later that week, when Dillon went over for the brief opening session of the new Parliament, he called at the Mathew's house and Elizabeth listened fascinated to his account of what had happened. What impressed her most was that he seemed to have 'not the least or remotest trace of bitterness against Healy'.[2] This is on the face of it unlikely and was probably wishful thinking. But if it was true, Dillon's Christian forbearance was soon to be stretched to the limit, for he had not yet heard the last of the 1895 election. The Member elected for South Kerry at the general election—Denis Kilbride, one of Dillon's faithful tenant-farmers—was also returned for North Galway, and as he chose to represent the latter seat a new candidate had to be found for South Kerry. At once the priests of the division held a meeting at which they came out in favour of William Martin Murphy, the Dublin businessman who was one of Healy's close associates. Healy's opponents could not ignore this challenge and pressed the claims of another candidate, a London-Irishman, T. G. Farrell. There is some evidence that the constituency itself was not pleased to have to choose between two total strangers, but this counted for little in face of the major clash which now developed.[3] Not only were two separate conventions held in South Kerry to nominate the two candidates, but these candidates, although ostensibly from the same party, proceeded to fight it out at the polls. Here at last was the open split which had been threatening for so long. And, as McCarthy pointed out in a manifesto he issued on 1 September, Murphy's nomination by an unofficial convention 'brings not only you [the electors of South Kerry] but the whole people of Ireland face to face with a momentous issue.[4] The forces of revolt against which my colleagues who are loyal to the party pledge, and myself, have been fighting for three years, have chosen a moment for forcing the decision between unity and disruption.' Against this Healy could argue, and did, that Murphy already had considerable support in the constituency, especially from the priests, and that the intervention of the party committee (which had summoned the convention nominating Farrell) was an intolerable infringement of the freedom of the constituency to choose its own candidate.[5] As if to emphasise the seriousness of the rupture, Healy himself and Arthur O'Connor left at once to give Murphy their support. Dillon remained in London, anxiously awaiting the result. But he need not have worried. Murphy was heavily defeated, receiving 474

[1] For this crucial meeting see Dillon to O'Brien, undated, but in envelope postmarked 17 Aug. 1895 (W. O'Brien Papers, N.L.I. MS. 8555/5); Dillon to Edward Blake, 18 Sept. 1895 (Blake Papers); F. S. L. Lyons, 'The Irish parliamentary party and the Liberals in mid-Ulster'.

[2] Diary of Elizabeth Mathew, 20 Aug. 1895 (D.P.).

[3] A local politician, who had had ambitions of becoming a candidate himself, wrote that 'there was great bitterness and discontent expressed by the people at having a stranger who knew nothing about agriculture appointed for the division against their wishes', David Doran to W. O'Brien, 26 Aug. 1895 (D.P.).

[4] *F.J.*, 2 Sept. 1895.

[5] T. M. Healy, *Why Ireland is not free*, pp. 129–31.

votes as against his opponents 1,209. 'If Tim had won,' Elizabeth Mathew noted in her diary, 'Mr. Dillon said there would be an end of the committee and of the pledge-bound party.'[1] As it had turned out, however, Dillon and his friends emerged from the struggle stronger than when they went into it.

Yet, although South Kerry was in a sense a mandate to take action against disunity and indiscipline, the balance of power both in the party and the Irish National Federation remained so evenly poised that it was difficult to make the decisive move against Healy. William O'Brien, from the comfortable remoteness of the west of Ireland, pressed insistently for Healy's expulsion. Dillon retorted that he had no idea of the difficulties involved. Apart from the weakness of the chairman, there were the usual agonising calculations to be made before even a precarious majority could be achieved:

> The absence of Sexton, Davitt and yourself [he explained] enorm-
> ously increases the risk of five or six weak men bolting. How can
> any sane politician overlook such considerations? With a strong
> wave of popular feeling behind one, there would be no need to calcu-
> late such matters too nicely. But as matters stand at present I think
> it would be extreme folly not to make the most careful calculation
> as to the majority that could be relied on before committing ourselves
> to any strong course.[2]

Nevertheless, the tide was slowly turning in his favour, and although, as he wrote to O'Brien next day, if a vote to expel Healy and his friends from the party were taken there and then it might well be defeated, he was beginning to consider the possibility of moving against him in the National Federation, though even this would be tricky.[3] In a further letter a few days later he estimated that on the council of the Federation each side had seventeen firm supporters with three waverers in the middle.[4] This was hardly the material for victory, but in November he was ready to take his courage in his hands and face the decisive battle. By then his own life had been transformed. He had become engaged to Elizabeth Mathew and they were to be married later that month.[5] The ending of his years of loneliness and neglect made a new man of him and he threw himself into the final stages of the struggle with a vigour he had not shown for a long time. On 7 November the Irish National League of Great Britain formally expelled Healy from its executive—a fairly simple manoeuvre, as he had not much following among the Irish in Britain and their organisation was firmly controlled by T. P. O'Connor. The real test came a week later at two crucial meetings in Dublin. On 13 November, after a long debate, Healy, Arthur O'Connor, W. M. Murphy and two other prominent Healyites, were all

---

[1] Diary of Elizabeth Mathew, 6 Sept. 1895.
[2] Dillon to W. O'Brien, 28 Sept. 1895 (W. O'Brien Papers, N.L.I. MS. 8555/5).
[3] Dillon to W. O'Brien, 29 Sept. 1895 (D.P.).
[4] Dillon to W. O'Brien, 3 Oct. 1895 (D.P.).
[5] For his married life see chapter 9 below.

expelled from the council of the Federation by forty-eight votes to forty-one, the reason given being their conduct at the South Kerry by-election. And the next day, at a private meeting of the parliamentary party, Healy and O'Connor were expelled from the committee by a majority of six, the ground again being that they had offended against discipline and 'endangered the existence of the parliamentary party' by their actions in South Kerry.[1]

(v)

The logical corollary to this clean sweep was a change in the chairmanship. No one was more in favour of this than McCarthy himself. 'He is fixed in the resolve that he must go', Dillon reported to O'Brien in December, 'and thinks he should announce his resignation about the middle of January. Thinks we are bound to offer the chairmanship to Sexton. I remain of the same opinion on the question—that I am impossible, and that the only course is to elect Sexton—though I am of course open to consider the views of others.'[2] William O'Brien also shared this opinion and in mid-January, having consulted various members of the party, he sent Dillon an elaborate plan of action based upon the assumption that Sexton would succeed McCarthy. But Sexton, a strange and solitary recluse who combined great talent with morbid sensitivity, was always unpredictable. McCarthy resigned on 3 February 1896 and the party unanimously offered the chair to Sexton. He, having taken a few days to consider the offer, in the end declined it, and although Dillon had earlier been ruled out both by himself and his friends as too controversial a figure, the party meetings at which the succession was debated were so dominated by his supporters that he would not have been human if he had not begun to think that the burden might fall upon him. It was a prospect that deterred him less than might have been expected. Whether it was because he was physically better and temperamentally more buoyant since his marriage, or whether it was because a quite natural ambition had reasserted itself, his tone altered markedly and his main worry now appeared to be that Sexton might change his mind and cause general confusion. If, for example, as he put it to O'Brien, 'someone of Healy's crowd were to get up and say that he was authorised to state that if certain guarantees were given by the followers of Mr. Dillon and the followers of Mr. Healy, Mr. Sexton would reconsider his position, so weak is the party that I believe they would fall into the trap'.[3]

These anxieties were groundless. Sexton did not change his mind; on the contrary, he chose this moment to retire from Parliament altogether.

---

[1] *F.J.*, 14 and 15 Nov. 1895; T. M. Healy, *Why Ireland is not free*, pp. 133–5, and *Letters and leaders of my day*, ii. 423.

[2] Dillon to W. O'Brien, 21 Dec. 1895 (D.P.).

[3] Dillon to W. O'Brien, 13 Feb. 1896 (W. O'Brien Papers, N.L.I. MS. 8555/6). Archbishop Walsh, on the other hand, though not unsympathetic to Dillon, thought Sexton's election would have made for unity. 'Dr. Croke and I', he wrote, 'would have come out again, just as of old, if Sexton had given us the chance of supporting him. His acceptance of the post would have put new life into the country. At present I can see nothing but strife all round.' Archbishop W. J. Walsh to Dillon, 21 Feb. 1896 (D.P.).

And in default of him Dillon came to seem more and more the obvious candidate. So much so, indeed, that when at the party meeting of 11 February Dillon was proposed as chairman by Justin McCarthy and seconded by Michael Davitt, he was elected by thirty-eight votes to twenty-one, a remarkable majority considering how evenly balanced the two sections of the party had been only six months before. At the same meeting, and taking advantage of an unexpectedly favourable situation, Dillon solved the intractable problem of the committee by simply abolishing it. Thereafter he conducted the party's affairs very much in the Parnellite manner, taking advice only from a small group of intimates of whom the chief were William O'Brien, Edward Blake, T. P. O'Connor and Michael Davitt.[1]

Dillon remained chairman for the next three years, but, although he never lost control of the party, Healy, while expelled from most positions of power, remained a member and had lost none of his capacity for mischief. He retained the support of many priests, and the *Irish Catholic* was Dillon's deadly enemy from the moment of his election. In March 1896 it launched a series of articles, 'The new Irish leader', which were a sustained and venomous attack upon his whole record as a Nationalist and which, in their combination of malice and artfulness, suggest the influence, if not the pen, of Healy. The paper continued the articles into the early summer of 1896, when they were taken over by the *Nation*, the newspaper owned by the Sullivan family with which Healy was connected by marriage. Since, just at this time, William Martin Murphy financed another daily paper with the object of attacking Dillon, it was clear that his critics were going to be as vocal as ever.

Partly because of this continuing hostility, partly because there was still no sign of peace from the Parnellites, what should have been the great event of Dillon's first year of office turned out to be something of an anticlimax. This was the so-called Convention of the Irish Race, which had first been projected in 1895. The impulse behind it was American and Canadian, the intention of its transatlantic sponsors being to use it as a possible means of restoring unity amongst the warring Irish politicians. The anti-Parnellite section was in favour of the idea, but it was not the best omen for its success that the party meeting which resolved to support it was also the meeting which expelled Healy and Arthur O'Connor from the committee. It was hardly surprising, therefore, that when the Convention of the Irish Race did eventually meet in Dublin on the first three days of September 1896 there were absent from it not merely the Parnellites, not merely the Healyites, but also the entire Roman Catholic hierarchy, with the exception of Dr. Patrick O'Donnell, the Bishop of Raphoe, who presided. The absence of the bishops was no doubt to be explained by their reluctance to become involved in something so controversial, but the boycotting by the rival politicians meant that the resolutions on party unity which took up so much of the Convention's time, wore a rather forlorn air. Dillon himself, it is true,

---

[1] T. M. Healy, *Why Ireland is not free*, pp. 142–8; F. S. L. Lyons, *The Irish parliamentary party*, pp. 61–2.

was well received, not only by the foreign delegates but by the Dublin crowd, which followed him up O'Connell Street in great numbers after the meetings were over.[1] His key speech came on the second day, when he had the delicate task of defending the record of the anti-Healyite wing of the party and the still more difficult function of defining the Nationalist role in Parliament as alliance with, but not dependence upon, the Liberals. As for party unity, he made one declaration which may not have had much impact at the time, but whose full significance was to be apparent eighteen months later. He would, he said, be only too willing to stand aside and make way for some other leader, if asked by the Irish M.P.s of all persuasions to do so. 'My personality', he continued, 'will never stand . . . in the path of Irish freedom, nor will it be allowed . . . to obstruct the reunion of Ireland.'[2]

But meanwhile he had still to grapple with disunion. Towards the end of 1896 it became apparent that Healy was striking out on a new path. He had begun to receive subscriptions from sympathisers—many of them priests —in various parts of the country. According to one of the most prominent of these, Father Matthew Ryan, it was intended that the money subscribed should be used 'in support of those members of the Irish parliamentary party who work with Mr. Healy and act with him outside as well as inside the House of Commons'.[3] Quite rapidly the sum contributed rose to £1,600, enough to earn the grandiose title of the People's Rights Fund. The subscribers held their first meeting in January 1897 and launched a new organisation, the People's Rights Association, with a twelve-point programme. Some of these were traditional enough—Home Rule, an independent Irish party, land reform, local government, amnesty for political prisoners and so on. But others followed very closely the line Healy himself had long been taking—that the real source of power in the movement should be the constituency, not the parliamentary party. The second point in the programme, for example, asserted that unity could only be restored on the basis of each constituency being free to choose its own candidate at conventions of delegates and clergy from each parish, appointing their own chairmen and themselves exacting the parliamentary pledge from successful candidates. The third point also struck directly at the Parnellite tradition by demanding that the 'indemnity' or salary paid to needy members to defray their expenses at Westminster should be provided either by the individual constituencies or from a central fund outside the control of the parliamentary party. And since point seven of the programme denounced 'the attempt to stereotype a "permanent chairman" or a "permanent majority" within the Irish party' as 'mischievous to national interests', it is clear that nothing less was aimed at than the destruction of the whole conception of the parliamentary party as it had hitherto existed.[4]

[1] Diary of Elizabeth Mathew, 16 Sept. 1896 (D.P.).
[2] *F.J.*, 3 Sept. 1896. For the background of the Convention see M. Banks, *Edward Blake: Irish nationalist*, pp. 165–77.
[3] T. M. Healy, *Why Ireland is not free*, pp. 174–5.
[4] Lyons, *The Irish parliamentary party*, p. 63.

Dillon reacted strongly to this threat, as he was bound to do. Davitt, indeed, who was temperamentally more inclined to bring on a direct conflict, had warned him of the consequences of drift a month earlier. 'I am more and more convinced', he had written, 'that this policy of doing everything from the point of view of what Healy and co. will say if you *don't* do it, or what Redmond and co. may do if you say something else, is the very negation of all spirit, manliness and consistency in politics and can only end, as it deserves to end, in our being crushed out of existence between these two extremes.'[1] But the nettle could not be grasped without due preparation and before the party meeting in the New Year Dillon had anxious conferences with his friends—with results that were immediately apparent. When the party met on 19 January he was re-elected chairman by a comfortable majority—thirty-three votes against the eighteen cast for Sir Thomas Esmonde, the Healyite candidate.[2] Then three more meetings were held in rapid succession—23, 25 and 26 January—at which the party considered, and in the end accepted, two important resolutions. The first laid down two new and far-reaching provisions affecting party discipline. One was that it was contrary to the duty of a Member to oppose publicly any decision reached by the party, or any step taken by the chairman in cases where he had to act swiftly without consulting the party. The other was that the fund recently started (the People's Right Fund), being in rivalry with the national subscription, was calculated to destroy the unity and efficiency of the party and that no member should associate himself with it. Should any Member do so despite this warning, a special meeting of the party would be called at a week's notice to consider the case for his expulsion.

This was a very strong resolution, extending as it virtually did the scope of the parliamentary pledge by obliging Members to support the decisions of the chairman and majority outside as well as inside Parliament. In his attack upon this 'unity and discipline' resolution Healy at once fastened, as well he might, upon the fact that these proposals struck at the freedom of the constituencies. In fact, he moved an amendment claiming that the only conditions binding upon the representatives of the people were those imposed by their constituents before election and that the chairman was now attempting to arrogate to himself 'new and unusual powers'. But this was anarchical doctrine and his amendment was decisively defeated by thirty-three votes to sixteen. The original resolution was then passed by thirty-three to twenty-one.

The second resolution dealt precisely with that question of Members' salaries which had prompted the initiation of the People's Rights Fund. It was proposed that during the week following the passing of the resolution the party secretaries should keep in the whips' room for signature by those Members concerned, a paper which was to have at its head the resolution on unity and discipline which the party had just passed and also a declara-

[1] Davitt to Dillon, 7 Dec. 1896 (Davitt Papers).
[2] Healy, *Why Ireland is not free*, p. 177.

tion affirming that the signatories had not before election undertaken to maintain themselves without indemnity, that they had not received and did not expect or intend to receive assistance from any other fund except the official one, and that they could not attend Parliament without indemnity.[1]

The fact that payment of a parliamentary salary was now made directly dependent upon acceptance of the resolution on unity and discipline marked a long step towards the reimposition of strict control over the party and it necessarily gave the party leaders a formidable weapon with which to keep the poorer members of the party in line. Before this financial resolution was passed the party adjourned for twenty-four hours, but when they re-assembled it was seen that most of Healy's following had decided to stay away. Consequently, this very remarkable tightening of the screw was passed by a majority of thirty-two votes to five. Healy himself simply ignored the whole proceedings and as he was still too powerful an individual to be brought down he was left alone. However, one of his friends, E. F. V. Knox, was more vulnerable. As soon as the resolutions were passed he wrote an open letter to his constituents denouncing them, promising to resign if they supported this 'new constitution,' but asserting that if they backed him he would still remain their Member. 'Under Mr. Dillon's management there is no real consultation at party meetings,' he wrote. 'A permanent majority mechanically registers decisions already arrived at.' This letter brought him swift retribution. On 2 February he received from the party secretaries a letter informing him that his case would be con-sidered at a party meeting two days later. At that meeting *pour encourager les autres*, he was duly expelled.[2]

(vi)

In this ruthless fashion unity and discipline were restored and for the next two sessions Dillon ruled unchallenged, except for the continuing but in-creasingly ineffective protests of Healy and his surviving followers. This, however, was not in itself enough to re-establish in the country the respect which the party so desperately needed. Had Home Rule been in the offing things might have been different, but the election of 1895 had returned a solid Unionist majority to Parliament and Nationalists and Liberals alike had to resign themselves to long years in the wilderness. At first the relaxa-tion of tempo this implied was a welcome relief. 'John Dillon says he is truly thankful that the last three years are over,' noted Elizabeth Mathew in her diary soon after the election, 'for the Liberals had neither power nor courage to do anything and the alliance made it often necessary to tolerate or condone conduct on the part of the Irish Government which ought properly to have been objected to, while John Morley was a disappoint-ment from beginning to end.'[3]

[1] Ibid., pp. 177–80; Lyons, *The Irish parliamentary party*, pp. 64–7; M. Banks, op. cit., pp. 177–83.
[2] Healy, *Why Ireland is not free*, pp. 180–1.
[3] Diary of Elizabeth Mathew, 20 Aug. 1895 (D.P.).

But although it was true, as Dillon frankly admitted when the new parliament assembled, that there were some things which the Unionists could do in Ireland much more easily than the Liberals, even he could scarcely have anticipated in 1895 the implications of this fact. Yet they were very soon made clear when the Tories revealed that their recipe for ruling Ireland was not just the traditional 'resolute government,' but resolute government combined with a policy of remedical social legislation, the policy of 'killing Home Rule with kindness'. Such a policy was bound to present Nationalists in general, and Dillon in particular, with a difficult problem. On the one hand, it would be madness to oppose measures which could only benefit the Irish people. On the other hand, since these measures were only put forward with the declared object of stifling the demand for Home Rule, they could not be accepted uncritically in case they did precisely that. Dillon was well aware of the danger and, as we shall see, became almost obsessed by it a few years later. Its true proportions only became apparent after he had ceased to be chairman of the party, but in his very first session as leader he lost no time in warning the Government not to imagine that simple land reform would meet the needs of Ireland. 'It was a delusion,' he said, 'which had been hugged by successive Ministers for Ireland—and it had always proved in the long run, even to them, to be a delusion—that the Irish question consisted only of the land question. The question that interested Ireland and Irishmen all over the world more than every other question was the conviction that Irishmen ought to manage their own affairs, and could manage them better than any other people.'[1]

Nevertheless, in the circumstances of the time the Irish question could at best be 'only the land question' and that session produced a major piece of reforming legislation. It was a complicated measure, intended partly to adapt the complicated Act of 1881 to the changed conditions of the nineties, but partly also to accelerate the trend towards land purchase by setting aside the unprecedently large amount of £36 million for credit operations and by easing the terms of purchase for tenants. Dillon could not refuse such a Bill, but he reserved the right to criticise it in detail, and did so very freely during its laborious passage through the Commons. In the end he admitted that it contained 'a whole string of clauses' that were a marked improvement in the law, though he repeatedly made it clear that this could not be regarded as a final settlement of the land problem.[2]

But if the Land Act debates demonstrated how difficult it was to deal with English Tories bearing gifts, Dillon's embarrassment was intensified when Irish Unionists simultaneously began to do the same. This was not quite so surprising as it might seem. All classes and creeds in Ireland, however much they might disagree on other things, shared a simple faith in the virtue of despoiling the British Treasury. With Home Rule for the time

---

[1] Hansard, H.C. Debates, 4th series, vol. 39, cols. 829–37.
[2] Ibid., vol. 41, cols. 683–6, and vol. 43, cols. 951–4, for his speeches on the second and third readings respectively.

being out of the way, why should not Nationalists and Unionists combine
to extract the maximum benefit for their country? So at least argued that
remarkable man, Sir Horace Plunkett. Plunkett was a Unionist and made
no pretence of being anything else, but he was deeply interested in Irish
social conditions and in the nineties had begun to attract attention for his
pioneer work in Irish agricultural co-operation. In August 1895 he
published in the newspapers a 'proposal affecting the general welfare of
Ireland'. In this, while affirming his own continued opposition to Home
Rule, he called on politicians of all parties to work together for the material
and social advancement of the people. He suggested in the first instance
that a committee should meet during the parliamentary recess (hence its
usual title—'the Recess Committee') consisting of representatives
nominated by the various sections, together with other leading men who
could contribute to the common task. He received an encouraging response
from Redmond and his friends, from Liberal Home Rulers and from one
or two Liberal Unionists. But Colonel E. J. Saunderson, speaking for
orthodox Ulster Unionism, refused. So also did Justin McCarthy in a
public letter which made precisely the point Dillon himself might have
made had he not been preoccupied with the climax of his struggle with
Healy and with the crisis in his private life. McCarthy repudiated absolutely
the notion expressed in Plunkett's letter that, given sufficient social better-
ment, the Irish people 'would cease to desire Home Rule'. No amount of
material improvement could extinguish the demand for Home Rule, he
asserted, but all the same he could not take part in any organisation whose
declared object was to find some other substitute.[1]

This declaration naturally debarred the anti-Parnellites from what
rapidly became a highly effective pressure group. In due course the Recess
Committee threw up the idea that a new department be created to deal with
Irish social questions with a junior minister at its head, directly responsible
to Parliament. Eventually, and largely in response to this suggestion, the
Department of Agriculture and Technical Instruction was set up with
Plunkett as the responsible minister, and it was soon launched upon a
career of the greatest usefulness to the county. But the Nationalists never
forgot Plunkett's unregenerate Unionism, and eight years later, when he
had lost his seat in Parliament and was technically ineligible to continue in
charge of the Department, Dillon played a leading part in the demand for
his dismissal, 'the real issue', as Plunkett shrewdly noted in his diary, being
'my influence in England, Ireland and America in favour of economics
versus politics'.[2]

It was a curious and from the Nationalist point of view slightly sinister
coincidence that scarcely had the Recess Committee got under way than
another opportunity arose for inter-party co-operation in Ireland. In 1893,
partly to meet Irish objections to the financial clauses of the Home Rule

[1] Sir H. Plunkett, *Ireland in the new century* (Dublin, 1904), p. 216. See chap. 8 for the
history of the Recess Committee as a whole.
[2] Margaret Digby, *Horace Plunkett* (Oxford, 1949), p. 115.

Bill, Gladstone had promised a Royal Commission on the whole question of Anglo-Irish financial relations. This was appointed in 1894 and contained, in addition to various English fiscal experts, representatives of Irish Unionism as well as Parnellites and anti-Parnellites. Two years later it produced a report fortified by massive statistical evidence, which indicated that Ireland had been seriously overtaxed during the Union. There was some difference of opinion among the commissioners and a litter of minority reports, but these did not affect the public view of the matter—that after intensive survey of the field a highly competent commission had confirmed the case so often made by Irish M.P.s that their country was too heavily burdened. The immediate outcome of these findings was that during 1896 mass meetings were held in various parts of Ireland at which all classes and political persuasions united to protest against their overtaxation. By February 1897 this agitation had given birth to an All-Ireland Committee which, when the Government showed signs of evading the issue, summoned a conference of Irish parliamentarians to discuss what immediate action could be taken. The circular calling the conference was signed by Colonel E. J. Saunderson, by the ubiquitous Plunkett, by John Redmond and by T. M. Healy. The most notable absentee from this list was John Dillon, who let it be known that while he would advise his friends to attend the meeting he could not sign the circular—his reason being that he distrusted this kind of collaboration, which served only to blur the natural lines of division, etched too deeply by history to be thus casually obliterated.

However, when the conference finally met Dillon, despite his misgivings, was present. Characteristically, he pressed for a strong line to be taken in Parliament, demanding early legislation to implement the report. This would certainly have been resisted by the Irish Unionists delegates and it was opposed also by John Redmond, who considered it impracticable. A committee was set up to find a satisfactory formula, but Dillon, who already smelt compromise in the air, refused to sit on it. When the main conference reassembled he found his forebodings fully justified, for the committee's formula merely stated that there was 'a disproportion between the taxation of Ireland and its taxable capacity as compared with other parts of the kingdom which deserves the immediate attention of parliament'. But 'attention' was not legislation and after a long and in the end contentious discussion no formula acceptable to all could be found. Dillon and his friends were much criticised for their attitude, which, it was said, prevented an impressive expression of Irish solidarity in this important matter. His argument, however, of which much more was to be heard in the years ahead, was that the conference had revealed precisely the danger he had always feared—that in a well-meaning attempt to co-operate with Irish Unionists who were themselves unyielding, Nationalists were only too likely to end by accepting something short of what ought to be their full demand. In the debate which followed in the Commons the anti-Parnellite case for immediate legislation was made by Edward Blake in one of the major speeches of his career. But it was all to no purpose. In the end the commission's report was quietly shelved and the question of Anglo-Irish financial relations remained to plague parliament for many years to come. [1]

This policy of non-cooperation with Irish Unionists and critical reserve towards Government measures would have been difficult enough for a united party to persuade the country to accept. For a divided party it was almost impossible. We can see now the logic behind Dillon's position— that he was trying desperately to preserve at all costs some vestige of parliamentary independence so as to prevent the movement from sliding into mere opportunism and losing sight of the fundamental objective of Home Rule. But even at the best of times this austere doctrine was un-palatable to many people who asked nothing of life but that it should be a little less laborious and uncertain for them than for their fathers. How could Irishmen, looking at the three angry factions quarrelling impenitently in the teeth of a massive and apparently benevolent Unionist majority, be expected to forgo immediate reforms for the sake of an increasingly hypothetical self-government? More and more of them, it seems, thought the price asked of them too high and the party funds, always the most sensitive barometer, registered the extent of their disenchantment. The years between 1895 and 1900 were the leanest years recorded in the sur-viving party ledgers. The number of members receiving parliamentary 'indemnities' fell from thirty-five to twenty and the amount each was paid dropped from the standard £200 p.a. to £60. [2] This was a desperate situa-tion and could not have continued much longer. That it did not do so was, by a curious irony, the result precisely of the country being more interested in social benefits than in political manoeuvres. For, while Dillon and his friends were locked in battle with Healyites and Parnellites, and while they were resisting Unionist blandishments in and out of Parliament, William O'Brien, who had been watching these developments with a more and more detached eye, suddenly emerged once more in his familiar role of agrarian prophet and agitator. The embers of the land war had begun to glow again, and from the far west, as 1897 drew to a close, came the summons to yet another new departure.

[1] The episode is discussed in detail in M. Banks, *Edward Blake: Irish nationalist*, chap. 6.
[2] F. S. L. Lyons, *The Irish parliamentary party*, pp. 206–8.

7
Reconciliations

'Distress'—the official euphemism for famine or near-famine—occurred so frequently in the far west of Ireland right up to the end of the nineteenth century as to be almost endemic. Heavy rains in July and August could, and often did, damage the potato crop, which was still the staple diet of most of the people, and as surely as this happened, so, with equal inevitability, poverty, want and actual starvation began to appear by Christmastime, continuing usually until the following spring. The fact that the country-folk depended so heavily upon the potato—eked out with Indian meal—certainly made them vulnerable to the bad seasons so common along the Atlantic coast, but it was not the root cause of their difficulty. The root cause was that in certain districts (especially Mayo and Connemara) too many people were trying to subsist on too little land. It was not, however, simply a problem of overpopulation, but rather a problem of maldistribution of population. These districts were 'congested', again the official phrase, not because they contained perhaps half a million people, but because a high proportion of these people were restricted to patches of bog or stony mountain land from which it was impossible to do more than scratch the barest minimum necessary to keep body and soul together.[1]

Arthur Balfour, when Chief Secretary, had recognised the existence of the problem, and in his Land Act of 1891 had taken an important step towards dealing with it by setting up the Congested Districts Board. Its object was partly to lessen the dependence of the peasantry upon their subsistence agriculture, by helping them to develop auxiliary resources—such as fishing or cottage industries—and partly to relieve the pressure in the most crowded areas by encouraging and initiating schemes of resettlement and migration. This, indeed, went to the heart of the problem, but as a permanent solution it was vitiated by the fact that the Congested Districts Board could only achieve such redistribution by long and complicated negotiations. It lacked compulsory powers and, as Dillon pointed out in the House of Commons at the beginning of 1897, when drawing attention to the existence of severe distress in the west, the Board, though

---

[1] *Congested Districts Board, First Annual Report, 1893*, H.C. 1893–4, lxxi, 526–46, gives the total population of the area under its control as 549,516 in 1891. The counties included were Donegal, Leitrim, Sligo, Roscommon, Mayo, Galway, Kerry and Cork.

within its limitations working well enough, had not yet succeeded in over-coming congestion.[1]

Dillon, as representing East Mayo, a constituency where poverty and congestion were common, was in a position to speak with first-hand knowledge. But his friend William O'Brien was even better placed to observe this tragic situation at close quarters. After his departure from Parliament he and his wife had made their home in a house just outside Westport, which they renamed Mallow Cottage. Facing Clew Bay, and under the shadow of Croagh Patrick, it commanded one of the loveliest views in Ireland. But, as he himself observed, 'it would take a hard crust of selfishness, indeed, to enable a man to settle down in the Mayo of that day without being shocked by its sorrows and incited to redress them'.[2] To him the remedy was 'as luminously self-evident as the disease'. It was to redress the balance between the peasants clinging to their patches of inhospitable land and the graziers who owned large stretches of rolling grass-land, often close by the impoverished villages. 'To look over the fence of the famine-stricken village', O'Brien wrote, 'and see the rich, green solitudes which might yield full and plenty spread out at the very doorsteps of the ragged peasants was to fill a stranger with a sacred rage and make it an unshirkable duty to strive towards undoing the unnatural divorce between the people and the land.'[3]

Despite the tone of excited hyperbole into which O'Brien's epiphanies always betrayed him, he was perfectly right in thinking that redistribution was the crux of the problem. He himself plunged into negotiations with the Congested Districts Board and, after intensive bargaining, had the satis-faction of seeing the Board purchase Clare Island at the mouth of Clew Bay and hand it over to the peasants who inhabited it. Dillon, visiting Mayo in December 1897, was impressed, both by the example of Clare Island, and even more by the fresh onset of famine which seemed as if it might be even worse this winter than last. Indeed, one old priest in the mountains beyond Kiltimagh told him he did not remember such bad conditions since the dreaded year of '47 and that 500 out of 800 families in his parish would be absolutely destitute after Christmas.[4] At the beginning of the next parliamentary session therefore he made two attempts to get emergency action from the Government. Speaking, first, in support of an amendment to the Address moved by Michael Davitt in order to call attention to the existence of famine in the west, he told in graphic detail what he himself had seen of the reality of hunger and of the diseases of malnutrition which inexorably followed in its train. And a fortnight later, supporting a Private Member's Bill to give the Congested Districts Board compulsory powers to acquire land for resettlement, he referred specifically to the Clare Island experiment as the model which ought to be followed.[5]

[1] Hansard, H.C. Debates, 4th series, vol. 45, cols. 157–69.
[2] William O'Brien, *Olive branch*, p. 85.
[3] Ibid., p. 86.
[4] Diary of Elizabeth Dillon, 3 Dec. 1897 (D.P.).
[5] Hansard, H.C. Debates, 4th series, vol. 53, cols. 162–80, 1475–80.

Both the amendment and the Bill were predictably defeated and from this O'Brien at least drew the moral he had so often drawn before, that only a thoroughgoing agitation could evoke an effective response from the Government. Indeed, even before these debates, he had begun to lay the foundation for such an agitation and in January 1898 had succeeded in tempting both Dillon and the Parnellite, Harrington, down to Westport to a meeting which launched a new body destined to become famous—the United Irish League. According to O'Brien, and there is no reason to doubt that this was his original intention, however much it may subsequently have changed, 'no political object entered into the first conceptions of our movement in the west'. It was, in fact, to be an agrarian movement with a *local* programme—'transplanting the people from their starvation plots to the abundant green patrimony around them'.[1] On the other hand, O'Brien was involved from the start in a contradiction which was ultimately to lead him far afield and indeed to end for ever his intimate friendship with John Dillon. Although the programme was local, and the grievance to be remedied one that primarily affected the congested districts, O'Brien maintained that 'a great accumulation of national strength' alone could solve the problem. If this meant anything, it meant that his organisation would soon become much more than what Elizabeth Dillon, who distrusted it from the outset, called it—'Mr. O'Brien's West Mayo League'. Moreover, the name he gave it was significant. It was to be a 'United Irish' movement which, in 1898, with the centenary celebrations of the 1798 rebellion looming up, carried unmistakable overtones. But not only this, a 'united' movement by its very existence would be a pointed comment on the disunity prevailing among the politicians, and O'Brien, with a vigorous organisation at his back, would be ideally placed to resume his favourite role of *deus ex machina* bringing peace to the suffering land. Certainly, his attitude, at the private discussions Dillon and Harrington had with him on the occasion of the Westport meeting, was ominous. Harrington had come armed with all sorts of proposals for a peacemaking convention or conference at which all sections would be represented, but O'Brien swept these contemptuously on one side. Harrington, reported Dillon to Blake, 'vehemently declares that reunion can never be reached through war. O'B. more vehemently declares it never will be reached except thro' war.'[2]

Whether the new, and as yet infant, League was regarded as the herald of another agrarian movement on the grand scale, or as a potentially unifying force to knock the politicans' heads together, it bristled with difficulties and dangers for a parliamentary leader in Dillon's position. And O'Brien always failed to grasp—with consequences that were to be fatal to his own career—that a parliamentary leader was what Dillon intended to remain. Of course, in his frequent moods of pessimism he bewailed his lot, lamented

[1] W. O'Brien, *Olive branch*, p. 89. O'Brien mistakenly gives the date of the first meeting to promote his new agitation as 16 January 1898; it was, in fact, January 23 (cf. the police report in S.P.O. 17425/S, 'United Irish League; its origins and history', 10 Oct. 1898).

[2] Dillon to Blake, 26 Jan. 1898 (Blake Papers).

the material he had to work with, and threatened to abandon the whole miserable business. O'Brien has graphically described the minute and agonising calculations the anti-Parnellites went through 'to give somebody or anybody authority enough to do anything', and there were certainly times when Dillon, himself the most fastidious of men, was nauseated by the conduct of M.P.s for whom, as their chairman, he felt directly responsible.[1] Here, for example, are two incidents in the House of Commons, as he described them to O'Brien a few weeks after the Westport meeting:

> That unfortunate wretch X is a great cause of anxiety to me. He appeared yesterday in a horrible state of intoxication and voted in the wrong lobby. And it was with great difficulty that he was prevented from making a public explanation in the House. Y also disgraced himself, he has been drunk for several days and was in a most beastly condition while I was moving the adjournment yesterday. When I had finished speaking I had to go and sit beside him to prevent his getting up and covering us with ridicule. It is very painful to have to deal with such men.[2]

No doubt only a very small minority of Irish Members misbehaved in this way, but the fact that even a few of them were liable to cast all dignity and decorum overboard was a constant worry to their leader. 'I am very sorry to say', he reported to O'Brien later that session, 'that an increasing number of them are prepared to throw themselves into oceans of whiskey and into nothing else.'[3]

A party such as this offered, it might be thought, little enough inducement to go on leading it. Worse still, those who did give it weight and authority were precisely those who were most often tempted by resignation. One was Davitt, who had never really adapted himself to parliamentary life, both because routine House of Commons business irked him and because, for a man of his antecedents, entry into Parliament represented a drastic—and in an important sense, damaging—break with his past. 'Remember', he wrote to Dillon later that year, 'I have all but alienated *almost all* of my staunch American friends through entering the British parliament. What was a serious sin in others becomes a mortal one when committed by yours truly.'[4] He was, indeed, becoming increasingly restless, and when the Boer War broke out in 1899 he seized the chance to shake the dust of the House off his feet for ever after a dramatic speech against what he regarded as naked British aggression. Scarcely less influential, and certainly more practised in the technique of resignation, was Edward Blake, who, apart from his own tendencies that way, urged Dillon at the beginning of the 1898 session to resign the anti-Parnellite chairmanship as a gesture towards unity. His pleas were not heeded, but this did not prevent him giving 'persistent advice' to the same effect through the session.[5]

---

[1] W. O'Brien, *Olive branch*, p. 91.
[2] Dillon to W. O'Brien, 25 Feb. 1898 (N.L.I. MS. 8555/15).
[3] Dillon to W. O'Brien, 8 July 1898 (N.L.I. MS. 8555/13).
[4] Davitt to Dillon, 29 Oct. 1898 (Davitt Papers).   [5] M. Banks, *Edward Blake*, p. 200.

Why, in the face of all these discouragements, did Dillon not take the advice and throw himself into the waiting arms of William O'Brien? The question is not easy to answer, especially as Dillon himself found it difficult to make up his mind and wavered from one course to another in these crucial early months of 1898. One factor which he had to take into account was that a renewed agrarian movement would very probably bring the familiar nemesis of arrest and imprisonment for those who led it. For a man in his late forties with notoriously poor health—in 1898 alone he had three separate attacks of influenza—this was a serious consideration. Even more serious was the fact that he now had a wife and a young family dependent on him. And Elizabeth Dillon, though she would never have stood between him and his duty, was increasingly worried about the danger of his becoming involved with 'that stormy petrel, William O'Brien'.[1] Indeed, later that year, when it seemed as if he might have to go to Egypt to recuperate from his recent illness, she reconciled herself to the separation precisely on the ground that it would also keep him away from William O'Brien, who, as she put it to Edward Blake, 'is in an alarming condition of excitement and irritability and is doing his best to torment John into adopting his own wildly aggressive policy'.[2]

But these personal considerations would not in themselves have been enough to hold Dillon back. What did worry him was the danger that, if he and O'Brien were to be imprisoned, the entire constitutional movement might go to pieces. And it was, after all, entirely possible that the reappearance in the field of the two Plan of Campaign veterans would affect the Chief Secretary, Gerald Balfour, in just the same way as his brother had been affected ten years earlier. Certainly, when on 24 February 1898 Dillon moved the adjournment of the House to call attention to words lately used by the Crown Prosecutor at a trivial case at Westport Petty Sessions, the Chief Secretary's reaction was ominous. The words Dillon complained of were these: 'And should the occasion for strong measures arise, he [the Crown Prosecutor] desired to say the authorities would be no respecter of persons, and that every person who broke the law, no matter what his position, would be treated as would be the humblest individual.' Against whom, asked Dillon, was this threat directed? Probably, replied Balfour, against Mr. William O'Brien and the Member for East Mayo, and he went on to cite passages from their speeches at the Westport meeting in January which, if one did not know their context, might have come straight out of the records of the Plan of Campaign. Both had urged the importance of organisation, and both had alluded to the possible use of boycotting to bring the graziers to their knees, though where O'Brien had called it 'picketing', Dillon preferred his old phrase, 'the mobilisation of public opinion'. But since Dillon had also remarked that the refusal of the Government to purchase and redistribute land in West Mayo was intolerable and that 'the time may come when the people, in their extremity, will

---

[1] Diary of Elizabeth Dillon, 22 Mar. 1898 (D.P.).
[2] Elizabeth Dillon to Blake, 7 Dec. 1898 (Blake Papers).

be driven to take the ranches, or know the reason why', it is easy to see that Balfour's attitude might cause him some uneasiness.[1] It is hardly surprising that in his letter to O'Brien the next day he warned him that the Chief Secretary was considering action against the League. A few days later he followed this with a prediction that Balfour was likely to 'proclaim' any meeting in West Mayo at which either of them was to speak and that if they disregarded this there would be a possibility of six months' imprisonment without appeal. 'And just consider', he added, 'the position in which I should be placed under those circumstances.'[2]

He was not thinking here of his personal fate, disagreeable as that would have been. Rather, he was speaking as the leader of the majority of the parliamentary party, and therefore as one burdened with responsibilities he could not jeopardise by throwing himself heart and soul into an agrarian agitation, unless that agitation showed itself likely to achieve more than could be gained by steady attendance at Westminster. And since the United Irish League was still at this stage a struggling local movement, it was obviously sensible not to sacrifice the whole to a part. On the other hand, the Government threat to the new League was not yet as grave as Dillon had imagined and even as late as the autumn of 1898 the Castle authorities, though watching O'Brien's progress with mounting apprehension, were still reluctant to afford him the priceless publicity of arrest and trial.[3]

It was hard to know what to do for the best and the more Dillon thought about the situation the more puzzled he became. Admittedly disgusted by the weakness of the parliamentary party, he yet clung to a deep, almost instinctive, conviction that an agrarian explosion at this stage would be a diversion and not a contribution to unity. That spring his mood seemed to change from week to week, though there were indications that he was beginning to weary of the long, unrewarding grind at Westminster. At the end of March, for example, after stubbornly maintaining to O'Brien that he had been right to hold on to the chairmanship, he admitted in the very same letter that once the session was over he might well resign, 'throwing upon the country the duty of restoring unity to the parliamentary ranks recommending that a convention be called for that purpose'.[4] Five days later—on 4 April—he repeated these views, though adding with characteristic scepticism that he did not really expect a convention to achieve anything. The impossibility of obtaining funds, the virtual collapse of the Irish National Federation, above all the counsels of Edward Blake, 'who, by his action in financing the party at a time when but for him I should have been obliged to abandon the struggle ignominiously, has acquired a peculiar authority for his advice'—these things together had convinced him that 'I am not

[1] Hansard, H.C. Debates, 4th series, vol. 53, cols. 1535–7; for the Westport speeches see *F.J.*, 24 Jan. 1898.
[2] Dillon to W. O'Brien, 25 Feb. and 7 Mar. 1898 (N.L.I. MS. 8555/15).
[3] S.P.O. Crime Branch Special Papers 17425/S, report of Assistant Inspector-General Allan Cameron, 10 Oct. 1898; W. O'Brien, *Olive branch*, pp. 99–100.
[4] Dillon to W. O'Brien, 30 Mar. 1898 (N.L.I. MS. 8555/15).

bound to continue labouring in what has become a hopeless position'.[1]

O'Brien might have been forgiven for assuming that Dillon was now at last about to throw off his parliamentary shackles and devote himself to the United Irish League. But nothing could have been further from the truth. Only four days after that *cri de coeur* a further letter revealed extraordinary reserves of optimism. He would go right on, wrote Dillon, if only he could be sure of £3,000 a year for the party and enough money to meet the demands of the next general election. 'For I do not by any means take a gloomy view of the general position of the Irish cause. On the contrary, I think it has gained ground within the last two years. And paradoxical as it may appear, I believe that the lull and apathy here have in some respects forwarded the Home Rule cause in Great Britain.'[2] To O'Brien this was the merest moonshine and he renewed his pressure on Dillon to come and speak at meetings in the west. But this the latter refused to do, insisting that he must still stick to parliamentary work, which, indeed, with the introduction of Gerald Balfour's important Irish Local Government Bill, had again become worth while.

Nothing could have been more cordial than the tone of their letters to each other (O'Brien was one of Dillon's few contemporaries who got on Christian-name terms with him), but we can easily see in retrospect what only gradually became clear to them—that already their interests and policies were diverging. As the summer approached Dillon was increasingly preoccupied with the question of how the '98 centenary celebrations might be used to promote the reunification of the party. Compared with this great aim, agrarian discontents sank into insignificance, and Dillon bent all his efforts to persuade O'Brien to take a more active part in the political campaign for unity. It had come to his knowledge that the Parnellite newspaper, *United Ireland*, was in financial difficulties. Just possibly there might be an opportunity to take it over, and who better to edit it than William O'Brien, its guiding spirit through all the exciting days of the Land League nearly twenty years before. But Dillon saw it in its projected new incarnation not as the mouthpiece of agrarian unrest, rather as an instrument for unity, exploiting the upsurge of national sentiment caused by the '98 celebrations. At the end of April, having discussed the matter with Davitt and with that most amenable of Parnellites, Harrington, Dillon wrote assuring O'Brien that he could dictate his own terms, though his success would depend not only on how far he could 'take hold of the '98 movement and influence it for good', but also 'to what extent you consider that you and I will be able to agree as to the best policy to be adopted in the near future'.[3]

The plan to remodel *United Ireland* had in the end to be dropped, since O'Brien's legal advisers warned him not to touch it under any circumstances.[4] But there remained the larger question of how far they could

[1] Ibid., Dillon to W. O'Brien, 4 Apr. 1898.   [2] Ibid., Dillon to W. O'Brien, 8 Apr. 1898.
[3] Ibid., Dillon to W. O'Brien, 30 Apr. 1898.
[4] W. O'Brien to Dillon, 1 May 1898 (N.L.I. MS. 8555/14).

co-operate in the future and the further they advanced into 1898 the more
uncertain was the answer. This was partly due to Dillon's own divided
mind, but O'Brien, who always grew demanding and unreasonable when
in the grip of some new enthusiasm, must bear some of the responsibility.
He did not, it soon appeared, want Dillon to surrender the chairmanship
precipitately (no doubt for fear the resulting chaos might damage his
Mayo League), but was quite unmoved by his friend's plea that without
funds the parliamentary party would soon be in a hopeless position, and
was in addition inclined to be critical of whatever the parliamentarians
attempted at Westminster.[1] Thus when Davitt bestirred himself enough to
ask awkward questions about recent disturbances in Sierra Leone, Dillon
had to write a defence to Westport. 'You look upon our proceedings with
a somewhat jaundiced eye', he observed with some bitterness. 'No doubt
Sierra Leone is not as important as Mayo, but it *is* a considerable advantage
to have drawn Davitt out of his shell.'[2] The Spanish-American war,
which erupted that summer, might perhaps have been regarded as rather
more important than Mayo, but it, too, revealed significant differences in
outlook. O'Brien reported that there was considerable pro-Spanish feeling
in Ireland and suggested the possibility that the Irish party should present
some kind of address to President McKinley. Dillon dismissed the idea
with total contempt. He did not believe that such feeling could exist in
Ireland, but if it did: 'Then the sooner someone else takes my place the
better, for I have no intention of concealing my opinions on the subject . . .
I shall see this session thro' and then they may get someone else.'[3]

(ii)

He kept to this resolve, though for him personally it was a very exacting
session. Apart from the shortcomings of the rank and file of the party,
which placed an unreasonably large share of the actual debating upon his
own shoulders, he was twice placed in the embarrassing situation of speaking one way and voting another. The first of these occasions was in February,
when John Redmond moved an amendment to the Address reiterating
the Irish demand for national self-government, but so phrasing it—no
doubt with malice aforethought—as to ask for 'an independent parliament
and executive responsible thereto for all affairs distinctly Irish'. The
amendment was designed to test the Liberal reaction, which, predictably,
was sharply negative. Sir William Harcourt spoke for most Liberals when
he denied absolutely that an 'independent parliament and executive' was
what he meant by Home Rule; he proposed, he said, to vote against the
motion. And, in fact, Redmond was only able to muster sixty-five votes
on the division, of which all, save three Liberals, were Irish. But Dillon's

---

[1] W. O'Brien to Dillon, 1 and 7 Apr. 1898 (D.P.); Lyons, *The Irish parliamentary
party*, p. 74 n. 3; Banks, *Edward Blake*, p. 201.
[2] Dillon to W. O'Brien, 12 May 1898 (N.L.I. MS. 8555/14).
[3] Ibid., Dillon to W.O'Brien, 21 May 1898.

dilemma was much worse than that of the Liberals. Redmond, in his speech, had made much play with the '98 centenary, and it was inconceivable that he should be allowed to monopolise national sentiment in this matter. On the other hand, his speech was obviously offensive to the Liberals and potentially destructive of the Liberal-Nationalist alliance. Dillon was thus in a position where he could not vote against the amendment without weakening his position in Ireland, but could not vote for it without alienating the English friends of Home Rule. There was no easy way out and the solution he did adopt, though the most logical one, involved him in much unpleasantness. He began by declaring that, of course, he must vote for the amendment, but then devoted most of his speech to criticising Redmond for introducing the phrase 'independent parliament'. This, as he pointed out, if it was more than Home Rule, was less than the full national demand, which was separation. And separation, he emphasised, was something that the Irish party, by its very presence in the House, had shown itself prepared to compromise.

How far did he realise that in saying this he was displaying the Achilles heel of the constitutional movement to the critical eyes of his fellow countrymen at home? Perhaps not at all, for at that time the separatist ideal seemed impossibly remote. On the other hand, Arthur Griffith was only a year away from launching the ideas of Sinn Fein upon the world and Dillon in this very speech admitted that hundreds of young men were turning to 'the old ways of 1865 and 1867'. Only recently, he said, he himself had been approached in Dublin by a group claiming the Parliament of 1782 as the national right of Ireland. 'How can you expect us [to accept such a programme],' he had said to them, 'who believe in the efficacy of parliamentary agitation, and who were standing on Parnell's platform, and were willing to accept the Gladstone Bill and the Gladstone policy as a full compensation and compromise for our national demand, and to stand loyally by that settlement?'[1] It was typical of him to face so boldly the consequences of the Parnellite doctrine which he and others of the left wing had accepted, but not even he, in his most pessimistic mood, could have guessed that in a sense he had pronounced the epitaph of the parliamentary party, although the funeral was still twenty years in the future. A party which stood confessed as having compromised 'the full national demand' must either succeed brilliantly or perish miserably. There could be no middle way. Meanwhile, Dillon's speech left an unhappy impression, not least on his most loyal and devoted admirer. 'I have just returned from the debate', wrote Elizabeth Dillon in her diary, 'and I am puzzled and worried by it . . . And—I hardly know why I am tempted to record it— for the first time since I belonged to him I feel a misgiving about the wisdom of his action. I wished he could have seen his way to *speaking* in the same sense as they voted.'[2]

Dillon's other dilemma arose out of the main Irish legislation of the

[1] Hansard, H.C. Debates, 4th series, vol. 53, cols. 388–95.
[2] Diary of Elizabeth Dillon, 11 Feb. 1898 (D.P.).

session. This was the Local Government Act, which marked a major
advance in Irish administration. It set up county councils, urban district
councils and rural district councils. These were to be elected every three
years, and though certain categories of people were ineligible to sit on them.
—for example, clergymen—the franchise was both broad and variegated,
extending to peers and to women. The councils were to take over the fiscal
and administrative, though not the legal, duties of the old grand juries.
The local rates payable by the tenants were to be lightened and the
government undertook to pay half the county cess and half the landlords'
poor rates. It was, in short, an opportunity for Irishmen for the first time
to take the main part in administering their own county affairs, and since the
councils were from the start dominated by Nationalists, this Act served
in a very real sense to prepare the way for self-government. It could,
indeed, be aptly described in the phrase Sir Henry Campbell-Bannerman
was to use some years later of a much less fortunate experiment—as a
measure consistent with and leading up to the larger policy of Home Rule.

   This, of course, was not what the Tory government intended, and
Dillon's criticisms of the Bill on its way through the Commons sprang
not only from disappointment with some of its details, but from an inner
feeling that this kind of legislation, however beneficial, was meant as a
substitute and *not* as a preparation for 'the larger policy'. Obviously it
was so useful that he could not reject it, but neither could he conceal his
doubts and hesitations. When it was first introduced he welcomed it in
general terms, but on the second reading, after digesting its full scope and
implications, he delivered a highly critical and probing speech. He thought
it would be an administrative nightmare because it was so complicated;
he disliked its financial provisions and especially (of course) the lightening
of the landlords' burden; he deplored the fact that police powers were not
given to the local authorities; and he considered the exclusion of clergy an
insult to religion and to the people of Ireland.[1] Nevertheless, he voted for
the second reading. And when the Bill was in its closing stages he conceded
that, apart from its 'blots', it was 'a great measure', *provided* one drew
from it the moral he was careful to point out to the House. 'Because it is
a great and liberal measure,' he said, 'amounting to a revolution . . . in
the control of local affairs in Ireland, I believe it will be followed, if the
Irish people use properly the rights about to be conferred upon them, by
the concession of larger and wider powers of national self-government.'[2]

   While this was the dominant issue for the Irish party in the session of
1898, in Dillon's own career that session has a particular significance in
that it evoked two of the most remarkable orations of his career, one of
them, indeed, described by his wife as the best he ever made in his whole
life.[3] This was the speech he delivered on 16 February, in moving an
amendment to the Address asking the Government to redress Catholic

---

[1] Hansard, H.C. Debates, 4th series, vol. 55, cols, 420–38.
[2] Ibid., vol. 62, cols. 163–8.
[3] Diary of Elizabeth Dillon, 22 Mar. 1898.

educational grievances by establishing a national university in Ireland. The question had a long history—which he gave—but had, as he claimed, recently become a burning issue in Ireland, about which Protestants and Catholics were both deeply concerned. His speech was very warmly received, and was supported both by Arthur Balfour, who years earlier had hoped to solve this problem when Chief Secretary, and by the Unionist members for Dublin University, Edward Carson and the historian W. E. H. Lecky. So warm was the reception that, at Carson's request, Dillon did not press his amendment to a division. Alas, the moment was not seized and the national university had to wait for ten more years, but Dillon's peroration is worth preserving, for it came more directly from the heart than almost anything else he said in Parliament. Towards the end of his speech he took up the objection that was sometimes made—that a poor country like Ireland would not produce enough students to make a university viable. But, he retorted, the object of a university is precisely to provide higher education for the children of the poor without interposing the barrier of expense, and he would answer those who put such a question by bringing them into the primary schools 'and bidding them look into the faces of our children'. And having, as he said, 'felt the bitterness of exclusion when young', he ended with this passage:

> Mr. Speaker, the wealth of Great Britain lies in her mines and minerals, her industry and her commerce. The wealth of Ireland lies in the brains of her children and the fertility of her soil. You have denied her for years the right to develop her wealth in either of these respects. Was there ever a race more passionately addicted to learning than the Irish? During ages of persecution and tyranny, they have sought for learning, and have been obliged to acquire it without a roof over their heads. In my youth it was no uncommon thing, in the wildest part of Mayo, to be introduced to some poor peasant whose clothes were in rags, and who had hardly a shoe to his foot, but who could repeat a book of Homer, and would show familiarity with the poems of Virgil. And if, as the right hon. gentleman the member for Montrose [John Morley] has so well said, you deny the right to look forward, they cannot avoid looking back. We cannot forget, when we look back, there was a day when the light of Irish learning shone brightly within the four seas of Ireland, and was carried through every capital of Europe by Irish scholars. And even to this day every scholar who wanders over Europe in search of manuscripts will find in Vienna, in the north of Italy, in Switzerland, and even in Rome itself, traces of those days when Ireland was recognised as one of the greatest seats of learning in the western world. I ask, was there ever a crueller injustice inflicted upon a nation than to deny the people the opportunity of learning? Speaking here to-day on this question, not only on behalf of the united Catholics of Ireland, but on behalf—and I claim it without fear of contradiction—of everything intelligent, liberal and broad-minded amongst the Protestants of Ireland—I demand that this grievance shall be forthwith redressed; that the barriers which for so many

years have stood between the people of Ireland and the acquisition
of university training shall be levelled to the ground, and that, as in
Scotland and in Germany to-day, the children of the poor in Ireland
shall be enabled to acquire that higher learning, the passionate love
of which throughout the ages that have gone by has so honourably
distinguished the race.[1]

Here, out of the darkness of a troubled and disturbed session, shone the
essential quality of the man. A couple of months later he revealed it again,
and though he himself thought this second speech would merely provide
food for his critics, it was soon reprinted as a pamphlet and may stand as
an eloquent example of the sympathy and love which the greatest Englishman of the day could evoke from the people whose cause he had made his
own. The occasion was the death of Gladstone, and Dillon spoke directly
after the moving tributes paid by Arthur Balfour and Sir William Harcourt.
Dillon spoke because, he said, the last 'and, as all men will agree, the most
glorious years of his strenuous and splendid life were dominated by the
love which he bore to our nation, and by the eager and even passionate
desire to serve Ireland and give her liberty and peace'. And he continued:

Above all men I have ever known or read of, in his case the lapse of
years seemed to have no influence to narrow his sympathies or to
contract his heart. Young men felt old beside him. And to the last
no generous cause, no suffering people, appealed to him in vain, and
that glorious voice which had so often inspired the friends of freedom and guided them to victory was to the last at the service of the
oppressed of whatever race or nation. Mr. Gladstone was the greatest Englishman of his time. He loved his own people as much as any
Englishman that ever lived. But through communion with the hearts
of his own people, he acquired that wider and greater gift, the power
of understanding and sympathising with other peoples. He entered
into their sorrows and felt for their oppressions. And with splendid
courage he did not hesitate, even in the case of his much-loved
England, to condemn her when he thought she was wronging others,
and in doing so he fearlessly faced odium and unpopularity amongst
his own people which it must have been bitter for him to bear; and
so he became something far greater than a British statesman, and
took a place amidst the greatest leaders of the human race. Amidst
the obstructions and the cynicism of a materialistic age he never lost
his hold on the 'ideal'. And so it came to pass that wherever throughout the civilised world a race or nation of men were suffering, their
thoughts turned towards Gladstone, and when that mighty voice was
raised in their behalf, Europe and the civilised world listened, and
the breathing of new hopes entered into the hearts of men made
desperate by long despair.[2]

Moments such as these come rarely, if ever, in the lives of most politicians
and for Dillon, certainly, there was no other occasion in his career when he

---

[1] Hansard, H.C. Debates, 4th series, vol. 58, cols. 754–81, especially cols. 780–1.
[2] Ibid., vol. 58, cols. 130–2.

was so much at one with the leaders of both the great English parties. But when the session was over and he came back to Ireland in a state of near-collapse through fatigue and overwork, the old nagging problems of disunity, poverty and impotence returned to plague him once more.[1] Outwardly, indeed, it was clear enough that the '98 celebrations were creating a mood in the country which was strongly favourable to reunion and, speaking in Dublin at a Wolfe Tone memorial meeting, on his way back from Parliament to join the family in Mayo, Dillon had an excellent reception. But he did not deceive himself. The future depended not on mass meetings but on whether he and O'Brien could agree about the future roles of the party and the United Irish League. And immediately he got home he began a systematic analysis of the situation, which, in one form or another, was to last through the autumn:

> Blake [he wrote to O'Brien in mid-August] is still strongly of opinion that I should resign this autumn. And as you know I have been for some time of opinion that in view of all the circumstances that is the course best calculated to give the country a chance of getting together. If I could see a chance of getting sufficient funds to keep the party in existence and to be ready for by-elections I should hold on without hesitation and with perfect assurance of success. But without some assured revenue it is impossible to hold on, and the prospect of an appeal to Ireland in support of the parliamentary movement does not at present look bright.[2]

This letter suggests that Dillon did not approach his friend in any penitential frame of mind; for him, clearly, the party was still *the* instrument of policy, and it was only because lack of money had rendered that instrument for the time being ineffective that he was prepared to consider other alternatives. But to O'Brien, by now totally immersed in the affairs of his still struggling League, all this talk of the party was irrelevant. Edward Blake, to whom Dillon sent a couple of O'Brien's letters at this time, was frankly appalled by what they revealed—'his mind is that you and all of us should be sacrificed, if need be, on the [altar of the] Mayo movement'.[3] These particular letters of O'Brien's have not come to light, but Dillon agreed with Blake's diagnosis. Unless O'Brien changed his attitude, he replied, he could not be counted on as a supporter of the party, or even of Dillon as chairman, and—here was the rub—'without his support I do not feel that I would be justified in attempting to carry on'.[4] Hard on the heels of this exchange came a warning from Davitt, all the more serious since he was himself much more attracted by what the League represented than were either Dillon or Blake:

> You will find [he wrote to Dillon on August 26] O'Brien unable to consider anything except the U.I.L. He is against *any* fund being

---

[1] Diary of Elizabeth Dillon, 30 Aug. 1898 (D.P.).
[2] Dillon to W. O'Brien, 17 Aug. 1898 (N.L.I. MS. 8555/13).
[3] Banks, *Edward Blake*, p. 201. [4] Dillon to Blake, 23 Aug. 1898 (Blake Papers).

raised for the party on the grounds (1) that the country ignores the existence of the party and (2) that the body which requires a fund is the U.I.L. . . . Unless you can change his view when you see him he will lend no aid whatever to any attempt to obtain, by public or private means, enough of money to keep the party together next session.

He is strongly opposed to the idea of your retiring, even while admitting that the want of a fund leaves you no alternative, but he argues that such a step, if taken before next year, would seriously injure the U.I.L.

Manifestly he has got convinced that the League is going to sweep the country and he thinks and talks on the line of the enthusiast—those who are not with him are against him.[1]

The beginnings of a serious divergence between Dillon and O'Brien are already apparent from these letters. If Dillon was, from O'Brien's view-point, obstinately pig-headed in still clinging to the party, then O'Brien, in Dillon's eyes, was hopelessly inconsistent in pressing him to remain chairman while insisting that only the United Irish League had a future. The trouble was that each was convinced that his own organisation was the key one and that, while the other might have a useful part to play, it must be a subordinate part. Obviously, the sooner they met to hammer out some sort of agreed policy, the better. Such a conference did, in fact, take place in Dublin on 6 September, when Dillon, O'Brien, Davitt and Blake all met at North Great George's Street. No formal record was kept of the proceedings (though O'Brien later published what purports to be an entry from his diary of that date), and the participants carried away rather different views of what had been agreed. Dillon, indeed, a year after had even forgotten altogether that the conference had ever taken place.[2] O'Brien's note of their conversation suggests that Dillon was at first worried about the threat posed by the new League to the existing Irish National Federation, instancing the recent decision of the Sligo branches of the Federation to affiliate instead to the League. He, says O'Brien, 'threw up his hands and cried, "another of our best counties lost". I asked had the Federation received £10 from county Sligo for the past twelve months. He admitted it had not, and that the Federation was in a state of total inanition. "Then", I asked, "where is the misfortune of having it turned into a real and live organization?" D[avit]t strongly took this view, repeated his own feeling of contempt and aversion for "the party", and agreed with me wholly that the United Irish League, such as it is, offers the only change of arousing a spark of enthusiasm in Ireland or America.' Dillon then—according to O'Brien—asked how far it was proposed to extend the new organisation, to which O'Brien replied with truth that he had found it

---

[1] Davitt to Dillon, 27 Aug. 1898 (Davitt Papers); the first paragraph of this letter is cited in Lyons, *Irish parliamentary party*, p. 74 n. 3. For further evidence of O'Brien's state of mind see Dillon's report to Blake of an interview with him just at this time in Banks, *Edward Blake*, p. 202.

[2] Diary of John Dillon, 26 Dec. 1899 (D.P.).

hard enough to get a footing in Mayo. 'He [Dillon] harked back upon the old cry that if he only had a fund the party would be all right . . . Upon the whole, the result of the interview staves off any immediate resignation and creates a better feeling, but I left with a heart-breaking feeling of being alone to struggle against all the myriad difficulties of giving the League a chance, even in Mayo.'[1] Although what strikes one chiefly about this passage is the inordinate vanity of the man, so monumental that even in the privacy of his diary he has to depict himself as the high-minded martyr plagued by the obtuseness of earthier and more short-sighted colleagues, it does reflect some at least of the realities of the situation. Dillon, as we have seen, was desperately worried about the whole future of the constitutional movement, and it is likely enough that he wanted to get from O'Brien a clearer picture of the potentialities of the United Irish League. O'Brien was right also in thinking that the conference had averted Dillon's immediate resignation of the party chairmanship, but he gives no inkling of what the other participants believed also to have been decided—that if Dillon was to stay in the chair, at any rate for the time being, O'Brien should give some help in the fund-raising which would be necessary that autumn. Davitt's recollection—and it seems to have been Blake's also—was that O'Brien had agreed that Dillon should launch a public appeal for funds and that various members should write privately to friends who might subscribe. Dillon himself, however, as he explained to Blake, a few weeks after the conference, had never expected that O'Brien's co-operation in fund-raising would go very deep, or indeed that it was anything more than a *douceur* to prevent him (Dillon) from creating alarm and despondency amongst Nationalists by a sudden or premature resignation. But as regards the future of the new League, and its relationship with the old Federation, there was a more serious difference of recollection. Edward Blake apparently had gone away from the conference under the impression that no move was to be made to spread the League outside the west of Ireland, and when later in September O'Brien spoke of its destiny as a truly national organisation, Blake wrote to Dillon in some perturbation that this marked an attempt 'to fix men's minds everywhere, not in 5, or 8, or 10 counties, on the League, and its purpose not as a lever for relief to congested districts, but as a unifying machinery in Irish national politics'. This was a little naïve of Blake—as well try to raise leviathan with a hook as to restrict O'Brien to the congested districts—and Davitt was probably nearer the mark when he told him that, although it had, he thought, been agreed at the conference that the Federation should be kept in being, the notion that the League should be confined to, say, ten counties had not been definitely accepted.[2] In September 1898, indeed, the question was premature, for the new movement was still essentially a Mayo one and real power was not yet within O'Brien's grasp.

Dillon himself seems to have taken little part in these exchanges. This was partly because he had a further bout of influenza that September and

[1] O'Brien, *Olive branch*, p. 103 n.   [2] Banks, *Edward Blake*, pp. 202–4.

partly for domestic reasons. His uncle, Charles Hart, in whose house in North Great George's Street he had lived for forty years, had now become frail and senile. That summer he had become involved in a lawsuit and was being sued for £2,000 for neglecting (of course, unwittingly) a trust. Since the family finances depended to some extent upon his contribution, the loss of even such a comparatively small sum was worrying and Dillon had to spend a good deal of time upon the business. It soon appeared, unhappily, that the old man was quite overwhelmed by his disaster and began to fail rapidly. On 12 October, while Dillon was away speaking in Glasgow, he had a stroke and died two days later. He was the last survivor of Dillon's mother's family and the breaking of the link affected him deeply. However, the house he had shared with his uncle for so long now became his absolutely and it was to remain his own home for the rest of his life.[1]

Dillon's absence in Scotland at this critical time was not just routine business. He did indeed make it a rule to speak at various centres during the recess, but what gave his Glasgow meeting a particular importance was that he used it to hold out to the Parnellites some hope of reconciliation by offering, admittedly in very general terms, to meet them in conference, five a side. Redmond did not take up the invitation, but all the same it had some unexpected consequences. The Limerick board of guardians—which had a strong Parnellite element—took the initiative in suggesting negotiations and circulated its proposals to other public bodies. Among these proposals was the notion that there should be a 'unity conference' of all Nationalist M.P.s. Dillon was prepared to accept this, but Redmond considered it unworkable and instead put forward a modification of Dillon's original offer to the effect that his suggested conference should be attended not just by five Parnellites and five Dillonites, but by five Healyites as well. This was unlikely to find favour with Dillon's supporters, since, as Blake publicly pointed out, it would be tantamount to recognising Healy as the leader of a separate party, and it seemed as if the effort at a tripartite reunion would peter out once more. However, again at the instance of the Limerick board of guardians, a convention of delegates from elective bodies in Munster met at Limerick and resolved to set up a committee to work for a conference of *all* Nationalist M.P.s in the spring of 1899.[2]

It seemed, therefore, that the ice was at last beginning to break up and that—formidable as were the obstacles—some progress might yet be made towards reunion. Dillon's own attitude was steadily hardening in favour of a conference. Up to October, it is true, he was still thinking wistfully of how he might raise funds for the party—he even suggested, a trifle disingenuously, to O'Brien that *he* should go off to the U.S.A. to raise money for the League, not specifying how that tender plant would survive the prolonged absence of its originator—but by November even Dillon had come to realise that the support he needed was simply non-existent.[3] This

---

[1] Diary of Elizabeth Dillon, 11 July and 4 Dec. 1898 (D.P.).
[2] Banks, *Edward Blake*, pp. 207–10.
[3] Dillon to W. O.Brien, 20 Oct. 1898 (N.L.I. MS. 8555/13).

must have been a factor prompting him to redouble his efforts towards reunion and on 16 November he wrote to Blake clearly stating that his policy was to bring on a unity conference and, once that was arranged, to resign the party chairmanship and leave it to the conference to choose the leader of the reunited party.[1]

But there still remained the vexed question of his relationship with the United Irish League. It was now, at last, beginning to take hold of the public imagination and O'Brien, whose sense of timing was highly developed, began to press his friend to attend a convention in the west in order to give the League a more permanent organisation, not just for Mayo, but for the whole of Connaught. This invitation led to an exchange of letters which was of the highest importance, not merely for the future of the United Irish League, but for their own personal friendship. Whether or not he could attend the congress, wrote Dillon on Christmas Day, would depend mainly on what O'Brien's view as to the development of the League really was. 'If you and I are not in accord as to the future conduct, not only of the United League, but generally of the national movement, I cannot see what good can come of my attending the provincial congress. And much mischief might result if any divergence of views between you and me were to become apparent. I confess I have observed with pain and anxiety that for the past year we seem to have been drifting rather far apart in our views of the general situation.' And, not mincing his words, he continued:

I have never for a moment supposed that it would be possible for me usefully to continue to occupy the position of chairman of the Irish party unless I could count on your active support. And the conviction that I could no longer count on this, and that the national organisation which is essential to the party from the electioneeering point of view, is doomed to death [he meant the Federation], has compelled me to adopt an attitude on the 'unity question' somewhat different from that which I would have adopted if I could have counted on a larger measure of support.

At least until the conference of 6 September, he reminded O'Brien, he had understood that after another two or three months the League could be considered to have had a fair trial and that 'it would probably by that time be possible to adjust the new movement to the conditions essential to the existence of an Irish party in the House of Commons'. But everything he had learnt since of O'Brien's intentions had made it clear that 'you contemplate a movement which, whatever may be its advantages, and I have no doubt there is much to be said for it, will be manifestly inconsistent with any attempt on my part to hold the chair of the Irish party'. The conviction, he added, grew upon him more strongly every day 'that I am bound to look out for the most suitable opportunity for getting out of my present position and into a position of greater freedom and less responsibility'.[2]

---

[1] Dillon to Blake, 16 Nov. 1898 (Blake Papers).
[2] Dillon to W. O'Brien, 25 Dec. 1898 (N.L.I. MS. 8555/12); part of this letter is cited in Lyons, *Irish parliamentary party*, p. 75.

The real sting in this letter was that it laid at O'Brien's door a large part of the responsibility for the resignation which Dillon was now pretty well determined to carry through. Not surprisingly, it evoked from Mallow Cottage not so much a letter as a bombardment.[1] At enormous length, and in his most vehement and excitable style, O'Brien poured out his side of the case. And, given his preoccupations of the moment, it was a case that had much to be said for it. He began by pleading with Dillon to reconsider his decision about the provincial congress—his absence would be little less disastrous than an open difference of opinion between them. 'The latter misfortune I, like yourself, should regard as putting an end to any hope of saving the movement in our time.' However, he was honestly quite unable to see why Dillon considered the growth of the League incompatible with his retention of the chairmanship or why he should have felt he was not being sufficiently supported. 'The only modification of the situation is that I (and, as I understood from many conversations you also) have come to the conclusion that the party can only be saved from outside —that is to say by creating a healthy public organization which at the right time would be in a position to cope with parliamentary mutineers and cranks.' In this, it must be said, O'Brien deceived himself. Dillon had indeed often lamented the parlous state of the party, but this did *not* mean that he thought it should be saved from outside—that his friend should have thought so lay at the root of the difference between them. And in a striking passage, which is so fundamental to his argument as to deserve reprinting here, O'Brien continued:

Then the frightful prospects in the west opened up another chance of creating a real and powerful public spirit. At the time of the West-port meeting [i.e. January 1898] I urged upon you that a mere isolated meeting ending in nothing could only destroy whatever spirit was left in the people. You acquiesced and spoke in that sense, and, as I supposed, quite agreed that a new organization, free from the narrow and depressing traditions of the Federation, and new methods of work, were the only ways of kindling any real spirit in the country. The United Irish League was then and there founded on the principle of an open door to all sections of nationalists. The idea in my mind, and I thought in yours, was to attract the rank and file of the Parnellites and Healyites (so far as there are any Healyites) to a fight under a common flag, and to put their leaders in the dilemma either that they must join in or efface themselves. In order to give the policy fair play it was necessary to keep the door genuinely open to all sections on an equal footing and to avoid all references to parliamentary disputes which could only have the effect of irritating and repelling, and were in no sense of the word questions of actuality until a general election was within measurable distance.

What I had hoped and calculated was that you and all our most

---

[1] The greater part of this very long letter has been printed in Lyons, *The Irish parliamentary party*, pp. 75–8.

9. T. M. Healy, from the portrait by William Orpen
(*Courtesy of the Municipal Gallery of Modern Art,
Dublin*)

10. John Redmond, from the portrait by Sir John
Lavery
(*Courtesy of the Municipal Gallery of Modern Art,
Dublin*)

influential friends would throw themselves into the movement on its own merits—that, there being an equal invitation to all, the men who kept aloof or kept on worrying about dissension would lose all influence in the country and could be safely left unnoticed—that a real fighting organization once firmly planted was sure to go on spreading and that then, whenever there was a reasonable prospect of a general election the time would come for discussing how the organization was to make its power felt in parliament, when you would have fifteen or twenty young fellows, divorced from all the bitterness and failure of the last few years, springing up to infuse new blood into the party and stand no nonsense in the way of mutiny.[1]

There is no reason to doubt that O'Brien was perfectly sincere in this exposition of the part he wanted the League to play in reuniting the party. But, as so often with him, attachment to one course of action led to intolerance of all other courses. The idea of unity by conference he dismissed with contempt—it would never be possible to deal with Redmond and Healy and their respective followers. And in conclusion he reverted to his *idée fixe* that unity could only come gradually by the formation of 'an outside public opinion'. 'Rightly or wrongly it was on the policy of postponing the question of parliamentary unity and practising rather than preaching it in the country that the United Irish League proceeded . . . Here, therefore, ready to our hands is what we have been pining for for the last eight years—a public opinion live, real and resolute, not depending upon the priests on the one hand nor the toleration of the *Independent* [the Parnellite newspaper] on the other for its existence or growth. I would urge you most earnestly to reconsider the matter carefully before we throw away such a chance.'[2]

It was an eloquent, but a vain, appeal. Dillon responded predictably— he would on no account give up his parliamentary work, nor could he, so long as he remained chairman, avoid the controversies in which the parliamentary party was immersed. 'I was under the impression', he replied with some asperity, 'that I had made it perfectly clear to you that I felt it quite impossible for me to do anything of the kind, that I felt absolutely bound to stick closely to the House of Commons; and that I was not prepared to commit myself to any line of action in Ireland which would make it impossible for me—for any cause—to give a close and steady attendance in the House.'[3] This was harsh, but it was not intended to produce a break —these letters were as usual addressed 'My dear William' and signed 'yours affectionately'—and in practice Dillon was not quite so unbending as he often seemed. Three days later he wrote promising that he would attend a League meeting in his own constituency and he kept this promise faithfully, going to Claremorris on 30 January 1899 and thus demonstrating, at

[1] Lyons, *The Irish parliamentary party*, pp. 76–77.
[2] W. O'Brien to Dillon, 26 Dec. 1898 (D.P.).
[3] Dillon to W. O'Brien, 27 Dec. 1898 (N.L.I. MS. 8555/12).

least to the man in the street, that the comrades of the Plan of Campaign were comrades still.[1]

(iv)

But by then the League was in reality only occupying a small part of his attention. After a brief holiday in Paris with Elizabeth in the New Year, he plunged directly into the complicated and arduous negotiations which eventually, by devious routes and after many setbacks, were to lead to unity—of a kind. The Irish party, at least that section of it which Dillon controlled, met first in Dublin to pass a resolution welcoming the initiatives taken in Limerick at the end of the previous year and declaring their readiness to co-operate. Then, in London on the eve of the new session, Dillon formally resigned the chairmanship. He proposed that the election of a successor be postponed until after the Easter recess—by which time he hoped the unity negotiations would be well advanced—but when the matter came up in April it was decided to leave the post vacant for the rest of the session, and subsequent meetings were presided over by the senior whip, Sir Thomas Esmonde.[2]

The next move now lay with the Parnellites and on 13 February they instructed their secretary—Patrick O'Brien—to open negotiation on the basis of a preliminary meeting between representatives of the different parties to find out whether enough common ground existed for a general conference to be held. This letter, inexcusably, was not answered until almost the end of March, and although Dillon explained it on the grounds that the senior whip had been seriously ill, this was scarcely convincing, since a party which contained Davitt, Dillon, Blake and T. P. O'Connor was unlikely to be overmuch influenced in its vital decisions by the state of Sir Thomas Esmonde's health. No satisfactory explanation for the delay —which provided Healy and his friends with some useful ammunition— was ever given, but it may well have been due to disagreement among the majority leaders as to what their reaction should be. And when that reaction did come it was unsatisfactory to the Parnellites, since the idea of a preliminary meeting was rejected and it was proposed instead to press on with the wider unity conference which had been suggested by the Munster convention and was due on 4 April.[3] Not unnaturally, the Parnellites as a party did not attend, since they would have been in a small minority and therefore very vulnerable. Two of them, admittedly, did turn up. One was J. J. O'Kelly, the veteran Fenian and war correspondent, who had been suggested by Davitt as a possible leader as far back as 1896, a fact which Davitt, with curious tactlessness, chose to make public on the eve of the conference. O'Kelly had, it seemed, been dropped from the *Independent* and was decidedly disgruntled. As a result he was now all for unity and the

---

[1] Ibid., Dillon to W. O'Brien, 30 Dec. 1898; for the meeting, a so-called 'Connaught convention' of the League, see *F.J.*, 31 Jan. 1899.

[2] Lyons, *Irish parliamentary party*, p. 79; Banks, *Edward Blake*, p. 210.

[3] For the Munster convention, see p. 194 above.

League. He did not, however, so Davitt had reported to Dillon, want the chairmanship for himself. 'He admits himself unfitted for it, but he is ready to do anything which will help to re-establish unity and to thwart the traitorous game of the *Independent*.'[1] The other Parnellite present was asked, perhaps as an ecumenical gesture, to preside. This was Timothy Harrington, who also had become very loosely attached to his party and, through his interest in the evicted tenants, had probably more in common with Dillon than with Redmond. Like O'Kelly, he was a journalist who was finding it hard to keep afloat, and the previous year Dillon, when toying with the idea of taking over *United Ireland*, had seriously considered keeping him on as business editor.[2]

Neither O'Kelly nor Harrington could therefore be regarded as truly representative of the Parnellites and the first business of the conference on 4 April was to try to make the all-essential contact with Redmond. Sir Thomas Esmonde proposed, and T. M. Healy seconded, that the conference should simply appoint a committee to meet a Parnellite committee for the purpose of discussing concrete proposals. But, since this was in effect what the Parnellites had originally suggested and the majority had rejected in March, it took matters no further forward and Dillon insisted, Harrington agreeing with him, that it was really for a conference to decide on the general terms of reunion, and that only *after* such a decision should the details be handed over to a joint committee. But he did not leave the matter there. In a speech which beyond question contributed much to creating a better atmosphere for unity, he elaborated a five-point plan, originally devised by Edward Blake and calculated to assuage the lingering doubts of most Parnellites. First, all Nationalists were to be reunited in one party on the principles and constitution of the old party as it had been in its prime, between 1885 and 1890. Second, this reunited party was to be absolutely independent of all English political parties. Third, its principal objective was to be a measure of Home Rule as ample as that of 1886 or 1893. Fourth, the party was to fight as heretofore for a whole range of other Irish reforms—in land, labour, taxation and education especially. So far so good—all these points were carried unanimously. The last proposal was more difficult to swallow—for two reasons. Partly because, with remarkable generosity, it pledged the anti-Parnellites to agree to support the election of a Parnellite to the chair of the reunited party. This occasioned some argument, but in the end there was only one vote against it, and nothing, it is safe to say, convinced public opinion of the urgency and reality of the desire for unity amongst the majority more than this single concession. But the other difficulty was more serious, since the resolution in question threatened to resurrect the danger of Healyite rebellion, by stipulating that 'the reunited party and its adherents should exert all legitimate influence' in favour of the principle that past service should be the only test of admission to the reunited party when candidates were being

[1] Davitt to Dillon, 4 Jan. '1898', error for 1899 (Davitt Papers).
[2] Dillon to W. O'Brien, 30 Mar. and 29 and 30 Apr. 1898 (N.L.I. MS. 8555/15).

selected for parliamentary and party offices. Some—especially Healy's father-in-law, T. D. Sullivan—were ready to suspect fresh designs against the freedom of the constituencies, until Blake averted an ugly collision by inserting the words 'fully recognizing the right of every constituency to select its own candidate'. This amendment was accepted unanimously.

But there remained the central problem of how to translate all these admirable sentiments into the reality of a union with the Parnellites. In the closing stages of the conference the idea of a joint committee was again brought forward and this time Dillon allowed himself to be persuaded, but—mindful of past history—only on condition that Healy would agree to serve on it. This Healy firmly refused to do, though adding politely that, of course, he would respect whatever decisions the committee came to. For Dillon, and for Blake, too, this was not nearly good enough and they at once declined to serve also. In the face of this treble boycott it was decided to drop the notion of appointing a committee and simply to renew the invitation to the Parnellites to attend a general conference. This was once more rejected and the unity movement seemed to have reached an impasse. It was not really so, however. The April conference, by defining the policy of a reunited party in terms which could only be satisfactory to the Parnellites, and still more by the magnanimity with which the vacant chair was reserved for a Parnellite, had created a situation so favourable to unity that Redmond could not hold out for long without putting himself and his followers in a hopeless position. All that was needed was a formula which would allow him and his tiny band of followers to march out, or rather into the camp of their opponents, with all the honours of war.[1]

This took longer than might have been expected and for Dillon that summer and autumn were an anxious time. On the one hand he had to keep open the line to Westport, and on the other hand he had to watch very carefully the manoeuvrings of his political rivals. Both tasks were vexatious, especially as William O'Brien—or 'the Tzar' as Michael Davitt had taken to calling him—showed very little appreciation of his difficulties. 'I feel bound in frankness to say', wrote Dillon to him early in June, 'that some passages in recent speeches of yours have seemed to me very unfair, and calculated to convey to many people that you had come to regard T. P. O'Connor, Blake and myself as equally responsible for the present state of the Irish party with Healy and Redmond, and that you regarded all of us who attended in the House of Commons as lending ourselves to a system of imposture and fraud.' If O'Brien went on conveying this impression, then, concluded Dillon gloomily, that would 'very seriously increase the difficulties of a situation which at best is not too promising'.[2]

The plain fact was, however, that events were so shaping themselves as to make him more rather than less dependent on O'Brien. Indeed, although he may not at first have realised it, he was in grave danger of becoming

[1] For the April conference and its antecedents see Lyons, *Irish parliamentary party*, pp. 79–83; Banks, *Edward Blake*, pp. 210–16.
[2] Dillon to W. O'Brien, 1 June 1899 (N.L.I. MS. 8555/11).

isolated. His position was based on the decision of the April conference that reunion should come from a general meeting of parliamentarians, and it was entirely consistent with this that when arbitration by Sir Charles Gavan Duffy, his father's old colleague of Young Ireland days, was suggested, he should have rejected the proposal. But it was ominous that Healy and Redmond, to whom the offer was also made, reacted very differently. Healy was in favour of the idea and Redmond, though more cautious, seized the opportunity to resurrect his original scheme of a small, intimate meeting between the leaders to decide whether a settlement, either through arbitration or on any other basis, was possible.[1] Worse still, though unknown to Dillon, was the fact that Redmond and Healy were passing beyond correspondence to personal contact from which an anti-Dillonite alliance might in due course emerge. And when in August both Redmond and Healy urged the reconvening of the April conference, that alliance seemed to be taking form very rapidly.[3] But since, almost simultaneously, Edward Blake was moving closer to O'Brien, it was clear that Dillon, if he was not careful, might find himself outflanked by the parliamentarians while he was still trying to make up his mind what attitude to take to the United Irish League. Blake took the plunge by writing to O'Brien (who promptly published his letter on 3 August) that he had ceased to hope for reunion by negotiation among the parliamentarians and that he had come round entirely to the view that the best hope for the future lay in the League. 'Its extension all over Ireland', he wrote, 'its development as the great national instrument, and the achievement by its means of a genuine, effective and organised union, should be the immediate aim.'[4]

Blake's instinct was sound. The growth of the League was not a figment of O'Brien's imagination, but a solid, ascertainable fact. The police had been watching it closely, and in August 1899 they supplied the Under-Secretary with a detailed analysis of its development during the previous six months. According to their reports—based partly upon intensive study of press accounts of meetings and partly upon mysterious, but usually well-informed local sources—they reckoned that the total of branches had risen from 175 on 1 February to 279 on 1 August and that the number of individual members had increased during the same period from just under 19,000 to slightly over 33,000. It was true that the heaviest concentration was still in the west (Mayo, Galway, Roscommon and Sligo had most branches—and Mayo with seventy-nine accounted for a little more than a quarter of the entire total), but twelve other counties and one city (Belfast) also showed some trace of League organisation; in fact, it appeared to be spreading north, south and east. Most of the energy of O'Brien and his friends seemed, however, to be going into the work of propagating the League rather than into actual agrarian agitation and although some

[1] Lyons, op. cit., p. 83; Banks, op. cit., p. 216.
[2] T. M. Healy, *Letters and leaders of my day*, ii. 435; Banks, op. cit., p. 218.
[3] Banks, op. cit., p. 219.   [4] Ibid., p. 217.

evidence (sixty-six cases) of intimidation was produced, it seems that between February and August 1899 only eight people and twenty-five farms were boycotted. The number of prosecutions during the same period was no more than nine and the number of meetings suppressed three.[1] The picture that emerges is of a movement growing fast, but apparently constitutional in intent and still well within the bounds of the law. How it might develop in the future was much more problematical, but at the time Blake threw his support behind it it was still eminently respectable. In these circumstances, it would have been suicide for Dillon to stand aside any longer, and although he was away in Germany for most of August and part of September, he made his peace with O'Brien even before he returned to Ireland. 'To me it is quite clear', he wrote at the end of August, 'that the time for negotiations has gone by. And that the only safe way in which we can look for unity is for all to unite without reference to the past on the platform of the United League.'[2]

When he returned to circulation in the autumn, however, he found that some parliamentarians at least had not given up the idea of unity through negotiation. The secretaries of the April conference had responded to Redmond's initiative by arranging a further session—it was to meet in November—for the purpose of choosing a committee to meet Redmond's followers. This placed the anti-Parnellite leaders in an awkward position. To abstain was to risk decisions being taken over which they would have no control, but which they might find it difficult subsequently to ignore. But to attend was to concede the very point they had resisted in April— that Redmond should have parity of representation on whatever body was eventually to decide the terms of reunion. Dillon, especially, found it hard to make up his mind. On the one hand Blake, who was absent in Canada, thought they should attend the conference, if only to keep an eye on what was happening. But on the other hand both Davitt and William O'Brien, whom Dillon saw soon after he got back from Germany, ridiculed the whole notion of a conference and urged him to throw in his lot completely with the United Irish League. Wrapped up as they both now were in the agrarian movement, the manoeuvrings of the parliamentarians seemed to them absurdly irrelevant. But Dillon could not, as he explained to Blake, take so irresponsible a view:

> When I put the possibility of combination between Redmond and Healy getting together majority of National representatives and agreeing on a neutral chairman such as Esmonde, thereby setting up rival centre to United League and affording rallying point for all those who feel their seats threatened by the United League and O'Brien's policy of a clean sweep, Davitt admitted that if such a state of things were brought about it would constitute great danger— no practical suggestion, but general denunciation of party, etc. etc.

[1] S.P.O., Crime Branch Special Papers, 19237/S, 'return of counties in which the United Irish League has appeared', 21 Aug 1899.
[2] Dillon to W. O'Brien, 29 Aug 1899 (W. O'Brien Papers, but not listed in the recent rearrangement of the O'Brien Papers).

As for William O'Brien, when Dillon asked him for his reaction to the idea of a renewed conference, 'I was met with explosions of wrath and had some difficulty in keeping him to the point'. However, when the dust had settled it was quite clear that O'Brien felt that any such conference should be ignored—there was, he added typically, no such body as the Irish party now existing—'the one service the party could do was by never meeting again'. Dillon himself felt that a conference would not only be useless, but even dangerous, for, as he pointed out to Harrington, there was a real risk that it would be dominated by a Healy-Redmond alliance. Harrington, who was too deeply committed to the conference idea to withdraw at this stage, countered with an argument calculated to carry a good deal of weight with Dillon—that even if a reconstituted party did emerge as a rival centre to the League, this in itself would be 'a very good thing'. In normal circumstances this might have been decisive. But circumstances were not normal and Dillon's disgust at, and distrust of, his parliamentary colleagues was such that he gravitated steadily towards O'Brien's camp, even though he did not approve of all O'Brien stood for. 'Substantially', he told Blake, 'everything that is honest and sound in Irish nationality . . . is either in the League or in sympathy with it, and all the dishonest element and those hostile to nationality in the country are drawing together in opposition to it. And I say this altho' I am clear that I cannot make myself directly responsible for the policy of the League until O'Brien modifies his attitude a good deal.'[1]

As the time approached for the conference to reassemble Dillon's attitude towards it hardened and, in telling his friend T. P. O'Connor that he had decided not to attend, he forecast that very few of his friends would go either. In this he was entirely correct, for in the end only nineteen members of the party turned up on 23 November and most of these were Healyites.[2] Dillon's attitude, as we have already seen, was conditioned partly by his suspicion of a burgeoning Healy-Redmond alliance and partly by his growing conviction that the future lay with the United Irish League, but it was not possible to explain his inner motives to the general public and, although Blake allowed himself to be persuaded into abstention, it is impossible not to sympathise with his criticism that non-attendance would be widely interpreted as non-co-operation and that they would be exposing a wide surface to attack.[3]

The immediate result, of course, was to restore the initiative to Healy. He seized it with his usual promptness and secured the immediate appointment of a committee to treat with the Parnellites. It was ingeniously chosen, for it contained not only the names of Healy himself, Harrington, Sir Thomas Esmonde and Jeremiah Jordan (an inoffensive Protestant Member), but also those of Dillon and Blake. Dillon at once realised—what, indeed, he had already half anticipated—that Healy had outflanked him and that unless he was very careful he would be involved in what he most

---

[1] Dillon to Blake, 2 Oct 1899 (Blake Papers)
[2] Lyons, *Irish parliamentary party*, p 84.   [3] Banks, *Edward Blake*, pp. 220–1.

wanted to avoid, a patched-up reunion of politicians entirely separate from
and independent of the United Irish League. He extricated himself from
the trap, therefore, by the only means open to him—he refused to serve on
the committee and brought the utmost pressure upon Blake to do the same.
Blake pleaded almost piteously that they should make some definite gesture
of goodwill at this critical moment, hinting even that now was the time to
reach a *modus vivendi* with Healy. 'I confess', wrote Dillon acidly in
December, 'I do not much believe in a negotiated *modus vivendi* as a means
of conducting a political movement, least of all an Irish political movement . . . But I may say that I think it not at all unlikely that something
closer than a *modus vivendi* may be very soon brought about between
Healy and John Redmond'. Their object, he was convinced, was 'to con-
struct an entrenched position from which the League could be successfully
resisted'. This being so, his own attitude remained what it had been. 'I am
resolved not to fight the League, nor to take part with any body of men
hostile to the League. I believe the United League movement, if wisely
directed, can save the political situation in Ireland, and make the Irish
question once more a living one'.[1]

By then, however, the situation had developed further. Redmond,
though unable to resist the temptation to make some capital out of the
abstention of Dillon and Blake, did agree to nominate a committee to meet
the anti-Parnellites. In doing so he was no doubt motivated to some extent
by the knowledge that his opponents were already committed to electing a
Parnellite as chairman of the reunited party, but also by the fact that the
outbreak of the Boer War in October had created a new political situation
in face of which it was essential that the Irish nationalists at Westminster
should speak with one voice. This added urgency to the meeting of the two
committees on 17 January 1900 and they had little difficulty in agreeing on
the five-point programme adopted at the April conference and in calling
upon all the Irish Nationalist members to meet together in London on the
eve of the parliamentary session to elect a new leader.[2]

These developments brought Dillon face to face with a crisis which
could quite easily have ended his public career. A joint meeting of the two
parties had been arranged, and a long stride made towards unity, without
any move from him. Everything seemed suddenly to have gone wrong.
After having held out for months against O'Brien's pressure upon him to
throw in his lot with the League because he still clung desperately to the
hope that reunion might come through negotiation, he had finally swallowed the League at the very moment when reunion through negotiation
at last became a real possibility. But, and this was the unkindest cut of all,
it was to be a reunion achieved by the very men who, within and without
his party, had been his bitterest opponents through the long years of the
split. Now, therefore, he had to choose between accepting the dubious gifts
of these highly suspect Greeks, or else, by standing aloof, risk forfeiting the

[1] Dillon to Blake, 21 Dec. 1899 (Blake Papers).
[2] Lyons, op. cit., p. 85; Banks, op. cit., pp. 223–6.

prestige of a lifetime and finding himself, perhaps, relegated for ever to the wings. At this crucial juncture he was deeply influenced, as so often before, by Edward Blake. Blake was no longer prepared to disregard his own judgement in order to spare his friend's susceptibilities, and, before Dillon had even had a chance to reach a decision, he wrote to the *Freeman's Journal* welcoming the decision to hold a meeting of the reunited party and announcing his own intention to be present. For Dillon, this seems to have been the turning-point. At any rate, having read the letter, he told O'Connor, his other confidant in the party, that Blake had separated himself from them and that this altered the whole situation. He had, in fact, at last drawn the conclusions Blake had for so long been wanting him to draw:

> If we were to remain away from the meeting on the 30th [he wrote] what would be our position during the session? Would we not hand over the whole parliamentary position absolutely into the hands of Redmond and Healy? And as we could not think of setting up any real parliamentary party—or of holding meetings of our friends— the tendency would in my judgment be irresistible for our friends to drift into the ranks of the men who were holding meetings and conducting Irish business.

There was, admittedly, an alternative—to abandon parliamentary attendance and concentrate on Ireland. 'This of course is what O'Brien is working for. But it is a course I am resolved not to take.'[1] O'Connor's view was similar. Blake's letter had forced their hands, no doubt, but 'it marks out the lines on which I think we should go'. Dillon's reply showed that all indecision was at an end. 'I agree', he wrote. 'Blake's letter makes it impossible for us to remain away from the meeting—and on the whole I am very glad he wrote it.'[2]

The decision to reunite had been taken on 17 January. On 30 January the reunion was ratified at a full meeting of both parties presided over by Harrington. Two further meetings—on 31 January and 1 February, also with Harrington in the chair—decided the order of business for the parliamentary session, and it was not until 6 February that the really crucial decision, the election of the new chairman, was taken. The period between 17 January and 6 February was filled, by the anti-Parnellites at any rate, with much anxious manoeuvring and correspondence. After all, though none of them could be a candidate, their numbers would determine the issue. But for whom should they vote? Dillon's own preference seems to have been for either Harrington or J. J. O'Kelly. The latter, however, was in poor health and would probably not have been acceptable to Redmond. As to Harrington, of whom he had been seeing a good deal, Dillon's guess, as he wrote to T. P. O'Connor, was that he would be 'willing to sacrifice himself on the altar of his country if pressed—but it is doubtful whether R[edmond] would agree. And from remarks of R's reported to me by H[arrington] last night, I think R has in his heart the possibility of getting

---

[1] Lyons, op. cit., p. 86.   [2] Banks, op. cit., pp. 228–9.

himself (Redmond) elected.'[1] Indeed he had, for, as we now know, he was assured of the support of Tim Healy, who was at that very moment arranging for William Martin Murphy to take over the almost defunct Parnellite *Independent*.[2]

Even despite this, and according to Healy's own last-minute calculations, it seemed as if Harrington (though his health was also suspect) would collect most votes.[3] That he did not do so seems to have been due to a decisive intervention by William O'Brien and Michael Davitt. Even though both of them were at that moment outside the parliamentary party, they carried very great weight, all the greater because it was obvious that as soon as the leadership question had been settled the next burning issue would be the relationship between the party and the United Irish League. And it was solely from the point of view of the League that O'Brien and Davitt looked at the leadership. To them Harrington was anathema because of his coldness towards the new agrarian campaign.[4] Just before the decisive meeting to choose the new leader Davitt wrote hastily to Dillon that O'Brien was '*most strongly*' against Harrington, whom he regarded as a man who could bring no strength or following to the League even if he wanted to. Redmond, on the other hand, though far from ideal, would be a better choice, partly because he might work with the League, and partly for tactical reasons. As Davitt put it:

> O'Brien thinks that if the country saw *you* either proposing Redmond or supporting him for the chair, it would do more to kill Healyism than anything you could possibly do in that way *now* by dividing against Redmond. Healy, in desperation, intends to down you by supporting Redmond. O'Brien is of opinion that your best plan is to turn the tables on Tim by proposing Redmond for the chair. I offer no opinion against this view. I have no confidence in Redmond, but I have less in Harrington. Undoubtedly, the election of Redmond would be more acceptable to the country than that of Harrington.[5]

And so the thing was done. With Healy, Dillon, Blake, O'Brien and Davitt apparently supporting his candidature, Redmond was borne to the chair which he was to occupy until his death eighteen years later. That he was proposed by Blake and seconded by Healy was no doubt intended as a symbol of unity, but it was a symbol that deceived none of those who had been behind the scenes. All of them, not least Redmond himself, knew that his election was due to a strange sequence of events which, almost fortuitously, had brought the right men into his camp at the right time. No one could pretend that it was a genuine union of hearts. Time alone would tell whether a marriage of convenience might not prove more durable.

[1] Dillon to T. P. O'Connor, 24 Jan. 1900 (D.P.).
[2] Healy, *Letters and leaders of my day*, ii. 443.
[3] Ibid., ii. 444.
[4] As recently as the previous October he had dismissed it as a mere Connaught movement with no national significance, Dillon to Blake, 2 Oct. 1899 (Blake Papers).
[5] Davitt to Dillon, probably 4 Feb. 1900 (D.P.), cited in Lyons, *Irish parliamentary party*, pp. 88–9.

8

Estrangements

(i)

Although Redmond's election had settled the question of the leadership, it had settled very little else. The party, indeed, was 'united', but union had been achieved only by plastering over the cracks. And, apart altogether from the nagging rivalries between the various parliamentary groups, there loomed the larger question of the future relations of the party with the United Irish League. The two issues were, in fact, connected, since the still-persisting hostility between Dillon and Healy was reinforced by the fact that Dillon was closely linked with O'Brien, whose organisation in Healy's eyes represented a threat to the party. But for Dillon himself the most immediate problem was the Redmond-Healy alliance. If the party were to be dominated by that alliance, then there would be no place in it for him. On the other hand, if Redmond could be weaned away from Healy, and persuaded to throw in his lot with the League, then a workable arrangement between League and party might very well be evolved and, if skilfully managed, might even lead to the isolation of Healy.

Redmond's position, with Healy and Dillon hanging threateningly on either flank, was certainly not enviable, but he began well enough, from the viewpoint of the Dillon-O'Brien axis, by writing to O'Brien four days after his election expressing a desire to work in harmony with him.[1] O'Brien was only too ready to accept this as a sign of grace and early in March wrote cheerfully to Dillon that he was sure Redmond realised that the future lay with the League. 'It is absolutely clear to me', he added, 'that the only hope for the country is to arrive at an understanding with Redmond to organise the country.'[2]

So far so good, but at this point Redmond suddenly committed a serious and totally unnecessary blunder. Acting apparently on Healy's advice, and also, according to Healy, on that of Blake, he rose in the House of Commons, the very day after O'Brien's letter, to make a fulsome speech welcoming the announcement that the aged Queen was shortly to visit Ireland.[3] Since anti-British feeling was already running high in the country because of the Boer War, the intended visit was regarded, and not only by extremists,

[1] D. Gwynn, *Life of John Redmond*, p. 95.

[2] W. O'Brien to Dillon, 'Wednesday', probably 7 Mar. 1900, copy in Sophie O'Brien's handwriting (W. O'Brien Papers, N.L.I. MS. 8555/11).

[3] Hansard, H.C. Debates, 4th series, vol. 80, cols. 402–3; Healy, *Letters and leaders of my day*, ii. 448.

as an insult. Dillon, who had been out of action for three weeks with influenza, erupted a few days later in a letter blaming O'Brien for saddling the party with such a leader:

> But for your interference he had no more chance of being elected than I had of being elected Lord Mayor of London. I considered then that your support of him was a great mistake, and I will confess that everything which has occurred since has confirmed me in that view.

So far as personal relations went, they were, he admitted on perfectly good terms, though Dillon had 'told him frankly' (and characteristically) that he had been entirely opposed to his election. He would give him fair play, he said, so long as he, Dillon, remained in the party. 'But more than fair play I cannot give him—for I have no faith in him.' Then, however, his sense of outrage at Redmond's speech boiled over:

> I confess I have never felt more disgusted and humiliated than by his crawling statement in the House on the Queen's visit, made on behalf not only of the party, but of 'our people'—a statement which was simply an outbreak of superabounding snobbery, which could not be contained . . . And this is the gentleman who is planted on our necks in the commanding position of first chairman of a united Nationalist party since the death of Parnell, a man whom no national instinct, nor even sense of danger to his own position, can prevent from falling on his hands and knees to crawl before the combined snobbery of Great Britain and Ireland.[1]

This did not augur very well for the future and the imbroglio could scarcely have come at a worse time. When the party reunited it had been agreed that a national convention should be summoned to set the seal on the policy of reconciliation. But there were serious differences of opinion both about the timing of this convention and about who should have the responsibility for summoning it. Redmond, naturally, wanted the process of legitimisation to be completed as soon as possible. Dillon and O'Brien, on the other hand, preferred not to rush matters, so that they could satisfy themselves completely that Redmond really was prepared to work with the United Irish League. Healy, for his part, while also wanting an early convention, was anxious above all things that it should not be a convention dominated by the League, and the newspaper which spoke for him—the *Daily Nation*—carried on an unceasing campaign denigrating O'Brien and his League.[2] In the end an uneasy compromise was reached whereby the parliamentary party appointed a committee to meet representatives of the League in order to arrange for the summoning of the convention under the joint auspices of the party and the League. It was to meet, if possible, at Whitsuntide, which still left plenty of time for manoeuvring and intrigue.

---

[1] Dillon to W. O'Brien, 14 Mar. 1900 (N.L.I. MS. 8555/11); see also Lyons, *Irish parliamentary party*, p. 91 and n. 1.

[2] For example, *Daily Nation*, 9 and 14 Apr. 1900.

Indeed, even this decision, though recorded as unanimous, was not reached without acrimonious debate. Dillon had tried to prevent a definite date being fixed, but had been overruled because Redmond was able to show that O'Brien had expressed no objection to Whitsuntide. Upon this Dillon wrote in some alarm to his friend, warning him that an early convention— that is, one held before the League was thoroughly organised—might well be dominated by Redmond and Healy.[1] O'Brien, naturally worried, replied at once that he had only agreed to a Whit convention on the understanding that Redmond would throw himself behind the League. If he did *not* do this, then 'it would be impossible for us to touch their convention'. But, he urged, not only must Redmond fall into line, Dillon, too, must give evidence of support by agreeing to speak at a League meeting in Ireland soon.[2]

Although the two friends were apparently in agreement about the future, yet in reality they were looking at it from different viewpoints. Dillon was still concerned essentially with the balance of power inside the parliamentary party and it was the effect of a Redmond-Healy coalition upon that balance which he chiefly dreaded. Knowing as he did the precariousness of Redmond's position, he could not bring himself to believe that the newly elected leader could shake off Healy's shackles, even if he wanted to. O'Brien was as usual more optimistic and, as usual, was so deeply involved in his own organisation that he had eyes for little else. He was convinced that the one way to separate Redmond from Healy was to show the former that the League had a real capacity for growth and for mobilising public opinion, and that by aligning himself with it he would at once cease to be dependent on those whose votes had brought him to the chairmanship of the party. But—and here was the rub—the League would be much more credible to Redmond as a living, expanding movement if Dillon could be seen to be throwing his weight behind it.

Such an appeal, however, left Dillon entirely cold. Not only did he not trust Redmond, he could not even fathom O'Brien's intentions. And that he should be asked to leave the party to look after itself while he crusaded in Ireland on behalf of the League was, he wrote, preposterous:

> The proposal astonishes me. How could I think of undertaking such a responsibility under present circumstances? When, as it seems to me, there exists a radical difference of opinion between you and me as to the conduct of the national movement, as to the meaning and effect of your action in putting Redmond in the chair of the party, and when I am utterly in the dark as to your intentions with reference to the future relations between Redmond and the organisation.[3]

Next day he returned to the charge. Did not O'Brien realise that by attempting to attract Redmond into the League he was laying up trouble

[1] Dillon to W. O'Brien, 24 Mar. 1900 (N.L.I. MS. 8555/11); Banks, *Edward Blake*, pp. 235–6.
[2] W. O'Brien to Dillon, 26 Mar. 1900, in handwriting of Sophie O'Brien (D.P.).
[3] Dillon to W. O'Brien, 27 Mar. 1900 (N.L.I. MS. 8555/11).

for himself? Did he really expect Redmond to identify himself with the
movement, or that he was free to do so? 'He is bound by the logical necessity of his position to nurse Healy and his gang and keep them on hand to
be used against any attempt on the part of the League to dictate to him.'
The significant weakness in Redmond's position, as Dillon was quick to
point out, was the fact that his newspaper, the *Independent*, would in future
be controlled by one of Healy's closest adherents, William Martin Murphy.
'And this will of course throw Redmond more than ever into Healy's hands.'
In short, with everything so uncertain, Dillon could not commit himself
further to the League without, in all probability, coming into conflict with
Redmond, and even possibly with O'Brien himself. 'Will you pardon me
for saying', he concluded, 'that in my judgment your appeals to Redmond
and his friends to help the work of the League . . . have a very bad effect
upon the party and I should imagine in the country also. On the party they
have the effect of creating the impression that the League is helpless without [? the smiles] of the party, and I need hardly tell you that any hold the
League has on the party is not based on love.'[1]

Lacking any convincing evidence that Redmond was prepared to work
closely with the League, O'Brien found it increasingly difficult to answer his
friend. And his embarrassment was aggravated by the fact that Dillon,
mysteriously, seemed to have become more O'Brienite than O'Brien in his
eagerness to preserve the League from contamination by the politicians.
In reality, however, there was no mystery. Dillon was still at heart a party
man and not a League man. That he leaned towards the League at this
juncture reflected not enthusiasm for O'Brien's movement, but disillusionment with his fellow parliamentarians. So long as the party was dominated,
as it seemed to him to be, by the Redmond-Healy alliance, so long did he
need the League as a counterpoise. Later, when he had recovered his position in the party, his old antipathy to the League as an esssentially
diversionary movement reasserted itself and it was O'Brien's turn to be disillusioned. In the meantime, however, Dillon lost no opportunity to warn
him that an early convention would be disastrous and that if Redmond
was allowed to manoeuvre himself into the presidency of the League, 'I can
only act as a private member according to my best judgment.'[2] The whole
object of 'rushing' the convention, he explained, was to secure the predomi-
nance of the party rather than the League at the general election. 'The
strength of the League is on the platforms—when it comes to committees
and conventions the Redmond-Healy alliance will be pretty strong.'[3] No
doubt this was perfectly true, but, as O'Brien was all too well aware, the
number of platforms open to the League was still not very large. In the west,
certainly, it was firmly based—the province of Connaught had now its own
governing body or 'Directory'—and O'Brien was poised to launch his
movement on a grand scale in Munster, but the plain fact was that the

[1] Ibid., Dillon to W. O'Brien, 28 Mar. 1900.
[2] Dillon to W. O'Brien, 5 Apr. 1900 (N.L.I. MS. 8555/10).
[3] Ibid., Dillon to W. O'Brien, 15 Apr. 1900.

League was still not *the* national organisation, even though there were no rivals in the field. A large convention establishing it as *the* national organisation would accelerate its growth more rapidly than anything else—a bandwagon only becomes attractive to the waverer after it has actually begun to move. For this reason, therefore, there was much to be said for O'Brien's anxiety to accept the party's invitation to help to organise an early convention. He put this point to Dillon forcibly and cogently:

> To reject an invitation under these circumstances would be to proclaim ourselves irreconcilable to any terms of agreement within the party. The result would be a horrible shock to the country and the beginning of a new civil war in which we would be hopelessly in the wrong. On the other hand, in accepting as the Directory did upon the terms I have stated (to which Redmond is clearly pledged) we either force Healy and Co. to swallow the public acknowledgment of our equal power or (as is always possible) force him into an open opposition in which he will be badly beaten, and so discredited, or else would beat Redmond and so completely justify (us) in having nothing further to do with the convention . . . Believe me, Healy's hold over Redmond has been your attitude of aloofness towards Redmond, and that feeling prevails among our very best friends here to an extent that would surprise you. The League is, and will remain, master of the situation, but its position is constantly subject to danger and anxiety owing to this suspicion giving Redmond an interest in keeping Healy on his hands.[1]

It did not seem at first that even this appeal would move Dillon. He replied coldly that he still intended, as he had said before, to give Redmond fair play, 'tho' I have not received, nor do I expect to receive, like treatment from him'.[2] And in his diary he noted that O'Brien's letter was very unsatisfactory, 'clearly showing that he [is] entirely in Redmond's hands—very *nasty* in its tone towards me. My aloofness from R. has thrown him into the hands of H. etc. etc. . . . I must now carefully consider whether I shall attend [the] convention. At present I am inclined to think better I should not.' A few days later—on 11 April—the two men met for an hour and a half's discussion, or rather monologue by O'Brien, in Dublin. 'He talked nearly all the time,' Dillon recorded, 'I do not know how he can stand it.' He found O'Brien 'very aggressive' and inclined to ask awkward questions —how would Dillon conduct the national movement, would he throw the League into open conflict with Redmond, and would he be prepared to take on the priests as well? They were probably rhetorical questions—Dillon certainly got very little chance to answer them—for O'Brien was clearly obsessed by the need to propagate the League and capture Redmond. It was useless to reason with him and, Dillon thought, impossible to work with him. 'I can only support the League and watch development of events.'[4]

[1] W. O'Brien to Dillon, 6 Apr. 1900 (D.P.); cited in Lyons op. cit., p. 95.
[2] Dillon to W. O'Brien, 8 Apr. 1900 (N.L.I. MS. 8555/10).
[3] Diary of John Dillon, 7 Apr. 1900 (D.P.).
[4] Ibid., 11 Apr. 1900.

Dillon maintained this attitude of detachment for some time longer, though it did not prevent him from following every detail of the struggle with fascinated interest. The burning issue was still the date and composition of the convention and Healy's attacks upon O'Brien in the *Daily Nation* grew steadily more bitter.[1] To Dillon these were 'amusing and satisfactory', but by satisfactory he meant, with his usual prescience, that Healy was yet again prejudicing his own case by his violent language. 'Once more', he noted, 'T. M. H. is making a *gross* blunder—and showing his want of tactical skill in writing these articles.'[2] O'Brien, naturally, could not be expected to appreciate these subtleties—he was desperately overworked, hard put to it to find reliable helpers, and anxious above all to pick the right men to meet the parliamentarians for the business of summoning the convention. In his extremity he wrote asking Dillon to be one of them.[3] It is difficult to believe that he expected an affirmative—what he got, of course, was a resounding negative.[4]

Yet, for Dillon to stand aside too long was to risk a second time the isolation from which Blake had rescued him at the time of the reunion. And Blake, having taken the plunge, made every effort to identify himself with the party, even going to the length of agreeing to be one of the parliamentary representatives on the joint committee for arranging the convention. If Blake thus committed himself so deeply, could Dillon continue to hold aloof? His other close friend in the party, T. P. O'Connor, was emphatic that he ought not. A few weeks later, early in June, when Dillon was still hesitating, O'Connor urged him to move closer to Redmond as a preliminary to a final clash with Healy. He had been sounding opinion in the party and had found a growing disposition to have it out with Healy once and for all. Those whom he had consulted took it for granted that Redmond would be offered the presidency of the League and thought this not only inevitable but desirable. 'The ground for this opinion is that Redmond is thereby detached from Healy and compelled in the coming fight to throw in his lot with the League.' O'Connor himself believed that Redmond would rapidly find that his interests and those of the League were identical, but if Dillon could bring himself to discuss the matter with him, that might make all the difference. 'I am sure he would be much more likely to act courageously and straightly if he had an agreed understanding with you.'[5]

This was sound sense and all the more attractive to Dillon because the political situation seemed at last to be improving. Just after receiving this letter he had another talk with O'Brien, who agreed with O'Connor's diagnosis that Healy was losing ground—he was, in fact, clinging desperately to what remained of his own organisation, the People's Rights Association, and the more he did so the more open and obvious was his isolation. In these circumstances Dillon felt able to move, very cautiously,

[1] See especially 'The O'Brien Ultimatum' in *Daily Nation*, 13 Apr. 1900.
[2] Diary of John Dillon, 13 Apr. 1900 (D.P.).
[3] W. O'Brien to Dillon, 13 Apr. 1900, in handwriting of Sophie O'Brien (D.P.).
[4] Dillon to W. O'Brien, 15 Apr. 1900 (N.L.I. MS. 8555/10).
[5] T. P. O'Connor to Dillon, 13 June 1900 (D.P.).

in the direction O'Connor had indicated and on 16 June wrote to O'Brien that if the committee responsible for calling the convention decided to put Redmond in the chair, and if Redmond and the committee wished it, he, Dillon, would be prepared to second his nomination.[1] It was an important concession, for it meant in effect that if the general trend of opinion was in favour of Redmond becoming head of the United Irish League as well as chairman of the party, then Dillon would not stand in the way.

The long-awaited convention was now at hand and in two crowded and productive days, 19 and 20 June 1900, it registered the triumph of the United Irish League. It was recognised as the national organisation and an elaborate constitution provided both central and local machinery for getting out the vote and for discussing major political and economic issues. Redmond was elected chairman—he did not assume the title of president until December—and to the delighted delegates Irish nationalism seemed once more one and indivisible.[2] Or almost one and indivisible. Healy virtually ignored the convention and his friends refused to dissolve the People's Rights Association. This in itself was of no great consequence, as the P. R. A. was on its last legs anyway, but it was an outward and visible sign of dissent, and with the tide now flowing so strongly towards conformity, dissent was dangerous. Tim Healy, in fact, had fallen into the very trap which Dillon had only just avoided at the beginning of the year. Dillon, when isolated by a *fait accompli* largely brought about by his own friends, had, albeit after much heart-searching, accepted it. Healy, when confronted by his former ally, Redmond, with a similar *fait accompli*, chose not to accept it and so condemned himself to the political wilderness.

This, it is true, was not immediately apparent. Redmond did not break openly with him as the result of the June convention. Indeed, he could not afford to do so, for he was still negotiating the sale of the *Independent* to William Martin Murphy, and this was not completed until August, the first issue of the new *Daily Independent and Nation* appearing on 1 September.[3] What really decided Healy's fate was the general election in October. It was fought with great efficiency through the local machinery of the United Irish League and the outcome was a decisive defeat for practically all of Healy's friends and supporters, including even his brother Maurice, who came bottom of the poll at Cork City where, with a kind of poetic justice, William O'Brien swept back to Parliament as the senior Member.[4] Tim Healy only scraped in for North Louth after a very savage fight and himself summed up the results of the election in a single phrase when, early in the new Parliament, he remarked that 'the hon. member for Cork has created two united Irish parties—of which I am one'.[5] Retribution soon followed

---

[1] Dillon to W. O'Brien, 16 June 1900 (N.L.I. MS. 8555/10).

[2] *F.J.*, 20 and 21 June 1900; the constitution of the League is analysed in Lyons, *Irish parliamentary party*, pp. 149–54, 193–6.

[3] Diary of John Dillon, 23 Aug. and 1 Sept. 1900 (D.P.); Healy, *Letters and leaders of my day*, ii. 449.

[4] O'Brien, *Olive branch*, pp. 129–30.

[5] Ibid., p. 130 n.

and after a further national convention in Dublin in December he was formally expelled from the parliamentary party.[1]

(ii)

It has been necessary to dwell upon these painful and sometimes squalid
details of the personal relationships of the leaders in the months after reunion, partly to emphasise what should never be forgotten, that the nine
years of the split had done almost irreparable damage to the constitutional
movement, but partly also because the pattern which began to emerge in
these months was to be the pattern of a large part of Irish politics for the
next fifteen years. The motives of the various protagonists were involved
and the results of their actions often unexpected. But the key to the puzzle,
and to much of the future, lay in the United Irish League. Dillon's instinct,
as we have seen had initially been to hold the League at arm's length because, as he rightly sensed, it was an organisation competing with, if not
actually antipathetic to, the parliamentary party which, ever since his
return to politics in 1885, had been for him the centre of Irish political life.
Tim Healy, also essentially a parliamentarian, had likewise distrusted the
League, and—from his point of view—had certainly been right to do so.
Redmond, no less a House of Commons man than the other two, only drew
close to the League in his extremity, and even then, as O'Brien so frequently
complained, was evasive and difficult to pin down. It is significant that the
only major figures of the time who really believed in the League were William O'Brien and Michael Davitt, both of them men ill at ease in Parliament
and both with their roots deep in agrarian agitation.

So long as Healy remained a danger Dillon, O'Brien and Davitt, though
differing in emphasis and approach, shared substantially the same ground.
Their suspicion of Redmond derived, as we have seen, less from his Parnellite antecedents than from the fact, as it seemed to them, that he either would
not, or could not, escape from Healy's embrace. Indeed, even after the
June convention, and before Healy's expulsion in December, this suspicion
still persisted, fanned into fresh life whenever Redmond made a speech indicating a reluctance to throw Healy overboard altogether. One such speech
in August, stressing the freedom of the constituencies to choose their own
candidates, Dillon, who interpreted it no doubt as a genuflection towards
the moribund People's Rights Association, found 'mean and dishonourable
towards me and the other members of the old majority party'; and another
in September, rebuking his anti-Parnellite colleagues for their continuing
internecine quarrels, he described as 'most insolent, gratuitously offensive
and treacherous'.[2] But Redmond's critics were probably overemphasising
the extent of Healy's influence, which in any event was largely dissipated by
his poor showing at the general election in October. Once he had been

---

[1] *F.J.*, 12 Dec. 1900.
[2] Diary of John Dillon, 9 Aug. and 10 Sept. 1900; the offending speeches are in *F.J.*,
8 Aug. and 10 Sept. 1900.

disposed of, the real issue had to be faced and that issue was nothing less than a struggle for supremacy between the parliamentary party and the United Irish League. O'Brien, of course, was perfectly clear where he stood. He made it plain at the June convention that he regarded the party as subordinate to the League and in intention (though not, subsequently, in practice) the League's constitution was designed to demonstrate its superiority, especially in the clauses assigning the selection of parliamentary candidates to local conventions organised by the League, and in the proviso calling for an annual national convention to review the progress of the cause and in effect to call the party to account.

In his preoccupation with the League O'Brien looked to Davitt for support and, initially, he got it. But it was always a conditional support, depending on the right conduct of the agrarian movement and upon Davitt's own capacity to put up with O'Brien's egocentricity. Already by September 1900 there were signs that this was proving intolerable and Davitt was writing to Dillon that the gap between him and the 'Tzar' was 'too wide to be bridged over'.[1] If O'Brien were to desert the hills and bogs of Connaught for the lusher pastures of parliamentary politics, that gap would certainly grow wider. But even the provisional support that Davitt might feel free to give was much more difficult for either Redmond or Dillon. Redmond, though he had become president of the League, was first and foremost chairman of the parliamentary party. With his undoubted political aptitude, his fine bearing, his magnificent voice, he was an admirable spokesman, and in that role steadily enhanced his reputation as the years passed. Moreover, as the leader of a political party, he had to be free to meet parliamentary contingencies as they arose; he could not possibly have his hands tied by having to refer back to an organisation in Ireland which was necessarily ignorant of, and incapable of dealing with, the difficult and sometimes highly secret questions which a party leader had to decide upon with, at most, the advice of a small group of colleagues. These same considerations were bound to govern Dillon's attitude towards the League also. He, by reason of his seniority, his experience and his high standing in the House, was the most obvious candidate for Redmond's confidences and, once Healy's shadow had ceased to hang over them, relations between them began slowly to improve. Although they were never to become intimate friends, there gradually developed a mutual understanding and respect, based upon the habit of close consultation and, on Dillon's side at any rate, extremely plain speaking. This dialogue, which relates to almost everything of permanent value in the work of the party from the reunion until Redmond's death eighteen years later, gives a peculiar fascination and flavour to a correspondence that has ever since remained one of the principal sources—perhaps *the* principal source—for the later history of the Home Rule movement.

The immediate political crisis confronting them after the reunion was of a kind to bring them together more rapidly than might otherwise have been

[1] Davitt to Dillon, 22 Sept. 1900 (Davitt Papers).

the case. The outbreak of the Boer War in the autumn of 1899, while the Irish party were groping their way towards unity, had evoked in Britain a wave of war hysteria. The Tories were, of course, solidly behind the war, while the Liberals were deeply divided—some falling in with the national mood, others earning hatred (and in some quarters admiration), as 'pro-Boers'. But for Irish nationalists there could not be any hesitation. All, whether Redmondite, Healyite, or Dillonite, joined in condemning what they regarded as an unjustified and brutal attack by a great power upon two tiny states. As the war dragged along on its slow and inefficient course, some of them—including Healy and Dillon himself—took a sombre satisfaction in exposing the shortcomings of the War Office. But their main concern was not to score debating points, it was rather to take a definite moral stand at a time when such a stand was unpopular in many places and when it required real courage to do so.

Courage was a quality not even his worst enemies had ever denied to Dillon, and his repeated attacks upon the war between 1899 and 1902 became so famous (or notorious) that even the Boers recognised him as one of their most passionate defenders. 'Tell Mr. Dillon we are all grateful to him for his speeches in Parliament,' said Christian de Wet to Michael Davitt, adding with characteristic caution, '*but see that no one else is present but you and he.*'[1] Dillon's was, in fact, the first Irish voice raised in the House of Commons against the war when, on the recall of Parliament in October 1899, he moved an amendment to the Address condemning British intervention in the affairs of the South African Republic as a violation of the 1884 convention and demanding that the Government seek independent arbitration. 'I am proud,' he said, 'to be in the position of declaring that in Ireland the overwhelming majority of the people condemn this war as unjust, unnecessary and cowardly.' He condemned it particularly as a war for which it was difficult to discover any adequate cause. It was not, he asserted, about the franchise for the Uitlanders; it was about gold, it was about power, it was about revenge for Majuba—'you goaded this unhappy people into war for the purpose of robbing them of their country'.[2] And a few months later, when the House was again debating the Address at the beginning of the 1900 session, he took up a remark that a member of the Government had made during the recess, to the effect that the British race would be predominant in South Africa, and delivered this solemn and in some ways prescient warning:

We know from long and bitter experience what that means. Predominant race! that is what you are fighting for—to put the Dutch under your feet in South Africa; but allow me to tell you you will never succeed. It is an infamous object; the conscience of humanity will be against you in this struggle, and although for a time you may beat down these people by overwhelming numbers, you are but creating for yourselves, as a result of this war, far away in the south-

---

[1] Ibid., Davitt to Dillon, 24 Aug. 1902.
[2] Hansard, H.C. Debates, 4th series, vol. 77, cols. 93–100.

ern seas, 7000 miles away from your shores, another Ireland, which will be infinitely more difficult to hold down than the Ireland which is so close . . . These people will rise and rise again, and my conviction is that even if you conquer the Transvaal the ultimate result will be the loss of South Africa to England.

These passages, which are typical of many, many speeches delivered by him in these years, convey adequately Dillon's detestation of the war and of the policy which, he believed, lay behind it. Inevitably, they brought him face to face once more with Joseph Chamberlain, who, as Colonial Secretary, had had so much to do with the antecedents of the war and who was, of course, one of its most deeply committed apologists. In March 1902, when the fighting was nearly over, the two men clashed as bitterly as at any previous moment in their careers. Chamberlain was trying to show that Boer opinion was divided and cited a certain General Vilonel as saying that the real enemies of the Transvaal were those who wanted to continue a hopeless struggle. Dillon interjected: 'He is a traitor.' 'Ah!' retorted Chamberlain, 'the hon. member is a good judge of traitors.' Dillon appealed to the Chair, but the Speaker told him that if he did not interrupt he would not be subject to retort. Whereupon Dillon, who, as he afterwards admitted to his wife, was feeling the onset of influenza and therefore not in the usual control of his temper, rose and said to Chamberlain: 'You are a damned liar.' For this he was 'named' by the Speaker, and, on refusing to withdraw, was suspended from the House.[2] He went home to Ireland, where he was ill for three weeks, but in May the Irish party initiated a motion (said to be the first of its kind for more than eighty years) charging the Speaker with not having afforded proper protection to Dillon and with having failed to ask Chamberlain to withdraw the provocative remark. It was partly a personal issue—'the man who killed Home Rule' was the object of intense hatred by Irishmen and seemed to revel in the fact—but there was a deeper principle involved. As Redmond put it, was there to be one rule of order for a member of a majority and another for a member of a minority? A Parliament excited by war was not, however, the best place to ask such a question and the motion was defeated by 398 to sixty-three votes. Dillon himself was unrepentant. 'I confess', he said, 'that in this instance I left the House with a bitter sense of injustice which I still feel . . . When I used language which I frankly admit is intolerable in any legislative assembly, I was punished, but the original cause and author of the scene was allowed to go scot free.'[3]

But it was not only personal injustice that moved Dillon to wrath and indignation. He was deeply stirred by the suffering and grief which the war was certain to bring to many homes and families. He included in his compassion the bereaved on both sides, but, as he pointed out reasonably enough, only a very small proportion of English people would be directly

[1] Ibid., vol. 78, cols. 654–62.
[2] Ibid., vol. 105, cols. 591–2; diary of Elizabeth Mathew, 4 Apr. 1902 (D.P.).
[3] Ibid., vol. 107, cols. 1020–50.

affected, whereas in the Boer Republic men, women and children were all
exposed to hardship and danger. In the later stages of the war, when the
British military authorities had adopted the practice of bringing the families
of Boer commandos into 'concentration camps', it was the plight of the
women and children especially which shocked many in England. The
motives for incarcerating these families were not wholly military, nor
wholly bad, but the camps themselves proved an almost insoluble administrative problem. They were overcrowded, insanitary, and nurseries
of disease; supplies were lacking, medical resources were inadequate and
great misery undoubtedly resulted. This was a cause to excite Dillon's
anger and sympathy, and before the 1902 session opened he wrote to
Redmond suggesting that if the 'pro-Boer' Liberals did not raise the
question, he should.[1] Accordingly, on 20 January he moved an amendment
to the Address condemning the whole policy of concentration camps as
contrary to the recognised usages of war and denouncing the methods then
being used as 'barbarous'. As he pointed out, the concentration camps were
a necessary corollary to the policy, first extensively carried out in 1900, of
burning farms. 'You deliberately set about the policy of reducing the whole
of the Transvaal and the Orange Free State to a howling wilderness and
therefore you had thrown on your hands this vast multitude of women and
children.' The House, he complained, had been led to believe that farm-
burning had ceased at the end of 1900, but this was quite untrue—and he
produced evidence to show that it had continued right up to the end of
1901. He then seized eagerly upon Balfour's admission that it was still
being carried on 'in those places where it is a military necessity'. 'Yes,' said
Dillon scornfully, 'the plea of military necessity without any qualification
would cover every conceivable atrocity practised in war. I say that one of
the things prohibited by the laws of war is the devastation of an enemy's
country for the purpose of rendering that country uninhabitable to women
and children and other non-combatants. Therefore I say that the whole
policy of the concentration camps has sprung up, as far as it was a necessity
at all, from your wholesale violation of one of the best-recognised usages of
modern war, which forbids you to desolate or devastate the country of the
enemy and destroy the food supply on such a scale as to reduce non-
combatants to starvation in the open country.' He made it clear he was
not attacking the men responsible for running the camps—they were doing
their best in impossible conditions. 'It is the system which is barbarous and
intolerable, and I believe it was instituted to bring pressure upon the men
on commandos to surrender—that you have found it impossible to overcome them by fair force of arms, and that you resorted to this barbarous
method of endeavouring to bring the war to an end.'[2] His amendment fell
on deaf ears, however, and he mustered a mere sixty-four votes, attracting

---

[1] Dillon to Redmond, 11 Jan. 1902 (R.P.).

[2] Hansard, H.C. Debates, 4th series, vol. 107, cols. 397–413. For earlier protests by
Dillon against the policy of devastation see vol. 83, cols. 1145–66, and vol. 96, cols. 858–
71.

the support of only a handful of pro-Boer Liberals, among them Henry Labouchere and David Lloyd George. He continued his criticism whenever occasion offered, but when the war finished in May his task was done.

(iii)

One consequence of the war which affected Ireland directly was that since South Africa occupied an increasing amount of parliamentary time and ministerial energy the pace of Tory reform began to slacken. In 1899, it is true, Gerald Balfour had carried through the act setting up the Department of Agriculture and Technical Instruction, but its first head was Sir Horace Plunkett, and Dillon at least was not impressed, since he regarded Plunkett as the supreme embodiment of a type—the constructive Unionist— dedicated to the killing of Home Rule by kindness, and therefore constituting a more or less serious threat to Nationalist aspirations. The ending of the war was expected to produce a spate of domestic legislation and George Wyndham (who in 1900 had succeeded Gerald Balfour as Chief Secretary) did indeed introduce a Land Bill, but it was a mere shadow of the one he was to pass the following year and had to be withdrawn. Wyndham was eager, charming and cultivated, with poetic as well as political talents. He had Irish blood in his veins (he was descended from Lord Edward Fitzgerald, the United Irishman who had been mortally wounded while resisting arrest in 1798) and his great ambition was to do something for Ireland. His time, however, was not yet. The attention of the House was concentrated that session on the adoption of important new rules of procedure and upon a vital and contentious English measure—the involved and difficult Education Act of 1902. The details of the latter are not central to Dillon's biography, but since the Act, while intended to create a national system of education, also endeavoured to safeguard the position of denominational schools (or 'non-provided schools' in the terminology of the act), the Irish members were under pressure from Catholic opinion, and especially from Cardinal Vaughan, to do what they could to help.

This, however, involved them in a difficulty. To vote for a Tory measure would in any circumstances have been painful, but to vote against the Liberals on this issue of all issues was, or could be, dangerous, since some of the more radical zealots for non-denominational education were so furious at the special terms accorded to religious schools under the Act that there was a real risk that they might be swayed from their none too steady allegiance to Home Rule by a Nationalist vote cast on obviously Catholic lines. The main debate came on the second reading in the middle of May and it fell to Dillon to explain the Irish position. He spoke particularly, he said, for the Irish Catholics in Britain, who were mostly poor, but who had subscribed magnificently to their own voluntary schools. His task—and a very difficult one it was—was to convince the nonconformists that he understood and sympathised with their grievances, while at the same time objecting to their solution. Their grievances, so far as he understood them, were based on the assumption that since in many parts of England and Wales there was but a single school, and this school was under church management, their children were of necessity exposed to Church of England teaching. If this was true (it was, in fact, an oversimplification), it was, he said, monstrous. But why did nonconformists propose as their solution 'the total destruction of the denominational character of the denominational schools'? Any other solution would, he promised, be warmly supported by the nationalist members. But then he put to them a key question. 'Are the nonconformists of this country anxious to banish Christian teaching of every kind from the schools'? There were cries of 'No'. Then, he asked, what kind of Christian teaching did they want? It was no good nonconformists complaining that denominational schools were sectarian in their religious instruction. Christian teaching of any kind was bound to be sectarian and dogmatic:

> Do you mean to tell me that the teaching of the divinity of our Lord is not one of the greatest dogmas? It lies at the root of our whole religion . . . Do you believe in the inspiration of the Bible? Do you believe in the sacred character of the Bible? Is not that dogma? Is it not a dogma to say that the Bible is a sacred book? The moment you make that assertion you are teaching dogma . . . The position of many of the non-conformists, so far as my limited intellect enables me to comprehend it, is this: 'Nothing is dogma in which we believe, but the moment you touch anything which the Church of England teaches, and still more which the Church of Rome teaches, you get into the region of dogma.' A more illogical or preposterous position was never taken up by rational people. If you are logical, the moment you break with the principle of sectarian teaching, you must banish Christianity and you must banish the Bible, or else you must bring the Bible in, as it was brought in some of the foreign schools, in the days of the French Revolution, as a beautiful poem to be placed beside the poems of Shakespeare and others.

Turning more specifically to the case of the Catholic schools, he made the important point that the kind of situation nonconformists complained of—one school, one parish—was essentially a rural one. But Catholic schools were mainly in cities and towns and there was no question of non-Catholic children having to go to them. What a melancholy thing it was, he said, that because Protestants could not settle their differences 'we should be dragged into the storm and made to suffer for their alleged offences against each other'. Nevertheless, although the Catholic schools to some extent stood apart in this controversy, there was one sense in which they were very deeply involved. For them, the teaching of their religion in their own schools was vital, and it was even more vital that whatever changes came about through the institution of the new education authorities, Catholic schools should remain Catholic in influence and atmosphere. He himself was not convinced that as it stood the Bill was wholly satisfactory in this regard—he was worried especially about Catholic representation on the new authorities and about the likelihood of poor schools being committed to increased expenditure in order to conform to a national average—but since it at least represented an effort to safeguard the position of denominational schools he and his colleagues were prepared to vote for it.[1]

Dillon's position on the education question was perfectly logical and defensible, but this did not save him from attacks by anti-clericals, even by Irish anti-clericals. Such a one was Michael Davitt, who in August wrote to him indignantly, inflamed both by Dillon's efforts on behalf of the Bill and by a congratulatory resolution the Irish party had just passed on the occasion of the Pope's jubilee. 'I really don't know where we are drifting', he complained. 'What with your own exertions for Vaughan and co., and the growing clerical treason against the national cause all over Ireland, and now the making of the Irish "national" party a Catholic party (for that is how the resolution will be understood everywhere) it begins to look as if we were drifting into a modern imitation of the historic "brass band".'[2] This was, of course, an extreme view and, knowing Davitt as he did, Dillon was probably able to make the necessary allowances. His reply, if he ever sent one, has not come to light, but in a letter he wrote in the following year to James Bryce—an opponent on the educational question, but in all else a Liberal ally and a scholar whom he much respected—Dillon revealed something of his difficulties. On the one hand he had to support the Tories as champions of the denominational schools; on the other hand he detested working with English Catholics whose leaders were not only antipathetic or hostile to Home Rule but who could not even be relied on to make the best bargain for their own schools:

The education question [he wrote] is getting more critical each day. You know from various conversations we have had on the subject how much importance I attached to it and how deeply I feared the consequences of the policy adopted by our people in England under the inspiration of Cardinal Vaughan. Since the act of 1902 I have never felt any doubt that this policy would lead ultimately to the total loss of the Catholic schools and to universal secular education on the American model. But the spiritual guides of the Catholics in England are in politics the blindest of the blind. And now passions have been aroused on both sides which will I fear make it more difficult than ever to get a hearing for any proposal of reasonable compromise. But you may count on me as always ready to do my best to promote a compromise and not afraid to oppose the views of the leaders of the Catholic church in England, if I were convinced that a good workable scheme were attainable through compromise with the Liberals.[3]

[1] Ibid., vol. 107, cols. 997–1009.
[2] Davitt to Dillon, 1 Aug. 1902 (Davitt Papers). The 'brass band' was a reference to the influence wielded by Archbishop Cullen over the Irish party of the late 1850s, which was known in consequence as 'the Pope's brass band'.
[3] Dillon to James Bryce, 24 Dec. 1903 (Bryce Papers, Box E).

Such, indeed, remained his attitude. Certainly no enthusiast for clericalism in education, and temperamentally inclined towards Liberalism, he wished only that extremists on both sides could bury a quarrel which, he asserted in his House of Commons speech, had brought English education below the level of that 'of the rest of civilisation'.

(iv)

Although in the debates on the Education Act and in his forays into South African affairs, Dillon had spoken as an Irish Member, these were, of course, large British and imperial issues which were, on the whole, remote from the Irish electorate. And his preoccupation with these issues has to be seen against a background of growing unrest in Ireland which was to have profound consequences for his own future. Once again the key lay with the United Irish League. It had from the beginning been an agrarian organisation and an agrarian organisation it remained. But, as it spread over the country between 1899 and 1902 the basis of the agitation changed. It could never have had the kind of appeal it came to have if it had continued to restrict its efforts to fighting for the transfer to needy peasants of plots carved out of the rich grasslands of the west. There were other places besides the west, it is true, where such a policy had its attractions—Meath, Tipperary and parts of Cork are obvious examples—but what really gave the League its hold upon an increasingly large section of Irish opinion was that for many tenant-farmers it came to be identified with a hunger that was as old as the Land League, the hunger of the tiller of the soil to become the owner of the soil. And as the League took hold, this hunger sought to express itself through the traditional channels of public meetings, protests against evictions, boycotting of graziers and of 'land-grabbers' who were rash enough to rent farms from them.

Yet, although the familiar signs and portents were plain, and were read anxiously by the police, the storm itself was curiously slow in breaking. Partly perhaps because of the restraining influence of the clergy, many of whom had early identified themselves with the movement in the west, partly because Tory remedial legislation had begun to have a pacifying effect, the League remained relatively law-abiding for a surprisingly long time.[1] Even as late as January 1900, the Under-Secretary had before him a secret report indicating that while boycotting had been openly advocated at League meetings, the movement had 'no doubt been carried on without "crime" in the sense of outrage or overt acts of violence'. Boycotting, the report conceded, had indeed had considerable effect in the west, but, although individual meetings had occasionally been proclaimed, 'until within the last two or three months, prosecutions have not been instituted

---

[1] Both these points were made as early as October 1898 by Assistant Inspector-General Allan Cameron, who thought that even within the congested districts people would hesitate to plunge into agitation for fear of hindering 'the beneficent intentions' of the Congested Districts Board (S.P.O. Crime Branch Special Papers, 17425/S).

unless under circumstances which rendered a prosecution unavoidable'.[1] At the time this report was written, admittedly, the League had not spread far outside the west, but after it had become *the* national organisation in June 1900, it began to grow very rapidly and to appear correspondingly formidable. The police estimated that in June 1900 there were 653 branches with nearly 63,000 members, whereas exactly a year later the number of branches had risen to 989 and the total of members to nearly 100,000.[2]

Such growth presented Dillon with a difficult problem. Even though, at the time of the party reunion and afterwards, he had looked upon the League mainly as a new and complicating element in Irish politics, the fact remained that its essential role was agrarian. This was something he, of all men, could not disregard, and hence arose his dilemma. On the one hand, his concentration on parliamentary business (especially during the years of the Boer War) was so intense that the work of the League seemed an almost intolerable intrusion. On the other hand, he was himself still an agrarian at heart and it was not in his nature to hold aloof while the land war entered a new phase. His first reaction, therefore, was to try to fuse both kinds of activity and to put his main energy into presenting the parliamentary case for urgent and far-reaching land reform. For him, as he soon made clear, this meant nothing less than a scheme of compulsory sale. The programme of the League, he pointed out in May 1900, doubtless was, so far as the west was concerned, to enlarge the holdings of tenants shut out by graziers, but in the rest of the country it was 'to abolish dual ownership and buy out the landlords'. If, he said, the Chief Secretary really wanted to check the League, 'let him get up and announce as the policy of the Government that they are determined to bring in a compulsory sale bill to enable the lands of Ireland to be bought out at a fair price by the tenant farmers'.[3] Although the time was not far distant when the Government would come much closer to meeting this demand than Dillon could then have imagined, his demand was still premature. Instead, the result of the general election later that year indicated that conflict rather than conciliation might soon be the order of the day, for not only did it confirm the Tories in office with a majority big enough to allow them to take a strong line if necessary, but it also demonstrated the power of the League in Ireland, personified by the return to parliament of its only begetter, William O'Brien.

The scene was now set for a clash between a strong Government which, with constructive ideas of its own to pursue, was in no mood to allow an Irish land war to deflect it, and a strong organisation which was pledged to attack landlordism and which, inevitably, turned more and more to the traditional weapons of boycott and outrage. In such circumstances a return to coercion was merely a matter of time and during the autumn of 1900 Dublin Castle's attitude hardened to such a degree that O'Brien himself moved

[1] S.P.O., Crime Branch Special Papers 23614/S, minuted by D.H. (the Under-Secretary, Sir David Harrel), 31 Jan. 1900.

[2] S.P.O., Crime Branch Special Papers, 24995/S, report by District Inspector E. V. W. Winder, 7 Aug. 1901.

[3] Hansard, H.C. Debates, 4th series, vol. 83, cols. 1354–61.

an amendment to the Address in January 1901 condemning this resort to
the methods of Arthur Balfour. It was an unavailing protest and a steady
stream of 'proclamations' and arrests continued, so that between 1901 and
1902 some thirteen Irish M.P.s or former M.P.s were imprisoned under the
Crimes Act and by the spring of 1902 the following areas had been proclaimed—the counties of Cavan, Clare, Cork, Leitrim, Mayo, Roscommon,
Sligo, Tipperary and Waterford, together with the cities of Cork and
Waterford.[1]

Yet, although coercion seemed once more in the ascendant there were
significant differences between this crisis and those of 1879 and 1886. It
was curious, for example, that at no time were any of the real leaders
arrested—neither O'Brien, nor Davitt, nor Dillon himself. It was strange,
also, that both Davitt and O'Brien were able to go abroad for considerable
periods and leave the agitation to take care of itself. And perhaps the most
striking thing of all was that neither the Chief Secretary nor the leader of
the Irish party seemed to believe in coercion. Wilfred Scawen Blunt saw
them both (separately) on St. Patrick's Day 1902—and from Wyndham
learned that he had had to threaten resignation rather than go in for the
extreme repression some of his Cabinet colleagues were pressing for, while
Redmond told him an hour or so later that he was obliged 'to be fierce'
with Wyndham in public, 'but I know he is with us in his heart and we all
know it'.[2]

Was the coercion of 1901 and 1902, then, a kind of elaborate shadow-
boxing? Not, certainly, for those who went to prison under the Crimes
Act, nor even for the leaders who had always to face the possibility that
some isolated incident might precipitate a serious clash between Government and people and so frustrate the undoubted goodwill which existed on
both sides to achieve a peaceful settlement of the land question. Moreover,
although Redmond and Wyndham might see eye to eye, there was little
likelihood that Dillon would be disposed to join such a mutual admiration
society. On the contrary, as coercion intensified, all his instincts drive him
to align himself once more with the tenants whom he knew and understood
so well. But while the parliamentary session of 1901 continued he was able
to resist O'Brien's pressure to come and speak at League meetings, and when
he got back to Ireland he was too exhausted to do anything. 'I am *really*
played out,' he explained to his friend. 'The last few weeks, with continuous
late sittings, etc, have left me quite limp and very dyspeptic.'[3]

Nevertheless, contact with the countryside roused him, as so often
before, to furious condemnation of landlordism. After two months of quiet,
he emerged from seclusion and during November and December made a
series of speeches of precisely the kind O'Brien had long been hoping for.
The theme of these speeches was very much the same theme that he had

---

[1] Lyons, *Irish parliamentary party*, p. 99.

[2] W. S. Blunt, *My diaries*, p. 434 (17 Mar. 1902). Later in the year Wyndham explained that 'coercion . . . was the price he had had to pay for obtaining a free hand
from his colleagues in the cabinet' (ibid., p. 445).

[3] W. O'Brien to Dillon, 9 Aug. 1901, and Dillon to W. O'Brien, 19 Aug. 1901 (D.P.).

developed so often in other days—the need for organisation, for discipline, for unrelenting hostility to the landlords. At Roscommon, Newry, Tipperary, Wexford, it was always the same message—the tenants must combine under the aegis of the League to end landlordism for ever. One of these meetings, at Frenchpark, was to have unexpected and serious consequences. Even before he went to Frenchpark in November 1902 there had been friction between tenants and landlords on a group of estates, of which the most important were those of Lord de Freyne, whose wife, curiously enough, had been a close friend of Elizabeth Dillon's before her marriage. Dillon in his speech not only encouraged the tenants to demand rent reductions but told them roundly that 'my object in coming to this meeting to-day . . . is not for the purpose of winning a beggarly reduction, whatever it may be, for this year, but for the purpose of driving every landlord out of the country'. This was quite in his usual vein, but the tenants of Roscommon took him very much at his word. Led by local men, notably John Fitzgibbon of Castlerea, an old I.R.B. man with a record of agitation reaching back to the Land League, they began to organise into what came to be called the 'associated estates' (de Freyne, Murphy and some others) and within a few months had arrived at the point where they were plotting a 'no rent' campaign of their own.[3]

It is not surprising that George Wyndham that autumn began to think that Dillon was about 'to try a fall' with him and force his hand to bringing on a direct confrontation between the Government and the people.[4] But in reality this was not the case. Elizabeth Dillon, recording the incident a few weeks after the Frenchpark meeting, noted that Dillon had warned the local leaders that joint action by the tenants must be their responsibility and that he could not himself become identified with this particular campaign. What he really wanted to do, she wrote, was to use the agitation as a lever for extracting a measure of compulsory purchase from the Government.[5] That this was so is borne out by his speech at the National Convention of the United Irish League in 1902. Referring specifically to the de Freyne and Murphy estates, he pointed out that while the tenants were entitled to support in their struggle, how far they would go must in the end depend upon themselves. And, as if to reduce this incident to its proper scale, he devoted most of his remarks to the larger issues of compulsory sale and the reinstatement of evicted tenants. Nevertheless, when Lord de Freyne soon afterwards took an action for damages against the U.I.L. leaders, it seemed for a while that Dillon might be involved in such serious financial difficulties that he might have to retire from politics. 'But I always told you', he wrote to his wife in June 1902, 'it needed to be a brave woman to marry an Irish agitator, and now you will have to show your bravery again by cheerfully facing whatever is before us and cheering up

---

[1] *F.J.*, 2, 4, 11 Nov. 1901, 9 and 16 Dec. 1901.
[2] *F.J.*, 19 Nov. 1901.
[3] *W.F.J.*, 8 Mar. 1902.
[4] J. W. Mackail and Guy Wyndham, *Life and letters of George Wyndham*, ii. 429.
[5] Diary of Elizabeth Dillon, 31 Dec. 1901 (D.P.).

others.' The threat hung over him for two years, since it was not until June 1904 that the claim for damages was dropped.[1]

While Dillon's sudden prominence in the agitation during the winter of 1902 was thus no doubt prompted by a genuine desire to foster the land agitation as a means of bringing pressure to bear upon the Government, more work fell upon him than would otherwise have been the case, because O'Brien, who had driven himself to the verge of mental and physical breakdown, went abroad for several months. Upon his return in the early summer of 1902 he again took charge of the League and at once resumed his career of violent and provocative speeches. 'His policy', wrote Elizabeth Dillon apprehensively, 'is to "fill the gaols"—but he does not explain what is to happen after that, and some of us think if the gaols are filled with the leaders and the organisation suppressed, the whole movement will crumble away.'[2] 'Some of us' also included T. P. O'Connor, who a few days later wrote O'Brien a long and in some ways brutal letter reproaching him for his recklessness:

> Without beating about the bush then [he wrote] I want to convey to you as clearly as I can that most of your colleagues are not in sympathy with your desire for a violent and rapid movement. They are of opinion that such an appeal to the country will not meet with the response that you expect; and that therefore, there may be much suffering and loss to the movement in the hunting down of its leaders and especially of yourself, without the corresponding advantage such sacrifice should obtain.

O'Brien, he added, seemed to be under a false impression about the mood in England and Ireland. 'You think Ireland is too quiet; here we have the impression that Ireland is utterly disturbed; that coercion is once more rampant; and that every Liberal must once more pledge himself against coercion and fight it.' 'We do not', he warned him, 'want thunderclaps in Ireland to arrest English attention; it is arrested already.'[3]

O'Brien replied in a friendly enough tone, but it was obvious that he was deeply hurt. 'Of course,' he said, 'no human being could stand the strain [of carrying on the movement] if I were to encounter the more serious discouragement that the principal men among my colleagues think I am only doing mischief.'[4] Later, in his memoirs it suited O'Brien to represent this letter as a round-robin from O'Connor, Davitt and Dillon (with all of whom he had quarrelled in the interval), but at the time he was so far from identifying Dillon with injurious criticism that he continued to urge him to address meetings in Ireland.[5] And Dillon was so far from identifying himself with the criticism that he continued to respond to these invitations by delivering

[1] *W.F.J.*, 11 Jan. 1902; Dillon to Elizabeth Dillon, 18 June 1902 (D.P.), *F.J.*, 28 June 1904.

[2] Diary of Elizabeth Dillon, 27 July 1902 (D.P.).

[3] T. P. O'Connor to W. O'Brien, 12 Aug. 1902, typed copy (D.P.).

[4] W. O'Brien to O'Connor, 14 Aug. 1902, typed copy (D.P.).

[5] W. O'Brien, *Olive branch*, p. 138.

during August two slashing attacks on landlordism and coercion. He was so outspoken that Elizabeth Dillon feared imprisonment for him and she looked forward with dread to a meeting O'Brien wanted him to attend at Claremorris in September. The appearance of both these veterans of the land war on the same platform would certainly have attracted the attention of the police and, given O'Brien's known excitability, could well have led to ugly consequences. However, Dillon was prevented from going by family preoccupations. Elizabeth was expecting a child—their son James was born on 26 September—and Dillon was anxious to be with her as the time approached.[1] Since he had undertaken to go to America with Davitt and Redmond immediately afterwards to help establish the United Irish League there and also to raise funds for the movement at home, the risk of arrest was thus for the time being postponed.

(v)

Indeed, it was postponed much longer than anyone could have anticipated. After two strenuous months in the U.S.A., Dillon fell suddenly and mysteriously ill, so ill that Elizabeth, taking her courage in her hands, left her young family in Ireland and set off to join him. The story of that illness will be told later, but it had one very important political consequence.[2] Dillon's health was so seriously affected that, after only a short spell at home in the New Year of 1903, he and his wife went to Egypt, from which they did not return for several months. This meant that from October 1902 until late April 1903 Dillon was to all intents and purposes out of Irish politics, except for a brief interval between his American and his Egyptian expeditions. By one of the strangest chances of his career this was precisely the moment when the whole land question underwent a revolutionary transformation. In September 1902, just before Dillon left for America, Captain John Shawe-Taylor (a nephew of Lady Gregory's and a landowner in the west of Ireland) published what was to become a celebrated letter, appealing to representatives of the landlords and the tenants to meet together in conference to attempt a satisfactory solution of the land problem. Although not all the landlords named in Shawe-Taylor's letter agreed to act (many of the more reactionary were, in fact, deeply suspicious), four reasonably representative figures were found—the Earls of Dunraven and Mayo, Colonel Hutcheson-Poe and Colonel Nugent-Everard. On the tenants' side John Redmond, William O'Brien, Timothy Harrington and T. W. Russell were chosen to negotiate. The conference had George Wyndham's blessing and on 20 December it met at the Mansion House, Dublin. After only a fortnight's discussion it produced a unanimous report recommending land purchase on the grand scale. It was not to be compulsory, but the landlords were to be guaranteed a fair price through state aid in the form of advances to purchasers who would repay by annuities extending over 68½ years. The

---

[1] Diary of Elizabeth Dillon, 11 Sept. 1902 (D.P.).
[2] For details of this critical illness, see chapter 9.

report also recommended that land purchase should be accompanied by a satisfactory settlement of the evicted tenants question and that the landlords' appetite to sell should be whetted by a treasury bonus on every sale.[1]

The Irish party had met in Dublin on the eve of the delegates' departure to America in the autumn and Dillon had there moved a resolution approving the action already taken by Redmond, O'Brien and Harrington in expressing their willingness to meet the landlords' representatives—*provided* the latter were truly representative and that the conference, if it took place, should contain nothing detrimental to 'the unity and the interests of the peoples' organisation'.[2] This expressed at best a tempered enthusiasm —a few days before Shawe-Taylor's original letter had appeared Dillon had publicly expressed his familiar view that the best way to deal with landlords was not to confer with them, rather to make life uncomfortable for them[3]— but by the time he had returned with shattered health from America the conference had already taken place and the scene seemed set at last for real progress. Just a few months earlier Wyndham had appointed as his Under-Secretary Sir Antony MacDonnell, an Irishman with allegedly Home Rule tendencies who had acquired a formidable reputation as an administrator in India. MacDonnell now approached Redmond, O'Brien and Dillon with a proposal that they should meet him to discuss certain points in connection with the Land Bill Wyndham was about to introduce in the new session and which, it was generally assumed, would follow closely the recommendations of the Land Conference. It was at this point that Dillon began to diverge from the line taken by his friends, with consequences which in the long term were to be momentous. Resisting the pressure of both Redmond and MacDonnell, he refused to enter into negotiations, partly, as he told the Under-Secretary, because he had not had time to consult Redmond since his return from America, and partly 'for other reasons'.[4]

What were these 'other reasons'? There is nothing in Dillon's correspondence at this time to suggest that he was being more than merely cautious, and certainly nothing to show that, as O'Brien was later only too ready to imply, he was piqued at having been excluded from the original Land Conference. But there are several straws which indicate the way the wind was beginning to blow. One is the fact that before he wrote declining to attend the meeting with Sir Antony he had had a visit from Davitt, who had made it clear that if asked (he wasn't) he would not go.[5] Now, Davitt was soon to emerge as an opponent of the Land Bill of 1903, not just because he was obsessed by his own solution—land nationalisation—but because he regarded the terms offered to the landlords as far too favourable. Of all men, Davitt was the one to whom Dillon was closest in his agrarian attitudes and Davitt's evident hostility was bound to carry great weight

[1] Lyons, *Irish parliamentary party*, pp. 100–1.
[2] W. O'Brien, *Olive branch*, p. 146.
[3] *W.F.J.*, 30 Aug. 1902, speech at Mullingar.
[4] Redmond to Dillon, 3 and 5 Feb. 1903 (D.P.); Dillon to Sir A. MacDonnell, 5 Feb. 1903 (D.P.).
[5] Diary of John Dillon; 5 Feb. 1903 (D.P.).

11. Michael Davitt, from the portrait by William
Orpen
(*Courtesy of the Municipal Gallery of Modern Art,
Dublin*)

12. Lord Justice Mathew
Drawing by Paul Renouard

with him. Another factor pointing in the same direction was the attitude of the *Freeman's Journal*, which, under the direction of Thomas Sexton (still widely regarded as the keenest financial mind among the Nationalists) had, almost from the moment the Conference report was issued, taken the line that the landlords were being too tenderly handled. At all events, when Redmond called at North Great George's Street after his meeting with MacDonnell to tell Dillon how things were going, Dillon informed him 'fully' about his views on the whole conference policy.[1] What these views were he did not confide to his diary, but that they were expected to be unpalatable is clear from a letter O'Brien wrote him, apologising for not having visited him after the MacDonnell meeting. 'I am afraid,' he wrote, 'differing as we unfortunately indeed do upon questions of national policy, nothing could be gained by discussions which could lead to nothing except irritating differences as to our points of view.'[2] Dillon, for his part, regarded O'Brien's evident enthusiasm for the Conference policy with deepening suspicion, and recorded in his diary that the public expression of this enthusiasm (in a letter to the Press) showed 'a most unjust and contentious frame of mind'. 'Every day', he noted shortly afterwards, 'I grow more strongly convinced that the Conference and its result was a mortal blunder.'[3]

For the time being, however, he held his hand. True, at a party meeting in London just before he left for Egypt he tried, according to O'Brien's admittedly hostile testimony, to argue that the Irish amendment to the Address which was to be moved a few days later should include no reference to the work of the Land Conference, but since he got no support for this suggestion he did not press it and resumed his convalescence immediately afterwards.[4] For the next two months he was out of reach and to a large extent out of touch, though perhaps it is significant that his most regular correspondent seems to have been Michael Davitt. Davitt's own distrust of the Conference policy was intensifying, but it was not until Wyndham introduced his long-awaited Bill in March that he had anything substantial to go upon. Compared with all previous attempts to solve the intractable land question, this was daring, generous and ingenious. In the barest outline his proposals envisaged that landlords should be encouraged to sell estates—not just individual holdings—and that proceedings for sale could be begun if three-quarters of the tenants involved were acquiescent. The prices to be paid would range from $18\frac{1}{2}$ years' purchase up to $24\frac{1}{2}$ years' purchase on first-term rents (that is, rents settled by the Land Courts under the Act of 1881) or from $21\frac{1}{2}$ to $27\frac{2}{3}$ years' purchase on second-term rents. The money was to be advanced to the purchasers by the State and repaid over $68\frac{1}{2}$ years by annuities at the rate of $3\frac{1}{4}$ per cent.[5] In order to stimulate sales the landlord was to receive a bonus which, however, was to be paid

[1] Ibid., 9 Feb. 1903.
[2] W. O'Brien to Dillon, 7 Feb. 1903 (D.P.).
[3] Diary of John Dillon, 9 and 12 Feb. 1903 (D.P.).
[4] W. O'Brien, *Olive branch*, pp. 208–13.
[5] J. E. Pomfret, *The struggle for land in Ireland* (Princeton, 1930), pp. 291–6.

for out of Irish revenues. This particular provision aroused nationalist resentment from the outset, but there were also some other features of the scheme which even its supporters disliked. They considered, for example, that the higher maxima (24½ years' purchase on first-term rents and 27½ years' purchase on second-term rents) were excessive. And they were even more incensed by the complicated 'zoning system', whereby the amount the tenant was to repay each year was fixed within certain 'price zones', i.e. 10 to 30 per cent less on first-term rents and 20 to 40 per cent less on second-term rents than the rent he would actually have been paying to his landlord if the estate had not been sold. Their contention was that under a system of free bargaining rents would fall lower than the reductions scheduled in the zones, and that if this were to happen under normal conditions the end result would be that the purchase price (x years multiplied by the lower rental) would itself be diminished. In short, they argued that the zone system could only serve to perpetuate a high average purchase-price. It was not surprising that Davitt, who had gone to London specially to watch the debate, was able to report with some satisfaction to Dillon that O'Brien had been much cast down, muttering that it might be necessary to reject the Bill. Davitt, who was always fascinated by the variations of O'Brien's mercurial temperament, suggested that this would be dangerous without making a big effort to improve it. 'He eagerly agreed and he went away.'[1]

Whether or not the Bill could be improved, or even supported, depended upon the verdict of an important National Convention of the United Irish League, to be held in Dublin in April. For Redmond and O'Brien, indeed for the whole Conference policy, it was a critical moment. Davitt was known to be hostile and it was difficult to know whether his presence at, or absence from, the Convention would be more damaging. Even worse, because of its wide influence, was the raking fire the *Freeman's Journal* had been directing against the Bill since its introduction. Sexton maintained not only that it gave too much to the landlords, but also—with a prescience time was to justify to the full—that the financial clauses were unsound and probably unworkable. As it turned out, however, Redmond and O'Brien were able to keep the Convention on an even keel and, despite some anxious moments, they secured solid endorsement for the line so far followed by the party. Davitt did after all attend—there ought to be someone there to suggest amendments, he told Dillon—but he did not create open dissension and, in fact, amendments came thick and fast.[2] Provided the party could persuade Wyndham to accept some of the more important of these, the measure might have a smooth enough passage.

Such was the situation when Dillon returned home at the end of April. While in Egypt he had met Wilfred Scawen Blunt and told him of his misgivings about the co-operative mood of the Irish party which, he said, would lead people to suspect some secret understanding between Wyndham and Redmond.[3] This suspicion that the new-found friendliness between the

[1] Davitt to Dillon, 29 Mar. 1903 (Davitt Papers).
[2] Ibid., Davitt to Dillon, 4 Apr. 1903.   [3] W. S. Blunt, *My diaries*, p. 458 (23 Mar. 1903).

Irish party and the Chief Secretary had some unsavoury foundation in fact was deepened by the first letter he had from Davitt on his return, which warned him that O'Brien and Wyndham had come to an understanding through the good offices of Lord Dunraven and that this would be concealed from Dillon. '*You ought to keep a free hand as far as you possibly can, and not fall in with whatever arrangement is made behind the scenes unless you are taken into Redmond's confidence in these matters and you find that honest things are going to be done.*'[1] Davitt was not far wrong about there being an understanding, but he had got the *dramatis personae* mixed. It was Redmond rather than O'Brien who was in contact with Wyndham and, ironically enough, the means of contact was provided by none other than Wilfred Scawen Blunt, to whom Dillon had just confided his doubts about secret diplomacy. Indeed, during the early days of April—before the Convention—Blunt acted as a kind of post office whereby Redmond conveyed privately to Wyndham his projected amendments and Wyndham sent back an indication of how far he would be prepared to accept them.[2] And it was Blunt also to whom Redmond confided the difficulties he expected to have with Dillon. Even before the latter had come back Redmond had been apprehensive that he would join forces with Davitt and Sexton and so create a powerful combination against the Bill. And when Dillon had returned Redmond reported at once that he was 'very much opposed' to it. 'He does not want a reconciliation with the landlords', Blunt recorded Redmond as saying, 'or anything less than their being driven out of Ireland.' On the other hand, he would not, Redmond thought, do anything 'shabby' in opposing the Bill.[3]

It is against this background of uncertainty and suspicion that Dillon's speech on the second reading of the Land Bill must be seen. That speech, which was his first public pronouncement on the measure, was one of the most critical and difficult of his career, for he had to steer a course between two alternatives, either of which would be disastrous. On the one hand, he could scarcely oppose the Bill outright—especially since it had been endorsed by the National Convention—without risking a serious split in the party and possibly jeopardising the whole reform. On the other hand, given his deep-seated and notorious views about landlords, he could not restrain his criticisms without being false to his friends and to his own deepest instincts. He began, cautiously enough, with an historical survey. This was, he said, the forty-first Irish Land Bill to be introduced into the house in forty years. Of all those measures the only one he regarded as an unmitigated success was the Ashborne Act of 1885, and even it owed its virtues to the fact that the Government of the day had taken advice from the Irish party. But he had also—and this marks the distance he himself had travelled in twenty years—something to say in favour of the Land Act of 1881 which Lord Dunraven (the chairman of the Land Conference) had recently described as having caused the demoralisation of the Irish people:

---

[1] Davitt to Dillon, 29 Apr. 1903 (Davitt Papers).   [2] Blunt, *My diaries*, pp. 459–66.
[3] Ibid., pp. 464–5 (25 and 30 Apr. 1903).

What a travesty of the truth [cried Dillon]. The act of 1881 had demoralised the people of Ireland! One would suppose . . . that
Ireland was a paradise of peace and of social and industrial prosperity
before the passing of that act. It was a hell; and I say that the act of
1881 was the first step taken in the emancipation of our people, who
before that act was passed were nothing but serfs. It is from the act
of 1881 that dates the emancipation of our country from agrarian
crime, and if today a considerable section of Irish landlords has
happily attained to a more reasonable frame of mind it is due in large
measure to twenty years' experience of that act.

This outburst was intended no doubt to make it clear that Dillon at
least did not feel himself bound by the events of the past few months to
treat Irish landlords (especially Conference landlords) with kid gloves, but
it also served to lead up to a statement which defined in two sentences the
gulf now opening between him and his old friend William O'Brien. The
success of the Land Conference had kindled O'Brien's imagination and he
was at this very moment well on the way to convince himself that what he
came to call 'conference plus business' was the key to Irish politics in the
future. It was, in its way, a noble conception, but it involved the danger that
the nationalist movement might be slowed down, or even diverted from its
fundamental aims by co-operation with those who, by definition, were
pledged to the maintenance of the Union. For Dillon the danger far out-
weighed the possible advantages. It was a point he was to make brutally
clear during the months ahead, but in the debate he confined himself to
relating it to land purchase. 'After all', he asked, 'where did the policy of
land purchase as the only and final settlement of the land question really
take its origin? It took its origin from the Land League.' The implication
was unmistakable—the revolution in land policy owed its success not to
conference and conciliation but to sustained pressure and agitation.

From this he turned to the, for him, delicate ground of the National
Convention, which he described as 'an absolutely authoritative expression
of the will and opinion of the Irish people in regard to this Bill'. This, however, did not prevent him from planting his banderillas with exquisite skill.
Taking into account, he said, the fact that the Convention had been
summoned by an organisation 'the foremost plank in the platform of
which was the application of compulsion', and also the fact that they had
been called upon to examine a Bill 'which appeared to many of the
delegates to contemplate an extreme price being paid for the land', it
would have been 'not unnatural' to expect strong language and strong
resolutions from the Convention. Instead, he continued with an irony that
must have seemed almost palpable to some of his hearers, he had been
impressed 'by the sobriety and conciliatory manner of the Convention'.
Even so, the sense of that body had been that the Bill could not, as it stood,
be accepted as a settlement of the land question. 'The principle and objects
of the Bill had the warmest sympathy of the Convention, and, without
waiving their views as to the possible necessity of compulsion, the members

of the Convention evidently were determined to give credit to the Government for their honest intentions and for a genuine desire for peace.' But for this very reason, he urged, the government must recognise that the amendments emanating from the Convention 'honestly represent the minimum of the popular demand'. He did not himself take the amendments in detail, but simply indicated where improvements seemed to him most obviously necessary—the maximum limit for rent reductions must go, the concept of a minimum price for farms must be abandoned, the prices envisaged in the Bill were certainly too high, future tenants and rural labourers should be looked after, the evicted tenants ought to be restored, the grazing ranches were to be broken up and the powers of the Congested Districts Board reinforced. 'The object of the Congested Districts Board is good,' he said, 'but if you pass the Bill in its present state the people of Connaught will be driven back again to commence agitation.'

He ended by confessing that in the short time he had been abroad the whole situation had changed so much 'that when I came home I sometimes asked myself whether, like an historic character, I had not been asleep for a century, and I wondered whether we had not reached the year 2000. To complete my bewilderment I found myself described by the Chief Secretary for Ireland as belonging to a chivalrous nation, the members of which are chiefly characterised by their ardent desire to pay their debts.' Again, the irony was unmistakable, for there was no Irish politician living who less resembled Rip van Winkle than Dillon. However, he ended on a constructive note, with an appeal 'to my Radical friends' not to oppose the Bill, but to help the Irish Members to obtain those amendments 'which will make it a real benefit and the means of restoring peace to Ireland'.[1]

As a feat of political balancing this speech must rank among the great achievements of his career. Within the space of about half an hour he had preserved his own integrity by restating the case against landlordism, had drawn attention to the deficiencies of the Bill, had reminded Irishmen at home that the resolutions of the Convention were not the last word on the subject, and yet, despite this steady undertone of criticism, had made it clear that in his view the measure, suitably amended, should be allowed to pass. But it cost him a great deal even to go as far as this and in private conversation with Blunt next day he revealed his true motives for speaking as he had done:

> He spoke last night in support of the bill [recorded Blunt] but he tells me that but for loyalty to his party he should be inclined to oppose it in committee and vote against it on the third reading. His view is that it is useless trying to get the landlord class on the side of nationalism, that they would always betray it when the pinch came, that the land trouble is a weapon in nationalist hands, and that to settle it finally would be to risk Home Rule, which otherwise *must* come. For this reason he was opposed to the Conference with the landlords, and

[1] Hansard, H.C. Debates, 4th series, vol. 121, cols. 1300–13.

was opposed now in principle to the bill. He should, however, of course support it, since it had been decided to do so, for the one thing in Ireland was union in the parliamentary party.[1]

Within the parliamentary party, it is fair to say, he was almost alone at this time in taking so extreme a view of the dangers implicit in the Conference policy. But as it was not the first time he had found himself isolated in an unpopular position, so it was not the first time that he bowed to the majority decision and rigorously abstained from wrecking tactics. By 7 May the Bill had passed its second reading by 443 votes to twenty-six, a personal triumph for Wyndham. Broodingly, Dillon watched the Irish reaction closely, noting with perhaps exaggerated alarm that the Lord Lieutenant had just had a very favourable reception in the west. 'This is a further striking illustration', he noted, 'of the deep laid plot to capture Ireland out of the hands of the national party which has been developing for the past few years, and especially during [the] last eight months.'[2] In this mood he might have been better out of the House altogether; his wife certainly thought so, though it was his health rather than his politics that worried her. On 17 May, swallowing her distaste, she wrote to Redmond (whom she could never bring herself to like), explaining that both she and Dillon's doctor were anxious about his health, because he had really returned from Egypt too soon. He was quite unfit for work and should not be allowed to take part in the committee stage of the Bill. 'He is, himself, naturally anxious to take his part and I do not think he likes to admit to himself that he is not equal to the strain.'[3] Redmond probably wished nothing better than that Dillon should retire again to Egypt—or even to Ballaghaderrin —but, in fact, Elizabeth's plea came too late, for her husband was already bombarding his chairman with suggestions about the committee stage and warning him very plainly to mind how he comported himself with the landlords:

> . . . I feel I ought to say to you [he wrote] that I am very uneasy about your having any deal with the landlords' representatives on these amendments. It is not conceivable to me that they will make any concession on points touching their own interests without demanding from you some *quid pro quo*, either in the shape of some concession in regard to our amendments or, what would be even worse, some understanding from you as chairman of the national organisation which would limit the freedom of the organisation in its attitude towards the working of the act in the future.[4]

The unfortunate Redmond was in a difficult position. His chief ally, O'Brien, although he spoke on the second reading, was looking wretchedly ill and at the very moment when Mrs. Dillon was urging the chairman to send her husband away Dillon was suggesting that he send O'Brien to the

---

[1] Blunt, *My diaries*, p. 468 (5 May 1903).
[2] Diary of John Dillon, 15 May 1903 (D.P.).
[3] Elizabeth Dillon to Redmond, 17 May (1903) (Redmond Papers).
[4] Dillon to Redmond, 13 May 1903, copy in Dillon's hand (D.P.).

South of France. 'I would write to him myself, but just at present I have no influence with him in any respect, on account of my invincible heresy on the Land Conference.'[1] Redmond replied as reassuringly as he could—Dillon could be perfectly easy in his mind that there would be no secret bargains.[2] Whereupon Dillon again pressed his suggested amendments, but with the saving clause that if he found himself in a minority, 'I shall either keep silent on the subject or content myself with stating my view and saying at the same time that I am in a minority and therefore will make no attempt to press my view on the House.'[3]

This bargain he faithfully kept and the committee stage, though hard fought, did not in any sense jeopardise the Bill. Most of the controversy, reflecting a hardening of opinion in Ireland, centred round the price zones. The Nationalists wanted them abolished, but Wyndham would not accept this, nor would he raise the maximum limit of reduction, though he did agree to exempt non-judicial tenancies (farms where rents had not been fixed by the Land Courts) and in other ways to increase the range of exceptions to the zones. The fiercest arguments came in mid-June. Thereafter, things ran more smoothly and by 21 July, the third reading had been passed. The Bill was only modified in minor ways by the House of Lords and by the middle of August it had become law. Almost immediately land purchase was enormously accelerated. Up to 1903 a total of nearly £20 million had been advanced for the purchase of 2½ million acres. Under the Act of 1903, and the consequential Act of 1909, the position was completely transformed. When in March 1920, the Estates Commioners looked back over the years they found that these two acts had led to a total of £83 million pounds being advanced (another million was put down by purchasers in cash payments), while sales totalling £24 million were pending; in that same period nearly 9 million acres had been transferred and another 2 million acres was in process of being sold. Indeed, the Act may almost be said to have been too great a success in that the sudden rush of landlords to sell and of tenants to pay created serious financial difficulties which, as we shall see, brought on a fresh crisis in 1909.[4]

(vi)

But although the Act did result in vastly extended sales—and to that extent deserves its revolutionary reputation—informed opinion in Ireland had already, even before it had begun to operate, done much to create a climate of disillusionment. Few readers of the *Freeman's Journal*, no doubt, were able to follow the financial intricacies in which Sexton delighted, but when

---

[1] Ibid.
[2] Redmond to Dillon, 14 May 1903 (D.P.).
[3] Dillon to Redmond, 23 May 1903 (R.P.).
[4] *Irish Land Acts, 1903–1909. Report of the Estates Commissioners for the year from 1 Apr. 1919 to 31 Mar. 1920 and for the period from 1 Nov. 1903 to 31 Mar. 1920*, H.C. 1921 [Cmd. 1150], xiv, 663–6.

they were told over and over again that the Act was a landlord's victory and
that they were being asked to pay too much for the land which was rightfully
theirs, it was only human nature that they should begin to regard the whole
policy of conference and conciliation as in some manner—which was felt
rather than comprehended—a threat to the full national demand. And
indeed it was this, rather than the details of the Wyndham Act, that lay at
the root of the quarrel which was fast developing between O'Brien on the
one hand and Dillon, Davitt and Sexton on the other. The issue was really
this—could any self-respecting national movement co-operate on a broad
front with a minority who, although also Irishmen, were so much separated in
interest, background and political allegiance from their fellow countrymen?
O'Brien said 'yes', and looked to the Land Conference as the precursor
of a more extended and fundamental partnership between nationalists
and Unionists. Dillon, and those who thought like him, maintained that
the differences were too great to be bridged by conferences and that the
national demand would only be fulfilled in the future, as it had been in the
past, by unrelenting pressure and organisation. Thus emerged the strange
paradox that although three years earlier O'Brien had been in the van of
agitation and had created the United Irish League to carry on the war
against the landlords, now it was Dillon, formerly sceptical, who was zealous
for the League, and O'Brien, at one time so fanatical, who was all for the
lion lying down with the lamb.

This divergence, which in a few short weeks was to turn the two old and
once intimate friends into mortal enemies, came to a head in the autumn of
1903. Within a fortnight of the Land Act becoming law Dillon went down to
his constituency, where he delivered at Swinford a speech which the *Freeman's Journal* described as 'the keynote of the autumn campaign'. He spoke
mainly of the new Act, and though he conceded it had certain good points
and promised he would give it a fair trial, he reiterated the view, already hammered home by the *Freeman's Journal*, that the landlords were getting an in-
flated price for their land. But what he was most concerned with, and what
precipitated the clash with O'Brien, was the whole policy of which the Act
was a symbolic gesture and upon which he then delivered a slashing attack:

> We hear a great deal about conciliation. To the amazement of some
> of us old campaigners, we hear Irish landlords talking of conciliation,
> and of intention to go into conferences with the leaders of the Irish
> party. That is the new feature, and some men are asked to believe it
> is due to what the Methodists describe as a new birth or infusion of
> grace into the landlord party. I don't believe a word of it, I believe the
> origin and source of it was the fact that the landlords of Ireland
> were behind the scenes, and they knew that the whole policy of coer-
> cion was going to topple down about their ears . . . When the land-
> lords talk of conciliation, what do they want? They want 25 years'
> purchase of their land . . . for my part . . . I am so far sceptical
> that I have no faith in the doctrine of conciliation.[1]

[1] *F.J.*, 26 Aug. 1903.

This was clear warning that the Wyndham Act was not going to have an easy passage in Ireland, and as a declaration of policy it was the more serious since a meeting of the National Directory of the United Irish League was due to be held on 8 September precisely for the purpose of advising the farmers how to get the best out of the new situation. For some inscrutable reason, which has never been satisfactorily explained, Dillon, up to two days before the meeting, received no notice of it, nor any letter from Redmond or O'Brien to explain what was to be decided at the Directory, though, as he noted in his diary, he was well aware that the programme had been in Redmond's hands for at least a week. He had been in two minds whether or not to go even before he had in a measure burnt his boats at Swinford, but this neglect helped to decide him finally against attending, even though he was in Dublin on the day the meeting was held.[1]

If he had gone, of course, he would almost certainly have run head-on into collision with William O'Brien on the whole question of conciliation. And on this subject Dillon's suspicions were sharper than ever, since he had just received a letter from Captain Shawe-Taylor canvassing the possibility of another conference, this time with the aim of reaching an agreed settlement of the university question. It is significant that Dillon showed this letter in the first instance to Sexton, who, characteristically, advised him to return 'a procrastinating answer', but at the same time told him that if there was to be a conference he ought to be in it.[2] While Dillon was conferring with Sexton the Directory meeting was actually in progress. That body was still sufficiently under O'Brien's spell to pass various resolutions approving the recent legislation, but it did throw out the suggestion that tenants were not to offer more for their land than 'the substantial equivalent of prices under the Ashbourne Act', in effect an average of twenty years' purchase.[3] At the same time, according to O'Brien's own account, the Directory laid plans (for obvious reasons, in private) to test the Wyndham Act by summoning conventions in each county, to be presided over by M.P.s, which, after a public meeting, would secretly choose test cases in the light of local knowledge. The intention was that the mass of tenants should hold aloof until it was seen whether the Act could produce rapid and reasonable sales on these test estates.[4] The scheme recalls the device suggested by Parnell after the Act of 1881 had been passed and it suffered from the same defect— that once the farmers had become possessed by the idea that the new legislation offered them a worthwhile bargain, no power on earth could prevent them rushing in to take advantage of it.

In his memoirs, while he was naturally concerned to make the best case

[1] Diary of John Dillon, 6 Sept. 1903 (D.P.). Redmond and O'Brien seem to have taken the line that after the Swinford speech he would not want to be involved in the Directory's proceedings (O'Brien, *Olive branch*, pp. 257–8).

[2] Ibid., 8 Sept. 1903; later that month Shawe-Taylor published a letter proposing a further conference on the university question (*F.J.* 25 Sept. 1903).

[3] For an analysis of conditions prevailing under the Ashbourne Act of 1885, see Pomfret, op. cit., pp. 228–31; the public proceedings of the Directory are in *F.J.*, 9 Sept. 1903.

[4] W. O'Brien, *Olive branch*, pp. 260–3.

he could for his own actions, O'Brien undoubtedly overemphasised the enthusiasm of the Directory for the Act. Equally, he underestimated the opposition in some quarters, especially the *Freeman's Journal*, and was wrong to dismiss it as that of a factious minority. So far as the Wyndham Act itself was concerned, it is probably true that most farmers in the first flush of enthusiasm were dazzled by the undeniable fact that purchase was at last an actuality and did not give as much attention as they should have done to the price they were paying or the burden of debt they were assuming. But this did not mean that they all at once jumped to the conclusion that the golden age had come round again, or that they accepted the further implications of O'Brien's policy of conference plus business—one step enough for them, provided that step made them the owners of their holdings. It follows, therefore, that public debate and criticism, as it was carried on in the *Freeman's Journal*, had a valuable, indeed necessary, part to play in the country's political education. O'Brien was utterly unable to grasp this. Always prone to interpret coolness towards his enthusiasm of the moment as *lèse-majesté*, on this occasion, as on others, he overreached himself. Before the Directory met at all, he tried to persuade Redmond to lay before it a resolution calling upon the national Press for 'loyal and cordial support of the policy of the national leadership'. Redmond, as even O'Brien admits, was 'staggered' at the suggestion and refused absolutely to adopt it.[1] Well he might, for any such manoeuvre would certainly have raised an outcry that the Press was being subjected to intolerable interference. But that O'Brien should have pushed as hard for this resolution as he did was an alarming index of his frame of mind, about which Dillon was receiving independent evidence, equally disturbing, just at this time. On 14 September, for example, Joseph Devlin (a rising Belfast nationalist who owed much to Dillon and was to repay much) wrote complaining of O'Brien's intolerance towards his critics, and Davitt, to whom the letter was sent for his comment, returned it with a diatribe which, though exaggerated, showed the bitterness that lay below the surface:

> You are right in thinking [he wrote] I believe the constitutional movement—that which has struggled through the treacheries and tensions of the past twenty-five years—is dead. It died in the Mansion House, Dublin, poisoned by O'Brien with a big dose of Dunravenism. I believe it is beyond your power to revive it, because the best proof of its demise is the position *you* now hold in it; you who have been its most loyal leader among all the men who followed Parnell. O'Brien would be delighted to see you driven out, and this being so, how are you with your broken health going to resist the policy which has already (in my view) knifed the movement. There is no man in the party to stand up to O'B. but you, not one. No-one out of the party will fight him but your humble servant, and I no longer wish to do this to save a movement which he has with Redmond's aid, killed in its truly national character and purpose.[2]

[1] Ibid., p. 264.
[2] Davitt to Dillon, 'Wednesday', probably 15 Sept. 1903 (Davitt Papers).

Davitt put the case with characteristic vehemence. Dillon did not go so far, but he was perfectly well aware of the danger in which he stood. And it was entirely typical of him that so far from throwing up the sponge, as Davitt's letter seemed almost to suggest, he chose instead to carry the war into the enemy's camp. His first step was to write a warning letter to Redmond at the beginning of October that Shawe-Taylor had just called on him to renew pressure for a conference on the university question. 'I, as you know, have all along been opposed to the policy of allowing the initiative on, and the direction of, large Irish questions to be taken out of the hands of the Irish party and handed over to conferences summoned by outsiders.' This was unpromising enough, but worse still was the intimation that Redmond's failure to show him the resolutions to be put to the Directory the previous month had seriously affected their political relations. 'While I shall, of course, as long as I remain a member of the party, abide by party discipline and accept the decision of the majority,' Dillon bleakly concluded, 'I cannot now accept the same share of responsibility for the policy of the party as I was glad to do up to December last.'[1]

To refuse responsibility was a merely negative reaction. But Dillon's other manoeuvre in this critical autumn was much more positive. Three weeks after writing that letter to Redmond he presided at the East Mayo Convention at Swinford. This was one of those summoned by the National Directory of the League to plan the testing of the act. Dillon used the occasion not only to reiterate the arguments made familiar by the *Freeman's Journal*—that the grant of a bonus to the landlord on each sale, plus the fact that he was being paid in cash rather than in depreciated land stock, meant that several years' purchase was in effect being added to his nominal price—but also to launch a deliberate and powerful attack upon the conference policy. He did this partly by attacking one of the conference landlords individually—Talbot Crosbie, who was alleged to have said that if he did not receive twenty-six years' purchase he could not afford to live in Ireland. 'They are welcome to stay if they like; but I deny that one single, suffering tenant should be called upon . . . to pay one single half-year's rent more to keep the landlords in this country.' But much more devastating than this, and what must—one cannot doubt—have brought the final break with O'Brien very close indeed, was the peroration of his speech in which, with passion and prescience, he warned his fellow countrymen of the dangers of conciliation:

> Some people [he said] believe . . . that all the obstacles in the path of Irish freedom are now levelled . . . that all that remains for us to do is to clasp hands in affectionate friendship with Lord Dunraven, Lord Mayo, and Mr. Talbot-Crosbie and co., and advance more or

[1] Dillon to Redmond, 2 Oct. 1903, cited in O'Brien, *Olive branch*, p. 258 n. Up to the time of writing I have been unable to trace the original of this in either the Redmond or the O'Brien Papers, though the former are still in process of being catalogued and it may yet turn up there. Although O'Brien was using the letter to demonstrate what, from his point of view, was Dillon's wrecking policy, there is no reason to doubt its authenticity. Alike in style, tone and content, it reflects very faithfully the Dillon of 1903.

less under their inspiration along the smooth and easy and short road
to that goal of Irish freedom for which we have so long and so
arduously struggled. I wish I could share that view . . . but I do not
believe it . . . And I say, beware of doctrines of conciliation which
may drive out of our ranks those young men who, although they
may, perhaps, in my old and colder blood and colder imagination,
be mistaken in [their belief in] the possibility of force, are the salt of
any movement they come into, because they are ready for sacrifice,
and I say, therefore, that in my opinion until our foot is firmly planted
on the last rung of that ladder in the effort to mount which so many
have fallen, until we have again the flag of liberty flying over the capital of our country, let us maintain the perennial tradition of struggle
and of fight so that we may rally round us when our necessity arises
the fighting young blood of the country.[1]

The lines of conflict were thus being clearly and inexorably drawn.
From O'Brien's point of view, Dillon was wantonly attacking a policy
which had been approved by the party and the League and which had already begun to produce solid advantages for the country. To Dillon, on the
other hand, no amount of benevolent legislation, no amount of co-operation with Irish Unionists, could justify any weakening of the national demand, and weakening he was convinced there would be if Nationalists
laid down their arms to fraternise with their hereditary enemies.

Why, then, it may be asked, if the difference between the two men was so
crucial, did not O'Brien, who had up to this held the initiative, use his
influence to crush the opposition of Dillon, Davitt and the *Freeman's
Journal*? The short answer is that he tried to do just this and he failed.
Despite repeated complaints to Redmond, he could not get the chairman
to move. O'Brien, in his spleen, subsequently ascribed Redmond's reluctance to the fact that in that same month of October 1903 the newspapers
had published a report that an estate Redmond had inherited from his
uncle had been sold *above* the price envisaged by the Land Conference as a
norm. This report was at once denied—its falsity has been demonstrated
by Redmond's biographer—but it is possible that for a time it may have
caused him some embarrassment.[2] There were, however, far stronger reasons for his inaction. It was all very well for O'Brien to dismiss the opposition as factious, but no leader in his senses could ignore the weight of
opinion represented by Dillon, Sexton and Davitt—all veterans of the Land
War and all deeply respected in the country. Again, on the purely personal
issue, Redmond must have known very well that while Dillon would always be a tower of strength in the party and in Parliament, O'Brien would
never be. And finally, the Irish crisis has to be seen against the broader
background of great events in England—Chamberlain's campaign for
Tariff Reform, the highly critical report of the Royal Commission on the
conduct of the South African War, and the growing conviction everywhere

---

[1] *F.J.*, 21 Oct. 1903.
[2] W. O'Brien, *Olive branch*, chap. xiv; D. R. Gwynn, *Life of John Redmond*, pp.
103–4.

that the Government had not long to live. This political uncertainty was of necessity reflected in Ireland. There, George Wyndham had been hoping against hope that he might be able to attempt a settlement of the university question, but by the middle of November he was in despair at the difficulty of governing Ireland.[1] If the Chief Secretary could not see his way, then the leader of the Irish party might be excused for not sharing O'Brien's passion for conciliation. Indeed, if a general election were really as near as people thought, it was extremely important that Redmond should be free to bring pressure to bear on the Liberals to take up again the Gladstonian policy of Home Rule. Coquetting with Irish Unionists would not help him to convince English Liberals that he was in earnest.

In this situation, with Dillon on the warpath, Redmond holding back, the Chief Secretary discouraged, and O'Brien still pressing for more and yet more of the conciliation policy, something, somewhere, had to give. And quite suddenly it did. On 4 November O'Brien wrote to his constituents explaining that as he was making no headway with his policy he was resigning his seat in Parliament, and his position on the Directory of the League, and was also ceasing publication of his newspaper, the *Irish People*. On the morning of 6 November the news was in all the papers and the party leaders, only three years after their reunion, were face to face with another split.[2]

Their immediate reaction was to try at all costs to minimise the shock to the public. Redmond was naturally very perturbed, since this totally unexpected *démarche* deprived him at one blow of his favourite position of balance. O'Brien, he explained to Dillon, had given him no warning until 5 November, and had written then only to say he had sent his resignation to the Press. 'I feel sure he has taken this action because he and I differed as to the *Freeman*, I objecting to attack it. His resignation is, of course, a very serious thing and will have very serious consequences in the country.' He suggested that a meeting of the party, and possibly also of the Directory, should be called to express regret and to invite him to reconsider. 'I have no belief', he added revealingly, 'that such a resolution would have any effect on O'Brien. I am not thinking of that, but of the steadying effect upon the mind of the country of such a meeting and of the proof it would afford of our continued solidarity.'[3]

Dillon, who was in London when the blow fell, agreed that O'Brien's resignation was 'a *very* serious thing', and bound to have a bad effect on the country. As to Redmond's proposal for meetings of the party and the Directory, he was not so sure. There was a real danger that such meetings would lead to angry debates about personalities and so leave matters even worse than before.[4] However, the next day Davitt wrote urging him to accept Redmond's suggestion, at least to the extent of attending a party

---

[1] Mackail and Wyndham, *Life and letters of George Wyndham*, ii. 472–3.
[2] W. O'Brien, *Olive branch*, pp. 289–90.
[3] Redmond to Dillon, 6 Nov. 1903 (D.P.).
[4] Dillon to Redmond, 7 Nov. 1903 (Redmond Papers).

meeting. 'At a meeting of the parliamentary party R. and yourself would control the action to be taken, while the fact that he and you were together on the question of O'Brien's return and on the *general* policy of the party would steady the country.'[1] Dillon decided to accept this advice and on 9 November wrote to Redmond that he would attend both meetings, if he could be assured that only a resolution regretting O'Brien's resignation and asking him to reconsider it would be proposed. If, he added darkly, he did not get this assurance he would consider himself at liberty either to attend or to stay away.[2] What he was really afraid of, so William Redmond reported to his brother, was that O'Brien's friends might launch an all-out attack on the opponents of his policy, which would almost certainly be disastrous to the unity of the party.[3]

Redmond, of course, could not give the sort of categorical guarantees that Dillon wanted, though his own prognostication was that there would be no recriminations or angry scenes—therefore, he wrote again, Dillon must at least agree to the meetings being summoned.[4] And since Davitt also renewed his pressure—'as you are the only force in the party that can save it, it seems to me that you should show the country you are really desirous that O'B. should come back'—Dillon at last agreed to go, though still reserving his freedom of action if wide-ranging discussion (he meant about the conference policy) was allowed at the meetings.[5] Redmond accordingly went ahead with the arrangements, though further broadsides from O'Brien in the Press on 12 November greatly increased his difficulties. Davitt, especially, was highly incensed and Dillon had hard work to hold him in. 'Of course,' he wrote bitterly to Dillon, 'there is no chance now of this gentleman being induced to reconsider his action, unless Sexton hands him over the *Freeman*, and you and I take a plunge into Dublin Bay.'[6] A few days later he was still boiling with rage, mingled with deep depression at his own parlous financial situation. Davitt had always lived close to the margin and latterly, having been entirely absorbed in his book, *The fall of feudalism in Ireland*, now nearing its end, his earning power had fallen off. His wife and he had agreed—so he told Dillon—to move to America, as there was no prospect of earning a living in Ireland, though to Dillon this despondency seemed really a reflection of his 'disgust and despair' at the political crisis, and he could not refrain from an acid comment: 'This is Davitt's contribution to [the] situation now that some have mustered up courage to act.' However, he persuaded him not to rush into print without consulting him, and even got him to promise not to attack either O'Brien or Redmond in the final chapter of his book.[7]

[1] Davitt to Dillon, 8 Nov. 1903 (D.P.).
[3] Dillon to Redmond, 9 Nov. 1903 (Redmond Papers).
[3] Ibid., William Redmond to John Redmond, 'Monday' (9 Nov. 1903).
[4] Redmond to Dillon, 10 Nov. 1903 (D.P.).
[5] Davitt to Dillon, 10 Nov. 1903 (D.P.); copy of telegram, Dillon to Redmond, 11 Nov. 1903 (D.P.).
[6] Davitt to Dillon, 12 Nov. 1903 (D.P.).
[7] Diary of John Dillon, 18 Nov. 1903, recording a conversation on November 16 (D.P.).

The next day—7 November—Redmond himself called and Dillon at last heard from him something of the circumstances of O'Brien's withdrawal. The latter, said Redmond, had constantly been pressing him to attack the *Freeman's Journal* for the line it was taking on the Wyndham Act, and had finally issued 'a kind of ultimatum' that if Redmond did not take issue with the *Freeman* and its abettors, O'Brien would have to consider his position. Redmond still maintained that it had never crossed his mind that by this he might mean resignation, and that O'Brien's action had taken him completely by surprise. Dillon asked him if he thought there was any hope that O'Brien could be induced to make peace. 'He said quite the contrary, that he had received a long and hysterical epistle from O'B., saying that he (O'B.) had taken the *only* step which would save the movement in view of R's refusal to come out against the *Freeman*.' Altogether, the interview left Dillon with the strong impression that Redmond was thoroughly disillusioned with O'Brien, with a further, and from Dillon's viewpoint gratifying, consequence. 'Redmond', he noted laconically, 'appears to [be] waking to the fact that conciliation policy is not a success.'[1]

If this was really so, and if the meetings of the party and the Directory did not lead to some unforeseen explosion, the end result of the crisis might even be beneficial. Dillon's main doubt concerned Davitt. He had some influence over him, but not enough to be quite sure he could stop him from becoming involved in public controversy which might sooner or later engulf them all. One way to keep him in check might have been to persuade him to come to the Directory meeting, but Davitt, whose own influence over Dillon had helped the latter to make up his mind to attend, refused flatly to go. 'An almost hopeless man to work with', Dillon recorded sadly. 'Certainly an Irish crowd is not an easy one to keep together.'[2] Nevertheless, when the party and the Directory did meet on 24 November, all went off peaceably—'far beyond my expectations', noted Dillon. Redmond had been 'as usual, admirable in the chair', and though Davitt had stayed away, he had allowed it to be known that he would not resign from the Directory.[3] All in all, things seemed to be shaping better than could have been hoped. Resolutions begging O'Brien to reconsider his position were passed, but his angry repudiation of these olive branches merely had the effect of isolating him still further. It is true that this was not immediately apparent and Dillon still believed, as he told Redmond, that his power for mischief remained 'enormous'.[4] Captain Donelan, one of the party whips, had shown him the original of O'Brien's reply to the peace offer and to Dillon's appalled eye it seemed 'the letter of a man full of fury against old colleagues and I should say determined to starve out and wreck the party in vengeance for their refusal to deal with his "assailants" '.[5]

However, there was nothing to be done but to ride out the storm and,

---

[1] Ibid., under same date.
[2] Ibid., 21 Nov. 1903.
[3] Ibid., 25 Nov. 1903; *F.J.*, 25 Nov. 1903.
[4] Dillon to Redmond, 26 Nov. 1903 (Redmond Papers).
[5] Diary of John Dillon, 26 Nov. 1903 (D.P.); O'Brien's letter is in *F.J.*, 27 Nov. 1903.

as the days passed without the heavens falling, it began more and more to seem only a storm in a teacup. Dillon and Redmond were soon able to shake off their anxieties about a counter-attack which never came, and turned to what were, after all, their two main tasks—to reassert their control over the movement, and to cast a critical eye at the Irish policy of the Government. So far as the first of these was concerned, Dillon very characteristically drew immediate profit from the crisis. O'Brien had attacked the *Freeman*, and in effect Dillon himself, for having frustrated his grand design. Though repudiating the grand design, Dillon recognised that the accusations against the *Freeman* were not without point. Just before Christmas he wrote to Redmond pointing out that the tenants, in deciding how to grapple with the Wyndham Act, had had to rely 'to a disastrous extent' upon the *Freeman* and the priests. As for the latter, some had done well for the tenants, and some for the landlords, but in either event they were, of course, outside the control of the party. The newspaper, however, was another matter. 'And while, as you know, I have all along been a warm admirer of the attitude and work of the *Freeman*, I think it is not a good thing for the party or the organisation that the people should be left to lean too absolutely on it for guidance'.[1] This was not a situation which could be remedied overnight, but remedied it eventually was, partly by more direct leadership from the public platform by Redmond and Dillon, and partly by more direct influence upon the editorial policy of the newspaper. In time the *Freeman* became again, what it had been in the past, the mouthpiece of the parliamentary party and of the United Irish League, just as the League itself, instead of assuming, as O'Brien had intended, a position separate from, and in some senses superior to, that of the party, fell increasingly under the domination of the parliamentary leaders. Neither the League, nor the *Freeman's Journal* had quite finished with O'Brien, nor he with them, but the control of Redmond and Dillon over both the organisation and the newspaper was never again to be seriously shaken so long as the constitutional movement lasted.

It was not, in the immediate aftermath of the crisis, so easy to see how pressure upon the Government was to be resumed. And in fact the session of 1904, so far as the Nationalists were concerned, was to be almost entirely barren. This was partly because for one reason or another their resources were drastically reduced. Of the leading figures, O'Brien had resigned. Blake was increasingly incapacitated by illness and coming towards the end of his service to the Irish cause, while Dillon, on medical orders, left for Italy in the New Year and was away for almost the entire session. This meant that the 'front bench', so to speak, was represented only by Redmond and T. P. O'Connor, the former described by the latter as 'shortsighted and living from hand to mouth politically', while O'Connor himself was deeply involved in journalism and, without Dillon at hand to guide him, excessively naïve in parliamentary matters, as he was indeed the first to admit.[2]

[1] Dillon to Redmond, 18 Dec. 1903 (Redmond Papers).
[2] T. P. O'Connor to Dillon, 19 Dec. 1903 (D.P.).

But the frustration of that year was not alone due to internal divisions and difficulties. It was at least as much the consequence of the political situation in England. It did not seem possible that Balfour could stay much longer in power—at the end of 1903 it would have been a bold man who would have prophesied that he would be there for two years more—and it was inevitable that Unionist policy in Ireland should lose its momentum. The Chief Secretary himself was harassed and increasingly out of humour with his office. Redmond wrote courteously to him at the beginning of the session that he intended to raise the question of the inefficiency of all the Irish governmental departments and much of the time spent on Irish business during the session consisted of just such wearisome and non-productive debates.[1] The idea of a University Bill, or even of a conference to prepare the way for one, had had to be incontinently dropped. Wyndham's other cherished reform, a Labourers Bill, which might have done something to meet one of Dillon's criticisms in the second reading of the Land Bill the previous session, ran into difficulties with his own party, and in March Wyndham was protesting angrily that the Irish landlords 'cannot combine the advantages of peace and war'.[2] But, despite his protestations, the Bill did not get beyond a second reading and it is not surprising that by May he had entered a phase of 'nausea at politics, nostalgia for poetry'. By the end of the session he was worn out and his private secretary counted him fortunate to have escaped a nervous breakdown. 'Artificial stimulants and bursts of violent physical exercise', his biographers discreetly observe, 'only ran up the overdraft.'[3] But payment in full was soon to be exacted, and before long the career of the author of the Wyndham Act was to lie, with the policy of conciliation, in irretrievable ruin.

[1] J. W. Mackail and G. Wyndham, *Life and letters of George Wyndham*, i. 90.
[2] Ibid., ii. 477–8.
[3] Ibid., i. 191; ii. 478.

9
A Short Happy Life

For most of his early career John Dillon had seemed an extreme example of the patriot so dedicated to the cause as to have crushed out of existence all the appetites and passions the flesh is heir to. There are signs, however, that this chastity was not achieved without effort. As a medical student he had, as his diaries indicate, endured—and resisted—temptation, and even as late as 1890, during his Australasian tour, when he had been immersed in politics for a dozen years, he could be deeply stirred by the sight of Maori girls diving naked for pennies thrown into a pool. 'The whole scene', he recorded, 'was so strange and gave rise in my mind to infinite thoughts which I wish I could give expression to. I can understand now better than before how these brown girls with their flashing black eyes could set men on fire.'[1] Nevertheless, such delights, he appears to have decided right from the beginning, were not for him. This was not because he was un-popular with women—quite the contrary, he suffered almost from an excess of admirers—but because he had made up his mind very early in his politi-cal life that devotion to Ireland must be set above private happiness. This bleak doctrine of political celibacy without doubt contributed to his recurring melancholy. Wilfrid Scawen Blunt, travelling to Cambridge with him in 1886, found him deep in one of his depressed moods and tried to cheer him up by telling him that he had never known what it was like to enjoy life till he was 40. 'Then there is hope for me', replied Dillon gloomily (he was then 35), 'for I have never enjoyed life.'[2]

There were, of course, good reasons why he should be anxious to avoid intimacy with women. First and most important was his precarious health; so long as the threat of tuberculosis hung over him he was unlikely to ask any girl to be his wife. But no less important a deterrent was the kind of life he led during the seventies and eighties. A man who spent such a large proportion of his time either agitating at home, travelling abroad, or in and out of prison, was hardly an ideal husband. Also, the fact that Dillon had little money of his own, and that his full-time commitment to politics was likely to prevent him from ever making any, was a further bar to marriage.

Yet no doubt there were many who would have been ready to take the risk. When he first entered public life, and indeed for a long time after-

[1] Diary of John Dillon, 15 Jan. 1890 (D.P.).
[2] W. S. Blunt, *The land war in Ireland*, p. 144.

wards, he was a striking figure. Tall, slender, olive-skinned, with black hair and beard and dark, burning eyes, he was undeniably handsome. The touch of extremism in his nature, his courage, his sincerity, his obvious compassion for the poor, the very fact that he belonged to a revolutionary tradition—these things made him at once conspicuous and desirable. And, such is human nature, his remoteness from human contacts, his dedication to politics, even the periodic rumours that the family curse of consumption was about to claim him—all increased rather than diminished his appeal.

He himself seems to have been genuinely unaware of the image of the romantic revolutionary he was creating, and continued on his solitary, fastidious and dedicated way until in 1886 he first met the girl who was to change his life. Elizabeth Mathew's family, as we have already seen, was Irish on her father's side and it was their custom to spend part of the judge's long vacation in Ireland. In the late summer and early autumn of 1886—when Dillon was about to launch the Plan of Campaign—they had rented Killiney Castle, not far from another house, Mount Mapas, where lived their friends, the Murrough O'Briens. Killiney, of course, was Dillon's own second home and he, too, knew the O'Briens very well. Nothing was more natural, therefore, than that Mrs. O'Brien should arrange for Elizabeth and 'our languid hero', as she rather deflatingly called him, to meet. It was settled, therefore, that he should come to luncheon at Mount Mapas on 9 October. The day before he was due to appear Elizabeth and her sister May were in 'desperate excitement'. 'Mr. Dillon's fame and *handsomeness*', Elizabeth noted apprehensively, 'make him interesting politics, and I believe that great numbers of young ladies are in love with him.'[1] Next day they met and Elizabeth—already, one suspects, quite ready to be carried away—was completely overwhelmed. There is a certain innocent abandonment in the picture she drew of him in her diary, but there are features in it one can recognise. Here is how she describes their first encounter:

> Well, he is the first person who has *awed* me. I feel quite equal to keeping up a conversation with all the bench of judges and any number of Lord Chancellors, but Mr. John Dillon made me feel what a poor, dull miserable thing I am after all. His appearance is very striking, but that is not the point on which I wish to dwell. There is a *je ne sais quoi* of earnestness and *majesty* about his whole demeanour the like of which I have never met. His manner is quite different to anyone else's; he evidently does not care a bit whether people are impressed with him or not, nor does he desire to make himself agreeable to them. He knows about everything, but does not start a conversation on anything; we did not refer to a single subject last night on which he could not give us the fullest information; who wrote a book, what opera a song came from, the climate of a foreign country, the different dialects of Italy, the peculiarities of American speech, the resources of the colonies, statistics of every kind; and

[1] Diary of Elizabeth Mathew, 8 Oct. 1886 (D.P.).

then at last he began to tell us about the evictions on the Clanricarde property and the history of the landlord oppression in that part of the country, and then his eyes glistened and his voice rose to that softly eloquent tone I have heard in the House, and we listened quite breathlessly; he had quite ceased to be 'languid' then.[1]

The next day he came to luncheon at Killiney Castle and this time was deep in conversation with her father, the judge, about prisons and prison sentences—subjects on which they were both, in their different ways, experts. Elizabeth could only listen to these exchanges and that night recorded despondently that 'Mr. Dillon, with all these charms that so attract ladies, seems to be anything but a "ladies' man". I doubt whether he can ever condescend to care for anyone, and as for the story of a broken heart I certainly don't believe it.'[2]

It would be easy to conclude from these passages that Elizabeth Mathew was simply a moon-struck, romantic girl who could only see her hero through a sentimental haze. But this would be far from the truth. Certainly, she never to her dying day ceased to regard John Dillon, in the phrase she used after her first meeting with him, as 'altogether remarkable and quite unlike ordinary beings', but there was nothing of the lovelorn maiden about her. When she met Dillon she had already passed her twenty-first birthday (she was born on 2 March 1865) and had mixed a great deal in society. Moreover, she was a highly educated woman in the Victorian mode. That is to say, she was well read in several languages, used to Continental travel, a frequent attender in the ladies' gallery in the House of Commons, and combined all this with a simple piety which expressed itself not only in regular attendance at Mass, but in wide-ranging charitable work. Thus, in her personal religion—to those who knew her, her most striking characteristic—in her interest in politics, and in her passion for literature and the arts, she had much in common with Dillon from the beginning.

Yet it was long before their acquaintance showed the least sign of blossoming into friendship, let alone anything deeper. That winter of 1886-7 he was completely preoccupied with the Plan of Campaign and when he did meet her once in the House of Commons he had apparently forgotten her completely.[3] She, however, followed his career with breathless interest and at dinner one evening found James Bryce, whose conversation was usually too encyclopaedic for her taste, quite charming, because on this occasion he was prepared to talk about Dillon, though not, of course, without the usual historical disquisitions. 'He told me', she wrote, 'much that was interesting about Mr. Mazzini, compared to Mr. Dillon, for instance, praising both highly as men not like the rest of mankind.'[4] This was in March, but it was not until July that Dillon paid his first visit to the Mathews' house, 46 Queen's Gate Gardens. She found him then 'most

[1] Ibid., 10 Oct. 1886.   [2] Ibid., 10 Oct. 1886.
[3] Ibid., 1 Mar. 1887, referring to a chance encounter on February 10.
[4] Ibid., 9 Mar. 1887.

gracious, confidential and friendly and *most* interesting', but still, obviously, immersed in the Plan of Campaign.[1] For this reason, although the Mathew family were again at Killiney in August and September, and discovered that Dillon, too, had rented a house there, they saw very little of him while they were in Ireland. Elizabeth, meeting him accidentally at Mass one morning, thought he looked 'dreadfully ill', but he told her there could be no letting up.[2] Not long after this came the horrific news of Mitchelstown and with it more worry about his personal safety. It was not therefore until October, when they were about to leave for England, that 'the patriot' could be persuaded to come to dinner at the O'Briens to renew their friendship of the previous year. Fortunately he was in a relaxed mood. 'Mr. Dillon', Elizabeth recorded, 'was quite merry and very chatty, enjoyed May's singing extremely, told us all kinds of amusing anecdotes of his experiences with American interviewers and really seemed to enjoy light and trivial conversation.'[3]

This was certainly a fond exaggeration. At no time in his life did Dillon take easily to light and trivial conversation and in the winter of 1887–8 he had other preoccupations. It was a critical phase in the Plan of Campaign and, with William O'Brien in Tullamore jail, the burden of leadership fell almost entirely upon him. It was essential that he, too, should not be arrested, and for this reason he spent the winter mainly in England, trying to rally working-class support for the Irish experiment in agrarian collective bargaining. Since London was his base, it was natural that he should begin to see more of the Mathew family. They, for their part, were able to provide him with more than hospitality, for it was at their house that he now began to make his first contacts with the rising generation in the Liberal Party. In December, for example, he was invited to a very splendid dinner-party they gave for her brother Theobald's twenty-first birthday. Among the guests were John Morley, Asquith, Haldane, Alfred Lyttelton, Lord Justice Bowen and the Chief Justice, Lord Coleridge. The Chief Justice was so taken with the Irish agitator that he invited him to dinner a few days later. This, too, was a glittering affair, with Augustine Birrell and Matthew Arnold and his wife present, as well as Elizabeth and her parents. Matthew Arnold took her into dinner, 'an honour which I would fain have exchanged for being near my hero who was placed quite at the other end of the table'. Dillon's partner was Mrs. Arnold, but she was not at her best, being petrified lest he should discover that she was related by marriage to William Forster, and that this would bring back awkward memories of Kilmainham.[4]

Dillon was still in London at the end of the year and to Elizabeth's delight he came to dinner with them on Christmas night. He showed them a side of his nature few even of those who knew him well would have believed to have existed at all. 'Mr. Dillon', she faithfully recorded, 'zestfully threw himself into all the merriment—pulled crackers, played loo, encouraged

[1] Ibid., 14 July 1887.   [2] Ibid., 22 Sept. 1887.   [3] Ibid., 12 Oct. 1887.
[4] Ibid., 5 and 23 Dec. 1887.

everyone to gamble wildly and himself recklessly took *3* new cards in order
to play'. It was all so agreeable that she could even begin to persuade herself that if he stayed in England long enough he might escape arrest
altogether.[1] It was an illusion, of course. Political reality, urgent and brutal,
kept breaking in, and Dillon was soon again totally involved in the fight
against Balfour and coercion. His arrival in Ireland in the spring of 1888
was, as he had forecast, the signal for his arrest. Between then and his actual
imprisonment in June he had, as we have seen, to face the first major crisis
of the Plan of Campaign, the crisis of which the papal rescript and Parnell's speech at the Eighty Club were the climactic events. Elizabeth
Mathew was at the Eighty Club and listened to Parnell's condemnation of
the Plan with dismay. 'I fear Mr. Dillon may have a feeling of being deserted,' she noted in her diary, 'but that would not be a true feeling.' She
herself was introduced to Parnell and, loyal though she was to Dillon, was
quite overwhelmed by his leader—'he, looking like a king, and more than
a king, accepting the homage with passive acquiescence'. She was thrown
off balance by his good looks, still more by his 'cold, impassive majesty',
but she managed to tell him something of her love for Ireland. 'Ireland,' he
replied coolly, 'is a delightful country from June to October, but on the
whole England is a pleasanter place to live in, at any rate now.' Unusually,
he made some effort at conversation himself, recollecting her family connection with Father Mathew, but giving the association an entirely characteristic twist. He only wished there was another such apostle of temperance
now, he told her, since a crusade against whiskey would 'put the Government in a difficulty, besides being good for the people, by diminishing an
enormous source of revenue'.[2] Temperance as an instrument of politics
may not have been exactly Father Mathew's ideal, but this pragmatic
approach to the question could not have been more typical of Parnell.

Yet all the leader's magnetism could not compensate for the fact that
he had publicly disowned the Plan of Campaign, and when soon afterwards
Dillon received his sentence of six months' imprisonment Elizabeth's
compass returned immediately to its true bearings. Dillon was in London a
few days before he was due to go to jail and called at 46 Queen's Gate
Gardens. 'I never was so much charmed with him as on that day,' Elizabeth
recorded, 'he was so gentle, so genial and so simple and talked so kindly
about all we wanted to hear, assuring us that if his sentence were confirmed
he would all the same be well looked after, and not allowed to get ill.'[3] It
was duly confirmed on 20 June and he entered Dundalk prison forthwith.
But the previous night he sent her a small present and with it a letter which
she treasured all her life and which he found among her papers after her
death. It ran thus:[4]

My dear Miss Mathew,
    Would you kindly allow me to continue the work of demoralisa-
tion which I commenced on last Christmas night, when I initiated you

[1] Ibid., 30 Dec. 1887.   [2] Ibid., 11 May 1888.   [3] Ibid., 24 June 1888.
[4] Dillon to Elizabeth Mathew, 19 June [1888] (D.P.).

into the iniquities of unlimited Loo. I now beg to present you with a pack of Euchre cards and treatises on the noble games of Euchre and Poker,

Sincerely yours,
John Dillon

It was, perhaps, a rather odd gift for a Victorian young lady of good family to receive, and the letter accompanying it could by no stretch of the imagination be called a declaration of love, but Elizabeth was probably right in thinking that he intended more than a mere gesture of courtesy. It seemed to her that 'he meant by it to tell us—or perhaps I may as well be simple and say me—to be brave and cheerful and remember that good times would come again, and moreover that he meant to show me he did not forget our friendship'. And she continued, in a passage remarkable for the clarity of its self-awareness:

> I cannot define the effect that Mr Dillon's presence has on me—I never met anyone who so absolutely embodied my ideal. For a long time this feeling was only one of hero-worship to which all young women are liable and I treated it and myself as such, but lately I have thought that he really does like us all, and perhaps especially *me*, and the worship has become more or less human as well as heroic. The books and the cards have done much to emphasise this change.[1]

Nevertheless, it was difficult to be sure and on one of the last occasions they met before his imprisonment he gave her a glimpse of that innate solitariness which was an essential part of him. His brother William's *Life of John Mitchel* had just been published and, discussing it, Elizabeth observed that transportation after 1848 had broken Mitchel's heart. John Dillon's reply, as she noted it down, reveals little about Mitchel, but a good deal about himself. 'Happiness, we must remember, must always be within a man and need not depend on his surroundings. Mitchel found Van Diemen's land unbearable, but I question whether I myself would not have spent a happier life had I been these last five years in Van Diemen's land rather than in all this struggle. "But", said I, "where would the country have been without you?" "Ah, well", he said, with a touch of bitterness, "according to the Pope apparently, the country would have been happier too." '[2]

While he was in Dundalk Elizabeth anxiously followed every fluctuation of his health, and seems indeed herself to have had some sort of nervous breakdown. However, she was in Ireland when he came out in September and was overjoyed to receive from him another gift—the *Memoirs* of Miles Byrne, the almost legendary hero of the United Irishmen of County Wicklow in the 1798 rising.[3] It was one of his own favourite books and that she could appreciate it was another bond between them—perhaps it was no

---

[1] Diary of Elizabeth Mathew, 24 June 1888.   [2] Ibid., same entry.
[3] Dillon to Elizabeth Mathew, 11 Oct. 1888 (D.P.).

coincidence that one of their children was later to bear the name Myles. They met several times before she had to go back to England and it was then that she heard about his projected Australasian mission which the shattered finances of the Plan had made essential. She was, naturally, horrified at the prospect. 'He looked very ill though,' she noted, 'and it was easy to see that he was so and not at all equal to the work of a parliamentary winter, so it would be selfish to regret that he is planning to start on a voyage to Australia and that he will probably be away for nearly a year. I don't know what the country and his friends will do without him, but it is imperative to his health that he should go.'[1]

(ii)

The year of his absence was a critical period in their relationship. He was, of course, wrapped up in public affairs and in the intermittent diaries he kept during his tour her name does not once appear. True, he sent her copies of Australian and New Zealand papers which told her something of how he was getting on, but his covering letters meant so little to him that when he came upon them after her death he was astonished to find that he had written to her at all. However, they met at the House of Commons in April 1890, immediately after his return, and a few weeks later chance threw them together on a crossing from Holyhead to Kingstown. But it was not the most romantic of occasions, as rough weather soon obliged her hero to retire precipitately below. 'He left me', she noted in almost the only sentence she ever wrote of him which betrayed feminine impatience with the frailty of man, 'quite lonely and deserted till we were within half an hour of Kingstown when he returned and we watched the Irish hills grow clearer together.' To be in Ireland with him was the summit of happiness for her and when a few days later he invited her to his house in North Great George's Street, took her into his holy of holies and showed her his superb collection of books, she could be forgiven for thinking that perhaps, after all, absence *had* made the heart grow fonder.[2] But this was, in fact, an illusion. With the Plan of Campaign once more in crisis, he had no time to spare for the pleasures of private life. Moreover, as so often under stress, his dyspepsia had returned to plague him, and with it that black depression which was so habitual with him at this time. Even that very study which charmed her filled him with disgust. 'I come into the study', he wrote in his diary just a week before she recorded her delight at being there, 'with immense arrangements [sic] and do simply nothing. Great God—cannot I arrange matters so as to pursue some continuous work . . .'[3] The mood persisted and even Killiney could not help him, could only remind him of the difference between then and now. 'Always think,' he wrote a few days later, 'when I see Killiney shore again after an interval, of time when I used

---

[1] Diary of Elizabeth Mathew, 9 Nov. 1888.
[2] Ibid., 1 June 1890 (the crossing was on May 21).
[3] Diary of John Dillon, 24 May 1890 (D.P.).

to walk on it with fire in my blood, and dreaming dreams—what a black gulf there is between that time and now. Twenty golden years ago, only they have not been golden for me, only leaden.'[1]

This was not the language of a man in love, but it was the language of a lonely man who desperately needed a settled home and married happiness. Indeed, he was more ripe for conquest than he knew. Back in London on parliamentary business in July, his attention was caught by 'a bright American girl' as he described her in his diary.[2] This was Kathleen Emmet, a granddaughter of Thomas Addis Emmet, the United Irishman who had emigrated to America at the beginning of the nineteenth century. Soon he began to see more and more of her. He met her at a reception where, although Elizabeth Mathew was present, she seemed to him 'the most brilliant-looking girl in the room'.[3] Two days later he gave a dinner at the House of Commons for Miss Emmet, but this time there was no Miss Mathew.[4] Then there was tea on the terrace, there were other meetings and finally a coaching-party at which both girls were present. Dillon enjoyed himself thoroughly, and as for Miss Emmet, 'I like her more the more I see of her'.[5] To Elizabeth this was painfully obvious. She hardly saw anything of Dillon on the picnic—'if anything he rather avoided me, which was rather wounding to my *amour propre*, though no doubt salutary'. 'I am feeling restless and unhappy and angry with myself', she added miserably. 'I wish I saw my way to leading a useful existence.'[6]

The plain truth was, though she could hardly bring herself to face it, that she was in danger of losing Dillon altogether. Shortly afterwards he left for Ireland without saying good-bye and though she was there herself in the late summer he made no sign. On the contrary, he wrote to her mother (not to her!) explaining that he would be too busy to come and see them before leaving for the fund-raising tour in America that he and O'Brien were to undertake in September. Unfortunately, Elizabeth herself had heard from Mrs. Deane that Kathleen Emmet was also in Ireland and had gone with Dillon on an expedition to County Wicklow—'so Mr. Dillon is not too busy for *some* amusement'.[7] A few days later insult was added to injury when the triumphant Miss Emmet came in person to pay a call. Elizabeth's reaction was predictable. 'I am sorry to say that the visit considerably modified my enthusiasm [never, surely very great] for Miss Emmet. I think her head was a little turned by all the attention she received in Dublin and I got very tired of her loud, assertive voice and thought her too full of herself altogether.'[8]

But at this point Arthur Balfour rescued Dillon from what looked like becoming a very awkward situation. On 18 September both Dillon and O'Brien were arrested and a few days later their trial began at Tipperary. On 9 October the Mathew family were in Cork attending the centenary cele-

[1] Ibid., 1 June 1890.   [2] Ibid., 14 July 1890.   [3] Ibid., 19 July 1890.
[4] Ibid., 21 July 1890.   [5] Ibid., 29 July 1890.
[6] Diary of Elizabeth Mathew, 3 Aug. 1890 (D.P.).   [7] Ibid., 24 Aug. 1890.
[8] Ibid., 9 Sept. 1890.

brations of the birth of Father Mathew. That same day Dillon and O'Brien, having made their break for freedom, were at sea *en route* for France, and for a whole new chapter of adventures, culminating in the Parnell split and in their return to Ireland in February 1891 to serve the sentences outstanding against them. Dillon's private life virtually ceased to exist and the brilliant Miss Emmet disappeared abruptly from his diary. So, too, indeed, did Elizabeth Mathew, but she, all jealousy forgotten, followed each phase of the crisis intently, judging everything by its effect upon John Dillon. Her immediate anxieties were relieved when the travellers reached France. A little later, when they were leaving for America, Elizabeth had word of them from Mrs. Kenny (Dr. Joe Kenny's wife), who had just seen them off from Paris. 'They were all in very good spirits', Elizabeth recorded, 'and Mr. Dillon looking very well in spite of all he endured on the passage to Cherbourg, when he was so dreadfully ill that he several times begged to be put on shore and allowed to travel with his beard shaved off, but on dry land.'[1]

Of all that followed Elizabeth was only a spectator at a distance. She had become a strong anti-Parnellite from the moment of the divorce-court revelations, but, like so many other people, had pinned all her hopes on the triangular negotiations in France between Parnell, Dillon and O'Brien. When these failed and Dillon and O'Brien went to prison—it is possible that a hint dropped by R. B. Haldane at Elizabeth's request may have been responsible for their being lodged in favourable circumstances in Galway rather than in the notorious Clonmel jail—she could only look on horrified at the increasing savagery of the duel between Parnell and Tim Healy. So terrible was the spectacle, indeed, that her main hope during the sad summer of 1891 was that Dillon, when he came out of prison, would retire from politics altogether. But this could not be. After he and O'Brien made their momentous declaration against Parnell in August 1891 both men were plunged into the thick of the struggle. Elizabeth Mathew was in Dublin for Parnell's funeral and was overwhelmed by the bitterness she found there. Dillon, she thought, was looking ill and strained and he was far too busy for more than a few hasty minutes with her on the rare occasions when they met.[2]

It was not until the parliamentary session opened at the beginning of 1892 that the old pattern, broken since his tour in Australasia three years earlier, was again resumed, and that he began once more to use the Mathew house as his second home. In February he came to luncheon 'and captured all our hearts anew'.[3] A couple of weeks later he was the principal guest at her birthday party (having left the invitation unanswered for ten days) and when he sat beside her at dinner her bliss was complete.[4] Or was it? True, their friendship seemed completely restored and he paid her the highest compliment he knew by talking to her seriously about politics, but his life was so busy, and so much of his energy was drained away by the endless

[1] Ibid., 31 Oct. 1890.   [2] Ibid., 11 and 17 Oct. 1891.   [3] Ibid., 13 Feb. 1892.
[4] Ibid., 21, 28 Feb. 1892.

internecine rivalries in Ireland that he had, or seemed to have, nothing left for private happiness. For him it was apparently enough that there should be in London a house where he could relax with a family which he liked and which welcomed him. But for her, as the years rolled inexorably on, friendship without love became a torment, and proximity without intimacy a burden he had no right to inflict upon her.

At last in 1895 came the crisis. Early that autumn she crossed once more to Ireland to stay with the Murrough O'Briens at Killiney before going on to spend a few days in Donegal. And once more—as so often before—John Dillon was staying in the neighbourhood. They met, they walked and all seemed as it had been.[1] But in reality it was very different. Their private friendship, as frequently happens in such cases, was becoming public property and tongues were beginning to wag. Unhappily, some of this gossip reached Elizabeth's ears just before she left Killiney for her journey to the north. Her reaction was swift and characteristic. On the night of 16 September she wrote to Dillon explaining delicately but firmly that her position was becoming impossible and that in the circumstances she could not—as she had originally intended—come back to Killiney for the end of her holiday.[2]

For Dillon this letter posed an excruciatingly difficult problem. The soul of honour himself, the very last thing he wanted was to place her in a compromising position. Yet now it appeared that this was precisely what he had done and how best to answer her letter was quite beyond his powers to decide. There is a family legend that just at this time Mrs. Deane came late to bed night after night, explaining to her maid who was waiting wearily to brush her hair, that she was trying to persuade Master John to commit himself. Part of the difficulty sprang from his own innate humility. He could not, it seems, bring himself to believe that Elizabeth, who had always in his eyes been at the centre of a glittering circle, actually preferred him to all the other men who would have jumped at the chance of marrying her. But even if she did prefer him, there were still awkward questions to be faced. Could he—should he—break the established pattern of his life so long dedicated to politics and to politics alone? Ought he to ask a girl who had led a sheltered and happy life in society to share his turbulent existence and live on a small income? Dare he, whose health was so suspect, marry at all? These were hard and difficult choices and it is not surprising that, day after day, he hesitated, torn between unbelief, bewilderment and a desperate longing for the happiness that had revealed itself to him only at the moment when it seemed likely to vanish from his life for ever.

Meanwhile Elizabeth, with that capacity to go outside herself and extract interest from her surroundings which was one of her most endearing characteristics, made the best of her visit to the north. Even Derry she found tolerable and half persuaded herself that that bleak city would resemble Siena 'if it were a little different and medieval instead of comparatively

[1] Ibid., 15 Sept. 1895.
[2] Elizabeth Mathew to John Dillon, 16 Sept. 1895 (D.P.).

modern'.[1] She spent the next few days with friends at Port Salon, walking and driving in Donegal. There, in the solitude and immensity of that superb landscape, she recovered her sense of proportion. Even Dillon's silence, as she told him in a letter of 21 September, she interpreted as an admonition not to allow herself to be made unhappy by ill-natured gossip.[2] So she decided—and it must have needed a great deal of courage—to return to Killiney. This time, however, she took lodgings in the neighbouring village of Ballybrack, where she prepared to receive her brothers, Theo and Charles. 'It will be rather amusing', she wryly recorded, 'to play at being an old maid for a few days.'[3] It was a role she played for just ten days. Under 11 October her diary has these simple sentences:

> This afternoon John Dillon told me that he cared for me. We hope to be married, please God, next month.
>
> I cannot write about what is so sacred, but joy, awe and thanksgiving, overwhelm me. May I always render thanks to Almighty God for his supreme goodness to me, and may my happiness be always sanctified by His grace.
>
> I was spending the day with them at Chesterfield. And so it has come to me in my beloved Killiney, and just nine years—within a few days—of the first time I met him.[4]

One of their first cares was to inform Sir James and Lady Mathew. Elizabeth's letter to her mother was, as can be imagined, ecstatic. Dillon's was severely formal and it was utterly characteristic of him that, at this moment of supreme happiness for both of them, he should have felt bound to present their future in terms of uncompromising realism. 'Dear Lady Mathew,' he wrote, 'I have asked your daughter to be my wife and she has consented. I cannot promise her a peaceful home or a prosperous future, but she knows the conditions of my life and has agreed to accept them. Please show this letter to Sir James Mathew. Yours sincerely, John Dillon.'[5]

Almost at once they settled that the wedding was to be on 21 November. Since for most of the intervening weeks Dillon was taken up with urgent political business in Ireland—it was precisely the moment when he was administering the *coup de grâce* to Tim Healy—their time together was very brief and they had to bridge the gap as best they could by letters. She usually wrote twice a day, he, naturally, less often, but when he did write the tone was utterly unlike anything he had ever used before. It was as if the ice of years had broken and the springs of his natural affection, powerful and pure, were unsealed. He went about in an ecstasy of bewilderment, almost afraid to savour his happiness and content, characteristically, to come upon it little by little. 'I cannot hardly [*sic*] realise that you love me', he wrote on 24 October. 'And yet I do realise it most intensely, for my

---

[1] Diary of Elizabeth Mathew, 18 Sept. 1895 (D.P.).

[2] Elizabeth Mathew to John Dillon 'Saturday' [25 Sept. 1895]; Diary of Elizabeth Mathew, 30 Sept. 1895 (D.P.).

[3] Diary of Elizabeth Mathew, 30 Sept. and 1 Oct. 1895 (D.P.).

[4] Ibid., 11 Oct. 1895, 11 p.m.

[5] Information supplied by Professor Myles Dillon.

whole being is changed. Every room in the house and every bit of furniture speaks to me of you. The mere fact that you exist in the world makes it impossible for me to feel lonely, as I used to feel . . . I have suffered so much and had such little pleasure in my life that I am not over eager to rush on a pleasure and take it all at once. I love to linger over each stage of it and to take out of it all the joy it will give . . . I wake up in the morning and thank God that you care for me.'[1] He sent her, as his first gift, a pocket Testament that he used to take to Mass, marked in many places with his own hand. Nothing could have pleased her better. 'What made you know', she asked, 'that I should love your little Testament more than any gift money could buy? It has *you* on every page and I stroke the pages softly and think that your hand has rested on them too.'[2]

A few days later he wrote again, even more ecstatically: 'My own darling, I cannot go to bed without writing you a line to tell you again that I love you and that it is delicious to me to hear it in every different form in which you tell it to me that you do really and truly love such a battered old campaigner as I am. I thought of last Sunday week . . . I shall never forget that day and night . . . And so you really do love me and you call me lord and master. And this even I love—altho' I hate to be petted and adored—because I know and feel that it comes from the fulness of your overflowing love, which makes it sweet to you to bow your neck and submit to the delicious tyranny of love . . . Do you know that most wonderful of all love songs?

> O wert thou in cauld blast
> On yonder lea, on yonder lea
> My plaidie to the angy aist
> I'd shelter thee, I'd shelter thee.[3]

This crossed with one from her which moved him more, he said, than any she had written, but which in time to come he was to read again with bitter anguish. On Sunday, 27 October, she had been to church as usual and had read the Epistle to the Romans, noting the verses he had marked. 'You have marked in the fifth chapter, "perhaps for a good man some one would dare to die", and I wish to point out that *you* are that man and that I, if I had to would thankfully give my life in exchange for the love you have given me . . . And I will ask you, in the future, to apply that text to me.'[4]

From him this evoked a no less passionate response. 'Yes—now that I really begin to know you, your love is a glory to me. More than a glory because it has transformed my life. Sometimes, when I try to think over the change, it recalls to me the wonderful transformation I used to wonder at when I was a boy, when a damp sea fog suddenly rolled away from Killiney and all its beauty was revealed, sparkling in an April sun.'[5] 'My dear', she

[1] John Dillon to Elizabeth Mathew, 24 Oct. 1895. This series of engagement letters is not in the Dillon Papers; I am grateful to the Dillon family for permission to use it.
[2] Elizabeth Mathew to John Dillon 24 Oct. 1895.
[3] John Dillon to Elizabeth Mathew, 'Monday' [28 Oct. 1895].
[4] Elizabeth Mathew to John Dillon, 27 Oct. 1895.
[5] John Dillon to Elizabeth Mathew, 'Tuesday' [probably 29 Oct. 1895].

replied, 'I can hardly feel my love is a glory to *you*, but yours is a crown of light to *me*, making everything else in the world dim and unreal because of its strength and brightness.'[1] These exchanges soon gave place, of course, to more prosaic details about banns, wedding presents, carpets, curtains and a thousand other details, but happiness kept breaking in. Elizabeth, for example, on 30 October, rebuked him gently for objecting to her calling him lord and master, 'but you guess aright why I like using the title—you see I knew all along that you were the only earthly lord I ever *could* obey and now it rejoices me to feel that I am yours at last.'[2] It was a title she first used in her letters to him on 1 November and she used it almost invariably for the rest of their life together. 'If I am your lord and master,' he conceded, 'I am so by the grace of your own sweet nature which has taught you the great lesson that to obey when there is no coercion but the delicious coercion of love is one of the highest and purest of human pleasures. And you know that I will never ask you to obey me unless your own dear heart coerces you to do it and makes the obedience sweet.'[3]

On 4 November he arrived in London bringing the first jewellery she ever received from him—a diamond and sapphire ring, a shamrock brooch and a greenstone cross given to him in New Zealand. They had a week together, but it was not—could not be—all wedding preparations, since the climax of his conflict with Tim Healy was now at hand. During that week he had the satisfaction of seeing Healy expelled from the Irish National League of Great Britain, but on 10 November he had to return to Dublin for the crucial meetings of the Irish National Federation and the parliamentary party which would finally decide the issue between them. By 14 November Elizabeth knew that victory was at last in sight and she turned her mind happily to the future—'My dearest lord and master', she wrote, "will have sunshine and peace to look forward to, and he will remember that in future contests his wife will be waiting for him at home, trying to smoothe the rough places in his life's journey as far as power is given her to do so.'[4]

This could well stand as the epitaph for their married life, which began, as they had planned it, on the morning of 21 November. They were married at eight o'clock, by the Bishop of Galway, in Brompton Oratory. It was a quiet wedding and the only people present were Elizabeth's parents, her sister Kathleen, her two brothers and—on Dillon's side—his uncle, Charles Hart, and, of course, Mrs. Deane, whose generosity in settling a large sum of money upon her cousin had made his marriage financially possible.[5] They left at once for the Continent and were away for a month, going by way of Paris and Avignon to Cannes, thence to Florence and finally, as a climax, to Rome. There, in mid-December, they had an audience with the Pope, whom they found amiable but a little inaccessible, since their only

---

[1] Elizabeth Mathew to John Dillon, 28 [a misdating for 29] Oct. 1895.

[2] Elizabeth Mathew to John Dillon, 'Wednesday' [30 Oct. 1895].

[3] John Dillon to Elizabeth Mathew, 31 Oct. 1895.

[4] Elizabeth Mathew to John Dillon, 14 Nov. 1895.

[5] *F.J.*, 22 Nov. 1895. The amount is not known, but Professor Myles Dillon recalls his old nurse mentioning the figure of £30,000.

common language was French, in which Elizabeth was considerably more fluent than her husband. They asked the Pope's blessing on Dillon's future work as well as on their marriage. 'He said "mais oui, mais oui" to everything,' Elizabeth noted, 'and fondled my hair with his tiny cold hand, and laid his other hand on John's black, smooth head.' So far so good, but the interview which followed with his Secretary of State, Cardinal Rampolla, was not so happy. Their sponsor, Bishop O'Donnell of Raphoe, had warned them that Catholic education was the great topic of the moment at Rome and that they should lose no chance of explaining that the best safeguard of Catholic interests was the Irish party, not the English laity. The Cardinal's opening gambit—'Vous connaissez, sans doute, le duc de Norfolk?'—was not, therefore, very encouraging, especially since Dillon's views on the Duke were not repeatable, at least within the Vatican. Hastily they explained that they represented the Irish element in the Catholic forces, whereupon Cardinal Rampolla floundered even deeper. 'Ah,' he said ingratiatingly, 'vous êtes ami alors de l'Archevêque Walsh. C'est un fort habile homme . . . C'est un excellent homme, mais très irlandais.' The Dillons, who had long considered the Archbishop's fault to be that he was not nearly 'Irish' enough, replied coldly, 'Nous sommes tous hautement irlandais, Eminence', and there the interview ended.[1] Soon afterwards they turned for home and by Christmas-time they were back in Dublin.

(iii)

The process of settling in was for both of them delightful. The house had been completely redecorated and a cook and parlourmaid provisionally engaged by Mrs. Deane. For a few weeks, before the parliamentary session started, they had a brief interval in which to come to terms with married life. To Elizabeth it was a peculiarly difficult adjustment and one that anybody else, lacking her charm and gentleness of spirit, might well have found impossible. John Dillon was a man already set in the habits of middle age and, though a devoted husband, was continually beset by political responsibilities and problems. Inevitably, therefore, most of the adjustment had to come from her side and it is a measure of her extraordinary tact and skill and readiness to efface herself that he probably never realised how great the adjustment was. For one thing, she was mistress of a house which was not hers, nor even her husband's. It was owned by Charles Hart, and since the old man, now becoming senile, still lived there, he had to be looked after. Apart from that, Dillon for most of his life had been watched over and cared for by Mrs. Deane, and for both women the new relationship bristled with difficulties. Elizabeth had conceded much in advance, the carpeting and redecoration having been done perforce by Mrs. Deane, who was, after all, on the spot. But after the honeymoon was over it was the latter's turn to yield ground. She retired to her business at Ballaghaderrin and thenceforth came only on special occasions to Dublin, though it

---

[1] Diary of Elizabeth Dillon, 13 and 29 Dec. 1895 (D.P.).

was part of the unwritten covenant that the Dillon family should spend some of each year with her in Mayo. Some idea of the magnitude of Elizabeth's task can be grasped if it is remembered that in addition to these personal problems she had to begin life in what was virtually a strange city, married to a husband who was at the very centre of political controversy and surrounded by a large circle of acquaintances, many of them kind, some of them envious, most of them embarrassingly articulate, and all of them consumed by curiosity to see what 'the patriot' would make of marriage and it of him.

On the whole they got through the first difficult months very well. There were, of course, trials and tribulations. Visitors kept calling in an unending stream and no amount of entertaining ever seemed to catch up with the hospitality they owed; Elizabeth had trouble with her housekeeping accounts and had to borrow from her own private sources, which were not plentiful; they had to cope with a visit from her family; above all there was a state visit to be paid to the constituency in East Mayo. There, Elizabeth had her first experience of being played by a brass band from the station to Mrs. Deane's house in Ballaghaderrin. She had also to undergo the scrutiny of fifteen priests who came to dinner, but survived this unnerving ordeal with flying colours. Best of all, however, was direct contact with the people and her first real understanding of her husband's influence on them and of his mastery of large audiences. After Mass nothing would satisfy the crowd but that they should present addresses of goodwill and, of course, Dillon had to reply. 'So picturesque it was,' she noted, 'to have the church porch behind us and the great crowd in front, and I loved to see John standing tall and commanding over the people with his head bare and his beautiful voice ringing through the air and penetrating everywhere. The addresses wished us all kinds of blessings and that we might have heirs to perpetuate the noble race. No beating about the bush with the people of East Mayo.'[1]

Shortly after this they travelled to London for the opening of the parliamenary session—and, incidentally, for Dillon's election as chairman of the anti-Parnellite section of the parliamentary party. Then began a pattern of life which they tried to preserve during the next decade, though once children began to arrive—and by March 1896 Elizabeth knew she was pregnant—it proved increasingly difficult, and in the end, impossible, to carry out in detail each year. Normally, they would come over together for the parliamentary session and Elizabeth would stay long enough to see Dillon settled in a hotel or lodgings. She would then return to Dublin and he would rejoin her whenever parliamentary business made that possible. Sometimes, if the session was a long one, she might pay a second visit to London, but in any event, when the House rose for the summer recess they would head for Ballaghaderrin; occasionally, they might manage an autumn holiday at Killiney, but this depended on the financial situation, which, though never desperate, was usually fairly tight.

[1] Ibid., 3 Feb. 1896.

Even this simple, humdrum life, however, had to be fought for. The complications were endless, but the three that Elizabeth most dreaded were the speaking tours which so frequently took Dillon away from her even during the recess, the demands of their rapidly growing family, and above all the ever-recurring anxiety about his health. She could do nothing about the meetings—except to warn him repeatedly not to become entangled with William O'Brien again—but the counter-claims of husband and children form the constant theme of her diary, itself reduced by domestic preoccupations to a shadow of its former self. Their first child—a son, baptised John Mathew, but known almost from the start as Shawn—was born in August 1896, and others followed at frequent intervals during the next ten years—their only daughter, Anne Elizabeth (Nano) in 1897; a second son, Theobald Wolfe Tone, born, as his name suggests in 1898; Myles Patrick in 1900; James Mathew in 1902 and Brian in 1905. At first this growing family did not make overmuch difference to their way of life and in the session of 1897, when there was still only one child, they all—together with an Irish nurse—put up at the Westminster Palace Hotel for the new parliamentary session. Dillon himself, however, was far from well, and feeling the strain of leadership. Both he and Elizabeth, therefore, went abroad for a brief second honeymoon at Nice, only returning for the later part of the session. With the birth of their daughter in the autumn, of course, such flights into the blue became more and more difficult to arrange and Elizabeth herself was increasingly immersed in the responsibilities of the household.

Nevertheless, she still tried to keep to the pattern they had marked out in the beginning and usually managed to spend some time with Dillon in London. But the sacrifice was becoming too great. Even in 1898, when there were two children to look after, she suffered agonies at leaving them. 'After all,' she scribbled in her diary, 'I must be very thankful that it is possible for me to be with John and what I feel is that nothing can make me unhappy while I am with him who is the source of my happiness—only, it is an *unnatural* thing to be away from the children God has given us and I can't help yearning after them.'[1] Sometimes, it was possible to bring the children to stay with their grandparents in Queen's Gate Gardens, but as the number grew the old people blenched at the prospect and Elizabeth had to make up her mind to leave them at home. 'It does seem a great pity', she wrote regretfully, 'that it should be so difficult in fact to do what ought to be only delightful.'[2] And even to leave them at home became more and more difficult. 'This separation between us', she wrote at the beginning of the 1902 session, 'is very, very hard for us both to bear, and seems so unnatural as to be *wrong*, and yet it is very hard to see a way out of it. The children must not be left for long at a time. And the more I think over it the more sure I am that it is a *fatal* mistake for an Irish politician to go to live in London—besides I could not bear (and strange to say I feel this more keenly than John) to bring up the children in an English atmosphere.'[3] What made it worse was that the children themselves were now getting old

[1] Ibid., 11 Feb. 1898.   [2] Ibid., 2 Feb. 1901.   [3] Ibid., 18 Feb. 1902.

enough to be conscious of the dual lives their parents were leading. 'I wish father would give up the profession of being in Parliament,' said Shawn at the end of that 1902 session; 'it makes too much going away from home.' 'And indeed it does', his mother added in her diary. 'And people who have five lovely children ought not to be asked to leave them.'[1]

These entries, and there are many others like them, throw some light on the kind of sacrifices most married Irish parliamentarians and their families had to make while the union between the two countries persisted. The transformation of the party, during the Parnellite period and afterwards, into a middle-class body, composed mainly of men without private fortunes and under the necessity of earning a living, placed a very heavy strain on the members, both financial and psychological. They had to live in London during the annual session, or sessions, of Parliament, but could not, as Elizabeth Dillon perceived, transfer there altogether without being cut off from their own country and their own kind. On the other hand, to exist in London, even as many of them did on a very meagre scale, cost money, as did the constant travelling to and fro, and since only the poorest received an allowance or 'salary'—usually about £200 p.a. when funds were plentiful, but often less—this heavy expenditure meant for most married members a solitary, bachelor existence so long as the House was sitting, and for their families a lonely and often impoverished life at home. Dillon, of course, was more fortunate than most. Not only was his wife's house available as a refuge when he or any member of the family was in London, but his own circumstances gradually improved as time passed. With the death of his uncle, Charles Hart, in October 1898, the house in North Great George's Street at last became his own. He did not inherit much else from the old man save some vexatious litigation, but it was different when Mrs. Deane died a few years later, after a lingering illness. She left him the business at Ballaghaderrin, and although he had absolutely no experience of commerce, it soon became plain that, barring accidents, he would be very comfortably off.[2]

Yet, although separation from wife and family may have been less of a financial burden for him than for many other members of the party, there was another sense in which it could be said to have been, quite literally, more dangerous. As a bachelor, he had, as we have already seen, found life in London lodgings intolerable, and it is quite possible that the frequent crises in his health in the late eighties and nineties were due, at least in part, to simple neglect and the lack of anyone to look after him. With his marriage that state of chaos disappeared overnight, and whenever he was at home, either in Dublin or in Mayo, he was watched over with unceasing care and tenderness. But when he was on his own again in London, even though his lodgings were now chosen for him by his wife and were much superior to what he had formerly put up with, his old vulnerability to the notoriously unhealthy conditions under which the House of Commons did its business

[1] Ibid., 5 Dec. 1902.
[2] Elizabeth Dillon to Edward Blake, 21 July [1905] (Blake Papers).

reappeared. The result was that almost every session he was attacked, often severely, by influenza, and that once more, as years earlier, his lungs became suspect. The trip to Nice in 1897 was an attempt to get him into the sun at all costs, but it was only a palliative, and in 1898 and 1899 there was talk of sending him for a prolonged stay in Egypt. In 1898 this was certainly not possible, for at that time he was still leader of the anti-Parnellite section of the party, but in 1899, when he had resigned the chairmanship, there was less to keep him and the pressure on him to go was very great. Elizabeth herself, though dreading the prospect of such a separation, recognised that he was thoroughly run down—'tired, tired, tired'. 'Now that he is no longer chairman', she noted in her diary, 'there is no need for him to martyrise himself and sometimes I feel disheartened about it all. When God has sent us such happiness I *do* want to enjoy it—and life is passing.'[1]

But it was one thing to resign the chairmanship, quite another to slip unnoticed out of politics. Indeed, with the centenary celebrations of 1898, the rise of the United Irish League, and the onset of the Boer War, Dillon seemed to be as heavily involved as ever. The threat of Egypt in 1899 dwindled to a week at Herne Bay at Whitsun, and though Dillon did go on his own to Kissingen that summer, this was only a short break and not the real holiday he needed. He was packed off to Switzerland, again by himself, in the summer of 1901, but it was disheartening that none of these expeditions seemed to give him more than a temporary relief. When, therefore, Elizabeth learnt next year that there was a probability that he would have to go out to the United States in October on a fund-raising mission, she was horrified. Her horror, it is true, was mitigated by the reflection that if he did not go to America he might well end once more in prison, caught up in the tempestuous agrarian campaign William O'Brien's United Irish League was then waging. On the other hand, their fifth child was expected just at that time and she shrank from the thought that he might have to leave even before it was born. The American tour, she wrote in her diary in September, 'presses like a nightmare on my mind', though she added, 'in philosophic moments I feel myself that America is a better place for John to spend the autumn than gaol'.[2]

But was it? On 26 September the new baby was born and ten days later Dillon left for the United States with Michael Davitt. At first all went well and he stood up not only to the voyage, but to the more extreme rigours of American hospitality remarkably well. So much so, indeed, that he agreed to extend his tour and not leave for Ireland until 13 December. But then came a change. On 24 November Elizabeth was shocked to get a cable from him from Chicago, which said simply: 'Confined room slight chill, no cause uneasiness.' She cabled back: 'Anxious, send daily message', but heard nothing for thirty-six hours until she received a cable from Dillon's brother William (now living near Chicago): 'Steady improvement, will wire every other day.'[3]

[1] Diary of Elizabeth Dillon, 7 Apr. 1899 (D.P.).   [2] Ibid., 11 Sept. 1902.
[3] Ibid., 5 Dec. 1902.

What had happened was explained by Michael Davitt in a letter he wrote her from Chicago on 24 November, but which she did not receive until over a week later. From this it appeared that Dillon had caught a chill in the course of a long night journey he and Davitt had had to make from Philadelphia to Toledo. On 19 November Davitt had called in a doctor, who confined Dillon to his room. The illness, added Davitt, had led them to cancel a proposed visit to Canada, but he still expected Dillon to be well enough to speak at a meeting at Washington before returning home.[1] He wrote again next day, intending only to relieve her anxieties, but in fact aggravating them. Not only did a newspaper clipping he enclosed allege that Dillon had had a high fever, but he himself revealed that the patient had been removed to hospital. True, he added that this was because their hotel was too noisy and because his brother William's house was too far out of Chicago to be within easy reach of medical help, but this in itself was hardly reassuring.[2] Two other letters reaching her about the same time were no more comforting. Both were from William Dillon. In one he suggested that what John had had was an attack of malaria and in the other he admitted that there *had* been fever, though it had abated.[3]

From the very first cable Elizabeth's imagination had led her to picture the worst. 'I had become obsessed with apprehension', she wrote later in her diary, 'and pursued with the feeling that I ought to go to him, and Mrs. Deane thought so too—still, I did not want to do anything rash and it seemed a terrible undertaking to leave the children.' But then came the news of his having been removed to hospital. 'Mrs. Deane and I were nearly out of our minds—and I decided that I must just come as quickly as I could.' No sooner had she cabled her intention than replies came from William saying his brother was better, and from John himself begging her not to come. This, she says, 'staggered' her a good deal, but, urged on by Mrs. Deane, she nevertheless persisted with her plans, which needed, it must be said, a kind of heroism. 'I was nearly out of my mind leaving the children', she noted in her diary aboard ship, and 'my first three days on this vessel were like an awful nightmare between apprehension for John and apprehension for them and wondering had I done right'. Later, she grew calmer and allowed herself to hope that he really was recovering, though '*any* illness is serious to him'. The whole frightening episode, she wrote, was 'a ghastly fulfilment of the horrible forebodings which made this American tour overshadow my thoughts like a black cloud ever since it was projected. I pray that God may grant a happy outcome but in all my life I have not shed so many tears as in the last ten days.'[4]

When she arrived a letter from John was waiting for her. It contained the scolding she had expected—'I cannot pretend I am glad you have come, I think it was a terrible thing to do'—but at least it indicated that he was

---

[1] Michael Davitt to Elizabeth Dillon, 24 Nov. 1902 (D.P.).
[2] Michael Davitt to Elizabeth Dillon, 25 Nov. 1902 (D.P.).
[3] William Dillon to Elizabeth Dillon, 20 and 25 Nov. 1902 (D.P.).
[4] Diary of Elizabeth Dillon, 5 Dec. 1902, on board *S.S.* Umbria.

better, for he was planning to meet her in New York. Moreover, he was emphatic that though he had had what he called 'a persistent low fever' which kept him in bed for eight days, his temperature had never been excessively high and there were no serious symptoms. The fever, he thought, had been brought on by his chill coupled with an attack from his old enemy dyspepsia, and aggravated by overexertion and travelling. His main concern was for Elizabeth, who was new to the harshness of the American winter and with whom he found it impossible to remain severe for long. 'I hope to see your dear, dear face on Sunday,' he ended, 'and altho' I am rather mad with you for coming our meeting will be a very happy one if I only find you safe from all the perils of your wild expedition.'[1]

They did indeed meet in New York, at Grand Central Station, but the moment Elizabeth set eyes on him she realised all was not well. 'His white drawn face frightened me.' When they got to their hotel she summoned a doctor, who found that the fever had returned and that Dillon had a temperature of 101 degrees. This was, inevitably, enough to revive the suspicion of lung trouble, but the most searching medical examination revealed nothing, even though both the fever and the dyspepsia continued for several days. The only diagnosis to which their New York doctor would commit himself was that the fever was due to some kind of internal poisoning caused by acute dyspepsia and made worse by the chill caught from travelling in adverse conditions. His prescription was rest and yet more rest. Sadly, therefore, they resigned themselves to Christmas in America.[2] In fact, they spent it pleasantly enough on Long Island with Bourke Cockran—one of the leading Irish-Americans of the day—and his wife, but on 31 December they finally left New York, rejoining the children in Dublin early in the New Year.

(iv)

To all appearances, therefore, the adventure ended happily. Nevertheless Dillon's illness, mysterious as it was, left its traces upon him for years to come. Indeed, his doctors peremptorily forbade him to face the new parliamentary session, and as soon as he had built up some strength he and Elizabeth went on their travels again, this time—and at last—to Egypt, where they stayed until April 1903. It was a critical time in Irish affairs with the land question, it seemed, on the point of solution, but since Dillon's views on that matter were so much out of line with those of his most influential colleagues, it was perhaps as well that he was removed from the scene. However, before they left Ireland he had arranged with Davitt that the latter should send for him if he was urgently needed for the Land Bill debates. And on 21 April, when they were at Athens on their way home, there duly arrived the telegram with the ominous word 'Come' which

[1] John Dillon to Elizabeth Dillon, 3 Dec. 1902 (D.P.).
[2] Diary of Elizabeth Dillon, 21 Dec. 1902.

Elizabeth had so long dreaded. But it was not so easy to change their plans overnight, and they returned in a leisurely fashion via Corfu, Venice and Vienna. In the end Dillon did, as we have seen, get back in time for the second reading of Wyndham's Land Bill, but he had still to take life easily and for the sessions of 1903 and 1904 he was virtually an absentee member.[1] Even in the summer of 1903, within a few weeks of his returning home, a London consultant was urging him to go away again at all costs. His idea of a restful holiday for his patient was to persuade him to go by sailing-ship to Australia or South America—a remedy which, for Dillon, would infallibly have been worse than the disease. 'I demurred,' he told Elizabeth, 'and he agreed that I should go to the east—Egypt and Palestine —on the understanding that I was to take the world easy, not to go in for any sight-seeing, and cut myself off from politics altogether and stay away for about six months.'[2] Ten days later he saw the specialist again and this time reported not advice but an ultimatum—he must have '*at least* six months of absolute rest from politics and all kinds of work.'[3]

It seemed almost as absurd to go straight back to Egypt as to go round the world on a sailing-ship, so he compromised by spending the summer and autumn of 1903 lazily at home—to Elizabeth's great contentment. At the beginning of 1904 he was still not fit enough for parliamentary work and in January left for the Mediterranean, spending most of his time in Sicily. In April Elizabeth managed to join him and they met at Naples. She found him sunburnt and better than when he had started, but still lethargic and easily tired.[4] They wandered slowly northwards, pausing at Monte Cassino, and then on to Rome, where, as on their honeymoon, they fell quickly and completely under the familiar spell. As before, they were granted an audience with the Pope, which, to Elizabeth's mind, was less impressive than the one they had had nine years before with Leo XIII, while a Papal Mass to which they were invited left her strangely untouched —'or is it that ten years have made me less susceptible to spiritual emotions?'[5] Perhaps they had, but they had not diminished her capacity for happiness. 'Here in Rome', she noted in her diary, 'I find myself constantly recurring to the joys and blessings that have fallen to my lot in the nine years since I was last here. How every moment of my life with John has been intensely happy save those in which we were separated.'[6]

From Rome they travelled by easy stages to Perugia and Assisi, and from there to Florence and Siena. By this time it had become very hot and they turned towards home, Elizabeth pining for the children, John restless after his long absence from politics. They reached London early in June and with great difficulty Elizabeth managed to steer him away from the House of Commons and back to Ireland. In vain, since that same summer

[1] Diary of Elizabeth Dillon, 12 Mar. to 14 May 1903; W. S. Blunt, *My diaries*, p. 458.
[2] John Dillon to Elizabeth Dillon, 18 June and 13 July 1903 (D.P.).
[3] John Dillon to Elizabeth Dillon, 23 July 1903 (D.P.).
[4] Diary of Elizabeth Dillon, 22 Apr. 1904.
[5] Ibid., 28 Apr., 1 and 6 May 1904.
[6] Ibid., 1 May 1904.

saw the mounting attack on devolution and the entire policy of conciliation which earned him the undying enmity of his old friend William O'Brien. Perhaps it was this recrudescence of political activity and all the worry and strain it entailed, perhaps it was the burden of another pregnancy, perhaps it was the fact that Mrs Deane was seriously ill towards the end of the year—but whatever the reason or reasons, Elizabeth's diary in 1904 began for the first time to have frequent references to her own deteriorating health and especially to attacks of asthma which left her shaken and exhausted.

Not surprisingly, therefore, when in 1905 Dillon decided to resume regular attendance at the House of Commons, she was filled with foreboding. 'I alternate', she admitted, 'between bravely telling him to go and a feeling of horror at the bare thought of his going.'[1] In fact, he had to come home almost at once, as their sixth child and fifth son, Brian, was born on 13 March. That same day, Mrs. Deane, who had been in and out of hospital for months, came to them from a vain attempt at convalescence in Lucan and the house seemed once more like its old self. But it was not to be so for long. In July the old lady died in her seventy-seventh year and Elizabeth suffered a sharp and inevitable reaction. Immediately after the funeral she had what she described as an attack of laryngitis. 'I really thought I was dying . . . Well, I wasn't dying, but I was very ill for three days.'[2] No sooner was this trouble past than news came that her father had had a serious stroke. For more than two months his life hung by a thread and her mother, too, fell ill, overwhelmed by this trouble—so ill that Elizabeth herself had to go to London early in 1906 in case of the worst, leaving John to look after the children at home.

With these cumulative demands her life was so busy that she did not open her diary at all between October 1905 and November 1906. In the interval there had been great changes. The Liberals had won their landslide victory in the general election of 1906 and Redmond and Dillon were testing just how far the old Gladstonian commitment to Home Rule had survived in this new and very different party. An old friend, James Bryce, had become Chief Secretary for Ireland, though, as Elizabeth shrewdly commented, he proved to be 'nearly as feeble an administrator as John Morley was'.[3] Nearer home, both of them were saddened by the death of a dear friend, Michael Davitt. 'To John,' Elizabeth recorded, 'it was the loss of one dearer than a brother. And what can I say of the desolation of his wife and children. That week when he lay dying was like a nightmare and remains in my recollection as a dream of misery.'[4] But politics pressed in upon them relentlessly, and that autumn both went over for the extra session devoted mainly to the Liberal Education Bill, which the Irish party were obliged to oppose on denominational grounds, but which embarrassingly aligned them with Catholic English Tories against their usual Liberal allies, much to Dillon's disgust. While they were in London Elizabeth was

[1] Ibid., 5 Mar. 1905. [2] Ibid., 5 Oct. 1905. [3] Ibid., 5 Nov. 1906.
[4] Ibid., same date.

confined to bed with what was probably bronchitis. As usual she was home-sick for the children, but reluctant to leave her husband alone in London, and the last sentence but one that she ever wrote in her diary returned once more to that perennial theme. 'John is well, thank God, though there is a good deal of influenza about. And the children are all well. How glad I shall be to be back with them all. But I am happy, too, in not having had to leave John alone.'[1]

She came over once more—and it was the last time—for the beginning of the session of 1907, but as on so many other similar occasions she could not stay long, partly because the family needed her, but partly also because a seventh child was soon to be born. 'I wish I could divide myself into two not halves but wholes', she wrote on the boat coming home, 'and be a devoted mother and an intelligent wife at the same time *and* in two places at once.'[2] She remained in fact, an intelligent wife, as well as a devoted mother, to the end, and the letters she wrote in the early months of 1907 were as well informed and acute as always. But though her accounts of domestic happenings were determinedly cheerful she was lonelier this time than at any previous separation and seems even to have been haunted by some strange presentiment of disaster. 'There was a really terrible storm last night', she wrote to Dillon on 18 March, 'and I awoke in a fright, having dreamt so vividly that I was clinging to you for protection from some mysterious danger, that I was quite disappointed to find myself alone.'[3] Nevertheless, she kept him regularly informed about local politics, about the vagaries of William O'Brien, even about the business at Ballaghaderrin, which she seemed to be handling as competently as she did everything else.

Ominously, however, her letters towards the end of April began to refer again to her old enemy, asthma, though by resting in bed for part of the day she seemed to be able to control it.[4] She retained all her interest in politics and, like everyone else, watched with the utmost eagerness for the introduction of the Irish Council Bill which was to be the Liberal Government's first great gesture towards self-government for Ireland.[5] Like Dillon himself, she was sceptical about it from the start, but as he had promised to come home to Dublin immediately after it had been introduced in the House, she had a double interest in its revelations, both for what they themselves might contain and because they would bring him back to her. 'I certainly wish ardently I could be at the centre of so much interest even for a few days', she wrote, 'and I have been, thank goodness, so *very* well for the last week that I feel almost as if I might have been. But I daresay that is a mistake, for of course I *am* leading a very quiet life.'[6] It was indeed tranquil, though the weather remained so atrociously stormy that she was wakeful at night and once again had a strange experience—'a

---

[1] Ibid., 10 Dec. 1906.
[2] Elizabeth Dillon to John Dillon, 11 Mar. 1907 (D.P.).
[3] Elizabeth Dillon to John Dillon, 18 Mar. 1907 (D.P.).
[4] Elizabeth Dillon to John Dillon, 21 Apr. 1907 (D.P.).
[5] For the Irish Council Bill and Dillon's attitude to it, see chapter 10 below.
[6] Elizabeth Dillon to John Dillon, 2 May 1907 (D.P.).

most vivid dream of suddenly finding myself with you, T.P., Mr. Blake and one or two others, and I was conscious that you were under some great anxiety and disappointment about public affairs which, however, I could not quite understand. I awoke in the greatest anxiety while I was trying to get you to explain it all to me. And I still see your anxious face when the dream comes back to my mind.'[1] Perhaps for this reason the last letter she ever wrote her husband (May 7) was a prayer 'for you all and for good to come' on that day which saw the introduction of the ill-fated Irish Council Bill.[2]

What happened then is best told in the account which Dillon himself wrote between 3 and 11 June 1907 and which he called 'A short narrative of the last illness and death of my dearest love.'[3] It opens with this poignant statement:

> In my awful misery since my love left me—turning over and over again in my mind the strange and inexplicable circumstances of her illness and death—it has occurred to me that I ought to write down those circumstances while they [are] fresh in my memory, that doing so might be some relief to me now, and in the future might spare me bitter regrets, if I were to find that owing to failing memory I could not recall the circumstances of her illness and death.

His narrative began with his return at 8.30 on the evening of Thursday, 9 May. She and the four eldest children were in the hall to meet him and 'my heart danced for joy to see my love once again, and be again in my dear, bright home'. But when the children had gone to bed and they were alone, he noticed that although she was looking 'fairly well' she was breathing much too rapidly. She dismissed it as a touch of asthma, but he—and, after all, he had been trained as a doctor—was not convinced. She then confessed that she had overdone things the previous day, and had been out to lunch and tea, only getting back to the house at about seven o'clock. It had been damp and cold and she had felt chilly; moreover, at lunch she had eaten something that disagreed with her and that night (Wednesday) she had suffered severely from heartburn and asthma. Indeed, as she admitted to John, it had been 'the worst night she had had for a very long time'.

Accordingly, on Thursday they went to bed early and although she slept fairly well Dillon noticed that her breathing was still not right. Next day he urged her to stay in bed, but she refused and actually went out, although it was again a miserably cold, wet day. That afternoon she looked tired; after supper she went up to the nursery as she usually did every night, but came down 'laughing' and told John that while she was up there she had had 'a most dreadful fit of shortness of breath'. At his urging she went to bed before him, but had such a bad second attack that she had to hold

[1] Elizabeth Dillon to John Dillon, 'Thursday night', 2 May 1907 (D.P.).
[2] Elizabeth Dillon to John Dillon, 7 May 1907. (D.P.).
[3] John Dillon, 'A short narrative of the last illness and death of my dearest love', 3–11 June 1907 (D.P.).

on to the bed to regain her control. Dillon now began to be alarmed and, though the night of Friday was not as bad as some she had had in the past, she coughed a good deal and—'what frightened me most'—the catch in her breathing never stopped. Dillon had already written to their friend Dr. Cox to come and see her and on Saturday she stayed in bed until he arrived. Dillon explained the symptoms and asked him to examine Elizabeth's lungs very carefully. Cox did so, reporting that but for slight bronchial catarrh there was nothing wrong with her lungs and no ground for uneasiness. Her temperature, however, as Dillon later found, was just 100 degrees and, though she slept well, the mysterious catch in her chest still persisted.

On Sunday, 12 May, Cox saw her again. He thought, and she herself asserted, that she was much better and she came down to tea to the drawing-room on the first floor. Dillon thought she looked 'very exhausted', but he had to leave her for a while, as W. F. Bailey (the Land Commissioner and an old friend) called to see him. It was then that she scribbled in pencil the last words she ever wrote to her husband—that if he wanted Bailey to stay to supper she would have coffee upstairs. But Bailey left before long and Dillon went to bring her down to the dining-room. They had supper and it was the last time they were to sit at table together. Going up to the drawing-room afterwards, she seemed exhausted. The shortness of breath was most noticeable and Dillon pressed her to go to bed. She agreed reluctantly, saying with a little laugh: 'The truth is I am afraid to face the stairs.' He urged her to make the effort and helped her as much as he could, but it was such an immense labour that it was only by 'what seemed a desperate effort' that he got her to the bedroom, where she collapsed on to the bed without undressing. Immediately she began to shiver and although he placed hot-water bottles at her feet and gave her brandy the 'rigor' (as he described it) continued for nearly an hour. Dillon sent at once for her gynaecologist, Dr. ——.[1] 'I was horrified', wrote Dillon afterwards in a revealing passage, 'when I saw his juvenile appearance.' He was not reassured when the doctor came downstairs at once to go to Merrion Square —right across the city—for an instrument he had not brought with him. Dillon sat with her while the gynaecologist was away, holding her hand and trying to soothe her, for she was now suffering 'the most cruel agony' and 'in a condition of extreme terror'.

On his return the doctor was able to give her some relief, and although she herself thought the birth was imminent, he assured Dillon that this was not so. On the other hand, he could offer no explanation of the rigor and he admitted that her temperature had gone up to 103 degrees. Dillon, now 'desperately alarmed', wanted to call in an obstetrician, but Dr. —— persuaded him to wait until her own doctor, Cox, had seen her in the morning. 'To this advice', Dillon later recalled, 'in an evil hour I yielded.'

However, on Monday morning Elizabeth seemed a little more comfortable. The gynaecologist came again and found no cause for uneasiness

[1] He is named in Dillon's narrative, but it seems an unwarrantable intrusion upon privacy to disclose his identity here.

and this was also Cox's verdict, even though Dillon, worried by her coughing, urged him particularly to examine her lungs. But there was apparently no sign of congestion or pneumonia. That afternoon, indeed, she was 'joyous' and apparently over the worst. 'Those doctors,' she told John, 'have worked a miracle on me—in fact I feel as if I were in paradise.' This progress continued throughout the evening—so much so that the doctors told him he could go to bed without fear. Being, as he says, worn out with the strain and now free from anxiety, he went to bed and slept soundly.

At seven o'clock next morning (Tuesday, 14 May) he was awakened by one of the maids in tears, who told him that the mistress was bad again and that the child was coming. 'I jumped up in an agony of alarm', he wrote, 'and rushed downstairs to send servants off for doctors.' After what seemed an interminable delay, he succeeded in getting Dr. Paul Carton from Rutland Square near by, while the gynaecologist was being summoned. Carton reached the house just in time for the arrival of a still-born baby girl—'the child we had so often talked of and had longed for so much'. Dr. —— then arrived and shocked Dillon by telling him that he thought the child had died during the Sunday night, as he had not been able to detect any sign of life or movement since. 'Why', wrote Dillon bitterly afterwards, 'did he tell me on Monday that there was no ground for uneasiness?' Probably from a wish not to burden a distraught husband, but, however that may be, once the dead baby had been delivered, he still maintained there was no reason for anxiety. This time, however, Dillon demanded and obtained his agreement to a second opinion from the obstetrician, Sir William Smyly.

The crisis had now come and both Dillon and Dr. Cox, who arrived that same morning, were shocked by the change in Elizabeth's appearance. Cox could still not find anything wrong with her chest, but her breathing had become more difficult and she had begun to have attacks of faintness. Cox and the other doctors paid a second visit shortly afterwards and this time they were upstairs for a long time. When they came down Cox said that the moment had arrived when it was his duty to suggest that she should have the Last Sacraments. The priest was sent for and while he was coming Dillon went up to her room again. She had actually rallied a little and, while herself suggesting the Last Sacraments, tried to reassure him. 'I have no intention of dying,' she said; 'I *mean* to get well and stay with you all.' 'I kissed her dear arms', wrote Dillon, 'and a ray of hope crept into my heart again.'

Shortly after this Father Conmee arrived—a Jesuit from Belvedere College a few yards away, the same Father Conmee on whom James Joyce was about to confer a dubious immortality.[1] From him Elizabeth received the Sacraments with perfect composure. This was in the early afternoon, just before three o'clock. Soon afterwards she began to sink very rapidly,

---

[1] Father John Conmee, formerly rector of Clongowes College, then prefect of studies at Belvedere College, and later Provincial of the Jesuit Order in Ireland (c.f. Richard Ellman, *James Joyce* (London, 1959), pp. 27–8, 35).

with frequent fits of faintness, and always, with every breath she drew, there was an ominous rattle in her chest. Once more the doctors came, once more they stayed long upstairs. When they came down to the study Sir William Smyly broke it to Dillon that there was now practically no chance. 'I said it was an awful message, but what I had expected—"but can you tell me what is killing her?" Sir William Smyly said, "Mr. Dillon, it is very hard for us doctors to give it a name" and I think he muttered something about influenza.'

It is possible that Dillon, in his anguish, did not take in fully what the doctors had to say. Certainly, it was in the highest degree unlikely that at that late stage in the case they would suddenly, and for the first time, have diagnosed influenza. And it is proper to add that later, when all was finished, Dillon had a further conference with Dr. Carton, who had been brought in at the crisis, and from him learnt that the probable cause of death was, after all, pneumonia, and that it was the high temperature of the mother's body arising from this which had killed the child on the Sunday night. 'He said', noted Dillon the day after this conversation, 'that cases of pneumonia generally did result in the death of the child and miscarriage and were very frequently fatal'.[1] Perhaps this, though it does not explain the strange complacency of the earlier diagnoses, is the nearest we can get to a true medical verdict on this baffling and tragic illness.

The end was not long in coming. The doctors tried all they knew to revive her with oxygen and injections of strychnine, and although she was by then mostly unconscious she had one last lucid moment in which she said quite clearly: 'Yes, yes, it is our duty to try everything, oxygen and everything else.' After this she lapsed into a coma and died at 5.30 in the evening, apparently without any further suffering. Dillon ended his narrative with these words:

> Two hours before she died I noticed large purpuric spots coming out on her arms, the dear sweet arms that I loved to kiss, the arms that had rescued me from misery and unhappiness and for eleven years had sheltered me and given me a taste of happiness which I did not believe was in the world for me. And now it is all over—and I am alone.

[1] John Dillon, 'Memorandum of conversation with Dr. Carton, 24 June 1907', in Dillon's hand, dated 25 June 1907 (D.P.).

10

The Liberal Alliance

By the beginning of 1905 it had become clear that the days of the Tory Government were numbered. Deeply divided by the tariff reform issue, chafing under Balfour's seemingly negligent leadership, and inevitably weary after ten years of uninterrupted office, Ministers and party were played out. Certainly, they were in no condition to meet the storm which sprang up suddenly out of a clear sky in Ireland. There, Lord Dunraven, the presiding genius of the Land Conference, had gone on from that triumph of conciliation to found an Irish Reform Association which, while reflecting primarily the views of progressive landlords like himself, was intended to be a rallying-point for all, regardless of political affiliation, who wished to see the 'conference policy' applied to other spheres of Irish life. In the course of 1904 this body had produced a scheme of 'devolution'— that is, for granting to Ireland limited powers of local self-government. What gave this scheme a peculiarly sinister significance in Unionist eyes was the fact, which gradually became public knowledge, that no less a person than the Under-Secretary, Sir Antony MacDonnell, had had a hand in drafting it. The Ulster Unionists, especially, who had scented a conspiracy from the moment the proposal was published, were outraged that a permanent official should have dared to tamper even to this extent with the sacred British connection. When attacked, Sir Antony naturally defended himself in the only way he could—by explaining that at an early stage in the proceedings he had written to his superior, George Wyndham, informing him that he had been helping Dunraven 'in this business'. Wyndham, however, had failed completely to realise the implications of this letter and when his fellow Unionists launched their onslaught, at first repudiated all knowledge of the scheme. Ulster resentment grew almost from day to day and when parliament met in February 1905 both Under-Secretary and Chief Secretary came under fire. Sir Antony stoutly resisted all pressure to resign, basing his position partly on his letter to Wyndham and partly on the ground that, when first appointed, he had been led to believe that he would have a degree of power in initiating policy not usually granted to permanent officials. In the end it was Wyndham, nerve and health both broken, who was driven from office into lasting and ignominious obscurity.[1]

[1] F. S. L. Lyons, 'The Irish Unionist party and the devolution crisis of 1904–5', in *I.H.S.*, vol vi, no. 21 (Mar. 1948) pp. 1–22. For the general situation of the Government at this time, see A. Gollin, *Balfour's burden* (London, 1965).

Retrospectively this fiasco can be seen as simply one more nail in the coffin of the Unionist Government, but when the Irish Reform Association's proposal first appeared it took the Nationalist leaders by surprise and produced very diverse reactions. Redmond, who was in America collecting party funds, was initially inclined to greet the devolution scheme as 'a declaration for Home Rule' and 'quite a wonderful thing'.[1] Dillon, on the other hand, saw it in a very different light. He distrusted its parentage, he disliked its contents, he feared where it might lead, and in a speech at Sligo that autumn he roundly asserted that 'any vote of confidence in Lord Dunraven, or any declaration of satisfaction at the foundation of the Irish Reform Association would tear the ranks of the Nationalists of Ireland to pieces'. And in another speech shortly afterwards (31 October) he drove the point brutally home by observing that 'conciliation, so far as landlords are concerned, was another name for swindling the people'.[2]

In one sense this was, of course, a continuation of his old quarrel with William O'Brien over the whole field of co-operation with landlords, and the bitterness between them was intensified as a result. But in another and more important sense his outspoken opposition to the Irish Reform Association was prompted by a profound—and surely correct—instinct that the Irish parliamentary party could only maintain its hold upon the country if it remained pledged absolutely to Home Rule. Anything less than the full demand, however tempting, was dangerous, because acceptance might postpone true self-government indefinitely. When Redmond returned, it was Dillon's view which prevailed, and the two leaders bent all their energies to making whatever political capital they could out of the situation. More particularly, since the Government really did seem to be tottering, they concentrated on trying to find out how the Liberals now stood on the Home Rule issue.

To find out how the Liberals stood on anything had not been easy in the decade that had passed since Gladstone's retirement and least of all had it been easy to find out how they stood on Home Rule. In the immediate aftermath of the failure of 1893 there had been a natural reaction away from Gladstone's policy, and by a curious irony it was Gladstone's son, Herbert, who eventually (but not until a year after his father's death in 1898) set the tone for the party as a whole by advocating that they should 'stand and wait'. There was not much else, indeed, that they could do in their long exile from power, and at that very time the attention of the leading Liberals was much more taken up with the struggle for the succession, and later with their acute disagreements over the Boer War, than with the murky future of Ireland. But expel Ireland with a pitchfork as they might, she was always liable to return, and between 1900 and 1905, as difficulties thickened round the Unionist Government, it became all too clear that the Liberals must somehow or other resolve their internal differences and emerge with a coherent Irish policy. There were, in fact, three possible policies. At one

[1] D. R. Gwynn, *Life of John Redmond* (London, 1932), p. 106.
[2] Cited in W. O'Brien, *Olive branch*, pp. 326, 339.

extreme there was simple loyalty to the original Gladstonian concept of Home Rule. Some of the old guard—including Campbell-Bannerman, John Morley and Lord Spencer—still held themselves bound by this loyalty, but there was no denying that among rank-and-file Liberals Home Rule had come to be regarded as a major electoral hazard and even its most devoted adherents could scarcely regard it as more than an academic issue at the dawn of the new century. At the other extreme was the viewpoint most forcefully represented by Rosebery and explained by him with devastating clarity in a celebrated speech at Chesterfield in December 1901. Calling upon Liberals to discard the 'fly-blown phylacteries' of the past, and to face the future with a 'clean slate' in domestic affairs, he left no doubt in the minds of those who heard or read him that in his opinion Home Rule was dead, and that it was high time for Liberals to unchain themselves from the corpse.

There remained, however, a third possibility. This was the policy Campbell-Bannerman was later to make famous as 'step-by-step' on the eve of the 1906 election, but it had been adumbrated by Asquith and Sir Edward Grey as far back as 1901. In a speech at Ladybank in September of that year, Asquith, while observing that he hoped the Liberals would never again take office depending upon Irish support for their majority (a high-flown sentiment he had no difficulty in shedding in 1910), had declared himself in favour of two principles of Irish government—maintenance of the supremacy of the imperial Parliament and 'as liberal a devolution of local powers and responsibilities as statesmanship can from time to time devise'. Or, as Grey put it when reporting to Campbell-Bannerman his and Haldane's agreement with this doctrine: 'Things must advance towards Home Rule, but I think it must be step by step.'[1]

At first sight it was not easy to determine which of these various policies, if any, would provide the basis for agreement the Liberals so badly needed. A simple adhesion to Home Rule was honourable but unpopular. A simple repudiation of Home Rule might—in some quarters—be popular, but in others it would certainly be regarded as dishonourable. Nevertheless, such was Rosebery's personal prestige that if he had followed his outburst at Chesterfield (subsequently repeated in private and in public) by the determined bid to regain the party leadership which his friends were urging him to make, the policy of repudiation might have gained formidable support. Even as it was Asquith, while still at heart convinced that 'step-by-step' was the right policy, agreed, together with Haldane and Grey, to join the Roseberyite Liberal League when it was founded early in 1902, although it was clearly an anti-Home Rule organisation.[2] But Rosebery, while refusing to identify himself with Campbell-Bannerman's leadership, refused equally to campaign for the leadership himself, and by 1902 it was plain that Liberal-

---

[1] H. W. McCready, 'Home Rule and the Liberal Party, 1899–1906', in *I.H.S.*, vol. xiii, no. 52 (Sept. 1963), pp. 316–48.

[2] In March 1902 Asquith devoted a major speech largely to an exposition of the step-by-step policy (McCready, op. cit., p. 335).

ism, which had just begun to recover from its Boer War wounds, was once more in schism. It was true that the Government had too many worries of its own to be able to exploit the Opposition's disunity, but this was cold comfort, for the nearer Balfour staggered to resignation or dissolution the larger loomed the prospect—at once enticing and embarrassing—of the Liberals having to take office. To do this, however, without having first resolved their internal differences would be suicidal, and it is not surprising that as 1904 drew to a close the search for a formula became frenetic.,

But when the session of 1905 opened with the Ulster Unionists in full cry after Wyndham and MacDonnell no formula had yet been found. And this was the moment chosen by the Irish leaders to test the intentions of the Liberals. The initiative was taken by Dillon, who on January 19 wrote to John Morley at Redmond's request asking if the Liberals, 'or at least the bulk of the party', would support an amendment to the Address condemning the existing system of Irish government as one under which the Irish people were denied all effective voice in the conduct of their own affairs. The suggestion was ingenious for, as Dillon pointed out, anyone who was not prepared to support 'the present system of Irish government' could vote for the amendment 'without being committed to any particular scheme for the reform of the government of Ireland'.[1] On the other hand, as Dillon himself realised, Liberals who did vote for such an amendment might well have to face the awkward question—what would they put in place of 'the present system of Irish government'? Morley, and Campbell-Bannerman and Spencer, whom he consulted, were only too well aware of the dangers inherent in this seemingly innocuous proposal and Morley, when he replied a week later, fell easily into his familiar role of wet blanket. In principle sympathetic, the Liberals would need to see the terms of the amendment before they could commit themselves:

> Personally [added Morley] I see immense disadvantages in a motion, because it may easily set back the movement from the Unionist camp. On the other hand, it is inevitable that the Liberal leaders should make frank declarations before the election comes. Only, *the longer it is before the Irish question interrupts the swing in our direction*, the better for all of us.
>
> I understand that there is to be a debate on Sir A. MacDonnell and the Dunraven move, raised by an Orange amendment. This will open the whole question of Irish government. Perhaps that might be handled so as to make your motion superfluous.[2]

Redmond did not think so. On the contrary, as he wrote to Dillon after seeing Morley's letter, 'it would be fatal if the only amendment raising the question of Irish government came from the Orangemen'. The Liberal leaders, he conceded, might well be nervous, but they had nothing to lose by supporting a moderate amendment and it would do no harm at all to

---

[1] Dillon to John Morley, 19 Jan. 1905, copy in Dillon's hand, (D.P.).
[2] John Morley to Dillon, 26 Jan. 1905 (D.P.); Gwynn, *Redmond*, p. 108.

'force their hands a little'.[1] Accordingly, a few days later Dillon sent the terms of the proposed motion to Morley, with a covering note explaining that he and Redmond had considered the question fully and were both of opinion that an amendment was necessary.[2] Redmond himself was at some pains to allay the anxieties of those whose goodwill he might soon be needing, and when Parliament opened he assured Herbert Gladstone in conversation that he fully recognised the difficulty of the Liberals' position and that he thought Home Rule would come 'by degrees'.[3] Nevertheless, the amendment was introduced on 19 February and, as anticipated, was largely taken up with an extended debate on the Wyndham-MacDonnell affair. It was notable for the savagery with which Wyndham was attacked by his fellow Unionists and it was therefore quite easy for the Liberals to go into the lobby with the nationalists.[4] The Government was not defeated, but Wyndham was broken irretrievably and on 7 March he sent his resignation to Balfour.

Dillon's own view was that so long as Sir Antony MacDonnell remained in office and the mystery of the terms of his appointment was unresolved, they should leave the running to be made by the 'Orangemen'. And that was in fact what happened until a new Chief Secretary of impeccable orthodoxy—Walter Long—had taken over and Sir Antony's position had been suitably redefined. This had been done by the end of March, but by then, so severe had been the criticism of the Government, it was widely expected Balfour might be obliged to resign at any moment. It therefore became urgent for the Nationalist leaders to take up the running themselves and especially to come to close quarters with the Liberals. On 30 March Morley saw Redmond and told him—apparently quite categorically—that Balfour had decided to go immediately after the budget (that is, early in June), that Campbell-Bannerman would form a government, ask for supplies and then dissolve. 'He sd. Rosebery would not be in this government', Redmond reported to Dillon. 'He also said they did not know where to turn for a Chief Secretary.'[5] Dillon's political professionalism was outraged by this news. If a dissolution did take place, he wrote by return, Campbell-Bannerman should refuse to form a government until after the general election. 'If he attempts the task the Roseberyites are sure to insist on terms, or render the formation of a government impossible. Think of the effect on the situation of an interregnum of wrangling between the Liberal leaders before the dissolution, leading either to a failure on Bannerman's part to form a government or the (secret) acceptance of the terms of Asquith and co.' Moreover, an immediate change of government would affect their own position. 'The moment the Liberals take office before the election the pressure on us to demand categorical pledges from them as a condition of our support will

[1] Redmond to Dillon, 28 Jan. 1905 (D.P.).
[2] Dillon to John Morley, 4 Feb. 1905, copy in Dillon's hand (D.P.).
[3] McCready, op. cit., p. 341.
[4] Hansard, H.C. Debates, 4th series, vol. 141, cols. 622–32, for Redmond's speech; voting figures are in cols. 875–80.
[5] Redmond to Dillon, 30 Mar. 1905 (D.P.); Gwynn, *Redmond*, p. 111.

be irresistible.'[1] The letter is remarkable both for its anticipation of what
was actually to happen at the end of the year, and as evidence of the deep
distrust Dillon felt for Asquith, whom he assumed—too readily as it turned
out—to be still a devoted Roseberyite. The dangers of a false step by these
dubious allies seemed to him so great that a couple of days later he wrote
again in deep agitation lest the Liberals by their own clumsiness might bring
about a dissolution. 'I do not think', he said, 'the Liberal leaders ought to allow
Balfour and co. to know anything of their intentions—God knows, perhaps
they have been fools enough to take Balfour into their confidence already.'[2]

In fact, these hopes and fears were premature. The Government hung
on doggedly until Parliament rose in August and Balfour, who had his own
deep concern for questions of defence to preoccupy him, did not resign
until the beginning of December.[3] The intervening months were filled with
manoeuvre, but from the Irish point of view there was really only one question to be settled—how far could they commit the Liberals to a satisfactory
declaration on Home Rule? It was hardly to be expected that Home Rule
would become an issue in the election, but the casting of the Irish vote in
Great Britain, and indeed the prestige of the Irish party in their own country, would depend upon the answer to this question. It was, however, desperately difficult to predict what the answer might be, since apparently
even the Liberals did not know it themselves. All that could be done to
edge them in the right direction was to make the Irish demand as plain as
possible. It so happened that in the autumn—well before Balfour had
announced his decision to resign—Redmond was due to make several
speeches in Scotland, and before setting out he consulted Dillon about the
line he should take. Dillon jotted down some notes of this conversation and
both these and a copy he sent the chairman have survived. From this evidence it is clear that they discussed two possibilities—either that Redmond
should press for a specific clarification by the Liberal leaders of their attitude, or that he should content himself with stating 'our resolve by every
means in our power to push on the cause of national self-government'. The
first course would have been disastrous—only a few days earlier Asquith,
though renewing his loyalty to the step-by-step policy, had made it plain
that Home Rule in the full sense could not be part of the programme of the
next Liberal Government, and in so doing had provoked a counter-state-
ment from Morley which showed that the Liberals were still at sixes and
sevens.[4] Accordingly, the Irish leaders decided in favour of the second
course, Dillon suggesting that Redmond, having defined the Irish demand,
should then ask how the Liberals, who earlier in the year had voted for the
amendment to the Address condemning the existing system of government
in Ireland, could possibly continue to sanction such a system when they
came to power. And not only this, he should go out of his way to allude

[1] Dillon to Redmond, 31 Mar. 1905 (R.P.).
[2] Ibid., 2 Apr. 1905; Gwynn, *Redmond*, p. 112.
[3] Blanche E. C. Dugdale, *Arthur James Balfour* (London, 1939), i. 319–22.
[4] My attention has been drawn to this exchange by Mr. A. C. Hepburn of the
University of Kent at Canterbury; see also McCready, op. cit., pp. 341–4.

to Asquith's recent speech and make it clear that if his section of the Liberal Party continued to say that the Liberals were unable to set up a statutory parliament in Ireland, then 'the consequences to the Liberal party will be very disastrous and they will find before many months are out that the Irish question will be with them with all the insistence of 1881 and 1886'. Much of this, of course, was mere manoeuvring for position. What counted in the last resort was votes, and Dillon's memorandum concerned itself with this also, at least with the Irish votes which would soon be cast in Great Britain. There was, it seems, agreement between the two leaders that where possible these votes should go to a Labour supporter of Home Rule, unless he was standing against an old and tried friend of the Irish cause. In general, the Irish vote should be given 'irrespective of all other considerations' to any candidate supporting the full Gladstonian policy of Home Rule and where such did not exist, the responsibility for deciding how the vote should go should be left to the Standing Committee of the United Irish League of Great Britain.[1]

(ii)

In making these dispositions Dillon and Redmond were probably both under the impression, as many others were at the time, that the general election would be close and the Irish position correspondingly strong. 'If the Liberals quarrel with us after the election', Dillon wrote to Redmond a week later, 'we shall have it in our power to make their position an impossible one.' At the same time, he added, almost with an air of condescension, that 'unless absolutely driven to it by the conduct of Asquith and Rosebery I do not think we should do anything calculated to make a sweeping defeat of the Unionist party and the formation of a strong Liberal government impossible'.[2] The upshot of all this discussion was that in Scotland Redmond felt able to take a firm, but not intransigent, line, dismissing the 'ridiculous and unmeaning policies' known as 'administrative Home Rule' or 'devolution' and stating the Irish case in unequivocal terms.[3]

Yet the big question remained—could the Liberals settle their internal differences before Balfour caught them unprepared? The omens were not propitious. Apart from the contrasting public positions of Asquith and Morley, there was still doubt about where Campbell-Bannerman stood and this could not be resolved until he came back from the Continent, where—deliberately—he was lingering later than usual. But, if there was doubt about Campbell-Bannerman, there was none about Rosebery, who, near the end of October, once more demanded some positive and official Liberal statement on Home Rule. 'Any middle policy—that of placing Home Rule

---

[1] 'Memorandum for John Redmond', copy in Dillon's hand, Oct. 1905 (D.P.); original, dated 26 Oct. 1905, in Redmond Papers.

[2] Dillon to Redmond, 2 Nov. 1905 (R.P.).

[3] Speech at Glasgow, 10 Nov. 1905, cited in J. A. Spender, *The life of the Right Honourable Sir Henry Campbell-Bannerman, G.C.B.* (London, 1923), ii. 180.

in the position of a reliquary, and only exhibiting it at great moments of public stress, as Roman Catholics are accustomed to exhibit relics of a saint—is not one which will earn sympathy or success in this country.'[1] As a general description of the Liberals' attitude this was uncomfortably accurate though, as a short-term prophecy, it was woefully astray. Within three weeks of that speech the reliquary was indeed to be furbished up for public exhibition, but with the assistance of a new acolyte—Asquith—whom Rosebery still fondly believed to stand with him outside the tabernacle. On Campbell-Bannerman's return to London on 12 November, he saw Asquith among his very first callers next day. Their conversation was mostly concerned with the possible composition of a Liberal government and although Asquith had previously concluded with Grey and Haldane the 'Relugas compact' of September 1905, whereby they all agreed not to take office unless Campbell-Bannerman went to the House of Lords, it was plain from that meeting that if Campbell-Bannerman resisted this pressure—as he ultimately did—the trio would be faced with an unpleasant choice between the sweets of office and the austerities of Relugas. How they reconciled it with their consciences to opt for the former is no part of this story—what is relevant, however, is that Campbell-Bannerman, having to a degree taken Asquith into his confidence, went even further at a second meeting a few days later and accepted the step-by-step policy in regard to Home Rule with which Asquith (and to a lesser extent Haldane and Grey) had for so long been associated.[2]

In the meantime—on 14 November—Campbell-Bannerman secured his lines of communication with the Irish. At breakfast with John Redmond and T. P. O'Connor he contrived to reassure them of his continuing loyalty to Home Rule while at the same time pointing out the difficulties in the way of any rapid and satisfactory solution. 'His own impression', noted Redmond afterwards, 'was that it would not be possible to pass full Home Rule, but he hoped to be able to pass some serious measure which would be consistent with and lead up to the other. He would say nothing, however, to withdraw the larger measure from the electors . . .'[3] This was the formula which he repeated in public at Stirling on 23 November and which at last allowed most Liberals to fall into line behind him, with the eminent but forlorn exception of Lord Rosebery, whose ill-timed denunciation of Home Rule in any shape or form two days later left him entirely isolated and, politically, a spent force. It may seem surprising that the Nationalist leaders should have accepted, apparently with reasonable equanimity, a formula which was much more designed to paper over Liberal cracks than to satisfy Irish needs. One reason why they did so may simply have been that they liked and trusted Campbell-Bannerman who, they knew, had remained loyal to the Gladstonian conception of Home Rule through all the changes

[1] R. R. James, *Rosebery* (London, 1964 impression), p. 453.
[2] R. Jenkins, *Asquith* (London, 1964), pp. 147–9.
[3] Gwynn, *Redmond*, p. 115.

and chances of the last few years. That he still remained loyal to that conception Redmond and T. P. O'Connor were evidently prepared to believe after their meeting with him on 14 November, and because they believed this they believed also his diagnosis that Home Rule would have to wait. Indeed, and this no doubt was the main reason for their acquiescence, they were in no position to demand anything more than he was prepared to promise them. They were realists, after all, and they had been watching both the Liberal divisions and the mood of the country very closely—they must have understood perfectly well that in the context of 1905 the only appropriate comment on Home Rule was the comment Gladstone had once used of Parnell's bid to retain the leadership in the much more unpromising circumstances of 1890—'it'll na dae, it'll na dae'. On the other hand, the acceptance by the Irish leaders of the step-by-step policy had in it the seeds of danger. For one thing, their dependence on one man—Campbell-Bannerman—was too great, since that man, had they but known it, had little more than two years to live. And for another, while it was reasonable to adopt a patient attitude towards their allies so long as there was a possibility of the general election being so close that the Liberals, if they took office, would be heavily dependent on Irish support, and therefore amenable to Irish pressure, the position was very different when, as actually happened, the Liberals swept back to power after a landslide so vast as to give them a clear majority over all other parties in the house.[1]

Indeed, even before Balfour had resigned and in the immediate aftermath of Campbell-Bannermans' Stirling speech and Rosebery's repudiation of it, Dillon was already expressing characteristic doubts about the reality of the Liberals promises, such as they were. All might be well, he conceded, if Campbell-Bannerman ignored Rosebery and stuck to his guns—and if he did do this Dillon was in favour of the Irish vote being thrown behind the Liberals at the election, but even as late as 12 December, he was still uneasy about the Liberal leader's relations with, and possible concessions to, Asquith and Grey.[2] By that time, however, Campbell-Bannerman was almost out of the wood—he was not only Prime Minister, but had been able to circumvent the Relugas compact and to form his Government with remarkable rapidity. His choice as Chief Secretary was James Bryce. Bryce was an Ulsterman by birth, internationally known as an historian, widely travelled and an omniverous reader in Dillon's own style. Dillon liked him as a person, distrusted him as a politician and grew to detest him as an administrator. He had grave doubts about Bryce's fitness for the post, but when the latter wrote to him expressing the utmost eagerness to have close

---

[1] For an earlier summary of my views on this question see *The Irish parliamentary party*, pp. 111–13. I there refer to Campbell-Bannerman's undertaking to Redmond as a 'guarantee', which is probably too strong a word, though Professor MacCready, in questioning this word ('Home Rule and the Liberal party, 1899–1906') is in error when he reads into my remarks that the so-called guarantee was 'with respect to home rule's imminence in the new parliament'. This is not deducible either from Redmond's record of the Campbell-Bannerman interview or from my account of the incident.

[2] Dillon to Redmond, 27 Nov., 8, 9 and 12 Dec. 1905 (R.P.).

contact with the Irish leaders, Dillon decided to test his sincerity.[1] On 19 December he wrote him a long analysis of the situation which Bryce thought important enough to have a section of it copied and sent to the Prime Minister. The part which reached Campbell-Bannerman ran as follows:

> My idea of an Irish policy for the Liberal party [wrote Dillon] is that until they are able to propose their legislative proposals for the better government of Ireland they ought to govern the country, so far as the present system allows, in accordance with Irish ideas—ascertaining those ideas from the representatives of the majority of the Irish people. And when attacked in the House or in the press, that they ought boldly to proclaim this policy, saying at the same time that the great evil of the present system is that under it it is not possible to carry out fully the government of Ireland in accordance with Irish ideas, because the men who are entitled to speak for the Irish people cannot be fixed with the responsible and sobering influence of power.

> If then the government of Ireland were carried on on these lines and a bold avowal made of these principles, the whole situation would be easier for us, and it would be made possible for us to give the government time to mature their proposals for reforming the system of Irish government and to approach the consideration of those proposals in a friendly and tolerant spirit.

> Finally, I think I ought to say that it is absolutely *vital* that Bannerman's Stirling speech should be allowed to stand as the definition of the position of the Liberal party on the Irish question. Any attempt to explain away that statement by the Prime Minister himself, or by you, would lead to the most disastrous results. We are content with that statement, although it was, as the Prime Minister said, a moderate statement. And I would strongly urge you to take the opportunity the first time you are speaking in public to express your agreement with the Stirling speech.[2]

It was a friendly enough letter, but it contained nevertheless a hint of menace and Bryce's reply, with the opening of the election campaign only a few days away, was full of sweet reasonableness. He was, he said, quite at one with the Stirling speech, and not only that, was also in agreement 'with most, perhaps indeed with all' that Dillon had said about Irish government. 'I am fully sensible of your difficulties, and desire to ease them as much as possible. You know ours also; and I do not doubt will desire to ease them. The more smoothly things go in Ireland, the greater the prospect of making substantial progress in the direction we desire.'[3]

[1] James Bryce to Dillon, 17 Dec. 1905.
[2] James Bryce to Campbell-Bannerman, 19 Dec. 1905, and enclosure (B.M. Add. MS. 41211, f. 331); I have not so far been able to trace the original of Dillon's letter in the Bryce Papers.
[3] Bryce to Dillon, 25 Dec. 1905 (D.P.).

However, when the two men met in Dublin nearly a month later Bryce was much more strongly placed. The Liberals had won an overwhelming victory in the election and, with a majority of 132 over all other parties, seemed to be in an unassailable position. Even so, Dillon took a firm line with the new Chief Secretary from the start. Several years later, speaking in Parliament, he recalled that he had said to Bryce: 'In the name of God let us have a Land Act immediately, because there is peace in Ireland now, and you never had such a chance of showing the Irish people that the government will be just without disturbance; but if you postpone dealing with this question you will have a disturbance of the most serious character . . .'[1] However, a letter he wrote Redmond a few days before he saw Bryce suggests that he intended to demand not merely a Land Act but also a Labourers Act and the repeal of the Coercion Act, while the notes he made for use in his actual conversation with Bryce on 26 January indicate that he went further even than this. Despite the fact that he was playing from weakness (a situation which never worried him unduly) it seems that he told Bryce bluntly that if there was not in the King's Speech 'a passage sufficiently strong to draw bitter attack from [the] Unionist party, it will be almost impossible for us to avoid moving an amendment, or at all events adopting [a] critical and hostile attitude'. He then went on to list a variety of items on which the Irish party would need to be consulted, including the finances of the Development Grant, the dubious official position of Sir Horace Plunkett (who had lost his seat at the general election of 1900, but was still at the head of the Department of Agriculture and Technical Instruction), the use of Irish in schools, the personnel of the Land Commission and the fate of the remaining evicted tenants. 'If we start off with a difference of opinion,' he warned darkly, 'the breach will widen rapidly . . . The Liberal party cannot afford to govern Ireland by coercion, and the *only* alternative is to govern with our support. But in order to give support we must have something substantial to offer the people.'[2]

Redmond, too, had been in contact with Bryce and also with the formidable Sir Antony and did not altogether like what he heard. The Government, it was true, was apparently preparing a scheme for the reform of Irish administration, but this would not see the light until 1907 (it was ominous for the future that Redmond carried away from his interview with MacDonnell an altogether exaggerated idea of the scope of this proposal) and in the meantime there was even a risk that Ireland would not be mentioned in the King's speech at all.[3] Dillon became more anxious than ever and on 6 February, having seen Bryce again, he wrote to Redmond that it now seemed as if they would have to stage some sort of protest during the debate on the Address, especially if, as he feared, the King's Speech contained no promise of a Land Bill. And next day he complained

[1] Hansard, H.C. Debates, 5th series, vol. 8 (1909), col. 766.
[2] Dillon to Redmond, 20 Jan. 1906; 'Notes used in conversation with Bryce on Friday, 26 Jan. 1906' (D.P.).
[3] Redmond memorandum of interview with Sir A. MacDonnell, undated, but probably end of December 1905 (R.P.); Gwynn, *Redmond*, pp. 120–1.

that they had not even got a firm promise of a Labourers' Bill, so that they must speak out.[1] In the end, however, the Speech included not only a Labourers' Bill, but also a statement that the Government had plans for 'effecting economies in the system of government in Ireland and for introducing into it means for associating the people with the conduct of Irish affairs'. This was vague enough in all conscience, but since the Ulster Unionists moved an amendment ingeniously designed to draw the Government into a premature disclosure of their plans Dillon felt obliged to refrain from the criticisms he would clearly have liked to make. Instead, he remarked only that he and his friends accepted the passage relating to Ireland in the King's Speech 'as a broad declaration in principle' and were prepared to give the government 'reasonable time' in which to work out the details. But he could not refrain from adding a veiled threat. The government, he said, would find in the Irish party 'old and tried politicians, practical men, reasonable men, men not difficult to deal with, men with whom it was easy to carry on a transaction so long as they were convinced that those with whom they were dealing were honest and in earnest'.[2]

The reluctance of the Government to commit themselves to far-reaching Irish legislation was only partly due to their own internal difficulties about the content of such legislation. It was due at least as much, and probably more, to the fact that their supporters expected from them a whole range of social reforms many of which had been promised or foreshadowed in the election campaign. The ministerial programme for 1906 set out over twenty different measures of which two at least were certain to arouse controversy—to revise the law relating to trade unions and to amend the Education Act of 1902. The first of these reflected the growing importance of the Labour Party in British politics and the Irish party could be expected to be sympathetic to it. But the Education Bill was a different matter and was certain to place them in a delicate situation. The Bill, inevitably, would be aimed against the denominational schools and would be condemned by the Roman Catholic Church. The Irish Members could not but be sensitive to this kind of pressure, yet they dare not risk alienating their powerful English allies by too vigorous opposition to legislation which had such a weight of Liberal opinion behind it. The one saving grace was that Archbishop Bourne of Westminster recognised the dangers of a head-on clash with such a powerful Liberal Government and in an interview with Redmond and Dillon on the eve of the session took a moderate line which surprised Dillon as much as it impressed him.[3] He would have been even more surprised, though possibly less impressed, had he heard the opinion of the Marquess of Ripon, who was the chief Liberal negotiator with the Church, that Dillon carried more weight in educational matters with the Archbishop than did Redmond.

Whether this was so or not, Dillon certainly worked hard on the Educa-

[1] Dillon to Redmond, 6 and 7 Feb. 1906 (R.P.); Gwynn, *Redmond*, pp. 120–21.
[2] Hansard, H.C. Debates, 5th series, vol. 152, col. 435.
[3] Gwynn, *Redmond*, p. 123.

tion Bill all that year. He spoke up for the Catholic case on the second reading and although many of his co-religionists might have found it hard to go all the way with him when he declared that if Catholics were faced with the choice between a purely secular system and a purely Bible-reading system, 'we will unhesitatingly accept the purely secular', no one could have denied that the analysis of 'essential points' he drew up for the Government in November was an admirable statement of the Catholic case, particularly in everything pertaining to the appointment of teachers. Since, in the end, the Education Bill was one of the first casualties in the running war that soon developed between the Liberals and the House of Lords, it is not necessary to follow his campaign in detail. It is enough to make the point that much as he detested having to side with English Catholics (many of them die-hard Tories) against his Liberal friends, he clearly recognised that the issue was one which transcended party affiliations and did the best he could for the denominational schools, knowing how many poor and devoted Irish families depended on them to counteract the disintegrating effect of life in the big cities. 'All we ask for', he said, 'is that our schools should be secured, and for liberty to build new schools for our people as centres of population spring up. I will not, and I cannot, believe that it is the purpose of this government to take from us the schools which, whatever can be said of any other section of the population, have undoubtedly been reared by the sweat and labour of the toiling millions of our population'.[1]

(iii)

With the Liberals thus heavily involved in their major English legislation it rapidly became clear that the Irish members must wait patiently in the wings. Wait they did, but not patiently. Tempers soon wore thin and Irish exasperation found a sitting target in the unfortunate Chief Secretary, James Bryce. Despite his great personal distinction, and the high regard Dillon and Redmond both had for him as a man, Bryce was completely miscast as Chief Secretary. He seemed quite unaware of the complex cross-currents that swirled around almost every public issue in Ireland, he was a poor administrator, he carried too little weight with his own colleagues, and worst of all, he showed signs of falling helplessly under the sway of the formidable Sir Antony MacDonnell. Almost immediately the Irish leaders had two illustrations of his inadequacy. One concerned the composition of the Land Commission, the body which handled the practical details of land purchase. Dillon and Redmond had hoped that with the advent of the new Government it might be possible to alter the personnel of the Commission so as to include more members sympathetic to the tenants. Bryce *appeared* favourable, but turned out to be as wax in the hands of his senior officials, with the result that Dillon had to report in disgust to Redmond that

[1] Marquess of Ripon to Augustine Birrell, 15 June 1906, and Dillon to Augustine Birrell, 29 Nov. 1906 (P.R.O., Education Office Papers, Ed. 24/111, B.11). For Dillon's speech on the second reading, see Hansard, H.C. Debates, 5th series, vol. 156, cols. 1326–36.

twenty-two out of twenty-seven subcommissioners had been reappointed.[1]

The other example of the Chief Secretary's shortcomings was more serious. Bryce was deeply interested in university education and dearly wanted to do something for Ireland in this regard. What most nationalists wanted, of course, was an entirely independent Catholic University. Bryce, however, while not ruling this out as a possible objective, turned his attention first to Trinity College, Dublin, then at the height of one of its periods of academic glory, but still very much a citadel of Unionism and, so far as its administration was concerned, decidedly in need of reform. Bryce's idea was to appoint a Royal Commission to look into the affairs of Trinity and among other things to make suggestions of a more general character concerning Irish higher education as a whole. Dillon, who early in the 1906 session had criticised the university as unfriendly to Catholics and 'the centre and fortress of all that was narrow and bitter and hostile to the national life of Ireland', was quite content that its administration should be minutely scrutinised.[2] He saw dangers, however, in the suggestion that the Commission's terms might be broadened to include the Catholic aspect of the question. If Bryce persisted in this course, he told Redmond, he ought to be warned that 'we shall feel obliged to repudiate the Commission and disown it as a scheme to strengthen the position of T.C.D. in resisting the Catholic claims'.[3]

Unfortunately Bryce, besides transgressing in the matter of the terms of reference, had also ignored Nationalist warnings about the personnel of his Commission and had nominated as one of its members Christopher Palles, Chief Baron of the Exchequer. Palles was indeed a Trinity man and a Catholic (as, for that matter, both Dillon's own father and, to a limited extent, John Redmond had been), but he was also a quite unrepentant Unionist. Dillon was mystified by such hamhandedness and leaped to the conclusion—probably in this instance unjustified—that stupidity of this order must have some sinister explanation. Not only Bryce, he began to think, but also the Viceroy, Lord Aberdeen, and even, conceivably, Sir Antony himself, must have been in some strange way bewitched. The Aberdeens (the plural was necessary, for already Irishmen were beginning to discern in 'Ishbel' the predominant partner) and MacDonnell, he assured Redmond, were 'in the hands of the enemy'. As for Bryce, 'he is being stuffed with the idea that the proper policy is to conciliate the landlords, T.C.D., etc. etc.' And he continued:

> Antony MacDonnell is beginning to get a little uneasy—his constant cry is, I understand, that these minor matters do not count, that the great thing is to make the way easy for the grand scheme. I am extremely sceptical as to this grand scheme, and I am *quite* sure that the present method of procedure is the way to block any scheme of Irish government.[4]

[1] Dillon to Redmond, 29, 30 and 31 Mar. and 1 Apr. 1906 (R.P.).
[2] Hansard, H.C. Debates, 5th series, vol. 154, cols. 666–77.
[3] Dillon to Redmond, 26 Mar. 1906 (R.P.).   [4] Ibid., Dillon to Redmond, 4 Apr. 1906.

Yet, even though in May the Irish leaders were so dubious about the Commission that they were threatening to wash their hands of it in disgust, Bryce's scheme—which in essence was to create a federal system based on a University of Dublin with two colleges, of which T.C.D. should be one and a new Catholic college the other—went a long way towards meeting the Nationalist case. However, when the much-abused Commission reported in this sense early in 1907 not only had the opposition of Trinity to any such proposal hardened ominously, but Bryce himself was in the throes of handing over his office to Birrell, whose ideas about—and eventual solution of—the problem were very different.

But although these disappointments might be, in Sir Antony's phrase, 'minor matters', they had to be seen against an Irish background which, from the viewpoint of the parliamentary party, was disturbing. Part, but only part, of the trouble was that William O'Brien was still hovering on their flank. He was at this time attempting to use yet another organisation—the Land and Labour Association, launched a few years earlier by his henchman, Daniel Sheehan—as a means of winning a following amongst the agricultural labourers and small tenants.[1] This never, in fact, became a formidable threat, but Dillon (who knew how O'Brien's enterprises could grow from small beginnings) took it seriously enough to propose to Redmond that the labour representatives within the Irish party should infiltrate the Association and set up branches wherever they could, 'so that we could recognise their League as *the* genuine Land and Labour League [*sic*] whose branches would be entitled to representation at our conventions'.[2] This ruthless policy, reminiscent of the bad old days of the nineties and a reminder to anyone who might have forgotten it that when it came to political infighting Dillon could be as ruthless as anyone, seems never to have been put into full operation (though there *was* a split in the Association soon afterwards) and the leaders contented themselves with the expulsion of Sheehan from the party.[3]

The real danger at this time came less from O'Brien himself than from the fact that the party's inability either to come to terms with him or to liquidate him offered a wide surface for attack. And the number of critics ready and willing to take advantage of such opportunities was growing. Some of them, notably the leading members of the Young Ireland branch of the United Irish League, belonged to the rising generation of able young Nationalists who, although on the whole supporters of the constitutional movement, were irked by the tendency of the leaders to keep matters very much in their own hands and who also felt—which was largely true—that these same leaders were out of touch with the exciting cultural renaissance which had changed so much of Irish life in the generation since Parnell's

[1] David Sheehan, *Ireland since Parnell* (London, 1921), chap. 14.

[2] Dillon to Redmond, 27 Mar. 1906 (R.P.).

[3] W. O'Brien, *Olive branch*, pp. 389–92. In his memoirs O'Brien makes much of the fact that he was not, in strict fact, a member of the Association, but it is plain, even from his own account, that his influence over it was very great, if not predominant. For Sheehan's expulsion from the party see Lyons, *The Irish Parliamentary Party*, p. 120 n.

death. But such critics, though sharp-tongued, were in the last analysis
friends. Far otherwise was the group, or groups, to which the generic name
of Sinn Fein was coming to be attached. Their spokesman and inspiration,
Arthur Griffith, was still unknown to most people, although he had been
using his journalistic genius to attack the party and advance his own alternative policy since 1899. That alternative policy—which he first described
as 'the Hungarian policy' and later (and more intelligibly) as 'the Sinn Fein
policy' was aimed directly at what he considered the farce of Irish representation at Westminster. Taking as his model the stubborn refusal of the
Hungarians after the revolution of 1848 to participate in any kind of imperial diet or parliament, he hailed the Austro-Hungarian Ausgleich of
1867 as the ideal solution for Ireland. If achieved, it would have the effect
of creating—or rather restoring—a dual monarchy of Britain and Ireland
such as he imagined the constitution of 1782 had embodied. It was a strange
conception, owing perhaps as much to ignorance of history as to knowledge
of it, but it contained a direct menace to parliamentarianism, nevertheless.
If Griffith was right, and if the proper course for Irishmen was to avoid
Westminster like the plague, then what need was there for the Irish parliamentary party?

Griffith, of course, argued that if the party had ever had any utility it
had long outlived it and should go. Even in 1906 this was still reckoned wild
doctrine and although his definitive statement of it, *The Sinn Fein policy*,
dated from this very time, his appeal was to a very small minority. But that
minority was sufficiently vocal for Dillon, whose ear as usual was close to
the ground, to view this new development with some alarm, the more so
since the constitutional organisation—the United Irish League—was in a
dilapidated condition with funds falling off, fewer local affiliations and
general apathy aggravated by absurd jealousies amongst the permanent
officials. Part of this was due to the temporary absence abroad of Joseph
Devlin, the mainspring of the League. Devlin had risen in the ranks from
being a local Nationalist organiser in Belfast to becoming the only newcomer to the parliamentary party who was accepted politically, (though
perhaps not socially) as an equal by the established leaders. He was devoted
to Dillon who, indeed, had helped him greatly in his rise to eminence, and
Dillon in his turn had come to rely heavily upon him, not only for control
of the United Irish League and of the Catholic organisation, the Ancient
Order of Hibernians, but also because he was the outstanding representative of Ulster Nationalism. Even Devlin, however, would have found it
hard to combat the vague, but nevertheless perceptible dissatisfaction which
spread through both the League and the parliamentary party at the end of
the almost barren session of 1906. 'An effort must be made', Dillon wrote
to Redmond in August, 'to put some life into the movement. At present it
is very much asleep, and Sinn Feiners, Gaelic League, etc. etc., are making
great play.'[1] And a month later, in a letter mainly devoted to urging Redmond to steal O'Brien's thunder and move the Government to settle the

[1] Dillon to Redmond, 22 Aug. 1906 (R.P.).

evicted tenants' question, he threw out this comment which curiously combines the ability to penetrate the meaning of Sinn Fein and the tendency to underestimate Griffith which he was to show over and over again in the years ahead. 'I have always', he wrote, 'been of the opinion that this Sinn Fein business is a very serious matter and it has been spreading pretty rapidly for the past year. But if the party and the movement keep on [the] right lines it will not become very formidable, because it has no-one with any brains to lead it.'[1]

The uncomfortable corollary of this summing-up was that if the party did *not* keep on the right lines there would be trouble. It therefore became all the more necessary for the Irish leaders to extract from the Liberals some inkling of how they proposed to put the 'step-by-step' policy into action. During the recess Redmond began to apply pressure, speaking publicly of the absolute necessity for the Government to meet the Irish demand in full and referring slightingly to rumours of 'administrative Home Rule'.[2] In October Bryce came over to Ireland to reveal to him the tentative proposals (themselves the results of long-drawn-out labours by MacDonnell and others) his colleagues hoped to translate into legislation the following year. What he had to offer was a Council of fifty-five members, two-thirds indirectly elected and one-third nominated, the whole to be charged with only very limited administrative functions.[3] Redmond's first reaction, as he reported to Dillon was that the scheme seemed 'beneath contempt'.[4] Soon afterwards the draft was shown to both Dillon and Sexton who were equally dissatisfied. The impasse was so complete that when the various parties to the discussions had returned to London for the autumn session it was Lloyd George and not the disconsolate Chief Secretary who was deputed to explain to the Irish leaders that intransigence would get them nowhere, since their affairs were only part of the much larger crisis caused by the apparently deliberate policy of the House of Lords in repeatedly rejecting Bills that had come to them from the Commons and thus stultifying the huge Liberal majority in the Lower House. When Redmond met him alone on 1 November, Lloyd George told him that the best the cabinet might be able to do in 1907 would be to promise in the King's Speech both an Irish Land Bill and a Bill for the better government for Ireland; as a matter of tactics they would first concentrate their efforts upon an English Land Bill, but if the Lords rejected the 1906 Education Bill and the 1906 Plural Voting Bill, and also in 1907 rejected the English Land Bill, then the Government would dissolve Parliament and fight an election on the specific issue of the House of Lords. The consequence of this for Ireland, of course, would be that the Irish measures promised for 1907 would not, in fact, be reached that year—in short, that the Irish party, so

---

[1] Ibid., Dillon to Redmond, 29 Sept. 1906.

[2] See especially his speech at Grange, County Limerick, at the end of September (Gwynn, *Redmond*, p. 133).

[3] The various drafts of the scheme have been carefully collated and analysed by Mr. A. C. Hepburn in a chapter of his doctoral thesis 'Liberal Policy in Ireland, 1906–1909'.

[4] Banks, *Edward Blake*, p. 310.

far from being in any position to demand full Home Rule, might have to face the prospect of a second almost barren session.[1]

Redmond, in recording this interview, noted that he had 'expressed no opinion', but as the weeks passed and no satisfactory way was found of meeting Irish objections (which, at this stage, were mainly concerned with the inadequacy of the electoral element in the proposed Council) his attitude and those of his advisers grew more and more critical.[2] It was becoming clear that Bryce had no hope of making headway and at the end of 1906 he seized with both hands the opportunity of shaking off his Irish troubles by accepting the Embassy at Washington. Dillon remained on amicable terms with him to the end and even broke his standing rule of social non-co-operation by agreeing to dine at the Chief Secretary's Lodge before Bryce left (though only, as Lady Bryce wrote subsequently, 'as a great concession to years of friendship'), but the ambivalence of his letter of congratulation and farewell suggests that he could not in all honesty pretend that Bryce's translation was not a benefit to all parties. 'You are leaving a most tangled, difficult and cross-grained problem', he wrote, 'and going to one of the greatest centres of human interest, where your work and character will be fully appreciated by one of the kindest and most sympathetic peoples in the world . . . but even in Washington you will often find it possible to put in a good word for Ireland, and it may fall to your lot as ambassador to the United States to do effective work for the redemption of Ireland.'[3]

(iv)

Exit Bryce—enter Augustine Birrell. Birrell was to be Chief Secretary for nearly ten years and though his term of office was to end in tragedy, during the early years he was popular with the Irish leaders and was able, despite the background of the conflict with the House of Lords, to pilot through several valuable Irish measures. He was scholarly, as Bryce was, but unlike Bryce was both witty and relaxed. He was shrewder than appeared on the surface and certainly more effective in the House and in the cabinet than Bryce had ever been. As minister in charge of the Education Bill, he had had a good deal to do with the Irish members in the session just past and they had found him sympathetic. That Bill, having run into the usual trouble with the Lords, had been finally abandoned just before Christmas, and Birrell was ready for a change. Campbell-Bannerman hesitated before appointing him, but by the end of December the decision had been taken, though conflicting rumours continued to reach the Irish leaders well into the New Year.[4]

[1] Gwynn, *Redmond*, p. 135.

[2] Ibid., pp. 137–8; Banks, *Edward Blake*, pp. 310–16.

[3] Dillon to Bryce, 27 Dec. 1906 (Bryce Papers); H. A. L. Fisher, *James Bryce* (London, 1927), i. 341.

[4] T. P. O'Connor to Dillon, 29 Dec. 1906 (D.P.); Dillon to Redmond, 17 Jan. 1907 (R.P.).

The change of Chief Secretary was no doubt an improvement, but the central problem remained—how to devise a scheme of governmental reform for Ireland which would satisfy the Irish Members and not precipitate a crisis with the House of Lords. From the Irish point of view the crux of the problem was still the composition of the Council—ideally, they would have liked it to be a local version of the Irish representation at Westminster, together with a small nominated group to protect minority interests, though they were prepared to consider other possibilities. Their ideas were embodied in a memorandum drawn up by Redmond, Dillon and T. P. O'Connor in December 1906 and this was apparently discussed at the cabinet on 15 December, together with the inevitable counter-stroke from the ubiquitous MacDonnell.[1] The details are not relevant to this biography, especially as no immediate action resulted, but Dillon's own attitude to the critical situation that was now developing is well expressed in a letter he wrote John Morley only a few days after the Cabinet meeting. In this he complained that the Irish leaders were 'much oppressed by a gentleman of whom you know who moves in an Indian atmosphere, quite aloof from the facts of the situation . . . His idea appears to me to be to break up the Irish party machine and dominance in Irish politics and get a kind of Indian Council composed of that favourite abstraction of amateur solvers of the Irish problem—non-political businessmen—and so turn Ireland into a loyal and peaceful country, very subservient and manageable, purged of politics and devoted to the breeding of pigs and the making of butter.' It would, he continued, be very dangerous to put up a weak scheme to the House of Lords which could then butcher it with a light heart. On the other hand, if a really strong scheme were put forward, although it would be likewise rejected by the Lords, it would enable the Irish party to share in the conflict which was obviously coming and—very important—it would enable them to face their constituents with the consciousness of a good session's work behind them.[2]

Such counsels, however sound from an Irish point of view, cut very little ice in London. The Liberals, it seemed, were bracing themselves for a struggle with the Lords, but it would embarrass them, not strengthen them, if that struggle were complicated by the Irish issue about which Liberals themselves held so many divergent views. At any rate, T. P. O'Connor, writing to Dillon of a recent conversation with Lloyd George, warned him that there would certainly be nothing resembling Home Rule next session.[3] Hard on the heels of this came a reply from Morley, characteristically gloomy. They were, he thought, approaching 'the most serious crisis in your business since 1891'. He personally thought that an Irish Bill (he meant one conferring any kind of self-government) would be 'an ugly and dangerous issue' on which to try conclusions with the House of Lords, and he

[1] I am indebted for this information to Mr. A. C. Hepburn; the reference is to Cabinet Paper 37/85/97, Dec. 1906.
[2] Dillon to Morley, 19 Dec. 1906 (copy in Bryce Papers).
[3] T. P. O'Connor to Dillon, 29 Dec. 1906 (D.P.).

suggested, more than a little disingenuously, that if the Irish party were to give a year's hearty co-operation to Liberal measures during 1907, then English support for an Irish Bill in 1908 would be correspondingly greater.[1]

Dillon's reply to this has not survived, but, as summarised by Morley for Campbell-Bannerman's benefit a few weeks later, it was a resounding—and surely expected—negative. Further delay, he insisted, would be most dangerous to the Irish party, now being assailed by extremists, and would provoke a rupture between the Liberals and the Nationalists.[2] Not surprisingly, Dillon's speeches in Ireland during the next few months reflected both his intransigence and his awareness of the extremist threat. Thus at Ballinrobe at the end of January 1907, he used language curiously reminiscent of that used by Parnell and himself nearly thirty years before, when he warned his hearers that the effectiveness of the Irish Government Bill soon to come would be the measure of their unity. It would not do, he said, hitting impartially at William O'Brien and Sir Antony, to have some artificially constructed council composed of the dispossessed landlords of Ireland under the name of conciliation, and they must make sure 'that it shall be no Greek horse introduced into our camp, and that under the cloak of a measure of devolution no audacious attempt shall be made to break up that army which has been enrolled during the last twenty-five years . . . and which the people ought never to allow to be weakened or disbanded until complete liberty is restored to our country'.[3] A week later at Foxford he echoed Morley's phrase when he warned his constituents that 1907 would be 'the most critical and fateful year' since 1890. What they would get in 1907 would not be 'the larger policy', but it must be a substantial instalment.[4] And in April he went out of his way to warn the people against the temptation to turn from constitutionalism to violence, again in terms very similar to those he had used in his youth:

> I am sometimes accused of being too much given to constitutional action . . . But why am I for peaceable methods and for constitutional action? Because I want to win . . . When we have recourse to open violence then they are too strong for us, but we have hit upon a method by which, inch by inch, and yard by yard, we are beating them to the ropes. I say once more that you require no weapon stronger than . . . the force of public opinion.[5]

By the time this speech was delivered the Government's proposals for the Irish Council Bill had been thrashed out over and over again and the date for the Bill's introduction was less than a month away. Dillon, from the beginning of the year, had been extremely anxious. Birrell, no doubt, would be an improvement upon Bryce, but could he discipline his terrible Under-Secretary about whom Dillon had heard (and for a panic-stricken moment almost believed) that he might become Chief Secretary himself?

[1] John Morley to Dillon, 29 Dec. 1906 (D.P.).
[2] John Morley to Sir Henry Campbell-Bannerman, 20 Jan. 1907 (B.M. Add. MS. 41223).
[3] *W.F.J.*, 26 Jan. 1907.   [4] *W.F.J.*, 2 Feb. 1907.   [5] *W.F.J.*, 13 Apr. 1907.

That nightmare had no foundation in fact, but this apart, the future still looked black to him. 'In view of all that has happened, and all that has been said during the last year', he warned Redmond, 'a postponement would be intolerable and could land us in terrible difficulties, making a conflict with the government inevitable.'[1] However, things, though bad enough, were not as bad as he feared, and by the end of January Redmond was able to tell him that Irish legislation *would* figure in the King's Speech.[2] Soon after this Birrell produced an amended version of the scheme for the Irish leaders' inspection. As it then stood there was to be an Irish Council of from eighty to ninety members, of whom about three-quarters were to be elected and the remainder nominated, the Under-Secretary being a member *ex-officio*. The Lord Lieutenant, through the Council, was to have complete control over all matters relating to local government, agriculture and technical instruction, public works, primary and secondary education, and the Congested Districts. He would have considerable powers of veto and there was also provision for appeal to the Judicial Committee of the Privy Council. The key financial provision foreshadowed the creation of an Irish fund paid over by the Imperial Exchequer, out of which would be met the expenses of the various departments involved.[3]

This was meagre enough and the temptation to reject it out of hand must have been very great. But, given the Liberal preoccupation with the House of Lords, to do this would be to risk an indefinite postponement of Irish legislation. It was better, however disagreeable, to persevere with Birrell and try to get him to raise his offer before it saw the light of day and was submitted, as the Irish leaders were determined it should be submitted, to the verdict of a National Convention of the United Irish League in Dublin. Birrell, to do him justice, did his best (usually with his Under-Secretary pulling in the other direction), and although the battle ebbed and flowed, he was at least able, by the end of March, to tell Redmond hopefully that he was trying to extract one million pounds from the Exchequer over and above the cost of the departments and that the Chancellor, Asquith, was inclined to be 'generous'.[4]

Dillon remained sceptical about the Government's intentions. He found Birrell as unreliable as Bryce on his favourite topic of Land Commission appointments and in April was complaining to Redmond that the way that business was handled was 'an outrage'. 'And what I am infinitely more concerned about than the personnel of the appointments is the danger that a vigorous attempt will be made to adopt the same methods in dealing with the Irish Govt. Bill.'[5] Redmond replied soothingly that Birrell was hoping to provide them with full details in a few days, and in fact from then until the introduction of the Bill on 7 May they were locked in close negotiation with the Government.[6] It is not necessary here to follow out the bewildering

---

[1] Dillon to Redmond, 17 Jan. 1907 (R.P.).   [2] Redmond to Dillon, 31 Jan. 1907 (D.P.).
[3] Gwynn, *Redmond*, p. 142.   [4] Redmond to Dillon, 29 Mar. 1907 (D.P.).
[5] Dillon to Redmond, 9 Apr. 1907 (R.P.).
[6] Redmond to Dillon, 10 Apr. 1907 (D.P.).

combinations and permutations of clauses, paragraphs and subclauses, but the fact that debate about these continued right up to the very day on which Birrell introduced the measure in the House of Commons indicates how hard it was to find ground common to the Nationalists and their Liberal allies. And, although it may have been true that its political doom was sealed in advance by the conflict between Lords and Commons, it could be argued that a measure about which even its friends found it hard to agree ought never to have been introduced at all. On the other hand, there is evidence that Redmond and Dillon, by sheer tenacity and stubbornness, did extract considerably more from the Cabinet than the original author of the scheme, Sir Antony MacDonnell, thought decent. They did not gain all their points by any means, but on what was to them one of the vital issues —the composition of the new body—although they did not succeed in converting the existing Irish parliamentary representation into the elective element of the Council, they managed to increase that elective element very substantially to eighty-two out of one hundred and seven seats, and they also ensured that these seats should be filled by direct, not indirect, election. As against this, the Lord-Lieutenant was left with very wide powers of veto and the overriding control of Irish affairs by the cabinet and, ultimately, the imperial Parliament, remained intact.[1] It is not surprising that, as the end of the marathon came in sight, Dillon's views were mixed. Writing to his wife on 3 May, immediately after a crucial interview with Birrell, he reported that they had won three-fourths of their battle. 'But there was a pretty hard fight in the cabinet, and we have not got all. The Bill as it now stands is so much improved that it bears no resemblance to the original scheme. Nevertheless it will not be easy for us to decide on our attitude towards it.'[2]

When the Bill was finally introduced on 7 May its Liberal sponsors went out of their way to stress its moderate character—probably for the tactical reason that they wanted it to pass the House of Commons with the minimum of trouble so that it could be offered to the House of Lords as an innocent lamb for the slaughter. Campbell-Bannerman, indeed, described it, in a speech at Manchester, in language that can hardly have been palatable to Redmond and Dillon, as a 'little, modest, shy, humble effort to give administrative powers to the Irish people'.[3] Birrell, stressing that Parliament would be 'majestically unaffected' by the Bill, explained that the new Council would not have authority for 'the levying of a single tax or the striking of the humblest rate'. It was merely intended to control the functioning of eight departments of Irish government—Local Government, Agriculture and Technical Instruction, Congested Districts Board, National Education, Intermediate Education, Reformatories and Industrial Schools, and the office of the Registrar-General. The necessary funds to service these departments were to be transferred to the new authority, together with a

[1] These points are fully brought out by Mr. Hepburn in the thesis mentioned above.
[2] Dillon to Elizabeth Dillon, 4 o'clock, 3 May 1907 (D.P.).
[3] Spender, *Campbell-Bannerman*, ii. 339.

bonus of £650,000 (so much for Birrell's million!) from the imperial exchequer.[1]

In the debate that followed Redmond, who spoke for the parliamentary party as a whole, was critical of many details of the scheme and declined to take any responsibility for it, but he left the issue deliberately in doubt, agreeing to support the Government in the lobby until the Irish Convention, due to meet on 21 May had given its verdict.[2] It became therefore, a matter of urgency for him to know how opinion in Ireland was reacting to the measure. On May 9 Dillon left for Dublin, partly to carry out these important researches, but partly also to rejoin Elizabeth who, it will be remembered, was expecting another child. There was, of course, no inkling of the terrible tragedy which was less than a week away, but he had been absent in London for nearly a month and was anxious to be with her again. Dillon had not been home more than three days before his wife's fatal illness began and this meant that his efforts to gather information were severely circumscribed.[3] But even as early as 9 May, although he devoted part of a letter to Redmond to discussing ways in which the Bill might be improved, he had already formed the opinion that it would be wrong to submit any official resolution to the Convention approving of or accepting the Bill.[4] This warning crossed with a letter from Redmond in which the chairman admitted that he was in doubt how best to proceed at the Convention, adding significantly: 'I am quite clear, however, that if the Convention decides that we ought *not* to support the second reading, the Bill will not be proceeded with at all.'[5]

Clearly, the situation was critical and Dillon's next report, two days later, indicated that he had been working hard, particularly with the *Freeman's Journal*, to obtain, as he put it, 'fair play' for the Bill.[6] In this, however, he was for once overoptimistic. The *Freeman*, although in effect the party newspaper, remained very hostile. Nor was it untypical of the country. Dillon zealously collected what evidence of approval he could find, but it was clear that amongst the provincial newspapers and the various public bodies, and also within the ranks of the parliamentary party, there was much disappointment, a great deal of bewilderment, and little enough support, even that seeming to spring rather from loyalty to the leaders than from any real liking for the Bill.[7] Inside the parliamentary party, indeed, there was so much confusion—and vociferous opposition from a minority —that Dillon advised against the holding of a party meeting before the Convention, a sure sign with him, though a rare one, that he was doubtful of their ability to control it.[8] Now at last the secrecy and delays of the past months were beginning to take their toll. For reasons which were largely

[1] Hansard, H.C. Debates, 4th series, vol. 174, cols. 78–103, for Birrell's speech.
[2] Ibid., cols. 112–28, for Redmond's speech.
[3] For details of the illness, see chapter 9.
[4] Dillon to Redmond, 9 May 1907 (R.P.); Gwynn, *Redmond*, p. 143.
[5] Redmond to Dillon, dated by Dillon 9 May 1907 (D.P.).
[6] Dillon to Redmond, 11 May 1907 (R.P.); Gwynn, *Redmond*, pp. 143–4.
[7] This view is based upon Mr. Hepburn's intensive analysis of the reaction of Irish public opinion between the first reading and the meeting of the Convention.
[8] Dillon to Redmond, 11 May 1907 (R.P.).

beyond their control, the Nationalist leaders had not been able to take their followers into their confidence (they had been very much in the dark themselves until April) and the result had been a massive failure of communication.

Meanwhile, Redmond, though still in London, was, almost as if by telepathy, adjusting himself to the mood of the moment, and he sent Dillon, probably on 11 May, a draft resolution for submission to the Convention which expressed deep disappointment with the failure of the Cabinet to propose a proper measure of self-government for Ireland and categorically stated that the Irish Council Bill was not a Home Rule measure and 'is not calculated to promote a settlement of the Irish question'.[1] This, as Dillon said when he replied on 12 May, was certainly a strong resolution, though he did not think it a bit too strong for the situation and (having clearly had more time in which to gauge the strength of the opposition) he was sure it, 'or even a more uncompromising declaration against the bill', would be carried at the Convention. While any attempt at curtailing or influencing free discussion at the Convention would, he felt, be disastrous, he was prepared to try his hand at an alternative:

> I should very much like [he continued] to see some form of words devised which would meet as much as yours the undoubted hostile feeling of the country in regard to the Bill, and would yet avoid the actual killing of the Bill by the Convention, a task which I think, if at all possible, we should leave to the Irish Unionists and the House of Lords.[2]

At the same time, though obviously much engrossed in the purely tactical aspect of the situation, Dillon suggested that it would be a bad mistake to confine the resolutions at the Convention to this single topic of the Irish Council Bill. 'It would disappoint priests, farmers, etc. etc., and would tend to create the impression that our work in parliament this year has been completely barren of results, except the introduction of the Council Bill, which your resolution would condemn.' What he wanted, in fact, was a whole series of resolutions dealing with some of his own favourite topics, including land purchase, the evicted tenants and education in all its branches.

Next day Dillon wrote twice. Once to enclose a rough draft of his own resolution, condemning the Bill, but leaving the door open for amendment, though he doubted if the Convention would be tractable enough to swallow it. But even if their hands were forced, he argued, it was their duty to lay this 'common-sense policy' before the delegates.[3] At that point, however, all thought of the Convention was wiped from his mind. Elizabeth's health,

---

[1] Gwynn, *Redmond*, p. 144, where the date is misprinted as 1 May. I have not so far been able to trace the original of this draft in the Dillon Papers, but internal evidence suggests that the date was 11 May.

[2] Dillon to Redmond, 12 May 1907 (R.P.); most of this is printed in Gwynn, op. cit., pp. 144–5, but wrongly dated 13 May.

[3] Dillon to Redmond, 13 May 1907 (R.P.); Gwynn, *Redmond*, pp. 145–6.

which had been worrying him since his return to Dublin, now deteriorated rapidly, and his second letter that day began thus: 'My wife was suddenly seized with a most serious illness last night. Doctors and nurses are in charge and we were up all night. You may imagine I am not in a very good condition for drafting resolutions'.[1] Within two days she was dead and he, shattered by this grief almost beyond recovery, was removed completely from the scene. It was several weeks before he could bring himself to write about politics again, and many months before he was able to throw himself fully into the fight.

Meanwhile the fate of the Irish Council Bill was speedily settled. Redmond arrived in Dublin immediately after Mrs. Dillon's death, conferred with Devlin and even, it appears, had an interview with Dillon himself. The consequence was, as he wrote to Edward Blake, that they had 'practically come to the conclusion that the best thing for the party and the movement is to reject to bill'.[2] It is clear from all the discussion and correspondence between the leaders in the weeks preceding the Convention that the decision to reject was in no sense a snap decision, nor even one dictated by the pressure of public opinion. Public opinion no doubt was an important factor—indeed, few issues in these years produced such unanimity amongst so many different groups. Sinn Fein, of course, ridiculed the Bill, but the ginger-group of the constitutionalists, the Young Ireland branch of the U.I.L., were equally derisive. The Church, too, was strongly opposed to the scheme, mainly because it seemed to portend a fresh intrusion by the Castle into the control of education, while the Unionists detested it simply as a further instance of the devilish malignity of Sir Antony MacDonnell and his friends. All this turmoil created an electric atmosphere when the Convention met, and Redmond, even had he felt otherwise, would scarcely have been able to avoid doing what he did do with tremendous effect—denouncing the Bill in the most vigorous terms and thereby in effect ensuring that it would be incontinently dropped by the Government. Perhaps he was to blame for not speaking out clearly against it during the debate on the first reading, but his position—and that of the Irish leaders generally—was very difficult. On the one hand, this was the first attempt made by the Liberals to redeem Campbell-Bannerman's promise of a reform consistent with and leading up to the 'larger measure'. To condemn it out of hand would have been to put a heavy strain on an alliance which was fragile enough as it stood. On the other hand, although, as we have seen, the Irish leaders were deeply dissatisfied with the Liberal proposals from the start, it would have been difficult for them either to reject or to accept them without taking counsel with their fellow countrymen through the medium, which since 1900 had become almost traditional (and for which there were even earlier precedents) of a National Convention. In the event, of course, they fell between two stools. At one level they were negotiating privately with the Liberals to improve the measure, not because they liked it, but because it

[1] Dillon to Redmond, 13 May 1907, second letter (R.P.).
[2] Redmond to Blake, 18 May 1907; Banks, *Edward Blake*, p. 323.

could be thrown into the 'cup' which the Lords were busily filling up. This certainly was Dillon's policy towards the Bill, and his influence—only apparently weakened after his wife's death—was one factor which clearly weighed very heavily with Redmond. But at another level they were committed to exposing public debate and ridicule a scheme which fell far short of Irish expectations, without being able to reveal the tactical situation of which the Irish Council Bill was only a part. In short, ahead of their time, they contrived with the best intentions to produce a grotesque *mélange* of old diplomacy and Wilsonian idealism. 'Open covenants secretly arrived at' seemed to have been their maxim and it would be hard to imagine one more disastrous. It is not surprising that the crisis was for all of them a traumatic experience, deeply affecting their attitudes and actions a few years later when they came face to face at last with a real and not a dummy Home Rule Bill.

(v)

Birrell for his part received the news philosophically, though the fact that the Church *and* Sinn Fein had, as he thought, influenced public opinion towards rejection seemed to him the most serious legacy of the episode, since, with these forces—either actually or potentially formidable—hanging on their flanks, the Irish party would find it very difficult in future to yield an iota of the full Irish demand. He gave his Prime Minister the option of his resignation, but Campbell-Bannerman would not hear of it and Birrell himself was still much too interested in Ireland to want to go. Indeed, before the session was out he had met one of Dillon's standing demands by passing rapidly through the House of Commons a Bill for the restoration of the evicted tenants. The aim of the Bill—which in its original form Dillon himself approved—was to empower the Estates Commissioners to acquire land, by compulsion if need be, for the resettlement of several thousand evicted tenants and to declare the land so acquired to be an estate within the meaning of the Land Purchase Acts. Occupying tenants dispossessed for this purpose were to be compensated or given as good land elsewhere. The Bill was only passed under the guillotine procedure and the Lords did their best to minimise the compulsory clause (and some others as well), with the result that the Irish party walked out of the last stages of the debate. Nevertheless, even this gesture of protest could not disguise the fact that a contentious issue with a history stretching back over thirty years had at last been effectively removed from politics. As a direct result of the act 26,000 acres were purchased, and 3,500 evicted tenants or their representatives either reinstated or given new holdings. It was truly the end of a long, sad chapter, even though the actual business of reinstatement dragged on until the final surrender of the Marquess of Clanricarde in 1912.[2]

[1] J. A. Spender, *Campbell-Bannerman*, ii, 341–2.
[2] Dillon to Redmond, 30 June 1907 (R.P.); J. E. Pomfret, *The struggle for land in Ireland*, p. 406.

Meanwhile, however, Redmond, deprived not only of John Dillon but of Edward Blake, who had suffered a stroke in May 1907 and retired from the party, had to deal with the repercussions of the Irish Council Bill, and with growing disillusionment, not merely amongst the 'Young Turks' of the U.I.L., but even within the party itself. Writing to Dillon in June, Redmond reported on a meeting at which, he said, 'there was plenty of plain talk, but no disorder whatever'. A group of members had proposed what Redmond called 'a silly resolution' to withdraw temporarily from Parliament and to seek reunion with William O'Brien and Tim Healy. Historically, this was a far more important resolution than Redmond could ever have imagined, for it was the first sign of the permeation of the party by Sinn Fein doctrines. At the time, it is true, the group—which consisted apparently of Thomas O'Donnell, James O'Mara, C. J. Dolan, Patrick White and Edward Barry—was so much in a minority that the resolution was withdrawn, though Redmond's own guess was that Dolan would soon leave the party.[1] In this he was perfectly correct. Dolan not only resigned, but stood for his old constituency as a Sinn Fein candidate. He was duly defeated, but it was the first time that the central political idea of Sinn Fein—abstention from Westminster—had been put before the electorate, and the contest attracted a great deal of attention.[2]

Other resignations—of James O'Mara from his seat in South Kilkenny and of Sir Thomas Esmonde from his post of senior whip—emphasised the low morale of the party, and led Redmond to attach more importance than he might otherwise have done to the evidence which was now beginning to accumulate that William O'Brien would be prepared in certain conditions to rejoin the party. Obviously, if losses on one wing could be compensated on the other by the return to the fold of a man of O'Brien's acknowledged influence and calibre, this demonstration of unity would go far to wipe out the unsavoury memory of the past few months. Dillon, although still in retirement, watched the situation with scepticism. His own instinct was to fight both O'Brien and the Sinn Feiners wherever they showed their heads and he tried hard to screw Redmond's courage to the sticking-point. 'The one real difficulty and danger', he wrote in October, in terms that recall the way he used to write to O'Brien ten years earlier, 'is the difficulty of raising money . . . If the party funds can be kept strong, O'Brien and Sinn Fein can be easily worn out . . . It has been and will be a hard year with you, but politics are a merciless game at best—and Irish politics are *not* the best.'[3]

It was one thing for Dillon to offer advice from the wings, quite another to have the actual responsibility for holding the party together. And in the exercise of that responsibility Redmond decided towards the end of the year to enter into conference with O'Brien. Their discussions centred mainly round the vexed question of the parliamentary pledge—the pledge taken by

[1] Redmond to Dillon, 12 June 1907 (D.P.).
[2] Gwynn, *Redmond*, pp. 150–1; Lyons, *Irish parliamentary party*, p. 117.
[3] Dillon to Redmond, 1 Oct. 1907 (R.P.).

every member to 'sit, act and vote' with the party and to resign if a majority
of the party voted that he had not honoured his commitment. During the
Parnellite period (from which it dated) the parliamentary pledge had been
an effective instrument of discipline, but after the split, and especially in the
middle nineties, when the party was divided into three warring factions,
different interpretations were put upon the pledge to satisfy different needs.
On the face of it, it was a weapon for use by the parliamentary party against
difficult or recalcitrant members. But on the other hand, and as a matter of
normal practice, it was actually taken in the constituency at a county convention by the candidate selected at that convention to stand for the seat
at the next election. Was it therefore really a party pledge, or a pledge to the
constituency, or did it, perhaps, in some mystical way form a kind of bond
between the two?

The problem went much deeper than a wrangle about mere terminology,
because, if the pledge was, in fact, to the constituency and if a Member
then broke with the party, there would clearly be no onus on him to resign
even if actually expelled by his parliamentary colleagues. This had been the
basis of Healy's political existence in the nineties and it is significant that
when in 1900 the party drew up a resolution on 'unity and discipline' as a
prelude to reunion, the pledge was interpreted to mean an obligation binding Members to support the policy of party *in and out* of Parliament. A
large part of O'Brien's quarrel with Dillon over the Wyndham Act of 1903
had been his conviction that Dillon had gone against the majority of the
party and of the national organisation, and had therefore been guilty of
breaking the pledge. Dillon's position, in essence, had been that while there
had certainly been agreement to negotiate with the landlords, this did not
absolve the party leaders from examining critically the Government's
legislation, however closely modelled on the Land Conference recommendations, or from warning the people of the threat to Home Rule implicit in
O'Brien's policy of co-operation with moderate Unionists. What O'Brien
now sought in 1907 was to establish whether or not the 1900 interpretation
of the pledge would be observed in the future. Redmond had no hesitation
in saying that it would be—naturally, since he did not agree with O'Brien
that it had ever ceased to be observed—and the scene seemed set for reconciliation. At the last moment, however, O'Brien, who always attached
excessive importance to vast representative gatherings, demanded the summoning of a National Convention to ratify the agreement. To this Redmond,
who had been specifically warned by Dillon to keep his hands free, would
not agree, and the conference thereupon broke down.[1]

O'Brien's intention, it seems, was to use this latest collision with the
parliamentary party to promote his idea of a broad-based movement to
bring together well-disposed Irishmen of all kinds. 'I am confident', he
wrote to Lord Dunraven, 'that it is now quite possible to start a
national movement which will very soon bring the irreconcilables to their

---

[1] Dillon to Redmond, 1 Dec. 1907 (R.P.); Redmond to Dillon, 9 Dec. 1907 (D.P.);
F.J., 24 Dec. 1907.

senses by leaving them "on the bleak shore alone" ."[1] From his own correspondence it appears that he sought, through the medium of that indefatigable correspondent, Captain Shawe-Taylor, to open negotiations with Sinn Fein, and with his usual capacity for unlimited optimism, he assured Dunraven that 'they jumped at the idea'.[2] The notion of a combination between progressive landlords and Sinn Fein, with, presumably, himself as a balance-wheel in the middle, was the oddest by a long chalk that O'Brien had evolved in the course of his eccentric career. No one, except O'Brien, seems to have taken it seriously and it came to nothing.[3] But since in the New Year both the parliamentary party and the United Irish League came out strongly in favour of the line taken by Redmond in the negotiations, O'Brien had to face the unpalatable fact that it was he, not his adversaries, who was likely to be left 'on the bleak shore alone'. Fortunately for him, the party left the back door open. At the party meeting no less a person than Dillon himself held out an olive-branch by moving a resolution that, as the principal obstacles to agreement had been removed at the conference, there was no valid reason why those who had been excluded in the past should not now take the pledge and rejoin their colleagues.[4] Like many another politician in a similar position, O'Brien's sense of self-preservation came to his aid and with an abrupt—and entirely characteristic—change of policy he wrote at once to Redmond that 'the summons to the next meeting of the party can be sent to every colleague on the basis of their acceptance of the parliamentary pledge as defined at our recent conference and on the principles then agreed between us'. Redmond replied cordially and O'Brien, D. D. Sheehan, John O'Donnell, Augustine Roche, Sir Thomas Esmonde and T. M. Healy all duly appeared at the sessional meeting of the parliamentary party.[5]

Perhaps the most extraordinary feature of this precarious peace was that it extended even to Tim Healy. A decade earlier Healy and O'Brien had been as deadly enemies as O'Brien and Dillon now were and it was difficult to see what they had in common except exile from the parliamentary party. The initiative in this particular reconciliation was taken by O'Brien, who earlier in 1907 had employed Healy as his counsel in a nominally successful libel action against the *Freeman's Journal*. When reunion seemed likely O'Brien urged Healy to act with him. But Healy, it seems, was genuinely reluctant to leave his lucrative practice at the Bar, partly because he was, he said, 'no longer confident about the future of this generation politically', and partly because he doubted if a clash between Dillon and himself could be avoided. Indeed, he even offered to remain outside, if by so doing he could smooth

---

[1] W. O'Brien to Lord Dunraven, 26 Dec. 1907, cited in the unpublished thesis by F. K. Schilling, jnr., William O'Brien and the All-for-Ireland League, p. 61.

[2] Ibid., W. O'Brien to Lord Dunraven, 28 Dec. 1907.

[3] For an interesting account of this curious episode see F. K. Schilling, jun., 'William O'Brien and the All-for-Ireland League', pp. 60–4.

[4] *F.J.*, 16 and 17 Jan. 1908.

[5] *F.J.*, 18 Jan. 1908; O'Brien, *Olive branch*, p. 432.

the way for effective parliamentary action by the party.[1] O'Brien would not hear of this, however, and in the event the stormy petrel was accepted, if not precisely welcomed, back into the party. But at least one of Dillon's correspondents had no illusions. Richard McGhee, a former Nationalist M.P. who had been one of Michael Davitt's closest friends, wrote in the New Year expressing his disgust that Redmond should have condescended to treat with O'Brien at all. 'There is one man in Ireland', he said, 'who must be enjoying to his heart's content the whole business and that man is our dear, dear friend, T. M. Healy. To Tim it must be a real joy to see that screeching fanatic O'Brien howling over the country for the return of Tim to the ranks of the Irish party'.[2]

The omens for a happy reunion were not, therefore very favourable and although, according to O'Brien's version, he accosted Dillon in the House of Commons with the plea that they should let bygones be bygones, Dillon, while agreeing to shake hands, could only summon up a few frigid words.[3] O'Brien's accounts of his personal relationships are always suspect, but this one rings true enough, because Dillon detested public displays of emotion, and also because, for a man of his deep reserve and intense feeling, too much water had flowed under the bridge for the old comradeship to be so easily recaptured. And unfortunately there was more to come. By a curious irony the land question, which had divided O'Brien from his colleagues in 1904, on his return to the party in 1908 immediately raised its head again. It had been obvious for some time that the financial provisions of the Wyndham Act were breaking down, partly because the demand from the tenants for advances in aid of purchase had greatly exceeded the original estimates, but also because the market price of the land stock which had been used to buy out the landlords had been steadily falling. For these reasons the pace of purchase had begun to slacken alarmingly and it was the aim of the Irish party to extract from the Government sufficiently generous financial concessions to set it going again. In April 1908, therefore, an important party meeting was held in Dublin to decide what attitude to adopt. Before it met Dillon had agreed with Redmond, though rather reluctantly, that they should set up a committee on Land Act finance, but urged him on no account to allow O'Brien to become a member of it.[4] The reason for this warning immediately appeared. No sooner had the party assembled than O'Brien, true to form, proposed the summoning of a new Land Conference on the lines of the original one of 1902. Redmond evidently had the party well in hand, for this was rejected by forty-two votes to fifteen. Thereupon Dillon moved for the appointment of the committee foreshadowed in his correspondence with Redmond, and this resolution was passed by the same majority as that which had defeated O'Brien's motion.[5]

[1] T. M. Healy to O'Brien, 10 Oct. and 10 Nov. (W. O'Brien Papers, N.L.I. MS. 8556/2.).

[2] R. McGhee to Dillon, 3 Jan. 1908 (D.P.).   [3] O'Brien, *Olive branch*, p. 432.

[4] Dillon to Redmond, 22, 23 and 26 Apr. 1908, letters in the possession of Professor Myles Dillon.

[5] O'Brien, *Olive branch*, p. 432–6.

This vote of the party was regarded by O'Brien, quite correctly, as a fresh rebuff to his policy of dealing with the moderate Unionists in order to win agreed social and economic reforms. He saw in it a blind refusal to work for co-operation between Irishmen of all creeds and classes and forthwith refused to attend meetings of the party. But what he failed to realise was that the Irish party must be a Home Rule party or nothing. As a bare necessity of survival it had to keep its eyes on the main question and treat all others, however desirable in themselves, as subsidiary. In the circumstances of 1908, and especially in view of the fiasco of the previous year, it was more than ever essential that they should bring the maximum pressure to bear on their Liberal allies. All the signs were that the Liberals were heading for a decisive conflict with the House of Lords and from this the Irish parliamentary party could expect to benefit—either electorally, by hoping to hold the balance between the two main parties, or in the longer term, and if the Liberals were victorious, in the destruction of the Lords' power to veto Home Rule. This, then, was no time to coquette with Unionists, who, however progressive, were still Unionists and who anyway only represented a section of their class. It was not, therefore, as O'Brien was only too ready to believe, a double dose of original sin on Dillon's part but inexorable political pressures that drove the two men apart once more and for the last time.

Whatever his faults and eccentricities it could never be said that O'Brien was not a fighter. When in the next year (1909) Birrell finally introduced a Land Bill to deal with this very question of the finance of land purchase, the United Irish League, following its usual practice, held a National Convention in Dublin. O'Brien resolved to put his ideas of 'conference plus business' once more to the test and had the shattering experience of failing to obtain a hearing from the organisation he had himself created. Ever afterwards he maintained that he had been the victim of deliberate rowdyism and he laid the blame mainly upon Devlin, who as general secretary of the U.I.L. was the responsible official. Devlin was also Grand Master of the Ancient Order of Hibernians (which could be loosely described as the Catholic counter to the Orange Order) and O'Brien alleges in his memoirs that it was Devlin's over-zealous henchmen—the Board of Erin—that had provided the hard core of Belfast hecklers who had made life impossible for him and his friends. There is probably some truth in this, but it is not the whole story. For one thing Dillon himself, as we shall see, had a very rough passage at that Convention; and for another, there can be no doubt that opinion at the meeting was overwhelmingly against O'Brien and his policy.[1] His own reaction was entirely characteristic. Shaking the dust of the 'baton Convention' off his feet, he withdrew to Cork, where he still had a strong following and one month later (March 1909) set about launching yet another would-be popular movement, the All-for-Ireland League, dedicated to the crusade for 'conference plus business'.[2]

[1] *F.J.*, 10, 11 Feb. 1909; O'Brien, *Olive branch*, pp. 441–56.
[2] *Cork Examiner*, 20 Mar. 1909.

Inevitably this new departure drew down upon O'Brien's head the thunders of the parliamentary party. Redmond at once denounced the League as an attempt to set aside both the party and the U.I.L. and as heralding a new split which might have disastrous consequences. Shortly afterwards the O'Brien organisation was condemned at a party meeting as 'hostile and subversive' and Members were warned, on pain of expulsion, not to identify themselves with it. But before either the League could establish itself or Redmond's excommunication take effect, O'Brien had already paid the penalty for the furiousness with which he burned his frail candle at both ends. Suddenly, as so often before, his health collapsed and, without even notifying Healy of his intention, he resigned his parliamentary seat and absented himself abroad for the rest of the year.[1]

(vi)

These tiresome squabbles were on the surface reminiscent of the worst years of the nineties, but although both Dillon and Redmond found them extremely vexatious, their importance—except to O'Brien—should not be overrated. The bulk of the party remained loyal, the dissidents were strong only in the county and city of Cork (with isolated pockets of support elsewhere), and best of all, the Liberal alliance was beginning to bear fruit. But not, however, in the direction of Home Rule. When in the spring of 1908 Asquith succeeded Campbell-Bannerman as Prime Minister, his response to an Irish Home Rule resolution was so frigid that Dillon was moved to describe the debate as 'in every sense a failure'.[2] This was an opinion widely shared in the country and one of Redmond's most valued supporters, Alderman Stephen O'Mara of Limerick, a trustee of the parliamentary fund and father of the Member for South Kilkenny who had resigned in disgust the previous year, best expressed it when he wrote to him urging that the party ought either to withdraw from Parliament altogether or else try 'by all means, fair or foul' to drive 'this government of frauds' from office. Redmond's answer was that he could not by any such irresponsible action jeopardise important beneficial legislation which was then pending.[3] And indeed it is only fair to set against the constant stream of criticism to which the parliamentarians were subject in these difficult years the undeniably substantial reforms they succeeded in winning. A year later the National Directory of the U.I.L. found it necessary to issue a circular outlining the work of the party in the previous three years and the list of achievements was certainly impressive. It included, besides the Evicted Tenants Act already noted, very considerable improvements in both rural and urban housing, the protection of tenants in towns, increased payments to national school-teachers and grants for school-building, the renewal of

---

[1] *F.J.*, 28 Mar. 1909; O'Brien. *Olive branch*, p. 455; Healy, *Letters and leaders*, ii. 484–5.

[2] Dillon to Redmond, 23 Apr. 1908, in the possession of Professor Myles Dillon.

[3] Gwynn, *Redmond*, p. 155.

the grant in aid of the study of the Irish language, the application of the Old Age Pensions Act to Ireland, the repeal of the Arms Act, the virtual cessation of coercion and, brightest jewel of all perhaps, the Irish Universities Act.[1] This last concession, the demand for which had consumed so much energy and roused such great passion over so many years finally established not one but two new universities in Ireland. Leaving Trinity in more-or-less splendid isolation, it converted the Queen's College of Belfast into the Queen's University, Belfast, and grouped the university colleges of Dublin, Cork and Galway into a National University which, although technically non-denominational, was in fact the Catholic University Nationalists had campaigned for so strenuously.

Although the cause of a Catholic University had been close to Dillon's heart from his student days, he welcomed the new Act in a speech less eloquent and more combative than was usual with him on this subject, but he was surely right when he saluted it as 'one of the greatest services to the Irish nation which it has ever been given to an English statesman to render'.[2] Yet curiously enough this very reform was shortly to involve him in one of the strangest controversies of his career. No sooner had the Act been passed than a powerful agitation was set going, with the Gaelic League in the van, to make Irish a compulsory subject for matriculation. The agitation was eventually successful, but not before Dillon, whose attachment to the language revival went back as far as his attachment to the idea of a Catholic University, had taken his stand firmly against compulsion. The climax of the debate came at that same National Convention in February 1909 which had treated William O'Brien with such scant ceremony. Dillon, too, had to face a hostile audience, but with great courage and persistence succeeded in presenting his unpopular case despite many interruptions. He began by deprecating the tactics of those who represented the quarrel as a quarrel between pro- and anti-national factions. Was it not rather, he asked a question of how best to secure the place of honour all desired for Irish studies? Those who argued for compulsory Irish claimed that without it the National University would not be a truly Irish university. But compulsory Latin did not make a Latin university any more than compulsory arithmetic made an arithmetic university. Again, it was said that if Irish were not made compulsory it would occupy an inferior and degraded position. Did that mean, then, that theology and Christian doctrine were to be made compulsory subjects, and that if they were not so made then they would be degraded and the university become agnostic or anti-Christian? 'Take care,' he said in one of the most prescient sentences he ever uttered, 'that in making Irish compulsory you may not take the fine edge off the

[1] *W.F.J.*, 17 Apr. 1909.
[2] Hansard, H.C. Debates, 5th series, vol. 188, cols. 835–40. Curiously enough, his papers yield almost nothing on the university question at this time. This is all the more disappointing since there was one school of thought which held that Birrell had been deeply influenced by Dillon in the framing of his scheme. See especially the letter of Sir Horace Plunkett to James Bryce, 21 Dec. 1907 (Bryce Papers). I am indebted to Mr. A. C. Hepburn for this reference.

enthusiasm of the Gaelic revival and bring down the study of Irish to the level of the study of Latin.'

He had equally little patience with the argument that if Irish was not on a par with other compulsory subjects the poor man's son from an Irish-speaking district would be at a disadvantage.

> There is only one respect [he said] in which making Irish compulsory could advantage an Irish speaking student . . . and that is by limiting competition for prizes in the university through the operation of compulsory Irish in excluding from the university a number of students who would otherwise enter it, and I cannot conceive any course more calculated to injure and lower the Gaelic movement itself than by a process of exclusion to make the winning of prizes more easy for the Irish-speaking students.

His own solution to this particular problem was the common-sense one of allowing candidates to substitute Irish for any of the compulsory subjects on a basis of equal marks, but it is clear from the whole tenor of his speech that his opposition to compulsion went much deeper than a mere question of methodology. It was partly temperamental, partly political. Temperamentally, he loathed compulsion of any kind, and in this sphere especially he dreaded the demand (which was, in fact, already being made) that it should be extended to the schools. 'I think the tendency in education for a long time has been towards too much compulsion, and my own inclination has always been towards more variety and more liberty.' Indeed, with that readiness to follow his logic wherever it led him, which was one his most attractive intellectual characteristics, he freely admitted that if he had his way there would be no entrance examination at all—simply registration, on the old German model—'and then you could not fight over the question to have Irish compulsory'. But behind this essentially liberal argument there was a more fundamental political purpose. All his life he had resented exclusiveness—whether religious, racial or linguistic—as tending to make more difficult that union of Irishmen of all creeds and classes which he saw as the most urgent task facing the nation when Home Rule should have been achieved. Consequently, he was bound to oppose to the uttermost any campaign to extend Irish,—still, after all, the possession of only a very small minority—to schools or other universities is such a way as to alienate those whom they must accept and live with in the future:

> I am deeply concerned [he concluded] that any attempt to force compulsory Irish on the Protestant schools of this country or on the universities of Belfast or Dublin would be a most outrageous and intolerant proceeding, and would effectively check the movement in favour of the Gaelic revival which has been going on slowly amongst the Protestants of Ireland. And any attempt to put coercive pressure on the Protestant schools or on the universities of Belfast or Dublin would have far-reaching effects in other directions which I need now not specify.[1]

[1] *W.F.J.*, 20 Feb. 1909.

He was, of course, defeated, by two to one on his own estimate, but he remained unrepentant and as late as 1913 incurred the censure of the Ard-Fheis of the Gaelic League for remarking in the House of Commons that if a policy of compulsory Irish were to be introduced in an Irish Parliament it would meet with such opposition that a normal Unionist minority would be converted into a majority on that question.[1] Since an all-Ireland Parliament has never yet met there has been no opportunity to test this interesting prediction, but it was one more provocation which his enemies duly noted and for which payment would eventually be exacted. It made no difference to Dillon, however; he had made clear once more a cardinal axiom of his political life—that he could never subscribe to the doctrine, already popular in some quarters, that the only true Ireland was an Ireland both Catholic and Gaelic.

The Irish Universities Act was perhaps the most glittering of the prizes won from the Liberals, but it was not the last. There remained the eternal land question, still posing its apparently insoluble problems and still demanding the expenditure of more and yet more money. The breakdown in the finances of the Wyndham Act and the consequent slowing of the pace of land purchase have already been mentioned. In 1907 and 1908 the Government made tentative and unenthusiastic efforts to promote a settlement, but by the latter year it had become obvious to Redmond that the question had simply become an acute embarrassment which Ministers wanted to avoid for as long as possible. 'I have been trying', he wrote to Dillon in July 'to arrange a conference with Lloyd George and the Prime Minister until I have given up the attempt in utter disgust. It is quite clear these men do not want a conference, do not see any importance in it, and are trying to let the whole question drift. I feel really humiliated in having run after them in the way I have done and I will ask them for no more interviews.'[2] However, the next year Birrell tried again, introducing a Bill which went much nearer the solution advocated by the Nationalists and which, of course, aroused corresponding opposition from the Unionists. In Nationalist eyes the essential points to be achieved were compulsory purchase, further relief for the congested districts and an assurance that Irish ratepayers should not be made liable for the heavy costs inherent in the flotation of land stock. They did not get quite all they asked for—amongst Birrell's economies was an increase in the tenants' annuity—but they had the satisfaction of seeing the landlords' bonus sharply reduced (somewhat compensated for by more favourable investment terms for their purchase money), they secured a larger grant for the Congested Districts Board and, above all, they obtained the crucial principle of compulsory sale. True, this applied essentially to the Congested Districts Board and was reduced in effectiveness by the inevitable Lords' amendments, but the breach once made was capable of being widened in the future.[3] The Bill only passed

[1] B. O'Cuiv, 'Education and Language' in T. Desmond Williams (ed), *The Irish struggle, 1916–26* (London, 1966), pp. 159–60.
[2] Redmond to Dillon, 22 July 1908 (D.P.).
[3] These points were made by Dillon in a notable defence of the Act at Kilteely, County Limerick, the following year (*W.F.J.*, 4 June 1910).

through the Commons under closure and, apart from the question of compulsion, at once attracted radical, or rather reactionary, amendments in the Upper House. Birrell, under Nationalist pressure, moved their rejection *en bloc*, and a deadlock, very similar to the one at that same moment developing over the budget, seemed inevitable. But rather than complicate the main constitutional issue with this further problem, which was incomprehensible to all save a few experts, the Liberals conceded some of the Lords' demands, leaving open loop-holes for the survival of large estates or the creation of new large farms.[1] Nevertheless, land purchase began once more to be accelerated and although a final phase of the problem still remained, it would be an Irish Parliament that would settle it—the Imperial Parliament had said its last word on this thorniest of all Irish questions.

Important as the 1909 Act was, it was carried through in an atmosphere almost of unreality, so preoccupied were both the English parties with the great constitutional crisis, so long impending and now at last precipitated when in 1909 Lloyd George brought in what seemed, for those days, a revolutionary budget. It was certainly much larger than the norm, partly because social reforms such as Old Age Pensions had to be paid for, and partly because the clamour for increased naval building meant that more money had to be found for defence. All through the early spring of 1909 the Liberal Cabinet worked at the budget, bracing themselves to swallow the Chancellor's radical proposals. Lloyd George was himself very much the architect of his budget and whether or not he framed it deliberately to provoke the House of Lords (the question is still much debated), there is no doubt that many of his colleagues were apprehensive about the way in which it hit again and again at the propertied classes. Lloyd George was looking for an additional sixteen million pounds and he sought to get it by an increase in income tax (from 1s. 0d. to 1s. 2d.) and by introducing a super-tax (at the rate of 6d. in the pound on the amount by which incomes of £5,000 or more exceeded £3,000). In addition he increased death duties, liquor licences and the taxes on spirits and tobacco. Finally, and most controversial of all, he introduced a series of land taxes, striking particularly at the unearned increment in land values, and at undeveloped land or minerals.[2]

The passage of the budget through the Commons was a long agony not completed until the beginning of November. During all that time the Irish party was stretched upon the rack. On the one hand, the budget was intensely unpopular in Ireland, especially the liquor licences and the tax on spirits, which hit distillers and publicans. The party depended upon both these highly articulate groups for financial and local support and anything that adversely affected them would be bound to have unpleasant

---

[1] For a succinct account of the legislative history of the bill, see *Annual Register*, 1909, pp. 71, 196–8, 205–6, 218–19, 223, 242, 256–7.

[2] The best recent description of the framing of the budget is in Jenkins, *Asquith*, pp. 194–7.

political repercussions. On the other hand, if the budget did produce the long-awaited crisis which would limit or end the veto of the House of Lords, then Home Rule might reasonably be expected to be a residuary legatee. There were opportunities here, but there were also dangers. There had still been no satisfactory Liberal pledge on Home Rule and Redmond and Dillon had a clear duty to do all they could to extract one. But they could not go to the length of siding with the Lords to throw out the budget, because if they did that the whole basis of the Liberal alliance would collapse. Perhaps the best description of what they eventually decided to do was given by Dillon in the House of Commons early in 1910, when their policy seemed to have been magnificently justified by results. 'From the beginning,' he said, 'we said that even in its original form, as regards its general purpose and its general scheme, we were not opposed to it; but as regards many of its clauses, it hit Ireland with intolerable injustice.' What the Irish party had done, therefore had been to bring these clauses to the notice of the Government. True, as Dillon had to admit, they had not got all the concessions they had asked, so on the crucial third reading of the Finance Bill they had abstained from voting. If they had voted, they would have had to vote against the Liberals, but this they refused to do, partly because they did not wish to embarrass their allies, but mainly because in the struggle between Lords and Commons they did not wish in any way to be identified with the Lords.[1]

This was accurate enough so far as it went, though it skated very delicately over what had been, in fact, a very serious crisis in Anglo-Irish relations. All through the summer Redmond had been in touch with Lloyd George, pressing on him the amendments necessary to placate Irish opinion. To lend point to his arguments he had even gone so far as to take the Irish party into the lobby *against* the Government on the second reading of the Finance Bill, anxious though he was to come to terms. By the end of August he thought (vain illusion!) that he had pinned Lloyd George down. A month later he found that this was not so and wrote indignantly to the Prime Minister. He explained that on 26 August, he, Dillon, Devlin and two other Irish Members had met the Chancellor of the Exchequer at Downing Street. Lloyd George had told them that he would accept the Irish amendments as to land valuation and, more important that he would abolish the minimum limit for licence duty, even though this had not been specifically requested. It had been agreed that these amendments should be moved by the Irish party in the House, but just before the debate Redmond had been astonished to learn that the Cabinet was not going to carry out what he and his colleagues had considered to be a firm understanding. On 17 September, in company with the same Irish Members, his statement continued, he had again seen Lloyd George and had, of course, protested. To this the Chancellor had simply replied that he was not in a position to meet their demands.[2]

[1] Hansard, H.C. Debates, 5th series, vol. 16, cols. 2103–16.
[2] Gwynn, *Redmond*, pp. 162–4.

The real danger in this situation was not just that it caused bad feeling within the Liberal-Nationalist alliance (though it certainly did do that), but that the failure of the parliamentary party to protect the Irish distillers and publicans was seriously weakening their position. By contrast, the dissident Irish Members who with O'Brien's departure had begun to separate themselves from the main body, even though not yet formally expelled, lost no opportunity of making political capital by uninhibited attacks upon the budget. They numbered no more than ten or eleven, but they included Tim Healy, who, in O'Brien's absence, had reverted to his natural element —political anomaly. Still technically a member of the party, he was so little amenable to its discipline that, by his own account, the leaders were bracing themselves to eject him again, but hesitated for fear of further offending the liquor trade in Ireland.[1] It was partly to combat these attacks and to present the official party line that Dillon spoke as frequently as he did in Ireland that summer. In these speeches, and they averaged more than one a month between February and October, he dwelt upon the positive achievements of the party, but most of all on the need for unity at this critical moment, trying to bring home to his audiences what indeed was the truth, though it was hard for simple people to see it, that the budget fight was only part of a much greater issue and that the final battle for Home Rule might only be a few months away. It was for this reason that he made very little attempt to defend the budget, except to make the best case possible for the reduced licence duties for publicans which, though he could hardly say this in public, were what Redmond had had to accept to his chagrin in place of the abolition of the minimum limit. On the contrary, Dillon was concerned rather to stress the fact that this *was* a thoroughly bad budget for Ireland and to draw from this the conclusion that the only way to avoid such impositions in the future was to have Home Rule.[2]

But although he might, and did, repeat this doctrine all over Ireland in his most uncompromising tones, he was privately much concerned at the dissatisfaction he encountered everywhere. T. P. O'Connor, who was his most regular correspondent, used his reports, and similar ones from Devlin, to try to warn Lloyd George of the effects of his intransigence. 'You will understand', he wrote in September, 'how far the feeling has gone when Joe Devlin—one of the most sanguine, ablest and truest men in our party— said to me on Friday night that Healy was right; and that we ought to have fought the budget from first to last. Of course I remain of the opinion that from the Irish point of view that would have been a foolish policy . . . but it is an indication of Irish opinion; and when I wrote to Dillon about it his reply was that it faithfully reflected the depression in our ranks in Ireland.'[3] O'Connor's view, and he was probably right, was that for Ireland the issue really narrowed down to the licence duties and a few weeks later, just before the third reading of the Finance Bill, he wrote imploring the Chancellor not

[1] Healy, *Letters and leaders*, ii. 488–9.
[2] For examples of his line on the budget see *W.F.J.*, 15 May, 21 Aug., 14 Dec. 1909.
[3] T. P. O'Connor to Lloyd George, 25 Sept. 1909 (L.G.P., C/6/10/1).

to jeopardise the whole alliance on this relatively trivial point. 'Why in Heaven's name you and your colleagues stick to these wretched licence duties in Ireland—on the one side adding to the forces against us another force which may turn the balance against us in our effort to support you in the election, on the other side bringing you in neither finance nor reputation —I am unable to understand.' O'Connor feared—wrongly as it turned out— that the Irish party would have to vote against the Government on the third reading, but the conclusion he drew from their dilemma was inescapable. 'It is quite true that you can beat down our opposition both by closure and in the division lobby; but what a prologue to the great life-and-death struggle we have to wage in the country, which we ought to wage together.'[1]

There is no denying that the budget, and the failure of the party to remove the worst of the Irish grievances against it, did seriously weaken the standing of Redmond and Dillon in the country. What the end might have been if the Lords had not rejected the budget, it is difficult to say, but the signs were certainly ominous. However, the fact that they did reject it transformed the situation almost miraculously. By late November such a rejection already seemed on the cards and a general election began to appear a certainty. At once the Irish leaders commenced their pressure for a declaration on Home Rule. As Dillon wrote to Redmond in late November, if there was nothing from Asquith before the election, 'the effect on our position will be most serious'.[2] Next day Redmond sent a strong letter to Morley, virtually demanding a declaration, preferably in Asquith's forthcoming speech at the Albert Hall, if the Irish vote was not to be thrown against the Liberals in the coming fight. On 30 November, the Lords finally did reject the budget and a dissolution of Parliament followed immediately. On 10 December, came Asquith's declaration, stating categorically that the Irish problem could only be solved in one way—'by a policy which, while safeguarding the supremacy and indefeasible authority of the imperial Parliament, will set up in Ireland a system of full self-government in regard to purely Irish affairs'.[3] Time was to tell whether the reservation contained in this statement was more important than the affirmation, but the Irish leaders were surely right in thinking that Asquith had made an important step forward and that Home Rule had once again entered the realm of practical politics. With this hope to sustain them they could now look forward confidently to the election, though even they could not have anticipated that after it was over Redmond would occupy a more pivotal position than Parnell in his palmiest days had ever been able to achieve.

[1] T. P. O'Connor to Lloyd George, 'Saturday', probably 30 Oct. 1909 (L.G.P., C/6/10/2).
[2] Gwynn, *Redmond*, p. 166.
[3] Ibid., p. 169; J. A. Spender and Cyril Asquith, *Life of Lord Oxford and Asquith* (London, 1932), i. 268–9.

11

Towards Home Rule

(i)

Although, as it eventually turned out, the fate of Home Rule hung upon what was happening in the British constituencies, the Irish party were of necessity preoccupied with the dour fight they had on their hands at home. Essentially, it was a fight against the massive dissatisfaction created in the country by all the delays and disappointments of the previous four years, of which the last and worst example had been the almost universally detested budget. In more practical terms it was a fight against the strange but undeniably effective partnership of O'Brien and Healy, resurrected by O'Brien's sudden reappearance after nearly a year of illness in Italy. Once back in Ireland he hurled the All-for-Ireland League into the fray with characteristic abandon, and in so doing presented the party leaders with the threat they most wished to avoid, a fresh split in the Nationalist representation at the very moment when unity, or at least the appearance of it, was their greatest need. The chief burden of combating this threat fell upon Dillon and he was, for him, optimistic about the outcome. Writing to T. P. O'Connor on New Year's Day, he forecast that O'Brien would win five or six seats, which would not be enough to make it difficult to deal with him. 'When the party is being reformed after the election *all* his gang should be rigidly excluded. And if that is done the faction will rapidly die out. O'Brien himself will of course resign again in about 6 months—and that will be the end of him.' As for Healy, Dillon had hopes that he might at last be beaten in North Louth, especially if Cardinal Logue withdrew his by now traditional support for him.[1] But this was too sanguine. The Cardinal, though refraining from actually nominating Healy, allowed it to be known that he intended to vote for him.[2] What effect this had upon the electors in terms of votes it is impossible to say, but no doubt the faithful, with a long experience of His Eminence to guide them, were able to recognise a hint when they saw one. At any rate, Healy was once more elected and survived to carry his long vendetta with Redmond and Dillon one stage nearer finality.

The overall results were not unfavourable to the majority, though scarcely as emphatic as they would have wished. The majority section—to revert to the terminology of the split—accounted for seventy out of 103

[1] Dillon to T. P. O'Connor, 1 Jan. 1910 (D.P.).
[2] Healy, *Letters and leaders*, ii. 491.

Irish seats, or seventy-one if T. P. O'Connor's Liverpool seat is included. There were, in addition, eleven Independent Nationalists (eight belonging to the Healy-O'Brien group and three others with private grievances of their own), one Liberal Home Ruler and twenty-one Unionists.[1] Dillon, who considered the result as generally satisfactory, was even able to persuade himself that O'Brien's hold on Cork was weakening and that next time Healy could be beaten in North Louth. But there was an ominous reservation. 'In spite of all we could do', he wrote to O'Connor, 'to stem the torrent of lies about the budget, they have left a considerable effect upon public opinion and there is a considerable undercurrent of hostility to the budget, and dislike and distrust of our toleration of it and of the government.' In addition to this he had noted with some alarm that friction was growing between the labourers and very small farmers on the one hand and the substantial farmers and graziers on the other, thus adding another complication to the rural constituencies. 'The truth is', he added, with a perception more profound than he could possibly have realised himself at that moment, 'that Irish politics is and has been for a considerable time, a much more complex problem than it used to be.'[2]

Yet, superficially at least, the election had left the party in a strong position. The great Liberal majority of 1906 had melted away and Liberals (275) and Unionists (273) were now neck and neck. The consequence was that the Labour representatives (40) and the Irish immediately assumed an importance out of all proportion to their numbers. Redmond, indeed, with his seventy-one votes, could make or break the Government. Obviously this was a position of great leverage, but it was also subject to grave disabilities. One was that if he used his power to turn an unsatisfactory Liberal ministry out, there would be an end to Home Rule in the foreseeable future. And the other was the danger, which soon proved real enough, that the two main parties would react so strongly against Irish influence at Westminster as to draw closer together and try to resolve their differences by some compact from which Redmond would be excluded.

The problem, therefore, was to bring pressure to bear upon the Liberals without driving them into the arms of the opposition, but it was a problem complicated for the Irish leaders by that deep hostility to the budget which had caused Dillon such anxiety during the election. The Irish party, in short, could only swallow the budget if they could demonstrate to their people that in doing so they had secured real guarantees of Home Rule. What this meant in practice, as Dillon explained to O'Connor in the letter of 1 February already quoted, was that the party could not allow the budget to pass unless Asquith could convince them that he would be able, *that session*, to pass a measure limiting the veto of the House of Lords. T. P. O'Connor made the same point, more forcibly, to Lloyd George on 9 February, the day before the Cabinet met to plan its policy in the light of

[1] For an analysis of the Irish results, see Lyons, *The Irish parliamentary party*, pp. 130, 136–7.
[2] Dillon to T. P. O'Connor, 1 Feb. 1910 (D.P.).

the election results. 'I have grave news to give you', he wrote from Dillon's house in Dublin. 'I have seen all our friends here and I find them unanimous in saying that they must *oppose* the budget unless it be preceded by the announcement of a measure limiting the legislative and financial veto of the House of Lords', this to be linked with a guarantee that it would pass into law that same year. 'I am certain', O'Connor added, 'that no other policy is possible to the Irish party in the present condition of Irish opinion.'[1] This demand was repeated publicly, and sharply, next day by Redmond,[2] who crossed to London immediately afterwards and was summoned, with O'Connor, to meet Lloyd George on the morning of 12 February, by which time the Cabinet had already had two sessions. It was quite evident that a major crisis was at hand and Redmond wrote at once to Dillon (still in Dublin) to explain what was happening:

> T.P.'s letter was read to the Cabinet. They came to the conclusion that it meant an end to the government and an immediate dissolution. After the Cabinet, George Grey, Haldane, Churchill, Samuel, McKenna and some others had a meeting and they *all* agreed to a proposal put forward by George to the following effect.
>
> 1. Whole time up to Easter to be devoted to necessary supply. Debate on address, etc. etc. etc.
>
> 2. Immediately after Easter Recess first business to be introduction of Veto Bill.
>
> 3. Interval between 1st and 2nd reading of Veto Bill, a budget to be introduced in which very substantial concessions on whiskey duty etc. to be made to Ireland. The old budget would thus disappear altogether. It would be a budget for 1910–11.
>
> 4. Veto and new budget to run *pari passu*, but *Veto* bill to go first to Lords.
>
> 5. On rejection of Veto Bill by Lords, but not till then, the king to be asked to appoint peers. On his refusal (which is taken for granted) Parliament to be dissolved—about July. After his meeting with Grey etc., George saw Asquith who would not commit himself but seemed not unfavourable. Cabinet meets at 3 o'c. on Monday *to decide this question*.[3]

This was clearly a situation full of menace for the Irish leaders. The salient fact to emerge from the discussion was that the Government had *not* got the guarantees from the King which Redmond and Dillon believed to be essential. Moreover, it was perfectly clear that the Liberals were in a state of disarray and it looked as if they were not getting a firm lead from Asquith. The Cabinet duly met on Monday, 14 February, but decided nothing, and met again every day that week except Friday, still without result. The consequence was that when Asquith spoke in the House of Commons on 21 February he had to say not merely that he had no

[1] T. P. O'Connor to Lloyd George, 9 Feb. 1910 (L.G.P., c/6/10/3).
[2] Gwynn, *Redmond*, p. 173.
[3] Redmond to Dillon, 12 Feb. 1910 (D.P.).

guarantees but had not even asked for any. It was, his Chief Whip dis-passionately observed, 'the very worst speech I have ever heard him make'. No wonder the Prime Minister found Redmond 'cold and critical' when they met next day.[1] The situation in fact had become so bad that by the end of that week some members of the Cabinet were preparing to take refuge in resignation as the only dignified exit left to them. Asquith, however, was far from sharing this view—he had not abandoned hope of hammering out some sort of compromise on the constitutional conflict. But Redmond once more pressed for action. On 24 February he saw the Master of Elibank (the Chief Whip) and told him that the Government would have to reckon on Irish opposition unless they promised (1) to introduce a veto resolution into both Houses at once; (2) if the resolution were rejected or 'hung up' in the Lords, to ask the King at once for guarantees; (3) to postpone the budget in any case until after the two previous conditions had been ful-filled. But all he got in reply was a curt intimation that the Cabinet were not prepared to give any assurances and that 'he must act on his responsi-bility as they would on theirs'.[2]

Clearly someone's bluff was about to be called. On the one hand, the Government, by refusing to give assurances to the Irish, was testing the reality of Redmond's threats. On the other hand, Redmond, in making his threats, was testing the firmness of the Government. But it is clear from his correspondence that Redmond was absolutely in earnest. It was essential, he explained to Dillon on 5 March, that the veto resolutions should be introduced simultaneously in both Houses. Otherwise, the budget would be upon them before they could know what the Lords' action on the veto resolutions was going to be. If *that* happened, he could not see how the Irish party could avoid voting against the Liberals, since there seemed no likelihood of real concessions on the items that had caused most trouble in Ireland. 'And thus the resignation of the government will be forced, not on the veto at all, but on the budget, an absolutely fatal position for them, and, of course, an injurious one for us.'[3]

Neither side would give way—yet neither side was quite sure if it could afford the luxury of intransigence. Negotiations, therefore, continued and on 8 March Redmond had another conversation with Lloyd George. The latter told him that the Government was still determined to deal with the budget in the interval between the veto resolutions being considered first by the House of Commons and then by the House of Lords. 'He held out no hope whatever of a change in this plan, and, on my side, I held out no hope whatever of an alteration of our attitude .' Lloyd George then let fall—what O'Connor was at that very time passing on to Dillon—that O'Brien and Healy had been in touch with the Cabinet through the Chief Whip, and that they were offering to support the Government if the budget was amended so as to remove the worst Irish grievances. Lloyd

---

[1] Jenkins, *Asquith*, p. 207.
[2] Gwynn, *Redmond*, p. 174; Jenkins, *Asquith*, pp. 207–8.
[3] Redmond to Dillon, 5 Mar. 1910 (D.P.).

George—in a very characteristic manoeuvre—having revealed this information to Redmond, then offered him virtually the same concessions as the price of Irish support:

> The conversation [wrote Redmond] ended in this way: I told him I stood by 'No veto, no budget'; but, at the same time, I said I felt it my duty carefully to consider the offer he had made, and I am to see him again in a few days.
>
> To be quite candid with you, I do not trust George in this matter. I do not believe he could get the cabinet to agree to these terms; but I felt bound to, at any rate, say that I would carefully consider them; and I am far from saying that, if they could be carried out, they ought not to be accepted.[1]

Meanwhile Dillon remained in Ireland trying to keep track of, and to influence, the movement of public opinion. He himself held firmly in public and in private to the 'no veto, no budget' line and warned T. P. O'Connor that feeling in Ireland was growing more hostile—'Asquith is looked upon as a traitor—utterly unreliable'.[2] He crossed to England to speak at a St. Patrick's Day meeting in Birmingham and once again came out strongly for 'no veto, no budget', emphasising that he and Redmond and Devlin were all at one in standing by this policy.[3] Nevertheless, when he got to London next day and had a long conversation with Lloyd George and the Master of Elibank he came away, so he told his friend C. P. Scott of the *Manchester Guardian*, 'feeling that the situation is almost desperate'. He could see no way out of the dilemma. On the one hand there was the state of feeling at home which had clearly impressed him deeply—'our attitude', he said, 'is bound to be influenced by this state of feeling in Ireland'. On the other hand, he knew very well what the consequence of turning out the Liberals might be. 'I believe it would result in the Tories winning the next election by a majority of anywhere from 100 to 200. The situation is a tragical one, but it is not of our making. And in the last resort we should be bound at all hazards to retain the confidence of our own people.'[4]

Fortunately, the Liberals were at least equally aware of impending disaster and on 21 March Dillon and Redmond were summoned for yet another conference with Lloyd George, who was accompanied this time by Birrell. The main purpose of the meeting was precisely what Lloyd George had previously foreshadowed to Redmond, to explore ways and means of making the budget palatable enough to allow the Irish to support it and so end the crisis. It seems that this proposal did in the end reach the cabinet, that it was discussed there exhaustively, but that ultimately it was decided—as Asquith informed the King on 13 April—that 'to purchase the

---

[1] Redmond to Dillon, 8 Mar. 1910; T. P. O'Connor to Dillon, 7 and 9 Mar. 1910 D.P.).

[2] Dillon to T. P. O'Connor, 15 Mar. 1910 (D.P.); *F.J.*, 4 Apr. 1910, for a very strong speech along these lines at Athlone.

[3] *W.F.J.*, 26 Mar. 1910.

[4] Dillon to C. P. Scott, 19 Mar. 1910 (D.P.).

Irish vote by such a concession would be a discreditable transaction, which they could not defend'.[1] As against this, however, it seems that Redmond had at last convinced Ministers that he meant what he said, for the very same Cabinet which took such a high moral tone about buying his support, also decided on action which would in effect give him what he wanted. Asquith explained to the King that the Government now felt that if the House of Lords rejected the veto resolutions about to be put to them, it would be his duty to ask the King for a dissolution, with guarantees that if the Liberals came back to office after the next election he would create enough peers to overcome resistance in the Lords; failing such guarantees the government would be obliged to resign.[2] This, as it proved, was the breaking of the ice. The next day Asquith announced his solution in the House of Commons, and since his veto resolutions were now accompanied by what seemed to the Irish leaders to be adequate guarantees they made no further difficulties about the budget, which by the end of April had passed through both Houses. Thereupon Parliament adjourned with every prospect that the Lords, faced by the possibility of a wholesale creation of peers, would surrender at discretion and thus leave the way open for Home Rule at last.

(ii)

But all these hopes were checked by the sudden death of King Edward on 7 May. Asquith's reaction, and indeed that of most English politicians, was that the new King, inexperienced and unsophisticated, ought not to be plunged headlong into the midst of a major constitutional crisis. At once the search for a way out began, some form of compromise which would either end the crisis altogether, or at least delay a collision until a decent interval had elapsed after Edward VII's funeral and George V's accession. From the Irish point of view this disposition to 'pile arms', as Asquith put it, was full of danger. If a compromise did result, it would almost certainly be at Redmond's expense, and as the rumours of a conference between the two main parties to solve the constitutional problem began to take more definite shape at the beginning of June, frequent and agitated letters flew to and fro between the Irish leaders. Dillon, though at this time remote in County Mayo, was, as early as 2 June, disturbed at the prospect of a conference and particularly apprehensive that Lloyd George's appetite for reforming the House of Lords would deflect him from the veto question in its strict form. He was beginning also to doubt that the Liberals would win the next election. 'But that', he wrote to O'Connor, 'as we agreed long ago would be a matter of no importance compared with the collapse and utter ruin of the Liberal party if they split up and quarrel with us before the election as a result of this infernal conference.'[3] The very next day, as it happened, O'Connor dined with Lloyd George and the Chief Whip and on June 4 he sent a full account to both

---

[1] Jenkins, *Asquith*, p. 209.   [2] Ibid., p. 210.
[3] Dillon to T. P. O'Connor, 2 June 1910 (D.P.).

Redmond and Dillon. As regards the budget, and the concessions which the Irish leaders were still, even at this late date, trying to extract from him, Lloyd George seemed adamant and would not hear of dropping the whiskey tax. On the veto question he had admitted that the Government had still not decided whether it was better to press ahead immediately, thus precipitating a clash with the Lords in July and a general election in September, or wait until the autumn, with the probably inevitable election in, say, January 1911. Lloyd George himself, it appeared, was quite convinced that there *would* be a conference, and clearly was not prepared to commit himself in the meantime on the veto question. This was discouraging, to say the least, and as O'Connor pointed out to his friends, the question facing them was 'whether we shall make definite objection . . . to the postponement under any circumstances of the veto campaign till the autumn session.[1]

O'Connor ended his letter with an urgent plea from Lloyd George that the two leaders should come at once to London, and at first sight it does seem extraordinary that at this crucial moment in the history of Home Rule Dillon should have been sitting quietly at home in Mayo and Dublin, and Redmond in County Wicklow. But their absence was almost certainly by design—a manoeuvre they were frequently to repeat in the years ahead, by which they deliberately removed themselves from Liberal pressure. Having once stated their case, it was their policy to vacate the stage and leave it for others to accept or reject what they had offered. And in this instance, for Dillon at least, absence was probably the wisest course—the more he thought about the conference the more irritated he became. Had he been in London some kind of explosion would probably have occurred —even as it was, his letters to his colleagues show that his natural inclination, which was always to take the offensive when in difficulties, was reasserting itself. The proper policy, he wrote to Redmond on 5 June, was still to precipitate a clash with the House of Lords in July and to bring on an election in November or, at latest, January.[2] And to O'Connor, in a letter recalling that in a previous conversation with the Liberal Chief Whip, they had been prepared to consider an election late that year or early the next provided the veto crisis came to a head in July, he continued in a passage which conveys better than anything else his attitude to the Liberal alliance at this vital moment:

> If the veto crisis is postponed to the autumn, and it is proposed now to proceed with this year's budget [it will be remembered that the budget passed in April had been the 1909 budget], we will be absolutely obliged to resume perfect liberty of action. And my *firm* conviction is that a disaster would result.
>
> If the government were to attempt to come to an understanding with the Tory front bench and carry thro' such a programme in spite of us, we should of course be driven into active opposition and the

---

[1] T. P. O'Connor to Dillon, 4 June 1910 (D.P.); Gwynn, *Redmond*, pp. 175–7.
[2] Dillon to Redmond, 5 June 1910 (R.P.); Gwynn, *Redmond*, pp. 177–8.

result could only be the complete demoralisation and ruin of the Liberal party.

The proposal for a conference between the leaders of the two parties I regard as absolutely fatal—taken in connection with the description given by L.G. of the present state of the government, it would mean the complete triumph of the Roseberyite section, who would unite with Balfour and co. And of course the moment a conference is agreed to, we and the fighting section of the radical party are shut out from exercising any influence whatsoever on the result.[1]

This was an extreme statement—and characteristically pessimistic—but events had an uncomfortable habit of conforming to Dillon's gloomiest predictions. Soon it appeared that this might be going to happen yet again. On 6 June T. P. O'Connor met the Liberal Chief Whip and lunched with Lloyd George and Winston Churchill. He carried away the impression that both the Chief Whip and Lloyd George would have liked to take the veto resolutions in July, but that they would be overruled in the Cabinet, with the necessary consequence of a constitutional conference.[2] In face of this ominous news the leaders in Ireland adhered stiffly to their original position. Redmond, echoing Dillon, insisted that the whiskey tax must be dropped, and in any event threatened active Irish opposition if the Government proceeded with the 1910–11 budget, without at the same time bringing the veto question to a head.[3] Dillon, writing to him next day (9 June), surmised that O'Connor might not have put their views sufficiently firmly to the Ministers', but took refuge in the hope that even if a conference did take place, it could not succeed. 'One thing I am very much afraid of', he added, 'is that Balfour, who is an extremely astute dodger, will manage to . . . drag out the negotiations to such an extent that all heart will be taken out of the fight.'[4]

This was, on the short term at least, precisely what happened. The conference began to meet in mid-June, the Government members being the Prime Minister, Lloyd George, Lord Crewe and Birrell, the opposition being represented by Balfour, Lord Lansdowne, Lord Cawdor and Austen Chamberlain. It continued to meet fairly frequently until the end of July, adjourned until October and finally broke up on 10 November. The Irish leaders, though informed from time to time of what was happening, were, as Dillon had anticipated, very much shut out. He himself remained nervous about the outcome. On 14 June, just before the conference began its sittings, he wrote to O'Connor in semi-apology for the 'somewhat brutal frankness' of his recent letters, explaining it by the fact that in the matter of conferences, 'I confess I have always had present to my mind a certain other conference which took place in 1902 [he meant, of course, the Land Conference], the methods by which its decisions were made the decisions of the party, and the consequences to the party which ensued.' In this instance, he agreed, once the Liberals had committed themselves, 'it would have been

---

[1] Dillon to T. P. O'Connor, 5 June 1910 (D.P.).   [2] Gwynn, *Redmond*, pp. 178–80.
[3] Ibid., p. 180.   [4] Dillon to Redmond, 9 June 1910 (R.P.).

idle and mischievous in the highest degree for us to attempt to stop the conference'. But, on the other hand, 'it is absolutely essential for us to be free to say that we had no kind of responsibility, direct or indirect, for this conference, and, if we consider it desirable or useful, to say further that we objected to it from the outset'.[1]

As it turned out, Dillon's fears as to what might result from the conference were unjustified. In its earlier stages it had seemed to make some progress, but the breaking-point was the question of Irish self-government. On this, the opposition had nourished hopes of inducing the Liberals to agree to a special constitutional procedure. But Home Rule by steeplechase was not a practicable proposition and Asquith could not, dared not, entertain it, since had he done so, the Irish would have gone into full opposition immediately and the Liberal Government would have collapsed. For Dillon, these prolonged meetings were an anxious period, but as there was nothing he could do to influence the outcome he retired to Ireland and divided his time as usual between Dublin and Ballaghaderrin. For others it was a more strenuous recess. Redmond and Devlin went to the U.S.A., and T. P. O'Connor to Canada, to raise funds for the election which they were sure was on its way. These tours were brilliantly successful and between them brought in 100,000 dollars—not a moment too soon, for on the voyage home in early November Redmond heard by wireless that the conference had indeed broken down and that the fight was on again. Irish intransigence had had its reward and although the perils of another general election now lay ahead, at least the bogy of a compromise settlement at his expense had for the time being disappeared.

(iii)

Parliament was prorogued on 28 November and the general election, no less bitterly fought in Ireland than the previous one, followed immediately. The results reproduced those of January with remarkable fidelity. This time, Liberals and Unionists were exactly equal with 272 seats each, while Labour had gone up from forty to forty-two. The Nationalists, on the other hand, increased their total from eighty-one to eighty-three and since one Liberal was also returned, the total Home Rule representation in Ireland was eighty-four. Of the eighty-three Nationalists, seventy-three belonged to the majority party and there were ten Independents. County Cork remained faithful to William O'Brien and, although the party ousted T. M. Healy from North Louth by a great effort, that effort was rather too uninhibited and the victorious candidate was unseated on petition. Healy himself received the gift of a seat in North-East Cork from William O'Brien and reappeared in the House, as irrepressible as ever, later in the session.[2]

---

[1] Dillon to T. P. O'Connor, 14 June 1910 (D.P.); there is a typed copy of this letter in the Elibank Papers in the National Library of Scotland.

[2] Healy, *Letters and leaders*, ii. 502–4; Lyons, *The Irish parliamentary party*, pp. 130–1.

It was a session dominated by the Parliament Bill, limiting the veto of the House of Lords in such a fashion as to ensure that legislation passed by the House of Commons in three successive sessions should become law even if previously rejected by the House of Lords. For the Irish party it was a period of mingled anxiety and anticipation, but beyond the necessary task of delivering the Irish vote in the lobby—which they did with exemplary regularity and precision—there was little that they could do to influence the result or sway the debates. For them the crisis had largely resolved itself into a matter of close attendance in the House of Commons. And this may be why 1911 is so sparse a year in Dillon's correspondence and archives. Scarcely a single letter relevant to the major issues of the day has come to light among his papers. Indeed, even in the House itself, some of his most forceful interventions were made not on Irish questions at all, but in the related spheres of naval building and foreign policy. As early as February 1911 he was confiding to C. P. Scott of the *Manchester Guardian* his apprehensions about the Naval Estimates. 'Grey's foreign policy', he observed, 'is coming to an utter smash. My thesis is that this policy—which is really the policy of Sir Charles Hardinge and King Edward—has already cost the country about 8 million a year in naval estimates. And it looks as if we were in for another 8 or 10 before we are done with it. And all this to make England the ally of Russia and the enemy of freedom in the East.'[1] A month later, in the House of Commons, he took his argument much further, launching a general attack on Grey's conduct of affairs. Earlier in the session Grey had made a notable speech in favour of international arbitration, but Dillon now riposted by asking how far this could be assumed to apply to struggling nationalities. Would it apply to Egypt if that country wanted arbitration against British occupation? Would it apply to Persia, if she protested against partition by the Anglo-Russian agreement? 'I should like to hear that side of the question, belonging, as I do, to a conquered nation, before I could give my adhesion to it.'

What really worried him, however, was that arbitration would never secure the full consent of the powers so long as the armaments race continued. Britain's share in that race was mainly confined to naval building, but, Dillon insisted, this was itself a part of a general—and he thought indefensible—involvement in power politics. Had the old two-power standard, he asked, now been replaced by a three-power standard? Originally, as he understood it, Britain's naval building had been aimed at matching the combined forces of France and Russia. But now they had the Anglo-French entente and 'a most iniquitous agreement' with Russia which 'rested largely upon the partition of a perfectly inoffensive and defenceless country'. Did this then mean that British naval-building must be such as to match the Triple Alliance? And what of the entente with France—what of the military conversations to which the French Foreign Minister had recently referred? 'I say there is a very uncomfortable feeling among many non-members that there is a secret alliance with France, or some understanding

[1] Dillon to C. P. Scott, 3 Feb. 1911 (D.P.).

which is not known to the members of this House . . .' In this estimate, despite all Grey continued to say to the contrary right up to 1914, he was not, after all, very far wide of the mark. As for the naval building itself, he accused the First Lord (at that time Reginald McKenna) of yielding to influences which no Liberal Minister ought ever to yield to. The Government, he asserted, by promoting a 'scare', had stampeded the Liberal Party into agreeing to a scale of naval expenditure which was entirely unnecessary and excessive. The country must have the weapons it needed for defence, this he entirely agreed with, but the present proliferation of dreadnoughts was, he claimed, out of all proportion to the threat from abroad. The Naval Estimates, he concluded—and who at this distance of time can say that he was altogether wrong—if allowed to continue at this rate 'may be the ruin of the Liberal party'.[1]

Interventions such as this—and there were others in the course of that session when he criticised British policy in Persia and Egypt[2]—of course did nothing to advance the Irish cause and Dillon (after the retirement of Edward Blake) was virtually the only Irish Member to concern himself with such esoteric matters. If criticised on that score he would have replied, without doubt, that these were not, or ought not to be, esoteric matters, but matters of life and death in which all men of conscience should concern themselves. In these debates he was, naturally, at the usual disadvantage of a private Member trying to interpret policy in an age of so-called secret diplomacy, and some of his views may seem in retrospect to have been excessively *simpliste*. But against this two points need to be made. One is that in certain areas—notably Egypt and Persia—he was quite exceptionally well-informed and spoke with some authority. The other is that in such matters he saw himself not as an Irish Member temporarily imprisoned at Westminster until Home Rule should set him free, but rather as one of that group of Liberals (admittedly a minority) who were deeply concerned about the peace of the world and the growing likelihood of a clash between the armed alliances. Indeed, he was more deeply concerned than most, since the quarrels of the great powers seemed so often to centre round small and oppressed nationalities with which he felt an immediate and instinctive kinship.

But while Dillon thus ranged over the globe, the affairs of his own little island were slowly progressing. With the passing of the Parliament Act in the autumn of 1911 the ring was cleared for what everyone knew would be the main conflict, the head-on collision between the Unionists and the Liberal-Nationalist alliance. Dillon took no part in the last stages of the Parliament Act debates for the good reason that he was suddenly and violently removed from the scene. On Sunday, 4 June, he was being driven by motor car to Carnlough, near Dundalk. Not far from the foot of Slieve

---

[1] Hansard, H. C. Debates, 5th series, vol. 22, cols. 2530–40.

[2] Ibid., vol. 23, cols. 632–9; vol. 28, cols. 1858–64. In addition, he asked twenty-one parliamentary questions (nine on Persia, six on Morocco and six on the Italo-Turkish war) between August and December 1911. (For this information I am indebted to Mr. Richard Langhorne, of the University of Kent at Canterbury.)

Gullion the road crossed a stream where the culvert was so steeply arched that as the car went over it Dillon was thrown against the roof, cutting his head very badly. At first, indeed, when he had been carried into a neighbouring house, it was feared that his injuries might be even more serious and he was given the Last Sacraments. Happily, this turned out not to be the case and he was moved to the County Infirmary. By a curious coincidence the last occasion on which he had been unavoidably detained in Dundalk had been in the prison hospital in 1888, but times change and his second stay was graced, as his first emphatically had not been, by a visit from no less a person than Cardinal Logue. There is unfortunately no record of what took place between them, but in all the circumstances it could scarcely have consisted of more than an exchange of platitudes—pious on the one hand and, no doubt, polite on the other. Dillon, however, had been severely shaken by his accident (he was in his sixtieth year) and he remained out of politics until October.[1]

(iv)

It was significant that when he did reappear in public his first large meeting was in Ireland, as were most of those he addressed during the winter of 1911–12. Significant, because it was just at this time that an unplanned, almost instinctive differentiation of function began to develop among the four men who to all intents and purposes were *the* Irish party. Redmond, naturally, was their chief spokesman, and in the Home Rule negotiations which lay ahead nearly all the important public speeches and private memoranda came from him. He conferred regularly with his colleagues, especially Dillon, but nevertheless the centre of the stage and the limelight were his. T. P. O'Connor, whose contact with Ireland by this time was minimal, served two quite different functions. In the first place, he was extremely influential amongst the Irish in Great Britain and could generally be relied upon to rally them solidly behind the policy of the party. His other function was, at this point, almost more important. He was the chief link between the party and the principal Liberals. More precisely, he was the chief link with Lloyd George. 'T.P.' belonged to that group—many of them able, hard-driving journalists—who formed Lloyd George's circle of friends and who, from time to time, were invited to golf at Walton Heath, or even, as O'Connor himself was, to holidays at English wateringplaces or further afield. This access to the corridors of power (he never really penetrated to the inner sanctum) was very precious to O'Connor; perhaps too precious, for, as Dillon had already surmised, he occasionally succumbed to the temptation to tell Ministers what they wanted to hear, and it was certainly true that in his reports back to the party he sometimes forgot that what seemed common sense at Westminster was totally unacceptable in Ireland.

To bridge the gap between Westminster and Ireland was, however, the main task of the third of the four leaders, Joseph Devlin. Although a

[1] *W.F.J.*, 10 June 1911.

comparative newcomer to national politics Devlin had rapidly reached the top by the skilful and unremitting use of two remarkable talents. First, although diminutive in size, he was a most persuasive, and sometimes a very powerful, orator. The 'pocket Demosthenes' was one of the few Irish Members who could hold the attention of a full House. Secondly, he was, as we have already seen, a great organisation man, deriving his influence not merely from his position as general secretary of the United Irish League, but because he also dominated the Ancient Order of Hibernians and was largely responsible for mobilising this powerful, sectarian body behind the party and delivering at elections a solid Nationalist vote wherever the A.O.H. was established. It was, in fact, based mainly upon Ulster and Devlin's control over it sprang largely from his pre-eminence among Ulster Nationalists, by whom, it is fair to say, he was loved as few politicians are ever loved. On the debit side, however, had to be set the fact that the prominence of the A.O.H. had already begun to excite hostile comment, not merely from Unionists, or the aggrieved O'Brienites, but within the ranks of the party's own supporters. One contributory factor to the restlessness of the Young Ireland branch of the U.I.L., and its impatience with the parliamentary leaders, was undoubtedly the dislike they felt for the Hibernians.[1] Dillon himself, though he took no part in the affairs of the A.O.H., nevertheless defended it in public as 'the greatest association of Catholic Irishmen in the whole world' and claimed for it that it was perfectly tolerant of other points of view.[2] No doubt he made this speech in all sincerity—he was certainly not the man to suffer sectarianism to make its way in politics unchecked—but in the light of the discontent which undeniably existed it is impossible to acquit him of a degree of *naïveté* surprising in so experienced a man. It is possible, of course, that he took this line out of simple loyalty to Devlin, but it was probably just as much a product of that fastidiousness he had shown throughout his political career and which had sometimes blinded him to the seamier side of Nationalism. Because he himself had always instinctively taken a high, moral tone he found it difficult to believe that other, earthier men might not be able, or desire, to live on that exalted plane. From time to time, of course, political grossness thrust itself inescapably upon his notice and whenever that happened the vials of his wrath were opened. But even so, it is noteworthy that his indignation was mainly directed against those who should know better—a Healy, an O'Brien, a Bishop of Limerick—rather than against the simple peasant meting out rough justice to a land-grabber, or the docile voter marching meekly to the polls at the behest of village priest or ward politician.

Dillon's own part in the scheme of things at this climactic moment in the Home Rule struggle was not so clearly defined as those of the other

[1] One of the survivors of the Young Ireland branch, Professor Thomas Dillon (incidentally, himself a member of the Dillon family) has been kind enough to show me an unpublished memoir he has written about the Young Ireland group within the U.I.L. and about their clashes with the A.O.H.

[2] Speech at Limerick, 11 Sept. 1910 (*W.J.F.*, 17 Sept. 1910).

three leaders, though the fact that he had a very special relationship with each of them, which they did not have with one another, made him in certain important respects indispensable. His role in Ireland was quite different from Devlin's—though they overlapped—and far more significant than either Redmond's or O'Connor's. Dillon's personal experience of Irish politics was profound, not merely because it went back to the mid-'seventies, but because it came from the grass-roots. His long association with the Land War in all its forms had given him an immense knowledge of people and conditions all over Ireland and maintaining, as he did, a vast correspondence with Irishmen at home and abroad, he was much more *au courant* with the movement of opinion than even Devlin, who necessarily had to rely a good deal upon second-hand reports from his officials. Indeed, the very fact that, having such sources of information at his disposal, Dillon could still speak as he did about the A.O.H., suggests that its unpopularity may not have been apparent in the country at large and that its principal critics were among the small minority of intellectuals whom Dillon and the other leaders were—unwisely—inclined to dismiss as crude young men in a hurry. But Dillon, of course, was much more than a post office. Not merely was he a quite extraordinarily fertile framer of policy, on whose advice Redmond leaned more and more heavily, he was also the principal interpreter to Ireland of the policy followed by the party at Westminster. More than anyone else among the parliamentarians he was heard with respect and attention, not just because his range of political expertise was so great, but because of that fundamental integrity for which even his critics had ungrudging admiration. The time was soon coming when the honesty of 'honest John Dillon' would be the most precious asset left to the party, but even in 1910 it was remarked upon by F. Cruise O'Brien, of all the young men in a hurry perhaps the most penetrating in his attacks upon the party leadership. 'One conceives of him', he wrote in *The Leader*, 'as the Roman patriot transplanted into this modern time with all his rigidness and prejudice and severity untempered and unaccommodated.' But with this sternness went two virtues, honesty and enthusiasm. 'He has been all through an incorruptibly honest man . . . he has not always acted wisely, nor spoken wisely, he has often been narrow and bitter and perhaps ungenerous; but he has never been insincere or dishonest or disingenuous.' As for his other quality: 'Ireland has *felt* Mr. Dillon. The flame of his enthusiasm has crossed it in fire . . . He is what Anatole France called one (*sic*) "des hommes qui n'ont jamais ri", but Ireland will remember him for his enthusiasm and his honesty.'[1] There is much, though not all, of Dillon in this portrait of the austere, unsmiling, rock-hard incorruptible. It omits his courtesy and kindliness, his cultivation, his liberalism in the wide, non-party, sense, and Cruise O'Brien's broad strokes convey nothing of the loneliness and pessimism which had coloured so much of Dillon's life. Nevertheless, this conception of Dillon as an antique Roman corresponded closely enough to the public image of a man whose

[1] *The Leader*, 12 Mar. 1910.

political style was inimitable and who filled a place all his own in the life of his country.

In his relations with the other leaders Dillon occupied a curious but strategic position. One had been his enemy, one was almost his creation, one was his closest political friend. The former enemy, of course, was Redmond. Since the reunion Dillon, though on occasion differing sharply from him, and soon to diverge much more, had shown an exemplary loyalty which, characteristically, he had managed to combine with full and free criticism of the chairman's policy, whenever he felt this was called for. Redmond, on his side, was careful to consult him at every turn and there gradually grew up between them a grave respect, reflected in the cool formality of their correspondence. Devlin was a different case altogether. He had first begun to emerge in Belfast politics when Dillon was the anti-Parnellite leader, and had shown conspicuous loyalty and ability. Dillon had encouraged him in every possible way, and Devlin early developed the habit, which he never lost, of seeking help and advice from the older man in personal as well as in public affairs. Dillon, though normally the last man to involve himself in another's private life, had invariably taken immense trouble and Devlin repaid him with extravagant devotion. Yet even here there was a barrier. Devlin had started life working in a public house and for a long time his highest ambition had been to own one. Despite his many gifts, his background was too different for either Dillon or himself to be entirely unconscious of it. Dillon, indeed, had a strong affection for the little Belfastman, who was always welcome at North Great George's Street, but to the very end there was always something of the *protégé* about him.

For the last of the group, T. P. O'Connor, Dillon had a specially warm regard. 'My dear T. P.', as he always called him in letters, was the only politician of his own generation (except, ironically enough, William O'Brien and Tim Healy in the old days) who addressed him in correspondence as 'My dear John'. Their close ties went back to the beginning of the Parnellite period and O'Connor, with his student background (he had been at Galway) and literary talent—somewhat prostituted, Dillon would probably have felt, by his resounding journalistic success—appealed to the book-lover and inveterate reader in Dillon. O'Connor's appetite for life attracted his friend, even while it sometimes appalled him, and the ease with which T.P. got on terms with the young, bereaved family after 1907 endeared him to everyone in the house, where he normally stayed on his infrequent visits to Dublin. Dillon valued O'Connor's judgement and relied upon him for information as to what was happening in Government circles, but this never exempted him from criticism, sometimes extremely sharp. T.P. had his feelings and occasionally showed them. Dillon, whenever an aggrieved letter reached him, was first taken aback at this lapse from his own standards of political objectivity and then overcome with remorse. No one else received such apologetic letters as T.P. did from time to time, but then no one else came so near to filling the void at the centre of Dillon's life.

<hr />

[1] Dillon to Redmond, 14 Jan. 1912 (D.P.).

(v)

These intricacies of function and relationship within the Irish party have
an important bearing on Dillon's part in the fast-approaching Home Rule
crisis. In the early stages, when the lines of battle were being drawn at the
end of 1911, and when the Bill itself was being shaped and made public
in the spring of 1912, he remained in the background, watching events and
spending as much time in Ireland as was consistent with regular attendance
at Westminster. This third attempt to give Ireland self-government was in
some respects less generous than the earlier Bills and was certainly a very
modest concession to the Irish demand. It proposed to create a bicameral
Irish parliament with an executive responsible to it, but to reserve very
extensive powers to the imperial Parliament, including foreign affairs, war
and peace, the position of the Crown, and the general control of taxation—
the powers of the local parliament in this respect being limited to little
more than the right to levy 10 per cent on or off existing duties. Even
authority over the police was to be left in British hands for an initial
period of six years. On the face of it, a more innocuous measure could
scarcely be imagined, or one less likely to bring both Ireland and Britain
to the brink of chaos. In retrospect, indeed, it is difficult to see quite why
the parliamentary party and their supporters greeted it with such enthusiasm. The explanation may well be psychological. The introduction
of the Bill in 1912, when the Irish party were poised to drive it through to
a successful conclusion, seemed to be not merely the fulfilment of Gladstone's pledge a generation earlier, but also provided a compensation for
all the setbacks of the past six years. The immediate reaction of Home
Rulers, therefore, was to concentrate on the great fact that an Irish
Parliament had been conceded and to pay less attention to what that
Parliament might or might not be able to do. It is only fair to add, however,
that when details of the proposed measure where shown to the Irish leaders
from 12 January onwards they were prolific in criticism and suggestion.[1]
And one can scarcely doubt that if they had achieved Home Rule in actual
reality, circumstances would have driven them on to enlarge the scope of
their demand. Of course, it was precisely this that the opponents of the
Bill either feared or professed to fear. They were not so much concerned
with the modest, devolutionary content of the Bill, but regarded it rather
as a sinister portent for the future both of Ireland, and of the whole
Empire.

The resistance of the Ulster Unionists had begun to take shape as soon
as it became clear that the Parliament Act had deprived them of the protection of the House of Lords. Already in September 1911 they had announced their intention of forming a Provisional Government to safeguard
their position when, and for as long as, a Home Rule Bill should be

[1] See, for example, 'Memorandum on the clauses of the Home Rule Bill', with
Dillon's holograph notes, 24 Jan. 1912 (D.P.).

operative. As a counter-blast to this, the Nationalists decided to hold a National Convention in the spring of 1912 to mark their approval of the Government's action in bringing in the Bill. Dillon had been a little sceptical of this demonstration at first—with memories of the 1907 Convention obviously fresh in his mind, he feared either outright hostility or a plague of amendments which might 'very seriously injure the whole situation'. But in this, as he was the first to realise, he had seriously miscalculated, and as the time for the Convention drew near, he wrote to C. P. Scott that Ireland was 'in splendid form—*much* better than I had hoped for'. There was, he added, an overwhelming feeling 'of *enthusiastic* acceptance of the Bill and of whole-hearted desire to make peace with England without any reserves. I confess that I have myself been taken by surprise by the universality of this feeling.'[1] This was the line he himself took at the Convention a few days later when he pleaded for unity in support of the Bill, and warned against the criticisms of extremists—he was thinking especially of Clan-na-Gael—whose profession of hating England would cease when Home Rule came. 'They cannot tear out from their hearts—I do not blame them—they cannot tear out from their hearts the bitterness which all of us felt a few years ago. Their ideal is eternal war between the Irish race and the English people. That is not our ideal. We want to end this war in the only way it can be ended, by England giving justice to Ireland.'[2]

The Convention, in spite of his earlier misgivings, turned out to be a great success, voting unanimously to accept the Home Rule Bill. The real danger came not from critics or dissidents on the nationalist side, but from two quite different quarters—one obvious and expected, the other more insidious and not, apparently, anticipated. The open and obvious opposition came of course from the Ulster Unionists, who were not only headed by a most able and ruthless man, Sir Edward Carson, but were in process of acquiring an invaluable ally in the English Tory party, led since November 1911 by Andrew Bonar Law. By the time the Home Rule Bill was introduced in April 1912, Bonar Law had already followed Carson far down the road of contumacy, and feeling had begun to run high on both sides. Yet his threats, whatever they might mean in practice, would not have become as serious as they did had not the second danger to Home Rule begun to emerge more clearly—the disposition of the Liberal Government to bend before the storm. Indeed, as we now know, the Cabinet, as early as February 1912, had left open a line of retreat on the Ulster question by agreeing that while the Bill as introduced should apply to the whole of Ireland, the Irish leaders should, as Asquith reported to the King, 'be given clearly to understand that the government held themselves free to make such changes in the bill as fresh evidence of facts, or the pressure of British opinion, may render expedient'. What this might mean a further paragraph in the same report made clear:

---

[1] Dillon to Redmond, 14 Jan. 1912 (R.P.); Dillon to C. P. Scott, 19 Apr. 1912 (D.P.).
[2] *W.F.J.*, 27 Apr. 1912 (the Convention was on 23 April).

that if, in the light of such evidence or indication of public opinion, it becomes clear as the bill proceeds that some special treatment must be provided for the Ulster counties, the government will be ready to recognise the necessity either by amendment of the bill, or by no passing it under the provisions of the Parliament Act. In the meantime, careful and confidential inquiry is to be made as to the real extent and character of the Ulster resistance.[1]

Much depended, therefore, on the strength of the opposition and upon the degree of Liberal sensitivity to it. If noise, intemperate speeches and passionate meetings were a test of opposition, then the feeling in Ulster and in the Unionist party was intense indeed. It is not necessary here to retell the tale of mounting hysteria, except to recall the Unionist demonstration at Blenheim in July 1912 when Bonar Law gave virtually a blank cheque to Carson ('I can imagine no length of resistance to which Ulster can go in which I should not be prepared to support them, and in which, in my belief, they would not be supported by the overwhelming majority of the British people') and also the undeniably impressive gathering at Belfast in September of that year when a great concourse of Ulstermen, headed by their Dublin-born leader, Carson, signed the 'Solemn League and Covenant', pledging themselves never to recognise Home Rule. In the face of these pronouncements the parliamentary history of the Home Rule Bill has only a secondary importance, except to the extent that as it went through the various stages laid down by the Parliament Act it brought the moment of collision inexorably nearer, a collision potentially more dangerous after the formation of the Ulster Volunteer Force early in 1913.

The first two circuits of the Bill, which consisted of its being solemnly passed by the Commons and speedily rejected by the Lords in 1912 and 1913, have recently been described as 'dummy runs' and up to a point this is correct.[2] Nevertheless, during those two sessions, and particularly in 1913, the crucial issue of Ulster was more and more clearly being defined. As early as June 1912 a Private Member's amendment—not, of course, acceptable to either side—had pointed towards some form of partition. Carson at that stage refused to countenance such a suggestion, since he, and most Unionists with him, believed that if Ulster resistance were strong enough, then Home Rule would be impossible for any part of Ireland. Neither could the Nationalists contemplate partition. In their view Ireland, to use Asquith's phrase in his Dublin speech of July 1912, was 'not two nations, but one nation'.[2]

However, as time rolled on and the Bill neared the end of its first circuit, with little essential change by way of amendment, the Ulster Unionist strategy began to change and on New Year's Day 1913 Carson, in a speech perhaps deceptively mild, moved the exclusion of the whole of Ulster from the Bill. This was a concession impossible for Nationalists to make, but they had to recognise that it confronted them with a serious threat. Now for the first time an alternative to complete Home Rule had been put

[1] Jenkins, *Asquith*, pp. 276–7.   [2] Ibid., p. 279.

forward by the responsible Ulster leader and, however repellent this alternative might seem in Ireland, many in England might be tempted to think
that here was the germ of a reasonable settlement. But would the Liberal
Government fall into this temptation? There was at least a possibility
that they might, for although Carson's motion was rejected, Ulster
Unionists by repeated demonstrations did their utmost to establish their
case for separate treatment. From the Nationalist viewpoint the great
danger of these demonstrations (which the leaders consistently underestimated) was that they increased the pressure on Asquith to compromise.
And this pressure was mounting in many different quarters. During the
summer of 1913 he was bombarded by the King with worried inquiries
about what was going to happen, and was obliged to lecture him a little
about the constitutional duties of the sovereign. Then in the autumn the
former Liberal Lord Chancellor (Lord Loreburn), generally reckoned a
firm Home Ruler, caused a stir by publishing a letter in *The Times* calling
for a conference to bring about an agreed solution. Even within the Cabinet
there were dark undercurrents. In September Winston Churchill met
Bonar Law at Balmoral. Churchill, who was apt to be haunted by his
father's ghost where Ulster was concerned, was, it seems, relieved to find
Bonar Law ready to discuss a compromise on the basis of some form of
exclusion for Ulster. There followed meetings in October and November
between Asquith and Bonar Law (who had his own difficulties with Carson
and F. E. Smith) and at the second of these the Unionist leader suggested
the exclusion of six counties rather than the nine which constituted the full
province of Ulster. From Bonar Law's account it appears that he understood Asquith to have agreed to urge upon the Cabinet, and then upon the
Nationalists, a scheme for the exclusion of either four or six counties
from the operation of Home Rule, but Asquith's biographer makes it
plain that Asquith felt that all he was undertaking was to report back to
his colleagues in order to obtain their opinion.[1]

It is important to have this background in mind when judging the actions
and reactions of the Irish leaders during the critical weeks and months
which followed. Redmond spent the 1913 recess at Aughavanagh, his
Wicklow house, except for a brief speaking tour in England with Devlin.
Dillon, although he had attended Parliament earlier in the year and indeed
spoken in the Home Rule debates during the second circuit of the Bill,
had been for most of the time in Ireland. This seems to have been partly
due to the after-effects of a second serious accident. In October 1912 he
had been thrown from a pony-trap near Ballaghaderrin, and although he
escaped with only mild concussion, he was badly shaken and had to take
things easy for some months. But even apart from this, the necessity to
present the party's case to the people would have kept him at home. Most
of his speeches in 1913 were made to Irish audiences and all of them were
concerned with one or other of the two themes that obsessed him at this

[1] Robert Blake, *The unknown prime minister* (London, 1955), pp. 155–65; Jenkins,
Asquith, pp. 286–93.

time—that the Ulster threat was bluff and that the parliamentary party could stand on its record when it appealed for unity and support on the eve of the final struggle for Home Rule.[1] Preoccupied as he was with this campaign, he relied more than ever upon T. P. O'Connor for news of what was happening in the great world of politics and the faithful T.P. kept him remarkably up to date. As early as 30 September, for example, he was able to give him an accurate account of Churchill's Balmoral meeting with Bonar Law and of the mounting tide of opinion in favour of a conference. But on the conference theme he added two ominous paragraphs which Dillon heavily underlined when he read them:

> L.G. points out that, if there be a conference, it would involve the acceptance of the Ulster option: to refuse that and then to have to go to extremes in putting down even a small rebellion would place the ministry in a difficult position.
>
> I do not gather that there is any desire whatever on the part of the government to force us into acceptance of the conference or the Tory terms; they simply want to know where we stand.[2]

It was difficult for Dillon to tell him precisely where they did stand. He was in Mayo and Redmond was in Wicklow and at this crucial moment there seems to have been little or no contact between them, or—directly—between either of them and the Liberals. To O'Connor, in London, this seemed absolutely incomprehensible and it is hard not to sympathise with him. On the other hand, Dillon was profoundly uneasy about the attitude of the Government and not at all anxious that he or Redmond should be exposed to Liberal pressures. It is interesting, in the light of his later experiences, that his distrust should have centred on Lloyd George, whom O'Connor had represented as standing 'firmly' by the position that the Government must act 'in full accord with the Irish leaders'. 'I have heard that formula before', Dillon replied, 'that they must act in full accord with the Irish leaders, but I should like to know what his own attitude with his colleagues is.' He himself, he said, was in agreement with what Redmond had just said in a speech at Cahirciveen and thought that all they were called on to do at present was to sit tight and point out to Ministers that, having received no offers, they had no comments to make. But then he added this:

> If in the future we were faced with a real firm proposal of allowing the Home Rule Bill to go thro' with an option for the four counties, our position would be an extremely difficult one. But no such option

[1] See for example, the speeches at Swords on 27 April (*W.F.J.*, 3 May 1913); in County Tipperary on 18 May (*W.F.J.*, 24 May 1913); in County Mayo on 31 August (*W.F.J.*, 6 Sept. 1913). It is only fair to add, however, that as early as January 1913 he had told C. P. Scott, in the strictest confidence, that he would go to almost any lengths to give 'Home Rule within Home Rule' to four north-eastern counties, *provided* they were recognised to be a part of Ireland, not England. (C. P. Scott, record of talks with Dillon, 10 and 16 Jan. 1913, in B.M. Add. MS. 50901, ff. 74–6).

[2] T. P. O'Connor to Dillon, 30 Sept. 1913 (D.P.).

is offered now. You should be *extremely* careful what you write in
Reynolds'—any hint, no matter how carefully veiled, that a conference is likely to come off, or that the separation of the four counties
is a question to *be considered*, would be fastened on and might lead
to disastrous consequences. It might be used to force Redmond to
make some irreconcilable declaration on the subject which, as you
may have observed, he carefully avoided at Cahirciveen.[1]

It seems clear from this that Dillon, knowing the stresses to which the
Liberal-Nationalist alliance was being subjected, was anxious not to
strain it still further by a display of undue stiffness on the part of either
Redmond or himself. Whatever they might *feel*, they must at least give the
impression of sweet reasonableness, at least until they were face to face
with a definite offer. At the same time he was perfectly well aware that any
proposal either of a conference or of Ulster counties opting out would be
political dynamite. If one or both of these suggestions were broached
clumsily or prematurely Redmond *must* refuse it, and if he were ever to
accept it, which in the autumn of 1913 still appeared highly unlikely, it
would only be if his hand were forced. Not surprisingly, in subsequent
letters to O'Connor, Dillon emphasised that in his view Redmond was
quite right to keep out of reach at this juncture.[2] O'Connor remained unconvinced. He knew that Asquith wanted Redmond's views and T.P. felt
that he should have them. 'I see no reason whatever why Redmond should
not say quite frankly that he could be no party to the exclusion of Ulster
and that also he saw danger in a conference, and above all that the conference, if granted, should be on proper terms and that the initiative should
be a Tory one.' He agreed with Dillon's own view that if there was to be
a conference at all it should come late in the proceedings, but, he added
ominously, 'L.G. made the significant observation that if the leaders of an
opposition ask for a conference on any subject, the ministry is bound to
accept it . . . I think L.G. is right.'[3]

(vi)

At this point the situation was complicated, or perhaps clarified, by a
controversial speech of Winston Churchill's at Dundee on 8 October, in
which he went out of his way to suggest that the claim of North-East
Ulster for special consideration 'is very different from the claim to bar and
defer Home Rule and block the path of the whole of the rest of Ireland', and
as such 'could not be ignored or brushed aside without full consideration by
any government dependent upon the present House of Commons'.[4]
O'Connor had awaited this speech with great trepidation and one of his
reasons for wanting Redmond to be in contact with Asquith was the hope
that Churchill might be restrained or forestalled:

---

[1] Dillon to T. P. O'Connor, 2 Oct. 1913 (D.P.).
[2] Dillon to T. P. O'Connor, 5 and 7 Oct. 1913 (D.P.).
[3] T. P. O'Connor to Dillon, 6 Oct. (1913) (D.P.).   [4] *F.J.*, 9 Oct. 1913.

Winston [he wrote a few days before the speech was delivered] is thoroughly unsound on Ulster. If he make[s] statements repeating his real views we may be faced with the very perilous dilemma of either accepting his views—which I think impossible—or repudiating him publicly, which might involve his retirement from the ministry. That would be a result not altogether without benefit to the Liberal party, as his growing demands of gigantic expenditure may land the government in a difficulty, including new taxation. But from our point of view his retirement, followed by a vigorous support of the Ulster campaign, would be a very grave addition to our difficulties.[1]

When the speech came it did not disturb Dillon too greatly, merely confirming his views as to the instability of that particular politician. His own mind, moreover, had clarified considerably in the past few days. His reservations about taking up strong public positions had been purely tactical, not a sign of any inner weakening. It made perfectly sound sense to avoid alarming their Liberal allies by premature intransigence. No one would be more intransigent than Dillon when the moment arrived, but timing was all. However, if Churchill's escapade was going to spread alarm and confusion, then perhaps the moment had come to take up a strong position after all. He and Redmond, he wrote to O'Connor on the evening of the Dundee speech, were 'wholly against any proposal of, or assent to, a conference on the part of the government. If and when a proposal comes from the other side, of a conference based on granting Home Rule . . . it will be time enough to consider the position and the conditions by which such proposals might be limited.'[2] In fact, when the two leaders spoke at the same meeting in Limerick a few days later they each took pains to demolish Churchill's arguments. 'Irish Nationalists,' said Redmond, in a phrase that was to haunt him for years to come, 'can never be assenting parties to the mutilation of the Irish nation.' Dillon, for his part, poured scorn on the Ulster threats of civil war and declared that if they did set up their Provisional Government they would soon come begging to be taken over by the Irish Government proper.[3] And a week later, speaking at Navan, he made the same point more brutally still. The Ulstermen with their talk of war reminded him, he said, of nothing more than the drunken man who calls out, 'will none of you come and hold me before I go and kill the fellow across the street'.[4]

In the long run a high price was to be exacted for such levity, but at the time these speeches expressed accurately enough their intense conviction that the Ulster resistance to Home Rule was a gigantic bluff which had only to be called for its hollowness to be exposed. Certainly O'Connor,

[1] T. P. O'Connor to Dillon, 3 Oct. 1913(D.P.).

[2] Dillon to T. P. O'Connor, 8 Oct. 1913 (D.P.). It is not clear whether Dillon wrote this before or after seeing the text of Churchill's speech, but, of course, he knew already from O'Connor that the First Lord of the Admiralty was liable to steer an uncertain course on this question.

[3] *F.J.*, 13 Oct. 1913.

[4] *F.J.*, 20 Oct. 1913.

when he read the Limerick speeches, was immensely relieved, though still utterly baffled as to why the views there made public had not been conveyed privately to Asquith beforehand. There was wisdom as well as exasperation in the lecture he read Dillon:

> An additional difficulty [apart from giving the impression that they distrusted Asquith] created by this silence has been that many of the ministers were left without guidance as to what Redmond's views were; and wobbled; not from want of loyalty to us but because they did not like to take up a position which Redmond might afterwards repudiate. His silence might be interpreted as meaning that he did not want to close the door against the exclusion of N.E. Ulster. Remember that though the Liberals, all but Winston, are determined to stand by us, they would be more than human if they did not want to get Home Rule out of the way, and that the separation of the four Ulster counties—which is evidently the price which would get them Tory support—does not appear to them as it does to us. Remember also that the policy of L.G. was at the very beginning of the struggle to offer them this; it is true in the hope that it would be rejected; but all the same, the contemplation of such a possibility meant an entire difference from our point of view. L.G. is all right now; he thinks that the rejection of his policy by the cabinet created a situation which got rid of his suggestion; and that the main duty of the government was to go ahead. But still it would not take much to take him back to his old position about Ulster; and he felt very strongly that Redmond's silence might mean that Redmond might hold this solution open—after a perfunctory and official denunciation of it.[1]

In the light of what happened later this was a remarkable and prescient warning, which the leaders in Ireland would have been well advised to heed. Dillon, it must be said, gave it less attention than it deserved—for two quite different reasons. First, he was convinced—quite wrongly as it turned out—that Churchill's Dundee speech, by emphasising his isolation, had in effect killed the proposal for the exclusion of Ulster which, he admitted to O'Connor, would have placed them in a very difficult position. If Bonar Law had made such a proposal, for the exclusion of the four counties, at the beginning of next session, there might well have been a split in the Liberal party. 'Now I am convinced this most dangerous proposal is dead beyond all possibility of resurrection. And whatever Churchill's feelings towards the Liberal Party may be, believe me he will never go out on the Ulster issue. Besides, deserting your party for the second time is not an easy operation.'[2]

[1] T. P. O'Connor to Dillon, 13 Oct. 1913 (D.P.).

[2] Dillon to T. P. O'Connor, 15 Oct. 1913 (D.P.). In his speech of 19 October already referred to, Dillon publicly declared that 'the proposal to cut off the four north-eastern counties is absolutely dead . . . If it were workable, as it is not, it would simply be a confession that the policy of Home Rule as a remedy for Ireland's troubles was a dismal failure . . . We, of course, as Irish Nationalists, could never tolerate for a moment such an admission' (*F.J.*, 20 Oct. 1913).

But Dillon had another and more pressing reason for ignoring O'Connor's warnings. What was happening in England seemed for the moment far less urgent and serious than what was happening on his own doorstep in Dublin. In August simmering labour discontents had led to trouble with many different employers and the latter, led by that old and still bitter enemy of the party, William Martin Murphy, resolved, if they could, to smash the workers' organisation—the Irish Transport and General Workers' Union—created by James Connolly and James Larkin. By September, in a great variety of concerns, employees who were members of the union had been locked out and by October the dispute—which was to last until the men went back in the New Year—had already paralysed a large part of industrial Dublin. It might have been expected that Dillon would derive some satisfaction from the quarrel that Murphy had involved himself in. So perhaps he did, but it was more than counter-balanced by his detestation of the socialism of Connolly and the demagoguery of Larkin. Even from Mayo Dillon was horrified by what he heard. 'Dublin is hell', he wrote to O'Connor, 'and I don't see the way out. Murphy is a desperate character, Larkin as bad. It would be a blessing to Ireland if they exterminated each other.'[1] And in the letter of 15 October already quoted—when he was back in the city and could see things for himself—he admitted that so different were the worlds he and O'Connor lived in that for him the chief causes of anxiety were (1) the Dublin labour war (2) the problem of whether or not the party ought to contest the seat in North Cork controlled by O'Brien and (3) English by-elections. 'The Ulster question and the cabinet appear dim and distant and of minor importance.'[2] Next day he wrote even more emphatically about the labour dispute:

> As regards the situation in Dublin, nothing could be more mixed and mischievous. Larkin is a malignant enemy and an impossible man. He seems to be a wild international syndicalist and anarchist and for a long time he has been doing his best to burst up the party and the national movement.
>
> The employers have been led into a false position by Murphy. It is a devilish situation and I feel convinced that any attempt on our part to interfere in any way will do *nothing but harm*. One overwhelming objection to your attending the meeting called by the Gaelic League [a meeting of the London branch of the Gaelic League to which O'Connor had been invited] is that your action will immediately be commented on in Beresford Place by P. T. Daly, Larkin and co., and contrasted with the *brutal* attitude of Mr. Redmond and Mr. Dillon who, altho, on the spot etc. etc. . . .
>
> The English labour leaders have, it seems to me, acted in a most weak and contemptible manner. They all hate Larkin and condemn his methods, and he does not conceal his contempt for them, but openly denounces them as humbugs and traitors. Yet they are financing Larkinism in Dublin, and thereby prolonging this wretched strike

[1] Dillon to T. P. O'Connor, 1 Oct. 1913 (D.P.).
[2] Dillon to T. P. O'Connor, 15 Oct. 1913 (D.P.).

and threatening Dublin with absolute ruin. And sowing a horrible
crop of bitterness and hate which it [will] take years to get rid of.[1]

This, it must be admitted, was a harsh view of an upheaval which, apart
altogether from the personalities involved, had its roots in the miserable
conditions in which many thousands of Dublin working-men and their
families existed. It is, indeed, one of the most serious indictments of the
Irish parliamentary party, which had shown itself so solicitous for the
welfare of small farmers and agricultural labourers, that it consistently
neglected the slums of Dublin and the unfortunates who had to live in
them. Dillon was not unmindful of the hardships of the workers, and the
very next month, speaking at University College, he referred to Dublin as
'one of the most terrible sinks of iniquity and poverty on the face of the
earth'.[2] But when he went on, as he did, to explain that poverty in terms of
the economic decline of the city since the Union, he fell untypically into
the old, familiar trap of the historical fallacy, the time-honoured tendency
of nationalists to explain away local evils they had done nothing about by
blaming them on the iniquitous, but convenient, British connection. One
has only to imagine what Dillon would have said to a landlord who defended rack-renting on the ground that conditions had been hard since the
Famine, to expose the hollowness of the argument. No doubt it was true
that Dublin industry, like Irish agriculture, had passed through a difficult
era, but this did not exempt employers or landlords from the ordinary
responsibilities of decent citizens.

The fact is that Dillon's hostility to Larkin was instinctive and went
deeper, perhaps, than he was prepared to admit even to himself. He belonged, as did most of the parliamentarians, to the men of property
and in any class war, real or incipient, between them and the men of no
property, there was little doubt on which side he would be found. Then,
too, Larkin's movement represented a potential political threat, partly
because he had re-established the Dublin branch of the Independent Labour
Party in 1908, and partly because, more recently, Connolly had appealed
to the British working-classes to vote against the Liberals in the future,
even if this endangered Home Rule.[3] But most of all, Dillon hated Larkin,
whose methods were certainly reckless almost beyond belief, because in the
field of labour politics he stood for the same sort of thing that Clann-na-
Gael stood for in revolutionary politics—war *à l'outrance*, regardless of
risks and consequences. To Dillon this was the absolute negation of leadership. The very reason he had become a constitutionalist, as he had explained so many times in the past thirty years, was not because he did not
sympathise with war *à l'outrance*, but because he regarded it as impossible
in the existing circumstances. Anyone who led simple people, whether
peasants or dockers, into this kind of hopeless struggle was, he passionately
felt, guilty of criminal irresponsibility. And so, when O'Connor rebuked

[1] Dillon to T. P. O'Connor, 16 Oct. 1913 (D.P.).   [2] *F.J.*, 7 Nov. 1913.
[3] E. Larkin, *James Larkin* (London, 1965), pp. 63, 142.

him for his lack of sympathy, Dillon replied that if he knew the realities of the situation, he would take a different view. 'Larkin is a ruffian and the strike, in my judgment, will end in disaster for the workingmen, as Larkin's movements in Cork, Belfast and Wexford have done.'[1] On the short view, Dillon was undoubtedly right, for although Murphy did not succeed in destroying the union, the men had to return to work on the employers' terms after a grim winter of near starvation for their families, and their last state certainly seemed no better than their first.

(vii)

Long before this had happened, however, the attention of the Irish leaders had swung back again to Ulster. O'Connor continued to report the news from the Liberal front, so far as it reached him from Lloyd George. Writing in mid-October, he said that the Cabinet had still taken no decision, but that the trend of opinion had been against Churchill's wish to consider the exclusion of the four counties. From this T.P. drew the moral that they must themselves be firmer than ever. 'So long as the Cabinet is convinced that we mean business about the four counties and that rather than accept the policy of exclusion from the government [of Ireland] we would be ready to await Home Rule for some years yet, the cabinet will stand by us.'[2] O'Connor himself feared that the exclusion policy was still very much alive and that Churchill would air it again in another speech. Sure enough, at Manchester next day, he stated that he had nothing to add to or subtract from what he had said at Dundee and that for him the door was 'always open for a fair and reasonable settlement . . .'[3] Since, as we have already seen, Asquith had had one secret meeting with Bonar Law and was shortly to have another, O'Connor was not far wide of the mark. On 12 November Asquith reported the substance of these conversations to the Cabinet and next day informed the King that feeling in the Liberal Party was very much against compromise, though he added that Lloyd George had suggested as a possible basis for settlement the exclusion of Ulster (defined apparently as 'the Protestant counties') for a definite term of five or six years, with a proviso for automatic inclusion at the end of that time. 'This suggestion', he said, 'met with a good deal of support' and he had been asked to discuss it with Redmond when they met the following Monday.[4] That same day he wrote to Redmond expressing the hope that a speech the latter was due to make at Newcastle would not 'close the door to the possibility of an agreed settlement'. Redmond's reply was to deliver an uncompromising public attack on the 'gigantic game of bluff and blackmail' to which Parliament was being subjected and to come out as strongly as ever against the notion of any kind of exclusion for Ulster, though he did offer all possible safeguards for the civil and religious

---

[1] Dillon to T. P. O'Connor, 18 Oct. 1913 (D.P.).
[2] T. P. O'Connor to Dillon, 17 Oct. 1913 (D.P.).
[3] *F.J.*, 20 Oct. 1913.   [4] Jenkins, *Asquith*, p. 293.

liberties of Protestants and, in that limited sense, 'shut no door to a settlement by consent'.[1]

This was not quite what Asquith meant by an open door, so the omens
were not propitious for their meeting which, however, took place as
planned on 17 November. According to Redmond's own account, Asquith
went very fully into his conversations with Bonar Law and into the recent
deliberations of the Cabinet. Of Lloyd George's scheme Redmond received
from Asquith an impression rather different from that the latter had sent
the king. Redmond's version was that Asquith had said that in the opinion
of the whole Cabinet, and of Lloyd George himself, such a suggestion could
not form the basis of a settlement by agreement 'as Sir Edward Carson and
his friends could never agree to a proposal which would really mean the
giving up of the whole principle for which they had been contending'.
Lloyd George had, it seemed, put forward the idea really as a delaying
tactic, to prevent an immediate outburst in Ulster 'as men could not possibly go to war to prevent something which was not to occur for five years'.
Asquith, Redmond's account continued, told him that the Cabinet had
come to no decision about the proposal except to ascertain the Irish party's
views— but the Prime Minister had ended on a slightly sinister note,
warning Redmond that the Ulstermen had possession of 5,000 rifles and
that there was danger of numerous resignations from the Army in the
event of troops being used against an Ulster insurrection. They parted on
the understanding that Redmond was to take time to think over the situation and then to embody his views in a memorandum.[2]

That same afternoon Dillon had an interview with Lloyd George,
whose detailed account of it has survived. They met in the presence of a
witness, the Liberal whip, Percy Illingworth, and there is no reason to
doubt that Lloyd George was putting down what seemed to him a fair
statement of what took place. On the other hand, as will be seen, he
seriously miscalculated Dillon's true position—though this may well have
been due partly to Dillon's own obvious anxiety not to appear unduly
intransigent at this stage. Their meeting opened, it seems, with a diatribe
from Dillon against Larkin, but was almost entirely concerned with the
Ulster question. They talked of Redmond's interview with Asquith that
morning, and Lloyd George gathered from Dillon that Redmond was
'inclined to be difficult' about it and that if pressed for an immediate reply
'he would certainly send in a blank refusal'. Then Lloyd George's report
continued:

> Dillon was very anxious that the Irish leaders should not be pressed
> at this stage to offer any decided opinion, and he urged with great
> emphasis, and with constant repetition, renewed many times during
> the conversation, the great importance of not putting any proposal
> of that kind before the Tory leaders at this stage. He was anxious the

[1] Gwynn, *Redmond*, pp. 233–4.
[2] Gwynn, *Redmond*, pp. 234–6; there is a typed copy of Redmond's account of the
interview in the Dillon Papers.

Irish leaders should be free during the next few months to state that no proposal of the kind had been made to the other side, and that they, the Irish leaders, had not assented to such a scheme. He thought that if put forward at the last moment, when the Bill was going through, it might be tactically a very wise plan to propose, and that then the Irish leaders might carry it in Ireland, inasmuch as it was accompanied by the carrying into law of Home Rule for the rest of Ireland, thus enabling the Irish leaders to point to Home Rule as an accomplished fact, with Ulster only temporarily outside its operation.

Lloyd George further understood that Dillon much preferred this solution to another which had been mooted—the setting up of a separate Ulster Council for local purposes—but that he anticipated great difficulty with Devlin if exclusion of any kind were proposed. Lloyd George, for his part, agreed with Dillon that any offer should be held back until the last (and best) tactical moment and this section of his memorandum ended: 'Dillon quite approved of that plan. Throughout, his attitude was friendly to the proposal of the cabinet, and it was clear that if left to him to decide, there would be no difficulty in obtaining the assent of the Irish Nationalists.'[1]

Full of this quite unjustified optimism, Lloyd George went off at once to see the Prime Minister and find out what had passed between him and Redmond. 'Redmond's attitude appears to be much more hostile, but he seems to have been prepared to concede a large measure of local autonomy to Ulster, with powers to make bye-laws.' Lloyd George then told Asquith of his own interview with Dillon. Asquith agreed that no proposal should be communicated to Bonar Law at that stage, but he still wished for a memorandum from Redmond. Late that evening Dillon came again to 11 Downing Street to see Lloyd George, who told him of his talk with the Prime Minister and also informed him that the matter had not been raised at all at the Cabinet. 'Dillon agreed with me [says Lloyd George's note of this second interview] that from the point of view of Irish nationalism, Redmond's proposal was not as good as mine, inasmuch as it established a permanent separate organisation for the Ulster counties, and that as it must necessarily involve handing over the police to the Ulster Council, the position of the Catholic minority in Belfast would be deplorable.'[2]

This document throws a curious, and to some extent misleading, light upon the political relations between Redmond and Dillon. Normally they have been presented, and no doubt so appeared to their contemporaries, as a kind of Spenlow and Jorkins partnership. In the foreground Redmond, the agreeable, amenable Spenlow, his natural generosity held in check only by the rigid and implacable Dillon—Jorkins behind him. In a broad sense this, though something of a caricature, is not an altogether distorted picture. It is true that Redmond, with his instinct for conciliation, his deep commitment to the House of Commons, and his dangerous isolation from

[1] 'Interview with Mr. John Dillon, at No. 11, Downing Street, November 17th 1913', in secretary's hand, initialled by Lloyd George on 18 November (L.G.P., c/10/2/4).
[2] Ibid., 'Second interview with Dillon'.

the movement of opinion in Ireland, was generally more prone to engage in, and to hope for results from, negotiations with English ministers. In Dillon, on the other hand, there was more steel, a more irreconcilable temper. In his way as dedicated a House of Commons man as Redmond, he had yet never lost either his sensitivity to Irish opinion or his sympathy with Parnell's dictum that the only way to deal with an Englishman is to stand up to him. These differences in temperament and attitude were to become even more marked as the years went on and for Lloyd George to assume, as apparently he did, that Spenlow and Jorkins had for the moment changed roles, was very unwise. Dillon may have shown himself friendly and understanding, but all his private correspondence suggests that he did not at this time seriously think that exclusion would ever become a viable policy. If he welcomed Lloyd George's scheme, it was partly because it was an ingenious method of spiking the Ulster Unionists' guns, but even more because it was intended only to be temporary. Permanent exclusion was to him, then as always, unthinkable.

(viii)

In the immediate future, however, the next move lay with Redmond, who had still to provide the Prime Minister with the written answer he had asked for. On 24 November this was duly delivered. The keynote of this long document was that offers must not be made by the Government, but must come from the other side. For the Government to offer concessions now would be interpreted as truckling to 'Orange threats', and such an olive branch would anyway be treated with contempt by the Tory party, or would be made the basis for further demands which would destroy Home Rule. Moreover, from the purely party point of view, it would arouse violent resentment among the Liberal rank and file 'and still more in the case of our party, as our people, and especially in Ulster, would be shocked by the prospect of any exclusion of Ulster'. Such a policy, Redmond considered, would raise insuperable difficulties, not only administratively, but politically, since it would tend to perpetuate, even perhaps to accentuate, the sectarian differences they sought to root out. 'During the period of exclusion, the Orange leaders, flushed with this great victory, would devote themselves towards making what is temporary perpetual'—and this tendency, he thought, would certainly be supported by the Tories in Great Britain.

As against all this, Redmond felt that if the Liberals refrained from making offers, Bonar Law would, by his own difficulties, be forced into doing so. And if he were to come out for exclusion he would run into immediate difficulties with some of his own supporters and especially, of course, with the Southern Irish Unionists. In Redmond's view this would knock the bottom out of the Unionist argument and he ended with an admonition to Asquith, which, in the event, was to prove grotesquely over sanguine. 'Writing with a full sense of the seriousness of the situation, but also writing with a full knowledge of my country and its conditions, I must express the strong opinion that the magnitude of the peril of the Ulster situation is considerably exaggerated in this country.'[1]

Next day Redmond saw Lloyd George and learnt that his memorandum had been read to the cabinet, but not printed for fear of leakages to the Press, of which there had been several recently—the general feeling among ministers being, according to Lloyd George, that these came from Churchill. Lloyd George further told him that the Cabinet were 'quite unanimous' in agreeing with the argument in his memorandum, that the Government should make no offer at that juncture—though Lloyd George himself thought an offer might have to be made sooner than they thought. The authorities had recently discovered 95,000 rounds of ammunition in Belfast and had made up their minds to seize it. Further, if, as was believed, Carson was intending to hold a review of armed men, the Government was prepared to suppress this and use any force necessary for the purpose—but this would be the moment when they would need to be ready to make an offer. Under certain circumstances, Lloyd George hinted, if no offer were made, the ministry might lose Churchill, Grey, Haldane and possibly Lloyd George himself—which, said Lloyd George, would be a very serious thing for Home Rule and for Redmond personally. Not nearly so serious, rejoined Redmond, as for Lloyd George personally—'the *débâcle* would mean the end of his career and the end of the Liberal party for a generation—perhaps indeed, for ever'. 'He admitted this', recorded Redmond dryly, adding that what worried him most was the impression Lloyd George left with him of believing that, in the last resort, the Irish party would agree to anything rather than face the break-up of the Government.[2] This impression he conveyed to T. P. O'Connor, who at once passed it on to Dillon, with the comment that Lloyd George seemed bent on making an offer of temporary exclusion. T.P. also added, incautiously, that 'Redmond agrees with you that the temporary exclusion of Ulster would be better than the loss of Home Rule now; but he also believes that the Tories would not accept it . . .'[3] This produced an explosion from Dillon, valuable as giving his side of his interview with Lloyd George. Trying to drive into O'Connor's head what his attitude really was, he wrote next day as follows:

> I said that if we were forced to a decision now on [the] question of temporary exclusion of Ulster, our decision *must* be a flat negative. That was what I said to L. George, when he replied 'For heaven's sake don't put that in [the] memorandum or it means the resignation of Grey'. To which I replied—then why try to force us to [a] final decision on that question now, when according to your own idea the

[1] Redmond memorandum, 24 Nov. 1913 (typed copy in Dillon Papers); only the concluding section is printed in Gwynn, *Redmond*, pp. 236–7.

[2] Most of Redmond's notes of this conversation are printed in Gwynn, op. cit., pp. 237–8; a typed copy of the whole document, dated 27 Nov. 1913, is in the Dillon Papers.

[3] T. P. O'Connor to Dillon, 26 Nov. 1913 (D.P.).

question will not be ripe for settlement till after [the] 2nd reading of [the] Home Rule Bill. He assented to this view and said he agreed that no proposals should be made till after [the] opening of the session. Whereupon I stated most emphatically and repeatedly that he must clearly understand that so far as I was concerned, I kept a perfectly open mind to consider this proposition when the time came, and assent to it or reject it after giving full weight to *all* the circumstances of the time. And I let him understand that my own decision would be largely influenced amongst other considerations, by the prospect of obtaining good will and acquiescence by such a concession. You must, therefore, keep clearly in mind that I am not, and never have been, in favour of consenting to a proposal for temporary exclusion of Ulster being made to Tory leaders now or at any time.[1]

This is as definitive a statement of Dillon's views at this critical time as we are likely to get—made privately to a close friend, and therefore without any necessity for disguise. It reveals him as far more uncommitted than Lloyd George had represented him to Asquith, but since Lloyd George was similarly representing the Cabinet to Redmond as being more ready to make an offer than they really were, it is difficult to resist the conclusion that he had already embarked upon one of those manoeuvres for pushing his own policy which he resorted to from time to time—acting as middleman between two parties and telling each a different tale. At any rate when, on 27 November (the very day Dillon was writing his letter to T.P.) Redmond saw Birrell and told him frankly what Lloyd George had said, Birrell discounted most of it. 'He told me the cabinet had never even considered the adoption of Lloyd George's proposal and that he knew for a fact that there was very strong and bitter opposition to it amongst members of the cabinet.'[2] This was not, perhaps, calculated to strengthen Redmond's confidence in Lloyd George as a go-between, but since he already had received a letter from Asquith, written on 26 November, assuring him that there was 'no question' at this stage of making an offer to Bonar Law, he had reason to face the future with some confidence, although Asquith was careful to leave a loophole open for further negotiation by adding that they must keep their hands free, when the critical stage of the Bill was reached, 'to take such a course as then, in all the circumstances, seems best calculated to safeguard the fortunes of Home Rule'.[3]

Had he but known it, Redmond was safe for the time being, since Asquith, on having a third interview with Bonar Law on 10 December, found that the latter rejected outright the scheme for temporary exclusion. Asquith tried once more—this time to Carson direct—but was again met with an uncompromising negative.[4] And so the year ended and the third circuit of the Bill approached with the two sides still divided by an apparently unbridgeable chasm. Within the Liberal Government there was gloom and, if Lloyd George was to be trusted, some considerable disarray.

---

[1] Dillon to T. P. O'Connor, 27 Nov. 1913 (D.P.).   [2] Gwynn, *Redmond*, pp. 238–9.
[3] Ibid., p. 238.   [4] Jenkins, *Asquith*, pp. 294–5.

A week before Christmas, T.P. O'Connor, meeting Devlin in London and finding him as hot as ever against the temporary exclusion of any part of Ulster, brought him to see Lloyd George, who tried to impress upon them that there was a real danger of the Government breaking up on the Ulster question. T.P. retailed their conversation—or rather Lloyd George's monologue—to Dillon thus:

> Winston had stated openly in the cabinet that if coercion were applied to Ulster without her having received any reasonable offer, he would have to resign. In addition, L.G. repeated to me a conversation with Winston, the details of which I need not go into: it amounted to this, that Churchill was seriously thinking of the possibility of his having to go back to the Tories and had been laying his plans for that purpose. I heard from another source that Churchill had declared in a public room in a Tory club that the mistake of his life was to have left the Tory party; Churchill does speak with this startling imprudence. L.G. thinks it would be a great mistake to allow Churchill to leave just now, characteristically saying that to keep him was worth a million, a million, of course he meant, on the Navy Estimates. Others of the cabinet, I gathered, would be quite ready to shed Churchill; but L.G. insisted he was worth keeping, for the moment; though, as you see, he has no illusions about him.

Lloyd George himself, said O'Connor, was still anxious for an offer to be made to the Tories, if only to prevent them from committing themselves to so violent a line that it would be difficult for them to withdraw. 'But he wound up with the satisfactory statement that whatever we did he should not desert us; though we had to expect the resignation of Churchill to be accompanied by that of Morley, which would add respectability and seriousness to the resignation of Churchill.' On the other hand, it had also been Lloyd George's opinion, that if an offer were made and rejected, then Churchill would stand by whatever action the Government might be forced to take. 'When the shooting begins, Churchill said he would be ready to back it if the Orangemen refused a fair offer; and much more boldly, added L.G., than some of the men who are now for it,'[1] Dillon's own reaction to this news was simply to reiterate that they should keep their hands free. 'At present', he replied, 'I am disposed to think that I should close with such an offer. But on the other hand it is quite possible that the state of feeling in Ireland might be such as to make it clear that we could not afford to run the risk.'[2] And in these words he defined accurately and concisely the position of the Irish leaders at the end of a year as anxious and difficult as any in the history of the Home Rule movement.

[1] T. P. O'Connor to Dillon, 17 Dec. 1913 (D.P.).
[2] Dillon to T. P. O'Connor, 20 Dec. 1913 (D.P.).

12

Home Rule:
Climax And Anticlimax

(i)

It was not long, however, before the New Year emphasised what the old one had revealed all too clearly, that the Irish party were not the masters of their fate. The Home Rule issue had become so inextricably involved in British party politics that its solution, at least if there was to be a peaceful solution, could only come from some compromise between Liberals and Unionists, a compromise which the Irish leaders went in almost daily dread of having imposed upon them. The situation for them, as Dillon explained to C. P. Scott early in January, was indeed most serious. Up to the previous August, he maintained, there had been a 'slump in Carsonism', but all the talk about peacemaking had revived it. Lord Loreburn's letter asking for a constitutional conference, the confabulations at Balmoral and, finally, Churchill's Dundee speech, had acted 'precisely as a can of petroleum thrown on the dying embers of a fire would act. And the Ulster gang blazed out into full activity, now fully convinced that the policy of bullying was a complete success and that the Liberal party and its leaders were thoroughly frightened. The result has been that Carson's policy is now looked upon as thoroughly successful and justified'. The danger of such a game of bluff, he added with his usual perceptiveness, was that men who were not cowards might find themselves so far committed that they could not decently turn back.[1]

Unfortunately for Redmond and Dillon, while their Unionist opponents were now again on the attack, the Government seemed so disorganised as scarcely to be able to organise any defence. During the recess the old question of the Navy Estimates had boiled up once more and threatened a major clash between the two former 'economists', Lloyd George and Churchill. Lloyd George, as Chancellor of the Exchequer, was still an economist, but Churchill, in the congenial role of First Lord, had the bit between his teeth. T. P. O'Connor went off to Algiers in January on a holiday with Lloyd George, reporting from there to Dillon that the Chancellor had made up his mind to break with Churchill on the Navy Estimates and that he, Lloyd George, was sure Churchill was really looking for an opportunity to leave the Cabinet. Ministers in general, T. P. gathered, were behind Lloyd George,

[1] J. L. Hammond, *C. P. Scott* (London, 1934), pp. 122–4.

some of them apparently detesting the voluble and domineering First Lord. 'They think Ch.'s leaving now, on the Navy, can do no great harm, whereas if he left on Ulster in the critical moment of the H.R. fight, it would be much more serious. L. G. talks of resigning rather than submit to Ch.'s estimates, but if there be any resignation it must, I think, be Churchill's.'[1]

This particular clash was in the end resolved for the time being, Churchill getting a good deal of what he wanted and no resignations resulting. But in the meantime the King, in a state of constant anxiety about Ireland, was pressing Asquith either to make concessions or to have another general election. In his abortive negotiations with Carson at the end of December Asquith had, in fact, made a conciliatory proposal when he suggested that in the Home Rule Parliament Ulster should have a veto which would operate, if a majority of Ulster Members so decided, to prevent the application of important classes of legislation (fiscal, educational, religious, industrial or land tenure) to that area. Carson had contemptuously rejected the scheme—which, indeed, had almost everything to be said against it—but Asquith got the Cabinet to agree to it on 22 January. The King warned him that this would not satisfy the Unionists, but Asquith's main preoccupation was whether or not he could persuade the Irish leaders to look at it any more favourably.[2] On 2 February he saw Redmond, who, Asquith afterwards wrote, 'shivered visibly and was a good deal perturbed'—as well he might be. Redmond at once wrote to Dillon, setting out the main points which had come up.

Asquith is greatly harrassed [*sic*].

1. Navy. This is not settled and tho' he speaks hopefully of averting a split in the Cabinet, he seriously fears a dry rot in the House which might easily lead to accidents.

2. The King. He tells me the King is thoroughly frightened. He does not fear his dissolving or refusing assent to bill when passed, but he seriously contemplates the possibility in certain contingencies of the K. *dismissing Ministers* as was done in 1834. Such a contingency might arise over the Army Bill. He thinks the opposition certain to do *everything* to wreck it in H. of C. and thinks the Lords might reject it, if it succeeded in getting through the H. of C.

   In view of these facts he thinks it quite essential for him to make an explicit offer to Ulster at once—probably the first night of the session. He thinks his offer will be rejected but that the making of it will cut the ground from under the feet of the opposition and most probably avert any action by the K.

   He has seen Bonar Law and Carson three times. Their one demand is the total exclusion of portions of Ulster and they would not seriously discuss anything else.

---

[1] T. P. O'Connor to Dillon, 13 Jan. 1914 (D.P.).
[2] For the history of this curious scheme see Jenkins, *Asquith*, pp. 295–7, 300–1.

The Cabinet have *decided* nothing, but Asquith's idea is, and he is sure the Cabinet would agree, is [*sic*] as follows. He is against exclusion of any part of Ulster for any period whatever but he would

1. Give up the Post Office.
2. He would agree to administrative autonomy Education, Factory Acts, etc. etc. etc.
3. He would give the Ulster members in the Irish Parliament the power to appeal to British parliament against the application to Ulster of any Bill dealing with certain defined subjects.

After I have had time for consultation he wants to see me again or to receive a memo from me.

The matter is so very grave and so urgent that I think at whatever inconvenience you and Devlin (show him this) should come over.[1]

In a dictated note about the interview which he made on that same day Redmond traversed the same ground, but added that he had argued generally against making any proposals whatever at that time—that this would only lead to destructive criticism, would not satisfy the Unionists and would certainly not be acceptable to the Nationalists. Asquith, he recorded, had not counted on the latter. 'The most he expected from us was that we would be willing, on the condition of the other side allowing the Bill to be an Agreed Bill and pass by consent, to make large concessions, so long as they were consistent with the limits we ourselves had laid down—namely, the creation of an Irish Parliament, with an executive responsible to it, and the maintenance of the integrity of Ireland.'[2]

Dillon was naturally exceedingly perturbed when Redmond's letter reached him. He discussed it with Devlin and they arranged to cross at once to London. In the meantime, however, in his reply to Redmond, Dillon agreed (and so, he said, did Devlin) 'that it would be very mischievous for the P.M. to make any definite offers to Ulster at this stage. Even if there be serious danger of the King acting, we consider that it would be very much safer for us to face the consequences of such action than to be faced with the consequences which might flow from the P.M. making at this stage such a proposal as that indicated in your letter.'[3] The next day he and Devlin arrived and immediately conferred with Redmond. The outcome was a letter to Asquith in which Redmond repeated his objections to the making of an offer, reiterated his opinion that the Ulster resistance was exaggerated, and appealed to the Prime Minister to limit his commitment to a declaration in the House that he was ready to consider all proposals consistent with an Irish Parliament, an Irish executive and the integrity of Ireland.[4] Dillon, lunching with C. P. Scott a couple of days later, elaborated on the Irish objections to positive proposals being made by the Govern-

[1] Redmond to Dillon, 2 Feb. 1914 (D.P.).
[2] The memorandum is printed in full in Gwynn, *Redmond*, pp. 250–2.
[3] Dillon to Redmond, 3 Feb. 1914 (R.P.); Gwynn, *Redmond*, p. 252.
[4] Gwynn, *Redmond*, p. 253; Jenkins, *Asquith*, p. 301.

ment at this stage. In the first place, he said, it would create an impossible parliamentary position, since the Opposition would immediately say that the new proposals amounted to a completely new Home Rule Bill and that the country should be given a chance to pronounce upon it. And secondly, in Ireland itself the psychological effect would be disastrous. 'Already', noted Scott, 'on the mere rumour of concession, protests pour in. If they were announced on authority, meetings and resolutions would follow, especially from the Ulster Catholics.'[1]

From Asquith's point of view, of course, the Irish reaction—though surely not unexpected—was far from satisfactory. Even more vexatious was the interview he had with the King on the same day that Redmond wrote his letter of remonstrance. George V admitted that he was extremely nervous about army loyalty if a clash occurred in or over Ulster, and warned the Prime Minister that he must reserve his freedom to act as circumstances might indicate, meaning by this apparently either that he might consider withholding his assent to the Home Rule Bill even if passed by both Houses, or perhaps that he would dismiss the Government. Asquith's response was to remind him that the royal veto was, literally, as dead as Queen Anne, but also to urge that if the King felt it his duty to dismiss his Ministers, as was his constitutional right, it would be better to do so at once, before Parliament met. The King disclaimed any such immediate intention, and the meeting was perfectly friendly, but it underlined the difficulties of Asquith's position and it may perhaps have helped to incline him even more towards compromise.[2] Though what that compromise might be it seemed impossible to decide, for when on 9 February the Cabinet devoted a whole session to Ireland all that Birrell could report to Redmond was 'great difference of opinion disclosed.'[3] And, in fact, when the Address was debated two days later Asquith was still not in a position to make any pronouncement one way or the other.

Nevertheless, behind the scenes the search for a formula continued feverishly. All through February memoranda and counter-memoranda flew to and fro. At length, on 2 March, Redmond, Dillon, Devlin and O'Connor attended what proved to be a decisive meeting with Asquith, Lloyd George and Birrell. After it was over Redmond drew up a memorandum outlining the solution which had been pressed upon the Irish leaders by the Government. This was that individual Ulster counties might opt out of Home Rule for a period of three years, at the end of which they would automatically come under the control of the Irish Parliament. The proposal was agreed to with the utmost reluctance by Redmond and his friends as 'the price of peace' and only then provided it was fully accepted by the Unionists and that it was 'the last word of the Government'.[4]

Devlin and another Ulster Nationalist M.P. (Jeremiah MacVeagh) went

[1] C. P. Scott Papers (BM. Add. MS. 5091, ff. 108–9); J. L. Hammond, *C. P. Scott*, pp. 126–7. This was written after lunch with Dillon on 7 Feb. 1914.
[2] Sir Harold Nicolson, *King George V* (London, 1952), pp. 233–4.
[3] Gwynn, *Redmond*, pp. 253–4.
[4] Ibid., pp. 267–9.

immediately to Ireland to persuade their people to swallow this bitter pill. Devlin himself had already made perfectly clear to the leaders of his own party the risks that were involved, but he bent himself, with his usual ability, to securing the acquiescence of his fellow Ulster Catholics in what he and they believed would only be a temporary exclusion. Then, at the last moment, another turn of the screw was applied. The Cabinet having agreed to the scheme on 4 March, the essence of it was immediately leaked by one of the Ministers to the *Daily News* .The King at once wrote agitatedly to Asquith that he was sure a three-year exclusion would not do. Whether his influence was decisive or not it is difficult to say, but the fact remains that on 6 March Birrell saw Redmond and told him the price had now been raised from three to six years. Deeply mortified, but deeply conscious also of the immensity of the issues at stake, Redmond agreed.[1] It was then possible for Asquith, moving the second reading of the Home Rule Bill (now on its third circuit) to announce on 9 March the terms of the concession wrung with such pain and difficulty from the Nationalist leaders. The immediate result was a deliberate slap in the face from Carson, executed with all his flair for the dramatic. Ulster, he said, would not accept 'a sentence of death with a stay of execution for six years'. Since information was reaching the Government just at this time that the Ulster Volunteers were planning to move against arms depots in the province, Carson's rejection of the olive branch seemed particularly ominous. Even more ominous was his behaviour a week later when, after a slashing attack on the Liberals, he walked out of the House, declaring that his place was in Ulster at the head of his movement. He actually left that night and for a short time no one knew whether or not he had gone to establish a Provisional Government. He did not, in fact, do so, but suddenly, and even more dramatically, the limelight shifted from Belfast to the military headquarters at the Curragh, in County Kildare. There, the news that the Cabinet was at last about to take steps to meet possible violence in Ulster evoked a spate of resignations amongst officers and provided the extraordinary spectacle of a cavalry brigadier, General Sir Hubert Gough, proceeding to London and, aided and abetted by the Director of Military Operations, exacting a pledge from the Secretary of State for War, Colonel J. E. B. Seely, that the Government had no intention of using the army 'to crush political opposition to the policy or principles of the Home Rule Bill'. The resulting crisis led to the resignation of the Minister and a brace of generals. Asquith himself took over the War Office and managed to calm the apprehensions of the soldiery, though he had, of course, to repudiate the pledge given by Seely. But the affair left an ugly legacy—on the one hand a nagging anxiety about the loyalty of the forces, on the other hand a further loss of confidence in the ability of the Liberals to stand up to Ulster resistance.[2]

[1] Ibid., pp. 270–2; Jenkins, *Asquith*, pp. 305–5.
[2] The best account of the actual events of the crisis, though lacking in political insight, is Sir James Fergusson, *The Curragh incident* (London, 1964). A. P. Ryan, *Mutiny at the Curragh* (London, 1956), remains the best political analysis.

The Irish leaders watched these developments with growing dismay. Dillon had, of course, been in close attendance upon Redmond while the negotiations about the offer to Ulster had been going on and that probably accounts for the gap in his correspondence at this time. But there is no doubt that he was deeply worried by the turn events were taking. He had always been ready to suspect a Government deal with the opposition and though he had accepted the concession of county option as probably inevitable in the circumstances, this did nothing to improve his temper. Two short letters to C. P. Scott in this critical month of March betrayed his uneasiness. In one he deplored the attitude of the *Manchester Guardian* to the crisis and objected particularly to a suggestion, given some prominence in the paper, that the Ulster question should be dealt with by a referendum. To a world grown wary of plebiscites his comment has a more than Irish relevance. 'Personally, as you know', he wrote, 'I have always felt very strongly on this referendum question, from the point of view of the future interests of Liberalism in its widest sense, liberty and good government in this country. The referendum in all great nations has really been the refuge of tyrants and dictators and that is what I am convinced it would (?end] in if once introduced into England.'[1] And in his other letter, written two days later when the Curragh incident was at fever pitch, he was at his most despondent. 'There can be no doubt', he wrote, 'that we are faced with a widespread conspiracy amongst the army—encouraged, I fear, by the court.'[2]

Though things were not, perhaps, quite as bad as this, Dillon would certainly have felt his worst fears confirmed had he known that a fortnight later the King was again urging Asquith to bring pressure to bear on Redmond, this time to get him to agree that the six counties should be allowed to opt out without voting and for an indefinite period. Asquith resisted this, rightly believing that he had pushed the Nationalists to the limits of their endurance.[3] But the time for manoeuvre was running out fast and before any further negotiations could be undertaken the temperature of that hectic spring was sent up still further by the audacious action of the Ulster Volunteers in landing a cargo of rifles and ammunition at Larne on the night of 24 April and distributing them throughout the province with formidable speed and efficiency. There could scarcely have been a more direct or deliberate challenge to the authority of the Government, which now had to decide whether or not to take action against those responsible. After several agonised discussions the Cabinet decided to do nothing. They were influenced, it seems, not only by the King, but by Birrell and Redmond both the latter being convinced that a prosecution would magnify the offence into a martyrdom and end by making a bad situation worse. This was Dillon's view, too, as he explained to C. P. Scott when Scott suggested that the Liberals had perhaps made a mistake in not checking the Ulster

[1] Dillon to C. P. Scott, 21 Mar. 1914 (D.P.).
[2] Dillon to C. P. Scott, 23 Mar. 1914 (D.P.).
[3] Nicolson, *King George V*, p. 240; Jenkins, *Asquith*, pp. 315–16.

Volunteers sooner. 'He dissented', Scott noted, 'and strongly deprecated
any action even now which might lead to actual conflict between army and
volunteers—fearing effect on future of Ireland.'[1] Perhaps the Nationalists
were right to take this line—after all, they knew how easily sectarian passions could flare up and an Ulster pogrom would be the worst possible
introduction to Home Rule. But it is more likely that they were wrong and
that this was the moment for firmness. Every move towards appeasement
would be greeted henceforward as a sign of weakness and the Ulster resistance, fortified now by weapons, become fiercer and more intractable than
ever.

(ii)

Inevitably, these grave events had their effect upon the South. There, in
the previous November, and in direct imitation of the Ulster Volunteers, a
parallel movement had emerged under the leadership of the Celtic scholar,
Eoin MacNeill. In their early stages the Irish Volunteers, as they were
called, had not been a very large or very prominent organisation, although
the fact that among the founders were members of the Irish Republican
Brotherhood gave it a significance which many of the Volunteers themselves
were not to realise until much later. Dillon, however, without knowing
anything about the secret penetration of the Volunteers by the I.R.B., did
not like what he saw even above the surface. When it was first started he had
asked his colleagues, Devlin and John Muldoon, if it was necessary to take
steps to prevent 'this new army' from passing under dangerous control, but
they had both thought it would 'fizzle out'. 'I am not quite sure they are
right', he reported to Redmond. 'We must watch it.' Up to the end of 1913
it seems that the membership was only about 1,850, but by July 1914, no
doubt in response to the increasing tension of the political situation, it is
estimated that the numbers had shot up to 160,000. Since perhaps a third
of these were in Ulster, and since the nationalist leaders were receiving
more and more disquieting reports about friction in that province between
nationalists and Unionists, there was an obvious possibility of a clash between the two sets of Volunteers.[2]

In these circumstances Redmond was bound to consider the possibility
of bringing the Irish Volunteers under the control of the parliamentary
party, and he was the more inclined to do this because in April 1914, even
before the Larne gun-running, MacNeill had arrived in London, accompanied by Sir Roger Casement, to discuss the possibility of some junction
of forces between the Volunteers and the parliamentarians. Redmond
probably assumed—it would certainly have been natural for him to do so—
that MacNeill, as head of the Volunteers, spoke with the authority of the

[1] J. L. Hammond, *C. P. Scott*, p. 127; Jenkins, *Asquith*, p. 317.
[2] Dillon to Redmond, 26 Nov. 1913 (D.P.); *Royal commission on the rebellion in
Ireland: minutes of evidence and appendix of documents*, 1916 [Cmd. 8279], vol. xi, p. 45
n. 994; Gwynn, *Redmond*, p. 307; F. X. Martin (ed.), 'Eoin MacNeill on the 1916 rising',
in *I.H.S.* (Mar. 1961), xii, no. 47, p. 243 n. 15.

Provisional Committee which governed their organisation In fact, as we now know, the Provisional Committee had not been consulted and the approach was an unofficial one, undertaken on MacNeill's own initiative.[1] From this misunderstanding much bitterness was to flow, but for a while the negotiations, transferred to Dublin, were continued, and letters, exhibiting a certain coyness on both sides, passed between MacNeill and Redmond, the latter pressing for such representation on the governing body of the Volunteers as would allow the party and their supporters to have, as he put it, confidence in the organisation. Dillon, acting for Redmond, saw MacNeill on 28 May and found him vague and exasperating. He raised an objection to one of Redmond's nominees to the governing body (Michael Davitt, son of the Land Leaguer) and, reported Dillon, 'either is, or pretends to be, afraid of his committee. You had better be pretty stiff with him.' MacNeill had some reason to be afraid of his committee, because, as Dillon now learned to his amazement, he had spoken to none of them except Casement, Colonel Maurice Moore and the O'Rahilly, the last-named for the first time only the previous day. Later, Dillon returned to the same theme in a second letter to Redmond of the same date. 'My interview with MacNeill left me with the impression that he is extremely muddle-headed, not consciously inclined to make mischief, but hopelessly impractical and possessed with the idea that *he* ought to be trusted.'[2] MacNeill himself also wrote to Redmond asserting that he could not carry 'young Mr. Davitt' and that 'it would be a flagrant breach of trust on my part if . . . any person not committed to this programme (to make the Irish Volunteers a permanent and effective defence force) were to obtain a position of control.' This 'impudent epistle', as Dillon called it when he read it, did not help matters.[3] Redmond's tone began to harden. The Home Rule Bill had just completed its third circuit of the House of Commons and although the ordeal of the House of Lords had still to come, and it was by this time known that an amending Bill was to be introduced, his position was a very strong one.[4] Clearly it would be much stronger still if he could speak, as Carson had so long spoken, with a formidable array of Volunteers at his back.

Accordingly, on 9 June he took the drastic course of issuing a public statement explaining that he must control the Volunteers or take steps which would, in effect, either split the movement in two or break it up altogether. The Provisional Committee was at that time in no position to resist this pressure and yielded, though with an ill grace. Redmond, therefore, gained the formal control he sought for, but at the price of arousing great resentment among the members of the Committee. In the event it turned out that the cracks had only been plastered over, and before long the inevitable split occurred—the majority (the National Volunteers) staying with Redmond, but the minority, who retained the title Irish Volunteers,

---

[1] Bulmer Hobson, 'Foundation and growth of the Irish Volunteers, 1913–14', in F. X. Martin (ed.), *The Irish Volunteers, 1913–15* (Dublin, 1963), pp. 43–6.

[2] Dillon to Redmond (two letters), 28 May 1914 (R.P.).

[3] Gwynn, *Redmond*, p. 315.

[4] For the amending Bill, see below pp. 352–4.

falling increasingly under the sway of the irreconcilables and in due course providing a large part of the striking force for the Easter Rising.[1]

In their dealings with the Volunteers the parliamentary leaders certainly took a very peremptory tone and the charge has recently been levelled against them that they, and especially Dillon, displayed 'a fatal arrogance' towards MacNeill and his followers.[2] In retrospect this may well seem to have been the case, but in the circumstances of the time their impatience was natural enough. On the one hand, they had arrived at the climax of the Home Rule struggle and it was vital for them to show themselves as the dominant force in Ireland. And on the other hand, MacNeill himself, by leaving his Provisional Committee so much in the dark, had proved a very unsatisfactory person to deal with. Eoin MacNeill has so far received very tender treatment from historians. He was such an obviously good, sincere and dedicated man that just as contemporaries loved him, so posterity has cherished his memory. Even the fact that on the outbreak of the Easter Rising he found himself, through no fault of his own, in even more dangerous isolation than in 1914, has in a strange way been accounted to him for grace. Muddled and deceived he may have been, runs the argument, but he was an honest patriot doing his best to find a path through the minefield of revolutionary politics. Such an interpretation, which has a wide currency, owes a good deal to hindsight. No one disputes his integrity or his idealism, but the parliamentary leaders may be excused for condemning him in 1914 as impractical and confused. They were professionals, nerving themselves for the supreme moment of their careers—it is not surprising that they found it hard to take this high-minded professor as seriously as he deserved, or that they failed to penetrate the real meaning of the movement he had brought into being. No one could have foreseen then that this failure was to be their tragedy much more than his.

(iii)

Meanwhile the Home Rule Bill had been proceeding steadily towards its final stages. By the terms of the Parliament Act it would then automatically become law (unless the King withheld his assent), and there was increasing risk that the Unionists, once their last constitutional barrier had fallen, would be tempted to use the guns they had landed at Larne. To avoid putting them in this last-ditch position, Asquith, building on the concessions he had wrung from the Nationalists in March, decided to bring in an Amend-

---

[1] For the negotiations between the party and the Volunteers, see Gwynn, *Redmond*, pp. 307–22; F. X. Martin (ed.), *The Irish Volunteers*, pp. 43–53, 141–4. At the time of the Woodenbridge speech there were about 180,000 Volunteers. After the split about 11,000 (increasing within a few weeks to 13,500) sided with MacNeill. The remainder remained faithful to Redmond, but by October 1914 their numbers had fallen to 165,000 (F. X. Martin (ed.), 'Eoin MacNeill on the 1916 rising', in *I.H.S.* (March 1961), xii, 243 n. 15).

[2] Terence de Vere White, 'Mahaffy, the Anglo-Irish Ascendancy and the Vice-regal Lodge', in F. X. Martin (ed.), *Leaders and men of the Easter Rising: Dublin, 1916* (London, 1967), p. 26.

ing Bill to deal with the special problem of Ulster. As introduced in the
House of Lords on 23 June it provided for county option for a period of six
years—precisely 'the stay of execution' previously rejected by Carson. The
Bill was at once amended by the Lords to exclude the whole *nine* counties of
Ulster, without any preliminary vote and for an indefinite period. This, of
course, was totally unacceptable and Asquith, now nearly desperate, began
to think again in terms of negotiations which, indeed, the King had repeatedly been urging him to resume. Reluctantly and slowly—because he
feared the consequences of failure and no rational man could anticipate
other than failure—Asquith prepared the ground and by mid-July was able
to tell the King that a conference was feasible. George V agreed it should
be held at Buckingham Palace under the chairmanship of the Speaker and
it held its first meeting on 21 July. On the Home Rule side the representatives were Asquith, Lloyd George, Redmond and Dillon; the Unionist
Members were Bonar Law, Lord Lansdowne, Carson and James Craig. The
conference was a total failure, becoming bogged down in the complicated
religio-electoral statistics of individual counties, and losing itself eventually,
in Churchill's famous phrase, 'in the muddy by-ways of Fermanagh and
Tyrone'. The two contending Irish parties could come to no accommodation, but they left the conference apparently with considerable respect for
one another. Captain Craig, a most intransigent Unionist and in a sense
the residuary legatee of all the men seated round that table, was so moved
that he came up to Dillon as they were leaving and said: 'Mr. Dillon, will
you shake my hand? I should be glad to think that I had been able to give
as many years to Ulster as you have to the service of Ireland.'[1] We do not
know Dillon's reaction, but no doubt in deference to the occasion he refrained from the blistering comment such a distinction between Ulster and
Ireland would certainly have drawn from him in normal circumstances.

Dillon's own view, before the conference met at all, had been that if the
Amending Bill were rejected in the form in which the Irish party had agreed
to it, then the original Home Rule Bill should be put on the statute-book.
Only then, he thought, would the Tories realise that the Liberals meant
business and consent to a reasonable settlement.[2] There is no reason to
suppose that he had changed his mind in the days that followed and at the
conference itself, according to Lloyd George, his attitude was very unyielding.[3] But the problem was fast passing out of the conference room into
the world of action. On Sunday, 26 July, the Irish Volunteers emulated the
feat of their Ulster brethren by bringing ashore—this time in broad daylight
—a cargo of rifles and ammunition at Howth, on the north side of Dublin
Bay.[4] They marched back to the city bearing their weapons, only to be confronted by a body of troops accompanied by the Assistant Commissioner
of Police. This official demanded the arms, but his request was refused. The

[1] Jenkins, *Asquith*, pp. 321–2.
[2] Gwynn, *Redmond*, p. 333.
[3] D. Lloyd George, *War memoirs* (London, 1933) ii. 701.
[4] For the organisation of this *coup*, see F. X. Martin, *The Howth gunrunning, July 1914* (Dublin, 1964).

Volunteers for the most part slipped away with their rifles and the troops marched back to barracks followed by an angry crowd. The inevitable happened. The troops turned and fired and three people were killed and thirty-eight injured. It was a tragic, and totally unnecessary, disaster, but its political consequences were important because, in the storm of ill feeling which the incident aroused in Ireland, it became impossible for the Nationalist leaders to consider any further compromise.

The deadlock was complete and an explosion of some sort seemed inevitable. It was averted—or rather postponed—only by the fact that at this point the Irish crisis was submerged in the vaster tragedy of the European war. By 30 July that catastrophe was clearly imminent and on that day Asquith, after conferring with both Redmond and Carson, announced the indefinite postponement of the Amending Bill. In England the onset of the war was regarded, at least for the time being, as putting an end to internecine strife. It was not so clear, however, that this would necessarily be the case in Ireland. There, indeed, there was a mounting impatience which the parliamentary leaders dared not ignore. Redmond's position in all this was excruciatingly difficult. On the one hand, it was essential to his own position that the Home Rule Bill should not suffer the fate of the Amending Bill. War or no war, it must go on the Statute-book. On the other hand, at this crucial moment in the history of the world he felt strongly drawn to take his stand with other statesmen of the Empire and to throw his country behind Britain in the struggle that was coming. By a curious chance he had to make the most vital decision of his life on his own, since Dillon and Devlin were both in Ireland. On 3 August, in the debate in which Grey warned the House of Commons of the storm that was about to break upon them, the Foreign Secretary referred to Ireland as 'the one bright spot in this very dreadful situation'. Redmond, following him, took a momentous step. Speaking with emotion in a highly-charged atmosphere, he pledged Ireland's support for the war, and urged the government forthwith to remove its troops from the country, leaving it to the Volunteers—of North and South—to defend the Irish coasts.[1]

This gesture, which made an immense sensation in the House, was at the time, and long afterwards, assumed to have been entirely spontaneous. However, a passage in Margot Asquith's *Autobiography*, in which she recalled a letter she had written Redmond on 1 August, begging him 'to offer all his soldiers to the government', suggests that here may have been at least the germ of his famous speech. Redmond replied hoping he might be able to follow her advice after he had seen the Prime Minister next day. Whether or not he did see Asquith before intervening in the debate is not established, but the speech itself certainly met Mrs. Asquith's appeal in full measure.[2] In another sense, however, as having been made without consul-

---

[1] Hansard, H. C. Debates, 5th series, vol. 65, cols. 1828–9; Gwynn, *Redmond*, pp. 354–7.

[2] Gwynn, *Redmond*, p. 354; Margot Asquith, *Autobiography* (London, Penguin edition, 1936), ii. 124.

tation with his colleagues, it may truly be said to have been entirely spontaneous. But whether those absent colleagues would receive it as enthusiastically as the House of Commons was another matter. With Dillon especially it was bound to create difficulties, for it was the kind of utterance he could never have brought himself to make. And in this context it is perhaps significant that Eoin MacNeill, in a brief memoir he wrote about a year later, thought it worth recording the Dublin gossip that 'Mr. Redmond was met immediately afterwards by Mr. Dillon with the strongest reproaches for having made an unauthorised and unconsidered declaration of policy.'[1]

Eoin MacNeill, of course, was the last man to set up as an authority on the internal tensions of the parliamentary party, and in actual fact immediate reproaches were impossible, since Dillon was staying at Killiney and out of touch with Redmond. It is true that in later years he looked back on Redmond's identification with the war, of which this speech was the symbol, as a major blunder, even as a turning-point in the party's history, but this does not appear in his correspondence at the time. On the contrary, he seems to have been much more absorbed in the international situation than in Irish affairs. Thus, writing to T. P. O'Connor the day after war was declared, the burden of his letter was that this was the logical end of the diplomacy of recent years. 'The world is now reaping the bitter harvest of the Triple Entente and Grey's foreign policy which for years I have denounced to deaf ears.'[2] This was a highly individual, not to say idiosyncratic, view and characteristically running right against the grain of the current war hysteria, but in his forecasts of what the war would mean for Europe and for civilisation at large, he was as far-sighted as ever. On 6 August, for example, writing to C. P. Scott, he described it as 'horrible beyond the power of words'. 'It is the greatest crime against humanity perpetuated in modern times and I cannot help feeling that England must bear a considerable share of the responsibility.'[3] A few days later he amplified this theme. It was hard, he admitted, to apportion the blame—'no doubt the German war-party must bear a good share'. But, he added, he could not resist the conviction that the heaviest share of the guilt lay 'with the new English foreign policy identified with Rosebery and Grey'. By removing foreign policy to a large extent from party politics they had made the Foreign Office officials supreme, and these, in his view, were mostly Russophil and Germanophobe:

> I take it for granted [he wrote] that Germany will be beaten. But after a titanic struggle, and great Heavens—what a prospect for Europe. If Germany is beaten, Germany and Austria will be dissolved, and good-bye to peace in Europe for some generations.
>
> I must say that my experience in the House of Commons during the last five years in trying to interest Liberals in what seemed to me

---

[1] Eoin MacNeill, undated memorandum, probably 1915 (Bulmer Hobson Papers, N.L.I. MS. 13174(13). I owe this reference to Rev. Professor F. X. Martin, O.S.A.
[2] Dillon to T. P. O'Connor, 5 Aug. 1914 (D.P.).
[3] Dillon to C. P. Scott, 6 Aug. 1914 (D.P.).

the manifest and inevitable trend of Grey's policy has been the most disheartening and tragic in my long public life.[1]

Holding these views he could hardly be expected to receive Redmond's declaration with much enthusiasm. That he did not at once explode in protest may have been due to letters which Redmond himself and O'Connor wrote to him on 4 August. Redmond's letter, as giving a picture of his relations with Asquith at this crucial moment in history is worth quoting in full:

My dear Dillon,
    I saw Asquith yesterday and of course raised the question of the Bill being placed on the Statute-book immediately, and pointed out the perils of the situation in Ireland if that were not done. Asquith expressed his entire agreement with me, but he was at the moment so worried with the foreign situation—and indeed he looked very worried—that he represented [*sic*] he could not consider the question at the moment. He said neither he nor the government had considered this question at all, and that he had not heard the matter even discussed by one of them up to the present and that he did not know when they would be able to discuss it.
    He said also that when it came to be discussed it would have to be discussed also with Bonar Law, and that the opportunity for that had not come. He had no idea in his own mind whatever as to the course of the session, or how long the House would sit, or anything of that kind at all. He is simply living from hour to hour, with his mind filled with one thing only.
    I hope you will come over here as soon as you can, because complications may arise at any moment, and I am quite sure that the House will continue sitting at any rate for a week or more.
    We believe that the Radicals are quite sound in backing us for the Bill being put on the Statute-book, though some of the centre and richer Liberals, in their anxiety to save their money, may urge the government not to bring forward any contentious business.
                                                        Very truly yours,
                                                        J. E. Redmond.[2]

This was troubling news and O'Connor's letter, written in full knowledge of Redmond's, was not reassuring. O'Connor had seen Devlin, who was

---

[1] Dillon to C. P. Scott, 12 Aug. 1914 (D.P.). Part of the blame for war hysteria he also laid at the door of the popular newspapers, which particularly enraged him by a campaign of systematic vilification against his old friend Haldane. In 1915 Dillon defended him in the House in a characteristically fighting speech, but, replying to Haldane's letter of thanks, he observed, equally characteristically, that he regarded the gutter Press as 'almost a more menacing fact . . . than even the horrible madness of the present war'. 'I felt it as a personal humiliation and pain', he continued, 'to see you subjected to the brutal insults of an utterly corrupt and unscrupulous Press, and to realise that the Press had the power to break a government and drive you from the service of your country at a time like this' (Dillon to Haldane, 23 Nov. 1915, Haldane Papers, National Library of Scotland MS. 5912, ff. 121–4).
[2] Redmond to Dillon, 4 Aug. 1914 (D.P.). Unfortunately, Dillon's reply to this, if he ever made one, has not so far come to light.

Above

13. Elizabeth Dillon in 1890

Below

14. Elizabeth Dillon in 1900

Above

15. T. P. O'Connor, from the portrait by John H.
Bacon

Below

16. Augustine Birrell, from a chalk drawing by
William Orpen
(*Courtesy of the National Portrait Gallery, London*)

'raging'. 'He declares that our position in Ireland will be intolerable without the Bill, with Sinn Feiners and that crew denouncing the government
for treachery and calling for German success. Redmond does not take so
serious a view; and says he is willing to face the situation and point out
that we shall get the Bill this year which is what he promised.' O'Connor
himself felt that Asquith would be in trouble if Bonar Law and Carson
opposed the completion of Home Rule as being 'contentious business'. On
the other hand, Redmond's speech *had* greatly influenced Tory opinion,
some of them having thanked him afterwards 'literally with tears in their
eyes'.[1]

Redmond himself was only too well aware of the precariousness of his
position. On 4 August, the day of his letter to Dillon, he wrote also to
Asquith as follows:

> I want you to understand that in making the speech I did yesterday
> I took great risks and if I have to go back to Ireland with the enact-
> ment of the Home Rule Bill postponed for two or three months the
> result will be disastrous.
>
> My people will consider themselves sold and deplorable things
> will be said and done which may perhaps wreck the Irish cause.
> I would be unable to hold the people. Surely it is not too much to
> ask that the Bill should receive the Royal assent coupled with a
> definite promise not to put it into operation until an Amending Bill
> had been disposed of in the winter session.[2]

Unfortunately Asquith was being simultaneously assailed from the right.
The next day came a letter from Carson, hoping he was not being unreasonable in pressing for a continuance of the *status quo*, and the day after
that one from Bonar Law which, while admitting that his party would not
oppose the putting of Home Rule on the Statute-book, so as not to appear
factious, warned the Prime Minister that 'it will be impossible for us to
co-operate with the government.'[3]

For a few desperate days it seemed as if non-cooperation was to be the
Tory line. Redmond saw Carson on 5 August and found him absolutely
irreconcilable and indeed highly excitable, threatening even to obstruct the
second reading of the Appropriations Bill, which, of course, would have
jeopardised the whole war effort.[4] On August 10 the Cabinet discussed the
question anxiously and the meeting disclosed acute disagreement, some
Members wanting Home Rule to come into force, but in an area to be
immediately defined, others fearful of a collision with the Unionists at a
time when national solidarity was essential.[5] Before they could make up
their minds Parliament had adjourned for a fortnight. Redmond seized the

---

[1] T. P. O'Connor to Dillon, 4 Aug. 1914 (D.P.).
[2] Redmond to Asquith, 4 Aug. 1914 (Asquith Papers).
[3] Sir E. Carson to Asquith, 5 Aug. 1914; A. Bonar Law to Asquith, 6 Aug. 1914
(D.P.).
[4] Gwynn, *Redmond*, p. 363.
[5] Ibid., p. 368.

chance to pay a quick visit to Ireland, where he found remarkable enthusiasm for the war among the Volunteers, many of whom assumed that, in view of the tremendous impact of Redmond's speech in the House of Commons, his offer to use them for the defence of Ireland would be taken up at once. He told T. P. O'Connor, who on 21 August relayed the information to Lloyd George, that Irish feeling in favour of the war was running high, but that any hanging up of the Home Rule Bill would turn back the tide of opinion at once.[1] That same day, 21 August, Redmond was back in London and learnt of the various possibilities being considered by the Government. The one he himself preferred best was to put Home Rule on the Statute-book at once. To achieve this he was prepared to assent to it not being put into operation until there had been ample time for the discussion, and if possible the passage by agreement, of an Amending Bill, if such a Bill were still deemed necessary. But if Home Rule were not put on the Statute-book immediately there would, he warned Asquith, be serious trouble in Ireland.[2] It was not, however, until after another adjournment of Parliament that, in early September, Asquith began to see his way clear to a characteristic compromise. At long last he announced in the House of Commons that the Government would proceed to place the Home Rule Bill on the Statute-book, but that it would be accompanied by a Suspensory Act which would prevent its operation until after the end of the war. And not only that, he also gave an assurance that Home Rule would not come into effect until parliament had had an opportunity of dealing with the Ulster question by amending legislation. Even as it was this statement, which fell so far short of the Nationalist demand, provoked a bitter speech from Bonar Law and a mass withdrawal of Unionists from the House. However, the formalities were speedily concluded and on 18 September the royal assent was announced amid the cheers of Liberal, Labour and Nationalist members. These were strange reactions to such a lame and halting conclusion to all the years of struggle. It is difficult not to feel, in retrospect, that if the Unionists had stayed to cheer and the Home Rulers had left the House in protest this would have been a more appropriate comment.[3]

(iv)

Dillon had remained silently in the wings during these concluding stages of the negotiations. He had come over once to London, at Redmond's summons, just after the outbreak of war, and had gone with him to see Lord Kitchener, then just taking office as Secretary of State for War, about the best means of using the Volunteers. It was a depressing interview, for Kitchener made it abundantly clear that he did not take the Volunteers seriously and intended simply to launch a straightforward recruiting appeal

---

[1] T. P. O'Connor to Lloyd George, 21 Aug. 1914 (L.G.P., 0/6/10/10).
[2] Gwynn, *Redmond*, pp. 374–6.
[3] Hansard, H.C. Debates, 5th series, vol. 66, cols. 882–3; see also cols. 893–905 for Bonar Law's speech and cols. 1017–20 for the final scenes.

in Ireland.[1] Redmond, in even venturing on this interview, had risked trouble with the Volunteer organisation, for MacNeill has recorded that it was arranged without consultation with the Provisional Committee. According to what MacNeill called 'a verbal account' given to him some time later, Kitchener was interested only in recruits for the regular army. Mac-Neill's memorandum continues: 'Mr. Dillon understood him to propose that the Irish Volunteers or some proportion of them should be induced to join the army, and was indignant at the suggestion. "I hope you don't think, Lord Kitchener," he said, "that we are coming here as recruiting sergeants." '[2] This, no doubt, was just what Kitchener wanted them to be and it was, indeed, what Redmond ultimately became. But it was not what Redmond had intended in his speech of 3 August. Later that same month, when General Sir Bryan Mahon had been sent over to Ireland to survey the recruiting possibilities, he asked Redmond what was the best thing to do with the Volunteers. The Irish leader then made it clear that he imposed two conditions on their employment—first, that they were not to be required to take the oath of allegiance to the King, and second, that they were to be employed in defence of Ireland and *not* elsewhere. And, despite the general's protest that the fate of England and Ireland was at that moment being settled in Flanders, he remained, for the time being, adamant on these points.[3]

Within a month, however, his policy had radically changed. Whether this was due to his growing personal involvement in the war (which was certainly real enough), whether it was a chivalrous reaction to the placing of Home Rule on the Statute-book, or whether, as his biographer suggests, it was inspired by Carson's appeal to the Ulster Volunteers to enlist for service overseas, it is difficult to determine. Probably all three factors influenced him in the speech he made at Woodenbridge in County Wicklow, on 20 September—a speech apparently spontaneous and almost accidental, but serious in its consequences. In it he advanced deliberately beyond the line he had marked out to General Mahon, urging the Volunteers not merely to defend the shores of Ireland but to go 'wherever the firing-line extends, in defence of right, of freedom and of religion in this war'.[4] The immediate outcome was a split in the Volunteer movement, as a result of which a minority—perhaps 12,000—followed Pearse, MacNeill and others into a separate organisation, retaining, however, the name of Irish Volunteers, while the remainder, roughly 160,000, stayed with Redmond, but were known thenceforward as the National Volunteers.[5] On the short view this internal crisis may even have strengthened Redmond's position by enabling him to pursue his recruiting campaign without having to face hostile criticism within his own camp, but in retrospect it can only be seen as one more

---

[1] Gwynn, *Redmond*, pp. 366–7.

[2] E. MacNeill, Memorandum (Bulmer Hobson Papers, N.L.I. MS. 13174/13).

[3] L. Comyn (who was present at the interview) in letter to *Irish Times*, 16 May 1956, reprinted in F. X. Martin (ed.), *The Irish Volunteers, 1913–1915*, pp. 146–8.

[4] Gwynn, *Redmond*, pp. 390–2.

[5] Gwynn, *Redmond*, p. 392 and n.; F. X. Martin (ed.), *The Irish Volunteers, 1913–1915*, pp. 152–5.

step along the road to revolution and to the disintegration of the parliamentary party.

Dillon's attitude towards recruiting, and indeed towards Ireland's participation in the war, was superficially similar to Redmond's, but in reality profoundly different. On the one hand, he believed, like Redmond, that the passing of Home Rule, even in the castrated form in which it reached the Statute-book, imposed a debt of honour upon Irishmen which they could best discharge by loyal support of Britain. On the other hand, feeling as he did about Britain's share in the responsibility for the catastrophe, he could not become emotionally involved (as Redmond did) and he was entirely unmoved by war hysteria. Moreover, he took a more pessimistic view than Redmond about the Irish reaction to the events of August and September. At home in Dublin, while Redmond was wrestling with Asquith to ensure that Home Rule completed its final stages, Dillon found that the delay was causing much dissatisfaction. The situation, he reported to T. P. O'Connor, was 'a good deal worse than I had supposed' and the country was 'seething with suspicion and disappointment', greatly to the profit of Sinn Fein.[1]

Once Home Rule was safely over its last fence the tension relaxed for the time being and his public comments were clearly designed to reassure the people about the nature of the settlement that had just been reached. Interviewed at home on 20 September he dismissed the Suspensory Act as a merely temporary inconvenience—no rational man, he said, would expect the Government to set up an Irish Parliament while the war was raging. As for the promised Amending Bill, 'our hands are entirely free, except in so far as we are bound by the public undertakings given by us during last session'. If there was no agreement about the Amending Bill, he asserted, Home Rule would nevertheless come into effect. For himself he hoped there would be an agreed settlement between the Unionists and the Home Rulers, but he ended, very characteristically, with a warning he was to repeat more than once in the months ahead—the Irish people should immediately take whatever steps were necessary 'to secure that they may be, when the war is over, in a position to resist any attempt—if such should be made—to forcibly deprive them of the constitutional rights which they have won after forty years of struggle and sacrifice.'[2] This, with its clear hint to the Volunteers that their organisation was going to be as vital in the future as it had been in 1914, was not, after all, any different from what Carson had just been saying to his Volunteers in the north.[3] And just as Carson coupled maintenance of the Ulster Volunteers with enlistment for service overseas, so, too, did Dillon insist that while the Volunteers in the south were a necessary safeguard for Home Rule, the price of Home Rule was loyalty to England in the present struggle. He took the occasion of a great public welcome home to Ballaghaderrin to make this crystal clear:

[1] Dillon to T. P. O'Connor, 5 Sept. 1914 (D.P.).
[2] *W.F.J.*, 26 Sept. 1914.
[3] Gwynn, *Redmond*, p. 390.

I am England's friend in this war [he said], and as long as she stands
by that Bill [Home Rule] and keeps faith with Ireland, any influence
I can exercise in this country will be used to its uttermost to induce
our people to stand by England and keep faith with her and to prove
to England that the bond of Ireland is something more than a scrap
of paper.[1]

This was not, however, an unconditional support. Apart altogether from
the broad question of England's fidelity to Home Rule, Dillon's own attitude would continue to be strongly influenced by what he saw of English
policy in practice. During that autumn of 1914 two things worried him
particularly—the fear that the Government would, by undue attention to
their pro-Germanism, magnify the importance of the extreme men, and the
nagging anxiety about the mishandling of recruiting. So far as the first of
these worries was concerned, he was emphatic that the Government should
not take too much notice of the Sinn Fein newspapers, which, indeed, were
violently anti-British in tone, but few in number and, he believed, small in
influence. He put this strongly to the Under-Secretary, Sir Matthew Nathan,
who had only taken up office in October and who, in Dillon's view, needed
to be educated as to Irish realities. They met first, in November 1914, at the
house of Dillon's friend, that notable Dublin host, W. F. Bailey of the Land
Commission, and, as Nathan recorded afterwards: 'He [Dillon] thought
that the suppression of these newspapers would result in the formation of
secret societies which would be very difficult to deal with. He also dealt
with the difficult situation which would be created for the constitutional
Nationalist party who would be considered to have urged the government
to take this action.'[2] Dillon, indeed, was so wrought up on this subject
that he wrote Nathan a long letter next day which is striking evidence of the
extent to which he had already grasped the central dilemma of the parliamentary party, committed to support a war which was attacked by extremists and was likely to become even more unpopular, yet compelled also to
urge the Government to refrain from suppressing their rivals for fear they
should be thought to be playing the Castle game:

This war [he wrote], coming just before we finally secured Home
Rule, has created a position of terrible difficulty and embarrassment
for us. And up to the beginning of this month the War Office and
other government authorities have done nothing but add to our
difficulties. Yet we have retained the confidence and the leadership
of about 20 to 1 of the Nationalists of Ireland and secured their good
will to England in this war. And according to my information we
have completely paralysed the attempts of the Germans to secure
co-operation of the Irish in America in influencing American opinion
against England. I do *not* believe that the Sinn Feiners and pro-Ger-
mans are making any headway against us in Ireland.

[1] *F.J.*, 6 Oct. 1914.
[2] Interview with John Dillon, 27 Nov. 1914 (Nathan Papers, Memoranda of interviews, vol. 1, ff. 36–7).

But because certain Tory newspapers, and rabid anti-Irish Unionists in the House of Commons, clamour for coercion measures, the government are about, I fear, to embark on that dangerous course . . . My strong feeling is—and I speak only for myself in this matter—that so far from helping us, or promoting recruiting, the suppression of these wretched, scurrilous rags will only increase our difficulties and raise fresh obstacles in the path of recruiting from the ranks of Irish Nationalists.

Had it not been for the perversity of the War Office in treating with contempt every suggestion we made, a *very large* number of nationalists would have entered the New Army before now.

There is a considerable movement in favour of recruiting since the Irish Brigades were really put in working order, and I think that movement would be largely strengthened by other measures, if the War Office could be got to adopt them.

But I greatly fear that the suppression of the papers, with the consequences wh. will probably follow, may have a very evil influence on the whole situation.[1]

For Dillon, evidently, the two factors of wise government and recruiting were interrelated, and for a short period, in the hope that wise government would be what Ireland would get, he was prepared to take his share in the recruiting campaign. It had become known in September that Carson had obtained permission from the War Office that the Ulster Volunteers should be allowed to enlist under their own officers and formed into a separate Ulster division—the same that was later to be slaughtered on the Somme. Naturally, Redmond hoped that his own Volunteers would receive the same privileges and Dillon drew up a memorandum for him setting out some of the best ways to attract troops into what, it was hoped, were to be specifically Irish brigades—good camp accommodation, good bands, much publicity, above all a distinctive uniform.[2] The heart-breaking disappointments of trying vainly to bring the War Office to regard Irish recruiting as a special problem belong more to Redmond's biography than to Dillon's, but perhaps it was significant that Kitchener, who was the rock upon which most of their efforts foundered, while believing in Redmond's loyalty, was distinctly sceptical of Dillon's.[3] Dillon, for his part, was not the man to suffer military fools gladly, however grandiose their reputations, and by the end of 1914 had become so thoroughly disillusioned that he resolved to speak on no more recruiting platforms.[4]

He continued, indeed, to pledge his public support for the war, and to praise Volunteers for enlisting, but a speech he made in Belfast early in 1915 suggests that his mind was really running on the struggle that might come afterwards. The Volunteers, he said, 'have recognised that when the war is over, and when we shall commence to resume the thread of Irish

[1] Dillon to Sir M. Nathan, 28 Nov. 1914 (Nathan Papers, 450–1, ff. 218–23.)
[2] Gwynn, *Redmond*, pp. 387–8.
[3] L. O'Broin, *Dublin Castle and the 1916 Rising* (Dublin, 1966), pp. 25–6.
[4] Gwynn, *Redmond*, pp. 411–12.

politics, that section of the Irish nation which has done best on the battle-fields of France will be strongest in the struggle which may then be thrust upon us'. And there might be a struggle for, he promised them, 'we will never consent, and I say it here in the face of you, the Volunteers of Belfast, who may yet have to make good my words, we shall never consent to di-vide this island or this nation, and we shall never consent to allow any section, clique or faction, to rule the people of Ireland'.[1] Two weeks later, in his own constituency, he developed the theme that expediency, as well as honour, bound Ireland to Britain's side in the struggle. 'I can understand', he said, 'the position of those in Ireland and in America who can never forget the past, and whose whole politics consisted in the passion of revenge and the consuming desire to pay England back for all the injury she has inflicted upon Ireland. That is a logical position, though to my mind a stupid, narrow-minded and unchristian philosophy and bound to end in ruin and disaster for this country.' It was not, he insisted, the philosophy of the majority. On the contrary, the great mass of Irishmen 'are bound by every consideration of honour as well as of self-interest, to stand with England in this hour of desperate danger'.[2]

By the beginning of that year, it was true, the recruiting position had somewhat improved and Redmond, as he told Dillon, had been able to assure Asquith that it was going on at about 4,000 a month. This was satis-factory, but the Prime Minister had seemed more concerned about the government of Ireland. Birrell's wife lay dying and Birrell himself was once again begging to be relieved of office. Perhaps unwisely, Asquith per-suaded him to stay on, but suggested to Redmond that the essential work in Ireland could perfectly well be done by Nathan and that Birrell could be allowed to remain in London (which he normally did, anyway) 'and con-fine himself to a little parliamentary work'.[3] This, in fact, suited the Irish leaders well enough. In Dublin Dillon had begun to develop an amicable relationship with Nathan, who called from time to time at North Great George's Street (it was still against Dillon's principles to visit the Under-Secretary's Office), where occasionally they were joined by Redmond for the purpose of working out in advance details of the transfer of power when-ever the Home Rule Act should enter into force.[4]

This collaboration has a pathetic ring about it in retrospect; indeed, even then it must have seemed a trifle premature. The war was going badly and Asquith's position was being steadily undermined. At the same time, and despite Redmond's optimistic figures, the consistent mishandling of Irish recruiting had affected the popularity of the Irish leader at home. Kitchener still bristled with mistrust and, as O'Connor reported to Red-mond at the end of February, his opinion evidently was that 'there were revolutionary forces in Ireland which you could not control and of whose

[1] *F.J.*, 8 Mar. 1915.   [2] *F.J.*, 27 Mar. 1915.
[3] Redmond to Dillon, 5 Feb. 1915 (D.P.).
[4] See especially Memoranda of interviews with the Nationalist leaders, 16 Dec. 1914 and 4 Feb. 1915 (Nathan Papers, 467, ff. 69–72, 133–40).

existence perhaps you were not even cognisant'.[1] In this Kitchener may have been wiser than he knew, but assuming he was right, it was still an egregious error to withhold from Redmond the kind of recognition which alone could restore his position in the country. Dillon was completely disgusted and only refrained from direct disagreement with Redmond out of loyalty and through a doubt that his own hostility to British foreign policy might have warped his outlook. By the beginning of March 1915 he was confiding to O'Connor how profoundly he differed from 'the chairman' (the use of that neutral term was usually a storm signal with Dillon) about recruiting. 'I have always', he wrote, 'felt in a great difficulty in dealing with all these questions. Because, as I explained to you already, I hold views about the origins of the war, so different from those held by you and the chairman and the public generally, that I distrust my judgment to some extent and don't like to take as strong a line in discussing matters of this kind with the chairman as I otherwise would.'[2]

But these disagreements were soon to be dwarfed by the much more serious problem raised by the collapse of Asquith's Government. It had been reeling towards disaster for some months. What finally pushed it over the edge was a crisis in the munitions industry, combined with the appalling failure at Gallipoli. Asquith was driven to the dreaded expedient of a Coalition Government. This meant in general terms the admission of the Unionists to an approximate equality of representation in the Cabinet. In particular, it meant the inclusion of Sir Edward Carson. Here was a fearful portent for the Nationalist leaders. Realising this, Asquith, when the die was cast and the reconstruction of the Ministry proceeding, sent urgent messages to Redmond asking him to join the Government, or if not him, one of his senior colleagues. For the Irish party it was a cruel dilemma. To serve would be to break with their whole tradition of independent parliamentary action. Not to serve would be to see the leader of Ulster Unionism seated at the centre of power and able, when he so chose, to thwart any development that might favour the coming of Home Rule. Nevertheless, to maintain the essential integrity of the party was the first duty and neither Redmond nor Dillon showed the slightest disposition to yield to the arguments of Asquith and Birrell.[3] But Dillon for one was under no illusions as to what the coalition might mean. 'I consider', he wrote to O'Connor a few days after it had taken shape, 'that the situation that has arisen in England is the most disgraceful and humiliating that ever befell any nation in the midst of a great war on which her existence depended. And I greatly fear that among the results will be the hopeless discrediting of Asquith and others of the Liberal ministers.'[4] Events were soon to prove him right, and he was no less prescient when he forecast to Nathan a few days later that the formation of the Coalition would go hand-in-hand with an attempt to apply conscription to Ireland:

A great deal of mischief [he wrote] has already been done, from the

---

[1] Gwynn, *Redmond*, pp. 414–15.   [2] Dillon to T. P. O'Connor, 1 Mar. 1915 (D.P.).
[3] Gwynn, *Redmond*, pp. 423–4.   [4] Dillon to T. P. O'Connor, 24 May 1915.

recruiting point of view in this country, by the formation of the coalition government and the inclusion of Carson. If you are consulted as to the question of conscription, I think you should represent *strongly* that any attempt to enforce conscription in Ireland will have *most serious* and deplorable results.[1]

What Dillon had constantly in mind at this point was the undercurrent of sedition in Ireland. He was well aware that it existed, and also that the Government knew it existed, but he was still trying to determine just how serious it really was. During 1915 his views fluctuated, though for a while, in the summer, he was inclined not to estimate it very highly—always provided the Government did not inflame Irish opinion by some *bêtise*. They nearly committed such a folly when the Coalition was being formed and J. H. M. Campbell—Carson's fellow member for Trinity College, Dublin, and a very bitter Unionist—was being pressed by his fellow Unionists for the Irish Lord Chancellorship. Only after the most vigorous opposition by the Irish leaders was Campbell's claim withdrawn, but it had been a very near thing and, in fact, before long they had to accept him in the almost equally objectionable role of Irish Attorney-General.[2] The slight easement secured by this superficially petty triumph may have helped to raise Dillon's spirits. At any rate by July he reported to O'Connor that the state of Ireland was 'slowly improving', though he was careful to add his usual reservations. 'It was *very* bad, worse than I have known it since 1900. The Clan men [he seems by this to have meant Sinn Fein, though, like many others, he constantly confused Sinn Fein and the I.R.B. at this time] are exceedingly active, and have eight organisers traversing the country with plenty of money. Our men are disheartened and puzzled, an increasing number of the clergy are very hostile.'[3] This relatively euphoric mood lasted rather longer than usual and Nathan, a couple of weeks later, found him 'in a —for him—optimistic state of mind even to the extent of conceiving the possibility of the coalition government eventually coming to an agreement on the Irish question'.[4]

But the position was always precarious and soon he was warning the Under-Secretary that the funeral of the old Fenian O'Donovan Rossa, on 1 August would be a 'massive demonstration'.[5] In this he was perfectly correct, for, as we now know, Patrick Pearse used the occasion as a means to focus public attention on the separatist, republican ideal. Since the I.R.B. had determined on a rising during the war, and since they were receiving aid and support from John Devoy and the Clan na Gael in America, and were also in touch with Germany, the possibility of an outbreak was steadily coming closer. The Irish Government had its eye upon most of the Sinn Fein and I.R.B. leaders, and from time to time it swooped on Sinn

[1] Dillon to Sir M. Nathan, 28 May 1915 (Nathan Papers; 450–1, ff. 268–9).
[2] T. P. O'Connor to Asquith (copy), 3 June 1915 (D.P.); T. P. O'Connor to Dillon, 4 June 1915 (D.P.); Gwynn, *Redmond*, pp. 427–33.
[3] Dillon to T. P. O'Connor, 4 July 1915 (D.P.).
[4] Sir M. Nathan to A. Birrell (copy), 16 July 1915 (Nathan Papers, 463, f. 6).
[5] Sir M. Nathan to A. Birrell (copy), 27 July 1915 (Nathan Papers, 463, f. 154).

Fein newspapers, but the Castle authorities felt they had matters sufficiently under control. On the other hand, the war situation was so serious, and the wastage of manpower so terrible, that the danger of conscription was never far away. And given the intense hostility towards the war which was growing, as the news grew more depressing and the failures more alarming, any official attempt to apply compulsory service was bound to throw many waverers behind Sinn Fein, which, after all, had a consistent anti-war record. It was true that the circulation of Sinn Fein newspapers was not impressive. A return communicated by Nathan to Dillon of the circulation of five of the most extreme papers in September 1915 gave a total of 12,574, and even though each copy might be read by more than one person, this scarcely seemed a very formidable propaganda machine.[1] But conscription, as Dillon never ceased to emphasise, could transform this situation overnight. He said it publicly in July and he repeated it privately to O'Connor in the autumn. 'Make no mistake about it', he wrote, 'Conscription in Ireland is *impossible*.'[2]

As it turned out, the efforts and representations of the Irish leaders were successful and when general conscription came early in 1916 Ireland was, for the time being, excluded. But it was an ever-present danger, and Dillon, who was constantly in Dublin (with occasional trips to Mayo), was probably much more aware than Redmond of how support was steadily seeping away from the party. This was apparent, indeed, even to the Government, and Nathan, when Dillon asked him in November how he thought the rival sections stood in the country at large, had to reply that he thought Sinn Fein was gaining and the parliamentarians declining. 'He was in agreement with the former of these two propositions,' noted Nathan, 'but doubted the latter. At the same time he seemed to think that the extreme party were trenching on the large body of people who were wavering in their opinions.'[3] Writing to Birrell shortly afterwards, Nathan put it even more strongly. 'In my talk with Dillon he showed himself for the first time impressed with the real danger that the Sinn Feiners are becoming to his party and to the state. He painted lurid pictures of what might happen if conscription were attempted in Ireland.'[4] Yet despite this, Dillon still believed that any all-out attempt to crush the extremists would martyrise them, redound to the disadvantage of the parliamentary party and end by complicating a critical situation still further. It was a vicious circle and as the year closed there seemed no way out of it. 'We talked of the state of Ireland', recorded Nathan after another meeting in December, 'and the Sinn Fein movement which he now regards as very serious but still advised me to keep my hands off organisers.'[5]

[1] Sir M. Nathan to Dillon, 13 Nov. 1915 (D.P.).

[2] *F.J.*, 26 July 1915 (speech at Limerick); Dillon to T. P. O'Connor, 30 Sept. 1915 (D.P.).

[3] Memorandum of interview with John Dillon, 11 Nov. 1915 (Nathan Papers, 467, ff. 86–7).

[4] Sir M. Nathan to A. Birrell, 14 Nov. 1915 (Nathan Papers, 450–1, f. 312).

[5] Memorandum of interview with John Dillon, 3 Dec. 1915 (Nathan Papers, 467, ff. 130–1).

As the spring of 1916 approached signs of tension steadily increased, but the Government still seemed to feel secure, though this, as events were soon to prove, was a false security due in part to an inadequate intelligence system.[1] Thus in February 1916 Nathan could assure nervous Irish Unionists that 'the hostile movement' was being carefully watched, 'but I made it clear to them that at the present time we proposed no general action against it'.[2] It is true that a couple of weeks later a conference of high officials at the Castle did decide to deport two 'organisers', Liam Mellowes and Ernest Blythe, but they agreed to take no action against T. J. Clarke, the veteran Fenian, 'unless some new offence could be proved'—and this though his tobacconist's shop had long been a rendezvous for the extreme men, whose plans for an insurrection, had the Castle but been able to penetrate them, were already well advanced.[3] As for Dillon, with whom Nathan had another review of the situation just at this time, he seemed to be more concerned about attacks on the party by their old enemy, the *Irish Independent*, and by *The Leader* than about Sinn Fein propaganda, but he was nevertheless well aware of the state of the country. His attitude, Nathan recorded in his methodical way, 'was one of astonishment at the change of feeling that had taken place in late years in the generations since the introduction of Mr. Gladstone's first Home Rule Bill'.[4]

By the end of March, however, Dillon was becoming more deeply worried. He had had, he wrote to Nathan, 'some very disquieting news from the country'.[5] He did not specify what it was, but he followed this letter a few days later with the comment that it did not seem to him that deporting organisers or suppressing Sinn Fein newspapers had done much good. 'To me it appears that the tension has seriously increased.'[6] Immediately on the heels of this came the appointment of J. H. M. Campbell as Irish Attorney-General, which Dillon denounced as 'a very great outrage'. 'In my opinion', he went on, 'it has created a most serious situation which may lead to very serious and deplorable consequences.'[7] In addition, as he told Nathan at yet another of their interviews, he was much disturbed by proceedings being taken against Irishmen who had come home to escape the possibility of military service in England, but on this, naturally enough, the Government had its own views, which he was unlikely to be able to change.[8]

Nathan, and those whose business it was to keep him fully informed, had, it is now abundantly clear, seriously miscalculated the situation. The Under-Secretary's letters to Birrell in the first three weeks of April 1916 were, if

---

[1] L. O. Broin, *Dublin Castle and the 1916 Rising*, chap. 15.
[2] Memorandum of interview with Lord Midleton and Lord Barrymore, 28 Feb. 1916 1916 (Nathan Papers, 467, ff. 78–9).
[3] Ibid., ff. 317–21, 17 Mar. 1916.
[4] Ibid., ff. 307–8, interview with John Dillon, 15 Mar. 1916.
[5] Dillon to Sir M. Nathan, 26 Mar. 1916 (Nathan Papers, 450–1, ff. 305–6).
[6] Dillon to Sir M. Nathan, 31 Mar. 1916 (ibid., ff. 309–14).
[7] Dillon to Sir M. Nathan, 13 Apr. 1916 (ibid., ff. 320–21).
[8] Memorandum of interview with John Dillon, 27 Mar. 1916 (Nathan Papers, 467, ff. 350–1).

not optimistic, at least reassuring and seemed to show that he had matters well in hand. Dillon was still worried, it was true, but he felt equal to pacifying him and, for the rest, 'things are going better for the moment'.[1] Even on 22 April, when he had information of an imminent landing of arms and ammunition in the south-west, as the prelude to a general rising timed for Easter eve, Nathan was still able to express doubts about its accuracy. By that time Sir Roger Casement had, in fact, landed near Tralee and had already been captured, while the arms ship, the *Aud*, had just been intercepted by the Navy and then scuttled by its crew. 'The Irish Volunteers', Nathan added, and must ever afterwards have regretted adding, 'are to have a "mobilization" and march out from Dublin to-morrow, but I see no indications of a rising.'[2] It may be said in Nathan's defence that Eoin MacNeill's frantic cancellation next morning of that Easter Sunday mobilisation, might well have seemed to indicate that whatever insurrection had been intended had collapsed. But MacNeill was only the tip of the iceberg and the principal charge against the Castle authorities remains—that they were remarkably ignorant of where power lay in the revolutionary movement and what the younger, fanatical leaders intended. Dillon, however, did not share the Under-Secretary's illusions, and was, wrote Nathan in the letter to Birrell just quoted, 'in a bad humour'. Well he might be. Even though he seems to have had nothing definite to go upon, he was as sensitive as always to the ebb and flow of feeling, however subterranean, and he knew his fellow countrymen well enough to spend that week-end in a state of extreme anxiety and alarm. On Easter Sunday, when, unknown to him, the die had been cast which was to change so much both in his life and in the history of Ireland, he wrote these prophetic words to Redmond:

> Dublin is full of most extraordinary rumours. And I have no doubt in my mind that the Clan men are planning some devilish business. What it is I cannot make out. It may not come off. But you must not be surprised if something very unpleasant and mischievous happens this week.[3]

Next day all the world knew what that was.

[1] Sir M. Nathan to A. Birrell, 4 and 13 Apr. 1916 (Nathan Papers, 466, p. 604–5, 680–1).

[2] Sir M. Nathan to A. Birrell, 22 Apr. 1916 (ibid., pp. 734–7). I may take the opportunity here of clarifying a somewhat ambiguous reference I made to this letter in my essay 'Dillon, Redmond and the Irish Home Rulers' in F. X. Martin (ed.) *Leaders and men of the Easter Rising*, p. 30. Nathan's letter to Birrell was not based on the cancelled mobilisation (which was not public knowledge until 23 April), but it did seem to be confirmed or justified by the cancellation. The Under-Secretary's letter was only part of a general miscalculation for which the British intelligence service must surely bear a large part of the blame.

[3] Gwynn, *Redmond*, p. 471.

13
1916

When Patrick Pearse and James Connolly led out their detachments of the Irish Volunteers and the Citizen Army at midday on Easter Monday to occupy strategic buildings and so launch the long-awaited insurrection, they took not only the Castle authorities, but most of Dublin, by surprise. The children of the Dillon family, despite their father's forebodings, were, like many others, out and about in various parts of the city, and when the firing started were only able to reach home by devious routes and after many adventures. The first intimation John Dillon himself had that a rising was in progress was at 12.30 on the afternoon, when his son Myles rushed in to tell him that the insurgents had entrenched themselves in St. Stephen's Green and were attacking the Castle. He had followed them for some time, but when the fighting began had very wisely come away.

Later that afternoon Dillon began a letter to his mother-in-law, Lady Mathew, to which he added day by day and which in the end became a miniature diary of the rising extending to over 100 pages of his writing-paper.[1] What chiefly strikes one in reading it now is the strange unreality of life as it presented itself to those who were caught up in events of which they did not know the origin or the progress and who, cut off absolutely from reliable news, could only clutch at the wild rumours circulating constantly through the city. North Great George's Street was only a few hundred yards away from the General Post Office, where Pearse and Connolly had set up their headquarters and outside which Pearse had proclaimed the republic. Very soon the G.P.O. and the whole area surrounding it became the centre of fierce fighting and heavy destruction. The Dillons' house, which was near the corner of North Great George's Street, was not hit, though it was in a very exposed position and bullets were flying about in all directions. The family were virtually beleaguered there until the fighting stopped at the end of the week and were only able to make occasional forays for food or to try to find out what was going on. The firing was so frequent and violent—Dillon's narrative speaks of 'fusillades' on almost every page—that ordinary sleep was impossible and days and nights merged into one unending nightmare. Indeed, so difficult was it to keep count of time that Dillon's habitual accuracy quite deserted

---

[1] Dillon to Lady Mathew, Monday, 25 (in error for 24) April, to Monday, 1 May, 1916, in the possession of Professor Myles Dillon.

him. He began his letter by dating it Monday, 25 April, instead of 24 April, and repeated the error each day until on Friday he managed to regain his chronological balance.

Penned into the house as they were, they saw little or nothing of the actual fighting, but they were astonished in the early days at the large numbers of people who passed up and down the street on their way to and from the ruined shops in O'Connell Street. 'All yesterday afternoon', wrote Dillon on the Tuesday, 'and again this morning, a steady stream of women, girls and young children have passed up this street, laden with loot—clothes, boots, boxes of sweets, etc. etc. It is horrible to see some well-dressed respectable girls laden with loot. Just now a woman passed with a baby's perambulator piled with boots.' This was an aspect of the rising Sean O'Casey was later to use with great effect in *The Plough and the Stars*, but O'Casey could not put on the stage what to Dillon seemed the strangest feature of this crowd—its silence. 'A constant flow of people', he noted later that day, '. . . going and coming without *the slightest appearance* of excitement, more than double as many people as one would see in these streets on any ordinary day, the only thing remarkable being their absolute silence. No one seems to speak. In the intervals between the outbursts of firing there is almost eerie silence. You could hear a pin drop. Then after a few scattered shots . . . a firmer fusilado [*sic*], then again silence, and occasional shrieks and shouts in the distance.'

From time to time messengers managed to get through to the house. Usually they were connected with the United Irish League and were looking for instructions, but the news they brought with them was confused and contradictory beyond all hope of disentanglement. Some said the Castle had been taken, others not; some said there was fierce fighting in Cork and Kerry, others that Meath and Galway were the main centres of rebellion; some said that London had been half destroyed by a Zeppelin raid, others—anticipating reality by only a few weeks—that there had been a fierce naval battle in the North Sea. And always and inevitably there were rumours of a German landing, though whether it was at Tralee or Belfast Lough no one seemed able to agree. By Wednesday, however, some more reliable information was at last beginning to get through—for example, that Jacob's biscuit factory had been the scene of fierce fighting (it had been one of the strongpoints seized by the insurgents), that there was a gunboat on the Liffey and that Liberty Hall (Connolly's old headquarters) had been destroyed. Yet the ordeal was far from over. On Thursday, Dillon wrote nothing at all in his record—it was, he noted next day, 'one of the worst days we had'. They were woken at 4.30 in the morning by fierce firing, amongst which Dillon could detect field-guns, and soon it was clear that a large part of O'Connell Street was in flames. Dillon himself, from the steps of his house, could see troops moving about with fixed bayonets and there was a report that the occupants of the G.P.O. had been called on to surrender before the building was shelled. Later that same afternoon (about 4.30 on Thursday, 27 April) the shelling of the Post Office began in earnest, one of the big guns being stationed at the Parnell monument, only a few yards from the Dillons' house.

It was on that day also that John Dillon heard more details of what was actually happening. His informant was a courageous Jesuit priest, Father Fahy from the neighbouring Belvedere College, who had been a good deal around the city during the week, among other things organising a dressing-station in Dorset Street. What he had to say is interesting evidence of the state of mind of both sides during those terrible days:

> He confirmed the story of priests having gone into the G.P.O., heard the confessions of all the garrison, found them full of enthusiasm and confidence quite convinced that they were in the right fighting for Ireland and ready to die for the cause. One dying man was anointed and said to the priest who anointed him that he was proud to die for Ireland.
>
> Father F. told me that when he first met the officers and soldiers coming into Dublin they were in a great state of extreme nervousness, under the impression that they were coming amongst a solidly hostile population, that they would be sniped from every house and would be attacked by hostile crowds on all sides. He, Father F., had assured them that they were under a wholly false impression, that they would find the great majority of the population friendly, and he said that the officers had now come to realise that in this respect he was quite right.

Meanwhile, the destruction continued and on Thursday night the fires in O'Connell Street and over towards Dominick Street (on the opposite side of O'Connell Street from North Great George's Street) were so fierce that Dillon did not let the children go to bed in case the wind changed and the flames spread in their direction. The next day, Friday, was nearly as bad, and when Dillon had to leave the house to go a few yards away to telephone to Nathan at the Castle, he had to run for it between bursts of rifle-fire coming directly up the street. The reason apparently was that snipers were stationed in some of the houses; that night there was a regular battle until they were dislodged.

Next day came the surrender of Pearse and the gradual dying down of the fighting in various parts of the city. Father Fahy, who called at the house again on Saturday morning to concert with Dillon measures for getting bread and other supplies to the people, some of whom were now almost starving, had further tales to tell of his adventures. One of these impressed Dillon sufficiently for him to write it out in full and it is worth reproducing here as an example of the kind of evidence which, perhaps unconsciously, was helping to shape his attitude to the rising and to drive a wedge between him and those of his parliamentary colleagues who had not had his experience of living through a rebellion. This, then, was the story the Jesuit told him:

> A young man had stopped him during his morning round, saying 'I want to shake hands with you, aren't we doing splendidly?' He then

explained that he had been at home to spend the night with his family and was on his way to relieve guard. Father Fahy remonstrated with him, using every strategy, and in rather cruel language said he regarded their conduct as murder, asked him was he married. To which the man replied that he had a wife and three young children. 'And you are leaving them to fight for a lost cause,' said Father Fahy, 'a cause in which you can do no good, but a vast deal of mischief.'

At this tears streamed down the face of the unhappy youth. But he was quite firm, said he must do his duty, that spiritually he was alright and ready to die, as he had been to the Sacraments and was doing no wrong. 'And what object can you hope to achieve?' said Father F. 'Some of us must die. But we shall save Ireland from conscription.' Father F. then pressed him to come into Berkeley Street Church and say three Hail Marys. But this he refused to [do] and went on his way.

Although from the middle of the week a curfew had been imposed, the virtual cessation of the fighting brought the crowds into the streets again and the Dillon boys passed from group to group gathering a fresh crop of rumours. One of the most persistent, repeated several times, was that the cease-fire had been brought about by the efforts of John Dillon—'God bless him, sure he's a grand man, he went down to the G.P.O. and arranged for peace'. It was with these words that Dillon chose to end the narrative of the strangest week of his life. Perhaps he recorded this rumour ironically, but it had a far greater significance than even he could have realised. The fact was that a great many simple and bewildered people *were* looking to him for leadership and Ireland, in the grip of military rule after the collapse of the insurrection, was never more in need of that leadership.

(ii)

The outbreak on Easter Monday had found the leaders of the parliamentary party scattered far and wide. Redmond and O'Connor were in London, Devlin was in Belfast (where he was marooned for several days) and only Dillon was on the spot in Dublin. For nearly forty-eight hours no word whatever reached Redmond of what had happened to his principal colleague. Then, on the night of Tuesday, 25 April, by the government wire from the Viceregal Lodge, came a message from Redmond's secretary, Hanna, that Dillon considered it 'vitally important' that Redmond should remain where he was in London.[1] And there he stayed, in an agony of suspense, waiting desperately for news. To add to his difficulties, Parliament was reassembling and he had to make a statement of the Irish party's attitude. His statement was probably typical enough of middle-class conservative nationalism at that time—'the overwhelming mass of the Irish people', he said, regarded the rising, as he did, 'with a feeling of detestation and horror'.[2]

[1] Gwynn, *Redmond*, p. 472.
[2] Hansard, H.C. Debates, 5th series, vol. 81, col. 2512; Gwynn, *Redmond*, p. 474.

But while this was an obvious and, from Redmond's point of view, natural reaction to a development which seemed to threaten his whole life's work, the situation rapidly became too complicated for sweeping generalisations of this kind. How complicated Dillon's reports from Dublin were beginning to reveal. He wrote his first letter on 26 April describing the fierceness of the fighting and entrusted it to Miss Annie O'Brien, one of the secretaries at the United Irish League headquarters. She volunteered to try to take it across to London, but was not able to leave Dublin before the end of the week.[1] By then, on 30 April, Dillon had written a second letter which was concerned almost entirely with the line to be followed by the party in the days that lay ahead. Already, it is clear, he had begun to form opinions which the events of the next few weeks were to intensify and which ultimately were to divide him from some of his old colleagues perhaps as deeply as he had ever been. It was important, he wrote, for Redmond to be in London mainly because if he were in Dublin he might be held responsible for all the Castle and the military authorities were doing, but, of course, would have no influence over their decisions. Dillon himself was determined not to make any public statement until he had fuller knowledge. But then he went on to forecast with almost uncanny prescience what he feared might happen:

> You should urge strongly on the government the *extreme* unwisdom of any wholesale shootings of prisoners. The wisest course is to execute *no one* for the present. This is *the most urgent* matter for the moment. If there were shootings of prisoners on a large scale the effect on public opinion might be disastrous in the extreme.
> *So far* feeling of the population in Dublin is *against* the Sinn Feiners. But a reaction might very easily be created . . .
> . . . Do not fail to urge the government not to *execute any* of the prisoners.
> I have no doubt if any of the well-known leaders are taken alive they will be shot. But, except the leaders, there should be no court-martial executions.[2]

The next day Redmond, having seen Asquith, reported to Dillon that he had got (or so he thought) the Prime Minister's agreement that 'while the recognized ringleaders who may be captured alive must be dealt with with adequate severity, the greatest possible leniency should be shown to the rank and file'. Of these, he added, between two and three thousand had already been captured and were on their way to internment in England. As to executions, he had been assured both by the Prime Minister and Lord French (C.-in-C. in Ireland) that so far there had been none.[3]

But, although the rising as a military threat had been stamped out a week after it had started, its aftermath involved not only the problem of

[1] Dillon to Redmond, 26 Apr. 1916 (R.P.).
[2] Dillon to Redmond, 30 Apr. 1916 (R.P.); Gwynn, *Redmond*, pp. 474–5.
[3] Gwynn, *Redmond*, pp. 475–6; Jenkins, *Asquith*, pp. 395–6.

punishment but also the problem of government. For the moment, indeed, martial law reigned supreme, but clearly there was something very wrong with an administration which had allowed such a situation to develop. An obvious victim was the Chief Secretary, Augustine Birrell, who had tried to resign several times already. Now, even before the rising was over, he bombarded the Prime Minister with letters of resignation and Asquith, much moved, had to let him go.[1] The problem of who to put in his place was so vexatious that Asquith left the office vacant for the next few months while first he, and then Lloyd George, discharged some of the political responsibilities that would normally have been the Chief Secretary's function. Nathan went with Birrell, but though the Viceroy, Lord Wimborne, was triumphantly reinstated, these administrative comings and goings were of only marginal importance, since power rested, and for a considerable period was likely to rest, with the military authorities. Even Dillon, though like his colleagues ready to speculate about Birrell's successor, felt that in the immediate future strong government was essential. Curiously, in view of what was shortly to happen, he suggested in a letter of 2 May to Redmond that if Wimborne were to be replaced it should be by a soldier, either Lord French, or else General Maxwell, who had been directly responsible for the suppression of the rising and who, though Dillon was not to know this, was about to authorise the execution, after court martial, of Pearse, Tom Clarke and Thomas MacDonagh. Later that day, however, he had an interview with Maxwell which, though not unfriendly, was disquieting. The general denied that anyone had been shot without trial, but, as Dillon reported to Redmond, 'I gathered that he contemplated considerable further executions'. Maxwell was preparing to disarm the city and, he said to Dillon, 'After I have finished with Dublin I propose to deal with the country.' Perhaps it was not surprising in view of this that though Dillon still clung for a little longer to the belief that 'some strong military man' should be Lord Lieutenant, his considered choice was now French, not Maxwell.[2]

The next day—the very day on which Pearse, Clarke and MacDonagh died before a firing-squad—Redmond saw Asquith and urged him to stop the executions. 'He said some few were necessary,' noted Redmond, 'but they would be very few. I protested.' In the course of that day (3 May) Redmond issued his first considered statement to the Press about the events of the past ten days. It was a strong denunciation of 'this insane movement', but further than that, it was a determined attempt to identify the movement as in essence a German plot. Strangely inadequate as this explanation may now seem, it reflects not only a view that was natural enough in wartime, but also, and more importantly, Redmond's own signal failure to understand the motive force behind the insurrection. It was this failure more than anything else which marked the gulf between him and Dillon. Redmond, to be fair, seems to have sensed the danger and was acutely anxious to have his

[1] Gwynn, *Redmond*, pp. 475–6; Jenkins *Asquith*, pp. 395–6.
[2] Dillon to Redmond, two letters, 2 May 1916 (R.P.); Gwynn, *Redmond*, pp. 476–9.

old colleague by his side, writing yet again (on 3 May) to beg him to come over to London. Meanwhile, he renewed his pressure on Asquith to halt the executions, writing to him on the evening of 3 May and on 4 May—on the latter occasion going so far as to say that if any more took place, 'I would feel bound to denounce them, and probably retire'.[1]

For the time being, however, Redmond was left to fight his battle alone. Dillon could not or would not leave Dublin. He was naturally reluctant to be separated from his children while the city was still so disturbed, but apart from that weighty reasons of policy held him there. For one thing, he was the only senior and responsible member of the party in Dublin and he was rapidly becoming the main hope of hundreds of families desperate for news of husbands and sons and brothers who had disappeared without trace. In the second place, he still did have some links with authority and although it was becoming obvious that the military now had the bit between their teeth, Dillon represented the sole means, however slight, of exercising some restraining influence upon them. Indeed, one of Sir Matthew Nathan's last official duties was to impress upon General Maxwell that it was important that 'I should be able to send him [Dillon] a reassuring note from you as to the general lines on which the courts martial are working, and that I should be able to tell him that the particular cases which he has brought to notice will be inquired into'.[2] In addition to this essential public service, Dillon also had on his hands the resuscitation of the party newspaper. The *Freeman's Journal* had been one of the earliest casualties in the fighting, since its offices were near the G.P.O. and had been totally destroyed. This was especially serious because it left the metropolitan Press in the hands of the Unionist *Irish Times*, which was thirsting for blood, and the *Irish Independent*, as hostile to the rising as the *Irish Times*, and the bitter enemy of the parliamentary party into the bargain. For all these reasons, as Dillon explained in a letter to Redmond written late at night on 3 May, it was impossible for him to leave Dublin:

> I do not know the cause of this fresh urgent call from you. But I guess it may be the break-up of the government. If that be the cause, I have expected that for some time and shall not be a bit sorry when it comes.
>
> I feel so strongly as to the situation here that I must again impress on you my intense conviction as to the fatal result of any compromising policy on the part of the Irish party. Either we must have a Home Rule executive in Ireland, which will act on our advice, or we must go into active opposition.
>
> *Campbell* [the Unionist Attorney-General] *must go*, as a mark and sign that we are to be masters; failing that, we must be free to attack the government in and out of the House and to persistently criticise its policy.
>
> An argument which it seems to me could be used with effect is that

[1] Gwynn, *Redmond*, pp. 481–3.
[2] Sir M. Nathan to General Sir John Maxwell, 4 May 1916 (Nathan Papers, 466, p. 774).

if Birrell disappears and Campbell remains it will represent to the people here the triumph of the Ulster party and the coercion policy.

This is striking evidence of how quickly Dillon had grasped what was to be the key political problem of the next few months—how to prevent the reaction in favour of the revolutionaries from becoming also a reaction against the parliamentarians. The only safe role for the party, he had already concluded, was to be as intransigent as it was possible for them to be within the constitutional framework. Redmond, replying next day (4 May), tried to reassure him that he had already indicated in Parliament that the party's unquestioning support of the Government was at an end. But his next sentences showed how far he, and indeed the Prime Minister also, were out of touch with what was happening in Dublin. 'I am sure', he wrote, 'the rumours about anyone being shot without trial are untrue. Asquith solemnly assured me that no one had been shot, except the three men named yesterday, and he told me that, as soon as he read of these executions, he had sent word to the War Office that it should go slow. He intends that there shall be practically no more executions, although he did not pledge himself that there might not be one or two more in Ireland . . .'[1]

For Dillon, who knew how much grimmer the situation really was (four more prisoners were shot on 4 May, including Pearse's brother), this was not good enough. He wrote immediately to Redmond that same day explaining that it would be madness for him to leave Dublin for some days yet:

It is quite clear that the military officers in charge here do not allow the P.M. to know what is going on. This morning an Irish officer who is working on the courts-martial called here to tell me what is going on. Some young fellows *have* been shot, either without trial or after court-martial. The military tribunals have by threats of instant execution forced a great many to give up names of those implicated.

I am sure that there are many more dead and wounded lying about the city in private houses and in the streets and lanes. *Many* corpses have lain in houses and in streets for five days unburied. The killing of women and children does not by any means involve necessary blame to the soldiers, because the conduct of the people was most reckless. They persisted in walking about the streets while bullets were flying and a good many were hit while engaged in looting . . .

I have heard nothing from Devlin yet. He is in Belfast. I expect he may be here in the morning. The trains from Belfast do not yet come beyond Drogheda.

The news from Munster and Connaught, so far as it has reached me, is very satisfactory. Lundon[2] will give you full information about Limerick and Tipperary.

I had the heads of the *Freeman* staff here for two hours to-day. The result of our deliberations was that for a variety of reasons it will not be possible to bring out the *Freeman* to-morrow. We hope it may

---

[1] For these exchanges, see Gwynn, *Redmond*, pp. 486–7.
[2] Thomas Lundon, a member of the Irish parliamentary party.

be possible to publish it on Thursday morning. The difficulties appear to be great. I do not know whether the *Independent* will appear to-morrow. That office is intact, but the gas supply is cut off and may not be available for a day or two. And it seems they cannot print without gas. The *Irish Times* has a gas supply of its own. It has appeared yesterday and to-day. Its leaders are most bloodthirsty and wicked, and they ought to be dealt with.

My idea is that it will be best for me to remain here, watch developments and keep you fully informed of my views.

I do not know whether Devlin and I will find ourselves in agreement, but after we have discussed the situation I shall urge him to cross immediately . . .[1]

Next day Devlin duly arrived and Dillon hastened to report to Redmond that they seemed to be agreed on all points. Devlin did not attach so much importance to the removal of Campbell, but Dillon still remained adamant that it must be one of the conditions without which they could not continue to support the Government. Among the matters they had discussed was a suggestion Redmond had passed on to Dillon in his letter of 3 May. Asquith had read to him a letter he had received from Bonar Law in which the latter had said that he thought Carson would not object to the extension of the Volunteer Act to Ireland—this would mean in effect disarmament of the Ulster Volunteers as well as of the insurgents in the south. Redmond believed this would effectively dispose of the 'Carson Volunteers' as a revolutionary force in the future and was evidently prepared, as part of the price for this, to support a general disarmament in Ireland.[2] Devlin, wrote Dillon, accepted this proposal 'instantly', but:

> . . . I am not at all so clear as he is. I dislike it, and fear that a good deal of capital will be made against you and the party for agreeing to it. I do not believe that the Nationalists could ever be got to believe that the Ulster men had *really* surrendered *their* arms. Moreover I very much dislike the idea that the national leaders should make themselves responsible for a proposal to disarm the people. If the proposal is considered at all it should only be a temporary arrangement, and on the receipt of a binding pledge that no attempt will be made to impose conscription on Ireland. Unless this understanding is given you may take me as strongly opposed to the disarmament proposal. Any attempt to impose conscription now would justify the Sinn Feiners in the eyes of the people of Ireland and have utterly disastrous effects.
>
> I think it would be well for you to see Bonar Law at the earliest possible moment, and find out where he stands on: (1) the question of conscription; (2) the disarmament question; (3) the Irish situation in general.
>
> Ask him to speak frankly to you and tell him frankly our position, warning him that the situation here is terribly critical, and that if

[1] Dillon to Redmond, 4 May 1916 (R.P.).
[2] Gwynn, *Redmond*, p. 483.

some arrangement cannot be arrived at the results may be disastrous in the highest degree.[1]

This letter suggests that Dillon's attitude was hardening very fast. Not only was he, almost instinctively, seeking to use the Government's difficulties as a means of safeguarding the country against conscription—or in other words trying to make political capital out of the disaster—but, knowing what he did of the state of feeling in Ireland, he was becoming more and more convinced that at all costs the parliamentary party must avoid being labelled 'anti-national'. It was almost as if, even at this early stage in the crisis, he had intuitively recognised that Irish politics in the future was going to reduce itself to a straight competition between the constitutionalists and the physical force men, and this although in most people's eyes physical force must have seemed utterly discredited by the collapse of the rising. But as Dillon, virtually alone among the parliamentarians, had already understood, physical force was not dead but stunned, and needed very little to wake it into fresh life. Accordingly, when on 6 May he sent over to Redmond a draft resolution which he wanted the party to adopt at its forthcoming meeting, the burden of it was a protest against the executions. It did, indeed, condemn the rising as 'wicked, reckless and without justification', and it affirmed that the overwhelming majority of the Irish people were opposed to it. 'But', it went on, 'now that the insurrection has been completely put down, and order restored, we feel bound to protest in the most solemn manner against the large number of military executions of men, many of whom were not prominent leaders of the insurrection. And we solemnly warn the government that very serious mischief has been done by the excessive severities which have followed the suppression of the insurrection, and that any further military executions will have the most far-reaching and disastrous effects on the future peace and loyalty of Ireland.'[2]

While these exchanges were taking place all sorts of rumours were circulating in Ireland about military excesses in and out of barracks. Many no doubt were greatly exaggerated, but not all—and one in particular was too well authenticated to admit of any uncertainty. This was the cold-blooded shooting without trial of three prisoners at Portobello barracks on 26 April. One of the prisoners was a well-known and much-loved figure in Dublin, the journalist, Francis Sheehy-Skeffington. He was a dedicated pacifist and of all men the least likely to have been involved in violence. He was arrested on Tuesday, 25 April, returning home after having spent the day helping the wounded and trying to restrain his fellow citizens from looting. That night he was brought as a hostage on a raiding-party and witnessed the brutal murder of an unarmed youth. Next morning, with two other journalists, he was taken out and shot on the orders of the officer who had led the raid, Captain Bowen Colthurst, himself an Irishman. Colthurst

---

[1] Dillon to Redmond, 5 May 1916; the closing paragraphs of this letter are in Gwynn, *Redmond*, p. 487.

[2] Gwynn, *Redmond*, p. 488.

was subsequently court-martialled and an inquiry was held. Neither was conducted in a very satisfactory manner and Colthurst was found 'guilty but insane'. Not surprisingly, Dublin opinion, which was horrified by this incident almost more than by any other, registered the guilt, but ignored the insanity.[1]

And at this point, just when Dillon was about to cross to London came news that yet more executions were about to take place. On 7 May he wrote to Redmond in fury and despair:

> Father Aloysius of the Capuchins called this afternoon to say that he had been summoned by the police to attend at Kilmainham Barracks to-morrow morning at 3 o'clock, and that of course meant more executions, and begged me to do what I could. He told me that the feeling among the working-classes in the city is becoming extremely bitter over these executions and that this feeling is strong even amongst those who had no sympathy whatever with the Sinn Feiners, or with the rising. Rumours are circulating and are widely believed that a large number have been shot without trial.

Dillon, doing his best to restrain the authorities, went first to the Castle and then to the Viceregal Lodge, where he saw Wimborne. Wimborne was no help. He had, he said, no authority, but, Dillon's letter continued, he had told him that two men were to be executed next morning—'Kent, and another whose name I forget'. 'Connolly', he wrote, 'can't yet be tried, his wound disables him from defending himself. The government think he ought to be executed. There are two or three others who murdered policemen, officers etc. I said I was not concerned personally to save Connolly or Kent—still less for the men who had committed cowardly murder, but that I could not find words to express sufficiently strongly my conviction that the policy of dribbling executions, going on for days was fatal and that the tide of exasperation was steadily rising.' Dillon urged upon Wimborne that 'whatever was the ultimate decision of the government as to Connolly, Kent, and those accused of cold-blooded murder, there ought to be no more executions for the present, and a final decision ought to be put off till Connolly could be tried'. The most he got from Wimborne in reply to this passionate protest was that he was dining with General Maxwell that night and would talk the whole thing over with him.[2]

Next morning there were not two executions but four—Kent (Eamonn Ceannt), who had signed the proclamation of independence, and three others—Michael Mallin, Con Colbert and Sean Heuston—who had all figured prominently in the fighting. Dillon, who had purposely postponed his departure for fear of precisely this development, wrote furiously once

---

[1] T. M. Healy, *Letters and leaders*, ii. 562–3; R. McHugh, 'Thomas Kettle and Francis Sheehy-Skeffington', in C. Cruise O'Brien (ed.), *The shaping of modern Ireland* (London, 1960), pp. 137–8. I am grateful also to my friend Owen Sheehy-Skeffington, the murdered man's son, who has allowed me to see a memoir he has written on this subject. See also my preface to F. Sheehy-Skeffington, *Michael Davitt* (London, new ed., 1967).

[2] Dillon to Redmond, 7 May 1916 (R.P.).

more to Redmond. 'This is really infamous and intolerable after what the
P.M. has been saying to you.' When the party did meet, he insisted,
Redmond must secure the passing of a strong resolution against the executions and if necessary move the adjournment of the House. As for the other
issue of general disarmament, he was now more than ever sceptical and felt
it should only be considered if the initiative came from Carson.[1]

(iii)

At last, however, a lull seemed to be descending in Ireland. On 9 May
Asquith assured Redmond that the previous day he had sent a strong telegram to Maxwell and that he hoped the executions—unless in some quite
exceptional case—would cease.[2] The reservation was to be significant—
Thomas Kent, no relation of the Kent just executed, was shot in Cork
that very day and Connolly still lay seriously wounded in prison, his life
hanging by a thread. Nevertheless, Dillon could no longer delay in Dublin
and on the 10th he arrived in London in time for the party meeting. A
resolution was passed, less strong than the one he had suggested, but still
demanding a sweeping inquiry into the causes of the insurrection. Asquith
peremptorily rejected that demand, though he promised there would be an
investigation of the circumstances leading to the rising, and of the responsibility incurred by the civil and military authorities in Ireland.[3] Such was the
position when on 11 May Parliament at last turned to debate the Irish
crisis. The situation was extremely tense and when Dillon rose to speak the
atmosphere was already highly charged. On the Irish side was mounting
resentment at the Government's apparent inability to control the military
authorities, combined with the growing fear that the policy of simple
repression now being followed out remorselessly in Ireland would bring
about such a *bouleversement* of Irish opinion that the executed men would
become martyrs and that there would be an end to the constitutional demand for Home Rule. But on the English side the position was hardly less
critical. This was, after all, one of the crucial phases of the war. A great
battle—the Somme—was about to begin and the prevailing attitude towards
the rising was one of outrage against a treacherous stab in the back which
had led to British troops being killed and which many people believed (as Redmond himself had publicly declared) to have been engineered by Germany.

Dillon's purpose was to move this resolution: 'That, in the interest of
peace and good government in Ireland, it is vitally important that the
Government should make immediately a full statement of their intentions as
to the continuance of executions in that country carried out as a result of
secret military trials, and as to the continuance of martial law, military
rule, and the searches and wholesale arrests now going on in various districts of the country.' He began by asserting that the Prime Minister was
being kept in the dark by the military authorities as to the true number of

[1] Dillon to Redmond, 8 May 1916 (R.P.).   [2] Gwynn, *Redmond*, p. 488.
[3] Ibid., pp. 488–9.

executions and he declared—'the primary object of my motion is to put an absolute stop to these executions. You are letting loose a river of blood and make no mistake about it, between two races who, after three hundred years of hatred and strife, we had nearly succeeded in bringing together'. He then referred to a speech Lord Midleton (a leading Southern Irish Unionist) had recently made in the House of Lords pointing out that this was the first Irish rebellion in which the Government had had a majority of Irishmen on their side:

Is that nothing . . . ? It is the fruit of our life-work. We have risked our lives a hundred times to bring about this result. We are held up to odium as traitors by the men who made this rebellion, and our lives have been in danger a hundred times during the last thirty years because we have endeavoured to reconcile the two things and you are washing out our whole life work in a sea of blood.

Ireland at that moment, he went on, was virtually ruled from the Kildare Street Club (the traditional meeting-place of Irish landlords and therefore always an object of Dillon's special detestation) and the Unionists were openly demanding the extension of martial law. Meanwhile, Dublin itself was seething with rumours about the secret executions and about what was going on in the military barracks. Trying desperately to get through to the House what the situation in the city was really like, he recalled an incident, just one incident from the many of the past two weeks, but as it led to an outburst which reverberated for years to come, it is worth giving his account of it in full:

I recall [he said] the case of a boy of 14 who was brought in as a prisoner and the officer looked at him. 'What on earth am I going to do with you'? The boy said to him: 'Shoot me, for I have killed three of your soldiers.' That may horrify you, but I declare most solemnly, and I am not ashamed to say it in the House of Commons, that I am proud of these men. They were foolish; they were misled. (Hon. Members: 'Shame.')

Major Newman: Now you have shown your hand. Mr. Dillon: Did I ever fail to show my hand in the House of Commons or conceal anything? I say I am proud of their courage and if you were not so dense or stupid, as some of you English people are, you could have had these men fighting for you, and they are men worth having. (Hon. Members: 'You stopped them.') That is an infamous falsehood. I and the men who sit around me have been doing our best to bring these men into the ranks of the army.

Passion was now running high, but the House fell silent when Dillon turned to describe in detail the Sheehy-Skeffington case and when he read out the short, poignant statement written for him by the murdered man's widow. Nothing but a public inquiry would satisfy Irish opinion in this matter, he said. As to the executions in general, after all the Irish party had done to keep not only the Irish themselves, but the Irish-Americans also, loyal to the Allied cause, they were entitled to have been consulted 'before this bloody course of executions was entered upon in Ireland'. Not, he added bitterly, that there was much chance of this, since they had been consistently flouted since the formation of the Coalition. However, he appealed once more to the Prime Minister to stop the executions. He was not defending murderers, he said—they should be brought to trial, *open* trial:

> But it is not murderers who are being executed; it is insurgents who have fought a clean fight, a brave fight, however misguided, and it would have been a damned good thing for you if your soldiers were able to put up as good a fight as did these men in Dublin—three thousand men against twenty thousand with machine-guns and artillery. (An Hon. Member: 'Evidently you wish they had succeeded.') That is an infamous falsehood. Who is it said that? It is an abominable falsehood. I say that these men, misguided as they were, have been our bitterest enemies. They have held us up to public odium as traitors to our country because we have supported you at this moment and have stood by you in this great war, and the least we are entitled to is this, that in this great effort we have made at considerable risk . . . to bring the masses of the Irish people into harmony with you, in this great effort at conciliation, I say we are entitled to every assistance from the members of this House and from the government.[1]

When Dillon sat down he had succeeded in outraging many English Members and in shocking some at least of his own colleagues, including his closest friend in the party, T. P. O'Connor. His speech had been vibrant with passion throughout and he himself in after years admitted that the tone of it had been very bitter. This bitterness, this passion, need to be explained, because from this moment onwards they set him apart from the general body of constitutional Nationalists. The fact that he had spent the last two weeks virtually imprisoned in the inferno of Dublin undoubtedly affected his attitude—alone in the House he had first-hand experience of what was happening in that city. He knew of the destruction, he knew of the exultation of the Unionists, he knew of the swift courts-martial and of the dangers of a repetition of the Sheehy-Skeffington incident—above all, he knew of the powerlessness of the civil arm in the face of the military government. No wonder, therefore, that he came to the House, seething with indignation, and that he was so easily provoked into extreme language.

But that is not the whole explanation. It may not have occurred to many of his hearers, but they were listening to a man who in his fiery youth had been very close to the Fenian tradition and who, in the struggles of the land war, had lived much on the frontiers of the law and sometimes beyond them. Eventually, as we know, he had made his choice and committed himself heart and soul to the constitutional movement. Temperamentally,

[1] Hansard, H.C. Debates, 5th series, vol. 82, cols. 935–51.

however, he was of a kind to feel an instinctive sympathy for men who had taken their lives in their hands and gone into the streets to add yet one more chapter to the history of insurgent Ireland. Logically, rationally, he believed they were wrong; intuitively, he could not bring himself to condemn them utterly. Yet, at the same time, as an experienced politician he had to recognise the mortal danger in which the parliamentarians were being placed by the Government's policy of blind repression. And when, on top of that, the fatuous interventions of English M.P.s showed all too clearly that even after thirty years of constitutional agitation some of them were still unable, or professed themselves to be unable, to distinguish the moderate from the physical force movement, it is not surprising that his fury broke all bounds.

Even so—shocking as the outburst appeared to so many of his hearers— it is arguable that it was largely responsible for securing for the parliamentary party the short time for manoeuvre that still was to be left to it. In his private correspondence for the summer of 1916 are many letters from constitutional Nationalists up and down the country, thanking him for having spoken as he did. Even the chairman of the *Freeman's Journal* company, who was at that very moment taking the decision to resign because of political differences with Dillon, wrote to him that he thought the speech correctly interpreted the views of 'the great majority of Irish Nationalists', and from America came a well-informed opinion (that of Shane Leslie) that Dillon was the only member of the party who could last ten minutes on an Irish-American platform.[1] A few months later Leslie, who was trying to launch a pro-Irish paper in the U.S.A., wrote that after the executions they had been about to give it up. 'Then came your speech which, however useful to your enemies in England, gave the Irish party and the non-German Irish here a new breathing-time.'[2]

(iv)

On the short view, of course, the speech seemed to have had little effect, for, as if by way of ironic comment, further executions took place next day, including that of Connolly, who only four days earlier had been pronounced too seriously wounded to be tried. Now, still so ill that he could not stand, he was taken out seated on a chair and then shot—an incident of heedless brutality which added fresh fuel to the indignation already raging in the city. However, as it turned out, these were the last of the Dublin executions and Asquith himself was sufficiently roused by the crisis to cross to Ireland on the night of 11 May. It may be true, as his latest biographer has said, that he went over because he could not find a suitable person to send as Chief Secretary, but his visit—apart from enabling him to cut through

[1] Walter Nugent to Dillon, 15 May 1916, and Shane Leslie to Dillon, 16 June 1916 (D.P.); for a typical example of the sort of letter Dillon's speech evoked from his admirers, see J. T. Donovan to Dillon, 19 May 1916 (D.P.).
[2] Shane Leslie to Dillon, 15 Sept. 1916.

military red-tape and release a number of wrongfully arrested prisoners
(whose names were supplied to him by Dillon)[1]—helped to bring home
to him the urgent necessity of grappling once more with the political aspect
of the Irish problem, which indeed he had promised to do when announcing
his departure for Dublin.[2] Since, however, he had coupled that promise with
a request to all parties to refrain from discussing the Irish question or
doing anything to increase the Government's difficulties, Redmond awaited
his return with impatience. So long as he was absent the Irish party were
in effect condemned to silence whatever happened in Dublin. And from
Dublin, where Dillon had returned to work for the release of prisoners,
the news was grim:

> It really would not be possible (he wrote to Redmond on May 17) to
> exaggerate the desperate character of the situation here. The execu-
> tions, house-searching throughout the country, wholesale arrests . . .
> *savage* treatment of prisoners, including a very considerable number
> of those who had no more sympathy with Sinn Fein than you have,
> have exasperated feeling to a terrible extent. I have not the slightest
> faith in Asquith's inquiry which appears so far to have been strictly
> [? limited] to the military and a mere circle of officials, Sir H. Robin-
> son, Horace Plunkett, etc. etc.[3] The city is full of the most horrible
> rumours as to wholesale murders in the various barracks, and in the
> houses, and altho' I have no doubt the rumours current are grossly
> exaggerated, I very much fear that there is a very considerable founda-
> tion for them. The distress is terrible and is very much aggravated by
> the dismissal of employees of all sorts who are suspected of Nationalist
> demands [*sic*].[4]

On 18 May, when Asquith returned to London, Redmond wrote to
him asking for an early interview, at the same time impressing upon Dillon
that they must do nothing which might exasperate opinion either in England
or Ireland, but that on the contrary they ought 'to do all that we can to
assuage the bitterness of the moment, and see whether it is possible to bring
about some settlement or other. If this is impossible, I have very grave
doubts as to the future of the Irish party'. 'I quite admit', he added, 'that
a policy of merely marking time may be impossible. On the other hand,
to fall back on a policy of open aggression and exasperation seems to me
a policy of despair, and certain to destroy any hopes for Ireland for,
perhaps, a generation.'[5]

This argument was reinforced by a letter from T. P. O'Connor written
the same day and conveying the results of a conversation he had had with

---

[1] On 14 May Dillon wrote out for the Prime Minister in his own hand a twenty-five-
page account of some of the worst incidents (including the Sheehy-Skeffington case) and
Asquith noted on it that he wished these to be investigated at once and the reports sent
to him (Asquith Papers, box 43, ff. 57–82).

[2] Gwynn, *Redmond*, p. 493; Jenkins, *Asquith*, pp. 397–9.

[3] This was not quite fair. Asquith did visit a number of the prisoners and was very
impressed by them (Jenkins, *Asquith*, p. 398).

[4] Dillon to Redmond, 17 May 1916 (D.P.).

[5] Redmond to Dillon, 18 May 1916 (D.P.).

both Redmond and Devlin. O'Connor himself was emphatic that this was 'the golden moment' for a final settlement:

Assuming we let the occasion pass; first, that we mark time. That we all three agree is fatal. Secondly, that we enter into actual criticism of the government. That appears to me to be a hopeless policy, because it must mean that we embarrass the government in the prosecution of a great war, and that thereby we [lose] all we have gained by our attitude towards the war, and confirm the opinion already well started by the Sinn Feiners, that Ireland is irreconcilably hostile. Redmond, Devlin, and many of the rank and file to whom I have talked . . . are of opinion that without reaching an arrangement now the party is dead, and that Ireland will relapse into a party consisting partly of men with Sinn Fein tendencies and partly of a new brass band,[1] with semi-revolutionary tendencies outside the party. This is a prospect none of us can contemplate without horror and despair.

The failure of a settlement, he urged, might mean the estrangement of America, the election of a pro-German Congress in the November elections and even the possible loss of the war. This, no doubt, was exaggerated, but there was no mistaking O'Connor's zeal for a peaceful solution, and a man with his contacts could not be ignored. He had, he disclosed later in the letter, already been in touch with Lloyd George, who was sympathetic, but so far not directly involved in the problems of Ireland. This, said O'Connor, was partly because he was tired, partly because he was absorbed by the Ministry of Munitions and partly because he was chafing impotently under Asquith's inactivity. But whoever made a peace move, T.P. was imperative that the move should be made. And he added one last ominous note calculated to touch Dillon very closely:

Redmond is very depressed. This is partly due to his son going to the front, but of course largely to the political situation. He seems to me tired out and sick of the whole position and has again and again referred to the possibility of his retiring from politics. This of course is one of the very serious aspects of the situation which is present to my mind.[2]

Next day he renewed his pressure on Dillon to return to London. The news reaching him suggested that various Tory leaders—he mentioned Bonar Law, Balfour and Walter Long—were anxious for a settlement. Redmond, moreover, had just seen Lloyd George and asked him to intervene. Lloyd George had said he could not do so while the matter was still in Asquith's hands, but he had added: 'If I am allowed to make some arrangement about Ulster I can promise to get you Home Rule for all the rest of Ireland.'[3]

---

[1] For the historical significance of the 'brass-band' see p. 221, *n* 2.
[2] T. P. O'Connor to Dillon, 18 May 1916 (D.P.).
[3] T. P. O'Connor to Dillon, 19 May 1916 (D.P.).

Dillon's reaction to this was entirely characteristic. Feeling as he did that the only safe course for the party was to resume open and active opposition in the House of Commons, he was filled with doubt and alarm at the prospect of yet more negotiations and would admit no arguments in their favour. He could unburden himself more freely to O'Connor than to anyone else, and to him, on 20 May, he replied: 'I differ *profoundly* from Redmond's action [in approaching Lloyd George] and am afraid that it will lead to disaster.' He would much prefer, he said, not to be present at whatever discussions Redmond and Asquith might have, 'as I am almost certain I should feel compelled to dissent and object'.[1] Nevertheless, the pressure on him was very great and go he did in the end, only to have, on 27 May, a stormy meeting with O'Connor and Lloyd George, when apparently he was so rude to his old friend that he had to write that evening to apologise. 'The truth is', he admitted, 'I am in a frame of mind wholly unfitted for conference or negotiations.' 'My own impression would have been', he added disarmingly, 'that I was *much* more rude to L.G. than to you.'[2]

Fortunately, perhaps, others had calmer nerves and less irritable temperaments. Asquith and Redmond went steadily on with their efforts to lay the basis for an agreement and on 25 May 1916 Asquith was able to announce to the Commons that Lloyd George had agreed to undertake negotiations to bring about a permanent settlement. Meanwhile, the Prime Minister renewed his plea that all those concerned should refrain from provocative language while Lloyd George was making his attempt. But since this self-denying silence was *not* accompanied by the end of military rule in Ireland, the Irish party were put in an extremely difficult position. If the negotiations went well, of course there would be no trouble. But if they failed, after having been dragged out for weeks or even months, then they would be in the dire situation of having allowed valuable time to be frittered away without having anything to offer their unhappy country. Despite this, however, and although he recognised the obvious dangers ahead, Redmond accepted this crucial limitation of his freedom of action and staked everything on the success of the negotiations. In doing so he went nearer than perhaps even he knew to a split with Dillon. The latter, in conversation with C. P. Scott a few days earlier, had bitterly lamented Redmond's 'complaisance', saying the leader had lost most of his influence in Ireland. He himself, Dillon had added, might be compelled ('deeply as he should regret it') to break with Redmond unless he took a stronger stand. And on 25 May, meeting Dillon in the House immediately after Asquith's announcement, Scott noted that he 'never saw a man look so black with suppressed passion'.[3]

[1] Dillon to T. P. O'Connor, 20 May 1916 (D.P.).

[2] Dillon to T. P. O'Connor, 27 May 1916 (D.P.).

[3] C. P. Scott, 'Memoranda of interviews', 22–26 May [19]16 (C. P. Scott Papers, B.M. Add. MS. 5093, ff. 10–22); Gwynn, *Redmond*, pp. 499–500. Dillon's temper can scarcely have been improved by the news, which reached him a few days later, that Eoin MacNeill, the Volunteer leader, had been visited after his arrest by Major Price

They were from the start very peculiar negotiations. Although in essence they took up the tangled problem where it had been dropped by the Buckingham Palace Conference in 1914, they differed from that Conference in one very remarkable way—this time the rival parties did *not* meet round the same table. Instead, they bargained separately with Lloyd George— Redmond, Dillon, Devlin and T. P. O'Connor representing the Nationalists, Carson and James Craig acting for the Ulster Unionists. This meant in practice that each side was dependent on Lloyd George for its information about the attitude of the other, and since the Nationalists at least had had previous cause to mistrust Lloyd George, this was hardly an auspicious beginning.[1] As a method of procedure it could, however, be defended on the ground that if the two sets of Irish negotiators *had* met face to face they would scarcely have been able to avoid falling into the same bickering over intricate detail which had brought the previous Conference to a halt. And, after all, what now faced the negotiators was not so much questions of detail as the determination of two major issues. First, if the Government of Ireland Act of 1914 (the form in which Home Rule had eventually reached the Statute-book) was to be brought into operation at once, or as soon as practicable, could Redmond persuade his followers to accept the exclusion, not just of this county or that county, as in 1914, but of the six counties of the north-east? And, if Nationalists could be persuaded to swallow this, the second major issue to be determined was how to deal with the excluded area.

Lloyd George's proposals were contained in a document entitled 'Headings of a settlement as to the government of Ireland'.[2] From this it appears that while the Government of Ireland Act was to be brought into operation as soon as possible, the six counties (Antrim, Armagh, Down, Fermanagh, Londonderry and Tyrone) were to be excluded and were to be administered by a Secretary of State, assisted by such officers and departments as might be necessary, these 'not to be in any way responsible to the new Irish government'. The Irish Parliament (i.e. the Parliament set up under the

---

(Director of Military Intelligence, Dublin), who told him his life would be spared if he implicated others higher up than himself. MacNeill asked who these others might be. 'He said Mr. Dillon, who was "bitterly anti-British" and also Mr. Devlin. I said I could not connect them with the matter in any way.' The notion that Dillon or Devlin might be involved must have seemed ludicrous even to Price, but as a means, however crude, of discrediting MacNeill, one can see it might have had its attractions to the military mind (Papers relating to the court-martial of Eoin MacNeill, including MacNeill's (undated) memorandum of the interview and a copy of his wife's account of it, sent to Dillon and Devlin on 27 May 1916, in MacNeill Papers, N.L.I. MS. 11,437/1).

[1] Not the least curious feature of these transactions was Lloyd George's remark in the very inadequate account he gave of them in 1933, when he said that Asquith had asked him to negotiate a settlement 'with the Irish revolutionary leaders' (D. Lloyd George, *War memoirs* (London, 1933), ii. 698–708). Since General Maxwell had already dealt with *them*, this was a strange slip—there could hardly have been a more grotesque misnomer for the quartet of constitutionalists with whom he had to deal.

[2] It is printed in full in Appendix I, pp. 485–6 below. There was, it appears, more than one draft. I have used the version (typed and undated) in the Dillon Papers.

Government of Ireland Act) was to consist of the existing Irish Members in the House of Commons, minus those representing the excluded areas, but the number of Irish representatives at Westminster was to remain un-altered at 103. Subsequent clauses then dealt with the technicalities of setting up, in effect, two separate administrations in Ireland, but, by an omission which seems almost incredible in the circumstances, it was not made clear whether the exclusion of the six counties was to be made per-manent or not. According to clause 14, the legislation that would be required to exclude Ulster was to remain in force for the duration of the war and for twelve months thereafter, but if Parliament had not by that time made 'further and permanent provision for the government of Ireland', the period for which the excluding act was to remain in force was to be extended by Order in Council until Parliament had made such provision. Finally, the pious hope was added that when an Imperial Conference met after the war 'the permanent settlement of Ireland should be considered at that Conference'. All this looks remarkably like an elaborate attempt to put off as long as possible the really crucial decision as to whether or not the country was to be permanently partitioned. Redmond could not face Irish —and especially Ulster—Nationalists on any other platform save that of temporary exclusion, and even that he would find difficulty in carrying. Carson could not face Irish—and especially Ulster—Unionists with any-thing less than permanent exclusion, and even this they would be reluctant to accept. But there was a difference in the negotiating position of the two men which was not generally known at the time. It was simply this—that whereas Redmond, so far as is known, did not obtain any firm assurance that exclusion was to be temporary, Carson received the proposals with a covering letter from Lloyd George in which the latter stated: 'We must make it clear that at the end of the provisional period Ulster does not, whether she wills it or not, merge in the rest of Ireland.'[1] Thus, the familiar chasm, deep and unbridgeable, still yawned and Lloyd George was apparently as far as ever from spanning it.

(v)

Much of the bitterness that followed might have been avoided if this had been realised at the outset and the negotiations discontinued. But Lloyd George, that supreme master of political blandishment, was able to keep the rival parties in play week after week, and for a time all but the most sceptical were able to hope against hope that at last a settlement really might be possible. The terms were not made public until mid-June, but already before then Nationalists and Unionists alike were taking soundings among their supporters. For both, of course, the reaction in Ulster was the

---

[1] H. M. Hyde, *Carson* (London, 1953), p. 403. As early as 23 June the *Irish Times* published a report to the effect that Carson had received a written promise from Lloyd George that the exclusion of the six counties was to be permanent. Commenting on this next day, the *Irish Independent* noted that while Redmond had dismissed this story as a lie, neither Carson nor Lloyd George had said it was.

17. John Dillon in 1914

18. The Old and the New. John Dillon and Mr. de
Valera addressing an anti-conscription meeting at
Ballaghaderrin in May, 1918

crucial test. Amongst the Nationalist leaders the only man who could hope to carry Ulster was Joseph Devlin, and a memorandum he wrote at this time indicates not merely the maximum he thought he could persuade Ulster Nationalists to adopt, but how far that maximum differed in precision and concreteness from Lloyd George's altogether more ambiguous proposals. Here, in Devlin's own words, are the concessions he was prepared to recommend to northern Nationalists:

1. The arrangement was to be *temporary*.
2. Twenty-six counties would be given an Irish parliament in full working order at once.
3. The six counties temporarily excluded would be controlled by the Imperial Parliament pending a final settlement.
4. During the interval the Irish representation at Westminster would be retained in full strength.
5. There would be no separate parliament for the six counties.[1]

Even these terms were most unenthusiastically received, as Devlin reported despondently to Redmond and to Dillon. The latter, indeed, in retailing the news to Redmond, made no bones about it. 'He says that *everywhere* outside Belfast the proposed terms were rejected with contempt. Everybody absolutely refuses to discuss or consider them.'[2] Dillon himself was fast relapsing into pessimism. This was not altogether because he thought the terms impracticable—he was quite ready to give them a fair chance—but because, back in Dublin again, he was becoming obsessed with a problem that was to plague him incessantly for the next three years. This was the dire financial plight of the *Freeman's Journal*. It was functioning again, but the destruction of the offices and plant in the rising, together with papers relating to about £18,000 worth of bad debts, had left it in a parlous condition. It was urgently necessary to put more money into it, for without it, as Dillon explained to T. P. O'Connor, 'we may as well shut up shop'. What made the fate of the *Freeman* of such immediate concern was the fact, as Dillon pointed out, that at this critical moment, when they needed a newspaper to defend and expound the terms of settlement more perhaps than they had ever needed one before, what they actually had was totally inadequate. Consequently, concluded Dillon, 'I do not see how it will be possible to carry any settlement'.[3]

Perhaps T.P. was not the best man to consult about newspaper finance. In one sense, of course, he was *the* expert, because no other Irishman, and few other men in Fleet Street, had his experience in launching newspapers and making them pay. But this was precisely the trouble. Having diagnosed the *Freeman*'s difficulty, correctly enough, as capital deficiency, he saw the crisis simply as a rescue operation involving the transfusion of enough new capital to put the paper on a sound footing, quite regardless of where it came from. When he got Dillon's letter, therefore, his first impulse in all

---

[1] Gwynn, *Redmond*, p. 508.
[2] Dillon to Redmond, 5 June 1916 (R.P.).
[3] Dillon to T. P. O'Connor, 6 June 1916 (R.P.).

innocence was to get in touch with Lloyd George. He saw him on 7 June and that day wrote in great glee that Lloyd George had offered to help in finding the money.[1] Dillon—in a state of high indignation—replied at once that any such interference by Lloyd George would be fatal and that he for one would immediately cease to have anything to do with the paper. Characteristically, he was viewing control of the paper in purely political terms; no less characteristically, he was already looking ahead to a situation that might arise before long. 'I have always', he wrote, 'to keep before my mind the possibility that we—or at least I—may be in conflict with L.G. & Co.'[2]

Dillon's views were undoubtedly coloured by the fact that the position in Dublin was still very critical. Martial law had not been lifted, there was still no effective civil administration, and the city was racked by rumours that, despite all the promises that had been made, there might yet be more executions. So perturbed was he by this possibility that he wrote direct to Asquith, who replied (10 June): 'There is no question of there being any more executions, though there are I believe one or two cases of such a kind that in normal times they would have involved the capital penalty.'[3] At the same time the Prime Minister wrote to Lloyd George that he had 'constantly impressed on Maxwell and will do so again the necessity of going slow and of creating no "incidents". In particular I have told him that there are to be no more executions, however serious the cases may be.'[4] It was not, however, simply a case of whether there might or might not be more executions. It was rather that Maxwell had come to be regarded by all sections of Nationalist opinion as a symbol of harsh repression. As T. P. O'Connor explained to Lloyd George in a letter meant for the Prime Minister's eyes, 'the real root of all this atmosphere of apparently irreconcilable hostility to any settlement among the Nationalists are the presence and proceedings of Sir John Maxwell. Unless he is withdrawn and military rule in Ireland brought to an end, I feel very despondent as to our being able to push the settlement through.'[5]

Unfortunately it was not open to Asquith and Lloyd George to see the situation in quite such clear and uncomplicated terms. After all, if there was to be a settlement, it would have to be agreed by Unionists as well as Nationalists—and to many Unionists Sir John Maxwell was a symbol not of oppression, but of preservation. Indeed, even with the general still in the plenitude of his power, Carson was making very heavy weather with his followers. On 10 June Lloyd George explained his [Carson's] difficulties to Dillon:

> If he gets it at all it will be a grudging assent. The Southern Unionists
> are working hard and skilfully against settlement. They are bringing

[1] T. P. O'Connor to Lloyd George, 7 June 1916 (L.G.P., D/14/2/17); T. P. O'Connor to Dillon, 7 June 1916 (D.P.).
[2] Dillon to T. P. O'Connor, 8 June 1916 (D.P.).
[3] Asquith to Dillon, 10 June 1916 (D.P.).
[4] Asquith to Lloyd George, 10 June 1916 (L.G.P., D/14/2/23).
[5] T. P. O'Connor to Lloyd George, 9 June 1916 (L.G.P., D/14/2/23).

unwonted pressure to bear upon the Unionist members of the cabinet; they are sending paragraphs to all the London newspapers of the most gruesome character as to disloyal demonstrations in Ireland. I have succeeded in keeping these paragraphs out of some of the papers, but the *Morning Post*, which is out for your blood, cannot be influenced. I am convinced of this—that unless the settlement goes through quickly, nothing can be accomplished until the war is over. Heaven knows what will happen then . . . I shudder at what may happen meanwhile in Ireland. The country must be governed, and if it cannot be ruled through and with the assent of the Irish people, there is no doubt it will have to be governed by force. In the middle of a great war you could not tolerate a rebellious or a seditious Ireland. But nobody knows better than you what coercion would mean under these conditions. People are getting accustomed to scenes of blood. Their own sons are falling by the hundred thousand, and the nation is harder and more ruthless than it has ever been.

As to General Maxwell, he added, he had just written strongly to the Prime Minister about his 'fatuous administration of Ireland'. 'I cannot help suspecting that there is an effort to upset settlement by irritating the Irish people.' And he ended this cordial, but nevertheless ominous, letter with the warning that even if Nationalists and Unionists in Ireland agreed to accept his terms 'we shall have a deadly struggle within the cabinet'.[1]

The hint of steel in this letter is perfectly apparent and it helps to explain a good deal of Lloyd George's subsequent policy in Ireland. At the time however, Dillon did not deny its essential truth. 'It shews me', he wrote next day in reply, 'that *you* appreciate the desperate character of the Irish situation.' Nevertheless, most of his long letter was occupied in explaining once again the difficulties with which the Nationalists were confronted. Outside Belfast, he said, Devlin had so far been repulsed on all sides—in Tyrone there had even been an independent convention of Ulster Nationalists 'summoned without consulting us' to commit that county and the Ulster bishops against the terms before they were fully made public. So far as Ulster as a whole was concerned, all would depend first upon a meeting Redmond was to have with the bishops in two or three days' time, and then upon the conference of Ulster Nationalists which was to be held as soon as possible thereafter. 'Meanwhile the temper of the country is extremely bad—and the temper of this city *ferocious*.' Great demonstrations were going on almost every day at high masses for the souls of the executed men:

The relatives [he continued] are received on their leaving the churches by enormous cheering crowds, and gradually these crowds are developing into processions and demonstrations singing political songs . . . It is inevitable that accounts of these proceedings should reach England, and I fully appreciate the truth of all you say as to the possible consequences. Do you wonder now at the bitterness with

[1] Lloyd George to Dillon, 10 June 1916 (D.P.).

[which] I spoke, when I came over fresh from observing the executions.

When the fighting was over and the insurrection crushed, if there
had been no executions, the country would have been *solid* behind us,
and we could have done what we liked with it.

The tragedy of the situation—and it is one of the greatest tragedies
of all history—is that but for the blunders and perversities of your
government—Ireland would be today as loyal to your cause as
Canada, and you would have had easily double the number of Irish
soldiers fighting at the front, including many hundreds of those who
took part in the rebellion, and many thousands who are now cursing
England, and eager for her defeat.

Now, admittedly, there were no more executions, but there was still widespread searching of houses and there were still many arrests. Dillon had no
doubt that this was a deliberate attempt to make a settlement impossible
'by irritating the people to such a state of madness that our influence over
them will be wiped out . . . And the horrible irony of the situation is, that
by giving the soldiers and Price [Major I. H. Price, Director of Military
Intelligence and widely detested in Dublin as Maxwell's right-hand man]
a free hand you are making yourselves the instruments of your own worst
enemies to defeat your own policy.' Even so, he did not entirely despair
of the Ulster conference, for Devlin had come out very strongly for accepting the proposals. However, the forces against them were 'terrific':

The *Independent* newspaper.
The priests and bishops.
All the cranks and enemies of the party—and no strongly disciplined
political party can exist for a number of years without making many
enemies.
Honest popular sentiment—which is dead against a divided Ireland.
The madness of your soldiers and the present military dictatorship,
which has roused old historic passions of distrust and hate—which
we had spent the last 25 years in laying to rest.

To all this we have only to oppose the voice of reason and
commonsense, political prudence. And you are Celt enough to know
how unequal are the forces.

The one thing which would have enabled us to carry our people—
the prestige and influence of a trusted leader—has been lost to us by
Redmond's super-zeal on the recruiting platform, and by his refusal
to take a vigorous stand against conscription for Ireland.

I do not know whether you will have patience to plough thro' this
letter. But I felt bound to write at length in reply to your very frank
letter. And as it is a time for frankness on both sides, I shall do my
best to carry through the settlement. But I confess, even if it be
carried, I do not believe we shall be thro' our difficulties. You have
let Hell loose in Ireland and I do not see how the country is to be
governed.[1]

[1] Dillon to Lloyd George, 11 June 1916 (L.G.P., D/14/2/2)5.

This letter is important on several grounds. In the first place it disposes of the charge Lloyd George made long afterwards that it was Dillon by his intransigence who blocked a settlement.[1] On the contrary, he here pledged himself unreservedly to forward the negotiations as best he could. Secondly, the letter is an indication that, whatever his previous misgivings, Dillon at this crucial point was prepared to trust Lloyd George, even to the extent of indicating so fully to him the weaknesses of the Irish party's position—from which Lloyd George may well have drawn conclusions not at all intended by Dillon. And in the third place, the letter is important because it contains one of the few overt criticisms of Redmond's leadership which Dillon permitted himself in these years. Perhaps it was unwise that he should have chosen to unburden himself to Lloyd George of all people, but this may have been one of the side-effects of the strain he was feeling, and had been feeling, since the beginning of the war; equally, of course, it may simply have been an indication of the extent to which he was still prepared to regard Lloyd George as a fellow worker in a cause which transcended personalities. And if this seems excessively naïve in the light of previous experience, it has to be remembered that before returning to Ireland Dillon, Devlin and Redmond, at their last meeting with Lloyd George, had asked him whether, if they won Nationalist consent to his proposals, they could count upon him, and upon the Prime Minister, not to tolerate any further concessions being exacted of them. 'He gave us the most emphatic assurance,' recorded Redmond, 'saying he had placed his life upon the table and would stand or fall by the agreement come to.'[2]

Dillon's news was alarming enough, but it was reinforced by T. P. O'Connor's report, sent on the same day from Dublin, where he had gone to attend the meeting of the parliamentary party called to discuss the proposals. That meeting was held on 10 June and heard what O'Connor described as an irresistible speech from Devlin. But this was about the only crumb of comfort T.P. had to offer Lloyd George. Like Dillon, he was struck by the way in which religious occasions were being used virtually as political demonstrations, and like him he laid the main blame on the presence of General Maxwell and the continuance of martial law. His account of Major Price's sinister reputation also tallied with Dillon's and he urged Lloyd George that he should be withdrawn at once.[3] One thing that had particularly struck him was the extent to which the executed men were already passing into legend. After he got back to London he thought enough of this to try to explain it to Lloyd George. 'Nine tenths of them', he wrote, 'were men of good character and ardent Catholics and many of them were also life teetotalers.' As evidence of the former he instanced the fact that in the G.P.O., even at the height of the fighting, they said the Rosary twice a day, and to illustrate their abstinence he pointed out the fact—which to Dublin savoured almost of the miraculous—that although they occupied Jameson's distillery for a week they had not touched a drop of the whiskey

---

[1] Lloyd George, *War memoirs*, ii. 701.   [2] Gwynn, *Redmond*, p. 506.
[3] T. P. O'Connor to Lloyd George, 'Sunday' (11 June 1916) (L.G.P.).

there. And he gave this further illustration of the growth of what might be called the cult of the Easter Rising. 'A little girl walking with her mother through the street begged to be given a new hat. Her mother refused; then the child began praying to "St. Pearse" to herself. In the end, after some words, the mother changed her mind and bought the child a hat.'[1]

It may be doubted if these simple pieties carried much conviction to Lloyd George's mind, but perhaps he paid more attention to O'Connor's repeatedly expressed belief that a secret society on the lines of the old Invincibles was being formed and that the names of certain individuals—even including Redmond—were being freely mentioned as having been marked down for assassination. And he may have been even more deeply impressed by his friend's analysis of the forces in Ireland opposed to settlement, for, as O'Connor saw it, these embraced not only the obvious antagonists—Southern Unionists at one extreme, Sinn Feiners at the other—but also the subtler, and perhaps more deadly, enemies within the gates. 'I need not tell you what these forces are', wrote T.P. in the letter already quoted, 'other than to say that they consist—first, of professed Home Rulers who are really hostile to Home Rule; second, of the group led by Mr. O'Brien and Mr. Healy; third, of the *Independent* newspaper as representing both the first and the second group in the person of Mr. William Murphy as proprietor; and fourth, of a large body of the priests—some because they are Sinn Feiners, some because they have apprehensions of the effect upon their position of an Irish parliament. These forces at present have all rushed into the Cave of Adullam.'[2]

(vi)

All this was very discouraging, but Lloyd George had his own troubles on the other flank. That same day (11 June) on which Dillon and O'Connor dispatched their jeremiads from Dublin, one of his Unionist colleagues in the Cabinet—Walter Long—wrote to him stating categorically that in view of what he had heard of the existing state of Ireland this was not the moment to embark on any political experiment 'and unless I am wholly misinformed I don't think it would be possible for me to give my assent to any agreement including the adoption of Home Rule . . .'[3] Next day, recounting this to Dillon, Lloyd George asserted that his reply had been that in that case he would place his, Lloyd George's, resignation in Asquith's hands, as he felt absolutely committed to the proposed terms. Then, having flourished his loyalty in Dillon's face, he added once more the unmistakable note of menace. 'I gathered from Bonar Law that the Southern Unionists are moving heaven and the other place to thwart settlement, I am afraid

---

[1] T. P. O'Connor to Lloyd George, 13 June 1916 (L.G.P., D/14/2/28). The story evidently impressed O'Connor himself very strongly, for he repeated it to C. P. Scott a few days later (C. P. Scott Papers, B.M. Add. MS. 5093, ff. 51–2).

[2] Ibid.

[3] Lloyd George, *War memoirs*, ii. 703–4, where Long is not named. He is merely 'a prominent Unionist member of the Cabinet'.

that the northern bishops mean to help them; so that Home Rule may be defeated by a combination of its open and its secret enemies.'[1]

That the situation in the Cabinet was 'somewhat critical' Dillon heard also from O'Connor. T.P. had dined with Lloyd George on 12 June and the latter had told him that not only was Walter Long being difficult but Lansdowne would probably resign. On the other hand, Lloyd George had seemed very appreciative of Devlin's efforts in Ulster. When O'Connor told him that they looked on Devlin as the Lloyd George of Ireland, Lloyd George clearly enjoyed the comparison, remarking 'that of course they were alike in their perfect simplicity and freedom from all guile'.[2] Dillon, however, was in no mood for pleasantries and took the situation so seriously that he wrote twice to Lloyd George on 16 June, partly to explain why it was taking so long to consult the Ulster Nationalists (the ground had first to be cleared with the bishops) and partly to emphasise yet again the unprecedented state of affairs in Ireland:

> Since the executions, we have a *new Ireland* to deal with—seething with discontent and rage against the government. Old historic passions have been aroused to a *terrible* extent. For the moment the party does not speak for Ireland. And there is *no leadership* in the country . . . And if we were to ignore it, and attempt to answer for the country, or to commit the country, the result would be utter chaos and disaster.

As to the condition of Dublin, it was, said Dillon, still *'extremely dangerous'*:

> I am accustomed to be set down as a pessimist, having repeatedly warned the Irish government during the last year of the dangers of Sinn Fein. But I feel bound to tell you that I am in daily dread of some horrid catastrophe in Dublin. One of the half mad officers of whom Dublin seems to have an inexhaustible supply might any day in connection with these Church demonstrations bring about a regular massacre, and the worst of the situation is that some of those who are working up the demonstrations—particularly the women— would I am convinced be well pleased if a collision took place.[3]

Later that day Redmond came to him straight from his ecclesiastical negotiations and Dillon in his second letter hastened to pass on the result to Lloyd George. The bishops had all been hostile and had forecast that the Ulster conference would reject the proposals by an overwhelming majority. The only alternative they had been able to suggest was to revive the old scheme of county option. 'Redmond said that would be useless. R. parted from the bishops on these terms.' The conference, Dillon added, would meet next week, and he could not see how there was any chance of their carrying the proposals. However, Redmond, Devlin and himself would attend and would recommend acceptance.[4]

[1] Lloyd George to Dillon, 12 June 1916 (D.P.).
[2] T. P. O'Connor to Dillon, 13 June 1916 (D.P.).
[3] Dillon to Lloyd George, 16 June 1916 (L.G.P., D/14/3/1).
[4] Dillon to Lloyd George, 16 June 1916 (L.G.P., D/14/3/2).

Ominous as the future seemed on the Nationalist front, Lloyd George was by this time well aware that the threat from the extreme Unionists was likely to prove at least as grave if not graver. Carson, admittedly, was doing his best, and it did seem as if the Ulster Unionists might be got to accept a six-county exclusion, though, of course, among themselves they took it for granted that this exclusion would be permanent. But it was the English Unionists within the Cabinet who were giving most trouble. And, as Lloyd George explained to Dillon, the Irish bishops and priests were 'playing the Unionist game to perfection'. 'If the Ulster convention decide to reject the proposals it will relieve the Unionists of all the responsibility for what happens. It is incredible that Home Rulers should play so completely the game of their enemies . . . But if the Irish parliamentary party and the Ulster convention accept the proposals, the Unionist members of the cabinet will be in the position of fighting not merely the Nationalist leaders but Carson and the Ulster members; and as Bonar Law (who, being in Paris, is out of this *émeute*) told me, that would be an impossible position for them.'[1] Three days later Lloyd George wrote again to Dillon, revealing very freely the divisions within the Cabinet:

. . . A number of Unionist members of the cabinet threaten to secede from the government if Home Rule is brought into operation under the suggested conditions. They are all in it except Balfour, Bonar Law and F. E. Smith. Long has behaved in a specially treacherous manner. He has actually been engaged clandestinely in trying to undermine the influence of Carson in Ulster by representing to the Ulster leaders that they were induced to assent to the agreement under false pretences. He told them there was no war urgency, no prospect of trouble in America, and that Carson's reasons for coming to terms were all false. I could not think it possible that any man, least of all one with such pretensions of being an English gentleman, could have acted in such a way.

However, he has met with a large measure of success and Carson will have a very difficult time—but Carson will stand firm.

It is quite on the cards that the government will go to pieces on the question of whether the Home Rule should be brought into immediate operation or not. Balfour, Bonar Law, and F.E. will stand by the Prime Minister and myself if Carson will adhere to his bargain. Carson swears he will not go back and he has intimated as much to the Unionist members of the cabinet.

I sincerely hope that the Ulster convention will not, by rejecting the proposals, play into the hands of these refractory gentlemen. They hate the idea of setting up an independent parliament in Ireland and, as they see it getting near, the prospect enrages them.

They are anxious to repudiate my proposals. Of course, if anything in the nature of a repudiation of my proposals or authority were to be published on behalf of the government I should have no alternative but to resign. To-morrow we meet to consider the situation.[2]

[1] Lloyd George to Dillon, 17 June 1916 (D.P.).
[2] Lloyd George to Dillon, 20 June 1916 (D.P.).

On the same day T. P. O'Connor also wrote, throwing a little more light on the tense situation inside the Government. Lloyd George, he said, was doing all he could to make Asquith stand firm, and was urging him to say to the dissident Unionists 'that if they insist on coercion for Ireland he can no longer take any responsibility for the government of that country and must put his resignation into the hands of the King and nominate Mr. Walter Long or some other person to carry on the government in his stead. If Asquith can be got to take up this position, and, of course, if Ireland do not reject the settlement, all will go well.' He added that when the Cabinet had met that day the Unionist members had wanted to publish a statement pointing out (what, in fact, was perfectly true) that Lloyd George's proposals had not been formally brought before the Government, much less approved by them. This had almost precipitated Lloyd George's resignation, for to make public any such statement at that stage would at once have undermined his authority in Ireland and brought the negotiations to a standstill.[1]

That extremity was avoided, but Lloyd George had nevertheless to agree to send a letter to Redmond making clear the Unionist attitude. The gist of it was that the Cabinet as a body had not yet considered any scheme, nor would it do so until the proposals were agreed to by Redmond and his friends. In a covering letter T. P. O'Connor explained that three of the Unionists in the Cabinet—Lord Selborne, Lord Lansdowne and Walter Long—had given notice of resignation and that the letter was really intended as a device to hold the Government together. What T.P. meant by this was that since there had been no formal proposal before the Cabinet, so there was, for the present, no need for the Unionists, now deeply divided among themselves, to take up hard-and-fast positions on one side or the other. Sending a copy of this letter to Dillon, T.P. added that Lloyd George thought that time, which had been gained by the letter, was on their side. 'Austen [Chamberlain], hostile on Tuesday, was friendly to-day; a row, which might have broken out to-day, is now postponed till Monday. If Belfast go right on Friday, things will be right here on Monday, except that the three will then go.'[2]

Time, it seemed, was on their side in Ireland, too. The Ulster Unionists had already by mid-June been reluctantly persuaded by Carson and Craig into acceptance, and letters reaching Lloyd George from both Devlin and Dillon showed that among the Nationalists the tide was slowly beginning to turn in favour of the proposals.[3] Even so, when the Ulster conference met in secret on 23 June it needed not only a virtuoso display of eloquence by Joseph Devlin, but also the knowledge that if the proposals were rejected

---

[1] Gwynn, *Redmond*, pp. 509–10.
[2] T. P. O'Connor to Dillon, and enclosures, 21 June 1916 (D.P.); Gwynn, *Redmond*, pp. 510–11.
[3] Joseph Devlin to T. P. O'connor, 19 June 1916, and Dillon to Lloyd George, 21 June 1916 L.G.P., D/14/3/15 and D/14/3/28; Ronald McNeill (Lord Cushendun), *Ulster's stand for union* (Dublin, 1922), p. 247.

Redmond would resign his leadership to bring about agreement.[1] This agreement, however, as registered at the conference, and at a meeting of the parliamentary party a few days later, depended entirely upon the supposition that the exclusion of the six counties from a Home Rule Ireland was to be *temporary*. Since the Ulster Unionists had only accepted the proposals on the basis that exclusion was to be *permanent*, it is hard to see how Lloyd George's ingenious scheme could have survived for five minutes if the two Irish parties had been allowed to meet round the same table.

In the end, however, the honour of cutting its throat was to be reserved to the Unionist members of the Cabinet, though, in this, as events soon proved, they were no more than representative of the views of many of their own backbenchers. One of the dissenting Ministers, Lord Selborne, indeed resigned even before the Cabinet formally took up the issue, but when it did take it up, at two long meetings on 27 June, Walter Long and Lord Lansdowne led a fierce resistance, arguing that the cession of Home Rule even to twenty-six counties at that moment would simply be regarded as a surrender to force which would invite more violence to extort further concessions. Other Unionists, however, including Balfour and Bonar Law (now back from Paris), firmly supported the proposals and a deadlock, with inevitable resignations and the possible break-up of the coalition, seemed in sight. At the last moment, and to avoid forcing a decision there and then, Asquith secured the appointment of a committee—it consisted of himself, Lloyd George, F. E. Smith and Lord Robert Cecil—to formulate any additions to the proposals that might seem to them necessary.[2]

Additions to the proposals—here was the danger Dillon had always feared, here was precisely the development both he and Redmond had believed Lloyd George to be committed to preventing.[3] And by a curious irony Dillon, writing to T. P. O'Connor the day after the Cabinet decision, but apparently before he had heard of it, chose just this moment to emphasise that the proposals must be accepted as they stood. Evidently he had been deeply impressed by the mood of the Ulster conference. 'We took our political lives in our hands', he said, 'and went within an ace of disaster . . . So far as I am concerned, I have gone to the utmost limit, and I shall not be a party to *any* further concessions.'[4] This was ominous, the more so since his letter crossed with one from O'Connor suggesting that certain concessions, which O'Connor himself did not regard as serious, would nevertheless be required. Within the Cabinet, he wrote, everything was trembling in the balance. Lansdowne and Long seemed certain to resign, but they might not be the only ones:

---

[1] *Irish Independent*, 24 June 1916; Gwynn, *Redmond*, pp. 511–12.

[2] Asquith to King George V, 27 June 1916 (Asquith Papers, Cabinet Letters, vol. 8, ff. 171–8); Jenkins, *Asquith*, pp. 399–401. Mr. Jenkins is in error in dating Asquith's letter 28 June.

[3] See p. 393 above.

[4] Dillon to T. P. O'Connor, 28 June 1916 (D.P.).

Bonar Law and Austen Chamberlain are wavering, so is Lord Curzon. The first straight but timid; the second sulky and reluctant; and the third one day for and the other day against. If the meeting of the Tory party had taken place today and if a majority had gone against the settlement, or if it had been carried by only a small majority, Bonar Law felt that his position would have been made impossible. The retirement of Bonar Law would have involved the retirement of all the rest, except Balfour, who has fought, as L.G. put it, for the settlement as if he had been a Home Ruler all his life; and it would be practically impossible for the wreck of the government thus left to carry the settlement.

At Lloyd George's request, T.P. added, he had telegraphed for Redmond and Dillon to come over, since London was now the place where the final decision must be made. Lloyd George had several times complained of being left to fight alone and questions were constantly cropping up which he could not answer without consultation with the Irish leaders. As an example, O'Connor instanced what he called 'the main argument that disinclines the Tories to agree to a settlement'—that was, whether a Nationalist Government would really be able to govern Ireland in the state the country was then in, and how far military forces would still need to be available in case of fresh disturbances. 'This suspicious state of mind also suggested', as O'Connor was quick to note, 'some precautions for the safeguarding of any military necessities in Ireland, such as taking ground for a camp, the use of ports and other things.'[1]

(vii)

It was obviously important that the Irish leaders should be in London and even Asquith himself was moved to send them a message that their presence was 'very desirable'.[2] But it was not easy for them to get away. For one thing they had still to submit the proposals to the directory of the United Irish League, and for another, both, and especially Dillon, were much preoccupied with the desperate financial state of the *Freeman's Journal*, still their only means of countering the intensive propaganda of the *Independent*. Dillon was in any case most reluctant to expose himself to governmental pressures. He was infuriated when he heard of the presence of General Maxwell at the Cabinet meeting of 27 June (though, in fact, Maxwell had been asked solely to report on the security position in Ireland and had scouted the notion that there would be any further violence, or that if there was, there would be any difficulty in dealing with it) and in the second of two letters he wrote to Redmond on 29 June Dillon was very refractory indeed. 'I have no doubt', he wrote, 'that this somewhat peremptory summons is for the purpose of demanding some large concessions from us, to enable the P.M. to keep the cabinet together. I am not disposed to go before Tuesday morning. I confess I resent being summoned over in

[1] T. P. O'Connor to Dillon, 28 June 1916 (D.P.); copy in L.G.P., 8/14/3/44.
[2] Gwynn, *Redmond*, p. 515.

this peremptory fashion, without a word of explanation. Since these
negotiations commenced the P.M. has not communicated with us, either
directly or indirectly. And now that the Tories have kicked, that we should
suddenly be summoned without a hint of what we are required for, is more
than I am prepared to stomach.'[1] Newspaper reports next day of a speech
of Lord Lansdowne's, saying that the Government was not bound by Lloyd
George's proposals and that the Unionists in the Cabinet had not accepted
them, inflamed him further:

> You know (he wrote to Redmond) that ever since the P.M. shovelled
> us on to L.G. and cut off all *direct* communication with us I have all
> along suspected treachery. But I certainly was not prepared for
> anything so cynically treacherous as Lansdowne's performance.
>   There is only one way of dealing with this kind of thing, and that is
> to let these gentlemen see that we are not so slavishly anxious for
> the settlement as to allow ourselves to be kicked about to suit their
> convenience and treated as if we were of absolutely no account.[2]

Nevertheless, the situation was too serious for them to absent themselves
from London any longer and on 3 July he and Redmond crossed together.
It was soon apparent that some degree of continuing British supervision
was part of the price that would be asked of them, and in an interview with
Asquith, Redmond agreed to accept a provision safeguarding British
military and naval rights for the duration of the war.[3] On 5 July Asquith
was able to announce this safeguard to the Cabinet and to report to the
King that the two chief opponents of the settlement—Lansdowne and
Long—had agreed not to resign, subject to imperial control of matters
relating to war and public order being secured as long as the war lasted
and—ominous proviso—'awaiting the form which [the settlement] might
ultimately take'.[4]
    It still remained, however, to win the assent of the Tory party as a
whole, and this was Bonar Law's unenviable task at a meeting at the Carlton
Club on 7 July. He fully admitted to his fellow Unionists there was a risk
in setting up a Home Rule Government in Ireland while the war was on—
'but there is a danger always with regard to Ireland: there is only a choice
of evils. It may be that to do this is a gamble but . . . there is not even a
gambler's chance if we do not.' 'If we go back on these negotiations now
as a party,' he warned them, 'we shall make a terrible mistake.' Even
despite this exhortation, however, there was so much support for the
views of Lansdowne and Long that Bonar Law dared not put the matter
to a vote and the meeting adjourned without coming to any conclusions—
but it was unmistakably a case where no news was bad news.[5]
    There was worse news yet to come. On 11 July in the House of Lords
Lansdowne at last succeeded in delivering the *coup de grâce*. Speaking of

[1] Dillon to Redmond, 29 June 1916, two letters (R.P.).
[2] Dillon to Redmond, 30 June 1916, two letters (R.P.).
[3] Jenkins, *Asquith*, p. 401.   [4] Spender and Asquith, op. cit., ii. 221.
[5] Robert Blake, *The unknown prime minister*, p. 287.

the recent proposals, he made it crystal clear that in his view, since the necessary legislation would involve 'a structural alteration in the Act of 1914' it would therefore be 'permanent and enduring'. 'We fully intend,' he added for good measure, 'that the Defence of the Realm Act which will remain in force, should, if necessary, be strengthened.'[1] The Irish leaders, naturally, were furious and Asquith had great difficulty in persuading them not to ask him point-blank in the House of Commons if Lansdowne's speech represented the policy of the Government.[2] Even as it was, Redmond could not be deflected from issuing an angry statement to the Press, and although this elicited from Lansdowne a slightly more conciliatory reply, it was clear that serious damage had been done.[3] Enough in itself to ruin the chances of a settlement, this blow was soon followed by another. Despairing of getting a clear, firm decision from the Government and fearing that continued hesitation would jeopardise the whole scheme, Redmond took the drastic step of publishing, on 21 July, a memorandum he had sent to Asquith and Lloyd George demanding an end to delay and asserting unequivocally that any departure from the terms agreed upon, and especially those regarding 'the temporary and provisional character of *all* sections of the bill', would mean the end of the agreement.[4] Here at last, with Lansdowne's speech and Redmond's letter, the two essential incompatibilities were made plain. The settlement, despite all Lloyd George's ingenuity, could not be both permanent and temporary and the Cabinet was brought face to face with the final decision. It met next day and did not leave matters long in doubt. The Unionist Members proposed and carried a major change in the proposals. The retention of the Irish Members at Westminster, which Redmond had regarded as a guarantee of the temporary character of the arrangement, was to be deleted and the settlement was to be treated as permanent. On 22 July these conditions were conveyed to Redmond and on 24 July in the House of Commons, in a speech full of rage and bitterness, he acknowledged that the end of the road had been reached and that all hope of a peaceful settlement was over.[5]

'That day', wrote one who at this time was very close to Redmond, 'really finished the constitutional party and overthrew Redmond's power. We had incurred the very great odium of accepting even temporary partition . . . we had involved with us many men who voted for that acceptance on the faith of Redmond's assurance that the government were bound by their written word, and now we were thrown over.'[6] This is a fair statement of a tragic situation. Tragic, not so much because the negotiations failed—it is difficult from this distance to see how something which was

[1] Hansard, H.L. Debates, 5th series, vol. 52, cols. 645–52, especially col. 646.
[2] Spender and Asquith, op. cit., ii. 222.
[3] These exchanges are in Gwynn, *Redmond*, pp. 518–19.
[4] *Irish Independent*, 21 July 1916; Gwynn, *Redmond*, p. 520.
[5] Hansard, H.C. Debates, 5th series, vol. 84, cols. 1426–34; Stephen Gwynn, *John Redmond's last years* (London, 1919), pp. 238–9; Gwynn, *Redmond*, pp. 520–2.
[6] Stephen Gwynn, *John Redmond's last years*, p. 239.

interpreted in such utterly opposing ways by the two contracting parties can ever have been expected to work in practice—but because of the way they failed. They failed not because of the divergent interests of Ulster Unionists and Ulster Nationalists, but because the Tory members of the Cabinet, spurred on both by their own rank-and-file and by the intransigence of the Southern Irish Unionists, of whom Lord Lansdowne was the acknowledged champion, wanted them to fail. In short, this great opportunity for reconciliation was sacrificed, and that at the crisis of a great war, to sordid party interest.

In the short term this negative policy succeeded, but the consequences were incalculable. A gulf, and one may say an unbridgeable gulf, was opened between the Irish party and both the major English parties. The long war of manoeuvre initiated by Parnell had come to this abject end, and two inevitable results followed. On the one hand, the Irish constitutionalists, convinced to their inmost core that they had been tricked and betrayed, were placed in the position where, even if they wished to do so, they dared not negotiate again with English statesmen. Redmond was so deeply wounded that for many months he would hold no communication whatever with Lloyd George, while Dillon was never again to enter into negotiations with English ministers. The other fatal result to flow from this miserable episode was that the position of the Irish party *in Ireland*, already precarious enough, was now compromised beyond recovery. If, after straining every nerve, and asking extreme sacrifices from their fellow countrymen, this was how the parliamentarians were requited in England, then the moral was clear. Sinn Fein had no better recruiting sergeant than Lord Lansdowne.

Against this double disaster Redmond, ailing, tired, despairing, had no defences. He was still to summon his reserves of courage for one more effort, but in reality he was a spent force. Dillon, though naturally weakened in the country like the other constitutionalists, was not quite so vulnerable. His record of scepticism and intransigence now stood him in good stead. Above all, his speech on the aftermath of the Rising, which at the time had seemed to many moderates almost suicidal, was suddenly realised to be invaluable to the party. While the negotiations were in progress he had kept his scepticism under control and, as we have seen, he had loyally taken his part in commending them to the Irish people. But, in the later stages of the tragedy, he had remained much more in the background. This was partly because it properly fell to Redmond, as chairman, to voice the outraged protest of his party, but still more it was because the differences between them had become increasingly acute. As the sorry fiasco moved towards its close, Dillon was reverting fast to the view he had held almost from the beginning of the war, the view, indeed, which he had never really quite abandoned even when the prospects of a settlement were rosiest. His argument had been, and was to be in the future, that the party should no longer give automatic support to the Government, that it should steer clear of entangling negotiations, and that it should devote itself to fighting against the two dangers which loomed largest in the minds of most Irishmen—subjection to military rule at home, liability to military service abroad. That autumn, having had time to move about and sound opinion in Ireland outside Dublin, he wrote this significant verdict to O'Connor:

> I realise more than ever how near we went to the total destruction of the party and the constitutional movement. The fact is that ever since the formation of the Coalition in June 1915 we had been steadily and rather rapidly losing our hold on the people, and the rebellion and the negotiations only brought out in an aggravated form what had been beneath the surface for a year. The average man—including a *vast* number of our loyal supporters—believes that since the formation of the Coalition our party acted in a timorous, weak manner, and that Carson proved himself more than a match for Redmond.

There was, he admitted, still some support for constitutional action, but 'our main strength is entirely of a negative character—the same kind of strength that has carried Asquith and the Coalition so far, the absence of any alternative either in leadership or policy. But enthusiasm and trust in Redmond and the party *is dead* so far as the mass of the people is concerned.'[1] It was, indeed, a true verdict—how devastatingly true Dillon himself was before long to find out.

[1] Dillon to T. P. O'Connor, 26 Sept. 1916 (D.P.).

14
The Downward Path

(i)

For Dillon the eighteen months after the breakdown of the 1916 negotiations were some of the most frustrating of his life. On the one hand, virtually alone among the leaders of the parliamentary party, he was fully aware of the mounting tensions in Ireland and of the dangers threatening the whole constitutional movement. On the other hand, since he was not the chairman, he could not initiate the policy which, he felt in his bones, represented the sole hope of survival. Only by competing with Sinn Fein in intransigence, by attacking the Government in the House of Commons and by opposing tooth and nail the threat of conscription, could the party avoid the fate which, all too clearly, he saw ahead. 'The situation in Ireland to-day', he wrote to T. P. O'Connor in August, 'is far worse than you can possibly realise. No-one can understand it who is not living among the people. Believe me, it is touch and go whether we can save the movement and keep the party in existence . . . Between Sinn Fein, the anti-exclusionists of Ulster and the *Independent* we are between two devils and the deep sea.'[1]

Nevertheless, although there were to be many occasions in the near future when to relapse into his habitual pessimism seemed the only rational reaction to a deteriorating situation, his instinct was to fight, and in his public utterances he was a long way from admitting defeat. Thus, in the same week as his *cri de coeur* to O'Connor, he was capable of writing to Shane Leslie in America in terms of subdued hope, obviously for circulation amongst Irish-Americans:

Personally I don't think *we* have lost anything by the breakdown of the negotiations and all the revelations which have come to light have convinced hundreds of our friends—who had been very suspicious and restive—that we acted for the best in agreeing to recommend the Lloyd George terms. The whole business has given the government a very bad shake and I am inclined to think that it will not long survive. And in the interest of the Irish cause I think the disappearance of this government would be a distinct gain . . .

You will have learned that all attempts at settlement broke down through the weakness and cowardice of the P.M. and Lloyd George, and the bitter prejudice of a section of the Tories. For the moment I

[1] Dillon to T. P. O'Connor, 19 Aug. 1916 (D.P.).

do not think there is any chance of settlement or of renewed negotiation. Nevertheless certain points have been gained, one being that *every one* in Great Britain and Ireland has come to regard Home Rule in some shape as quite inevitable and [that] is a great advance on the state of affairs in 1914.[1]

This was certainly putting a bold face on it, but in private Dillon was much less sanguine, because he was at this time completely in the dark about Redmond's plans for the autumn session of Parliament. It was known that Redmond was going to speak to his constituents at Waterford, but what he was going to say was shrouded in mystery. 'A speech from R. in the wrong key', wrote Dillon to O'Connor, 'would make [the situation] perfectly hopeless.'[2] Anything like an attempt to renew negotiations, he added a few days later, 'would finish the party—it would kill it as dead as Queen Anne'.[3] However, Redmond's speech proved much more satisfactory than Dillon had dared to hope. It was eloquent of his bitterness at the lost opportunity of the summer. 'We have taken a leap back over generations of progress', the chairman declared, 'and have actually had a rebellion, with its inevitable aftermath of brutalities, stupidities and inflamed passions.' The constitutional movement would go on, but he made it clear that he, as leader, would be no party to further private negotiations. As for the menace of conscription, he warned the Government that it would be resisted in every village in the country and that any attempt to enforce it would cause 'a scandal which would ring through the world'.[4] Such words were music to Dillon's ears and he reported to O'Connor not only that the speech had delighted him, but that the day after it he had had a long consultation with Redmond as a result of which they were 'in complete agreement' as to the line of action the party should follow in Parliament.[5]

It soon appeared what this was to be. On 18 October Redmond, in a speech of great power and dignity, moved a vote of censure on the Government with this resolution: 'That the system of government at present maintained in Ireland is inconsistent with the principles for which the allies are fighting in Europe, and has been mainly responsible for the recent unhappy events and for the present state of feeling in that country.' Dillon's contribution to the debate was an angry speech in which he deliberately took the tone that was to be heard from him increasingly in the months ahead. It was partly an attack upon the Irish Unionists, who, he alleged, had in effect patronised Sinn Fein in order to undermine the authority of the parliamentary party. It was the same old 'ascendancy party', he declared passionately, whose policy for a hundred years had been 'to foster and keep up bad blood between the Irish and the English people. These

[1] Dillon to Shane Leslie, 15 Aug. 1916 (Leslie Papers).
[2] Dillon to T. P. O'Connor, 1 Oct. 1916 (D.P.).
[3] Dillon to T. P. O'Connor, 5 Oct. 1916 (D.P.).
[4] *F.J.*, 7 Oct. 1916; Stephen Gwynn, *John Redmond's last years*, pp. 242–3; Gwynn, *Redmond*, p. 529.
[5] Dillon to T. P. O'Connor, 8 Oct. 1916 (D.P.).

gentlemen have on more than one occasion encouraged rebellion in Ireland, because they know perfectly well that rebellion works for them and kills constitutional movements in Ireland, and constitutional movements are the only things which they dread.' But partly also, Dillon was still desperately anxious to warn Englishmen about what might happen if the Irish party—which, he readily admitted, 'had got a very severe shock' from recent events—were to disappear altogether. Their power in Ireland, as he pointed out, had been shaken because of their general support for the war, and if they were wiped out at the next general election 'does any man in this House really believe that it would make any considerable advance towards a settlement of the Irish question'? Would it not, he suggested, be wiser to acknowledge generously the Irish contribution to the war effort, despite all the official obstacles to recruitment, and to match the comradeship of the battlefields with justice for Ireland at home. And he ended, without having said all he had meant to say, by quoting a moving poem of T. M. Kettle's, doubly moving since Kettle had recently been killed in action:

> Bond, from the toil of hate we may not cease;
> Free, we are free to be your friend,
> And when you make your banquet, and we come
> Soldier with equal soldier must we sit,
> Closing a battle, not forgetting it,
> With not a name to hide,
> This mate and mother of valiant 'rebels' dead
> Must come with all her history on her head.[1]

In the then temper of the House of Commons, and still more at that critical point in the war when Asquith's Government was reeling towards collapse, Dillon's warning fell on deaf ears. So, too, did urgent appeals to the Prime Minister to release the remainder of the prisoners interned after the rising. If it were not done soon, as Redmond anxiously explained to Asquith, a massive 'amnesty movement' would develop, and if this 'after months of furious and angry agitation' were *then* to lead to the release of the prisoners, it would not only further weaken the authority of the parliamentary party but would also be one more indication that the one thing the government understood was force or the threat of force.[2] But Redmond's letter, which was written on 30 November, came too late for Asquith to do anything about it, even if he had been so inclined. The dark, intense struggle for power inside the Cabinet was approaching its climax, and within a week of Redmond having sent his letter to the Prime Minister, the Prime Minister was no longer Asquith, but Lloyd George.

The change was a momentous one for the Irish party, but at first sight it was not easy to see what its immediate effects might be. Lloyd George's

---

[1] Hansard, H.C. Debates, 5th series, vol. 86, cols. 675–86. Dillon's rough draft for this speech is less elaborate, but if anything more outspoken. See the 'Notes of a speech in the House of Commons, 18 Oct. 1916, only half-delivered', in the Dillon Papers.

[2] Gwynn, *Redmond*, pp. 532–3.

mandate was essentially to prosecute the war more effectively and there can be little doubt that for him—and indeed for English opinion generally—the Irish question had come to seem peripheral. Yet there was one important reason why it could never be completely peripheral. The Irish question, after all, was not merely Irish. It had all sorts of overtones, and of these the American were the most important. Reports from the United States indicated that Irish-American opinion had been greatly inflamed by the executions after the Rising (especially, perhaps, by that of Casement in August 1916, in support of whose reprieve the U.S. Senate had actually passed a resolution), and the failure to reach a settlement in the summer had done nothing to improve the situation.[1] If the Allies were looking to America for salvation, and by the end of 1916 this seemed their best, if not their only, hope, then some effort must be made if not to settle Ireland, at least to keep Ireland quiescent. Accordingly, on 9 December Lloyd George sent for Redmond, and told him (so the Irish leader recorded) that he intended to release the interned Sinn Feiners, and to revoke martial law after consultation with his Unionist colleagues. As for conscription, he would not raise this issue himself, and if anyone else did so he would propose immediate Home Rule for all Ireland as a condition. 'On this matter,' Redmond commented, 'I told him we could never agree to conscription as a condition of Home Rule and that under any circumstances conscription was impossible in Ireland.' To this Lloyd George merely replied that he was not, in fact, intending to initiate any move for an Irish settlement, though he admitted that the military secretary to the War Council had put in a 'strong report' that the conciliation of Ireland was an imperative necessity as a war measure.[2]

Yet, despite this not unpromising beginning, Lloyd George's first speech on Irish affairs as Prime Minister was a profound disappointment to the Irish party. He did not announce the release of prisoners, he made no constructive proposals for Ireland, and he dwelt self-pityingly on his experiences of the summer. 'I was drenched with suspicion of Irishmen by Englishmen, and of Englishmen by Irishmen, and, worst of all, of Irishmen by Irishmen.' Redmond then replied in an uncharacteristically aggressive tone, accusing Lloyd George of evading his responsibilities to Ireland and delaying unnecessarily the release of the prisoners. Lloyd George rose, more than once, to interrupt him angrily, but Redmond would not be placated and demanded 'drastic, decided and bold action' by the Prime Minister.[3] But he spoke to a restless and depressed House of Commons which had had its fill of Ireland. Lloyd George, who was far from well and

---

[1] 'They have blood in their eyes when they look our way', reported the British Ambassador at Washington to Grey on 16 June 1916 (S. Gwynn (ed.), *The letters and friendships of Sir Cecil Spring Rice* (London, 1929), ii. 338; Arthur S. Link, *Woodrow Wilson and the Progressive era* (London, 1954), p. 218. For the curious incident whereby the Senate resolution arrived too late to be of value, see Charles C. Tansill, *America and the fight for Irish freedom, 1866–1922* (New York, 1957), pp. 202–14.

[2] Gwynn, *Redmond*, p. 534.

[3] For a vivid eyewitness account of their clash, see S. L. Gwynn, *John Redmond's last years*, pp. 246–8.

overwhelmed with his immense responsibilities, reacted in what was for him a very violent fashion. To O'Connor he described Redmond's speech as 'one of the most ill-conditioned utterances I have ever listened to in that House', and he claimed to draw from it the conclusion that Redmond was trying to force a quarrel with him. 'Ireland', he wrote, 'seems to be always doomed to lose her chances thro' the folly of one or other of her leaders.'[1] T.P. did his best to pour oil on the troubled waters and the prisoners were in the end released by Christmas, but that terrible year of 1916 closed with the gulf between Lloyd George and the Irish party still unbridged.[2]

Dillon had not been involved in these exchanges, but there can be no doubt that he would have approved Redmond's language as the only language a self-respecting Irish leader could use. T. P. O'Connor, however, who was still to a considerable extent hypnotised by Lloyd George, lost no opportunity of trying to restore cordial relations. He dined with the Prime Minister on 22 January 1917 and sent a memorandum of their conversation to Dillon, Devlin and, of course, Redmond. The news was not very good. Lloyd George still evidently thought of a settlement by partition, so far as he was seriously thinking of a settlement at all. What appeared to be much more on his mind was the pressure building up in England to apply conscription to Ireland. The Cabinet had recently had a report indicating an almost complete cessation of Irish recruiting and this, wrote T.P., 'of course produced a considerable sensation there'. O'Connor naturally pointed out to him the impossibility of enforcing conscription in Ireland, 'but he said that in the present temper of the English people, with so many of them sending their sons to the war and losing them, these perils would have to be faced; and he even expressed the opinion that on the issue of conscription he could be beaten in the House of Commons and a purely Tory government take his place.' When T.P. objected that to impose conscription on Ireland might mean the loss of a hundred lives, Lloyd George rejoined that the English people would not care if it were ten thousand. He assured O'Connor over and over again that he wanted to remain on friendly terms with the Irish party, but nevertheless it was clear that he was haunted by the spectre of Ulster Unionism and that because of this his thinking on Ireland was still governed by the necessity, as he saw it, for partition.[3] It did not augur well for the future that on the very day O'Connor was sending his memorandum to Dillon, Dillon was writing to O'Connor about the strength of feeling in the country against conscription and also warning him that any settlement, even temporary, based on the exclusion of Ulster was 'stone dead'.[4]

Dillon, at that moment, was feeling revitalised, as often happened with him, by contact with the country. He had just been in East Mayo, making his first speech to his constituents for two years and his tone had been

[1] Lloyd George to T. P. O'Connor, 19 Dec. 1916, typed copy (D.P.).

[2] T. P. O'Connor to Lloyd George, 20 Dec. 1916 (L.G.P., F/42/2/2).

[3] T. P. O'Connor to Dillon, 23 Jan. 1917 (D.P.); the memorandum is printed in full in Gwynn, *Redmond*, pp. 537–8.

[4] Dillon to T. P. O'Connor, 23 Jan. 1917 (D.P.).

confident and aggressive. His purpose was partly to defend the record of the party since the outbreak of the war and partly to deal with the question of recruiting. It was perfectly true, he said, that recruiting *had* fallen off, but whose fault was that? In 1914 it had been excellent and he himself—though denying that he had ever set foot on a recruiting platform properly so called—had said 'that those of my countrymen who saw their way to join the army . . . were, in my opinion, doing work and fighting for Ireland'. Even this encouragement, however, he had ceased to offer, after the War Office had failed to create a distinctively Irish army and, of course, since then the situation had become even worse. 'The people who killed enlistment were the British War Office and the Coalition Government.'[1] He was well aware that what he was saying would be highly unpopular in many quarters, but it is hard to believe that he did not get some satisfaction out of being able to say it in public at last. 'I have no doubt I shocked many friends', he wrote quite unrepentantly to C. P. Scott. 'But you know me of old—I believe in speaking out in time, and not trying to skim over trouble till some outbreak awakens people to the realities of the situation.'[2]

(ii)

He himself was about to be awakened to quite a different kind of reality. In the course of his speech he had boasted that despite all they had been through the party had not lost either a man or a seat. As it happened, however, a couple of weeks before he spoke the veteran Parnellite, J. J. O'Kelly, had died and his seat in North Roscommon had fallen vacant. Inevitably, this by-election, the first occasion on which it had been possible to test the party's hold on Irish opinion since the rising, became the focus of attention, and once it became known that one of the candidates was to be Count Plunkett, father of Joseph Plunkett, executed for his part in the rebellion, it was evident that the party was faced with a very grave threat. Even Dillon had not at first realised how grave, and his early forecasts had been fairly optimistic.[3] In reality the constitutional candidate stood no chance, Plunkett being elected by a large majority. Ostensibly an Independent, his victory was everywhere regarded as a victory for Sinn Fein, and he himself declared on election that he would not take his seat at Westminster. This result created an entirely new situation in Irish politics, to which the various parliamentary leaders reacted in different, but predictable, ways. T. P. O'Connor, as always, was prepared to sound Lloyd George to see if, in face of this rising tide of Sinn Fein, he might be prepared even at this late hour to propose a settlement, provided always that such a settlement did not involve partition. He would, he wrote to Joe

[1] *F.J.*, 17 Jan. 1917; *W.F.J.*, 20 Jan. 1917.
[2] Dillon to C. P. Scott, 24 Jan. 1917 (D.P.).
[3] For example, in the letter to T. P. O'Connor of 23 January cited above, though he had added 'there may be rough work if the Sinn Feiners go on with the candidature of Count Plunkett'.

Devlin, give Lloyd George 'full notice' that if he suggested partition 'it is the end of all compromise between him and us'. And he continued:

> If that should happen or if these negotiations should fail what are the possibilities for Ireland? Dillon is of course more pessimistic than I; at the same time he knows Ireland thoroughly and can see no end to these things in our present condition but the destruction of the party and the constitutional movement. He thinks, as I do, of course, that Ireland in time would revive her claim, would once more come to the front and would ultimately of course be successful; but I am too old a politician not to shrink with horror from another decade or even five years of violent agitation in Ireland, even if I thought that full self-government were to be at the end of it.[1]

Redmond, to whom a copy of this letter was sent, was even more despondent. He, indeed, had gone beyond all thought of negotiation. Sick, tired and full of despair, he was at that moment drafting a remarkable memorandum which, as he told Dillon when sending it to him on 21 February, he intended to give to the Press 'as a purely personal statement'. It was prompted, he said in the first sentence of the document, by 'the remarkable and unexpected result of the election in North Roscommon'. If that result was freakish, 'due to a wave of emotion or sympathy or momentary passion', then it might be disregarded, but if, as was being widely stated, 'it is an indication of a change of principle and policy on the part of a considerable mass of the Irish people, then an issue, clear and unequivocal, supreme and vital, has been raised, which must be decided as speedily as may be by the Irish people, who alone can decide it'. Next, after tracing the history of the constitutional agitation, culminating in the Home Rule Act of 1914, 'the crowning triumph of forty years of patient labour', he summed up the central dilemma of Irish politics as follows:

> These then are the results of the principle and policy pursued since 1873: the principle of an Irish parliament loyally within the Empire, and the policy of pursuing that end by constitutional and parliamentary methods.
> The alternative principle and policy which Ireland's enemies to-day assert, on the strength of the North Roscommon election, have been adopted by the Irish people are separation from the Empire, the establishment of an Irish Republic, withdrawal from Westminster, and the methods of physical force, which would mean, apart from inevitable anarchy in Ireland itself, not merely the hopeless alienation of every friend of Ireland in every British party, but leaving the settlement of every Irish question, big or little, material or political, in the hands of Irish Unionist members in the Imperial Parliament, a policy which was denounced as vigorously by Smith O'Brien as by O'Connell and has never found favour with any prominent leader of Irish public opinion in the last one hundred years.

[1] T. P. O'Connor to Joe [Devlin], 16 Feb. 1917, typed copy (R.P.).

He did not doubt, he said, that Ireland was at bottom sound and he hoped the day would come soon when the issue could be tested in every constituency, but he ended on a note which was beyond all question valedictory:

> If, as would perhaps be not unnatural, the people have grown tired of the monotony of being served for twenty, thirty, thirty-five or forty years by the same men in Parliament, and desire variety and a change, speaking for myself, I have no complaint to make . . . Let the Irish people replace us, by all means, by other and, I hope, better men, if they so choose. But, in the name of all they hold most sacred, do not let them be led astray by any passion of resentment or will-o'-the-wisp of policy into courses which must end in immediate defeat of their hopes for the present and permanent disaster to their country.[1]

To Redmond's appalled colleagues this memorandum came as a thunderbolt. Hurriedly they met to discuss it, agreed that to publish such a document would be virtually to destroy the party, and entrusted the universal peacemaker, T. P. O'Connor, with the disagreeable task of persuading Redmond not to release it. He accomplished this with the delicacy he often showed in personal relations and the memorandum did not go to the Press.[2] Nevertheless, it remains as evidence of how far the leader of the party had given way to despair that *one* by-election defeat could have elicited from him such a confession of failure. Dillon, on the other hand, though normally more prone to pessimism than Redmond, was always at his most aggressive when the news was worst. And the news was very bad indeed. Hard on the heels of the by-election the authorities began to re-arrest some of the men (who, certainly, had shown themselves quite impenitent Sinn Feiners) released at Christmas. Dillon, who came over from Ireland consumed with fury at this gratuitous gift of martyrdom to the party's enemies, was now convinced that nothing was to be hoped for from Lloyd George. A few days later, on 26 February, he delivered in the House of Commons a scathing attack on the policy of the Government. Complaining bitterly of the rearrests, he demanded why they had been made, whether there was or was not a state of martial law in the country, and why 'the Press have been ordered not to speak about Ireland'. 'For the last year and a half,' he declared, 'the British Government in Ireland have been manufacturing Sinn Feiners by tens of thousands, until they have nearly maddened the country now, and the country will listen to no reason.' Then he continued with great bitterness:

> Our party was built up thirty years ago and more by saying to our countrymen, 'We will show you a road by which you can trust British people and trust British statesmen'. The occurrences of last July have poisoned our people against us, and when we go back to Ireland we are asked by all the young men, 'What is the use of your telling us to

[1] Redmond to Dillon, 21 Feb. 1917, enclosing copy of the memorandum (D.P.); part of the document is printed in Gwynn, *Redmond*, p. 540.
[2] T. P. O'Connor to Redmond, 21 Feb. 1917 (R.P.); Gwynn, *Redmond*, p. 539.

trust British statesmen? One blast of Carson's horn is worth all your reasoning. And why is it . . . that the right hon. gentleman the member for Trinity College is an honoured member of the Government now, after he had boasted in this House that he would be a rebel and defy the King's authority and had flouted this House?' The answer of all these young men, who are joining Sinn Fein by thousands now, is that this is the only argument that British ministers understand, and they say: 'If you had acted like Carson, and if you had hurled insults across the floor of the House at British ministers, you would be in a very different position now from what you are in.'

We are, and I am not ashamed to admit it, in a sense between the devil and the deep sea. On the one side we have the Irish revolution and on the other side we have the Castle gang . . . Our task has been for a long while difficult, and you are making it impossible.[1]

This outburst, revealing though it was of Dillon's own almost total disenchantment with the traditional policy of his party, made absolutely no impact upon Lloyd George, except perhaps to confirm in his eyes what was steadily becoming more apparent to all beholders, that the constitutional Nationalists were going downhill fast and were ceasing to count for much in Anglo-Irish relations. Certainly, when a few days later T. P. O'Connor had an interview with him, the Prime Minister would offer no encouragement, making it clear that he could not move without Carson— in short, that the irreconcilable differences between Irishmen themselves made a settlement impossible.[2] Nor was this merely for private consumption. When on 7 March O'Connor moved a resolution in the House of Commons calling on the Government to give Home Rule to Ireland which evoked from Redmond's brother, Willie (soon to be killed in Flanders), a poignant speech pleading for reconciliation, Lloyd George's response was bleak in the extreme. Ulster, he said truly enough, could not be coerced, but he went out of his way to add that the province was 'as alien in blood, in religious faith, in traditions, in outlook, as alien from the rest of Ireland as the inhabitants of Fife or Aberdeen'. This deliberate deflation of the mood his brother had created angered John Redmond so intensely that then and there he led his party out of the House.[3]

Lloyd George's attitude was the more remarkable because, the day before the debate, O'Connor had written to him begging him to attempt a settlement at the right psychological moment. If he continued to hold out no hope, then, said O'Connor, all the news from Ireland indicated there would be such an outburst of resentment that the Government might be driven to coercion. 'What does that mean to your future political career?' 'Is it not,' asked T.P. shrewdly, 'the beginning of that necessary and inevitable dependence on the Tory forces which would paralyse your future work as a reformer?'[4] Lloyd George, however, was in no mood to discuss his

[1] Hansard, H.C. Debates, 5th series, vol. 90, cols. 1776–87.
[2] Gwynn, *Redmond*, pp. 540–1.
[3] Hansard, H.C. Debates, 5th series, vol. 91, cols. 425–42, 442–8, 459, 474–82.
[4] T. P. O'Connor to Lloyd George, 6 Mar. 1917 (L.G.P., F/42/2/3).

future with O'Connor. The present was demanding enough, since the war at sea was now at a critical stage and the submarine menace had somehow or other to be combated. The responsibility for this lay with Carson, who was not achieving at the Admiralty quite all that had been hoped of him. Already there was pressure to move him and Lloyd George was about to be faced with the awkward problem (which he eventually solved with his usual ingenuity) of relieving Carson of his post without losing him from the Ministry. The last thing he wanted in the midst of these delicate manoeuvres was a recrudescence of the Ulster problem.

Not indeed that the internal stresses of war politics were the sole reason for disappointing Irish hopes. There was also a growing feeling—which Dillon and Redmond could ignore only at their peril—that the parliamentarians were played out and were no longer in control of Irish opinion. In the course of debate a few days later Bonar Law made the significant remark that if a general election were to be held in the near future the Irish party might find it going against them—the obvious implication being that if this was likely to be the case then perhaps it was not the Irish party with whom the Government should be bargaining. Dillon lost no time in taking up the point. It might well be, he conceded, that they would lose some seats at an election, but nevertheless he would welcome one soon. And he went on to make a large admission:

> The reason why I am anxious for a general election is that it lies in the mouth of anyone to say to us of the Irish party, now for the first time in thirty years, that we do not speak for Ireland, that after the North Roscommon election we can no longer speak for Ireland until we get a new mandate. We want as soon as possible to put to the Irish people the question whether they have confidence in us and whether we are to continue to be responsible for their representation.[1]

Despite the rumours to the contrary, a general election did not, of course, come at that time, but the party were very soon to have another chance of testing opinion at a by-election in South Longford. While that was still pending, pressure upon Lloyd George to attempt a settlement began to increase in America. At the beginning of April the United States had entered the war and it was essential for Wilson to be able to placate Irish-American opinion. Almost immediately, therefore, through the American Ambassador in London, the President urged the necessity of 'a satisfactory form of self-government' for Ireland.[2] But still the omens were not propitious. Seeing Lloyd George just at this time, T. P. O'Connor found him 'quite hopeless'. He tried to impress upon the Prime Minister

---

[1] Hansard, H.C. Debates, 5th series, vol. 91, cols. 1837–42. He made the same point privately to Colonel Maurice Moore, but coupled with it an emphatic insistence that Irish parliamentarians must continue to attend at Westminster. 'I have no faith whatever', he wrote, 'in any attempt by the Irish party to reassert its position in Ireland by a feeble and—in my mind—contemptible imitation of Arthur Griffith's policy' (Dillon to Moore, 13 Mar. 1917, Moore Papers, N.L.I. MS. 10561/9).

[2] Gwynn, *Redmond*, p. 544.

that the Irish party could not accept any terms involving partition. Lloyd George, on the other hand 'seemed perfectly clear in his mind, or professed to be, that if he yielded to us Carson would break up the ministry'.[1] At this point, to complicate matters still further, Redmond fell ill and had to retire to Bath. This meant that Dillon was in effective control, a prospect which filled some members of the party with dismay. One of them, the former Parnellite, J. J. Clancy, wrote complaining that in his present mood Dillon could not be counted on to follow the party line. 'I believe,' he said, 'and so do many members, that a grave calamity may happen to us and to Ireland, if George's statement on Home Rule is made this coming week. The danger arises from the fact that Dillon is certain to speak. The great majority of the party are averse, in my belief, to having him make *any* pronouncement and would like you to be at hand.'[2] That Clancy had perhaps some grounds for apprehension emerges from a letter Dillon himself wrote Redmond the next day, when among other things, he mentioned that he had *twice* in the past few days refused to go to see to Lloyd George![3] However, after some difficulty, the Prime Minister did manage to make contact with Devlin and T. P. O'Connor. On 30 April the latter reported that Lloyd George still seemed nervous at the prospect of Carson leaving the Government and attacking whatever settlement might be proposed.[4] It appeared, in fact, as if Dillon's persistent scepticism was still justified. Earlier in the year, in the immediate aftermath of North Roscommon, he had warned his friend C. P. Scott that the Irish situation was again becoming critical. 'I don't believe', he had written, 'that L.G. has the slightest notion of attempting a settlement. Carson is still on top, and it is within the limits of possibility that we may have a period like 1795–98 before us.'[5] The last part of that remarkable prophecy was still some way from fulfilment, but Lloyd George certainly seemed to be running true to form, or at least the form that Dillon had come to expect of him.

Meanwhile, however, the responsibility still lay with Redmond whose reaction was to play for time. With the South Longford by-election reaching its climax, there was a good deal to be said for Lloyd George deferring his statement until after it was over. Moreover, he was convinced that pressure from America would intensify as time went on, and his mind was already turning towards the idea of an appeal to moderate Irish-Americans for financial and moral support sufficient to place the party in a position to fight the general election vigorously whenever it might come. For the present, therefore, he advised his colleagues to be very wary of Lloyd George. If he put forward any scheme involving the exclusion of the six counties that should be 'instantly and vigorously denounced', though, if he reverted to his old notion of county option, then, he suggested, it might be well to temporise, neither accepting nor rejecting it out of hand.[6]

[1] T. P. O'Connor to Dillon, 4 Apr. 1917 (D.P.).
[2] J. J. Clancy to Redmond, 29 Apr. 1917 (R.P.).
[3] Dillon to Redmond, 30 Apr. 1917 (R.P.).   [4] Gwynn, *Redmond*, p. 544.
[5] Dillon to C. P. Scott, 7 Feb. 1917 (D.P.).   [6] Gwynn, *Redmond*, pp. 544–5.

As it turned out, Lloyd George saved the Irish leaders the trouble of having to make up their minds. On 3 May Dillon and O'Connor dined with C. P. Scott and learned from him that the Prime Minister's proposal, when it came, would be for 'a clean cut' of the six counties. This, they agreed, would be 'the end of all things', and Dillon, more disillusioned than ever, went off at once to throw himself into the closing stages of the Longford election.[1] His report to Redmond a few days later suggested that the party organisers were confident of victory; this was a confidence he did not share, but he was well aware, none better, of the crucial importance of the contest:

> We have the bishop, the great majority of the priests and the mob and four-fifths of the traders of Longford. And if in face of that we are beaten, I do not see how you can hold the party in existence.
>   If we win there will be a fresh chance for the party. But I hold a very definite and strong view as to the only line on which there is the least prospect of success for the party and the movement. And when you get back to London I shall put my view clearly before you.[2]

Two days later he was in London, giving T. P. O'Connor—who duly passed it on to Redmond—a very gloomy account of the condition of affairs in Ireland.[3] As so often before, events soon confirmed Dillon's pessimism. South Longford was won by Sinn Fein, and though the margin was only thirty-seven votes, the blow was as heavy as if it had been a hundred times as much. To some members of the party this defeat seemed nothing less than a notice to quit and the idea began to circulate that they should resign in a body. Redmond still had enough authority to quell this panic, but the mere existence of such a feeling in the ranks of his own followers weakened his position still further—and this at the moment when Lloyd George was at last about to make his long-deferred proposal.[4]

(iii)

The story of that proposal is well known and need only be briefly told here. On 15 May, still far from well, Redmond attended a banquet in honour of General Smuts. He sat beside a Liberal peer, Lord Crewe, who told him that Lloyd George had written him (Redmond) a letter offering an immediate Irish Parliament on the basis of the exclusion of the six counties. Inevitably, Redmond retorted that this was quite unacceptable. What, then, would he suggest as an alternative, inquired his neighbour? Redmond answered—as apparently he had already been saying for some time privately among his friends—that the only hope lay in some Conference or Convention of Irishmen. If they could work out their own salvation and agree on a recommendation to the Government, then indeed there might be

[1] T. P. O'Connor to Redmond, 3 May 1917 (R.P.).
[2] Dillon to Redmond, 8 May 1917 (R.P.).
[3] T. P. O'Connor to Redmond, 10 May 1917 (R.P.).
[4] S. L. Gwynn, *The last years of John Redmond*, p. 260.

a chance of a permanent settlement. This was reported at once to Lloyd George and early next morning Lord Crewe was on Redmond's doorstep to get the suggestion in writing for immediate consideration by the cabinet. That same day Redmond received the promised letter from Lloyd George. It did indeed, as anticipated, proceed on the basis of partition (though it provided for a Council of Ireland in which north and south might participate), but in the closing paragraphs Redmond's own suggestion was taken up and Lloyd George stated categorically that the government was ready 'in default of the adoption of their present proposals for Home Rule, to take the necessary steps for the assembling of such a Convention'. Redmond replied at once, repudiating the partition scheme, but promising that the Irish party would place no obstacle in the way of a Convention. They would even recommend it to the country 'on condition that the basis on which the Convention is to be called is such as to secure that it will be fully and fairly representative of Irishmen of all creeds, interests and parties'. Finally, Lloyd George in his turn threw over the partition proposal and on 21 May announced in the House of Commons that a fully representative Convention would be speedily summoned. 'If', he promised, 'substantial agreement should be reached as to the character and scope of the constitution for the future government of Ireland within the Empire', then the Government would 'accept responsibility for taking all the necessary steps to enable the Imperial Parliament to give legislative effect to the conclusions of the Convention'.[1] Thus was launched on its chequered career the last attempt to find a peaceful and constitutional settlement of the Irish question.

Almost at once the wires began to hum with proposals and counter-proposals as to the size and character of the Convention. Dillon, though absolutely resolved not to serve on the Convention himself, took the proposal seriously enough to submit the composition of the body to repeated close analysis. He was joined in Ireland by Devlin and Redmond, leaving O'Connor (protesting as usual, and, as usual vainly, that he should not be left to bear the brunt of negotiating with Lloyd George) to serve as their intermediary in London.[2] From the start Dillon was suspicious of government attempts to pack the Convention. The earliest indications were that a fairly small body was in prospect, with twenty-five Nationalists, twenty Unionists, and a number of official nominees. 'If we attempted to defend such a body,' he wrote tartly to T.P. on 24 May, 'we should be charged reasonably with having betrayed the country.' If the Government were actually to adopt any such scheme, he added ominously, 'I shall feel coerced to protest publicly immediately'.[3] Next day, having had a chance to

---

[1] Lord Crewe to Asquith, 16 May 1917 (Asquith Papers, box 37, ff. 140–1); S. L. Gwynn, op. cit., pp. 257–8; Gwynn, *Redmond*, pp. 546–51. In Redmond's biography Lord Crewe is not mentioned by name—he is simply 'a Liberal peer'. It appears that C. P. Scott also had a hand in the drafting of the letter of invitation (Scott Papers, B.M. Add. MS. 5094, ff. 48–59).

[2] Telegrams between Dillon and O'Connor, 24–26 May 1917 (D.P.).

[3] Dillon to T. P. O'Connor, 24 May 1917 (D.P.).

confer with Redmond and Devlin, he sent O'Connor a memorandum on which, he said, they were all agreed, but which quite obviously reflected his own views very closely:

Memo. on proposed basis for Irish Convention.

    I Proposal, on assumption that Sinn Fein do not attend, works out at 20 Unionists to 25 Nationalists apart from government nominees. And with government nominees the most that could be expected would be an equality between Nationalists and Unionists, together with neutrals. A convention so composed would be immediately denounced as a shamefully packed body, and it would be impossible for us to say a word in its defence.

   II The proposed basis of representation gives *not one* representative to the Nationalists of Ulster, would enable the five Unionist co. councils to vote down the four Nationalist councils and so raise immediately a row in Ulster wh. would be an irresistable [*sic*] weapon in the hands of wreckers.

  III The proposed basis would result in a solid block of Unionist representatives from Ulster—a result which from more than one point of view would be fatal to all chance of agreement at convention.

  IV The proposal to offer 4 representatives to Sinn Fein is very unwise. The S.F's. will *not* come in. That is all the greater reason for seeing that they have no plausible excuse for staying out.

   V They ought to be offered equal representation with the Ulstermen and with the Irish party, i.e. 6.

  VI *Each* county council should be represented either by its chairman or by a specially elected delegate.

 VII The names to be nominated by the government should not be settled without consultation with us.[1]

For the next two or three days Dillon continued to bombard O'Connor with letters insisting on a large Convention with a preponderance of Nationalists. Redmond in the meantime had taken refuge in his Wicklow home, Aughavanagh, while Devlin was in Belfast. Eventually, the unfortunate O'Connor received three separate drafts from his three colleagues. 'What possible advice', he not unreasonably asked, 'can I give to Lloyd George under the circumstances?'[2] Unrepentantly, Dillon wrote that same day (28 May): 'I am *irreconcilably opposed* to our accepting full responsibility for composition of the Convention. Nothing will shake me in this determination. What I was prepared, and am prepared to do, is to let L.G. know what is the minimum which would enable us to tolerate the Convention as fairly representative. More than that he is *not entitled* to ask us for. If Carson is to dictate the composition of the Convention, then the game is up. I am afraid you do not yet realise the condition of Ireland.'[3]

[1] Dillon to T. P. O'Connor, 25 May 1917 (D.P.).
[2] T. P. O'Connor to Dillon, 28 May 1917 (D.P.).
[3] Dillon to T. P. O'Connor, 28 May 1917 (D.P.).

His alarm, in fact, was needless, for the scheme announced by Lloyd George
on 11 June conceded most of his points and, if implemented, would have
resulted in a Convention of 101 members. Owing, however, to the abstention of Sinn Fein, William O'Brien and his group, and the Dublin and Cork
trades councils, the number who actually participated when the Convention
eventually met fluctuated around ninety.[1]

While these preliminaries were going on the party and its organisation
had somehow to be kept together. Money was essential—money to keep
the *Freeman's Journal* from foundering, money to enable the party to fight
the next general election. Since it could only come from America, Redmond
now persuaded the long-suffering O'Connor to cut himself loose from his
multifarious newspaper commitments and undertake a comprehensive
fund-raising mission in the U.S.A. For some weeks before he went Dillon
devoted considerable effort to trying to inculcate into him the correct line
for America. The ensuing correspondence may not have helped O'Connor
overmuch, but it throws a very clear light on the extent of Dillon's disillusionment, not merely with the hopeless fight they had been carrying on
at Westminster, but also with Redmond's leadership. Thus, on 31 May,
after he had just heard of O'Connor's mission (the one hope of saving the
movement, Dillon thought) he offered him some suggestions. 'If any of
them seem to you absurd, extravagant or impertinent, put them down as
the extravagances of an Irish extremist, and take them in good part.' In the
first place, he warned T.P. not to be too enthusiastic about the war, but
simply to express the 'intense gratification' Wilson's speeches (on the rights
of small nations) had given in Ireland. Secondly, he was on no account to
appear as a champion of England, and he was to 'keep as clear as possible
of [the] British Embassy at Washington'. Above all, he was to confront
Irish-Americans with the dire urgency of the situation in Ireland:

> In explaining need for large sum of money, state that from *whatever
> source* obtained, the Republican leaders in Ireland have flooded the
> country with money—that the country is so disturbed and irritated by
> Maxwellism and martial law, and the government's breach of faith in
> July last that just at the moment we are unable to raise a fund and
> that a large fund is absolutely required to enable us to save the
> country from falling into the hands of the Irish Republicans and pro-
> German party. That a victory of the Irish party pledged to an Irish
> Republic separated from England must lead to another and much
> bloodier rebellion—and put an end for a very long time to any hope of
> a peaceful settlement of the Irish question.[2]

Such cold-blooded realism was very foreign to T. P. O'Connor's temperament, but it was entirely characteristic of Dillon. He had grasped the
two salient facts of the situation and he stated them quite flatly and un-
emotionally—first, that no Irish mission to the U.S. could afford to be pro-

[1] *W.F.J.*, 14 July 1917.
[2] Dillon to T. P. O'Connor, enclosing 'Notes on American mission', 31 May 1917
(D.P.).

British; second, that the Irish party, enfeebled and impotent though it seemed, was all that stood between the country and an Anglo-Irish war. It was his nature, having reached so far into the problem, to think it through to the end. Next day, therefore, he added a further note of warning:

> Do not be too enthusiastic about [the] Convention, or put all your money on its success. On the contrary, I consider you should emphasise the fact that the cabinet are *solely* responsible for this proposal, but that dangers and difficulties of the Irish situation are so great that we felt absolutely bound to give the proposal a fair and friendly trial and that we felt that if a settlement should be arrived at with general agreement and good-will—as a result of the Convention —it would be an incalculable blessing to Ireland, besides being an immense gain to the allies. If, however, the Convention failed to produce an agreed settlement, the Irish problem would remain in a more aggravated form than ever, and we should have to look to our friends and fellow-countrymen in the U.S. to help us to carry a national settlement.[1]

By the time he wrote this Dillon was in Mayo and clearly had no intention of involving himself further in the details of the Convention. Writing again to O'Connor a couple of days later, he admitted that if Redmond's health had been better 'I would have told him plainly that it was his business to remain in London and see this matter thro'.' As it was, he had been profoundly disturbed by Redmond's recent speech in the House of Commons, welcoming the Convention and offering, as it must have seemed to Dillon, extravagantly generous representation to the Unionists.[2] 'It has brought me nearer to the point of giving up the fight than anything which has yet occurred.' Dillon himself would not go to London. 'I have no doubt', he said with perfect frankness, 'I would immediately break up the whole business.' Then he went on: 'The condition of Ireland is *horrible*, even our own best friends are getting possessed with the idea that we have *no* backbone and are prepared to yield everything and always to L.G. and the government. And the time has come when we must either make a start and if necessary a fight—or get out.' O'Connor's mission, he was convinced, was the only chance left of saving the movement. 'With £50,000, or better £100,000, of American money and the moral support of the American Irish I think this country could be brought back to sanity and the constitutional movement saved.'[3] His immediate preoccupation remained, of course, the continuing financial chaos of the *Freeman's Journal*, and a few days later he was lamenting to T.P. that he needed a further £10,000 to carry it on through another year. On the broader issue of the lack of leadership he was, if anything, gloomier. 'The curse that is hanging over us in Ireland is that the great mass *of our friends* are bewildered and do not know where they are. They have got it firmly fixed in their heads that Redmond

[1] Dillon to T. P. O'Connor, 1 June 1917 (D.P.).
[2] Gwynn, *Redmond*, pp. 550–1.
[3] Dillon to T. P. O'Connor, 3 June 1917 (D.P.).

has no more fight in him'.[1] Not unnaturally, O'Connor reproached him with despairing too soon, but Dillon's response was again typical—realism not despair was his *forte*. 'I have *not* despaired. I have only endeavoured— perhaps in too rough and violent language—to bring home to you the terrible gravity of the situation here. I said, and now repeat, that given American money, the moral support of the American Irish, and even at the 11th hour a firm lead, this country could be redeemed. I am quite convinced of this. But you will admit that the three conditions are *serious* and without the three the situation is really quite hopeless.'[2]

(iv)

The leadership issue was at that very moment becoming even more serious than Dillon had imagined. On 7 June Redmond's brother Willie was killed in action at Messines and the tragic death of this much-beloved member of the party had two important consequences. First, it was a wellnigh mortal blow to John Redmond himself. He was deeply attached to his brother, valued his counsel and found in him a confidant far more congenial and accessible than any other member of the party, with the possible exception of the Chief Whip, Paddy O'Brien, whom death was also to remove in only a few weeks' time. In the second place, Willie Redmond's death caused a vacancy in East Clare. For this vacancy the Sinn Fein candidate was the most formidable there could well have been—Eamonn de Valera, the most distinguished survivor of the 1916 Rising, just at this point released from prison. Confronted with this challenge, and with their leader disabled by private grief, the party did virtually nothing, despite urgent appeals for help from the constituency. Local Nationalists then held an unofficial meeting at which they adopted a candidate—Patrick Lynch, K.C.—who in normal times would have stood a good chance. Against Mr. de Valera he stood no chance at all. 'We are faced here with desperate opposition', wrote one of Lynch's backers to Redmond. 'The bishop, and a section of the clergy, are arrayed against us, and the junior clergy in particular are moving heaven and hell to get de Valera elected.'[3] Redmond's attitude, however, as conveyed to Dillon by Devlin, was that they should on no account involve themselves in such a lost cause. Dillon accepted this, though reluctantly, since not to fight elections was in his view an abdica- tion of their whole position. Having accepted it, he would have wished to carry the policy of non-interference to its logical conclusion, but this proved impossible when appeals for help continued to pour in, and again he allowed himself to be overruled, to the extent of sending some speakers into the constituency. The consequence, as he was quick to point out to Redmond, was that they had the worst of both worlds, supporting a candi- date who had not been selected by the party, yet sharing the stigma of his

[1] Dillon to T. P. O'Connor, 7 June 1917 (D.P.).
[2] Dillon to T. P. O'Connor, 8 June 1917 (D.P.).
[3] John Moroney (vice-chairman Ennis U.D.C.) to Redmond, 4 July 1917 (D.P.).

defeat. 'You know', he wrote, 'I have always considered the abstention on the part of the party from elections as an impossible attitude. The result is this system of being dragged in without being consulted in the selection of the candidate.'[1] And when Mr. de Valera, who used the opportunity to state the separatist case in the most unequivocal terms, won easily, Dillon had only the melancholy satisfaction of being proved right after the event. 'I deeply regret', he wrote to his much-tried chairman, 'we ever consented to take any part in that election. Nothing would have induced me to withdraw my opposition, but the urgent appeals of loyal supporters in East Clare and Limerick city.'[2]

Perhaps the most extraordinary feature of the East Clare election was John Redmond's own almost total indifference to it. This was partly the after-effect of Willie Redmond's death, more the result of a serious deterioration in his health, but most of all because he had transferred all his hopes and his last reserves of energy to the Irish Convention, which was due to open at the end of July. With the history of that ill-fated body we are not here directly concerned, since Dillon adhered to his refusal to serve on it and continued to watch it sceptically from the wings. It is easy to see now that given the abstention of Sinn Fein and of important sections of the Irish labour movement, and in view also of the fact that the Ulster representatives had no intention of abating their resistance to being included in any general Home Rule settlement, the whole Convention was a gigantic irrelevancy. It was the last tragic irony, in an accumulation of tragedies over the past four years, that Redmond should have attached himself so strongly to the idea that the Convention was in microcosm an Irish 'parliament' which, if given a fair chance, might reach the degree of 'substantial agreement' that would enable Lloyd George to carry through a permanent settlement. So obsessed did he become with this conception that his usual skill in negotiation quite deserted him, and in the last days of the Convention, and in the last weeks of his own life, he went so far towards accommodation with the representatives of Southern Irish Unionism that he found himself subjected to the final humiliation of being opposed even by his own closest supporters, Joe Devlin and Bishop O'Donnell.[3]

This bitter conclusion to a great career took some six months—from July 1917 to January 1918—to unroll. In the meantime the real centre of gravity of Irish politics was the Sinn Fein movement. That movement did not, however, progress majestically from strength to strength. On the contrary, its fortunes fluctuated, and the record of the by-elections was by no means one of unmitigated disaster for the parliamentary party. Nevertheless, although the constitutionalists did retain several seats during 1917, their inner confidence had been undermined, and some, even inside the party itself, were beginning to grow restive. One sign of this increasing disillusionment with Redmond's leadership was the curious episode of the

---

[1] Dillon to Redmond, 26 June 1917 (R.P.).
[2] Dillon to Redmond, 3 Aug. 1917 (R.P.).
[3] Gwynn, *Redmond*, chap. 16.

'Remonstrance' which was circulated among members within a fortnight of the Clare election and on the eve of the meeting of the Convention. It was in the form of a letter to Redmond, drawing his attention to the rapidly changing situation in Ireland and pointing out that this, combined with the apparent paralysis of the Government's Irish policy, necessitated 'a review of our own policy and methods'. The decay of the party, the letter stated, could be traced from the moment when, under the threat of the Curragh mutiny and of rebellion in Ulster 'consent was given . . . to accept a measure of Home Rule which was not to apply to the whole of Ireland'. The new programme which they wished the party to adopt was:

1. Self-government for the whole of Ireland on South African and Australian models.
2. Adherence to constitutional methods.
3. 'In case the Convention which is to meet on July 25 comes to no decision within a limited period of say, one month or in case, by a majority, it declares for a constitution on the colonial model and the government declines to give effect immediately to that decision, then we should unite all Irish nationalists in an appeal to the United States, Russia and France, and finally to the International Peace Congress.'

This last proposal was an attempt to take a leaf out of the Sinn Fein book, but towards Sinn Fein itself the remonstrants were curiously ambivalent. They could not, they said, accept its full programme, partly because withdrawal from Westminster was simply a way of disfranchising Ireland, even more because they thought that another rebellion was the logical consequence of such withdrawal. All the same, they ended with this strange genuflection towards the policy of extremism:

> For the aspirations which now stir the young men and women of Ireland and their desire for the complete independence of our country, rather than that it should remain in its present humiliating position, we have full admiration. We believe that the manifestation of their indomitable determination to win for Ireland her true place in the sun is the most hopeful sign of recent years.[1]

This document does not seem to have attracted the support of more than a small minority of the party. The copy in Redmond's papers was signed by only six members—and one of his friends, Hugh Law, did his best to reassure him. 'I want you to know', he wrote, 'that a large section of us was firmly opposed to it; and we succeeded at any rate in dissuading the promoters from making it, as some of them apparently at first intended, a public manifesto.'[2] Although Dillon received a copy of the remonstrance, no comment of his upon it survives, though it must have provided him, no less than Redmond, with plenty to think about. There could be no question of his associating himself with it. Critical of Redmond he might be to his

---

[1] Typed, unsigned copy dated 24 July 1917 (D.P.).
[2] Hugh Law to Redmond, 17 Aug. 1917 (R.P.).

intimates, but he never wavered in his loyalty. So far as the document itself was concerned, he would probably have been contemptuous of its muddled thinking and of the evident disposition of its authors to placate the revolutionary spirit without exposing themselves to any of the inconveniences of actual revolution. But it did at least look forward, as he did, to what might happen if the Convention failed, and in one respect it advocated a procedure—appeal to the Allies and ultimately to the peace conference—with which he was coming to have some sympathy.

His own efforts, for the rest of that year, as the Convention dragged its slow length along, were directed partly to the not uncongenial task of fighting Sinn Fein on public platforms, and partly to finding an alternative solution to have ready if—or rather when—the Convention came to nothing. The most important speech he made in Ireland that summer was at Armagh and it was notable, not merely for his frank admission of the weakness of the parliamentary party, nor for his somewhat faint praise of the Convention, but for his profound insight into where the Sinn Fein policy was likely to lead the country. The Convention he described as 'the device of a hard-pressed minister to escape from a desperately difficult position', but he insisted that the Irish party were bound to give it a fair trial. If it succeeded, well and good—but if it failed, then the position would be more menacing than ever, for such a failure could only redound to the advantage of Sinn Fein. Sinn Fein, he warned his audience, was making a completely dishonest appeal to the passions of the young men of Ireland. Whatever they might say, an independent republic was impossible without fighting Britain, and a united Ireland would be impossible without fighting Ulster. Some Sinn Fein supporters, he said, were deluding the people by maintaining that these objectives could be won without the use of force, but in a striking passage he expressly excluded Mr. de Valera from this accusation:

> Personally, I am unacquainted with Mr. de Valera, but from all I have heard of him and judging from his actions and speeches since he emerged into the public life of Ireland, I should suppose him to be a brave and honourable man who would scorn to be a party to such a policy as is imputed to him by these whispers to which I have alluded. I take it Mr. de Valera believes in the policy that he preaches and while I profoundly differ from him and am of opinion that his policy is calculated to throw the whole country into terrible disaster, I cannot help having a great admiration for a man who, having risked his life and suffered imprisonment for the cause of liberty, is prepared now to throw the desperate die once more.[1]

This remarkable, if back-handed, tribute explains much of Dillon's own dilemma in these difficult months. Absolutely opposed to everything Sinn Fein stood for, the memory of his own passionate youth rose up to prevent him from joining the chorus of execration which was the usual reaction of

[1] *W.F.J.*, 18 Aug. 1917.

less complicated constitutionalists to their rivals. He could not find it in
him to condemn utterly men who had taken their lives in their hands once
and might do so again. Thus, he was curiously inhibited in his onslaughts
upon the party's enemies, even though no one knew better than he how near
the party was to extinction.

(v)

As summer merged into autumn extinction seemed indeed to be advancing
by giant strides. The Convention had become so immersed in detail that it
was hard to see how it could achieve anything except to add one more
chapter to the weary tale of Irish recrimination. Then in August, following
the death of Paddy O'Brien, W. T. Cosgrave captured his vacant seat in
Kilkenny, and Sinn Fein began to seem irresistible at the polls. More and
more the leaders of the party pinned their hopes on T. P. O'Connor's
mission to America, but even here the outlook was bleak. His initial reception in July had been unenthusiastic, and at the end of August he was still
complaining that he was sweltering in New York in a state of complete
isolation, if not of actual boycott.[1] 'I think', wrote Shane Leslie, 'Mr.
O'Connor will be wise to return without raising up too many hornets. Irish
feeling has perceptibly embittered since his arrival.'[2] And if all this were
not enough, the government had recommenced that pin-pricking policy of
arrests in Ireland which Dillon had repeatedly condemned as providing the
best possible publicity for Sinn Fein. In September this policy provoked,
as sooner or later it was bound to provoke, a serious incident. One of the
men seized, Thomas Ashe (who had played a prominent part in the Rising),
went on hunger-strike in protest against his arrest, and on 25 September it
was announced that he had died after forcible feeding. Immediately there
was a tremendous outburst of popular feeling and Ashe at once took his
place in the martyrology of Sinn Fein.

From Dillon's point of view this could not have happened at a worse
time. During September he had been engaged in furious controversy with
Arthur Griffith. Griffith had, of course, long been one of the most formidable critics of the party, and although Dillon had spoken on his behalf in
the House of Commons just after the Rising, he had referred to him even
then as 'a very bitter political enemy of my own'.[3] Now, in a speech in
Cavan, Dillon went out of his way to make against Griffith the very injurious charge that he was, as he put it, 'exploiting and trading on the fight and
death of the rebels of Easter week, although when the chance was offered
to him to stand by the side of these men and share their fight, he emphatically refused to do so'.[4] This was quite incorrect. It was true that Griffith had
refused to join the Supreme Council of the I.R.B., but not that he had
refused to join the Rising. He had been kept in ignorance of it until two days

[1] Shane Leslie to Dillon, 11 July 1917 (D.P.); T. P. O'Connor to Devlin, 31 July 1917
(D.P.).
[2] Shane Leslie to Dillon, 26 Aug. 1917 (D.P.).
[3] Hansard, H.C. Debates, 5th series, vol. 82, cols. 2965–6.
[4] *W.F.J.*, 29 Sept. 1917.

before it broke out and had heard the news with disapproval. Even so, once the fighting had started he had pleaded to be allowed to join, only to be told that his contribution must continue to be mainly propagandist.[1] Naturally, he was deeply incensed by Dillon's charges and met them with counter-charges, such as that Dillon had tried to entice both him and Eoin MacNeill into the parliamentary party, which Dillon denied with equal vehemence. It was an undignified and bad-tempered exchange on both sides, but as a tactical manoeuvre it had, from Dillon's viewpoint, something to be said in its favour. If he could drive a wedge between Griffith and the Republicans, then he might gain at least some breathing-space for the parliamentary party, even perhaps give it a fighting chance at the general election. And more and more he was coming to look on the general election as the key to the whole situation. 'If the people of Ireland', he said in that same speech in which he had insulted Griffith, 'are of opinion that the old leaders have led them wrong and are prepared to trust their fate, their fortune, their lives—because this is a matter of life and death—their lives, as well as the fate of this country, to new leaders who are untried, then let us meet at the polls, and if the people decide against us, for my part I shall have no bitterness in my heart, because the nation has the right to choose its own leaders.'

The notion of driving a wedge between Griffith and the men who had been 'out' in 1916 would probably have been a forlorn hope at best, but the death of Thomas Ashe, as Dillon himself realised immediately, wiped out whatever headway he had been making, or thought he had been making, in the country. 'Sinn Fein was on the decline until the new arrests and the death of Ashe', he wrote to O'Connor some weeks later. 'His death acted just like a can of petroleum poured over a dying fire. Since that event S.F. has gained enormously in strength.'[2] Indeed, by the time that letter was written, Griffith's movement and de Valera's had moved much closer together and, as the result of the Sinn Fein Ard Fheis in October 1917, de Valera had emerged as potentially the most powerful leader in Ireland, combining in his own person the presidency of the Volunteers with the headship of the Sinn Fein organisation.

It was hardly surprising in the circumstances that Dillon from this time onwards became possessed with the idea that the Government was nerving itself for an all-out campaign against Sinn Fein and that the fate of the parliamentary party had ceased to enter into its calculations. 'My own opinion', he told T.P. in the letter already quoted, 'is that the government cannot much longer resist the pressure of the military men, *Morning Post*, *Irish Times*, etc., etc., etc., and that we are on the eve of very grave events . . . R. does not seem to me to realise the situation any more than he did in the winter of 1915–1916.' The parliamentary party, he thought, would be kept dangling until the general election removed it from the scene, 'and

---

[1] S. O. Luing, 'Arthur Griffith and Sinn Fein', in F. X. Martin (ed.), *Leaders and men of the Easter Rising*, pp. 62–3.
[2] Dillon to T. P. O'Connor, 16 Nov. 1917.

then there will be nothing left in Ireland except Republican separatists and Ulster loyalists . . . It is a very pretty scheme.' This is the first appearance of what one can only call the 'conspiracy theory' to which Dillon was to become increasingly addicted as time went on. The parliamentary party, he believed, had become a nuisance to Lloyd George. On the one hand it stood in the way of a settlement based on the exclusion of Ulster. On the other hand, because it was a constitutional party, it could not be coerced. If, however, it became thoroughly discredited in the country, and was rejected by the Irish people at the next election, then the way would be left clear to deal with the Ulster Unionists—presumably on the basis of six-county exclusion—and to impose, by force if need be, whatever settlement of the rest of Ireland seemed desirable to Britain.

Because events were later to follow out this prediction with uncanny accuracy it is tempting to think that Dillon's theory of conspiracy was well founded. But in reality this Machiavellian interpretation of British policy—like all such interpretations—assumed too much. It assumed, in particular, two things that were conspicuously lacking in the British approach to Irish affairs at this time—consistency and resolution. Lloyd George, deeply immersed in the war as he inevitably was, could never spare for Ireland more than an intermittent and cursory attention; other Ministers, if possible, spared her even less. They moved blindly from one desperate expedient to another, endlessly improvising and never pursuing any course to a ruthless or logical conclusion. Hence the sudden arrests and the equally sudden releases, the long spells of indifference alternating with the feverish spasms of negotiation—hence, above all, the readiness to push the whole question off on to the Convention in the reasonable expectation that it might deliberate for months, during which time the government might cling, like a drunken man to a lamp-post, to the *status quo*. Yet, when all is said, Dillon had this much on his side—that the party had many enemies, who would be happy to see it disappear and who, no doubt, were being rapidly convinced by the by-elections that it was on its last legs. But this is still a long way from saying that it disappeared because of the machinations of those who looked for its destruction. The decline of constitutional Nationalism sprang not just from the imbecilities of British policy between 1916 and 1918, nor even from the Home Rule crisis between 1912 and 1914, but from a whole complex of causes reaching back to the Parnell split and its consequences. Nobody had to will the parliamentary party to perish; it was caught in an impossible situation and was perishing anyway of slow strangulation.

Many men in this situation would have been content to throw in their hand. Dillon's code of public conduct did not allow him to do so. When the general election came, and if the party were then defeated, *that* might be the time for a *nunc dimittis*. But in the meantime he and his colleagues were still the constitutionally elected representatives of the Irish people. As such, they had a double duty—to expose the mistakes of British policy in the House of Commons, and to explain to their fellow countrymen the dangers that would surely flow from a wholesale surrender to the seductions of Sinn Fein. During that winter of 1917–18 it was clear to Dillon that his most urgent work lay in Ireland and not at Westminster. Until the Convention reported, nothing was likely to happen in London, but at home the threat from Sinn Fein continued to grow. It may be argued that Dillon, with his undeniable admiration for the men of 1916, was not the best man to state the constitutional case. But, in fact, it was precisely his admiration, openly declared on the floor of the House of Commons when the rebellion had collapsed in the ruins of a largely hostile Dublin, that gave him—virtually alone among the parliamentarians—dignity and respect in Ireland. He could denounce Sinn Fein, not out of blind distaste and incomprehension, but because he could at one and the same time sympathise with the passions of the young men and warn them of the doom that awaited them. This comes out most clearly in a speech he made in Dublin in November just after the junction of forces between Griffith and de Valera, and when the demand for a republic seemed to be gaining ground. Recalling his own part in trying to stop the executions, Dillon admitted that 'I shrink from the condemnation of men who had the courage that these men had on that occasion. The words stick in my throat if I attempt to condemn it.' Nevertheless, he insisted, the Sinn Fein demand for a republic was unrealistic, because a republic could not be had without a full-scale victory over Britain, which he believed to be impossible. And he reiterated yet again the view he had consistently taken from his earliest years in politics, but now more ominously relevant than it had ever been in the days of the Land League:

> I have never in the whole course of my public life said—and I never will—one word against physical force when it was used in a just cause and with some hope of success, but to hurl the unarmed youth of a nation like Ireland, who have been throughout the whole history of the country signalised by martial courage, what I may describe as reckless courage, to hurl them unarmed up against the infernal machinery that has been devised for the destruction of human life in modern war, is a crime or an act of unspeakable folly.[1]

(vi)

Meanwhile, at the Convention, Redmond, in his desperate attempts to save something from the wreckage of his hopes, was drifting further and further away from his own supporters in a noble, but impracticable, effort to find some common ground with his opponents. As the discussions proceeded, it became clear that the Ulster Unionists were as unyielding as ever. Redmond therefore devoted all his efforts to trying to persuade Lloyd George to agree to put pressure upon them if the rest of the Convention could agree on a workable scheme. The Prime Minister was much

[1] *W.F.J.*, 10 Nov. 1917.

too wily to commit himself, but Redmond persisted nevertheless in his
efforts to reach agreement with the Southern Unionists. The crucial point
at issue was the control of customs and excise. On 18 December the Earl
of Midleton, on behalf of the Southern Unionists, laid down the terms on
which his group would co-operate with Redmond. Briefly, they envisaged
a Home Rule Act for all Ireland (for evident but very different reasons they
were no more anxious than the Nationalists to see Ulster excluded), but
insisted that the imperial Parliament should retain full control over customs
and excise as well as national defence. Unhappily, as Redmond was
isolated at Aughavanagh by a snowstorm, this crucial debate took place
without him, but the Bishop of Raphoe—a staunch friend of the party over
many years—made the obvious and orthodox Nationalist riposte that this
was too high a price to pay for Southern Unionist support unless Lord
Midleton could deliver the Ulster Unionist vote as well. That, of course,
he was in no position to do, whereupon both the Bishop and Devlin
decided to reserve their position until they heard what the Ulster Unionists
themselves thought of the proposal.

So the position remained over Christmas. At the turn of the year it
seemed even to improve, for Lord Midleton went himself to see Lloyd
George and came back with a pledge that 'if the Southern Unionist scheme
is carried by the Convention with substantial agreement—*i.e.* with the
opposition of Ulster alone—the P.M. will use his influence with his colleagues, the sympathies of many of whom are well known, to accept the
proposal and to give it legislative effect'.[1] As a pledge this was about as
watertight as a sieve, and if Redmond had been less desperate he would
have realised it. But instead he clutched at it gratefully and on 4 January
made a powerful plea to the Convention for agreement. It was in effect
his swan-song and it was fitting that it should have been one of the finest
orations of his career, but in the eyes of his colleagues it was vitiated by the
fact that he virtually accepted Midleton's position on customs and excise,
modified slightly to allow the Irish Parliament the right of collection,
though still not that of imposition, of duties.

There was to be a pause for consultation before the final and crucial
debate was held on 15 January. A week before that Dillon, who had been
spending Christmas in Mayo with his children, came up to Dublin and dined
with Devlin and Bishop O'Donnell. The result of their conversation he
reported to T. P. O'Connor on 10 January. They had told him that the
Ulster representatives were, if anything, stiffer than two years ago, and that
although the Southern Unionists had come a long way towards agreement,
the deadlock over customs still remained. 'Redmond', wrote Dillon, 'has,
I fear, gone too far on the road of concession and is I gather anxious to
agree with Lord Midleton . . . And I am *convinced* that if the Nationalists
were to agree with the Southern Unionists and surrender the customs, in
the present state of Ireland, we and the Southern Unionists would be swept
off the field in a few weeks. S.F., linked with Murphy and the *Independent*

[1] Gwynn, *Redmond*, p. 579.

and three-quarters of the priests, would carry the country hands down. The result would be that L.G. and the government would abandon any attempt to carry the Convention compromise. It would be the July negotiations over again in a much worse form.'

Dillon did add that they had all agreed that if the Ulster Unionists offered to come in '*heartily*', but making the surrender of customs a condition, they would be prepared to treat that as a new situation and reconsider their position, but he himself felt there was very little hope of this. If Redmond had been more militant, not only at the Convention but during the past three years, the Government might now have been disposed to listen to him. But what chance was there of that?

> The *only* chance of an agreement would be the exercise of really irresistible pressure by L.G. and the cabinet, including Carson, and that, I feel, will *not* be put in force. If R. had made himself more disagreeable and dangerous on previous occasions I think the cabinet might do what is needed to compel agreement. But unhappily they do not believe that R. will really, really [*sic*] show fight. If he did, the government could not hold out for three months. They are very much discredited and in a very shaky condition.[1]

Within a few days the crisis was reached. Feeling on the Nationalist side reached a high pitch and in the outcome Redmond, coming to the crucial debate on 15 January, found that he could not carry either Devlin or Bishop O'Donnell with him. Accordingly, in a short, bitter speech he announced that he could be of no further service to the Convention.[2] This was really the end, but a few days later he made one last despairing effort. On 18 January, and again on 21 January, he suggested to Lloyd George that the Prime Minister should write to the Convention urging that there should not be a breakdown until he had had a chance of conferring in London with the leaders of the various sections. But, although Lloyd George did write to the chairman, Sir Horace Plunkett, conveying such an invitation, the form of it suggested that this should only be done *after* the Convention had reached deadlock—that is, after the collision which Redmond had tried so hard to avoid had actually taken place. Lloyd George did subsequently have some quite fruitless interviews with several of the delegates, but since nothing remotely resembling general agreement emerged, the Convention, after a few weeks more of aimless debate, finally submitted conflicting reports and quietly expired early in May.[3]

By then Redmond had been more than a month in his grave. Dillon, following his manoeuvres at the Convention with deepening gloom, had been filled with mingled sympathy and anxiety, but had continued to perform his usual function of keeper of the chairman's conscience. In mid-January, for example, he had seen Redmond in an attempt to convince

---

[1] Dillon to T. P. O'Connor, 10 Jan. 1917 (D P.).

[2] Gwynn, *Redmond*, pp. 584–6.

[3] For the history of the Convention in detail, see S. L. Gwynn, op. cit., chap. 8; Lord Midleton, *Records and reactions, 1856–1939* (London, 1939), chap. 19; Gwynn, *Redmond*, chap. 16.

him that acceptance of Lord Midleton's proposal would be suicide for the party. 'I do not think I made much impression,' he reported to O'Connor, 'but the interview was perfectly friendly.'[1] He saw him again on 25 January, after the abortive exchanges with Lloyd George, putting his view to the already broken leader with, as he admitted, 'almost brutal frankness'. 'I said that if Lord Midleton's proposal were accepted by the Nationalists I did not believe the party would continue to exist for six weeks.' Once more the interview was 'quite friendly', but in describing the situation to T.P. he added a fresh and ominous note:

> What is really disturbing me and causing me to take a gloomy view of the situation is the state of R's health and his apparent helplessness in view of the failure of the Convention to agree. Meanwhile, the country is drifting rapidly to anarchy . . . Duke [H. E. Duke, appointed Chief Secretary after the collapse of the negotiations in 1916] is quite hopeless and will I fancy be cleared out immediately if the Convention fails. And then there will be nothing for it but vigorous coercion and courts-martial, unless the English make up their mind to evacuate the country and leave us to cut each other's throats in peace.[2]

Within a fortnight of writing this letter Dillon heard from Redmond himself that he was going into hospital immediately to have an operation for the removal of gall-stones. This would mean that he would be *hors de combat* for a considerable time. However, he felt that the party ought to proceed with its usual annual meeting and this raised the issue of the chairmanship. Even after the failure of the Convention, he wrote, he had hoped that he might have been able to continue as chairman until the general election, though he admitted that by then he would probably have found himself out of sympathy with the general views of the party. 'Now, however, it is quite clear that I can do nothing for some months to come, and I think it would be well for the party to hold a meeting soon, and to learn these facts, and to make up its mind about the chairmanship. It would be absurd for me to remain chairman when I am constantly absent and unable to do anything and, of course, in a position where I could have no share in guiding the policy of the party.'[3]

In the event, the decision was taken out of his hands. The operation itself was successful and the first accounts of his condition were optimistic. But then, on the night of 5 March, his heart began to falter and early the next morning the end came. His body was accompanied to Ireland by Dillon, his old opponent, loyal colleague and now predestined successor. And it was Dillon who, over his grave at Wexford, delivered his most fitting epitaph. He praised Redmond not only for his obvious virtues as an orator and House of Commons man, but more especially for what was perhaps his essential life-work, the re-establishment of unity in the party after 1900.

---

[1] Dillon to T. P. O'Connor, 22 Jan. 1918 (D.P.).
[2] Dillon to T. P. O'Connor, 13 Feb. 1918 (D.P.).
[3] Redmond to Dillon, 26 Feb. 1918; Gwynn, *Redmond*, pp. 593–4.

'He succeeded—I can say so with confidence, speaking here on behalf of my colleagues—in making himself a leader loyally followed by every man who belonged to that party, and sincerely beloved by every single one of them.' He praised the dead leader also for all he had sought to do in the last ten years of his life in his great work of reconciliation. This he had had to leave incomplete, but 'it was at least given to him to know that he himself, with his own right hand, had struck down all the obstacles to Irish freedom across the water which two or three years ago were thought to be insurmountable and impassable, and that he left the whole of England friendly to his country's freedom, and that now there remains but one obstacle'. His speech ended with this peroration:

> Is it too much to hope that the grave we have closed to-day may cry out with an irresistible voice to his countrymen to take and put into effect the lesson of his life, and to bury for ever the discords and dissension which have been the curse of Ireland throughout the centuries, and consummate the work of John Redmond's life by uniting all Irishmen to work for the good of Ireland?[1]

John Dillon asked the question. Upon John Dillon the answer greatly depended.

[1] Gwynn, *Redmond*, pp. 596–7.

15
Leader of a Lost Cause

(i)

The tone of panegyric which Dillon thought proper to use of his dead leader in public was one he found harder to maintain in private. Thus, although at his first big meeting after Redmond's death he referred to him as 'the greatest figure in the British House of Commons', to T. P. O'Connor he wrote two weeks later that the last two years 'have added one more great tragedy to the tragic story of Ireland and his fate is a terrible warning to all Irish leaders who have to deal with British statesmen'.[1] Refusing an invitation from C. P. Scott to write an appreciation of Redmond, he was even more outspoken. 'I feel so bitterly and deeply the tragedy of Redmond's fate', he wrote, 'that if I were to attempt to write about him just now I would be irresistibly dragged into a bitter attack on George, Asquith and British ministers in general, and into drawing the moral from his fate of the madness and folly of any Irish leader putting any trust in the promises of English ministers.'[2]

It was a moral he was himself determined to draw. From the moment of his unanimous election to the chairmanship after Redmond's funeral he put into effect the policy of opposition to, and criticism of, the Government that he had been urging on Redmond ever since the collapse of the negotiations in the summer of 1916. And it was curiously symbolic that his first major decision as chairman was to refuse Sir Horace Plunkett's invitation to take Redmond's place at the moribund Irish Convention. 'Most certainly I earnestly desire that the Convention shall not fail,' he replied politely, '. . . but there are more ways of failing than one. And I am not sure that you and I would find ourselves in agreement as to what would constitute success on the part of the Convention.'[3] But what if the Convention did

---

[1] *W.F.J.*, 23 Mar. 1918; Dillon to T. P. O'Connor, 6 Apr. 1918 (D.P.).

[2] Dillon to C. P. Scott, 6 Mar. 1918 (D.P.). Writing to Lord Murray (the former Master of Elibank) later that month, Dillon drove the point further home, observing that Redmond had 'faced great unpopularity and misunderstanding in Ireland in a high-minded and sincere attempt to reconcile the Irish and the British peoples, and to serve the Empire in a time of terrible crisis and danger, and his reward was to be snubbed and humiliated in the face of his own people. And finally, in July 1916, when he staked all in an attempt to bring about a settlement between the two nations, he was made the victim of the most scandalous and cynical breach of faith that I have ever heard of in my political life' (Dillon to Lord Murray, 28 March 1918, Elibank Papers, National Library of Scotland).

[3] Dillon to Sir Horace Plunkett, 25 Mar. 1918 (Plunkett Papers, box C–E).

fail? How were the parliamentary party to recapture the loyalty of the large numbers of Nationalists who were now, as he freely admitted, clamouring for the Republic? Trying to answer this question in a speech at Enniskillen in March, Dillon could not help revealing how much he and his friends had been thrown on to the defensive, because in essence his solution was no different from the one that Sinn Fein was advocating at that very time. If England did not give full justice to Ireland he would, he said, 'shame her before the nations of the world'. 'Speaking for a united Ireland, I will appeal to America and the president of the United States, and I will say "tell England that she must, before she can pretend to carry on this war for small nationalities . . . go home and set her own house in order.'[1]

As a statement of policy this was hardly one of his most impressive performances, lacking, as it did, any indication of how he proposed to reach President Wilson, how he was going to define 'full justice' in such a way as to satisfy both Home Rulers and Republicans, or how, for that matter, he ever hoped to be in a position to speak for a united Ireland. Yet, in the strangest fashion, unity of a kind was only just round the corner. Even by the time of Redmond's death it had become clear that if the Irish Convention failed to reach that degree of 'substantial agreement' which would allow Lloyd George to attempt a workable settlement, the pressure upon the Government to apply conscription would probably be overwhelming. And so indeed it proved. In the last days of March and the early days of April the wildest rumours were circulating in Ireland about the imminence of compulsory military service. They were by no means without foundation. Although the Convention did not meet for the last time until 8 May, it was already obvious at the beginning of April that it was not going to reach agreement and that it would submit not one, but two, or possibly more, reports.[2] Immediately, the Government acted. In the House of Commons Lloyd George announced that conscription would be applied to Ireland, but sought at the same time to sugar the pill by promising to introduce a measure of self-government before military service began to take effect. The Conscription Bill went rapidly through all stages and had passed the House of Commons by 16 April. Dillon, attacking it fiercely to the very end, warned the Government repeatedly that they would not get the slightest reinforcement in this way. 'All Ireland as one man will rise against you,' he said. And at the close of the debate he led his entire party out of the House and back to Ireland, where a few days later they resolved to abandon attendance at Westminster (another leaf out of the Sinn Fein book) in order to help the people in their fight against conscription.[3]

How any sort of Home Rule settlement could have been imposed on Ireland in view of the deep divisions which the Convention had exposed so

[1] *W.F.J.*, 23 Mar. 1918.

[2] M. Digby, *Horace Plunkett*, p. 235.

[3] *W.F.J.*, 13, 20 and 27 Apr. 1918; Dillon's speech moving the exclusion of Ireland from compulsory military service is in Hansard, H.C. Debates, 5th series, vol. 105, cols. 292–305.

thoroughly, it is difficult to see. Perhaps Lloyd George's promise was designed mainly for export, to reassure American opinion. In Ireland, certainly, this aspect of his speech was ignored and attention was concentrated from the start upon conscription. Within a few days a formidable public movement—easily the most impressive since the outbreak of the war —began to manifest itself in opposition to the impending threat. Apart from the north-eastern corner, support for the anti-conscription campaign came from all directions. It came from Cardinal Logue and the Standing Committee of the Irish bishops, from the trade unions, from the different parliamentary sections, and, of course, from Sinn Fein. The climax of all this furious protest was reached in the last week of April, when representatives of all shades of Nationalist opinion came together in a conference at the Mansion House, Dublin. Sitting round the same table were Dillon, Joseph Devlin, Mr. de Valera, Arthur Griffith, William O'Brien, T. M. Healy and various labour leaders. Not even in his most strenuous labours for an Irish settlement had Lloyd George ever come near producing such uniformity of views amongst so diverse a group of Irishmen as he did by this one action. Very rapidly the movement began to take practical shape. A National Defence Fund was to be launched to finance the movement, Irishmen were to be asked to take a pledge to resist military service and in every parish a 'committee of defence' was to be formed to organise this resistance. In addition, a statement of the Irish case was to be drawn up for presentation to the world at large, and the Lord Mayor of Dublin was to be sent to America, where, of course, it was particularly important, but also peculiarly difficult, to explain the reasons for this great upsurge of feeling.[1]

These developments confronted constitutionalists with a grave crisis. The Government move to impose conscription, though all too predictable, could not have come at a worse time. For a few weeks before the blow fell it had begun to seem as if the tide were beginning to turn again in the constituencies. In the three by-elections fought since the beginning of the year—South Armagh, Waterford City and East Tyrone—the parliamentary party had beaten off the challenge of Sinn Fein and more than held their own. But, as so often before, just at the very moment when the fortunes of Sinn Fein seemed on the wane, the Government had stepped in to revive them. For Dillon the situation created by the anti-conscription movement posed a terrible dilemma. On the one hand, he was utterly convinced that the party must be as outspoken in their opposition to military service as any other group or section in Ireland. On the other hand, he was perfectly well aware that the protest was a heaven-sent opportunity for Sinn Fein, and that by acting with the Sinn Fein leaders in the Mansion House Conference, he was only postponing the eventual clash, while at the same time helping to build up the forces which sooner or later would be used for his destruction.[2]

[1] *W.F.J.*, 27 Apr. 1918; Robert Brennan, *Allegiance* (Dublin, 1950), pp. 164–6.
[2] He did, however, consent to speak from the same platform as Mr. de Valera at an anti-conscription meeting in Ballaghaderrin on 5 May (*The Times*, 6 May 1918).

Not surprisingly, when he wrote to T. P. O'Connor just at the time the Conference was beginning, he was full of misgivings. To oppose British policy in Ireland while still maintaining an attitude of general support for the war was, he said, becoming almost impossible:

> One of the difficulties of the present situation is that the Britishers look upon me as a kind of half S.F., with a dash of Bolshevism thrown in, while the S.F. leaders are out for all they are worth to down me because they think I have *some* hold still on the masses of the people here. There can be no doubt that L.G. has let loose *Hell* in Ireland and with our knowledge of his political instinct and intelligence it is very difficult to resist the conviction that his action during the last year has been all of a piece—a Machiavellian plot to escape from the necessity of granting Home Rule and to do so at such a time and in such a way as will embroil us with the American government and the American people, and make it safe for England to have a regular quarrel and stand-up fight with Ireland.

Naturally, in the circumstances, he was uneasy about the kind of company he was having to keep, though it was some comfort, he said, to learn that some of de Valera's friends were very angry with *him* for going into the Conference. But Dillon doubted that the highly artificial unity achieved by the anti-conscription movement would last for long. 'All I can safely say is that enough has transpired already to make it quite clear that the purpose is to swallow us up and that the "tiger" should emerge from the Conference with the constitutional party inside, and followed by the blessings of O'B[rien] and T. M. H[ealy].' As for conscription itself, although he had had confidential information that Lloyd George was bent on going on with it, 'my own opinion is that we shall have neither Home Rule nor conscription'. Nevertheless, he remained convinced that he was right in his general analysis of the intention behind the Prime Minister's manoeuvre. 'Considering L.G's action in bringing forward his measure applying conscription to Ireland hot-foot on our three successive victories over S.F. at the last three elections . . . it is hard to escape from the conviction that he deliberately adopted the policy of destroying the constitutional party in Ireland and throwing the country into the hands of the revolutionary party. The purposes of such a policy are plainly apparent.'[1]

Clearly, Dillon, absorbed in the Irish crisis, was becoming even more obsessed than before by his favourite conspiracy theory, which, he assured C. P. Scott just at this time, was the 'universal opinion' in Ireland—that is that 'the whole business has been an elaborate plot by L.G. to put off the Irish settlement until he has got America so deeply committed to the war that American opinion will not support Ireland'.[2] Yet, if he had been able to lift his eyes from what lay immediately before him, he might have seen that Lloyd George's primary objective, after all, was the prosecution of a great war and that by comparison with the destruction of the German

---

[1] Dillon to T. P. O'Connor, 23–24 Apr. 1918 (D.P.).
[2] Dillon to C. P. Scott, 22 Apr. 1918 (D.P.).

armies, the destruction of the Irish parliamentary party occupied only a very small part, if any, of his attention. Dillon's old friend, C. P. Scott, tried hard to make him look at this wider horizon. Scott had been in person to see Lloyd George and had asked him point-blank why he had chosen this moment, when the fate of Home Rule hung in the balance, to introduce Irish conscription. The answer that Scott passed on to Dillon is so interesting that it is worth giving in some detail, complete with Dillon's own underlinings and marks of emphasis:

> His view is (1) that it is politically impossible for him to carry an adequate measure of Home Rule with the consent of his government, except by linking it with conscription.
> (2) He holds strongly that the power of imposing conscription, that is the power of determining the raising of armies is as essential to the authority of the Imperial Parliament as the power of determining their use. He therefore regards the denial of this as a denial of the necessary authority of the Impl. Parlmt. and in effect as converting the movement for H.R. into a movement for secession, *and he is prepared to meet it exactly as Lincoln met a similar movement. He knows that this may mean bloodshed, but he certainly does not desire, and will do nothing he can avoid, to provoke it.*[1]

This letter, as may be imagined, was far from satisfying Dillon. Indeed, he wrote by return, if Lloyd George had so clearly intimated to Scott that he contemplated civil war in Ireland on this issue of conscription, then the situation was even more serious than he had imagined. 'Now *Ireland will not accept conscription*', he warned him. 'And it will be resisted by the most effective means that can be devised. And on this matter you may accept it from me that nine-tenths of the nation are united.' If the military were to be allowed unfettered control, then he dared not think of the consequences. 'Surely', he said, 'Englishmen like you must realise that the moral position of England in the war goes absolutely if she embarks on a career of brutal military savagery in Ireland.' As for the motives behind Lloyd George's action, he held quite unrepentantly to his conspiracy theory. 'Surely if he had any sense of responsibility or true perspective of the actual values of the situation, he would have broken up his government a dozen times before he would have created such a Frankenstein. And after all his government, judged by results, has not proved such an invaluable asset to the Empire as to have established a claim to be indispensable.'[2]

Scott found it hard to counter these arguments, but as he was in close touch with Lloyd George and genuinely believed that the Prime Minister meant what he said about Home Rule, he tried once more to move Dillon, whose presence in the House would, he considered, be absolutely essential if a Home Rule Bill were actually to be introduced. Writing on 26 April, he began by agreeing that 'all the folly and wickedness of the course on which he (Lloyd George) appears to be embarked . . . would hardly seem

[1] C. P. Scott, to Dillon, 23 Apr. 1918 (D.P.).
[2] Dillon to C. P. Scott, 25 Apr. 1918 (D.P.).

credible, apart from some sinister design, did not one learn more and more every day of the almost limitless folly possible to governing men'. Nevertheless, he tried to improve on his previous analysis:

> As to accounting for L.G.'s action in raising this question now, apart from an intention to wreck Home Rule, I admit the difficulty, but you have to bear in mind
> (1) His love of, and exaggerated belief in, the use of force. (2) His eagerness for more men—conscription wd. at least give him 4 or 5 divisions from Ulster. (3) His conviction that only by imposing conscription can he carry his govt. for Home Rule. (4) His belief that the Home Rule movement has developed, or is developing, into a definitely separatist movement and that the question of the control by the Imperial Parlmt. of the armed forces of the Crown (which includes the raising as well as the use of them) is the touchstone of this.
>
> I am still quite clearly of opinion that the explanation of his policy is to be found in these considerations and not in any ulterior design, and that he intends quite definitely to force through both parts of his policy.[1]

This is probably as close to the truth about Lloyd George's motives as we are likely to get and it has to be remembered, in support of Scott's contention, that this was the moment of the German breakthrough on the Western Front, when the whole issue of the war hung in the balance. Given the exhaustion of Britain, the fearful casualties of the past four years, and the fear that American reinforcements might not be brought to bear in time, it is easy enough to see how powerful the pressures in favour of a conscription policy for Ireland must have been.

Dillon, however, remained unconvinced. He ridiculed the constitutional argument about the need for imperial control of the Irish forces by pointing out the absurdities this would create once an Irish Government was actually in being. Clearly, he still felt that at least the military authorities, if not Lloyd George, were eagerly looking for a Sinn Fein outbreak as a chance to impose a reign of terror and carry out conscription in the process.[2] As for the promise of Home Rule, he refused to take it seriously, telling O'Connor that the Irish party would not be in the House of Commons if or when it was introduced and that it was an open question whether they would attend for the later stages. 'I am inclined to think', he wrote early in May, 'our best course will be to stay in Ireland while the present crisis lasts and leave Lloyd George and Carson to fight the bill out between them.'[3]

(ii)

But at this point, and with the conscription issue still undecided, the precarious truce between the party and Sinn Fein broke down, less than a fortnight after the Mansion House Conference. The break came, predictably, over a by-election—caused by the death of the aged Samuel Young, who

[1] C. P. Scott to Dillon, 26 Apr. 1918 (D.P.).
[2] Dillon to C. P. Scott, 27 Apr. 1918 (D.P.).
[3] Dillon to T. P. O'Connor, 3 May 1918 (D.P.).

had represented East Cavan for some thirty years. Dillon, by his own account, tried hard to avoid a contest. His first suggestion, that while the truce lasted any vacancies should be filled by the party in possession, was rejected out of hand; not surprisingly, in view of the heavy preponderance of seats still held by the party. Alternatively, he put forward the idea that neutral candidates should either be elected as caretakers until the general election, or that they should occupy them until Dillon and de Valera agreed that the immediate crisis was over and that the rival sections could safely fall to cutting each others' throats again.[1] Since either of these courses would have given the parliamentarians a much-needed breathing-space, Sinn Fein quite naturally rejected them. But they did much more than that. By putting forward as their candidate none other than Arthur Griffith they made it perfectly obvious that they were spoiling for a fight. Dillon was almost in despair. It was impossible, he wrote to O'Connor, to exaggerate the dangers of the situation in Ireland 'and, if the storm breaks, there will be bloody chaos'. Then, in a passage which has no parallel in all his correspondence for its bitterness, he added: 'And lest Ireland should be false to her well-known history I am off to Cootehill, East Cavan, to denounce Griffith and Valera [*sic*] and there is very likely to be a row. Ireland is a great country. There never was in the history of the world any country or people quite the equal of our people.'[2]

At Cootehill, true to his word, he duly described Griffith as 'the most offensive and scurrilous critic of the Irish party' among their opponents and attacked his electioneering slogan that a vote for the party was a vote for conscription as 'an impudent and outrageous falsehood'. Remarks like these would probably have been fatal to the truce anyway, but Griffith himself hammered the last nail into its coffin when he declared that before any kind of united front between Sinn Fein and the parliamentary party could be established, the party 'would have to accept the Sinn Fein programme of absolute independence for Ireland, abstention from the British parliament and that the Peace Conference was the place where freedom was to be won'. This indeed would have been the 'tiger' walking off with the constitutional movement inside, and Dillon had no option but to fight for dear life. But even here the malign fate (he would have called it Lloyd George) which had dogged the party since 1916 stepped in once more. On the morning of 18 May the newspapers carried an official proclamation to the effect that it had come to the knowledge of the Government that Sinn Fein had been engaged in a treasonable conspiracy with the Germans. On the basis of this so-called 'German plot' the principal Sinn Feiners were at once rearrested (practically the entire leadership except Michael Collins), with the immediate result that since Griffith was, of course, among those taken into custody, his election in East Cavan was virtually assured. Few people outside official or Unionist circles believed in the reality of the plot at the time, and it has generally been scouted by historians since, the more

---

[1] *W.F.J.*, 18 May 1918.
[2] Dillon to T. P. O'Connor, 10 and 11 May 1918 (D.P.).

so as the Government refused to produce the evidence on which it had acted. It was true, admittedly, that Joseph Dowling, a former prisoner of war in Germany and a member of Casement's 'Irish brigade', had been seized after shipwreck on an island off the coast of Galway, and it appears to have been the case that he was carrying a code message indicating that if there was another rising Germany would support it. What has *not* been demonstrated, however, was that any further rising was being contemplated at that time, though, as always in these troubled years, the air was thick with conflicting rumours.[1] Dillon himself, for example, heard from one correspondent 'on fairly reliable authority' that the arrests (most took place on the evening of 17 May) were precipitated by the belief that a mobilisation of the Volunteers had been ordered for the afternoon of the 18th.[2] On the other hand, P. J. Hooper of the *Freeman's Journal* assured him a few days later that there was no evidence of a German plot worth considering to justify the arrests.[3] Dillon's own reaction was the common-sense one—if the authorities really had evidence, they ought to have brought those concerned to public trial. 'As it is', he wrote to C. P. Scott, 'between their conscription policy and this *coup* they have put Sinn Fein *on top* in Ireland for the moment.'[4]

Whether or not there was a plot was irrelevant to the East Cavan election. There, the only thing that mattered was that Griffith was in jail again and that in attacking him Dillon henceforward had one arm tied behind his back. The line he took in public was that the whole thing was a ridiculous fabrication. 'I ask', he said in one of his speeches, 'is it conceivable that the Government, knowing as they do that production of proofs of this charge would destroy the power of Sinn Fein in this country and justify their action in the eyes of all the great democracies of the world, would not produce the evidence?' At the same time, experienced campaigner as he was, he could not resist making a little capital out of the ease with which the arrests were made. 'In one brief twenty-four hours the whole of the leaders throughout the country who were going to burst up the British Empire were swept into the net without a drop of blood being shed.' More seriously, in that speech and in many others during the next few weeks, he developed three major themes. One was that the Sinn Fein policy of an independent, sovereign republic could only mean bloodshed and war with England which he believed—and at that time it was a perfectly reasonable supposition—must end in disastrous defeat. The second was that such a policy, combined as it would be with total abstention from Westminster, was something the parliamentary party could never accept—it was, he said in a speech just after the by-election, 'a policy of lunatics'.[5] And finally, he

[1] Dorothy Macardle, *The Irish republic* (American ed., New York, 1965), pp. 253–5. For the meagre evidence made public see 'Minutes of meeting of War Cabinet, 23 May 1918 (P.R.O., War Cabinet Papers, Cab. 23/6, 416 and appendix); also *The Times*, 25 May 1918.
[2] J. J. Bergin to Dillon, 18 May 1918 (D.P.).
[3] P. J. Hooper to Dillon, 22 May 1918 (D.P.).
[4] Dillon to C. P. Scott, 21 May 1918 (D.P.).
[5] *W.F.J.*, 1 June 1918; *W.F.J.*, 29 June 1918.

condemned the excesses of Sinn Fein not merely because they meant the end of the unity achieved at the Mansion House Conference, but because they were rapidly alienating responsible opinion in America at a time when Ireland should be looking to President Wilson to secure justice at the Peace Conference.[1]

It was difficult to be sure what sort of impact he was making. The by-election was a long-drawn-out affair (polling only took place a month after Griffith's arrest) and Dillon's own hopes and fears fluctuated. He threw himself heart and soul into the fight and in doing so recovered his spirits to a remarkable degree. He was not oversanguine, of course, but he did allow himself to think that the party had an outside chance of winning. Writing to the long-suffering O'Connor, who after nearly a year in the States was begging to come home, he urged him to stay for another few weeks, partly to combat the rising tide of anti-Irish feeling in America, but even more to collect further funds. 'It is almost entirely a question of money now. If I can raise another £30,000 I can see my [way] clearly to saving the movement.'[2] A fortnight later, with the issue in doubt, he wrote again—still by no means unhopeful, but assessing with his usual realism the difficulties by which he was surrounded. The *Freeman's Journal* was still his principal worry—its circulation had admittedly risen to 40,000, but it was constantly haunted by the twin spectres of paper famine and capital deficency. As for East Cavan, while there was evidence of solid support for the party and the Bishop was sound, the younger priests, many of them very influential, had largely gone over to Sinn Fein. Had it not been for the conscription issue and for the arrests 'we had S.F. absolutely beaten'. East Cavan would have been won decisively 'and that would have been *the end* of S.F. as a progressive and dangerous force in Irish politics'. But then he continued:

> To sum up my view of the situation in Ireland. We must look forward to six months at least of military rule and *severe* coercion. Whether it will be possible for us under such a régime, and with the extended franchise, to hold such a number of seats as would make it possible to carry on the party is doubtful. But it is quite conceivable that in six months, if the government do not commit some fresh atrocity, Ireland may have sobered down so much that we shall emerge from [the] election with say 40 seats. That would do very well. In my opinion our hope of survival depends on two things. Funds, and paper to print the *Freeman* in sufficient quantity.[3]

Hard upon this letter came the news of the result—Griffith had won by over a thousand votes.[4] Dillon's immediate reaction was that this was in effect a victory for the priests. 'I hear their conduct was outrageous', he explained to O'Connor—'the most violent spiritual intimidation. If they had [been] neutral we would have won. But the priests and the arrests

---

[1] *W.F.J.*, 1 and 29 June 1918.
[2] Dillon to T. P. O'Connor, 2 June 1918 (D.P.).
[3] Dillon to T. P. O'Connor, 17 June 1918 (D.P.).
[4] *F.J.*, 22 June 1918. Griffith's majority was 1,204 votes in a total poll of just over 6,000.

were too much . . . There was a good deal of physical intimidation also, but that did not affect the result so much.'[1] Next day he wrote again to T.P., recording 'great rejoicing all over the country over the Cavan result' and still attributing it to the priests, with, however, some assistance from outside. 'This, combined with the cry—who wants the blood of Griffith?—and the desperate hatred of L.G. and the Government formed an accumulation of forces which it was impossible to overcome.'[2]

These letters do not convey the impression of a beaten man, but rather of a man fully committed to what he knew to be a mortal combat, and watching every move and sign of the enemy to snatch what advantage he might from a desperate situation. What made that situation really impossible, however, was that he had to fight not one enemy, but two. He had to contend not merely with the frontal assault from Sinn Fein, but with the devious ways of British policy, or lack of policy. And what may seem to us in retrospect to have been simply convulsive and misguided improvisation, continued to strike Dillon as part of a preconceived plan. While the East Cavan election was still in progress, he had described this plan in detail to Shane Leslie in America. This, then, was how it still seemed to him:

> We are in for a little coercion campaign now and the Orange ascendancy party are more firmly in control of Dublin Castle than at any period since Catholic Emancipation. This is the result of the policy of Sinn Fein and this condition of things would have come into existence long ago but for the sittings of the Convention.
>
> L.G. is not a bit mad, but he is playing a very deep game, a game which necessitates the encouragement of S.F. up to a point sufficient to kill the parliamentary party and identify Irish nationalism with S.F. and pro-Germanism in the eyes of the world, and especially in the eyes of America. And he has played this game with immense skill and superb audacity. The S.F.s, being utterly devoid of political sagacity, and overcharged with poetic fervour and wild, unregulated enthusiasm, have played right into the hands of L.G. and Carson, who is now the practical dictator of Ireland. While the S.F. leaders loudly proclaim that *the* one great object for Irish patriots of the true brand is to 'wipe out' the Irish party.[3]

If Dillon's understandable bitterness led him to exaggerate Lloyd George's duplicity, his contempt for his Irish opponents led him to underestimate the potential strength of 'poetic fervour and wild, unregulated enthusiasm'. But, on the short term, his prediction that coercion was imminent was absolutely correct. On 3 July the Government 'proclaimed' as 'a grave menace' the various Sinn Fein organisations, the Irish Volunteers and the Gaelic League. Next day another proclamation prohibited all public meetings (and the playing of Gaelic games!) unless with police

[1] Dillon to T. P. O'Connor, 22 June 1918 (D.P.).
[2] Dillon to T. P. O'Connor, 23 June 1918 (D.P.).
[3] Dillon to Shane Leslie, 14 June 1918 (D.P.).

authorisation.[1] The effect of these measures was, of course, exactly what might have been anticipated. Sinn Fein, so far from being destroyed, was driven underground, where it became, if anything, even more dangerous than before.

This was precisely the 'fresh atrocity' that Dillon had feared, making the position of the party even more difficult than ever. On the one hand, they had to oppose Government policy—both the coercion measures and the continuing threat of conscription—if they were to keep any grip at all on Irish opinion. On the other hand, such opposition was steadily losing them valuable support overseas, especially in the United States, where war fever was reaching its peak. T. P. O'Connor, indeed, had done his best to keep some spark of sympathy alive, but he returned home in August just at the moment when feeling against Ireland was running dangerously high. 'Nobody loves the Irish any more', wrote Shane Leslie to Dillon from America, and he gave as the principal reason for this the resistance to conscription.[2] Three weeks later, while acknowledging that O'Connor had achieved much, he added: 'I am frankly not pro-party, but I am for Dillon, and I think this represents a good deal of the moderate feeling among the Irish here. You ask what has been the effect of the arrests, the German plot etc. The unthinking and, unfortunately, the patriotic American, has swallowed it whole.'[3]

The position was complicated by the fact that the war was now fast swinging in the Allies' favour, for although at the beginning of August it was still hard to predict when the end would come, it was clear that the German armies were beginning to crack. To Dillon's way of thinking this prospect could only militate against Sinn Fein, and his next public appearance—a much-advertised speech at Blackrock, near Dublin—was devoted to demonstrating the hopelessness (as he saw it) and the dangers of the Sinn Fein policy. The country, as he pointed out, had been disarmed, the right of public meeting had been suppressed, and the real masters of Ireland were the military authorities. What possible chance had the Sinn Fein policy of force of succeeding in these circumstances? And not only that, they had backed the wrong horse in the war. If they looked now to the peace conference, it would be the Allies they would have to woo, and what help would pro-Germanism be then? 'They believed,' he said, 'that the Germans were certain to win this war, and it looked very like it at one time, but I thank God the forces of democracy and justice are prevailing, and the Germans will not win this war.' By resuming their attendance at Parliament that summer, he claimed, the Irish party had put themselves in the position of being able to offer an alternative policy for Ireland, the old, true remedy—Home Rule. Never, he declared, was an alternative to the Sinn Fein demand more urgently needed. 'One thing you will not get, and you may as well make up your minds on that matter, and that is an independent Irish republic without fighting for it and beating England to

[1] *W.J.F.*, 13 July 1918.   [2] Shane Leslie to Dillon, 18 July 1918 (D.P.).
[3] Shane Leslie to Dillon, 9 Aug. 1918 (D.P.).

her knees, and every man in this room who is not an idiot knows perfectly well that that is not possible.'[1]

Meanwhile, however, he had still to reckon with the mysterious ways of the Government. On 15 August he was due to speak at Omagh. Shortly before he went there he was informed that, constitutional leader though he might be, since the promoters of the meeting had not sought police authority he would be refused permission to make a public speech. His reaction was to tell his friends to proceed with their arrangements, but when he arrived in Omagh he found troops in readiness and all the signs of an ugly incident evident. 'I really think', he wrote to O'Connor next day, describing the scene, 'the government reached the extreme limit of idiotcy [*sic*].' But he had been far from well when travelling and in all honesty he had to add: 'Truth to tell it was an immense relief to me that the military stopped the meeting as I was not fit to speak.'[2] He did, in fact, address a private meeting indoors, and took the opportunity of saying that if Ireland could unite on a policy it would still be possible after the war to obtain what he called a settlement 'within reason'. He defined this as follows: 'What I meant by saying a settlement "within reason", and it includes Dominion Home Rule, is a settlement giving Ireland full control over her own affairs, but such a settlement as will give to the people of Great Britain some assurance that we mean loyally to live with them, to co-operate with them, and not to separate from them.'[3]

From Omagh, Dillon returned briefly to Dublin, then setting off for Mayo to spend the usual summer holiday at Ballaghaderrin. From there he watched the general situation closely, connected with the great world only by T. P. O'Connor's frequent bulletins from London. O'Connor had not entirely shaken himself free from Lloyd George's magnetism, speculating often and sometimes wildly, upon what the Prime Minister might do, with the end of the war approaching and a general reorientation of party politics inevitable. Dillon, removed for the time being from the stress and strain of political in-fighting (though not from perpetual anxiety over the future of the *Freeman's Journal*) was able to indulge his flair for political forecasting. 'You may take it from me', he wrote, 'what L.G. will do will be, by a khaki election, to get a verdict for L.G. as a great war minister and then trust to his adroitness to keep in the saddle by various devices after the election is over.'[4] What the fate of Ireland would be in such a situation he had already begun to consider. Even before he had left Dublin he had been encouraging O'Connor to think that a complete revolution in Irish politics by Christmas might be possible. 'All that is needed is, 1st activity and faith on our part, 2nd money, and 3rd time.'[5] Each of course was lacking and Lloyd George might deny them time in particular. Dillon, as he revealed in another letter a few days later, was still convinced that the Prime Minister was bent on the destruction of the Irish party—certainly,

[1] *W.F.J.*, 17 Aug. 1918.   [2] Dillon to T. P. O'Connor, 14 and 16 Aug. 1918 (D.P.).
[3] *W.F.J.*, 24 Aug. 1918.   [4] Dillon to T. P. O'Connor, 30 Aug. 1918 (D.P.).
[5] Dillon to T. P. O'Connor, 18 Aug. 1918 (D.P.).

if the existing coercion persisted right up to the general election, it would, he felt, be impossible to save the party. 'Without meetings, and newspaper reports, we are paralysed . . . If we saved twenty-five or thirty seats we might occupy a very strong position after the election. But if the present regime continues I do not see how we can save ten.'[1]

T. P. O'Connor, always prone to take a more optimistic view, still evidently clung to the hope that Lloyd George might use the necessity of solving the Irish question as a lever to prise himself free from the Tory element in the Coalition. But this was far too *simpliste* for Dillon to take it seriously. If Lloyd George were an honest man, and genuinely anxious to settle the question, then this, he conceded, might indeed be the best thing for him to do, but since Ireland and Home Rule together had become intensely unpopular in Britain, 'largely owing to L.G.'s own manoeuvres', it was extremely doubtful if any Minister could win a majority on the basis of an Irish settlement. On the other hand, it was true that sooner or later Lloyd George was going to find himself in difficulties with the Tories, so the best thing the Irish party could do would be to hold off until the situation was a little clearer. 'I am *not* in favour of committing ourselves to a declaration of war on L.G. until we see how the present tug-of-war between him and the Tories ends.'[2]

(iii)

Meanwhile the election was coming closer and closer and the appalling difficulties confronting Dillon and the party were growing clearer and clearer. The *Freeman's Journal* was losing money hand over fist (£150 a week, even though the paper now cost 5*d*.) and Devlin, all his old drive and enthusiasm broken by the frustrations of the past two years, had up to the beginning of September still done nothing to prepare for the campaign, even though it was known that Sinn Fein were hard at work selecting their candidates.[3] By the middle of that month Dillon was becoming anxious as to the party's prospects, especially in view of the continuing uncertainty about Lloyd George's attitude. 'So long as he does not take up a hostile attitude on Home Rule', he wrote, 'I am convinced it would be *madness* for us to force that issue generally in the election. We would be utterly smashed. In the present temper of England it would not be listened to and L.G. would then *by our action* be furnished with a splendid excuse for dropping Home Rule. Our policy is to go on the assumption that Home Rule has been fully [? endorsed] by the whole nation and by Wilson and America, and the only question is how and when it is to be put into force.' The real difficulty, however, as he very well realised, was not so much the formulation of the Home Rule demand as the effect upon the country of continuing military rule and the not yet dissipated fear of conscription. 'If conscription is persevered with', he added, 'and the election comes in

[1] Dillon to T. P. O'Connor, 27 Aug. 1918 (D.P.).
[2] Dillon to T. P. O'Connor, 5 Sept. 1918 (D.P.).
[3] Dillon to T. P. O'Connor, 18 and 27 Aug. 1918 (D.P.).

November, I do not believe we shall have a chance. The people will vote for the prisoners. It will come to an issue between our policy and Sinn Fein and will simply be a question of how most effectively to give expression to popular hatred of this government.'[1] A week later, despondent about the lack of organisation on their own side and the growing popularity of Sinn Fein, he felt that if conscription was followed at once by the election, the party would not get ten seats, which, considering that at that time it still held upwards of sixty, was a very remarkable forecast. The root difficulty of dealing with Sinn Fein, he admitted in a revealing flash which recalled the Dillon of forty years before, was that it 'appeals to the hatred and distrust of the British government—a sentiment which is in the blood and marrow of all Irish men and women'.[2]

His mood continued for some time longer to see-saw, changing as conscription seemed nearer or more remote. As the war drew more rapidly towards its inevitable end, and as there was still no conscription, his spirits rose. Towards the end of September he paid a flying visit to Dublin for a two-day meeting of the parliamentary party. The purpose of the meeting was partly that they should go on record as being inexorably opposed to conscription and to coercion, but partly also to define Home Rule in the new context. This was 'the establishment of national self-government for Ireland, including full and complete executive, legislative and fiscal powers', thus very pointedly contrasting with Redmond's apparent willingness to abandon fiscal autonomy just before his death. What, in fact, the Irish party were now demanding was something virtually indistinguishable from dominion status, a striking indication of the way in which the advent of Sinn Fein had raised the stakes all round.[3] It was decided that a committee of the party (Devlin, J. J. Clancy, J. P. Hayden, R. Hazleton, W. A. Redmond and Dillon himself) should draw up a statement of the party's case to serve as an election manifesto, after which Dillon retired again to Mayo for the last few days of peace he was to know as a practising politician. He was more convinced than ever that if coercion were lifted and the party were allowed a fair field, they would win, though he was at the same time infuriated that the *Freeman's Journal*, which could have reached a peak circulation of 50,000, was restricted by the paper shortage to 20,000– 25,000, with disastrous effects upon their publicity.[4] But one has the impression from his letters that these difficulties faded into insignificance before the prospect of battle, by which, as so often in the past, he was exhilarated and rejuvenated. Writing just at this time to congratulate T.P. on his seventieth birthday, he observed: 'I don't like growing old. And if any friend were to send me a congratulatory telegram on attaining my 70th birthday—or my 67th birthday which I did attain on September 4—I should feel disposed to assassinate him.'[5] Two days later he wrote again,

[1] Dillon to T. P. O'Connor, 15 Sept. 1918 (D.P.).
[2] Dillon to T. P. O'Connor, 22 Sept. 1918 (D.P.).
[3] *W.F.J.*, 5 Oct. 1918.   [4] Dillon to T. P. O'Connor, 5 Oct. 1918 (D.P.).
[5] Dillon to T. P. O'Connor, 6 Oct. 1918 (D.P.).

convinced that the German collapse had demoralised Sinn Fein and as exuberant in his optimism as formerly he had been despondent in his pessimism. 'If we had our army mobilised', he said, 'and were in a position to attack, I believe there would be as great a *débâcle* as on the Western Front and in the Balkans.'[1]

From this point onwards events began to move very fast. Dillon was convinced that the election would come immediately the war was over, and in the last weeks before the Armistice he was hard at work trying to inject some semblance of enthusiasm into his followers. On 10 October the party and the United Irish League held a joint conference in Dublin, and from this emerged a statement of policy which formed the basis of the 'Appeal to the Nation', issued as an election manifesto only a few days before the war ended. Dillon put the case as bluntly as he could, making it clear that he was staking everything on the general election—the country would have to choose between the party and Sinn Fein. On the one side he placed the party, with its proud tradition and long record of service to the country— the source of every major reform in Ireland since the New Departure. On the other side stood Sinn Fein, politically inexperienced, and inhibited by its flagrant pro-Germanism from appealing successfully to the Peace Conference or, for that matter, either to English or American opinion.[2] This broadside was followed immediately by a published appeal to President Wilson, signed by sixty-three members of the party. It took up Wilson's favourite theme of self-determination for small nations and begged him to apply it to Ireland, because 'you are the ruler of more millions of men of our blood than any other ruler on earth, because your country, above all others, has been the asylum of our race, driven in hunger and by force from the land of their fathers; because we know it is the desire of you and all your people that men of our race shall find in their motherland the same liberties and rights that have made them so powerful, prosperous and loyal a section of your community'.[3]

These were fighting words and though Dillon was far too experienced to believe in mass conversion through published addresses, at least these manifestos showed that a far tougher and more aggressive leader was now at the head of the parliamentary party than had been the case for many years. Nevertheless, the difficulties were immense. The effects of years of neglect and discouragement could not so easily be swept on one side and, as he became immersed in the campaign, Dillon realised more and more clearly the extent to which his followers were already beaten in their hearts. One incident in particular indicated the kind of problem with which he was confronted. In Cork City one of the party's staunchest supporters was Mr. John Horgan, a solicitor whose father had been a friend of Parnell's and who was himself a devoted Redmondite and a pillar of the United Irish League. Mr. Horgan had been present at the conference of the U.I.L. and the party in Dublin on 10 October and had proposed a resolution en-

[1] Dillon to T. P. O'Connor, 8 Oct. 1918 (D.P.).   [2] *W.F.J.*, 19 Oct. and 9 Nov. 1918.
[3] *W.F.J.*, 16 Nov. 1918.

dorsing President Wilson's declarations in favour of the rights of small nations and looking for their application to Ireland. Afterwards, feeling that Ireland's case could only be successfully presented if the country would unite on a truly national policy, he wrote to Richard Hazleton, one of the younger M.P.s in whom Dillon had considerable confidence, suggesting an approach to Sinn Fein on the basis of a joint appeal to President Wilson or to the Peace Conference. This produced no result, so Horgan published a letter on the same lines in the national Press on 1 November. Ireland, he said, ought to be heard at the Peace Conference, but Sinn Fein, by reason of its previous support for Germany, had no hope of achieving anything there. Yet Sinn Fein and the parliamentary party were the only two effective nationalist forces in Ireland. 'Both have formulated their electoral programmes. The one asks for an Irish Republic, the other for 'the establishment of national self-government including full and complete executive, legislative and fiscal powers. The only real difference is a difference as to method—the question of attending the Imperial Parliament.' Why, therefore, he concluded, should they not build on the experience of the Mansion House Conference to combine in approaching the Peace Conference? This statement of the Irish situation, though it begged the vast question of the difference there could be between the republic and national self-government, elicited a not-discouraging reply from Eoin MacNeill on behalf of Sinn Fein, and Mr. Horgan was prompted to carry his initiative a little further. On 10 November he secured the passing, by 'a representative conference of Cork Nationalists', a resolution calling on all Irishmen to unite for the purpose of presenting Ireland's claim for self-determination to the Peace Conference. In order to forward such a united front, a conference of Irish Nationalists should immediately be summoned in order to avoid internecine strife at the general election. This resolution was forwarded to Dillon on 11 November and three days later he delivered—for publication —a crushing reply, which put an end to all hope of co-operation and which Mr. Horgan, recalling the incident years later, believed had sealed his fate.

Dillon began by pointing out that any proposals he had made for avoiding conflict at the general election (which was now known to have been fixed for 14 December) had been received not only with a negative 'but with insult and abuse'. He would still, he said, be glad to take part in a conference of Irish Nationalists *constituted on a fair and just basis*', but he then went on to define his own position in terms that indicated clearly enough how fruitless such a conference would have been in the scarcely conceivable event of it having met at all. First, he could not possibly agree to accept the policy of abstention from the House of Commons. The idea that during the protracted negotiations which were bound to follow the armistice the whole representation of Ireland should be handed over to Sir Edward Carson and his followers 'is to me an absolutely insane one'. In the second place, he thought there was much misconception as to what the Peace Conference would be really like. In effect, he pointed out, it would be an assembly of the victorious Allies before which the Germans would only appear as suppliants. Thanks partly to Sinn Fein's acts and words, and to the anti-Irish propaganda of the British Government, 'at this moment Ireland and her cause are very far from being popular with the Allied Nations'. As for the Sinn Fein boast that their leaders would enter the Conference with heads erect, 'there is not the slightest chance of representatives of Ireland being allowed to enter the Conference.' If they did, he added, their reception would be 'of a very painful, and to them, surprising character'. His own view, on the contrary, was that the one hope of Ireland obtaining any kind of recognition of her rights from the Peace Conference depended entirely upon President Wilson and upon the U.S.A.; all their efforts, therefore, ought to be brought to bear upon the President and the American people.[1]

Whether or not this uncompromising reply did seal the party's fate, it is difficult in retrospect to see how Dillon could have done other than he did. The position, as he outlined it, was indeed bleak, but Dillon at his bleakest was frequently most clear-sighted. The fact that Sinn Fein had become a genuinely formidable force naturally impressed Irish electors, but Dillon was surely right when he pointed out that this would cut no ice whatever at the Peace Conference. For the parliamentary party to go hand in hand, or rather cap in hand, to the Allies with their own most deadly enemies would not save them from annihilation, it would merely add ignominy to that annihilation. On the short run, it is quite true, the effects of this exchange were unfortunate, since Mr. Horgan and some of his colleagues resigned all their official connections with the constitutional movement and took no part in the election when it came.

This heavy blow from the south was serious enough, but it was surpassed by the news from the north that at this critical moment Joe Devlin had fallen ill—so ill that he was to be incapacitated for the whole of the campaign. This meant that almost the entire burden of fighting the election fell upon Dillon himself, aided by one or two faithful friends—notably Richard Hazleton and J. J. Muldoon. Together they dealt with all the correspondence at the central office, tried to answer the constant appeals for local organisers, provided speakers for the constituencies whenever they could be found.[2] And if this were not enough, some of the bishops, even the aged Primate, Cardinal Logue, were becoming apprehensive about the dangers of a clash, especially in northern seats with a strong Unionist vote, between Sinn Feiners and parliamentarians. Their solution was that the contending parties should divide the doubtful seats—there were eight of them—equally between them.[3] Dillon, therefore, found himself involved in the, to him, extremely distasteful task of negotiating a seats-deal with

---

[1] Dillon to J. J. Horgan 14 Nov. 1918 (Horgan Papers); J. J. Horgan, *Parnell to Pearse* (Dublin, 1948), pp. 345–52. The exchanges were actually more amicable than Dillon's letter might suggest; two days later he wrote, still in a friendly tone, discussing election possibilities with Mr. Horgan (Dillon to J. J. Horgan, 20 Nov. 1918, Horgan Papers).

[2] Dillon to T. P. O'Connor, 18, 22 and 28 Nov. 1918 (D.P.).

[3] *W.F.J.*, 30 Nov. 1918; Macardle, *The Irish republic*, pp. 264–5.

Eoin MacNeill, confiding to T. P. O'Connor that he thought it 'really rather indecent' that MacNeill, who was a candidate for one of the seats, should be participating in the negotiations.[1]

Worse even than divided seats were seats that went uncontested, and the evidence was beginning to pile up that there would be all too many of these. Several members of the party, after having given firm pledges that they *would* stand, had backed out at the last moment. Part of this, Dillon admitted to O'Connor, was due to faulty organisation, but part of it was 'sheer cowardice'.[2] However, it did not affect his will to fight on and he tried to extract from it what solace he could:

> The one comfort is that the men who showed such a spirit could be of no use to any party, and that we are well rid of them. Of course the large number of uncontested seats with no corresponding victories on our side will have a very grave effect on the country, and I do not think it is possible to save more than a few seats now . . . In point of fact, there are some things to be said in favour of a small minority. The more the responsibility is fixed on the other side to deliver the goods, carry out the promises they have made, the better and the more speedy will be their discomfiture and breakup.[3]

But even despite last-minute withdrawals and uncontested seats, the fact remained that many seats would be fought, and fought, in all probability, with a bitterness that had not been seen in the country for many years. To some, even among Dillon's closest associates, the prospect seemed too horrible to contemplate. On 7 December he received from Dr. Patrick O'Donnell, the Bishop of Raphoe (and one of his own oldest and warmest supporters), an urgent plea that in view of the strength of Sinn Fein and the inevitability of a savage struggle, Dillon should ask all his candidates to stand down. They could, the Bishop suggested rather cryptically, 'disappear to reappear'.[4] This evoked from Dillon a remarkable reply, which not only silenced the Bishop (who ended by meekly expressing the hope that despite the coming defeat Dillon himself would not retire), but revealed so strikingly the essential quality of the man that it must be given in full:[5]

> My dear Dr. O'Donnell,
> I have given the best consideration I could to the proposal contained in your letter received yesterday. The proposal is one of such extremely important and far-reaching character that I am sure you will agree with me that I was bound to take some time to think over it, before sending you a definite answer.
> Your proposal is that for the reasons stated in your letter, I should *at once* ask all my supporters to stand down. Such a proposal

[1] Dillon to T. P. O'Connor, 3 Dec. 1918 (D.P.).
[2] Dillon to T. P. O'Connor, 3 Dec. 1918 (D.P.).
[3] Dillon to T. P. O'Connor, 6 Dec. 1918 (D.P.).
[4] Bishop O'Donnell to Dillon, 7 Dec. 1918 (D.P.).
[5] Dillon to Bishop O'Donnell, 9 Dec. 1918 (D.P.); Bishop O'Donnell to Dillon, 10 Dec. 1918 (D.P.).

coming from you was of course bound to receive the most careful consideration. Any proposal coming from you, who have been such a faithful and generous friend in trying and difficult times, I would naturally be inclined to adopt if I could at all see my way to doing so. But I have come to the decision that it would be quite impossible for me to accept your suggestion.

This decision is based mainly on two considerations.

I It would be utterly inconsistent with my life-long conviction as a public man—to run away from one's principles because of a passing, or even a permanent, unpopularity would to my mind be an act of cowardice, and a betrayal of the trust which is placed on any one who accepts the responsibility of a public man. Moreover in the present instance I have so deep-seated a conviction of the disastrous results which may come to the country from the Sinn Fein policy and leadership that I could not reconcile it to my conscience to be a party, by requesting my friends to stand down, to handing over the people and the country to such a policy, and to such leaders.

II I do not think you have the least idea of what would be the feeling of my friends throughout the country if I were to take the step which you recommend.

If there is one thing more than another which the Irish people cannot tolerate in a political leader it is cowardice, and failure to stand and fight for the principles which he says he believes in. And in this I must say I heartily agree with the people.

How could I then, in view of the declaration I have quite recently made, run away from the fight and call on my friends to surrender at the very last moment to a policy which they and I, have denounced as ruinous to the best interests of the country?

You speak of 'disappearing to reappear'—could a political leader guilty of such conduct ever reappear, or show his face in public life? Could he reasonably expect the people to trust him or place any reliance on what he said?

If this policy of retiring from public life and leaving a clear field to S.F. was at any time a right one, the time for it was after the failure of the July negotiations of 1916 or after the Clare election. It was then carefully considered and rejected.

Now in my judgment it would appear to the people to be sheer cowardice and would only cover me and my friends with contempt. After the people have given their verdict on Saturday and the result has been announced, I shall of course carefully consider the position. And it will then be quite open to me to give the S.F's, who will have received a popular mandate, a fair opportunity of trying what their policy can do for Ireland.

As for my reappearance in Irish politics, that does not give me very much concern. But I am absolutely convinced that the only chance of my reappearing in such a fashion as would be honourable or tolerable to me lies in standing to my guns on the present occasion, and assuring the Irish people that I am not afraid to fight even a losing battle for a cause and a policy in which I believe.

In view of what I have written above I most earnestly request you *not* to mention this suggestion of yours to *anyone*, at all events till after Saturday.

About the Ulster seats I have done and shall do *all* in my power, but if you knew the intense bitterness amongst my friends in E. Down, Derry City and South Fermanagh at being asked to support S. Feiners, you would more keenly sympathise with the decision I have come to on your wider suggestion.

Yours sincerely,
John Dillon.

(iv)

In the midst of these preoccupations it was not easy for Dillon to give his own constituency the attention it deserved. Suddenly, after thirty years of cast-iron security, it was in jeopardy, for Sinn Fein, by nominating Mr. de Valera as his opponent, had deliberately concentrated the attention of the whole country upon what was clearly intended to be a symbolic contest between the two leaders. Dillon had paid a flying visit to East Mayo at the end of November and in his first speech there had marked out the line he was to follow consistently for the rest of the campaign. He dwelt upon the social and economic achievements of the party contrasted with Sinn Fein's virginal record, he reminded his listeners of the part he himself had played in stopping the executions in 1916 and, above all, he emphasised that Sinn Fein had fatally weakened the position of the country not only by shattering nationalist unity, but by poisoning world opinion, and especially that of America, against Ireland.[1] But his visit, brief though it was, was enough to show him that there was going to be, as he described it to O'Connor, 'a fierce struggle', due to what he called 'organised intimidation'. 'Young bands of roughs', he said, 'are going around the roads at night shouting that they will burn down any house that votes Dillon, and threatening to destroy cattle . . .'[2] Next day he returned again to the theme of Sinn Fein organisation, for which he could not conceal his professional admiration. He was by now quite certain that the party were going to lose heavily and, given the temper of the country, almost relieved that this should be so:

It would be difficult [he wrote] for me to make you realise to what extent the results of the election in Ireland are due to superb organisation—working against no organisation at all—bluff, and intimidation. My experience has convinced me of two things: first of all, that tens of thousands of strong supporters of ours went over to Sinn Fein in consequence of the anti-conscription campaign; and secondly, that if we had maintained our organisation in Ireland we could have saved at least forty seats.[3]

Back in Mayo again during the first two weeks of December, he found the situation if anything worse, and the air thick with threats and reports of violence. From one of his most devoted supporters, Father Denis O'Hara

[1] *W.F.J.*, 30 Nov. 1918. [2] Dillon to T. P. O'Connor, 6 Dec. 1918 (D.P.).
[3] Dillon to T. P. O'Connor, 7 Dec. 1918 (D.P.).

of Kiltimagh, the news was ominous, all the more so because it came from an expert in local opinion. On the day of polling, 14 December, he wrote: 'I am sorry to say we could not have done worse. I did think we might get something like half, but we are far from this. They were simply terrorised into voting Sinn Fein . . . The cry of "vote for the man in prison" and "vote for de Valera and no taxation" had the desired effect . . . it is sickening and disheartening to see what condition the country is in after forty years of uphill fight.'[1] Two days later he wrote again, with mounting bitterness: 'My men showed neither gratitude nor intelligence. All the old people voted as illiterates; they were terrorised, no doubt, by the young people, but one would expect some little gratitude and some little pluck.'[2]

Dillon himself was more philosophical. That defeat would be heavy he did not doubt, but he was still far from thinking it the end of all things. On 20 December, when the votes were in, but not yet counted, he set out his views for O'Connor in a long letter which, as an analysis of the contemporary Irish situation, was full of insight:

> The fight at East Mayo was a microcosm of the conditions all over the country—absolute lack of organisation and helplessness on our side against *the most* perfect organisation and infinite audacity on the other, backed by ferocious intimidation.
>
> All my experience during the contest has confirmed and deepened the conviction mentioned in a previous letter to you—that we had *plenty* of support in the country, including a very decided majority of thoughtful and intelligent men, but that during the last four years our machinery has been scrapped and cold water pumped on our supporters and the young men repulsed and driven wholesale into the Sinn Fein camp, and no effort whatever made to meet the poisonous propaganda of S.F.
>
> The bedrock of the situation is that the negotiations of July 1916 struck a deadly blow at the Irish party, and since that the party has been going downhill at an ever accelerated pace. The one chance we had since those fatal negotiations was last spring, and if L.G. had not forced thro' the Conscription Act for Ireland, we might have recovered the country. But even then it could only have been done by a complete and fundamental reform of our methods in Ireland. But after L.G's conduct in April and May last the position of the party became desperate and there was nothing for it but to put the matter to a clear issue and force the country to take the responsibility of coming to a decision.

Then, after a brief digression about the pressure he had been subjected to to stand down ('this of course I absolutely refused to do') and about Devlin's collapse, he continued:

> Now for the other side of the picture. I have never doubted since July 1916 that a catastrophe was inevitable. Carrying on a movement on

[1] Fr. D. O'Hara to Dillon, 14 Dec. 1918 (D.P.).
[2] Fr. D. O'Hara to Dillon, 16 Dec. 1918 (D.P.).

false lines and with the conviction that a catastrophe is inevitable is about the most horrible task a public man could be tied to. Now the worst has come. And before the crash came we got time to put before the country a sound, defensible policy, and clear issues.

Unless I am hopelessly mistaken, the Sinn Fein policy must end in failure and discredit, and if we have it still in us our time will come in a year or two. The number of seats we have saved at this election makes really very little difference. And while my defeat in East Mayo is undoubtedly a very severe blow to any hope of a revival of the constitutional movement in Ireland, it does not finally close the door.

One thing is perfectly clear—if there is to be any future for the constitutional movement it must be through a radical and fundamental reconstruction of the movement here in Ireland. Work in parliament would not, in face of present conditions, contribute in any degree to such a resurrection.[1]

Brave words, but when he wrote them Dillon, not usually prone to underestimate catastrophe, had not realised how complete the disaster to his party was going to be. At one time he had supposed that they might win nine or ten seats and that, although he would be defeated himself in East Mayo, the margin would not be more than about 1,000 votes.[2] In fact, when the results were known, at the very end of December, Mr. deValera had received 8,843 votes and Dillon 4,451, giving Sinn Fein a crushing majority of 4,392. Over the country at large the party was almost entirely wiped out. Under redistribution there were now 105 seats. Of these, Sinn Fein won seventy-three and the Unionists twenty-six. The once-proud party was reduced to only six, and five of these were in Ulster, four of them in seats where Sinn Fein had in effect not competed, and where the main fight had been between Unionist and Nationalist. The fifth, West Belfast, had been a personal triumph for Devlin, who, though too ill to do much for himself, had been returned with a majority of more than 3,000 over Mr. de Valera. The single, solitary seat won by the party in the south was Waterford City, which remained faithful to the Redmond tradition, re-electing Captain W. A. Redmond, though only with a majority of 474 over his Sinn Fein opponent.[3]

Such a massive repudiation of the parliamentary party could not simply be explained in terms of Dillon's thesis of superior organisation and unparalleled intimidation. Organisation and intimidation played a part, no doubt, but nothing could disguise the fact that the country had quite deliberately turned its back on the Home Rule movement and that the old tradition, which looked to physical force for the ultimate realisation of Ireland's dream of freedom, was once more in the ascendant. This being so, there was nothing Dillon could do but to stand aside and watch the situation develop. In a letter to T. P. O'Connor, part of which was written before the final results were known, and part after, he warned him to remain absolutely silent on the Irish problem for the present:

[1] Dillon to T. P. O'Connor, 20 Dec. 1918 (D.P.).
[2] Dillon to T. P. O'Connor, 19 and 24 Dec. 1918 (D.P.).   [3] *W.F.J.*, 4 Jan. 1919.

And if questioned on your attitude by friends, say that L.G. has by his policy, in the teeth of our warnings and protests, thrown Ireland into the hands of S.F. and the Republican party, and that for the present they—L.G. and the Republicans—have to find a way out. If they fail, our time will come again; and then we shall have something to say . . . There are dark forces at work in Ireland—I do not care to write details—and the situation is so full of menace that I do not think any of us ought to take the *smallest* atom of responsibility, even in the *most confidential* manner, as to the method of governing Ireland . . .

The wild young spirits have got it firmly fixed in their minds that the government is afraid of them, and their hatred of the British government is fully equalled by their contempt for it. I need not enlarge on what the consequences may be.

I have a good deal of information going to show that the Castle authorities winked at and deliberately abstained from interfering with the outrageous intimidation of the S.F. bands on the polling day.[1] And this, combined with the well-known fact that S.F. is riddled with spies and government agents will give you an idea of the devil's cauldron that L.G. has set going in Ireland.

You are perfectly right. *The only* policy for us to pursue is to give S.F. for the present an absolutely free hand, refusing to take the slightest share of responsibility for their policy, so that they shall not be able to charge us with any share of responsibility for their failure. If, as we must assume, the S.F's fail with Wilson and the Peace Conference, we shall have very serious happenings in Ireland and perhaps elsewhere.

At this point Dillon broke off his letter, resuming it next day when the results had come in. His mood was distinctly chastened. 'The landslide', he admitted, 'is a good deal greater than I had expected from my reports, and I confess some of the results have surprised me very much.' They would, he supposed, have to have some kind of meeting or conference to decide the future of their movement, whether in Ireland or in Great Britain. But he was worried by Devlin's continuing lethargy. 'Unless Devlin pulls himself together, and throws himself earnestly, in his old style, into an Irish movement, I do not see any possibility of keeping our friends together in Ireland. In any case after such a crushing defeat it would be no easy task.'[2]

Although Dillon did not yet quite realise the fact, and would probably have denied it indignantly had it been suggested to him, he had received his notice to quit, and was now to leave the stage on which he had played so important and distinguished a part for over forty years. But if the finality of his defeat had not fully come home to him, the magnitude of it was unmistakable and in those last, grim days of 1918 he looked back upon the recent past and tried to analyse, both for his old friend O'Connor and for himself, how it had all happened. His analysis, naturally, was highly sub-

[1] Whatever information he was referring to, no trace of it has survived in his private papers.

[2] Dillon to T. P. O'Connor, 28 and 29 Dec. 1918 (D.P.).

jective and coloured by animosities that went far back into his own career and into the history of the party. But introspection was one of his talents and what he wrote down is essential to the proper understanding of the tragic and squalid end of the Parnell movement. It is not the whole truth about that movement, but it has its own historic interest as being the nearest thing we have to an inquest upon the parliamentary party by one who, at the time of writing it, was still its greatest living representative. Written on Christmas Day 1918, it summed up as follows the causes of what he called 'the present chaos' in Ireland:

I The treachery and weakness of the government.

II The poisoning of the minds of the Irish people for *many* years by the *Independent*, the mosquito press and S.F. propaganda, without any effective effort on our part to counteract this poison.

III The folly and ignorance of the younger generation in Ireland, *who have not forgotten, but are ignorant of,* what our movement achieved for Ireland, and many of whom have grown up in the mephitic atmosphere of the Parnellite split, and Healyism.

IV The fury of a large section of the priests, who are most dishonestly using S.F. to carry out a purpose they have long nursed— the destruction of our independent lay party and the recovery of their own [? direct] power over Irish politics, which the Parnellite movement had to a very large extent *destroyed.*

V The outbreak in all its old savagery of the hatred of England, due to the executions and vile and idiotic policy of the government for the past five years.

VI And by no means least—our own blunders in not realising what was going on, digging a gulf between the party and the younger generation, making absolutely no effort to counteract the poisonous propaganda or to maintain our organisation and our movement. And Redmond's persistence in [? following] what has been called his imperialist policy long after it had become apparent to me that such a course would inevitably throw the country into the hands of S.F.

After the Rebellion in May [*sic*] 1916, the Irish party came to the parting of the ways. If we had then attacked the government and warned them of the results of their policy we could have rallied a partially united Ireland behind us. But we took the road which I felt sure would lead us to ruin and my instinct has been justified. Whether it will be ultimately possible to rescue the Irish cause in our life-time remains to be considered. But I am quite clear that for the moment our only course is to stand aside and let S.F. and L.G. fight it out.

L.G. will find that by betraying and killing the Irish party he has not got rid of all his difficulties.[1]

And with these prophetic words he withdrew into the wings.

[1] Dillon to T. P. O'Connor, 25 Dec. 1918 (D.P.).

16
At Rest

(i)

The declining years of a politician who has left public life under the shadow
of defeat are inevitably an anticlimax. Dillon was no exception to this
melancholy rule. The massive withdrawal of support indicated by the general election was, even if neither he nor others realised it at the time, final
and irrevocable. Henceforward, he was on the fringe of events, without the
power to influence them effectively. Nevertheless, right up to the end he
retained the full use of his faculties, and his passion for politics was un-
diminished. This gives his correspondence for these years a special character.
Less directly involved than ever before in his life, he was able to reflect,
to analyse, to criticise—in short to indulge himself at leisure in his favourite
pastime of intellectualising about politics. Moreover, the fact that a tiny
fragment of the old Irish party still hung on in the House of Commons for
a few years more, and that this fragment included Devlin and T. P. O'Connor, allowed him to keep in close touch with what was happening at Westminster. Ironically enough, although after 1918 he lived almost continuously
in Ireland, he was, if anything, less in touch with what went on there. He
still had his sources of information, indeed, and he was better than most at
reading between the lines of newspapers, but towards the new generation
of Republicans his attitude remained one of fascinated incomprehension,
lit now and then by flashes of penetrating insight. However, his intense interest in the revolution that was taking place around him never flagged and
his letters continued to give a remarkable, if increasingly an outsider's,
view of the Irish question long after he had officially done with it.

His own opinion, as he expressed it to Shane Leslie immediately after
the election, was that there was no possibility of Britain conceding the
Sinn Fein objective of a republic:

> I do not believe [he wrote] that this object is practicable, within the
> lifetime of this generation at all events, and I wholly disapprove of the
> methods used by Sinn Fein. I am convinced that if they are seriously
> attempted to be carried into effect the result will be disastrous failure
> and probably serious bloodshed.
>
> I am quite well aware that many of the Sinn Feiners do not mean
> what they say when they demand a republic. But that is the pro-
> gramme to which they have committed themselves, and on the faith of
> which they have carried the elections. And the I.R.B., which really
> controls the S.F. movement, does really mean a republic.

Many of the S.F. M.P.'s would, I am informed, like to take their seats in the House of Commons, but I do not see how they can do so in view of the pledges they have given and the language they have used. Moreover, I do not believe the I.R.B. would tolerate their going to parliament . . .

After the result of the election I consider that the S.F.'s are entitled to a fair field to try their policy. But, as I have said, I have no faith in their policy, and I am convinced their alleged object is unattainable. And if they seriously pursue it by the methods they propose [the setting up of their own parliament and government in Dublin], they will lead the country off in pursuit of a shadow and lose the substance —which was within our grasp—and lead the people along a path bound to end in a bloody morass similar to 1798.[1]

It was easy for Dillon to write of allowing Sinn Fein a fair field, but in practice, with the millstone of the *Freeman's Journal* still about his neck and the small group of Nationalist M.P.s at Westminster to succour and advise, he might have found it harder to cut himself off than he had supposed. Quite unexpectedly, however, the decision was removed from his hands. On 31 December he was taken seriously ill. His daughter Nano, writing to T. P. O'Connor, explained that up to that date he had been perfectly well and apparently not unduly depressed by the election results. Then he had suddenly become extremely unwell and had been in great pain. 'It was', she wrote, 'an attack of the old complaint, "internal inflammation".'[2] She was referring to what, thirty years before, his doctors had called 'intestinal catarrh', and which still returned to plague him occasionally, especially in time of stress. The trouble was, in reality, gall-stones and it was to kill him in the end, but this time he survived, though only just. The need for an operation was averted at the last moment, but though he was able to write to his old friend T. P. within a fortnight of being struck down, his progress was slow and it was several months before he was able to lead a normal, active life.

This setback—no doubt part of the price he had to pay for the severe mental and physical strain of the previous two years—relegated Dillon to the wings much more effectively than even the general election had succeeded in doing. But he could not isolate himself completely, and even before he was fully recovered had to plunge into the dark and tangled affairs of the *Freeman's Journal*. It had not been doing too badly in the second half of 1918, but then had come the election, resulting in a drop in circulation and in advertising, and on top of that his own illness. By the time he was well enough to look into the situation he found that although the price of paper had fallen sharply, the *Freeman* was making a loss of over £100 a week. This, he reckoned, was 75 per cent due to bad management and 25 per cent due to the changed situation after the election.[3] The position was, in fact, quite impossible. The newspaper had never really recovered from the de-

[1] Dillon to Shane Leslie, 29 Dec. 1918 (Leslie Papers).
[2] Nano Dillon to T. P. O'Connor, 'Wednesday' (2 Jan. 1919) (D.P.).
[3] Dillon to T. P. O'Connor, 20 Feb. and 10 May 1919 (D.P.).

struction of its premises in 1916, when, as a result of the burning of its records of debts outstanding, insufficient insurance and inadequate government compensation, it was saddled with so many liabilities that it could only operate at all with the aid of a crippling overdraft. It was only due to Dillon's influence that the bank had not foreclosed long ago, and it says much for his reputation that the overdraft was extended into the summer of 1919. But finally, by the end of July, even Dillon despaired of keeping it alive any longer and the whole concern went on the market. Shortly afterwards, Alderman Stephen O'Mara of Limerick, a former trustee of the party but now a declared supporter of Sinn Fein, made a bid which caused considerable heart-searching among the old parliamentarians. On the one hand, if he bought the paper, this would mean that it would pass lock, stock and barrel under Sinn Fein control. But on the other hand, if his offer were declined, it might well be that the *Freeman* would be bought up cheap by the *Independent*. To some of those connected with it, this seemed a fate worse even than Sinn Fein. Indeed, one of the consolations of selling out to Sinn Fein would be that at last the *Freeman* might be put into good fighting trim and be able to make some inroads upon William Martin Murphy's empire. Nevertheless, if any other buyer could be found this would obviously be preferable, and during August and September feverish efforts were made by P. J. Hooper, of the *Freeman* staff, and John Muldoon, the former Nationalist M.P., to find alternative backers. Lord Northcliffe was sounded so was Horace Plunkett, so, too, was Moreton Frewen, a compulsive backer of economic lost causes who was also—unpalatable thought!— a close associate of Tim Healy's. But in the troubled and uncertain state of Ireland none of these could be brought to the pitch of risking their capital on such a dubious proposition as the *Freeman*, and when O'Mara withdrew also, the prospect seemed hopeless. Eventually it was bought by an Irish merchant, Martin Fitzgerald, acting, so Dillon believed, in the liquor interest. One could hardly imagine a better prospect for a journalistic resurrection in Ireland, but the *Freeman* continued to be dogged by misfortune. The Anglo-Irish war, and then the civil war, added enormously to its difficulties and although it staggered on for some while longer, it was never financially healthy, and ceased publication in December 1924. As the final humiliation, the plant and premises were sold to the *Independent* in February 1925[1]. By that time, however, Dillon had long become reconciled to being without an organ, since he had neither a party nor, indeed, a policy.

But the detachment possible in 1925 was more difficult to achieve in 1919. Dillon found himself under constant pressure from those of his old colleagues who had survived the holocaust of the election, but who were so confused and pessimistic about the outlook that they could not make up their minds whether or not to take their seats. Devlin, at the outset, was

[1] The demise of the *Freeman's Journal* can be followed in two large envelopes of correspondence in the Dillon Papers, entitled 'The *Freeman* crisis'; also in Dillon's own letters to T. P. O'Connor, 9 and 10 May, 27 July and 22 Oct. 1919; and in T. M. Healy, *Letters and leaders*, ii. 613–14.

against returning to Westminster and in a letter to Bishop O'Donnell on the eve of the new session he marshalled an impressive array of arguments in favour of abstention. Six members in a House of over six hundred would, he said, be so feeble 'that we should only advertise our own weakness'. Being so few, they could not hope to influence Irish legislation and their impotence would be regarded 'as an absolute proof of the futility of parliamentary representation'. In addition, there was the further difficulty that if, as he thought likely, there was to be bloodshed in Ireland, a parliamentary group could not continue at Westminster without criticising the Government's Irish policy. But to do this would in effect be to defend Sinn Fein, and since Sinn Fein was bound to repudiate them anyway, this seemed a peculiarly pointless exercise. Apart from all this, Devlin was sure that the continuance of an Irish representation in the House of Commons, however minimal, would be used by the Sinn Feiners as at least a partial explanation of their failure to get a hearing at the Peace Conference, thus bringing odium on what was left of the constitutional movement. Devlin, had, therefore, consulted such of his colleagues as he could reach and had put these points to them. 'They were not impressed,' he told the Bishop. 'They stated that we were elected to go to Parliament and, that being so, it was our duty to act according to our mandate.' Logically, admitted Devlin, that might be right, but how could they disregard the 'practical unanimity' of the rest of the country in favour of abstention?[1]

This seems not to have been the Bishop's view—a year later, at any rate, he was urging Devlin to 'stick like glue' to his seat at Westminster. No doubt this was partly because the hierarchy wanted a responsible eye kept on British education policy, but it was also because, as a good Nationalist, he felt that the little group should be there to speak out on behalf of Sinn Fein prisoners, and he added a maxim of conduct of which Dillon would surely have approved. 'No matter how much an Irish leader or representative in the House of Commons may disagree with extreme men at home, he can never throw them over before a foreign assembly.'[2] Devlin himself conquered his initial reluctance and, with Dillon's warm support, decided to take his seat. He was never very happy there, however, and found the new Parliament (which, indeed, was to earn one of the most unsavoury reputations in the history of modern British politics) a very reactionary and unsympathetic body. He did not even find it easy to get on with his handful of Irish colleagues and although he acted more closely with T. P. O'Connor than with anyone else there was sometimes friction between them. What they had most in common, it seemed, was that they both relied heavily upon Dillon. 'You are very much missed here and we all feel very lonely without you', wrote Devlin at the beginning of the session, and he was echoed a few days later by O'Connor: 'I often long for your reconciling influence, as well, of course, as for your inspiration, in a somewhat forlorn position'.[3] Dillon

[1] Devlin to Bishop P. O'Donnell, 22 Jan. 1919, copy (D.P.).
[2] Bishop O'Donnell to Devlin, 20 Feb. 1920, copy (D.P.).
[3] Devlin to Dillon, 14 Feb. 1919, and T. P. O'Connor to Dillon, 22 Feb. 1919 (D.P.).

did his best to encourage and guide them from a distance and a whole series of letters bears witness to their gratitude, as also to their helplessness without him. Devlin, especially, not only sought his advice on parliamentary strategy and tactics, but was even indebted to him for financial help. He had only his parliamentary salary, plus a small sum from his post as general secretary of the almost defunct United Irish League, and he found that this did not go very far in postwar London. From time to time, therefore, Dillon came to his rescue with grants from the meagre funds still remaining under his control.[1] Even so, Devlin remained restless and miserable in the House of Commons and when, in 1920, Lloyd George's Government of Ireland Act led to the emergence of Northern Ireland as a separate entity with a Parliament of its own, Devlin was glad enough to go home to build up a whole new career and reputation as leader of the Ulster Nationalists at Stormont.

T. P. O'Connor presented Dillon with a different problem. For one thing, of course, his was not an Irish seat. His old Liverpool constituency (the Scotland division) remained faithful to him through all adversities and he was therefore less vulnerable in one sense to the changed conditions in Ireland. But in another sense he *was* vulnerable, since, as one of the longest-established Irish Members—and one known to be on friendly terms with the Prime Minister—he was under constant pressure to pronounce upon Irish affairs. In addition, he was still, as he always had been, deeply involved in the politics of the Irish in Great Britain. Since the *débâcle* of the election, their organisation, the United Irish League of Great Britain, had been disintegrating rapidly, some of its members turning towards Sinn Fein, and many others looking to the Labour Party as their hope for the future. The drift to Sinn Fein O'Connor fought as hard as he could, but the drift to Labour was another matter, since his own relations with some of the Labour leaders were so close that it would not have taken very much to attract him personally into that party. In dealing with his old colleague, therefore, Dillon had to take account of these two new factors in the situation—that O'Connor was, or believed himself to be, in the intoxicating position of being *the* parliamentary spokesman for Irish affairs, and that, at the same time, he was apparently becoming less interested in the preservation of a separate Irish organisation in Britain, and more concerned with securing for his fellow countrymen an influence in the Labour movement proportionate to their numbers. Dillon saw the dangers of both these tendencies and his correspondence with T. P. for the years after 1918 is full of warnings and instructions. It says a great deal for their friendship, and especially for T.P.'s forbearance, that these directives, which often contrived to be both peremptory and negative, did not lead to a breach between them. In fact, the opposite was the case; their relationship became if anything more affectionate as it drew towards its close.

What Dillon set himself to do was to be towards O'Connor very much what he had been towards Redmond between 1914 and 1918. Of course, the circumstances were vastly different, but the essential aim was the same—

[1] Devlin to Dillon, 2 Apr. 1919 and 1 Mar. 1920 (D.P.).

to try to convey to the principal Irish representative at Westminster the realities of the Irish situation as seen from close at hand. T.P. might play the parliamentary spokesman to his heart's content—*provided* he based what he said upon the advice and information liberally supplied to him by the man on the spot. At the very outset, when Parliament assembled at the beginning of 1919 and there was still no inkling of what plans, if any, the Government had for Ireland, Dillon warned his friend to steer clear of committing himself to any precise formula, even the seductive one of dominion status.[1] Feeling was running so high in Ireland, he wrote a little later, that it would be madness for anyone connected with the constitutional movement to put forward any kind of compromise:

> Nothing but a broad generous measure of full dominion Home Rule would have the slightest chance of affecting the Irish situation favourably at present, and it would be a *fatal* mistake for any of us to commit ourselves, even in private conversation . . . As for the S.F.'s, they will accept nothing short of separation and a republic. But if L.G. brings in a measure of dominion Home Rule they will do all they can to wreck it, by declaring that [they] will make no compromise and are resolved to secure an independent Irish republic. If, however, the bill were put through I am convinced Ireland would accept and work it.[2]

This was an accurate anticipation of what Ireland was eventually to accept in 1921, but before that could come about many terrible things were to happen. And in the spring of 1919 Dillon was almost daily expecting the catastrophe he so clearly foresaw. At the end of March he wrote that they had just been 'on the edge of another Easter week, of a much bloodier character. But for the enormous forces concentrated in Dublin by the authorities I have no doubt there would have been an outbreak.'[3] A few days later his alarm was, if anything, even greater. 'So far as I can learn,' he wrote, 'the extreme element are out of hand, and are determined to carry on what they are pleased to call war . . . the more moderate leaders are trying to run a counter-attraction in the Dail Eireann, which continues its absurd proceedings. But this body is drifting irresistibly towards a collision with the government. I do not see how a collision can be avoided. And when that comes—then the deluge!'[4]

The Irish situation, drifting, as Dillon rightly said, towards a head-on clash between the Government and Sinn Fein, was so full of danger and confusion that he had no advice to offer save to maintain an attitude of cautious reserve. 'The young people in Ireland', he told O'Connor, 'are quite intoxicated with this idea of a republic, and are more inflamed with hatred of England than I can ever remember to have been the case in

[1] Dillon to T. P. O'Connor, 28 Feb., 11 and 13 Mar. 1919 (D.P.).
[2] Dillon to T. P. O'Connor, 17 Mar. 1919 (.D.P.).
[3] Dillon to T. P. O'Connor, 31 Mar. 1919 (D.P.).
[4] Dillon to T. P. O'Connor, 11 Apr. 1919 (D.P.).

Ireland . . . And I need not say the young priests are the worst.'[1] Given
this temper in the country, he could not see how any proposal short of a
republic could stand a chance of success—but a republic was not on the
cards. All the more reason, therefore, he thought, for the constitutionalists
to be at the ready. 'If there is to be any chance of a settlement in our days
I think it will be absolutely necessary for us to appear upon the scene with
a definite programme before very long. Not just now, but when the lesson
of the total failure of the Sinn Fein methods has had time to sink into the
minds of the people in Ireland.' When that moment came, their programme,
he added, could not be less than full dominion status.[2]

(ii)

The inevitable outcome of this embittered temper in Ireland, combined
with the apparent inability of the Government to produce anything remotely resembling a solution, was a deterioration in public order and a
growth in all kinds of extremism. One form of this, though it can never
have attracted more than a tiny minority, was a disposition to look on the
Russian revolution as providing a model for Ireland, combined with a hope
that in some mysterious fashion the Soviet Union might bring influence to
bear in favour of an Irish settlement. The bare mention of such a possibility
evoked an outburst of wrath from Dillon. 'I am', he wrote to Shane Leslie
in June, 'a convinced anti-Bolshevist. I consider Bolshevism as it has prevailed in Russia for the last year to be one of the most horrible tyrannies
the world has ever been cursed with . . . The latest mad fancy of the
extreme S.F.'s and the Bolshevists in Ireland is that Russia is the *one
country* on which Ireland can confidently rely. In my judgment Russia
will prove an even more rotten reed to lean on even (*sic*) than "our great
European allies" . . . At this moment more than half the world is mad.'[3]

Much more relevant to the Irish situation, because so much more typical
of how the pattern was to develop in the immediate future, was the news
that began to appear with increasing frequency of the shooting of policemen. Scattered and apparently unconnected at the outset, these were, in
fact, the first shots in what was soon to become a veritable Anglo-Irish
war. 'Hatred of England is *the* dominant passion with the young of both
sexes in Ireland now', he observed bitterly to C. P. Scott. 'Murder of
policemen and soldiers is to them guerrilla warfare, and the men who do
these deeds are national heroes.'[4] Characteristically, Dillon seized at once
upon the significance of this portent:

> I am not pessimistic [he wrote to Leslie] about a few assassinations,
> but I most decidedly object to a policy approved of by public men
> which justifies what appear to me to be murder, on the grounds that

[1] Dillon to T. P. O'Connor, 11 July 1919 (D.P.).
[2] Dillon to T. P. O'Connor, 20 July 1919 (D.P.).
[3] Dillon to Shane Leslie, 10 June 1919 (Leslie Papers).
[4] Dillon to C. P. Scott, 21 July 1919 (D.P.).

it is carrying on a legitimate guerrilla warfare. I have never sanctioned the outcry against leaders of Sinn Fein for not denouncing these occurrences, but I most strongly object when public speeches are made calculated undoubtedly to encourage them, and to convey to the people the impression that they are approved of by responsible leaders as a legitimate method of war. You cannot quote anything from the leaders of the Land League similar to such speeches.

As for the demand for a republic which lay behind these outbreaks, his opinion on that had not changed in the slightest:

I regard that as lunacy, and no question can arise of my encouraging such a settlement; and I most certainly will not be any party to encouraging foolish, brave and enthusiastic young men to go out and get slaughtered in pursuit of such an ideal, believing as I firmly do that there is a powerful and influential gang in the government of this country who are carrying on their present system of government in Ireland with a view to producing such a catastrophe, and that this has been adopted as a deliberate policy, and as the safest method of killing the danger of Home Rule.[1]

This, of course, was the old conspiracy theory once more. We may feel that what Dillon attributed to deliberate policy was much more likely to have been due precisely to a lack of policy, but the end result was certainly the same. And as the summer of 1919 turned to autumn the possibilities of any sort of peaceful settlement seemed to him less and less. 'Here', he wrote to O'Connor in November, 'we have settled down to the business of murdering policemen and I expect that this will be the chief political activity of Irish patriots for some months to come.'[2] Not, as O'Connor hastened to inform him, that the situation was any easier across the water. 'I might tell you that our position here is getting pretty desperate. The Sinn Feiners have undoubtedly produced a tremendous impression among our people. The argument which is most cogent with our people here is that they should not put themselves up against Ireland, and that as Ireland has pronounced for Sinn Fein we should not go against Sinn Fein.'[3]

Nevertheless, Dillon still continued to point the same moral. The general election had placed the responsibility for finding a solution squarely upon the Government and upon Sinn Fein, who must be left to fight it out between them.[4] A little later, after having received the most despairing account from T.P. of the way in which the organisation in Britain was breaking up, he expanded this view:

Our only policy is to leave the matter for the moment between the government and Sinn Fein. The government and Sinn Fein have between them created the present situation and it is up to them to find a way out. A damned difficult job. I do not believe they can

[1] Dillon to Leslie, 24 June 1919 (Leslie Papers).
[2] Dillon to T. P. O'Connor, 4 Nov. 1919 (D.P.).
[3] T. P. O'Connor to Dillon, 5 Nov. 1919 (D.P.).
[4] Dillon to T. P. O'Connor, 7 Nov. 1919 (D.P.).

succeed. Both are in desperate difficulties and it is none of our business
to help them out, even if it were possible for us to do so. And at this
moment it is *not* possible. The only result of our interfering would
be that we should find ourselves once more in the bog-hole and L.G.
and Sinn Fein would climb out on our backs.[1]

O'Connor was only half convinced by this logic and when, in December
1919, it was announced that a Home Rule Bill was to be introduced in the
New Year he showed unmistakable signs of wanting to take part in the
debate. Dillon, however, remained adamant. They *must* not get involved
at this stage in what would probably turn out to be yet another round of
undignified and fruitless bargaining:

> For some time [he wrote] the S.F. leaders have been privately circu-
> lating the statement that the government here were about to make
> an offer far better than Redmond's Home Rule and that they, while
> declining to discuss it, would offer no opposition, but would use it,
> when established, for their own purposes. Our only sound policy is
> to leave them and the government to deal with this splendid offer.
> In the appalling muddle which will result our time will come if we
> only make ready to take action at the proper moment.[2]

Dillon's irony was only too well justified by events. The 'splendid offer'
turned out to be a proposal giving Home Rule on roughly the 1914 model
to the two parts of Ireland and creating separate parliaments for each. It
was true that Lloyd George's new scheme looked forward to the reintegra-
tion of north and south and that he proposed to set up a Council of Ireland
consisting of representatives drawn from each parliament, but since the
powers conceded to the individual legislatures fell far below dominion
status, which even Dillon now regarded as the minimum demand, there
was no real basis for a permanent settlement. The Government of Ireland
Act, as it passed into law during the 1920 session, was from the start unpopular on both sides. The north eventually accepted it as the least disruption of the British connection they could hope for, but in the south
Sinn Fein greeted it with open derision.[3] Dillon, looking at the situation
strictly from the viewpoint of the constitutionalists, saw the defects of the
scheme, but, for Machiavellian reasons, hoped nevertheless that it would
go through. 'If the bill passes,' he explained to O'Connor, 'the Sinn Feiners
will stand for the southern parliament and then proclaim a republic. But
they will not carry their party solid in that policy. And I feel confident that
the time would then come for us to come forward with a sane policy.'[4]

There was, of course, more than a touch of political Micawberism in
this attitude. The fallacy underlying it was the assumption that when some-

[1] Dillon to T. P. O'Connor, 21 Nov. 1919 (D.P.).

[2] T. P. O'Connor to Dillon, 24 Nov. 1919, 11 Dec. 1919 (D.P.); Dillon to T. P.
O'Connor, 10 Dec. 1919 (D.P.).

[3] For the background of the Act, see D. R. Gwynn, *The history of partition* (Dublin
1950), chap. 7.

[4] Dillon to T. P. O'Connor, 21 Mar. 1920 (D.P.).

thing turned up it might be to the advantage of the constitutionalists. Whereas, what did eventually turn up, as Dillon himself had prophesied more than once, was the long-awaited collision between Sinn Fein and the government. The great question of the hour was indeed to be decided by blood and iron, not by resolutions of majorities, still less by the wishful thinking of minorities. The real centre of gravity of the problem was no longer at Westminster but in Ireland. The most immediately important fact with which all parties had to reckon was not the Government of Ireland Bill, proceeding on its leisurely path through Parliament, but the steadily increasing intensity of guerrilla warfare fought with extreme bitterness and savagery by both sides. Dillon, watching this deterioration in fascinated horror, blamed the Government primarily, but Sinn Fein almost as much. His attitude towards extremists remained—as it had been since 1916—mixed. 'The organising skill, courage and audacity of the S.F.'s are admirable', he wrote to a friend that summer, 'but their methods are beastly and horribly demoralising . . .' They have absolutely *no* statesmanship or real leadership amongst them, and I very much fear that they are playing right into L.G.'s hands.' But it was the breakdown of law and order which horrified him most. 'The whole country', he had explained to T. P. O'Connor in May, 'is now held in the grip of a reign of terror, unparalleled, I believe, in the case of any country professing to be civilised.'[1] He was appalled particularly by the attacks of the Irish Republican Army upon the police, but when the government reinforced the latter with para-military units—the Black and Tans and the Auxiliaries—he reacted just as violently against their often barbarous reprisals. Living in Dublin, he was a witness to many of the scenes he described to O'Connor, but guerrilla warfare was, if anything, more extreme outside the capital. Even in Ballaghaderrin he could not get away from the threat of violence. The shopkeepers in that town were warned in June by the I.R.A. not to supply policemen with goods, or they would be treated as enemies of the Republic, whereupon the police retaliated by serving notice that if the shops did not supply them they would be occupied by the military. 'An agreeable alternative', commented Dillon.[2] Nevertheless, in the summer and autumn he paid his usual visit to Mayo and was actually at Ballaghaderrin in October when the town was in the hands of the Black and Tans. Despite a great deal of tension there were no serious incidents while he was there, but when he got back to Dublin in November he found the situation 'horrible beyond words'.[3] This was just after the events of 'Bloody Sunday' (21 November 1920) and the position seemed to get no better in the succeeding weeks. One got hardened to it in time, he wrote to T. P. in mid-December, but for anybody with sensitive nerves it was hardly possible to keep sane. 'It is difficult', he continued, 'to make up one's mind which side to condemn

[1] Dillon to J. F. Tuohy, 22 June 1920 (Letters of J. F. Tuohy, N.L.I. MS. 3883); Dillon to T. P. O'Connor, 14 May 1920 (D.P.).
[2] Dillon to T. P. O'Connor, 24 June 1920 (D.P.).
[3] Dillon to T. P. O'Connor, 29 Nov. 1920 (D.P.).

most. And the whole business is like a mad pandemonium of lunatics. *All* the forces which after years of patient toil succeeded in destroying the leadership of the Irish parliamentary party are now reaping the harvest of the seed they sowed—and they don't seem to enjoy it.'[1]

(iii)

The early months of 1921 brought no improvement. Indeed, the Government seemed more determined than ever to meet brutality with brutality. The area subject to martial law expanded inexorably; the possession of arms and the harbouring or aiding of rebels became a capital offence subject to trial in a military court; and in the spring the Government authorised the use of drumhead courts martial for men caught actually under arms. Dillon, watching all this at close quarters, found his thoughts turning yet again to the main architect, as he saw it, of his country's misfortunes. Lloyd George, he conceded to C. P. Scott (who still retained an affection for the Prime Minister even while castigating his policy in the *Manchester Guardian*), would no doubt like to settle Ireland on democratic principles, but Ulster had always stood in his way; besides, he could not bring himself to sacrifice his own appetite for power:

> In pursuance of his own ambition to secure a subservient House of Commons he *deliberately* killed the old National party and he did this with his eyes open, knowing well what he was doing. He did it because he knew us too well to suppose that he could secure such a House of Commons as he had in view so long as the National party was there.
>
> He succeeded in December 1918 in securing the most subservient and degraded House of Commons since the days of Robert Walpole. But he made one grave miscalculation—he utterly underestimated the forces he was letting loose in Ireland. I often warned him on this point, but like many very able men he thought he knew everything. And just as he has made a hideous mess of Europe, never having had any *serious* interest in foreign politics, so he has made a hell's cauldron of Ireland.[2]

Although Dillon was once again probably attributing too much malice aforethought to Lloyd George, he was surely right when he said that the Prime Minister had miscalculated the forces against him, and even more accurate in his forecast that after the fight had gone on for some time longer—his guess to C. P. Scott was six months—both sides would be ready for compromise. Meanwhile, however, the war continued, and since some of the shootings in the spring of 1921 involved women, Dillon began to suspect that the extreme element in the I.R.A. might be getting out of hand, with the possible consequence that Mr. de Valera might be all the

---

[1] Dillon to T. P. O'Connor, 16 Dec. 1920 (D.P.).
[2] Dillon to C. P. Scott, 18 Jan. 1921 (D.P.); for Scott's attitude to Lloyd George at this time, see J. L. Hammond, *C. P. Scott*, pp. 277–9.

more inclined to treat. We now know that during April and May peace feelers of various kinds were being put out, that Mr. de Valera had secret, if apparently abortive, interviews with Lord Derby, an 'unofficial' emissary from the British Government, and also with Sir James Craig, the Prime Minister of Northern Ireland.[1] Dillon, of course, was unaware of what was going on, but he tried hard to disentangle the problem for O'Connor:

> I have strong reasons to believe [he wrote during May] that Valera is very much alarmed at the situation and would gladly compromise and make peace. But I am still very doubtful whether he will find it possible to do so. He is not a strong man, and is I believe completely under the control of the secret executive. Whether *they* want peace or not, I do not know. The situation—so far as my knowledge goes— is this. Within the next six weeks Valera and his fighting crowd must make up their minds either to make peace on the basis of dropping the demand for a republic and letting Ulster alone, or to continue the war in face of a greatly intensified military régime.[2]

This, though betraying that Dillon was tending to underestimate de Valera as he had previously underestimated Griffith, was in some other respects a shrewd analysis, anticipating with remarkable precision the basis of the eventual settlement. On the short run, too, Dillon's prediction was accurate, for the truce did indeed come within six weeks—in fact, on 11 July 1921. But until it came the situation seemed to get worse, not better. Before May was out Dillon was able to write to T.P. that the past fortnight had been 'the bloodiest and most war-like since Easter 1916'.[3] Almost immediately after this came what seemed to him one of the most senseless incidents of the whole struggle—the burning of the Dublin Customs House, one of the finest of the city's Georgian buildings. It was justified by the Republicans as a blow against the British administration—through the destruction of countless official records and other documents—but it moved Dillon, who, with his daughter Nano, watched it blazing, to bitter and almost incoherent indignation:

> Later on [he wrote to T.P.] we walked across town and from O'Connell Bridge, on which a great crowd had collected, looked on at a most tragic and awful sight—the most beautiful building in Ireland a mass of flame and awful clouds of black smoke. The whole scene was one of the most [word illegible] and tragic I have ever witnessed. A *lovely* summer afternoon, the crowds of *silent* people, afraid to express any opinion, and the appalling sight of the most beautiful [building] of Ireland [of] our period of greatness, wantonly and deliberately destroyed by the youth of Ireland as the latest and highest expression of idealism and patriotism.[4]

[1] D. Macardle, *The Irish republic*, pp. 446–51; Randolph Churchill, *Lord Derby,* *'King of Lancashire'* (London, 1959), chap. 18.
[2] Dillon to T. P. O'Connor, 19 May 1921 (D.P.).
[3] Dillon to T. P. O'Connor, 23 May 1921 (D.P.).
[4] Dillon to T. P. O'Connor, 26 May 1921 (D.P.).

Nevertheless, the truce came at last and conditions of life in Ireland gradually became more tolerable. 'I cannot tell you', wrote Dillon to T.P. in August, 'how strange it has been walking through Dublin without Auxiliaries' lorries and the constant expectation of bombs, no curfew and peaceful nights without . . . hideous street battles.'[1] It was, of course, a precarious peace, from time to time broken on both sides, but the longer it lasted the more difficult it became for the I.R.A. to launch a full-scale guerrilla war again. On the other hand, that it *was* a truce for so long, without leading apparently to anything more permanent, indicated how difficult the negotiations for a settlement were proving. Difficult as between Britain and Ireland, since Lloyd George would only consider some form of Home Rule within the Empire. No less difficult among the Irish themselves, already beginning to be divided between the zealots of the republic and those who felt that peace was so necessary it must be bought by some kind of compromise. Dillon, although obviously unaware of the intricacies of the situation, knew enough about the problems involved to be for a long time sceptical about the continuance of a truce, let alone the conclusion of a genuine settlement. But it was significant that his tone, when he tried to describe the condition of affairs to O'Connor, was far more detached and resigned than it had ever been before. When his old friend wrote to him expressing a wish to intervene in a forthcoming debate on Irish policy, Dillon still had no advice but that he should sit silent, proffering that advice in the language of a man who has at last come to terms with the bitter truth that he no longer has, and need never again hope to have, any influence on the course of events:

> L.G. and the gentlemen in control here have studiously ignored us throughout the last three years. They have committed blunder after blunder and succeeded in bringing the country and the whole Irish question into an impossible position. Why in the name of com- monsense should we attempt to butt in now? We have no practical proposal to put forward and any action on our part either by speech or voting which would bear the appearance of putting our money on the present conference would in my judgment be fatuous.[2]

Detachment, however, brought no loss of interest and Dillon continued to follow the unrolling of the tragedy as intently as ever. When the 'Treaty', conceding dominion status but denying the Republic, was signed in December he watched the developing rift between the pro- and anti- Treaty sections with grim and, as usual, accurate, foreboding. 'Judging from the temper of yesterday's discussions' [in the Dail], he wrote to O'Connor in January 1922, 'it looks as if we were in for another split quite as ferocious as the Parnellite split, with this difference that bombs, revolvers and rifles will be substituted as arguments for sticks and stones used in 1890.' As for the Treaty itself, it was, he admitted, 'on the whole

[1] Dillon to T. P. O'Connor, 1 Aug. 1921 (D.P.).
[2] Dillon to T. P. O'Connor, 29 Oct. 1921 (D.P.).

. . . a very good settlement, and if well handled, could be made the basis of a truly united and free Ireland'—though even so, he did not envy Griffith and Collins their task in trying to make it work.[1] However, once it had been signed, he added a few weeks later, 'my advice to all who consult me is to support the new government and do all in their [power] to give it a fair chance to restore order and show what policy it proposes to carry out'.[2]

Yet, as the divisions between the zealots and the compromisers deepened, he began to wonder whether the Provisional Government would be able to carry out any policy at all. 'The country', he wrote to O'Connor early in February, 'is drifting into anarchy. Whether Collins and co. will be able to restore any kind of order, and civilised government, is still an open question. The news that is reaching me is sinister in the extreme. There is, I fear, the gravest danger that the I.R.A. is getting completely out of hand, and as it is the *only* power in Ireland now, if it goes, then there will be . . . absolute anarchy and chaos.'[3] Two days later he wrote that both the Republicans and the pro-Treaty party had been inquiring about what the parliamentarians were going to do in the general election to be held later that year. Dillon himself, he said, had received a 'friendly' warning (he did not specify from whom) that it was going to be a savage business, in which it would be wiser for him and his supporters not to intervene. Not, indeed, that he had any intention of doing so, for he saw all too clearly the way things were going. 'The real truth', he wrote, 'is that the departure of the Auxiliaries and the British garrison has gone very far towards killing the Treaty. Childers and co. have 40 organisers out, and it is being dinned into the people that the British government is utterly beaten and that there is no question of any more fighting. All they have got to do is to proclaim the republic and the job is done.'[4]

But there remained the fundamental divisions among Irishmen themselves. By March Dillon was convinced that the break was coming and he doubted if the Provisional Government would survive it. 'Collins', he wrote, 'has shown great courage, and a very considerable amount of ability, but I think he is lacking in political judgment . . . Without Collins Griffith would not last a fortnight.'[5] He was quite right in his forecast that a break was coming, for on 13 April the I.R.A. seized the Four Courts in Dublin and it was evident that a trial of strength was about to begin. What followed was not a pitched battle or an orderly campaign, but rather a dreary and savage repetition of the old round of bomb outrages, ambushes, burnings, murders, executions and reprisals—but with this difference, that since Irishmen were now killing other Irishmen on a

[1] Dillon to T. P. O'Connor, 5 Jan. 1922 (D.P.).
[2] Dillon to T. P. O'Connor, 27 Jan. 1922 (D.P.).
[3] Dillon to T. P. O'Connor, 6 Feb. 1922 (D.P.).
[4] Dillon to T. P. O'Connor, 8 Feb. 1922 (D.P.).
[5] Dillon to T. P. O'Connor, 23 Mar. 1922 (D.P.).

point of passionately held principle, the degree of ruthlessness was, if anything, intensified. Moreover, while the government forces operated on a
more or less disciplined and coherent pattern, the control of the Republican
leaders over their men was not, and in the circumstances could not be, as
tight as it had been during the Anglo-Irish war. The result was that on
many occasions it was perfectly innocent by-standers who suffered most
from the sudden, unpredictable outbursts of violence. Admittedly, a truce
of a kind, though often broken, was patched up to permit the holding of
the general election on 16 June. But once this had been held and had
demonstrated, so far as the unsettled state of the country allowed it to
demonstrate, a fairly large preponderance of votes in favour of pro-Treaty
candidates (486,419 for the Treaty, 133,864 against) the civil war was
resumed in all its ferocity.[1]

Dillon had never really believed that the electoral pact would lead to
any wider settlement. 'The only authority left in the country', he explained
to O'Connor, 'resides in the bands of armed men who call themselves the
I.R.A., and I fear that the murders and robberies will continue . . .'[2]
Immediately the election was over, however, the provisional government
did their best to prove him wrong. On 28 June they began to move against
the I.R.A. (or 'Irregular') forces in the Four Courts, whereupon the
struggle entered a more intensive phase. At various points in Dublin, one
of them just behind Dillon's house in North Great George's Street, furious
gun-battles broke out, and that same day he wrote to O'Connor that 'it
was quite as bad as, if not worse than, the hottest night of 1916'.[3] A week
later (in the course of which the Four Courts had been burnt out and the
garrison forced to surrender) he reckoned that Dublin was actually in a
much worse condition than in 1916. 'Yesterday the sniping round this
house was the worst we had during the fight. And at 12 o'c last night
O'Connell Street was a perfect sea of fire—an appalling spectacle. Looking
from our top windows, and listening to the explosions as the ammunition
dumps were reached by the flames, it seemed as if the whole city must be
destroyed.'[4]

All the same, despite the death of Griffith on 12 August and the killing
of Michael Collins in ambush ten days later, the Provisional Government
slowly began to make headway. Its new leaders, W. T. Cosgrave, Richard
Mulcahy and Kevin O'Higgins, were quite as ruthless as the old, and they

---

[1] In an attempt to reduce the number of contested elections Collins and de Valera
concluded a 'pact', which, however, was not very effective in its operation. In total it
has been estimated that fifty-eight pro-Treaty candidates and thirty-five anti-Treaty
candidates were elected; there were in addition seventeen Labour seats, seven Indepen-,
dents, seven Farmers, and four members from Dublin University (Donal O'Sullivan
The Irish Free State and its senate (London, 1940), pp. 61–63). Figures slightly more
favourable to the Republican side are given in D. Macardle, *The Irish Republic*, pp. 722,
982; the difference amounts only to the transfer of one Independent seat to the Republican total.

[2] Dillon to T. P. O'Connor, 6 May 1922 (D.P.).

[3] Dillon to T. P. O'Connor, 28 June 1922 (D.P.).

[4] Dillon to T. P. O'Connor, 6 July 1922 (D.P.).

resorted unflinchingly to courts martial, executions and reprisals. The two most bitterly resented incidents arising out of this policy were the execution of Erskine Childers on 24 November and of Rory O'Connor and three other prisoners early in December. Dillon's reaction to this new development was one of utter abhorrence. It is notable that whereas, in his letters to O'Connor, he had usually written of the Provisional Government under Collins and Griffith with some respect, his attitude towards their successors was far harsher. And when, in December, the Dail met amid extraordinary precautions for the safety of its members, his sarcasm knew no bounds:

> It certainly is not a very auspicious start for a new government—beyond the dreams we are told, of all previous patriots—to open its first sitting with all galleries closed, the street in which it sat barred by cordons of military, the ministers all imprisoned in government buildings under elaborate guards, upwards of ten thousand men and women in gaol without any charges made against them. And in spite of this, the capital in such a state that no member of parliament's life is safe for an hour without a personal guard. If this be liberty, I have no use for it.[1]

He had still less use for the execution of hostages and, after the shooting of Rory O'Connor and his fellow prisoners, he told O'Connor that public opinion had been deeply shocked. 'Even amongst supporters of the government I think the predominant feeling is hostile. And really so far as I can recollect there is no exact precedent for such a proceeding in the annals of any modern civilised government.'[2]

(iv)

But from this point—the end of 1922—onwards, the broad stream of Dillon's political correspondence, which had flowed so freely for over forty years, began to show signs of running dry. This no doubt was partly due to age—he was, after all, over seventy—but to judge from the letters he did write after 1922, it was even more because he had come to realise that the Irish situation had finally passed beyond the power of his generation to influence or, indeed, even to comprehend. It was a baffling and an increasingly alien world in which he found himself in these last years and that he felt this is indicated by the changed character of his letters. He still wrote long, friendly epistles to T. P. O'Connor—though apparently hardly at all to any of his other former colleagues—but they were much less frequent than formerly, and although they almost always contained political comment of one kind or another, they were notable chiefly for their increasing emphasis on family and private affairs. At last, indeed, Dillon was beginning to indulge himself a little in the vicarious joys of parenthood, taking pleasure from the doings and experiences of his sons

---

[1] Dillon to T. P. O'Connor, 8 Dec. 1922 (D.P.).
[2] Dillon to T. P. O'Connor, 11 Dec. 1922 (D.P.).

and daughter, no longer absorbed in the vicissitudes of his own political career.

And they gave him a great deal of pleasure. They were, of course, growing up fast and were more and more away from home, but they were devoted and lively correspondents whose letters he carefully preserved. The eldest, Shawn had entered religion and this inevitably withdrew him somewhat from the family group. But the others were all about him and were beginning to carve out careers and lives for themselves. They had taken the revolution in Ireland in their stride, having become, as their father remarked, 'absolutely hardened and go and come by day and night as if they were living in a civilised country'.[1] Theo—who had always shown considerable intellectual promise—had achieved in 1921 the rare feat of obtaining first-class honours in all subjects in his medical finals at the National University and had come first in the entire examination. He had gone on from there to post-graduate work on the Continent and, although this was interrupted by serious illness, his early promise was more than fulfilled. He was soon to come back to Dublin to a brilliant academic medical career, too early cut short by death. Myles also had shown great intellectual distinction in Celtic studies. After an outstanding career at University College, he, too, had left to study abroad. In 1925 he obtained his doctorate at Bonn and after a year in Paris embarked on a life of university teaching and extraordinarily fruitful research. James, who helped greatly with the business in Mayo, having spent a couple of years in America to broaden his knowledge, was already displaying the interest in politics which was to develop into his abiding passion and which was to lead him, as the third generation of his name, to make his mark on Irish public affairs. His father watched this evolution with fascination, but a little nervously. These were murderous times, after all, and James worried him by his outspokenness. 'But', as he wrote half-admiringly to T. P., 'he seems to get on well—he abuses *both* sides quite impartially. And by abusing both sides to their faces seems to be on the best possible terms with both Free Staters and Republicans.'[2] The youngest son, Brian, who later, like Shawn, first showed great promise in the law, delighting his father by becoming a Brooke scholar. Finally, his daughter Nano, who as she grew older stepped into the vacant places left by her mother and by Mrs. Deane, pleased him much by becoming engaged to a rising Dublin surgeon, Patrick Smyth. 'I am entirely satisfied with the marriage,' Dillon told T.P., 'and have every ground to hope that it will be a happy one.'[3] The fact that she would still be living in Dublin was, of course, a consolation, since he would continue to be in close touch with her.

The growing up and branching out of this young household, which it had been his heavy responsibility to bring up unaided since 1907, naturally occupied an increasing amount of his attention. But this did not mean that

[1] Dillon to T. P. O'Connor, 8 Feb. 1923 (D.P.).
[2] Dillon to T. P. O'Connor, 8 Feb. 1923 (D.P.).
[3] Dillon to T. P. O'Connor, 2 May 1923 (D.P.).

politics was crowded out of his life. When Dillon ceased to be interested in politics he would have ceased to breathe, and the link with T. P. O'Connor was one way of ensuring that that interest would continue to be intense. O'Connor, as a matter of fact, was causing him some trouble. He was still deeply concerned about the Irish in Great Britain, feeling, understandably enough, that in the new condition of things they should not be left without the guidance for which he, O'Connor, had been responsible for so many years. In practical terms this meant either resuscitating their old organisation or starting a new one. Dillon, in theory at any rate, agreed with him that there must be an organisation, and at the end of 1922 went so far as to draft for T.P.'s instruction certain criteria which any such organisation must fulfil. It must not, he said, be tied in any way to the Labour Party. It must not be just a federation of Catholic societies. Above all it must be run on different lines from the old organisation and—as if to show how ready to learn he was even at this stage of his career—he explained in more detail what he meant. 'It would be necessary to give far more attention to Irish language, literature, dances and games—in fact, to make a bold effort to capture the Gaelic revival movement and the social side of Irish life.'[1] At one point the idea interested him enough to make him consider breaking the fundamental rule he had set himself since 1918—not to speak in public. However, a day or two's thought convinced him that since he was so identified with 'implacable hostility to Sinn Fein', any movement that he helped to launch would inevitably be damned as anti-Sinn Fein, and perhaps even as a forlorn attempt to revive the constitutional movement.[2]

To T. P. O'Connor, however, looking at the question as he was bound to do, from the English standpoint, this seemed beside the question. For him, an organisation of the Irish in Great Britain was primarily an organisation which would help to make the Irish a force in *British* politics and which, in his view, would best achieve this object by allying itself as closely as possible to the Labour Party. To Dillon this seemed unrealistic. In the immediate future, he argued, any Irish organisation would surely be sensitive to Irish developments and therefore vulnerable to Republican influences. 'So long as Ireland is unsettled—organisation or no organisation—active politicians on this side will interfere, and more or less successfully interfere, in the direction of the vote of our people in Great Britain. And looking back over the history of the Irish organisations in Great Britain, I feel strongly that it is idle to suppose that any general organisation of Irish people in Great Britain can be formed so long as Ireland is unsettled, which will not take a live interest in Irish questions, and be influenced by whoever may be the prominent leaders of sections in Ireland.'[3]

Furthermore, he was disturbed by O'Connor's notion that the organisation should be tied to Labour. 'I never had any difficulty', he admitted, 'in working with the Labour party in the loose kind of alliance which existed

---

[1] Dillon to T. P. O'Connor, 4 Dec. 1922 (D.P.).
[2] Dillon to T. P. O'Connor, 8 Dec. 1922 (D.P.).
[3] Dillon to T. P. O'Connor, 28 Jan. 1923 (D.P.).

between them and our party. But I profoundly distrust some of their leaders, and their fundamental programme is all wrong and will, I am convinced, in the long run land them in a split and consequent disaster, before they have succeeded in ruining Great Britain.'[1] He agreed with T.P., however, that 1923, with Sinn Fein so bitterly divided over the Treaty, was a propitious moment for launching an organisation, and though he refused to come over himself to a convention of Irish societies, he went so far as to write notes which T.P. could use in addressing such a body. As might be expected, they were a reminder that while Irishmen in Britain must, of course, join English political parties, there would from time to time be occasions when they must intervene as Irishmen to defend specifically Irish interests. This was not to be interpreted as a plea to them to intervene *now*, but they should be alert 'to aid any *rational* attempts which may be made to secure the unity of Ireland'. In the meantime they should watch over Irish needs in education, doing all they could to foster the language and a general attachment to Irish culture. But to T. P. himself, Dillon repeated his warning about the Labour Party, giving it this time a doctrinal cast interesting from one who so often in his career had been at odds with orthodoxy:

> The Labour Party are pledged to Socialism and as always happens in such cases the extreme men are bound to get more and more control. The Catholic Church has definitely committed itself against Socialism.
>
> Personally I am entirely at one with the Church on this question, and while I clearly see that circumstances will draw the bulk of young Irishmen into the Labout Party for the present, a considerable section will *not* join Labour. And a time will come, and pretty soon, when issues will arise that will make it very difficult for Irish Catholics to work with that party.[2]

No more was heard for the time being about an Irish organisation—it was always, after 1918, rather a figment of O'Connor's imagination—but Dillon got a shock towards the end of 1923 when he heard that T. P. O'Connor had been urged to go to the House of Lords as a Labour peer. T.P., in fact, refused the offer (Dillon characteristically wrote that if he had accepted it he would have got no congratulations from him), but he did become a Privy Councillor during the period of Ramsay Macdonald's first government.[3] When that episode was over and ugly splits were beginning to appear inside the Labour movement, Dillon seized the chance to drive home once more to his friend the unreliability of his Socialist friends. Ramsay Macdonald, he admitted, had done better than he had expected, but he had not been tough enough with the Communists. 'He had not the steely fibre of Parnell, who did not fear or hesitate to fight the

---

[1] Dillon to T. P. O'Connor, 17 Feb. 1923 (D.P.).
[2] Dillon to T. P. O'Connor, 25 Mar. 1923 (D.P.).
[3] Dillon to T. P. O'Connor, 17 June 1924 (D.P.).

Fenians at the election of 1880, altho' it was they who created his movement.' It was true, he admitted, that the Labour Party was 'the natural
party for our people in Great Britain. None the less, I cannot help feeling
sorry to see them lost in it—because of my profound disbelief in the
British Labour party and because I fear that the national temperament of
our people will lead them—or at all events the most active spirits amongst
them—to join the extreme Bolshevik section.'[1]

The pessimism with which Dillon looked on the future of the Labour
Party was as nothing compared to the pessimism with which he regarded
the condition of his own country. It might reasonably have been thought
that the slow approach of peace in the spring of 1923 would have been
welcome to him. As a businessman, no doubt, it was, though his house in
Mayo continued to be occupied by Free State troops for another year or
more, but what was most apparent from his comments on Irish politics
from this point until the end of his life was his intense distaste for the
régime which Cosgrave and his Ministers were trying to set up. In this, it
must be admitted, he was—or rather appeared to be—somewhat inconsistent. On the one hand, he complained bitterly about the prevailing
anarchy. On the other hand, when the Government attempted to cure it
by harsh, repressive measures, he criticised that with equal asperity. But
this was a contradiction that can be explained. All his life he had been a
man of principle, and it had been the guiding rule of his political career
that, whatever unpopularity, loss of power or other penalty a man suffered,
it was dedication to principle that mattered most. It had been precisely this
dedication to principle which had impressed him in the first instance about
the men of 1916, and which had led him into his passionate defence of them
in the House of Commons. Now, some of the men who were still defending
the principle of the republic in 1922 and 1923 were the same men who had
fought for it in 1916. And while he hated the civil war as much as anyone,
he could not forget this fact, nor even restrain a certain contempt for those
who, having accepted the compromise of 1921, were trying to make it work.
In one of his letters to T. P. O'Connor, written at the beginning of 1923,
there is a passage which illustrates this very clearly. Among the members
of the government of the Irish Free State, Kevin O'Higgins was rapidly
emerging as one of the most ruthless and fearless, and probably also the
most able. In Dillon's eyes he was no doubt suspect anyway as a connection by marriage of the irrepressible Tim Healy, now just elevated to the
post of first Governor-General of the Irish Free State, but this, as the
letter to O'Connor makes clear, was not the main charge in the indictment
Dillon drew up against him:

> The men whom he denounces as wild beasts and mad dogs were two
> years ago his comrades—saints and heroes. The only difference be-
> tween him and them being that he has always kept carefully out of the
> firing line. And the methods for which they are now denounced are

[1] Dillon to T. P. O'Connor, 11 Dec. 1924 (D.P.).

simply those taught by Michael Collins and his comrades. They still believe in the republic, whereas Higgins and co. never did.[1]

This, it must be said, was an unfair criticism. Unfair to O'Higgins personally, who was a very brave man, and who paid for his actions with his life when in July 1927 he was shot down by gunmen near his home. Unfair also to the new government which, not less than the Republicans, was actuated by principle—the principle of *salus populi suprema lex* or, as they might reasonably have put it, that to survive as a dominion was preferable to perishing as a republic. The terms secured by the Treaty, which Dillon himself had admitted to be good terms, were honestly believed by those who accepted them to be the best that could be got from England at that time and in those circumstances. Emotion apart, Dillon would probably have conceded this as a rational proposition, but since the terms—in effect, dominion status—were precisely those he had nailed to the masthead of the parliamentary party in the 1918 election, it was only human that he should feel a deep resentment against men who had waded deep in blood to achieve only what he himself would have sought by constitutional means.

What would come of it all he had no idea. As he wrote to T.P. later in 1923: 'I, who know Ireland, and the forces at work, as intimately as any man living, am wholly unable to form any forecast as to the future. All I can say is that I think the fighting is over.'[2] In this, at least, he was perfectly correct, for on 24 May Mr. de Valera ordered his forces to call off the struggle and the civil war was at last ended. There followed in the summer a general election which gave the government party (Cumann na nGaedheal) a working majority, with sixty-three seats against forty-four for the Republicans, the remainder being held by Independents (17), Farmers (15) and Labour (14).[3] It was symptomatic of how far Dillon had drifted away from his supporters that, according to his own account, most of them voted for the Government of which he had such a low opinion.[4]

How low that opinion was became known to the general public by a curious accident. At the beginning of 1925 Dillon agreed to address graduates of the National University at a meeting of their club in Dublin. He did so in the belief that there were no reporters present and he therefore spoke with great freedom about the existing régime. The details of his speech have not survived, but there *were* reporters present who relayed some of his stronger remarks to an audience which, to his astonishment, grew bigger and bigger as newspaper after newspaper took up the story and gave it prominence. A large envelope of cuttings survives among his papers from which it is clear that, quite unconsciously, he had caused a furore. The occasion of his speech was a paper read by a former M.P., Thomas O'Donnell, attacking Irish Free State finance. Dillon joined in

---

[1] Dillon to T. P. O'Connor, 8 Feb. 1923 (D.P.).
[2] Dillon to T. P. O'Connor, 2 May 1923 (D.P.).
[3] Macardle, *The Irish Republic*, p. 982; O'Sullivan, *The Irish Free State and its Senate*, pp. 131–3.
[4] Dillon to T. O. O'Connor, 21 Sept. 1923 (D.P.).

this with Gladstonian zest, denouncing the 'extravagant taxation' which was driving the country to ruin. But what attracted most attention was what he had to say about the Government's measures to preserve law and order:

> The Irish party has been accused of bossing, but, my God, I thought that I would never live to see what is taking place to-day under an Irish government. When we look back on the days when we were oppressed by England it would look like Paradise if we could get the same sort of oppression now.[1]

This was an extraordinary conclusion to have reached at the end of a lifetime spent in opposing British rule in Ireland, and there can be little doubt that the speech embarrassed some of his friends. Dillon himself, however, was quite unrepentant, and to O'Connor professed himself highly amused by the whole incident.[2] Yet, beneath the bravura of this last public appearance, there lurked perhaps a trace of nostalgia. British 'oppression' might indeed seem to him more acceptable than what had happened in the past seven years, because, for most of the time he had known it, it had been applied within certain prescribed and clearly defined rules. Part of the very success of Parnell or William O'Brien, or Dillon himself, had lain in the skill with which they had been able to operate the rules for their own purposes. But after 1918 there were no rules, and for long periods no law save the law of the gun. Small wonder that the distant hills now appeared to him much greener.

(v)

It was widely believed at the time that this speech was the prelude to Dillon's re-entry into politics. In fact, it was nothing of the sort. It was an entirely isolated episode, for his own attention was soon concentrated much more upon a domestic worry. Early in 1925, along with many other employers, he found himself confronted with a strike of shop assistants. This was the sort of challenge on his own doorstep that he could understand, and he threw himself into the fight with a certain relish. He was not being wholly ironical when he wrote to O'Connor that he was 'enjoying all the delights of a prolonged strike, picketing, etc. etc.' 'The strikers', added, 'have absolutely *no* merits, and we are bound in self-defence to see the fight out to the bitter end. But you know what Irishmen are, once they get into a fight. And the truth is that the unions in this country have become largely Bolshevik, and are out to set up an intolerable tyranny, which would make the carrying on of any business impossible.'[3]

One wonders if the thought ever crossed his mind that his own rise to prominence in Irish politics had come largely from his success in persuading tenant-farmers to combine against their landlords in very much the

[1] 'Speech at the National Club, 9 Jan. 1925' (D.P.).
[2] Dillon to T. P. O'Connor, 16 Feb. 1925 (D.P.).
[3] Dillon to T. P. O'Connor, 25 Feb. 1925 (D.P.).

same sort of way as his shop assistants were doing against him. Perhaps it did, because when he next wrote he was at pains to explain the strike as really a part of the larger national predicament:

> It is indeed a strange irony of fate that in my old age I should be engaged in a fierce strike fight, and with a set of employees who had always been treated with quite exceptional kindness and indulgence. But the truth is that this is only one symptom of the terrible demoralisation which has been wrought in this country by the happenings of the last six years. The union of shop assistants—with which we are in conflict—has passed under frankly Bolshevist control and is avowedly out for the wiping out of 'the capitalists'. And, as I in-informed the organiser who called on me in February I propose to fight.[1]

Fight he did, and was amazingly rejuvenated in the process. The strike continued unabated into the summer, but he was not in the least dismayed. It was one consolation to know—or at least to believe—that the Government was staggering to a halt. It might hold on, he told O'Connor, for a year or two, but 'it will then collapse amidst universal execrations, leaving the country in a very impoverished and chaotic condition. If I were thirty years younger I would be getting ready to take the field. But as it is I can only look on at the ruin of the country and leave it to the younger generation to start afresh.'[2] Neverthelesss, he was still full of energy. That summer of 1925 he closed up the house in North Great George's Street and went to Mayo with James, determined to see the strike through to the end. By September its back was broken, and many of the workers were leaving Ballaghaderrin in order to try to find work elsewhere. Business, of course, had fallen away almost to nothing, but he reckoned that with a smaller staff in future he would be able to economise on wages by over £1,000 a year. One thing, however, the dispute had demonstrated beyond question —the fact that in all matters of business he had come to rely increasingly upon his son James. 'Without his help,' he readily admitted, 'I could never have carried through the strike fight.'[3]

With the strike behind him he set off on what was to be his last visit to the Continent, spending several weeks at the Italian lakes with Theo and Myles. Back in Dublin by Christmas, he had an attack of influenza just before the close of the year, but recovered quickly, remaining to all appearances no less vigorous. Certainly, his letters to T.P. were as pungent as ever; uncomfortably so, indeed, since he had now taken it into his head that his old friend was doing too much for his age—as he probably was. 'You go to too many entertainments,' Dillon admonished him, 'no-one could stand it, not even a much younger man than you are.'[4] Later in the year, when the news of T.P.'s health had not been good, he chided him again for his unaccountable addiction to public banquets—'one quarter

---

[1] Dillon to T. P. O'Connor, 12 Apr. 1925 (D.P.).
[2] Dillon to T. P. O'Connor, 15 June 1925 (D.P.).
[3] Dillon to T. P. O'Connor, 17 Sept. 1925 (D.P.).
[4] Dillon to T. P. O'Connor, 6 Sept. 1926 (D.P.).

[of T.P.'s commitments] would kill me in a few months'.[1] But then Dillon had always loathed banquets.

One special reason for his anxiety about O'Connor's health—apart from the natural concern these two old friends felt for one another—was that T.P. was at last grappling with his memoirs. Dillon kept encouraging him to finish them, hoping in this way that the partisan and prejudiced versions of past events given by, for example, F. H. O'Donnell and William O'Brien, would be corrected. As he grew older, indeed, Dillon became almost obsessed by the story of the parliamentary party—'the most remarkable and the most successful', as he proudly described it to T.P., 'in the history of Ireland, since the landing of Strongbow'.[2] He recognised, of course, that the memoirs would have some delicate ground to cover—including some that concerned Dillon personally—and, with characteristic caution, he suggested he might be shown those passages 'purely for the purpose of negative criticism'.[3] In fact, fate was unkind to him even here. T.P. laboured more painfully over these memoirs than over any other part of his writing and they did not appear until 1929, when Dillon was in his grave. But perhaps it was as well that he did not live to see them, for, although readable and containing occasional flashes of insight, they were incurably gossipy. Moreover, they were tantalising in that they only dealt with Irish affairs up to 1886 and very haphazardly at that. The 'negative criticism' from George's Street would without doubt have been formidable.

But now at last the end was approaching. In August 1926 Dillon had been quite seriously unwell for about three weeks, and although he did not say what it was, and seemed to recover from it well enough, it is probable that it was the first onset of his final illness. He spent most of that summer in Mayo and was back in Dublin by December. The following March he wrote to T.P. that he had been having recurrent attacks of sickness and had been advised by his doctors that a serious operation would be necessary.[4] At that time he had not made up his mind to face it, but when he next wrote in May his condition had become so much worse that he no longer had any option. Since this was apparently his last surviving letter to his old friend, it is given here in full. By a curious chance it combines the two themes —health and politics—which had dominated so much of the writer's life:

My dear T.P.,
     Your letter came this morning. There could not be the slightest objection to your attending a Trinity College dinner with an unobjectionable chairman. But I do think that your presence at a dinner with Lord Carson in the chair would do harm. The feeling here about partition and Carson's Ulster campaign is still very bitter.

---

[1] Dillon to T. P. O'Connor, 1 Dec. 1926 (D.P.).

[2] Dillon to T. P. O'Connor, 6 Sept. 1926 (D.P.). He had been urged by C. P. Scott to write his own memoirs but refused because of lack of materials and of skill (Dillon to C. P. Scott, 18 Apr. 1921, in *Manchester Guardian* collection of Scott letters). I owe this reference to Mr. D. Ayerst.

[3] Dillon to T. P. O'Connor, 17 Sept. 1925 (D.P.).

[4] Dillon to T. P. O'Connor, 24 Mar. 1927 (D.P.).

I cannot say much for my health. I have had two or three nasty attacks since I wrote last. What I am suffering from is gall stones —and the doctors tell me there is no remedy but an operation. As it is I am liable at any moment to be attacked by violent pain and sickness. I am thinking of going to London in June and consulting Sir B. Moynihan, and I have some notion of going on to Karlsbad if I feel equal to it, as my old enemy dyspepsia has attacked me with vigour as a consequence of this new trouble.

I was very glad to get your letter announcing your safe arrival in London—and saying you were better. Since you arrived, however, you have had an experience of the risks of returning from a warm climate to England early in May.

Yours sincerely,
John Dillon.[1]

Later in the summer—in August and not, as he had intended, in June— he went over to England for the operation to remove the gall-stones. It was the same operation which had proved fatal to John Redmond. Like Redmond, Dillon was reckoned to have a good chance of recovery. Like him, he seemed to come well through the initial stages, but like him, he suddenly collapsed. His heart proved unequal to the strain and on the evening of Thursday, 4 August 1927, he died, like Redmond, in a London nursing-home.

(vi)

By any standards John Dillon's life must be reckoned a tragedy, scarred by personal pain and grief, and ending in the ruin of all his hopes for his country. Yet he himself, though beyond question deeply hurt by his rejection in 1918, lived long enough to be able to reach a certain serenity and to look back with pride to the achievements of the great movement in which for forty years he had played so notable a part. What, at the end of all, were those achievements, and what precisely was his part? The list, though since 1916 it has been fashionable to ignore or to decry it, is undeniably impressive. It includes the creation of a famous parliamentary party—in its prime one of the most remarkable phenomena in modern political history—and its re-creation after the Parnell split; the building of successive popular organisations which gave to the Irish people, so long debarred from participation in government, valuable experience in the democratic process and in the business of managing their own affairs; the virtual solution of the land question and the reinstatement of the evicted tenants; the winning of other substantial reforms—chief among them the Congested Districts Board, the Irish Local Government Act and the National University; finally, and the *raison d'être* for the whole movement, the formulation of the demand for Home Rule, its elevation into a major issue in British politics and its eventual embodiment in legislation—a triumph of sustained pressure and negotiation which not even the later disasters can ever wholly obscure.

[1] Dillon to T. P. O'Connor, 2 May 1927 (D.P.).

In all these fundamental aspects of the Irish question from the time of Butt to the time of de Valera, John Dillon was constantly and intimately concerned. Yet it would be very misleading to define his special contribution simply in terms either of agitation or of legislation. It is important to remember that he was not an innovator in the sense that Parnell and Davitt, or Griffith and Pearse, were innovators. No new departure, no dramatic revolution, is associated solely with his name. Even the Plan of Campaign, perhaps the nearest he came to an independent initiative, was essentially a partnership with William O'Brien and Timothy Harrington. To say this is in no way to diminish Dillon's stature. It is rather to suggest that his real and lasting significance may be less in what he did than in what he was. What he was—to try to put it in a sentence—was the embodiment of a type or style of nationalism rare in any country and of incalculable value to the Ireland of his day.

It is difficult even now to define the quality of that nationalism, since so many different traditions went to its making. Dillon, we may say, was one part Young Irelander, one part Fenian, one part Land Leaguer and one part Home Ruler. But these labels do not help us very much. They refer to movements, whereas it was as an individual that Dillon impressed his contemporaries. He found Ireland impoverished and degraded, alternating between spells of hopeless apathy and outbursts of even more hopeless violence. Through his exertions, and no less by his unconscious example, he helped first to restore to his fellow-countrymen the basis of a decent livelihood, and after that to give them back their self-respect. He wanted desperately that they should show themselves worthy of self-government and so, in season and out, popular or unpopular, he preached to them the virtues which underlay his own code of public conduct—courage, tenacity, firmness, tolerance, dependability. He aimed, as his ultimate goal, at a society that should be religious, but not priest-ridden; progressive, but not official-ridden; mindful of a great past, but not fanatic-ridden. His ideal Ireland would be Catholic, but not exclusively so; Gaelic, without denying a place to Anglo-Irish culture; and, in the broadest and best senses of the term, it would be a liberal Ireland.

To this generous conception of nationality there was, however, one major reservation. At no stage in his career was Dillon ever prepared to come to terms with Irish landlordism. For him it was the root of most of the evil that had afflicted his people, and it was the principal business of a large part of his life to destroy it. This passionate commitment to agrarianism led him from time to time into what seemed excessively rigid or doctrinaire positions which cost him, among other things, the friendship of William O'Brien. His hounding of Sir Horace Plunkett, his rebuffs to Captain Shawe-Taylor, his belittlement of Lord Dunraven and other moderate landowners—how can these be squared with the doctrine of comprehensive nationality[1]? And how, to be even more specific, could a

---

[1] It is pleasant to record that in his last years Dillon's relations with Plunkett became very amicable.

man so essentially broad-minded take the absolutely negative line he did take towards the policy of conciliation initiated at the Land Conference? In fact, the answer is very simple. Dillon's doctrine of nationality was comprehensive, but, before everything else, it was a doctrine of *nationality*. There was no room in it for any continuing union with Britain, nor for any policy which offered the seductions of social legislation as a substitute for, rather than a complement to, Home Rule. Irishmen of all creeds and classes must certainly live together, but they must live together in an Ireland free to govern herself, free to redress the historic grievances that had flowed from all the conquests and settlements and plantations of the past. A landlord could live in this Ireland like any other man—*provided* he ceased to hanker after the Union and did justice to his tenants. Since these were conditions which, during his public career, most landlords seemed unwilling to fulfil, Dillon saw no reason to change his attitude and there is no evidence that he at any time regretted his lifelong war against them.

But, of course, it was not only landlords with whom Dillon had to contend. In presenting his enlightened but austere nationalism to his earthier fellow-countrymen, he suffered the usual fate of a prophet in his own land, finding himself more than once, and in the end permanently, alone in the wilderness. To some extent this was his own doing. Holding as he did such a high conception of patriotic duty, he was apt to be impatient with those —and they were numerous—who did not live up to his standards. Moreover, like many men of strong character, he was not easy to move from his own opinions, while tending to view others who clung to theirs as either fools or knaves, or both. Yet his very harshness was of a piece with the qualities he brought to Irish public life, qualities which were recognised even by his enemies to be remarkable. These were—absolute incorruptibility and integrity; iron courage and consistency; a hatred of servility, whether towards Church or State; an almost instinctive understanding of the needs and desires of Irishmen in general, and of Irish countrymen in particular; an extraordinary flair for political calculation and analysis; a fine intelligence, fortified by an unappeasable appetite for knowledge and information of all kinds.

A man endowed with so many gifts stands very much apart and, unless he has social ease as well, is likely to be lonely. This was Dillon's fate. For most of his life—except for his last years and the too brief happiness of his marriage—he led a solitary existence. Lacking completely the professional *bonhomie* of the run-of-the-mill politician, he made little effort to acquire it. Even to the majority of his own parliamentary colleagues he appeared distant and aloof. And it was quite true that he, who in private could be the kindest and most charming of men, found it painfully difficult to go through the routine motions of conviviality. He had no small-talk, he ate and drank sparingly, he was fastidious in his personal tastes and in his morals. All this might have seemed to set him down a prig, were it not that he made no attempt either to parade his standards or to impose them on others; and were it not also that he was so unmistakably dedicated to his public life that men grew accustomed to thinking he had no other. In this they were mistaken. There was a private life, but it was very largely a life of the mind rather than of the affections. He, who had suffered so many bereavements, gave his friendship hesitantly and infrequently. When he gave it, it was intense, warm and generally permanent, but this only a small circle of intimates ever knew.

Loneliness, then, was his fate—but it was not his tragedy. His tragedy—like that of the constitutional movement as a whole—had two aspects. In the first place, there was the tragedy of unrequited talent. It is difficult now to realise the sheer enormity of the fact, but Dillon was one of a group of gifted young men who entered Parliament under Parnell and sat there for thirty, thirty-five or forty years, doomed to perpetual opposition. Not many parties, not many individuals, could have survived this ordeal as the Irish Members did for so long. Most of them, no doubt, adjusted themselves to their grim situation by registering a mechanical attendance at Westminster, voting as they were told, and living their real lives elsewhere. But this was not Dillon's way. He loved and reverenced the House of Commons, of which after stormy beginnings, he became one of the most accomplished ornaments. More than that, he played a double role, being virtually the only Irish Member to occupy himself with major issues of state as well as with specifically Irish questions. In matters of colonial and foreign policy, indeed, he emerged, towards the end of his career, as one of the foremost critics of imperialism, rearmament, and *Machtpolitik* in general. So great was this impact that no less a Liberal than C. P. Scott, writing to him in his retirement 'with affectionate remembrance', had this to say: 'I can never forget the old times or your splendid advocacy. As a matter of fact you were not only about the best upholder of your own cause, but the best also of ours. I always said that you were the best Liberal in the House.'[1] That such a man should have gone through his entire political life debarred by principle and conscience from the high office he would certainly have attained in an English party, was a waste which surely deserves to be called tragic.

But this was only part of his burden. Even more stultifying was the total failure of successive governments to understand what he and his party stood for, or to realise that the Home Rulers, so far from being disruptive of the Empire, were a bulwark against other and far more destructive forces. The obstinate, and in the end successful, resistance of Ulster and English Unionists to the extremely moderate self-government which Parnell, Redmond and Dillon were originally prepared to accept will always remain one of the strangest mysteries of politics. No doubt they sincerely believed that Home Rule would lead to the break-up of the Empire. Since it was never allowed to operate we cannot know how it would have developed. But we can say with some confidence that under the direction of the parliamentarians its evolution would have been peaceful and probably conservative. In time, it is true, it might have been transformed into dominion status

[1] C. P. Scott to Dillon, 26 Oct. 1926 (D.P.).

which, as we have seen, was Dillon's own response to the challenge of Sinn Fein. But since dominion status had to be conceded anyway at the point of the gun, and with far more danger to the Empire than the parliamentarians had ever threatened, it is understandable that Dillon, having been regarded for so long as a wild man of the left, should have felt great bitterness in seeing far wilder men reaping the harvest he had sown.

This bitterness must have been intensified when he reflected on the course of his own career and especially on the crucial decision he had made at the outset—that he would turn his back on violence and preach to the people the virtues and effectiveness of peaceful agitation. It had been a difficult decision, taken not without regretful backward glances. All his life he would respond to bravery, however hopeless or misguided he might consider it to be, and his famous speech in 1916 bore witness to the fact that, although he had chosen the other road, he could never forget the powerful attraction of the Fenian tradition. Englishmen, hearing him speak up for rebels, naturally took him for a rebel himself. In a sense, of course, he was and never ceased to be a rebel, whose whole life was centred on the breaking of the Union between Britain and Ireland. But, having once made up his mind that to lead out eager, ignorant young men against the armed might of England in pursuit of a republic was to bring untold bloodshed and disaster upon his country, he never wavered in his condemnation of physical force and in his advocacy of constitutional action. It was the crowning irony of his career that his speech demanding leniency for the insurgents of 1916 should have been so completely misinterpreted in the House of Commons. That speech combined sympathy and admiration for men who had risked their lives for an ideal with absolute detestation of the ideal itself. His enemies recognised the sympathy and admiration, but ignored the detestation. Consequently, all the old doubts about his own allegiance were resurrected at the precise moment when the blindness of the Government and the intransigence of the Unionists were preparing an explosion of hatred which was to sweep away not only British rule but Dillon and the Irish parliamentary party as well.

So all was utterly changed. Ireland turned in a new direction and John Dillon was left alone and disillusioned, presenting to history the spectacle —melancholy but not without nobility—of a fiercely honest man who loved his country, but learned through harsh experience that patriotism was not enough.

Appendix

Headings of a Settlement
as to the Government of Ireland[1]

1. The Government of Ireland Act, 1914, to be brought into operation as soon as possible after the passing of the Bill, subject to the modifications necessitated by these instructions.

2. The said Act not to apply to the excluded area, which is to consist of the Six Counties of Antrim, Armagh, Down, Fermanagh, Londonderry, and Tyrone, including the Parliamentary Boroughs of Belfast, Londonderry, and Newry.

3. As regards the excluded area, the executive power of His Majesty to be administered by a Secretary of State through such officers and departments as may be directed by Order of His Majesty in Council, those officers and departments not to be in any way responsible to the new Irish Government.

   A Committee to be appointed on which both of the Irish parties are to be represented, to assist the Government in preparing the necessary Orders in Council.

4. The number of Irish representatives in the United Kingdom House of Commons to remain unaltered (viz. 103).

5. The Irish House of Commons to consist of the Members who sit in the United Kingdom House of Commons for constituencies within the area to which the Act applies.

6. A reduction to be made in the number of Irish Senators proportionate to the population of the excluded area. The Senators to be nominated by the Lord Lieutenant, subject to instructions from His Majesty.

7. The Lord Lieutenant to have power to summon conferences between the members for constituencies in the excluded area, and the members for constituencies in the rest of Ireland.

8. A deduction to be made from Item (a) of the Transferred Sum (cost of Irish Services) when ascertained proportionate to the population of the excluded area.

---

[1] Typed and undated copy in the Dillon Papers. The document was later published as a White Paper (*Parliamentary Papers*, 1916 [Cmd. 8310], xxii, 415–16) under the same title.

9. Provision to be made for permanent sittings of the Irish High Court in Belfast as well as in Dublin, or for the constitution of a new court in Belfast with the same jurisdiction as that of the High Court but locally limited.

All appeals, both from the courts in the excluded area, and those in the rest of Ireland, to go to the Appeal Court in Dublin, which is to be composed of judges appointed in the same manner and having the like tenure of office as English judges.

The appeals from the Court of Appeal in Dublin, whether as respects cases coming from the excluded area or from the rest of Ireland, to go to the same tribunal of appeal in England—whether it should be the House of Lords or the Privy Council is for the present immaterial.

10. Section thirty of the Government of Ireland Act to be extended to any disputes or questions which may arise between the excluded area and the new Irish Government.

11. His Majesty's power of making Orders in Council for the purposes of the Act to be extended so as to include power to make the necessary adjustments and provisions with respect to the Government of the excluded area and relations between that area and the rest of Ireland and Great Britain, etc.

12. Amongst the various questions to which attention must be directed in this connection will be the question of fixing fair rents under the Irish Land Acts. It is proposed that there should be two Commissioners specially allotted for fixing rents in the excluded area and appointed by the British Government.

13. All Orders in Council under the new Act to be laid before both Houses of Parliament in the same manner as Orders under the Government of Ireland Act. (See s. 48.)

14. The Bill to remain in force during the continuance of the war, and a period of twelve months thereafter, but if Parliament has not by that time made further and permanent provision for the Government of Ireland, the period for which the Bill is to remain in force is to be extended by Order in Council for such time as may be necessary to enable Parliament to make such provision.

It is also understood that at the close of the war there should be held an Imperial Conference with a view to bringing the Dominions into closer co-operation with the Government of the Empire, and that the permanent settlement of Ireland should be considered at that Conference.

Bibliography
SYNOPSIS

A. Sources

B. Secondary Works

This bibliography is not intended to be exhaustive, but it includes, in addition to manuscripts and printed sources cited in the text, other manuscripts and printed sources which have been consulted in the preparation of this book.

Except where otherwise stated, all books listed in this bibliography were published in London.

A. Sources

I *The Dillon Papers*

This vast collection forms the basis of the entire biography. It has not been catalogued at the time of writing, though I have deposited in the papers a brief hand-list which may serve as a guide until a more permanent record has been made. The Dillon Papers are relatively scanty for the earlier years of John Dillon's career, but they are voluminous from 1886 onwards and when opened to inspection will undoubtedly provide one of the main sources for the general history of the period. They are at present in the possession of Professor Myles Dillon of the Dublin Institute for Advanced Studies.

II *Other collections of private papers*

(*a*) In Ireland

    (i) Collections at present in the National Library Dublin:

        Blake Papers (microfilm of the originals in the Canadian National Archives, Ottawa)

        F. S. Bourke Collection (of documents relating to the history of the parliamentary party)

        Bryce Papers (a selection relating to James Bryce's term of office as Chief Secretary)

        Gill Papers

        Harrington Papers

        Horgan Papers (microfilm copies of the political correspondence of the late J. J. Horgan)

        Bulmer Hobson Papers

        Macdonagh Papers (letters of general political interest written to Michael MacDonagh, the biographer of William O'Brien)

        MacNeill Papers.

        Maurice Moore Papers.

        J. F. X. O'Brien Papers.

        W. O'Brien Papers.

        Redmond Papers.

        Tuohy Letters (letters from Dillon and others to J. F. Tuohy of the *Freeman's Journal*)

    (ii) Croke Papers, in the archives of the Archbishop of Cashel. Microfilm copy now in the National Library of Ireland

    (iii) Davitt Papers, at present in the possession of Professor T. W. Moody, Trinity College, Dublin

    (iv) Walsh Papers, at Archbishop's House, Drumcondra. I have drawn upon a previous acquaintance with the papers of Archbishop W. J. Walsh, but was refused admission to pursue my researches further for the purposes of this book

    (v) Archiepiscopal Archives, Armagh. I am grateful to His Eminence, Cardinal Conway, for sending me a photostat of a letter from John Dillon to Bishop (later Archbishop) Patrick O'Donnell, referring to the controversy over the Education Act of 1902

(*b*) *In Britain*

    Asquith Papers, Bodleian Library, Oxford

    Balfour Papers, British Museum

    Bryce Papers, Bodleian Library, Oxford

    Campbell-Bannerman Papers, British Museum

Dilke Papers, British Museum
Gladstone Papers, British Museum
Granville Papers, Public Record Office, London
Haldane Papers, National Library of Scotland
Harcourt Papers, Stanton Harcourt, Oxford
Lloyd George Papers, Beaverbrook Library, London
MacDonnell Papers, Bodleian Library, Oxford
Murray of Elibank Papers, National Library of Scotland
Nathan Papers, Bodleian Library, Oxford
Plunkett Papers, Plunkett House, London
Ripon Papers, British Museum
Salisbury Papers, Christ Church, Oxford
Scott Papers, British Museum

(c) *Miscellaneous*
  (i) Letters from John Dillon to Augustine Birrell and his wife, Liverpool University Library
  (ii) Correspondence between John Dillon and E. F. V. Knox in Public Record Office, Belfast

III *State Papers*
Chief Secretary's Office, Registered Papers, State Paper Office, Dublin
Crime Branch, Special Papers, State Paper Office, Dublin
Cabinet Papers, 1906–7, Public Record Office, London
Education Office Papers, 1906, Public Record Office, London

IV *Newspapers and periodicals*
Belfast Newsletter
Cork Examiner
Daily News
Dublin Daily Express
Evening Telegraph
Freeman's Journal
Insuppressible
Irish Catholic
Irish Daily Independent
Irish Times
The Leader
Nation
National Press
Pall Mall Gazette
Sinn Fein
'*Suppressed*' *United Ireland*
The Times
United Ireland
United Irishman

V *Contemporary works of reference*
     Dod's parliamentary companion, 1832—work still in progress
     Thom's Irish almanac and official directory, Dublin 1844—work still
      in progress
     Thom's Irish who's who, Dublin, 1923
     Who was who (1897–1916), 1920
     Who was who (1916–1928), 1929

VI *Memoirs, diaries and other contemporary narratives*
     Asquith, Margot, *The autobiography of Margot Asquith* (Penguin
      ed.), 1936
     Birrell, Augustine, *Things past redress*, 1937
     Blunt, W. S., *The land war in Ireland*, 1912
     Blunt, W. S., *My diaries* (one-volume ed.), 1932
     Brennan, Robert, *Allegiance*, Dublin, 1950
     Carter, Lady Violet Bonham, *Winston Churchill as I knew him*, 1965
     Chamberlain, Austen, *Politics from inside*, 1936
     Chamberlain, Joseph, *A political memoir, 1880–92*, ed. C. H. D.
      Howard, 1953
     Churchill, W. S., *The world crisis, 1911–18* (2 vol. ed.), 1938
     Davis, Thomas, *Essays and poems; with a centenary memoir, 1845–*
      1954, Dublin, 1945
     Davitt, Michael, *The fall of feudalism in Ireland*, London and New
      York, 1904
     Devoy's post-bag, 2 vols, ed. W. O'Brien and D. Ryan, Dublin,
      1948 and 1952
     Dillon William, *Life of John Mitchel*, 1888
     George, David Lloyd, *War memoirs*, vol. i, 1933
     Haldane, R. B., *An autobiography*, 1929
     Healy, T. M., *Why Ireland is not free*, Dublin, 1898
     Healy, T. M., *Letters and leaders of my day*, 2 vols., 1928
     Horgan, J. J., *Parnell to Pearse*, Dublin, 1948
     Kettle, A. J., *Material for victory*, ed. L. J. Kettle, Dublin, 1958
     Leamy, Margaret, *Parnell's faithful few*, New York, 1936
     Lucy, Sir Henry, *Diary of the Salisbury parliament, 1886–92*, 1892
     Lucy, Sir Henry, *Diary of the Home Rule parliament, 1892–5*, 1896
     Lucy, Sir Henry, *Diary of the Unionist parliament, 1895–1900*, 1901
     Lucy, Sir Henry, *Diary of the Balfourian parliament, 1900–5*, 1906
     McCarthy, Justin, *Reminiscences*, 2 vols., 1899
     McCarthy, Justin, *The story of an Irishman*, 1904
     McCarthy, Justin, and Praed, Mrs. Campbell, *Our book of memo-*
      ries, 1912
     Midleton, The Earl of, *Records and reactions, 1856–1939*, 1939
     Morley, John, Viscount, *Recollections*, 2 vols., 1917
     O'Brien, William, *Recollections*, 1905
     O'Brien, William, *Evening memories*, 1907

O'Brien, William, *An olive branch in Ireland*, 1910

O'Connor, T. P., *The Parnell movement* (1st ed.), 1886

O'Connor, T. P., *Memoirs of an old parliamentarian*, 2 vols., 1929

O'Donnell, F. H., *History of the Irish parliamentary party*, 2 vols., 1910

Oxford and Asquith, Earl of, *Fifty years of parliament*, 2 vols., 1926

Plunkett, Sir Horace, *Ireland in the new century*, Dublin, 1904

Rendel, Lord S., *Personal papers*, ed. F. E. Hamer, 1931

Sheehan, D. D., *Ireland since Parnell*, 1921

Sullivan, A. M., *New Ireland*, 1877

Sullivan, Donal, *The story of room fifteen*, Dublin, 1891

Sullivan, T. D., *Recollections of troubled times in Irish politics*, Dublin, 1905

Tynan, Katherine, *Twenty-five years: reminiscences*, 1913

West, Sir A., *Private diaries*, ed. H. G. Hutchinson, 1922

Yeats, W. B., *Autobiographies*, 1955

VII *Parliamentary debates and papers*

Annual Register, 1870–1927

Hansard, parliamentary debates, 3rd, 4th and 5th series, 1870–1918

Report of the commissioners appointed to inquire into the estates of evicted tenants in Ireland (c. 6935), H.C., 1893, xxxi

Special commission act, 1888; reprint of the shorthand notes of the speeches, proceedings and evidence taken before the commissioners appointed under the above-named act, 12 vols., 1890

Report of the Royal Commission on the Land Law (Ireland) Act, 1881, and the Purchase of Land 'Ireland') Act, 1885 (c. 4969), 1887

Royal Commission on the rebellion in Ireland: minutes of evidence and appendix of documents, 1916

B. Secondary Works

I *General histories*

Beckett, J. C., *The making of modern Ireland, 1603–1921*, 1966

Curtis, E., *History of Ireland*, 1936

Ensor, R. C. K., *England, 1870–1914*, 1936

Mansergh, Nicholas, *The Irish question, 1840–1921*, 1965

O'Hegarty, P. S., *A history of Ireland under the Union, 1801–1922*, 1952

Shearman, Hugh, *Anglo-Irish relations*, 1948

Strauss, E., *Irish nationalism and British democracy*, 1951

Taylor, A. J. P., *English history, 1914–45*, 1965

II *Biographies*

Abels, Jules, *The Parnell Tragedy*, 1966

Banks, Margaret, *Edward Blake, Irish Nationalist*, Toronto, 1957

Blake, Robert, *The unknown prime minister*, 1955

Churchill, Randolph, *Lord Derby, 'king of Lancashire'*, 1959

Churchill, Winston, *Lord Randolph Churchill*, 2 vols., 1906

Crewe, Marquess of, *Lord Rosebery*, 2 vols., 1930

Dictionary of national biography, and supplements, 1908–40

Digby, Margaret, *Sir Horace Plunkett*, 1949

Dugdale, Blanche, E. C., *Life of Arthur James Balfour*, vol. i, 1936

Fyfe, H., *T. P. O'Connor*, 1934

Gardiner, A. G., *Life of Sir William Harcourt*, 2 vols., 1923

Garvin, J. L., and Amery, J., *The Life of Joseph Chamberlain*, 4 vols. 1935–51

Greaves, C. D., *The life and times of James Connolly*, 1961

Gwynn, D. R., *Life of John Redmond*, 1932

Gwynn, S. L., and Tuckwell, G., *Life of Sir Charles Dilke*, vol. 8, 1917

Gwynn, S. L., *John Redmond's last years*, 1919

Gwynn, S. L., *The letters and friendships of Sir Cecil Spring-Rice*, 2 vols, 1929

Harrison, Henry, *Parnell vindicated*, 1931

Haslip, Joan, *Parnell: a biography*, 1936

Hyde, H. M., *Carson*, 1953

James, R. Rhodes, *Lord Randolph Churchill*, 1959

James, R. Rhodes, *Rosebery*, 1963

Jenkins, Roy, *Sir Charles Dilke, a Victorian tragedy*, 1958

Jenkins, Roy, *Asquith*, 1964

Larkin, E., *James Larkin*, 1876–1947, 1965

Macdonagh, Michael, *Life of William O'Brien*, 1928

Maurice, Sir Frederick, *Haldane*, 2 vols., 1937

Morley, John, *Life of W. E. Gladstone*, 3 vols., 1903

Newton, Lord, *Life of Lord Landsdowne*, 1929

Nicolson, Harold, *King George V*, 1952

O'Brien, R. Barry, *Life of Charles Stewart Parnell*, 2 vols. (3rd ed.), 1899

O'Hara, M., *Chief and tribune: Parnell and Davitt*, Dublin, 1919

O'Shea, Katharine, *Charles Stewart Parnell: his love-story and political life*, 2 vols. (1st ed.), 1914

Petrie, Sir Charles, *Walter Long and his times*, 1936

Petrie, Sir Charles, *The life and letters of the Right Hon. Austen Chamberlain*, 2 vols., 1939

Skeffington, F. Sheehy, *Michael Davitt: revolutionary leader and labour agitator*, 1908; new edition, 1967

Sommer, D., *Haldane of Cloan*, 1960

Spender, J. A., *Life of Sir Henry Campbell-Bannerman*, 2 vols., 1923

Spender, J. A., and Asquith, Cyril, *Life of Lord Oxford and Asquith*, 2 vols., 1932

Sullivan, M., *No man's man*, Dublin, 1943

Thorold, A. L., *Life of Henry Labouchere*, 1913

Walsh, P. J., *William J. Walsh, Archbishop of Dublin*, 1928

White, T. de V., *The road of excess*, Dublin, 1946

White, T. de V., *Kevin O'Higgins* (paperback ed.), Dublin, 1966

Young, K., *Arthur James Balfour*, 1963

II *Special studies*

Beaverbrook, Lord, *Men and power, 1917–1918*, 1956

Beaverbrook, Lord, *The decline and fall of Lloyd George*, 1963

Brown, T. N., *Irish-American Nationalism, 1870–1890*, Philadelphia, 1966

Caulfield, Max, *The Easter Rebellion*, 1963

Curtis, L. P., jr., *Coercion and conciliation in Ireland, 1880–1892*, Princeton, 1963

Fergusson, Sir James, *The Curragh incident*, 1964

Fogarty, L. (ed.), *James Fintan Lalor*, Dublin, 1918

Glaser, J. F., 'Parnell's fall and the Nonconformist conscience', in *I.H.S.*, xii (Sept. 1960)

Gollin, Alfred, *The Observer and J.L. Garvin, 1908–14*, Oxford, 1960

Gollin, Alfred, *Balfour's burden*, 1965

Gwynn, D. R., *The history of partition, 1912–25*, Dublin, 1950

Hammond, J. L., *Gladstone and the Irish nation*, 1938

Harrison, Henry, *Parnell, Joseph Chamberlain and Mr. Garvin*, 1938

Harrison, Henry, *Parnell, Joseph Chamberlain and the Times*, Belfast and Dublin, 1953

Henry, R. M., *The evolution of Sinn Fein*, Dublin, 1920

Howard, C. H. D., ed., 'Documents relating to the Irish "central board" scheme, 1884–5', in *I.H.S.*, vii (Mar. 1953)

Howard, C. H. D., 'Joseph Chamberlain, Parnell and the Irish "central board" scheme, 1884–5', in *I.H.S.*, vii (Sept. 1953)

Howard, C. H. D., 'Joseph Chamberlain, W. H. O'Shea and Parnell, 1884, 1891–2', in *I.H.S.*, xiii (Mar. 1962)

Hurst, Michael, *Joseph Chamberlain and Liberal reunion*, 1967

Hurst, Michael, *Parnell and Irish nationalism*, 1968

Jackson, J. A., *The Irish in Britain*, 1963

Larkin, Emmet, 'The Roman Catholic Hierarchy and the fall of Parnell', in *Victorian Studies*, iv. (June 1961)

Larkin, Emmet, 'Launching the counterattack: part ii of the Roman Catholic Hierarchy and the destruction of Parnell', in *Review of Politics*, xxviii (July 1966)

Link, Arthur S., *Woodrow Wilson and the progressive era*, 1910–17, 1954

Lyons, F. S. L., 'The Irish Unionist party and the devolution crisis of 1904–5', in *I.H.S.*, vi (Mar. 1948)

Lyons, F. S. L., 'The Irish parliamentary party and the Liberals in mid-Ulster, 1894', in *I.H.S.*, vii (Mar. 1951)

Lyons, F. S. L., *The Irish parliamentary party, 1890–1910*, 1951

Lyons, F. S. L., 'The machinery of the Irish parliamentary party in the general election of 1895', viii (Sept. 1952)

Lyons, F. S. L., 'The economic ideas of Parnell', in *Historical Studies*, ii, (1959)

Lyons, F. S. L., *The fall of Parnell, 1890–91*, 1960

Lyons, F. S. L., *Parnell* (Dundalk, for Dublin Historical Association), 1963

Lyons, F. S. L., 'John Dillon and the Plan of Campaign, 1886–90', in *I.H.S.*, xiv (Sept. 1965)

Macardle, Dorothy, *The Irish republic* (American ed.), 1965

McCready, H. W., 'Home Rule and the Liberal party, 1890–1910', in *I.H.S.*, xiii (Sept. 1963)

Macdonagh, Michael, *The Home Rule movement*, Sublin, 1920

McDowell, R. B., *The Irish administration, 1801–1914*, 1964

MacNeill, Ronald (Lord Cushendun), *Ulster's stand for union*, 1922

Martin, F. X. (ed.), 'Eoin MacNeill on the 1916 rising', in *I.H.S.*, xii (Mar. 1961)

Martin, F. X. (ed.), *The Irish Volunteers, 1913–15*, Dublin, 1963

Martin, F. X. (ed.), *The Howth gun-running, 1914*, Dublin, 1964

Martin, F. X. (ed.), *Leaders and men of the Easter Rising: Dublin 1916*, 1967

Moody, T. W., 'Michael Davitt and the "pen" letters', in *I.H.S.* (Mar. 1945)

Moody, T. W., 'The new departure in Irish politics, 1878–79', in H. A. Cronne, T. W. Moody and D. B. Quinn (ed.), *Essays in honour of James Eadie Todd*, 1949

Moody, T. W., 'Parnell and the Galway election of 1886', in *I.H.S.*, ix (Mar. 1955)

Moody, T. W., 'Michael Davitt and the British Labour movement', in *Transactions of the Royal Historical Society*, 5th series, iii (1953)

Norman, E. R., *The Catholic Church in Ireland in the age of rebellion, 1859–1873*, 1965

O'Brien, Conor C., *Parnell and his party, 1880–90*, 1957

O'Brien, Conor C. (ed.), *The shaping of modern Ireland*, 1960

ÓBroin, L., *Dublin Castle and the 1916 Rising*, 1966

O'Hegarty, P. S., *The victory of Sinn Fein*, Dublin, 1920

O'Sullivan, Donal, *The Irish Free State and its Senate*, 1939

Pakenham, Lord, *Peace by ordeal* (3rd ed.), 1962

Palmer, N. D., *The Irish Land League crisis*, New Haven and London, 1940

Pomfret, J. E., *The struggle for land in Ireland*, Princeton, 1940

Ryan, A. P., *Mutiny at the Curragh*, 1956

Ryan, Desmond, *The rising* (3rd ed.), 1957

Stansky, Peter, *Ambitions and strategies*, 1964

Stewart, A. T. Q., *The Ulster crisis*, 1967

Tansill, Charles C., *America and the fight for Irish freedom*, 1866–92, New York, 1957

Thornley, David, 'The Irish Conservatives and Home Rule, 1869–73', in *I.H.S.*, xi (March, 1959)

Thornley, David, 'The Irish Home Rule Party and parliamentary obstruction, 1874–87', in *I.H.S.*, xii (Mar. 1960)

Thornley, David, *Isaac Butt and Home Rule*, 1964

Wilson, Trevor, *The downfall of the Liberal party*, 1914–35, 1966

Index